CLUES, CHRISTMAS TREES AND CORPSES

A COZY MYSTERY CHRISTMAS ANTHOLOGY

HILLARY AVIS MOIRA BATES AUBREY ELLE BABS EMODI
JOANN KEDER PATTI LARSEN R.B. MARSHALL
ROSIE MELEADY MP SMITH CATHY TULLY
VICTORIA LK WILLIAMS CARLY WINTER

Collated by
R.B. MARSHALL

AN AYE ALBA COLLECTION

CONTENTS

First Edition: 2021
2nd Edition (this edition): 2022
Cover by Alba Covers

ABOUT THIS ANTHOLOGY

Secretive Santas, puzzling presents, dangerous decorations... and murderous mistletoe!

From a sparkling selection of amazing authors, including USA Today and Wall Street Journal best-sellers, comes this wonderful collection of 12 festive cozy mysteries.

Featuring poisonous poinsettias, corpses on Christmas trees and toxic tinsel, these fabulous stories will keep you entertained until Santa arrives.

Pour yourself a cup of something cheery, kick off your shoes, settle into a comfy chair and immerse yourself in these marvelous mysteries by your new favorite authors!

❄

Please note that authors from the United States, the United Kingdom, Australia, and Canada have contributed to this collection, so you may notice a slight variation in spelling and punctuation between the different stories.

CLUES, CHRISTMAS TREES AND CORPSES

THE SECRET SANTA MYSTERY

R.B. MARSHALL

This wasn't the secret she expected from her Secret Santa...

Note: British English

CHAPTER ONE

A bony elbow poked me in the ribs. "Izzy!" hissed my colleague Devlin Connolly, known to his friends as Dev. "Who did you buy for this year?"

"It wouldn't be a *secret* Santa if I told you, would it?"

He gave me what he thought was an innocent look. On a six-foot Irishman with wild black hair and two days worth of stubble, it had more in common with sinister than with sinless. "But you can tell me, sure you can. I can absolutely keep a secret."

I skewered him with some prime side-eye. "Suffice to say I didn't buy for you. Although you'd have been a lot easier to shop for than my *real* target. I could just have got you a catering-size box of Skittles."

Shoulders hunching, he had the grace to look shameful. "At least they're not addictive."

My eyebrows climbed towards my hairline.

"I could give them up anytime," Dev said, sliding an arm behind his back. I felt sure he was crossing his fingers.

In honour of the occasion, he'd ditched his usual outfit of superhero t-shirt and jeans, and was wearing beige chinos and a blue-checked shirt. He almost looked smart, for a change.

"Maybe that should be your New Year's Resolution." I grinned at him. "No more snacking on sweeties while sat at your desk."

"There's at least three weeks till—"

At the front of the room, Gordon Dempsey, our CEO, stepped ponderously to the microphone. "Colleagues!" he cried, interrupting Dev, and looking out at us in the slightly unfocussed way of someone who has overindulged at the free bar.

Despite having the money to dress in Armani, Mr Dempsey had this uncanny knack of making even designer clothes look shabby. With his tie hanging at half-mast and the silver buttons on his waistcoat struggling to contain his ample girth, he was not the ideal poster boy for our organisation.

"Uh-oh," I said, nudging Dev. "Dempo is about to speechify."

Dev rolled his eyes. "Pity save us."

The other six people at our table were also IT staff from Bleubank, one of the major financial institutions in the City of London. But Dev was the one I knew best, and the only one I'd call a friend.

Across from us sat Manda Kumar, the third—and

quietest—member of our team. We'd worked together for over a year, but I knew very little about her, apart from the fact that she liked to read celebrity gossip magazines, and had an overbearing mother who phoned, without fail, every lunchtime.

Four other seats were taken up with staff from the web and server section, and at the head of the table sat our team leader, Nicholas Spence. Thin face scowling and pale skin flushed, his thumbs jabbed like knives at the keyboard on his phone.

An exaggerated throat-clearing drew our attention back to the front. Mr Dempsey's pudgy lips curled into something approximating to a smile as he stepped closer to the microphone. "It's that time again. Time for Bleubank employees to show their ingenuity—and generosity," he added, with all the aplomb of an old-fashioned music hall master of ceremonies. "What goodies will Santa have for you this year?" With a flourish, he pointed to the side of the hall.

Our office Christmas lunch was being held in a restored corn exchange not far from the Tower of London. Oak-panelled walls soared to a beamed ceiling, and in a corner stood a towering evergreen adorned with red baubles and silver tinsel. The faint aroma of fresh pine needles reached us even at our table near the back.

Right on cue, a hidden door beside the tree opened to reveal a fat figure clothed in red and white, carrying a bulging sack. More North Pimlico than North Pole, Santa's tunic strained over a belly that was probably a result of too many business lunches. Not only that, but the red nose that peeked from under suspiciously white eyebrows looked like it owed more to malt whisky than mince pies.

The CEO ostentatiously delved into Santa's sack, pulled out a gift, and called the first name. "Iris Hooper! Come on down!"

A small, mouse-like woman, our CFO's secretary, scurried from her seat two tables away, and almost curtsied before the unidentified manager who'd dressed up as Father Christmas. He handed her a pink-wrapped present and leaned forward for a kiss before she could avoid him.

Dev got called up before I did and came back to the table clutching a gift bag decorated with frolicking penguins. Pulling the handles apart, he peered inside, then looked accusingly at me. "Why would you be lying to me?"

My forehead scrunched quizzically.

"Look!" He thrust the bag in my direction.

It was filled almost to the brim with rainbow-hued packets of Skittles.

I was still laughing at him when my name was finally called a minute later. Wiping quickly under my eyes with a tissue, I headed to the front of the room, suddenly feeling self-conscious.

Why was it I could confidently ride into a competition arena in front of ranks of spectators when sat on Leo, my dressage horse? But ask me to walk a few steps in front of my work colleagues and I'd be stumbling and tripping like I had two left feet.

It wasn't like I'd been drinking. Unlike pretty much everyone else here, I had work to do afterwards. Or perhaps that should be sport to do afterwards...

Murphy's Law dictated that the Friday two-and-a-half weeks before the world celebrated Jesus' birthday would not only be my work's festive do, but also the day of the Christmas party for the staff at the livery stables where I kept Leo. Which meant that I had to travel there after work, change my fancy clothes for jeans and leather boots, and clean out his box.

And sobriety was definitely recommended when negotiating a stinking muck heap with a dodgy wheelbarrow. Plus, I had a busy weekend coming up with a long drive on Saturday, so I needed all my wits about me.

Pulling myself together, I tried to channel confident horsewoman rather than introverted computer geek, and strode forward.

When I finally reached the surrogate Santa, he handed me a somewhat inauspicious envelope, then puckered up and leaned in. "Not tonight, buddy," I muttered under my breath, and deftly turned my head so his lips met my cheek.

Buoyed by this small victory, I was back in my seat before I'd had time to become embarrassed again.

"So what did you get?" Dev demanded.

I held out the envelope. "Just this."

"Open it, then."

Working with horses on a regular basis meant that I had no nails to speak of, so I plucked a clean knife from Manda's side plate, and sliced the packet open.

Inside was a voucher for a horse tack and feed shop in Richmond, near the livery stables. Obviously my Secret Santa knew at least *something* about me. I waved it at Dev. "I can get some treats for Leo." I glimpsed my nails again. "Or gloves for me."

The card that accompanied the gift had a quaint picture of a mare and foal on the front. But it was the inscription inside that caught my eye and piqued my interest. They had printed it on white paper, cut it out, then stuck it onto the card:

If mystery is your game
And honesty your aim
In dark places you should seek
The Secret you must keep

From foreign places go
And track both high and low
Try following the money
For clues will reveal the honey

Your route may lead to failure
And perils will assail you
But truth will always win
When bravery comes in
Robin Hood 1454

Sitting back in my chair, I puffed out a breath. *Robin Hood.* But the verse said nothing about his merry men or the sheriff of Nottingham. What could it mean?

I was about to show it to Dev, when the phrase *'The Secret you must keep'* jumped out at me. *Perhaps I'll just keep it to myself for now,* I thought. I slid the card back into the envelope, which was plain white and had my name written on the front in block capitals.

That was the only personalised thing about the gift, other than the fact that the giver knew I liked horses. But anyone that passed my desk at work would know that, since I used a picture of Leo as a screen-saver and had a dressage calendar pinned to the partition beside me.

At the front of the room, Santa handed out the final present, then Mr Dempsey clapped his hands. "Last orders at the bar, ladies and gentlemen." He pulled a device from his pocket and checked the screen. "We have the place for another twenty minutes." With a flourish like a demented magician, he pressed a button on the gadget. Irritating Christmas musak streamed from loudspeakers high on the walls, grating at my eardrums.

I took that as my cue to leave. It's not that I don't like Christmas. I enjoy being with my family in Scotland on Christmas Day as much as the next person. But the enforced jollity and tinsel-wrapped commercialisation that begins before autumn has properly ended just annoys me. Somehow, the festive period has become a retail juggernaut, and the real reason for the season has been lost.

Stuffing the gift voucher, envelope and card into my black messenger bag, I slid out of my seat. "See you on Monday," I said to Dev, and waved my fingers at the rest of the table. "Catch you later."

A minute afterward I stepped onto the busy street outside the corn exchange and hugged my jacket around me. There was a nip in the air, although in crowded London it seldom got cold enough for frost. I wrinkled my nose. The faint breeze smelled of overflowing bins and car exhaust. *Lovely*. If it wasn't for my work, I'd live as far away from London as possible.

Born in a small town on the outskirts of Edinburgh, I'd gone to school there, studied Computer Science at Glasgow University, then done a Master's degree at Dundee University. But it turned out that all the jobs I was interested in were in the capital city, so here I was, a country girl stuck in the middle of the largest urban area in Britain.

I coped with it because of the little 'villages' that you find even in the biggest municipalities. For example, there was a real community spirit at the stables where I kept Leo; and Putney, where I lived, had a homely feel about it. Shopkeepers knew your name and neighbours actually spoke to you—like the Steadmans, the retired couple upstairs who always stopped for a chat, or Mrs Lacey, a widow from downstairs who regularly pressed home baking into my hands.

Work wasn't bad either—it was a big organisation, but having friends there made it more enjoyable.

As I descended the last few steps leading to Tower Hill tube station, an unearthly screech almost caused me to jump out of my skin.

"When did Dev get hold of my phone?" I grumbled, as I fished it out of my pocket. It was his favourite trick, to change my ringtone for something entirely inappropriate. I reckoned he'd been a pickpocket in a former life, as I was sure I hadn't left it unattended at the party.

It was Nicholas, my boss. "You went before I had time to say," he started, without preamble, "I'm calling a team breakfast meeting for eight a.m. on Monday. Something important has come up."

I made a face at the phone. Why couldn't he just have emailed? "No problem, see you then."

My finger was about to hit the red button when his tinny voice came out of the speaker. "Bring your incognito laptop."

Taken aback, I brought the device to my ear again. "Okay. Any hints what it's about?"

"You'll find out on Monday." The line went dead.

Computer scientists aren't exactly renowned for their people-skills, but Nicholas Spence took it to extremes. He was all about the work, no play—and something of a dull boy.

Shaking my head, I slid the phone into my inside pocket and headed through the barriers of the tube station.

Time for some horse therapy.

When I made it to the stables an hour later, I found several of the other horse owners already there and up to their elbows in straw and hay. Someone had brought mince pies, Christmas songs were playing on the radio, and there was an impromptu karaoke sing-along competition in progress.

Apparently Suzannah, whose horse was housed next to mine, had killed it with a rendition of *The Fairytale of New York*, using her pitchfork as a make-believe microphone stand.

I opened the door to Leo's stable—or stall, as Veronica, the American lady on the opposite side of the barn aisle would call it—and checked the state of his straw bed. I groaned. It looked like he'd been having his own party in there last night.

As I went off in search of a wheelbarrow, *Last Christmas* by Wham came on the radio, and Kirsty, three stables down, took to the floor. In the central passageway between the stables, she turned up the collar of her jacket in true eighties style, used her fingers to smooth her hair over her eyes, and sang soulfully into a grooming brush.

Needless to say, with such entertainment going on, my time at the yard passed in a twinkling. Soon Leo was tucked up in a nice clean stable with plenty of hay to see him through the night, and I was ready to head home.

Even though it was barely nine o'clock when I got back to my cozy flat in Putney, I was ready for bed. It'd been a long day—all that socialising at the Christmas party, and then the impromptu shindig with my horsey friends was quite wearing for a person like me who was something of an introvert. I generally preferred animals to people.

Then, tomorrow I had to get up at stupid o'clock to

drive south for a training course. So an early night was in prospect.

It was only when I was almost asleep that I remembered the mysterious rhyme in my Secret Santa card. *It'll need to wait,* I thought groggily, then zonked out and headed for dreamland.

CHAPTER TWO

But I didn't get to think about the Secret Santa mystery until Sunday night. It was all Robert Redford's fault.

As a horsey teen, I'd watched his film, *The Horse Whisperer*, and become determined to learn to do some of the things he did. Through Pony Club and my long-suffering Connemara pony, Jangles, I'd experimented —with mixed results. But as an adult, once I got Leo, I'd realised I couldn't just muddle along. I needed to study it properly.

So I'd invested in a part-time course at a farm on the South Downs, which I'd been attending monthly for most of this year. This weekend had been the final part of the course, and I was now a fully qualified 'Horsemanship' Trainer, skilled in using natural methods such as body language to guide and work with the horse.

It had been an intense couple of days, with borrowed horses to train, final lecture sessions to attend, and an exam to pass, but it was done, and I couldn't wait to tell Leo—even though it was dark and I hadn't eaten dinner yet.

Driving along the streets of Richmond, I marvelled at the number of Christmas trees covered in twinkling fairy lights that sparkled in the windows of the flats and houses I passed. Shops and restaurants were decorated with fake snow or holly wreaths, the people on the street all seemed to be laughing, and my car radio was playing seasonal songs.

I smiled, feeling less like Grinch and more like Gonzo in *The Muppet Christmas Carol*. All I needed now was to sing carols at the Watchnight Service back home in Scotland, and I'd *really* be in the festive spirit.

With a sigh of satisfaction, I pulled my little red Corsa into the car park at the livery yard. Street lights gleamed orange on the road outside, but the lights were off in the stables, and all was quiet. Everyone else must have gone home.

Except—there was one car still parked up in the corner, a Mini, from what I could see. My good mood evaporated. Had someone had a riding accident and been taken off in an ambulance? *I guess I'll find out from the others tomorrow*, I said to myself.

Switching on the lights in the barn, I strode toward Leo's stable. A few sleepy noses turned my way, but most of the horses continued dozing or munching at their hay.

Leo was near the end of the building, and on the

way I passed an empty stable, then stopped abruptly. A flash of colour had caught my eye. What could it be? I peered over the half door.

Blinking up at me from a sleeping bag resting on a thick bed of straw was Trinity Allen, one of the part-time grooms who worked at the yard. Her long dark hair was all mussed up, and her sand-coloured skin looked pale.

"Trinity! Sorry to wake you up. Have you got an early start for a competition or something?" Even as I said that, I realised that tomorrow was Monday, and horse shows were usually run at weekends.

She rubbed her eyes and swallowed. "Don't tell, will ya? I'll get into trouble from Mrs B if she finds out. It's just..." She screwed up her face. "I had to leave the flat. I've left Dwayne. But there weren't anywhere else I could think of to go. An' I was too scared to sleep in my car. Thought it would be warmer in here."

"Oh no, that's terrible!" Something about her forlorn look tugged at my heart strings. Trinity was one of the people I liked best at the stables, always cheerful, kind to the horses and a real bundle of energy. It was strange to see her despondent like this. "But you can't stay here—it'll be freezing later. Grab your stuff and you can sleep on my couch. It pulls out to make a bed."

"Aw, bless you, Izzy. But I don't want to be any trouble to ya. I've got a six thirty start tomorrow morning at the yard." She pulled her phone out of a pocket. "So I've set an alarm so I can tidy up my things before anyone gets 'ere."

"And I've a breakfast meeting at *my* work. So I'll be

up at the crack of dawn too." I gave her a reassuring smile. "C'mon, you'll be much more comfortable at mine. Give me a minute to check on Leo and I'll be right with you."

Leo, to give him his due, stopped eating his hay and came over to the stable door. It was probably just greed, for he snuffled at my pockets, hunting for treats, but it made me feel like he appreciated my presence.

In an excited whisper, I told him about passing the course. He gazed at me with his soft brown eyes, then tilted his head, inviting me to itch his neck. Next thing I knew, my fingers were buried in the silky hair behind his ears, and he was bending into the scratch with an expression of pleasure on his face. With a laugh, I realised that my horse had probably trained *me* better than I had ever trained him—course or no course!

When Leo finally had enough of ear-rubs, I headed back to where I'd left Trinity. I gave her a sideways look. "Have you eaten? I was going to stop for a Chinese take-away on the way home."

Her brown eyes widened. Now that she was out in the light of the barn aisle I could see that they were red-rimmed, as if she'd been crying. "D'you know, that sounds good. I were too upset to be hungry earlier. But now me old stomach feels like me throat's had a knife taken to it."

Forty minutes later, we were sitting in the warmth of my rented flat, me devouring king prawn chow mien and Trinity scoffing sweet chilli chicken with egg fried rice.

On the middle floor of a three-storey apartment building in the district of Putney in London, my home was small but serviceable. It had an open-plan living/dining/kitchen room which you entered from the shared corridor. To the right, inside the door, there was a shower room, and beyond that a separate bedroom large enough for a double bed, a wall of built-in wardrobes and not much else. The thing that had sold the place to me was the light—the flat was south facing and painted in pale shades with a fawn-coloured carpet throughout, so it always seemed bright and cheerful.

"Had you been with Dwayne long?" I asked Trinity, biting into a greasy prawn cracker.

"It's only been six months. But he's always been one of those jealous types." She put down her fork. "Tonight he came along to one of my salsa classes, I think he only went to check up on me. Well, he caught me chatting to one of the clients—one of the male ones. And, oh my word, did he lose his rag!" Her hands flew up expressively, and she almost knocked over her plate of food.

"He were ranting and raving about how I shouldn't be talking to other men and how he couldn't trust me and that I was a right—" she glanced across at me, "—well, let's just say he was angry. Very angry. But Winston—the lad I was talking to—he's got a girlfriend. He's been having dancing lessons to surprise her, like. So there was absolutely nothing in it, I told Dwayne that. But he wouldn't listen. He went and lost the plot."

"Sounds like he's a bit possessive."

"You're not wrong. An' it's not the first time he's been like that, neither. So off I went home, packed up me stuff and left before he could stop me."

She picked up her fork again and took a mouthful of chicken. "A girl I used to know, something similar happened to her; her bloke got really mean and controlling and she ended up in hospital. So there's no way I was having that happen to me. But I was so angry with him when I left that I hadn't really thought it through, and I hadn't worked out where I'd stay. Really stupid of me, I know. I'll have to start flat-hunting tomorrow."

She grimaced. "Although goodness knows when I can fit it in. I've got work at Mrs B's till four, and then from four thirty until nine I've got dance classes."

"You could have a look at lunchtime? On your phone?" I paused for a moment, realising that she wouldn't just walk into a new flat with half a day's notice. "But you can stay here for a few days till you find something, as long as you don't mind the couch."

"You're having a laugh. I couldn't do that."

"Well, if you can find a flat to rent tomorrow, then that's great. But it'll probably take a day or two to find one, won't it?"

"Yeah, I s'pose it might," she mumbled through a mouthful of rice.

"So stay here till you get somewhere else. It'll be nice to have a bit of company—though it sounds like you work most of the time so I won't see much of you, anyway." I jumped up and went over to a shallow cupboard by the door and returned clutching a key.

"Here's my spare key. I go to the stables most nights after work, as you probably know; so I don't usually get back here until about eight. I'll cook a quick stir fry tomorrow and you can heat some up when you get in from dancing. After that you can just text me and we can arrange who cooks."

Her eyes glistened. "Aw, Izzy, you're so kind." She pointed at the cooker with her fork. "On a Tuesday I finish earlier, so it'll be my turn to cook *you* something. If I'm still here," she added.

"Deal!"

Stacking our plates together and grabbing the cutlery, Trinity headed for the kitchen nook, which was in a corner of the open-plan living area. "I'll wash up," she shouted over her shoulder, putting the dishes in the sink.

Unfolding my legs from under the dining table, I stood. "I'll dry then."

"Don't you dare! I'll be done in two shakes. You go and do what you'd normally do on a Sunday night."

"But you're my guest! You don't need to tidy up."

She threw her hands wide in an expressive gesture. "I do, y'know. I'm a compulsive cleaner. Blame my Italian mother. But it comes in handy when you work as a groom."

With a shrug, I turned on the TV. Flicking through the channels, all I could find were Christmas shows or Hallmark movies. "Do you want some escapism? Or shall I fire up Netflix?"

Wiping her hands in a dishtowel, Trinity squinted

at the screen. "Dwayne and me had Sky, not Netflix. Is there anything good to watch?"

"Lots. I've been working my way through all the CSI episodes. How do you feel about good-looking Americans solving seemingly impossible crimes?"

"Now *that* sounds like my cup of tea. I tell you, right at this minute, I'm fed up to the back teeth with romance."

Half an hour later, when the detectives were up to their eyeballs in suspects, clues and dead bodies, I found myself wondering what Grissom would do, if he'd been given a rhyme by his Secret Santa.

With the gift card in one hand, I pulled out my laptop, fired up a search window and typed in 'The Secret'.

Various books, films, and lacy underwear sites were listed, but nothing that looked like it was anything to do with my note. Next, I tried 'Robin Hood 1454', and once more found links to films plus various pubs in England. But from the Robin Hood page on Historic England's website, I discovered that the green-clothed vigilante had probably been born in the twelfth century, or perhaps in the thirteen hundreds. Not fourteen fifty-four.

So what was the rhyme all about?

I squinted at the signature again. Were those letter Os or zeros? Robin Hood with numbers instead of letters was more like a password than a username. Frowning, I typed *that* into Google, but the search engine decided I couldn't spell and gave me the same results again. I sighed.

Trinity looked across at me from the armchair. “Everything all right?”

“Just…” I hesitated, wondering what to tell her. “I got a card from the Secret Santa at our office party, and it had a strange poem on it.”

“Strange like weird, or strange like modern and not rhyming?”

Picking up the remote control, I paused Netflix. “Weird I suppose. I think it might be a clue to a mystery.”

Her eyes lit up. “Y’mean a real live mystery?” She pointed at the TV set in the corner. “Like CSI?”

I pursed my lips. “Hopefully not! Probably a colleague was just playing a joke on me.”

“Go an’ read it to me?”

Studying her briefly, I reasoned to myself that she didn’t work for Bleubank, so ‘the secret you must keep’ part probably wouldn’t apply to her. Plus, it would be good to have someone to discuss it with. Clearing my throat, I picked up the card and read out the verses of the poem, then looked up at her. “What d’you think?”

She wrinkled her nose. “You work at a bank, don’t you?”

I nodded.

“Well, what I think is, someone’s doing something dodgy, and your Secret Santa thought you was exactly the person to work out what was going on.”

“But why not just report whoever-it-is, if they know there’s wrongdoing happening?”

“Maybe they only suspect something’s going on.

Or maybe they're not in a position to get proof, but they know that you are. What's your job again?"

"I.T. Information Technology."

She tilted her head enquiringly, obviously expecting more.

"Computer Security Analyst. I test our systems," I raised a palm, "looking for weaknesses. Basically I'm a hacker. White-hat, they call us. Like in the cowboy movies, the villain always wore a black hat and the hero a white Stetson."

"Well, that must be it! There must be something in the security. Or the systems. Something that only *you* could find."

"But there's three on our team. Why not contact Dev? Or Manda?"

Trinity drummed her fingers on the arm of her chair. "P'rhaps they don't trust the others." She suppressed a smile. "You've an honest face. Or perhaps they *suspect* the others, but for some reason they've ruled you out."

I stared, unseeing, at my laptop, scrolling back through the last couple of weeks in my head, trying to remember when I'd been out of the office but the rest of the team were in. Or, conversely, when I'd been the sole person there. "Apart from lunchtimes, when we all dive out at different times to grab a sandwich, the only time I can think of recently that I wasn't at work but the others were, was last Friday afternoon when I took time off to wash and plait Leo ready for the dressage show at Windsor."

"P'rhaps that was it." She frowned. "Or maybe

they just want to give you a mystery to think about, to stop you finding something else."

"You could spend forever thinking about all the options if you head down that route. I'll have a dig around at work tomorrow and see what I find." I picked up the remote and waved it at the telly. "Let's finish this episode and head to bed. We've both got an early start."

CHAPTER THREE

Nicholas Spence's idea of a breakfast meeting was for us to bring our take-away coffees while he provided a single bag of pastries from the nearest supermarket. His stinginess was infamous within Bleubank, and Dev and I had quickly learned to bring muffins or porridge as well as a hot drink.

Manda, however, had never been seen to eat, which might explain her bird-like figure. Instead of coffee, she sipped at a clear glass mug filled with boiling water and a slice of lemon.

My love for coffee was also infamous within Bleubank. Tucked in a back street, half-way between the tube station and the office was Caffè Fiorio, which, in my opinion, made the best coffee in the whole of London.

Giovanni, the owner, who considered Starbucks a thing of the devil, had succumbed to my pleading, and would grudgingly make me a take-away in my 'keep cup', warning me every morning to "not tell any of the other customers that I let you take my precious coffee away with you when you rush in here like a scirocco." Hands would fly expressively in the air. "Coffee from Caffè Fiorio should be savoured. You should sit, taste, appreciate!"

So every morning I would reply that his coffee tasted like nectar from the gods, and that he must be the finest barista in all of London, but that if I wanted to be able to afford my coffee habit, I needed to get to work rather than sit in Italian cafés.

Clutching my double-shot cappuccino, I would hurry to the office, then sip reverentially while the caffeine kick-started my brain.

Today was no exception.

Grunting "Good morning," to Dev and Manda, I entered the small second-floor meeting room. Bleubank prided itself on having ergonomic and productive workspaces. But what that really meant in practice was that the interior designers had picked office furniture in the company colours of airforce blue and silver, and arranged everything—apart from the meeting rooms—in an open-plan layout.

My preference was to sit opposite the window, so I could see the sky, and dream a little. London could feel claustrophobic at times; all concrete and glass high-rises, narrow streets, and crowds of people hurrying hither and thither.

I lived for the weekends, when I could ride Leo in Richmond Park, and pretend I was in the country—for a couple of hours at least.

I put my laptop and my cherished coffee on the table, close enough that the bittersweet aroma of the Colombian beans could filter its way into my neurons. Then I pulled a container with a blueberry muffin out of my messenger bag.

Across from me, Dev looked spritely as a spring lamb. He was obviously a lark, and the owl in me hated him—just for a second. It was too much effort, this early in the morning, to be annoyed at him for longer. In front of him sat a take-out cup of black tea.

Manda was sipping her customary lemon water, and wearing her customary black—black boots, black slacks and high-necked pullover, topped by a sheet of raven-glossy hair falling over one eye and hiding half her face. All she needed was a gun and she could audition for a James Bond movie.

Wondering whether she'd be a villain, accomplice or love interest kept me amused, briefly, until I realised that I, too, wore a sort-of uniform to work.

At my first job in Oxford, I'd come to the conclusion that a smart jacket could make Cheapside appear more like Chelsea. So I generally wore dark chain-store trousers or leggings with a self-coloured t-shirt and toning designer jacket, which would give the whole outfit more class.

Today's jacket was almost military style, with double rows of brass buttons on a red, tartan-like wool weave. I'd bought it for next to nothing in the Jaeger closing-down sale last year, and it was one of my favourites for winter.

Dev started to ask how we'd enjoyed the Christmas

lunch, but before we could get into any chit-chat about our weekends, the blue-painted door opened and Nicholas stalked in, carrying a tablet computer and the expected cheapo croissants. He placed them in the centre of the grey-blue melamine table, sat down, then looked at us over the top of a pair of horn-rimmed spectacles.

New, I thought. *Must be reading glasses.* They made him look more hipster than ever, with his scruffy beard, slouchy blazer and flannel waistcoat.

"Good morning, everyone." He opened his tablet and pulled out a stylus. "Let's get right into it, so we can get back to our desks." With a forefinger, he pushed the specs up his nose, dabbed the stylus a few times at the screen of his device, then looked up at us again. "Can I get a quick update on where you are with your projects? Manda, let's start with you."

In clipped tones that were so quiet they had me wanting to push the 'plus' volume button, Manda told him that, "the work with the web team is going according to schedule; I am assisting them by testing the new forms for security issues. So far I have found twenty instances of insecure inputs for them to rectify."

Dev went next. "The phone app is getting close to having a release date, let me tell you." His voice rose in pitch. "It's looking amazing. The mobile team are pulling out all the stops. Me, I've been focussing on the encryption and the cellular traffic, making sure that malicious outsiders can't get access to the data. It's been pretty full-on."

Nodding slowly as his bony fingers pattered across his tablet screen, Nicholas pressed his lips together. "And Izzy?"

"I've been examining the network systems, searching for weak spots or external vulnerabilities that hackers could exploit. I've been coordinating with Rob Gosling."

"Progress?"

I shrugged. "How long is a piece of string? As soon as we find and patch one hole, another pops up. It's like painting the Forth Rail Bridge."

My Scottish idiom appeared to sail right over his head. "So you don't have any set milestones on that one?"

"I guess not. It's—"

He cut me off. "Okay, well I have a new task for you. Start date today." He glanced at Dev and Manda. "Thank you for your time. There's no need for you to wait while I explain this new project to Izzy."

Dev's bushy eyebrows crept up his forehead, but he meekly gathered his things and sloped out, followed by Manda.

Swivelling in his seat so he could face me better, Nicholas took off his specs and fixed his pale grey eyes on me. "We've received intel from our parent company in France that there have been some..." his mouth turned down, "irregularities in the internal systems. Nothing concrete, just a data delay here, a parity error there. There's concern that someone might have infiltrated our networks. There was a veiled comment on

Twitter from the 404 Hacker Group, which could have something to do with it."

My interest was piqued. "When was this?"

"On Friday when we were all at the party. You can check it out when you get back to your desk." He swiped the screen on his tablet, then raised his chin. "Any questions?"

"Um—do you have anything specific for me to go on?"

"I'm afraid not. You'll be looking for anomalies. Unexplained glitches. Inconsistent date tags."

"The ghost in the machine?"

For a moment he looked surprised. "Yes. You could call it that."

I chewed my lip. "Is there a deadline for my ghost busting?"

He scratched at his scraggy beard with a thumb. "Head office didn't say. But it would be helpful to have an answer for them before the holidays. After that I'll be busy with annual report data."

Two weeks. A fortnight to find a nebulous issue that mightn't even exist. *Joy.* "Couldn't it just be some rogue programming that's causing the errors?"

"Quite possibly. But it's your job to track it down."

Perhaps it was paranoia, but I was beginning to feel like the fall guy. "What happens if I don't?"

The stylus tapped emphatically on the edge of his tablet. "I have every faith in you."

In my head, I growled. His non-answer was typical management speak, and it annoyed the pants off me. I narrowed my eyes. "So I've fourteen days to find something that may or may not exist, that nobody else has been able to track down, with nothing really to go on? That's going to look good on my appraisal," I added sarcastically.

He had the grace to look sheepish. "This project is off the books, so you needn't worry in that regard. If you don't get any results by Christmas, then we'll reassess."

I blew out a breath. "Is there someone to liaise with at head office? Or can they send me screenshots of the issues they've seen?"

"I'll put you in touch with Antoine Lanier in our Paris IT team. But you'll report directly to me, and you've to say nothing to anyone else in the department. This is strictly on the QT." He lifted his chin, indicating my laptop. "And work only on the incognito. Okay?"

Stalling, I took a slug of my coffee. Despite how impossible the task sounded, I was intrigued. It would be like *CSI-Information Technology*. Forensic detective work on our computer systems, hunting for dastardly hackers. I *liked* a mystery. So this might be fun? "All right, I'm in," I said with a nod of my head.

He smiled for the first time that morning. "Good." Picking up his tablet, he pushed his chair back. "I suggest you start on the dark web. See if you can find any references to Bleubank there. I'll catch up with you on Wednesday."

And with that, he was gone, the door swishing across the grey carpet and closing behind him with a muted thunk.

Absent-mindedly, I picked up my coffee and the untouched packet of croissants, thinking that I should be wearing grey coveralls with a big black backpack. "Who ya gonna call?" I said to myself and then giggled. *Antoine Lanier, naturally.* I hoped my schoolgirl French would be good enough.

Monsieur Lanier turned out to have excellent English. He was also rather charming, and much more encouraging than my boss. "Of course, of course, Mademoiselle Paterson. Anything for you. You are doing the important work, and I am told you have the unique skills to offer."

"Really?"

"Oui. Monsieur Spence thinks very highly of your investigation skills."

I blinked. Several times. "He does?"

There was a chuckle at the other end of the line. "I suppose he *can* be rather difficult to read. How you say? Stone face?"

"Yeah." That about summed him up. I could actually see the back of his head from where I sat.

We each had a relatively generous U-shaped arrangement of desks and shelves, with waist-height partitions between us. Nicholas was at the end, then Dev, me, and Manda at the other side.

"Well, okay, so I will send you the information I have. Although there is not very much. It will appear in your secure file transfer folder within the hour."

"Thanks, Monsieur Lanier, I appreciate your help."

Yawning, I leaned back and stretched. It was just after nine o'clock, and it felt like I'd done a day's work already. Reaching for my coffee, I up-ended the cup and swallowed the last of the cappuccino. I made a face. It had gone cold. *Might need another of those at lunchtime to keep my synapses firing.*

Normally, in circumstances like this, I'd make some sort of project plan. But if I wanted to keep things secret, I'd need to think of some way of keeping covert notes. I daren't write anything down.

But first, I had to keep myself busy until Antoine's files appeared. I drummed my fingers on the desk. Perhaps I could check out the Twitter lead that Nicholas had mentioned.

Using the incognito laptop, which automatically opened a secure connection to the internet, I logged in to Twitter with a disposable account. It didn't take long to find the hacker group's page. Scrolling back to their Friday tweets took longer, but eventually I found it:

> *Things are not as they seem in the world of corporate networks. #bleubank #security #cybersecurity #banking #finance #followthemoney*

Like Nicholas had said, it was pretty vague. And they hadn't directed the comment directly at Bleubank as if they wanted a response, they'd just hashtagged them.

On a whim, remembering my Secret Santa rhyme, I tried searching for Robin Hood and Robin Hood. *Nothing*. I chewed a thumbnail.

Perhaps I should check out the dark web, like Nicholas had suggested.

The dark web is a part of the world-wide-web that can't be searched by normal search engines. Everything that happens there is hidden by spaghetti-like layers of encryption, so it's pretty much impossible to trace who anyone is, or who is hosting information.

Of course, that makes it a great location for criminals selling contraband, or for scammers and hackers. But it also has a positive side, providing anonymous communications channels for people in countries where free speech is criminalised, or where governments eavesdrop on their citizens.

None of that was my concern right now, though. I needed to search for references to Bleubank. With a normal web browser on the dark web, this would prove impossible. Even with a specialist browser it was difficult. But I had a secret weapon—something nobody at Bleubank knew about. *Gremlin*.

Round my neck and tucked under my t-shirt hung a quartz pendant, shaped like a teardrop. Taking it off, I flicked open the end, revealing a hidden USB flash drive that contained the Gremlin code.

Gremlin was an app I'd written as a university project; a search engine for the deep web. Exactly what I needed right now. It was versatile, too—it would also work like Google on the surface web, so, given the right keywords to look for, it would carry out a comprehensive search anywhere and everywhere. I inserted it into the laptop and set it going.

While Gremlin did its stuff, I had to keep busy, so I turned on the desktop computer, which I used for the majority of my work, and opened up my email program.

My sigh was so loud it earned me a sharp look from Manda.

In the space of one weekend, how could there be ninety-six questions or pieces of information so important that someone had sent or copied them to me? My shoulders sagged.

The next half-hour was spent answering or filing emails—usually in the round bin—until Antoine's data arrived, rescuing me from my Inbox infinity. But his files had me scratching my head.

Everything he'd seen, all the weird issues—they were all in our *internal* systems. Nothing external. Nothing on the internet. So why did Nicholas have me wasting time on the dark web? I massaged my temples, my brain hurting.

Was it only because of that tweet by the 404 group? Or was he trying to throw me off the scent? I shook my head. But why, then, would he have asked me to look into this in the first place?

I decided I was just being paranoid. His reasoning must be that if an external hacker group had somehow got into our network, perhaps there would be a reference on the dark web. That made sense. So I'd leave Gremlin to it, and see what it turned up.

In the meantime, I should concentrate on our internal systems. But where to start?

Frowning, I clicked back to the hacker group's twitter feed. There was something nagging me about that.

It took a few minutes, but finally it dawned on me.

Follow the money.

They had hash tagged that, and it was also in the Secret Santa rhyme. So, did the person who sent me the riddle somehow know about the issues Nicholas and Antoine had uncovered? I rubbed my temples again.

"You look like you need a coffee." A loud voice startled me. *Dev,* peering over the partition between us like a meerkat in the desert.

I nodded theatrically and faked a yawn, whilst surreptitiously sliding a piece of paper over the side of my laptop to cover the Gremlin USB. "Yeah. Is it that time already?" I checked my watch.

"I'll go and put the kettle on." He indicated the unopened packet of croissants on my desk. "You bring the eats."

Grabbing my mug and the pastries, I followed him to the kitchen area at the end of our floor. From the cupboard I produced my pack of espresso and over-cup coffee filter, spooned grounds into the filter then poured boiling water on top, to percolate through. It wasn't Caffè Fiorio, but it was miles better than instant coffee.

His mug of tea made, Dev took a bite of croissant, then leaned back against the counter and tilted his head at me. "So, what is this mysterious project that Auld Nick has you working on?"

I thought quickly. "Nothing much. He's got me looking for data for the annual report. Just until Christmas."

That seemed to satisfy Dev. He brushed a crumb off his t-shirt.

"How's the phone app going?" I asked, to distract him from asking me any further questions about my work.

He pressed his lips together and rolled his neck. "It's looking good. Think we'll be done by the new year."

"And then what?"

His eyes took on a far-away look. "Then I'm thinking about moving on. Maybe back home to Ireland. PayPal is recruiting for their mobile app team in Dublin." He gave me a sideways glance. "I've sent in my CV."

I puffed out a breath. "Wow. I didn't see *that* coming."

He shrugged. "It's time. I've been here two years. To be honest, that's more than enough time in this place." One of his big hands swept through the air, indicating the blue and grey business landscape around us. "And I've had my fill of London, too. D'you know, in my local, they're charging a *fiver* for a pint of Guinness?" He sounded genuinely shocked at that.

"So you're going to leave me to cope with Manda and Nick all on my own, just because of the price of beer?" I teased.

Green eyes swivelled sideways. "You could always come too. There's more than one opening."

Wow. I didn't see that coming either.

To give myself time to think of a suitable answer, I busied myself getting milk out of the fridge and stirring it into my coffee.

"There are plenty horses in Dublin," continued Dev, "you'd love it. And keeping a horse in Ireland has got to be loads cheaper than it is over here."

A sip of my drink gave me another few seconds thinking time. Or recovery time. Dev had never given me anything except friendship vibes. But this sounded... more, and it was a lot to take in.

"I've never thought about moving to Ireland," I said, truthfully. "But you make a good point. And I've heard lots of positive things about PayPal. Let me know how you get on."

From under my eyelashes while I sipped my coffee, I examined Dev. Today's t-shirt was emblazoned with the Batman logo. Baggy blue jeans and Nike trainers completed the ensemble. It was only on the worst days of winter that he added a denim jacket on top, seeming impervious to the cold.

Curling at the back of his neck, his black hair was messy as ever and slightly too long. On the plus side, Dev *did* have nice eyes and a friendly smile, but I'd never thought of him as anything except a colleague and friend, especially since relationships with people at work were usually a bad idea.

However, if I was reading his body language correctly, my non-answer seemed to have disappointed him. With feigned cheerfulness, he picked up his mug of tea and raised it in my direction. "I'll let you know. Now, I'd better press on."

"Me too," I said as he turned away.

I stared at his retreating back, wondering if I'd done the right thing. Did I want to stay in London, or would I consider a move to Ireland? Irish people always seemed lovely and friendly, in a 'talk the hind leg off a donkey' sort of way. And there was nothing in particular keeping me in the capital city, other than work opportunities.

But… Did Dev want more than friendship? It certainly felt that way, and any indication I gave that I was thinking about Dublin might encourage him, and that wouldn't be fair.

Wandering back to my desk, coffee in hand, I decided to put it behind me for now. I had enough else to think about—Secret Santas, temporary flatmates, horsemanship training and organising things so I could get home to Scotland for Christmas with my family. Not to mention mysterious data glitches at work. Surely that was more than sufficient for one person to be worrying about?

And then I smiled. Perhaps Gremlin would have found the answer for me already, and I could tie everything up with a nice neat bow, then hand it over to Nicholas in time for Christmas.

It was a nice dream, while it lasted…

CHAPTER FOUR

The caffeine in my coffee seemed to be doing the trick. Gremlin was still busy hunting through the nether regions of the internet, but while it was occupied, I'd put my thinking cap on. I had worked out that an old-fashioned paper notebook would work for my secret project notes, as long as I always kept it with me. Even if hackers were on our internal systems, they wouldn't be able to read my notes, so they wouldn't know I was after them.

To that end, and remembering the 'follow the money' exhortation, I was mapping out a diagram of where the money went within Bleubank. And how it got there. And then how it passed *out* of Bleubank. The page on my notebook soon filled up with lots of boxes, and even more arrows. But, basically, it gave me two choices of where to start: either inside or outside the company.

I tapped my pen against my bottom lip as I thought it through.

Inside Bleubank made more sense—it would be easier, for one thing, and it seemed more likely, from what I'd found in Antoine's files.

The right tool for the job was a 'network sniffer'—an app that would run in the background and monitor the information travelling between the computers in our company. I could see which devices were involved, and check if anything looked anomalous. Maybe that would be all I'd need.

From our company software library, I downloaded SmartNet, an app that promised to do just what I needed, and set it going. I'd probably need a full twenty-four hours of information to be sure I hadn't missed something, but I could extract the results hourly while I was in the office and at least get started.

Straightening my back, I pursed my lips and surveyed the technology around me. With the laptop busy, I needed to find something else to do, and I knew just what that should be. *The Secret Santa rhyme.*

It wasn't strictly a work thing, but the 'follow the money' coincidence had me wondering. Could the Antoine's Anomalies project and the Christmas Party Conundrum be related?

Pulling the gift card out of my bag, I stared at the verses, remembering my discussion with Trinity last night. Might something have happened on that Friday afternoon over a week ago, when I was away at the horse show?

Clicking on the Files app on my desktop computer,

I chose the top-level which showed all the files on our network, and arranged them in date order. I checked the calendar hanging on my partition to find the date I needed, then concentrated on files changed on Friday the first of December in the afternoon.

There were a lot. Too many to investigate quickly. But hadn't Trinity suggested it might be something to do with Dev or Manda? I cut my eyes right and left, to check they weren't looking at me, then filtered the results by username. It showed two files modified by Manda, and none by Dev.

I couldn't stop myself glancing at Manda again. It was illogical, since she'd have no idea what I was doing, and was probably busy with her own work, but I just wanted to be sure she wasn't watching me while I opened the files. She wasn't. Eyes fixed straight ahead at her screen, and frowning in concentration, her fingers flew across her keyboard.

Taking a deep breath, I clicked on the first of the files. It looked like it contained a bunch of test inputs for web forms, snippets of data similar to those a hacker might use.

The second file contained only streams of nonsensical letters and numbers. I scrolled through it, but could see no pattern, no rhyme or reason for the unintelligible contents. I was sure that file was unrelated, but, just in case, I used a USB flash drive to transfer a copy of it to the incognito laptop.

To my left, Dev was humming tunelessly under his breath, head bobbing slightly from side to side as he listened to music via a set of red Bluetooth headphones. Unfortunately, the absence of files by him didn't let my friend off the hook, as it was always possible they'd been edited again at a later date, therefore the date on the file would have been updated.

However, call me biased, but Dev didn't strike me as the sort of person who'd do anything nefarious. How could someone who looked like a cross between a brown bear and a character from *The Lord of the Rings* do something criminal?

I half-rose from my seat to attract his attention, then waited till he pulled the headphones off. "Sounds of the eighties?" I asked.

He made a clownish face. "I wasn't singing along again, was I?"

"You call that singing?" I teased.

If he'd rolled his eyes any harder, he'd have strained a muscle. "Do you not have a Christmassy bone in your body, Izzy Paterson? Surely even a philistine like you must like Band Aid?"

"Do I know it's Christmas?" I quoted the charity supergroup's Christmas song title.

He put one forefinger on his nose and pointed the other at me. "I see what you did there."

I tilted my head at him. "I'll have you know I was singing Mariah Carey karaoke on Friday night at the stables."

His eyebrows climbed under his fringe. "I didn't know you sang."

"I don't." I grimaced. "Normally. But all the other girls were singing, so it felt churlish not to." I didn't tell him that I'd done a duet with Emma, and that she had done most of the *actual* singing, while I did a brilliant job of lip-synching. Much as I love music, I can't carry a tune to save my life.

"That's it settled then." He waved over the partitions at Manda until she looked up. "Works night out. Friday. Christmas karaoke. You up for it?"

She did that shaky-noddy head thing that means maybe-yes, maybe-no.

Dev gave her a thumbs-up. "I'll check out which pub is doing karaoke and let you know where." He checked to his left, but Nicholas must've gone without us noticing. "I'd better ask Nick, too."

"And the web team. Won't be much fun with only the four of us," I added.

"Grand idea," he said. "Let's make it so."

It was my turn to roll my eyes. "You're such a Trekkie."

He grinned. "And don't you just love me for it."

Another hour later, Gremlin had uncovered nothing unusual or suspicious about Bleubank on the internet, dark web or otherwise. With a growl of frustration, I sat back in my chair. I hadn't really expected it to find anything, but it was still annoying.

Dev peered over the partition. "You look like you need lunch."

"Is it that time already?"

"Can be."

"What I want is coffee. Again. Caffè Fiorio for me."

"You need to get an intravenous drip of that stuff."

A smile crept across my face. "Maybe Santa will bring me one."

He rolled his eyes for about the ninetieth time that day. "Paterson, get your coat. You're getting delirious. I prescribe some caffeine. Stat!"

I went to the Italian café perhaps once a week for lunch. Sitting at one of the tiny round tables dotted around the room, I would people-watch the variegated representatives of humanity who rushed past the window. It was almost soothing.

In front of me would be a bicerin: layered espresso, hot chocolate and milk, or, in warmer weather, a macchiato: espresso with a dash of steamed milk. Something to taste and appreciate. Something to keep Giovanni happy. Today was a bicerin day.

Because it was mainly a coffee shop, the food menu was limited. But the Italian owner made a mean caprese panini with avocado basil pesto. I ordered one of those, while Dev, not being a vegetarian, went for the Tuscan chicken.

We found a table by the window and had just begun to eat when a familiar figure walked past.

Walter Oxley, our Chief Financial Officer, came into the café wearing a well-tailored grey suit, clutching a tablet computer in his hand, and carrying a raincoat over his arm.

My brows scrunched as I looked up at the sky outside. "No sign of rain," I said to Dev. "Oxo must be a Boy Scout."

Dev followed my gaze. "Or maybe he feels the cold. He's a bit of a stick insect."

"True. The man makes size zero supermodels look fat."

Mr Oxley gave his order at the counter, then found himself a table opposite, putting his coat on one of the two empty chairs. He didn't seem to have noticed us, but I doubted he would recognise us anyway—we were mere plebs to such an exalted executive in the company management.

Placing a pair of half-moon reading glasses on his long nose, he propped his tablet case open and started tapping on a little Bluetooth keyboard.

"Can't leave his work behind," I commented as I took another bite of panini, then licked a dribble of pesto off my finger.

"Well, I'm glad you managed to," said Dev. "You were looking a bit fraught, back there. Is it *that* difficult to find info for the annual report?"

I shook my head. It pained me to lie to him, so I tried to tell the truth without revealing my secret project. "It's not that, it's just a bit..." I twisted my lips as I tried to think of the right word, "frustrating. Well, I suppose identifying the data *is* proving to be a bit of a problem. But I've got a couple of weeks."

"Sure. When are you finishing for Christmas?"

"A week on Friday. I'm at a dressage competition on the Saturday morning, then I've got train tickets back up to Scotland late afternoon. What about you?"

"I'm finishing the Friday lunchtime, then flying from Gatwick to Dublin that afternoon." He lifted his cup, as if toasting invisible companions. "I should be in the Dancing Leprechaun with the boys by eight."

"Maybe you can organise an interview with PayPal while you're over."

"That's the plan," he said, cutting me a look.

Realising I'd moved the conversation onto difficult ground, I looked across at Mr Oxley again, hoping to change the subject. Then I jerked my head back in surprise. "Oxo has a friend."

Dev glanced over at the CFO's companion. "I don't recognise him."

"Me either."

The man that had joined the big boss was about half his age and half his height. Wearing a dark suit and tie, he had short auburn hair and a tidy beard, narrow eyes and a wide mouth. Something about him set my spidey senses tingling.

Mr Oxley had closed his tablet when the other man arrived, and now they were in earnest conversation, almost head-to-head across the table. They were interrupted when the waiter arrived with the CFO's order—a bowl of soup, from what I could see. After a few words with Oxo's companion, the waiter disappeared back to the kitchen, and the two suits resumed their pow-wow.

A loud 'ping' had Dev retrieving his mobile.

Across the room, two heads turned, and the CFO and his friend stared at us for a second, before continuing their conversation.

My jaw tightened, and I wriggled my shoulders. It seemed we weren't anonymous plebs after all.

Dev checked his phone screen, then stuffed the last bite of panini into his mouth. "We should get back to the office. There's a staff meeting at two, it totally slipped my mind. It's as well I set a reminder."

"I'd forgotten too." I set about finishing my food, drained the dregs of my coffee, then followed Dev to the door of the café.

Before I left, I looked across at Mr Oxley's table. He was on his own again, and slurping the remains of his soup. Presumably he was also heading back to the office for the two o'clock session. "I guess we'll see him there," I said to Dev's retreating back.

It turned out that Mr Oxley was one of the main speakers at the staff meeting. A monthly event that was supposed to help morale and communications within the company, they gathered nearly one hundred staff into the large atrium area on the ground floor of our building.

With grey marble floors throughout, boxy navy couches sat on each side of a square blue rug near the reception desk, then further over, a chrome staircase spiralled up to the higher levels. Apart from doors to the lifts, stairs and toilets, most of the rest of the concourse was open-plan, and ideal for a large gathering.

Mr Dempsey tapped the microphone, then cleared his throat. Behind him, our corporate logo was being projected onto a large screen that hung from the ceiling. "Colleagues," he said, calling the session to order, "welcome to our December staff meeting. You'll be pleased to hear it's a short agenda today. Now, I hope you all enjoyed the Christmas lunch on Friday?" Pinning a fleshy smile to his face, he waited for our murmurs of agreement, before signalling for the next slide.

Up popped one of those ubiquitous jaggy charts that looks like it's showing someone's heart rate, but is actually displaying profits. Or losses. This graph had a significant droop at the end. If it'd been my heart, I'd have been off to the hospital, with blues and twos going crazy!

"I'm going to call on our CFO, Mr Walter Oxley, to talk to you about company performance," continued Dempo, opening an arm to invite Mr Oxley to the mic.

"Ahem. Ladies and gentlemen, good afternoon." Oxo's voice was as thin and reedy as his body. He waved an arm at the graph behind him. "As you will see from this diagram, whilst profits were robust in the first quarter of the year, things have declined since then, and we are looking at a significant shortfall in this current period."

He was so tall that he had to hunch his shoulders to speak into the microphone. "We have a shareholder meeting next week, so you can rest assured that your management team is pulling out all the stops to address the issues before then."

"What *are* the issues?" Someone called from the middle of the crowd. It sounded like Rob Gosling, but I couldn't see.

A brief look of irritation crossed Mr Oxley's face. "Ahem. I'll take questions at the end. But, to answer your question, company performance has declined, and we are looking to improve it."

"Is that not what he just said?" I said under my breath.

"Obfuscation worthy of a politician," Dev whispered back.

At the front, Oxo signalled for the next slide. It was a pie chart, with a few large slices and one tiny sliver. "Now, as most of you will be aware, this is the time of year when we usually award staff bonuses."

That word, 'usually', caught my attention. Judging by the stirring and murmuring in the assembly, I wasn't alone in that.

"As you can see," the CFO used a pen to point at the pie chart, "once we have covered our salary commitments, fixed costs and shareholder remunerations, there is almost nothing left this year for bonuses."

The murmuring increased to muttering.

In most other areas of business, workers got paid every week or month, and were happy with that. But the financial services industry had a tradition of paying annual bonuses, and staff had begun to expect that—even to rely on it. For most of my colleagues, to hear that the payout would be reduced was bad news indeed. Especially this close to Christmas.

Since I'd not worked for Bleubank that long, I'd not begun to rely on the bonuses. Fortunately. In the last couple of weeks, I had to admit to drooling over websites with fancy new bridles for Leo, and smart competition jackets for me. But I didn't *need* them, so I'd be fine either way.

Mr Oxley cleared his throat again. "Your managers will meet with you in the next forty-eight hours and let you know individually what you can expect in your December pay packet." He lifted his chin. "Now, I thank you for your time. Let's all get back to work and get those profits rolling in again!" With that he turned away, hurried over to the lifts with Mr Dempsey, and they disappeared up to the management suite in the top floor like rats scurrying up a drainpipe.

Around us, more than a few jaws had to be lifted off the ground. "So much for taking questions at the end," I said, still trying to process what I'd just witnessed.

"I guess that's my new car out the window," said Dev with a mock sigh. "I'll not be able to impress the girls with my wheels after all."

"If all it takes to impress the girls is a fancy car, then they're probably not the sort of girls you'd actually want," my logical side replied before my tactical brain had time to approve the comment.

"You're so right," he said, flashing me a look from under his eyelashes.

Uh-oh.

"We'd better get back to work," I said brightly, unsubtly changing the subject, "and get those profits rolling in again, like the man said."

CHAPTER FIVE

The memory of the declining profits chart haunted me all afternoon as I examined spreadsheets filled with SmartNet results. Was the poor corporate performance the *real* reason behind the tricky task Nicholas had set me? Or were hackers somehow siphoning off our profits? I scratched my head. But surely the company auditors would pick up on that?

Unless... perhaps the hackers were getting to the money before it got as far as our accounts? Could they surreptitiously divert funds before we'd even counted them, and therefore our accountants hadn't missed them? I'd need to do some more research on that one. But it could wait until tomorrow.

With a start, I realised that the office around me was quieter and darker than usual. Several staff had already gone home, but I'd been so caught up in my analysis of the figures that I hadn't noticed.

Glancing at the clock in the corner of my computer

screen, I reckoned that, if I hurried, I'd be able to get to the stables by seven thirty. Then I could ride quickly before tucking Leo up for the night.

Locking the incognito laptop into the deep drawer at the bottom of my desk, I pushed my notebook into my cross-body bag, tucked the Gremlin necklace under my shirt, checked my phone was in my pocket, then grabbed my coat and rushed off down the stairs.

On my way across the concourse to the main doors, I was joined by Rob Gosling from the networks team. "You're not heading for the tube station, are you?" he asked. About the same height as me but significantly wider, he was the sort of man whose glass never even got to half full.

Working with him on the network security project, the only way I'd coped with his relentlessly negative attitude was to get him talking about one of his passions: birdwatching on the Norfolk Broads, or playing Fortnite on his PlayStation. He seemed a solitary man, obsessed with his gadgets and technology.

"Yeah. If I hurry, I'll catch the six ten."

He pushed up his sleeve and checked his Apple watch. "I'll probably miss my train. But I may as well walk with you."

"Of course." The automatic doors opened before us, and we strode out into the rush hour.

"Spence said you'd been reallocated." Street lights reflected off his large glasses as he glanced sideways at me.

"Yeah, he's got me gathering data for the annual report." A cold wind was whistling through the high buildings surrounding us. Fishing in my bag, I pulled out a black beanie, then wrapped my scarf tighter around my neck.

Power-walking to the nearest tube station, we joined hundreds of business-suited lemmings, dodging traffic and skipping round the occasional slow-moving tourist who blocked our way.

Overhead, multi-coloured Christmas decorations were strung across the street, and fairy lights twinkled in the windows of most of the shops we passed. It was a shame London seldom got snow, because, if it had, the whole scene would have become quite festive.

Rob pulled a shapeless dark green hat over his thick black hair. "I'm thinking about writing to the papers about them doing us out of our bonuses. It's just not good enough. Them executives in their fancy offices with their six-figure salaries won't suffer a jot. But us poor sods who work hard for a living, we're the ones who're out of pocket."

How could I respond to that? I risked a quick glance at him and nearly crashed into a lamppost. Staggering slightly until I regained my balance, I tried something noncommittal. "Um, does anyone still read the papers? I thought it was all online petitions and FaceBook memes these days."

His face brightened. "A petition might be an idea." I could almost see the cogs whirring. "We could present it at the shareholder's meeting. Embarrass the fat cats."

We. I hoped he meant the royal 'we', because I didn't want to get involved in organising his protest.

"There are plenty of online apps you could use to set up your petition." I said. I didn't emphasise the word 'your', but I hoped he'd take the hint.

"I'll look into it when I get home." He checked his watch again. "One hundred steps per minute." There was a brief pause while his lips moved silently. I guessed he was doing some mental arithmetic. "We need to increase to one-ten if you want to catch your train." With that he put on a spurt, dashed across a pedestrian crossing, and I almost lost him.

When we finally arrived at Monument Underground Station, I was breathing hard and had pulled off my hat and scarf. But I did catch the ten past six.

I never did find out if Rob made his train.

From my work to the stables it was about an hour's ride south west on the District Line, with a ten-minute walk at each end. To keep me entertained on the tube, I'd usually either read—if I got a seat—or listen to audio books if the service was busy and I ended up strap-hanging.

Recently, I'd been borrowing audio versions of the Hamish Macbeth mysteries from the library. They were well performed by the narrator and did a good job of describing the people and scenery in the far north of Scotland. But they also made me feel a little homesick for the open spaces and freedom of the Scottish countryside. I couldn't wait to be back with my family for Christmas.

When I arrived at the livery yard, I found my neighbour, Suzannah, busy grooming her horse,

Cracker. She had him tied outside her stable and almost blocking the central aisle.

Short and cuddly with a mop of curly brown hair, Suzie Wilks was one of those 'salt of the earth' people without whom the country would fall apart. Working shifts as a nurse at a local children's hospital, she would arrive at the yard at all sorts of odd times, so we didn't often see each other, despite having next-door stables.

Squeezing past, I kept an eye on the black horse's ears, which would give me the first warning sign of an impending kick. Not for nothing was he known in the barn as Cranky Cracker.

"Evening, love. How d'you get on at that course at the weekend?" Suzie asked, in her broad Manchester accent.

I reached Leo's stable without getting booted by Cracker. "Good, thanks. I passed." Leo came to the door, and I touched my hand to his nose in greeting.

"Oh, that were mint." Suzie brushed behind Cracker's elbow. Obviously it was a sensitive bit, as she did well to dodge his teeth. She growled at him to behave, then asked me, "What'cha up to tonight?"

"Practicing my dressage test. We've got the final competition in the Parkside League a week on Saturday." Opening my stable door, I gave Leo a pat on the shoulder then tied his head collar on.

She puckered her forehead. "How's that work, love?"

"It's a series of dressage shows. You get points each time depending on your placing, and they get added up to find who the overall winner is."

"Oooh. I'm on nights that weekend, otherwise I'd have come to watch. How're you getting on?"

"Pretty good thanks. We're second overall at the moment. But the lady in third place is only a point behind, so it could go either way."

"Excitin'." She put down the brush she was holding and picked up a comb for his mane. "Well, all the best. I hope you win."

"Unlikely," I said, stepping out of the stable. "But thanks." Rummaging in my own grooming kit, I hunted for a hoof pick. "What're you up to yourself, tonight?" Spying the implement I wanted, I grabbed it and went back into my stable.

"Oh, nowt. Just a bit of pampering for his lordship here." She looked fondly at the crotchety gelding. Suzannah was one of those people who seemed to spend hours fussing over her horse, giving him the best of care and attention, but never actually riding.

Me, I enjoyed riding Leo so much that I'd exercise him pretty well every day, even though it meant early starts, late nights and not much of a social life. But my friends at the stable yard made up for it. We were quite the little community, and I relished my time there.

"Actually," Suzie called me over, "go an' have a look at this for me?" She motioned at something on Cracker's shoulder.

Nodding, I went back out to the aisle, putting a hand on the dark horse's flank as I passed him so he'd know I was there. All of a sudden, I felt a cramping pain in my gut, which almost had me doubled over.

"You okay, love?" Suzie's forehead creased in

concern.

It took a moment to feel normal again. I breathed out heavily, then straightened. "Just a sore tummy. Must've been the panini I had for lunch." But that sparked an idea. Sticking my hands in my pockets, I contemplated Cracker's pinned back ears and swishing tail. "Suzie, did you ever think to get him checked for ulcers? That might explain his grumpy behaviour."

Her frown deepened. "You think?" She ran her eyes over her horse, as if trying to see beneath the surface. "You know, you could be right. That could be a reason for his quirky character." Her face cleared. "I'll phone the vet in the morning." Pointing at his shoulder, she added, "I could get them to look at that, too."

Glancing at the mark on Cracker's shoulder, I was able to reassure Suzie. "It's only a rub from his blanket. Often happens with sensitive-skinned horses in the winter. You don't need to bother with the vet for that—you can buy a shoulder guard for him to wear under his rug if it bothers you."

Once Leo was ready, I took him into the schooling area, mounted, then walked him round to warm us both up. After that I started working on exercises that would make him stronger and more supple, finally moving on to practicing the specific movements we'd have to perform at the competition.

Despite the cold, when we'd finished we were both sweating a little. Walking for five minutes helped to cool him off, then I took him back to his stable, gave him a feed, and wrapped him in a fleecy rug that would keep him warm overnight.

As the crow flies, it was only a few miles from the livery yard to my flat. The route went through Richmond Park, which, whilst very green and pleasant in the daytime, wasn't the safest place to walk alone in the dark. Because of that, I tended to drop my car at the yard in the morning so I could drive back safely at night.

After a short diversion via a local supermarket to pick up supplies for the stir fry I'd promised to make for Trinity, I arrived home. Throwing the ingredients into a wok, I sautéd the veg with one hand while the other used the remote to click through the channels on the TV. I finally settled on a re-run of a *CSI New York* episode.

When I at last heard Trinity's key in the lock, the delicious aroma of the Thai red curry sauce was making my stomach rumble.

"Good timing!" I said, pulling a couple of plates out of the cupboard. Then I caught sight of her face. "What's wrong?" I set the dishes on placemats before hurrying over to help her with the myriad of bags she held in either hand.

"Dwayne," she said, succinctly, a tear running down her cheek.

"Put those down," I inclined my head at her luggage, "take your coat off and sit yourself at the table. You can tell me all about it over dinner. You'll feel better with some food inside you."

She nodded mutely and did as I asked.

The whole sorry tale came out over the spicy vegetable curry. With a hitch in her voice, she told me how her final dance class of the evening had been cancelled because of a blocked toilet, of all things, so she'd decided to go to the flat she'd shared with Dwayne to pick up the remainder of her stuff.

Dwayne was out when she arrived, but returned just as she'd packed the last bag, reeking of beer and still wearing his work clothes. Barring the doorway, he demanded to know what she was doing.

Her hands flew in the air as she described their conversation. "'I'm getting my things,' I said to him. 'I told you I was moving out.'

"Then he said that I couldn't, that I still needed to pay half of next month's rent—my half. Well, I tell you, I could've seen him far enough. 'I've already paid for next month,' I told him. But he got all stroppy, like, an' shouted at me, 'Yeah but you have to give a month's notice.'

"Then he wouldn't listen to me when I told him it was four weeks' notice we needed to give, not a full month, and that it was only a few days ago that I paid a whole month up front. Apparently, he says I'm two days short of the four weeks' notice, and he just won't move an inch."

Her face crumpled. "And that's not the worst of it. If I 'ave to pay another month at that place, I won't have enough money left over to put down a deposit on a new flat."

I put my elbow on the table and tapped a thumb on my lip while I thought about it. "What job does he do?" I asked.

"He's a security guard at a store on Oxford Street."

"Does he use FaceBook?"

She nodded, swallowing another mouthful of curry.

"What's his full name and where's he from?"

"Dwayne Brooks. Dwayne Jeffrey Brooks. Born on an estate in Hackney I think."

"And his date of birth?" I grabbed a pen and paper so I could write it down.

She told me his birthday and age.

"And his mobile phone number?" I wrote that down too. "Okay, leave it with me and I'll see what I can find."

With the TV in the corner showing another CSI episode and the log-effect electric fire keeping the chill of night at bay, we sat in companionable silence in the living area. But I wasn't really paying attention to the telly.

Instead, I was curled on the couch with my laptop computer on my knee—my personal one, not my work one—doing some digging into Dwayne's background. With Gremlin's help, and the information Trinity had given me, I was doing a bit of social media snooping to find out more about my friend's ex.

It only took me about an hour to hit the jackpot. "Gotcha!" I cried, and grinned over at Trinity.

She creased her brow at me. "What's up?"

"Jasmin Alisha Freeman updated her relationship status on FaceBook."

Trinity shook her head. "And I should care because...?"

"Because she's Dwayne Jeffrey Brooks' new girlfriend."

"No!" Her eyes widened. "The rat." Her voice got louder. "The skunk. The total toad." She rocketed out of her chair and stomped around the room, muttering under her breath and calling him every name under the sun.

I let her work off some steam. Then I prepared to tell her the coup de grâce. "Not only that, Trinity, there's more."

She spun round to look at me, eyebrows at sharp angles.

"Jasmin posted a photo this evening, of 'her new pad'." I turned my laptop so she could see the screen. It showed a tower block flat in Kingston, with Dwayne leaning against the door jamb, a cocky expression on his face.

That set off a fresh round of name-calling.

Unfolding my legs, I went to put on the kettle while I waited for her to calm down again. By the time steam had stopped coming out of her ears, I'd made two mugs of hot chocolate. She came to join me at the kitchen counter.

"You know what, Izzy, you're a genius."

I pushed a mug in her direction.

She picked it up and took a sip. "Thanks. But, listen, you was so quick, it were no time at all, like the blink of an eye before you found that out. It were like magic." Brown eyes locked onto mine. "You should do that for a living, girl. Izzy Investigates. Richmond Research." Her lips twitched. "Or perhaps: Paterson's Probes."

Her last suggestion made me laugh out loud. "That sounds like something unmentionable they'd do to you in hospital."

She grinned. "Could be you're right. But, think about it. There must be millions of wives out there trying to find out what their rotten husband is up to. Or bosses wanting to check on new staff. You'd get loads of business."

"I like my current job." I lifted my shoulders. "But thanks." Placing my mug of hot chocolate back on the bench, I raised a hand. "We're not finished there, though. What time d'you finish work tomorrow? And when will Dwayne finish?"

"Now, let me think." She tapped her forefinger on her thumb. "The shops open late for Christmas shopping this week. So he should be at Macbie's till seven. Then home about eight if 'e don't go to the pub again. Me, I finish at six on Tuesdays. I said I'd cook, remember?"

I pursed my lips. "Okay, I'll ride Leo in the morning, then aim to get here maybe six-thirty after work. Once we've eaten, we're taking a trip over to see Mister Brooks."

"We are?" She opened both hands. "Why would we want to do that? The man's a rotten, two-timing, lowlife scum of the highest order."

"I'll tell you tomorrow." I tapped the side of my nose. "But keep it quiet—we don't want him to find out you're onto him."

CHAPTER SIX

Things at work the next morning were quieter than usual. Dev was away all day at an Apple developers' conference with the mobile app team, Nicholas was also out at some management briefing, and Manda had her headphones on and was engrossed in whatever she was looking at on her screen.

With my take-out coffee to oil the cogs in my brain, I spent most of the morning examining the SmartNet results. I was thinking about putting that to one side and doing some Secret Santa investigating, when Nicholas arrived back in the office and stopped by my desk.

"Any progress?" he asked, direct and to the point as usual.

I sighed heavily. "Nothing concrete so far, sorry. I've got a network sniffer monitoring our internal data traffic, which takes quite a lot of analysis, but it hasn't thrown up anything. Yet," I added.

"What about the dark net?"

"Drew a blank there. But everything Antoine sent seemed to be internal, so I think I need to focus here," I waved an arm in a circle to indicate the Bleubank building, "rather than outside."

A flash of something crossed his face, so quickly that I wasn't quite sure what I saw—possibly fear? But then his usual stony mask slipped back into place.

Keeping an eye on his expression, I added, "If there are hackers getting into our system, then the sniffer should pick that up."

He nodded, giving the briefest of smiles. "Yes. Sounds like you're on the case. Keep it up." And with that, he strode off to his desk.

I narrowed my eyes at his retreating back. Suspicion furrowed my brow. Could he have something to do with the hacking? But then, why would he have put me onto this task?

Unless... Could he have been ordered to allocate a member of his team to this project? Was I some kind of patsy?

Had he not told me specially to bring my incognito laptop to Monday's meeting? And yet none of the others had computers there. It was like he'd already decided, on Friday night when he phoned, that he'd give the job to me.

Perhaps he hoped I would fail, and he'd get away with—whatever it was he was up to. With a groan of frustration, I glowered at Nicholas' hunched shoulders and bent head, which was all I could see of him from here.

This task had me searching for shadows, suspicious of everyone and anything. What I needed was some kind of clue, or better still an answer, so I'd know what was *actually* going on and could work out who was responsible.

Maybe the thing to do was to have a break for lunch, clear my head, and then go through what I knew so far and try to make sense of it. Pushing myself up out of my chair, I headed for the kitchen area.

Once the kettle had boiled, I made a cup of coffee and headed back to my desk. Delving in my bag, I found the sandwich I'd bought on the way into work, ripped open the packaging and took a bite.

The tuna and sweetcorn roll was fairly unexciting, but while I ate it, I decided to check out Dwayne and Jasmin's social media again.

What I discovered nearly made me laugh out loud. Jasmin had posted another selfie of her with Dwayne, this time obviously taken in bed before they got up.

It amazed me that people would leave their Face-Book posts as public, in this day and age. Surely she should realise that *anyone* could see it? Anyway, there was no way Dwayne could deny their relationship now, so that would help Trinity's cause.

I spent a little while preparing some documents for our show-down with Dwayne that night, and then it was time to get back to work. Or rather, back to my investigations.

From my bag, I pulled out the Secret Santa card. It was starting to look somewhat dog-eared. I looked from the typewritten rhyme to the laptop screen, wondering, once again, if the two mysteries were connected.

On a whim, I opened the most recent file of SmartNet results, and searched for 'The Secret'. Nothing. Then I tried 'Robin Hood'. Still nada. 'Robin H00d' with zeroes was next, and suddenly I got a result!

Leaning forward, I stared at the screen, hardly believing my eyes. Did I *finally* have a breakthrough on this case?

"Hello?" said a loud voice.

I just about jumped out of my skin. Spinning round, I came face-to-face with Frank Varley. Well, face to chest, to be precise. I looked up, and realised that he was looking over my shoulder, at the laptop screen behind me.

A member of the computer support team, Frank had trouser hems hovering somewhere above his ankles, a check shirt covering a pigeon chest and a face that had been taken over by large black-rimmed glasses. He was the epitome of the IT geek.

"Hello Frank," I said, more loudly than I would normally speak, attempting to draw his attention to me, and away from my computer. At the same time, I scooted my chair back, so that my body would block the display. It also put some distance between me and Frank, who had an irritating habit of ignoring social mores regarding personal space.

Stubby fingers delved into his shirt pocket and pulled out a black tablet. He pushed the screen toward my face. "According to our records, you've downloaded some unauthorised software."

Resisting the impulse to check that Gremlin was still covered by the computer magazine I'd artfully placed at the side of my laptop, I shook my head. "I got something from the software library, that's all."

With a frown of irritation, he checked the tablet screen. "That's not what it says here."

"Let me see." I held out my hand for him to give me the device. What could I do to get rid of this idiot and back to my search results? I glanced at the display. "Yes. SmartNet. It's in the software library." I returned the gadget. "Go and check it yourself."

He planted his feet. "Show me." A finger waggled imperiously at my computer.

"Frank!" A sharp voice interrupted him.

We both turned, to see Nicholas facing us with his hands on his hips.

"Stop bothering Izzy. She's working on some data for me, and she's got a tight deadline." With a raised palm, he wiggled his fingers in the direction of the exit. "Let her get on with her work."

Frank jutted his jaw. "I just need—"

"No, you don't." My boss pointed at the door again. "She has my full authority, and if you delay her any further, I'll be reporting you to Pam." Pamela Emerson was Frank's boss.

With his tail between his legs, and muttering under his breath, Frank scuttled off.

"Thanks," I said, hoping that Nicholas wouldn't hang around, for he might see what was displayed on my screen. And had Frank seen it? It wouldn't make much sense if you didn't know about the issues I was investigating, but I was already suspicious of Nicholas.

Although... would he have defended me against Frank if he was the one doing the hacking? I smiled up at him and gave him a nod. Fortunately, he took the hint and strode away to his desk.

Mentally wiping my brow, I turned back to the laptop.

Someone had used 'RobinHood' to log in to a deposit account on one of our banking servers. I clicked onto the account details. Large sums of money—*exceedingly* large sums—came into and out of the account on a regular basis. The interest that accrued was significant and regularly withdrawn. But... there was something about the account that looked off.

It took me a minute to work out what was wrong, and then I sat up taller, my mouth open in disbelief.

"Izzy!" Nicholas' sharp voice called my name from a couple of desks down.

Suppressing a sigh of annoyance, I stood up and looked over the partitions. "Yes?"

"Can we go to meeting room two? I have the details of your bonus for this year."

The expression on his face was stony, and I didn't fancy my chances of arguing for another slot. "Okay," I said, inwardly groaning. "Be right there."

With a longing look at the interesting information on my laptop screen, I closed it down, so prying eyes wouldn't see what I was working on. After removing the Gremlin USB and looping the chain round my neck, I grabbed a notepad and pen, and followed him out of the office.

The meeting about my bonus was relatively short, and relatively unexciting. Rather than the five and six-figure sums I'd heard some of my longer-serving colleagues talk about in the past, this year I was to receive a relatively modest four-figure sum.

Being as I hadn't particularly expected it or relied on it, I was happy with that amount. It would be in my bank account by the new year, so I'd have a think between now and then about what I'd do with it.

It wasn't enough to make any significant purchase like a house or car, and not enough to be worth investing, so I would probably either spend or save. Or maybe a bit of both...

I was musing on that while I returned to the office. Nicholas had asked me to send Manda up next, and I was just passing my desk on the way to hers when something pulled me up short. My heart started to hammer in my chest.

Someone's been sitting on my chair. I felt like one of Goldilocks' three bears. The laptop screen, which I'd closed before I left the office, was sitting open, and my chair was facing the desk, when I'd left it facing outwards.

A chill ran down my spine. Was someone spying on me? Rounding the partition, I waved to get Manda's attention. She pulled off her headphones. "Hi Manda,

Nicholas wants to see you in meeting room two. But, did you notice if anyone was at my desk in the last wee while?"

She waggled her head. "No, nobody that I saw."

"You sure? I left my computer closed, and now it's open."

She craned her neck to see over the divider. "Could be you forgot," she said dismissively, then ostentatiously closed down her own computer, before gliding off to the meeting room.

I clenched my jaw. Who could have been at my desk? We weren't away that long. Trying to appear casual, I scanned the other desks around our pod. Nobody was paying any attention, and a lot of the seats were empty.

Nicholas was ruled out, I realised, since I'd been with him and left him upstairs before I came straight back. Between that fact and his intervention with Frank, I was starting to trust him again.

Could it have been Manda? She had a real brass neck if it was. And why would she? She always seemed too caught up in her own work—and her trashy gossip magazines—to be worried about mine.

Maybe Frank had come back and snooped, his jobsworth instincts compelling him to discover what was really on my computer? He was perhaps the most likely candidate.

Whoever it was, my hackles were up, and I couldn't let it go. Locking the laptop in my desk drawer, I hurried out of the open-plan area and down the stairs to the large Computer Support office where

Frank worked. If it had been him, I had an idea of how to winkle that out.

The first section on the left was the noisy one, where a lone guy and two ladies clacked away at their keyboards as they talked nineteen to the dozen into their headset microphones. Those were our phone support IT staff, a thankless task, if you asked me. They had constant targets and no real letup in the barrage of questions and help requests that came in to them, every minute of every hour, from random members of the public.

In the middle of the area was a large, almost square arrangement of desks with so many monitors and computers on it that the owner could have used a different one each day of the week. It was Pamela Emerson's workspace, but she wasn't there right now.

There were some empty seats at the far end of the room. Possibly Pam was also having a series of meetings about bonuses with her staff. Maybe that's what the management briefing Nicholas had been at this morning was all about—how to break it gently to your team members that they were getting very little in their Christmas stocking from Santa Bleubank. I clenched my fists.

Beyond Pam's desk was the main computer support area. Grouped there were the technicians who installed and fixed the hardware and software used in Bleubank's London offices. I was making a beeline for Frank's desk when I caught sight of a strange—yet familiar—face, which drew me up short.

It was the guy from the café yesterday lunchtime,

the one who'd been talking to Walter Oxley the CFO. What was he doing here?

Taking a minute to school my features into something other than surprise or anger, I pretended to study a leaflet on Pam's desk. Why would a mere computer tech be meeting a member of our board of directors for lunch? It seemed strange. Unless he wasn't a part of the support department? But then why would he be sitting here?

There was only one way to find out...

"Afternoon, guys," I said, then looked pointedly at Oxo's lunch date. "Is that you got a new team member?"

He stood up in a waft of lemony aftershave and held out a hand. "Lee Isaacson. I've been transferred from the Birmingham office." Gone was the suit from yesterday—presumably a first-day nerves thing—but he still appeared a little starchy in a blue shirt with all the buttons done up, a paisley-patterned golfing pullover and dark trousers with a crease down the front of each leg so sharp it could take your eye out.

I shook his hand. His grip was about as droopy as a daffodil after Easter, and I had to resist the desire to wipe my palm on the seat of my leggings. "I'm Izzy Paterson from the IT Security team. Nice to meet you," I said, pasting a fake smile on my face. "When did you start here?"

"Just arrived yesterday," he replied. I couldn't quite

place his accent, but it wasn't Birmingham, for sure. His voice was over-loud, almost as if he was slightly deaf.

At the third desk was Charlie Thwaite. With her part-shaved, part-spiky hair, skinny jeans, fitted grey t-shirt and black leather jacket, she looked far too 'street' to be working in IT. She was the most relatable member of their team, and I was always glad if it was her who answered any call-outs on our floor. I resolved to get her alone when I could find a chance, and ask her along to Friday's karaoke night. It would be good to have some more girls there. But I didn't want straight-laced Frank to get wind of the event. He'd be sure to put a dampener on things.

"I actually came down to see Frank," I said, turning to face the bespectacled technician. Watching his face closely, I continued, "I remembered after you left the office earlier. I *did* install another app on my laptop—some spy software that records keystrokes and timestamps them." I was lying through my back teeth, but I was hoping the threat of being logged by this software might flush out the person who'd used my computer.

There was no reaction from Frank other than a flaring of his nostrils, but out of the corner of my eye I saw a flash of movement from Lee. I glanced over, but he'd dropped his head and was studying something on his phone.

Frank, meantime, was pushing a piece of paper at me across his desk. "Software installation record form. SIRF. Fill it in and return it to us." He fixed me with a beady eye. "Next time, complete the form first," he commanded.

I grabbed the paperwork and turned to leave, stealing one last peek at Lee before I went. He lifted his head and gave me a sideways look, his jaw jutting. I couldn't work out if he was annoyed at me for not sticking to the rules, or if there was something else going on.

From his reaction, it didn't seem that Frank would have been the one to snoop on my computer. Could it have been Lee? But why? He only started yesterday and would hardly have had time to use his *own* PC, let alone be logging in to mine. And Frank was the one who'd been in our office earlier.

My feet dragged as I climbed the stairs. Who on earth was the baddie here? I seemed to have more clues than ever, but no idea who was hacking into our systems. Sadly, I was also clueless as to whether they were outsiders, or if it was an inside job.

However, I *did* now know what was going on.

Arriving back at our office, I seated myself at my desk and retrieved the laptop. Opening the lid, I stared at the figures on the screen before me.

Just before Nicholas had interrupted me, asking me to attend the bonus meeting, I'd worked out that the Robin Hood account I'd been looking at was being used as a temporary 'pass-through' account for large sums of foreign currency.

They'd be deposited in the account one day and transferred out the next. Nothing stayed in the account for any longer than twenty-four hours, which was very unusual. But that single day in a high-earning account was enough to amass significant amounts of interest.

It wasn't clear to me where the foreign currencies were coming from, but it mightn't matter. If only I could discover where that interest was being transferred to, perhaps I'd find our miscreant.

Flexing my fingers, I poised my hands above the keyboard, determined to discover who was receiving these large amounts of dosh. Was Robin Hood really taking from the rich to give to the poor, like in the legend? It was time to 'follow the money' and find out.

CHAPTER SEVEN

Two hours later, I was just about tearing my hair out.

The interest from the Robin Hood pass-through account was withdrawn and transferred to another deposit account, where it would stay for a day. Then it was siphoned off from there into a different account, and so on, and on, like a daisy chain, accumulating further interest along the way.

It reminded me of the anonymous shell corporations that shady businessmen used to evade tax—or the law. But, perplexingly, these deposit accounts had no beneficiary information associated with them. Not even the main Robin Hood account had an owner's name linked to it. And unless I could find the payee's name, I wouldn't be able to work out who had set up this elaborate scheme.

All I could think was that the accounts had been generated electronically by a computer program, because to have been set up manually by the normal channels, an account would have a name and address associated with it.

So that narrowed my list of suspects to people who had computer programming skills. The number of Bleubank staff with a background in writing software was limited. But an external hacker could do something like that with their eyes closed and their hands tied behind their back.

Pulling out my secret project notebook, I was about to start noting down names, when I noticed the time. *Rats.* I'd need to get a wiggle on if I wanted to arrive home for six-thirty like I'd promised Trinity. My list of suspects would have to wait.

Desk tidied and laptop locked away, I grabbed my stuff and hurried across the office, out into the hall and then through the door to the back stairs.

With an exclamation of annoyance, I pulled up short. For some reason the lights were out, and the stairwell was in darkness. It was so black that I couldn't even see the banisters I knew must be just a few feet in front of me.

Pulling out my phone, I flicked to the torch app, clicked a few buttons, and, like magic, a circle of light illuminated the wall to either side of the doorway. In common with other horsey girls who often had to negotiate dark barns or paddocks, I was a regular user of the phone's flashlight function.

Aha! I spotted the light switch and pressed it down. But nothing happened.

Frowning, I tried again—with the same result, of course—then berated myself for stupidly expecting something to change. Presumably a fuse had blown, and that was why the lights were out.

I looked from the black stairs to the door behind me, and contemplated going the long way round to the main staircase. But, since I already had the torch out, laziness won, and I decided to find my way down in the dark. Surely if I could negotiate a dark, muddy field, I could manage a few stairs.

But I'd only taken two steps down the first flight when the beam of light from my phone glinted on something thin and silvery. I gasped, and my foot stopped, hovering in midair. Carefully, ever so carefully, I put it back down. Was that...?

Reaching down, I played the light along the length of the tread. There was an almost invisible wire, positioned exactly where, if I hadn't spotted it first, it would've tripped me and sent me flying down the flight of concrete steps.

Had some saboteur put it there deliberately? My blood ran cold. Surely you wouldn't do this accidentally? And, had it been meant for someone else, or for me? Feeling paranoid, I shone the torch beam around, then up and down the stairwell, making sure I was alone.

Taking a deep breath, I took a tight hold of the banister and stepped very carefully over the wire. My pulse thumping in my ears, I negotiated the rest of the stairs with extreme caution, but there didn't appear to be any further booby-traps.

When I reached the ground floor, I almost ran across to the reception desk and gabbled at the security guard. "You have to come." I gestured wildly behind me. "There's a trip wire on the stairs and I nearly fell. The lights are out. We have to stop anyone else from coming down there."

A stocky, middle-aged man with a foxy face and thinning hair, Harry McPhail was an ex-policeman with designs on an easier life for his last few years of work, and plans to retire to the South Coast. To give him his due, even though I must've sounded like a total lunatic, he didn't try to have me committed. Instead, with raised eyebrows, he silently picked up his cap, reached under the desk for a torch, then walked around to join me.

"Lead on, Miss Paterson," he said, motioning toward the stairs, then pulled a radio out of his pocket. Pushing a black button on the top, he spoke into the handset. "Blue four to control. Investigating a report of an obstacle in our southwest stairwell." He switched it off and whispered to me. "Which floor?"

"Second."

Harry relayed that information, then pushed through the door to the stairs, with me following close behind. Reaching across, he flicked the light switch—and the lights came on!

My mouth hung open. "What?" I turned to him. "They were off a minute ago, I swear. I tried the switch on our landing."

His eyebrows raised again, then he shrugged. "Could be the switch is faulty." He jerked his chin up the stairs. "Show me where you saw this wire."

I led him up the dull grey steps until we reached the spot where I'd narrowly avoided breaking my neck. Except—there was nothing there. No tripwire, and no sign anything had *ever* been there. I gazed angrily around. Was someone playing tricks on me? But, as before, the stairwell was empty.

"It was here," I said, pointing across the step and indicating where the wire had been. "Three steps down. Honest it was. Tied round the metal railing on either side. It must have been moved."

Harry took off his peaked hat and scratched his head. "Now, Miss Paterson, I'm sure you're not one for flights of fancy. But, the facts are, the lights are working and there's nothing on the stairs." He gave me a level stare. "Could you have been mistaken?"

"I know what—" I stopped myself. I had been going to tell him that I knew what I saw. But there was no wire there now, and no evidence there ever had been. Berating myself for not taking a photo as proof, I sighed.

Voices approached the door above us, and a couple of staff members pushed through and clattered past down the stairs, wishing us a "Good night."

"Miss?" Harry prompted.

With a shake of my head, I took a step downwards. "Sorry to waste your time." My shoulders slumped. "I don't know what happened."

But as we descended, I grew more sure with every

stride that someone—presumably the Robin Hood hacker—somehow knew that I was onto them. And, because of that, they'd tried to incapacitate me. Or worse.

My mouth went dry. Things were getting serious now.

Strap-hanging on my way home in the underground, the situation at work kept going round and round in my head.

The stations on my route passed in a blur of white tiles, crowded platforms and bright lights. Lost in my thoughts in the jam-packed compartment of the tube train, I swayed and rocked and bounced as the carriage barrelled along the metal rails, oblivious to the chatter of the surrounding travellers, and the smell of soot and humanity that pervaded the air in these underground vehicles.

What I kept coming back to was: if the tripwire really *had* been intended for me—and the fact that it disappeared as soon as I'd gone into the main concourse supported that—then it pointed to the Robin Hood hacker being someone on the inside. One of my colleagues in Bleubank, not an external perpetrator. Which narrowed the list of suspects considerably, but scared the pants off me.

The attempt to nobble me must mean that I was getting close to an answer. But how would the hacker know that I was making progress with the investigation?

And how did they know that I was leaving the office, timing it just right to set the wire and fuse the lights? I wasn't the only person who used the back stairs. Could they somehow be spying on *me*, the way I was snooping on them via the network sniffer? Or was it someone nearby, who'd spotted me putting my things away?

The thought that I was being observed so closely chilled my bones.

CHAPTER EIGHT

The aroma that met me when I entered my flat was indescribably amazing. And the wave of relief that washed over me when I realised that I was safely home was also rather surprising. I puffed out a big sigh and let my shoulders relax.

After dropping my bag on the floor by the door and hanging my coat, I hurried through to the kitchen. "Evening. That smells incredible!" I said, craning my neck to see into the steaming pot that Trinity was stirring on the stove. "What is it?"

"It's Jamaican black-eyed pea curry. And it's ready now," she replied with a smile.

"Oh wow. I can't wait, it looks delicious."

Trinity spooned fluffy white rice onto two plates, then topped it with the fragrant, creamy sauce.

From the first bite, I was in heaven. "Trinity, this must be the best veggie curry I've ever tasted. Where d'you learn to cook like that?"

"Well now, I'd have to thank my Jamaican grandmother. She loved to cook, and she taught my dad, and then me when I was just a little thing." She tucked a lock of her long, black hair behind her ear. "It was Dad did most of the cooking in our house. 'E said it relaxed him."

"Feel free to carry on the tradition," I said with a wink. Preparing food was *not* my favourite pastime. Eating, yes. But if it took longer than twenty minutes to cook, I wasn't interested.

Trinity laughed. "What're you like! But I don't mind cooking when I've got the time. I find it relaxing too. Now, tell me," she put her fork down and leaned on her elbows, looking intently over the table at me, "how d'you get on today? Did you find the hacker?"

I made a face. "Nearly. But he—or she—must know I'm onto them. There was a tripwire across the stair when I came out of the office tonight, and all the lights were out. It's lucky I noticed it."

"Seriously?" Her eyes turned to saucers. "What did the police say?"

Colour rose in my cheeks. "We didn't call them. I got the security guard, but by the time we got back up the stairs, the lights were working and the tripwire was gone. I'm not sure he believed me."

"Men!" Trinity slammed her fist down on the table. "Does it need you to get a broken neck before they take you seriously?"

"Hopefully not!" I tried to lighten the atmosphere. The male of the species obviously wasn't at the top of Trinity's Christmas Card List at this moment in time.

"You should tell your boss."

I tapped my fork against my bottom lip. "Actually, I think you're right. This is getting too much for me on my own. I'll tell him tomorrow. But now," I pointed at her half-full plate, "let's eat up so we can go and sort Dwayne out. That guy needs to know he can't mess with my friend!"

I had to admit to feeling a little nervous as we climbed the stairs to Dwayne's second-floor flat. A bulb was out on the first-floor landing, which had me clutching at my bag, wondering if I could use it as makeshift cudgel if need be. In heels, tights and a business suit, I felt like an actor playing a part. Which I guess I was.

Someone had been cooking cabbage, and the metallic smell hung in the still air like a bizarre chemical weapon. In a flat down the corridor, another resident was murdering a cat. No, wait... they were practicing scales on a violin. The RSPCA could stand down.

Trinity stopped outside a dented white door. "Ready?" she asked.

Smoothing down my skirt, I took a deep breath. "Yep. Let's go for it."

She leaned on the rusty doorbell, and, somewhere inside the flat, tinny Westminster chimes announced our arrival. Half a minute later, Dwayne threw the door open with a belligerent, "Yeah?" before he even saw who was there.

I stepped forward, my heels clicking on the concrete hallway. "Dwayne Brooks? Dwayne Jeffrey Brooks?"

He crossed his arms and leaned against the doorjamb, just like he had in Jasmin's photo. "Yeah. What's it to you?" With a baseball cap crammed over his short black hair, three gold chains hanging around his neck, and the crotch of his trousers drooping somewhere around his knees, Dwayne looked like an extra in a rap video.

"I'm Isobel Paterson of Paterson, Paterson and Banks. I'm here on behalf of my client, Ms Trinity Allen." I swivelled my eyes over my shoulder at Trinity, then pulled a piece of letterhead paper—for my fictional company of lawyers, concocted this lunchtime—out of my bag and thrust it at him. "This is a cease and desist letter, ordering you to stop harassing my client for rental monies."

He shoved it back at me. "You can go take a hike."

Holding up my hands, I refused to accept the letter from him. "We have evidence that, firstly, you are contravening the rules of your tenancy by sub-letting to another party, and secondly, that you have already replaced my client with another tenant, namely one Jasmin Freeman, and therefore Ms Allen now owes no rent."

Pointing a finger at my face, Dwayne started to bluster, "But, but—"

I cut him off. "Should you bother my client again,

we will be forced to inform your landlord of the illegal sub-let." Signalling that our meeting was at an end, I clicked shut the catch on my shoulder bag. My frosty smile didn't reach my eyes. "Good evening, Mr Brooks." Then I turned on my heel and marched off down the corridor, followed quickly by Trinity.

We were almost at the bottom of the stairs when I could hold it in no longer. Leaning back against the wall, I let the laughter loose. "His face!" I cried, tears running down my cheeks.

Trinity was holding her sides. "Priceless, it was. Priceless! You should join the Royal Shakespeare, Izzy. That were some performance!"

Fishing a tissue from my pocket, I wiped my eyes. "Hopefully that's the last you'll see of him."

"An' good riddance too!"

On the way home, Trinity and I stopped off to buy some celebratory ice cream. It seemed counter-intuitive, since the weather was on the frosty side of normal, but we passed the drive-through outlet and both had a hankering at the same time. The plan was to make some hot chocolate, put our feet up in front of an episode of CSI, and gorge ourselves on delicious creamy dessert.

You know what they say about the best-laid plans...

As I turned the car through the short brick pillars flanking the entrance to my apartment building, I jammed on the brakes, gasping in surprise. Before us in the car park were crowds of people, a red fire engine with its blue lights flashing, and beside that a white plumber's van.

My pulse hammering, I craned my neck, looking for the fire. Or smoke. But I couldn't see any. There was just a throng of residents flanked by brown-uniformed firefighters wearing yellow helmets.

In the passenger seat beside me, Trinity was also gaping out of the window. "What's going on?" she asked, just as a dark-haired, chunky fireman strode toward us and motioned for me to roll down the window.

He leaned in to speak to us. "Evening, miss." He noticed Trinity and inclined his head at her, an appreciative glint in his eye. "Ladies, sorry. May I ask why you're visiting here this evening?" His breath smelled of peppermint and his voice sounded like chocolate.

"I'm not visiting. I live here."

"Ah." A radio crackled in Officer After-dinner-mint's top pocket, and he pulled it out and frowned at it. Then he turned back to me. "Which flat?"

"Two C."

"Ah." This time the simple word carried layers of meaning. My heart sank.

"Is something wrong, Officer?"

He tilted his head at a parking space near the road. "Park your car over there, and I'll get the super to have a word with you." He moved away and started speaking into the radio handset.

Starting the car again, I glanced over at Trinity. Her face was tight, her normally smiling mouth set in a line of concern. “I’ve not got a good feeling about this,” I said.

“Neither have I.”

With a growing sense of dread, we got out of the car and headed toward the entrance. I sniffed the air, but couldn’t smell smoke. This was a weird fire. If that’s what it was...

We were met by another fireman, this time a taller guy with a silver stripe on his collar, grey goatee and light blue eyes. “Ladies,” he greeted us, “Officer Yourdis tells me you live in apartment two C.”

I nodded, scared that if I spoke my voice would come out in a squeak.

“And your landlord is Mr Bashir Noorzai?”

“Yes.” Yep, I was right. I sounded like a mouse.

He sucked air through his teeth. Beside me I thought I heard Trinity whimper. Officer Yourdis hovered on the edge of the crowd in front of us, looking concerned.

“Has the flat burned down?” I asked, running through a mental checklist to try and think if we’d left any appliances on, or left something flammable next to a heater. But nothing came to mind. We’d not been home for long that evening, just enough time for dinner and then quickly getting changed before we went to Dwayne’s.

“No,” his chin jerked up. “Not that. But your neighbour in the flat above has gone on holiday.”

“Yes. The Steadmans.”

“The same.” He hooked a gloved thumb around the flashlight strapped below his right shoulder. “Unfortunately, they left a tap dripping in their bath, and the stopper was in. It overflowed this evening and took down part of the ceiling in your flat."

"Oh no!" My hand flew to my mouth.

Out of the corner of my eye, I saw Trinity start to sway. Before I could grab her, Officer Yourdis was there, propping her up and guiding her over to a bench at the entrance to the communal garden.

I had to leave my friend in the care of the firefighter, because at that moment I was confronted by my landlord, Mr Noorzai, all waving hands and rolling eyes and effusive apologies.

"Miss Paterson, Miss Paterson," he said, almost bowing before me, "it is so terrible what has happened, so terrible. I am so sorry. So very sorry. But," he raised a hand and smiled at me, showing a row of impossibly white teeth, "I have a proposition to make. A proposition for you."

I blinked. I hadn't been propositioned by a man for a long time. A *very* long time. Even one in a shiny brown suit, slip-on shoes and thin moustache.

"On the top floor," Mr Noorzai continued, "I have a flat for rent. A most lovely apartment. Fully furnished, with the two bedrooms, a bathroom with shower, and a kitchen with the built-in oven. Most excellent."

"That's good," I replied, not quite sure what he was expecting me to say.

"For you," he said, looking pleased with himself.

"For me?" I repeated, frowning.

"Yes. You must take that flat, you can live there

most comfortably while the builders repair your place. For no extra charge."

"No extra charge?" I repeated again, my eyebrows climbing my forehead.

"Yes, no extra. Until your place is ready. Just continue the bank payment every first of the month as you do now."

I flicked my eyes at the bearded firefighter, who was still beside me. He lifted his shoulders.

"Uh, okay," I said to my landlord, hardly believing my luck. A two-bedroom flat in London would usually cost a good few hundred extra pounds per month. Maybe several hundred. "Thank you. But," I glanced across at Trinity, who was sitting on the wooden bench, being ministered to by the younger fireman, "is it all right if I have a friend to stay with me? She's between places right now and had to move out at short notice."

Mr Noorzai followed my gaze. "Of course, of course. And," his mouth curved into a smile, "if you should both be deciding to continue on in the top-floor flat, I might perhaps maybe be persuaded to give you a most generous deal on the rental." I could almost see the pound signs scrolling before his eyes. Fishing in his pocket, he produced a keyring, placing it in my hand with a flourish.

"Great. Thanks, Mr Noorzai. We'll get moved in then."

I turned to the firefighter. "Are we able to get our things from the flat?"

He held up a finger, then said something unintelligible into his radio. A crackly voice seemed to reply in the affirmative, because he nodded at me. His eyes swung to the garden bench. "I'll get Officer Yourdis to accompany you and make sure everything is safe."

When we were finally installed in the new flat, I was almost falling asleep on my feet, and Trinity had a dinner date with a handsome firefighter on Thursday evening.

Leaning against the front door, I surveyed my new domain. Similar in layout to my old flat, it was just a little bigger all over—plus it had a second bedroom, so Trinity didn't need to sleep on the couch.

Everything was white or grey, with an accent wall in the lounge area which was decorated in a warm plum shade. Overall, the effect was quite restful. "I could get used to this," I said to Trinity, who had fallen into the grey leather couch with a sigh of contentment.

"I'm trying not to," she said, swivelling her feet back onto the floor and twisting round to look at me. "I'll need to start flat-hunting again tomorrow."

Pursing my lips, I stared at her for a moment.

"What?" she asked, looking alarmed.

"What if..." I was thinking aloud, which was not my normal modus operandi, being more of a planner. "What if we stayed on here? We've got the first month effectively for free. There are two bedrooms. You could save yourself a lot of hassle and move in here. With me. Then you don't have to find another place."

She scrunched her nose and waved an arm round the room. "Someone like me couldn't ever afford somewhere like this. It's way above my pay grade."

"Hmmm." I went over to the dining table, where

my computer stuff had been placed, temporarily, and switched on my laptop. A minute later, I'd found Mr Noorzai's advert for the flat. Like I'd thought, it was a chunk more expensive than the one downstairs. "How much were you paying at Dwayne's?" I asked.

When she told me, I did a quick calculation. "If you could afford to keep paying that, we could both stay here, and I'd actually save a little each month."

"Are you serious?" Her face brightened.

"Yeah. We could share the cooking, share the bills—that will probably make things even cheaper for both of us."

She came to look over my shoulder at the advert. "Oh, I can't have that. You'd be paying more than me. That's not fair."

"It's fine. It's less than I'm paying right now, and this is a nicer place."

She still didn't look convinced.

"Tell you what," I said, stifling a yawn, "since it's all paid for, let's give it to the end of the month." I shut the laptop down. "Or at least till I go home for Christmas. We can see how we're getting along, and how we like it here in the daylight, and then decide."

My yawn must've been infectious, because Trinity couldn't speak for a minute. She just bobbed her head, then mumbled. "Okay. Deal!"

Sleepily, I stumbled to my new bedroom, passing the forlorn tub of ice-cream melting quietly on the kitchen counter. I shook my head. This evening definitely hadn't gone the way I'd expected.

CHAPTER NINE

As soon as I arrived at work the next morning, I dumped my bag at my desk and made a beeline for Nicholas. "Can I get a word with you?" I asked.

He looked up at me over his glasses, frowning. I could see the annoyance in his face, but something in my demeanour must've changed his mind, because his expression altered to one of concern. He grabbed his tablet and stood. "Let's go and see if there's a meeting room free."

Five minutes later, I'd told him the story of the trip-wire and the intruder on my computer, and he appeared even more grave. "This all happened yesterday afternoon, you say?"

"Yes."

If he'd pressed his lips together any harder, they'd have disappeared. "Devlin was away all day at that conference, wasn't he?" Nicholas asked, rhetorically.

I nodded.

He picked up the grey phone in the middle of the table and dialled Dev's extension. "Devlin," he barked, "join us in meeting room three." Putting the handset down, he turned to me. "It can't have been Devlin, since he wasn't here."

"That's what I thought too. Rules him out." A smile flickered on my lips. I was glad it wasn't my friend. "And it probably rules out external hackers too."

"Which means someone internal." Nicholas' eyes narrowed, and his long fingers drummed on the table, as if he were going through a list of our colleagues in his head, just like I had yesterday.

When he walked in a minute later, Dev's eyes widened when he saw me. "Morning," he said, then pulled out the chair opposite Nicholas.

Our boss took his glasses off and put them down. "Devlin, Izzy has been working on a special project for me."

"The annual report, yes." Dev leaned back, glancing from one of us to the other.

Nicholas scratched his beard. "It's a little more than that." He glanced across at me. "And now it's got somewhat more... complicated. I need you to double-team on this. Literally. Izzy isn't to go anywhere alone—you'll go to lunch together, and please can you see her to the station after work."

"What about the toilet?" Dev asked, obviously thinking this was some kind of joke.

"You can wait outside. And if she takes longer than five minutes, you phone security."

Dev looked from one of us to the other. "Seriously?"

"Deadly serious." Nicholas stood up, abruptly. "Izzy, you can fill Devlin in on the details. Two heads should be better than one. Maybe you can get this solved today, and we can all stop worrying."

The door slammed behind him, and Dev turned to me, his mouth open. "What's going on?"

"Let's go get a coffee. Caffè Fiorio. I need some caffeine, and I think we need to get out of the office for me to tell you the story."

Dev put down his china cup with a thump and stared at me, his eyes like saucers. "You're never serious?" A couple of people in the café turned to look at him, and he lowered his voice somewhat before he carried on. "There's someone at work stealing money from our systems and now they've tried to kill you?"

My hand shook a little as I put down my own cup. "I suppose... I hadn't thought of it in as stark terms as that, but, yes, that about sums it up."

He banged his fist on the table and swore. Quietly. "We need to get them, Izzy, before they get us." Green eyes caught mine. "Did you make a list of suspects yet?"

"Only in my head."

"Okay, let's start with that. We need to know who we're dealing with."

Somehow, it made me feel better that he was

saying 'we'. The task of finding the hacker had seemed quite daunting when I was on my own, especially when there were so few clues. But with two of us on the job, surely we'd crack the case really quickly? It had to be easier... didn't it?

On our way back to the office, we passed a newspaper stand, and one of the headlines caught my eye. I stopped abruptly, which caused Dev to almost crash into me. "Look." I pointed.

'Bleubank profits slump', the sandwich board declared. *'Investors nervous.'*

My heart thumping, I turned to Dev. "We need to find this hacker, or none of us will have jobs come the new year."

I half expected him to argue, but for once he was silent, staring moodily at the newspapers in the kiosk. "You're right," he said after some moments. "This is serious."

We were both in a sombre mood when we got back to the office. The first thing I did was to scout around for a hidden spy camera, or something that would explain how the hacker knew my movements. But we didn't want them to know we were onto them, so I disguised my search by making it look like I was dusting my shelves and rearranging the items on my desk.

After polishing everything that didn't move, and possibly even a few things that did, I had found nothing. "Fancy a cup of tea?" I asked Dev, raising my eyebrows, so he'd know I wanted to talk—without being overheard.

He stood up with alacrity and grabbed his mug. "Sure thing."

I led the way to the kitchen area at the other end of the open-plan office. When we got there, two co-workers were in the process of making coffee, so Dev and I made small talk until they'd left.

When we had the place to ourselves, he filled the kettle and started it boiling. "So, did you find anything?" he asked, while he got his mug out of the cupboard.

"Nope. There's nothing on my desk. Unless I'm totally blind."

Dev stared intently at my eyes for a moment as if he was checking, then laughed when he saw my expression. "Gotcha!" he said. Then he leaned back against the counter so that he had a good view of the office. "Don't point," he said, "in case they're watching. But what about the bookshelves between our desks and the web team?"

Picking up my cup as if cradling a coffee, I went to stand beside him. "I see what you mean. That would give a perfect line of sight." I sighed. "But I won't get away with dusting there."

"No, probably you wouldn't." The kettle clicked off behind us, and Dev busied himself making his tea. "I could hunt for a book, though."

"True. And if it's not there?" I got my coffee things down from the cupboard.

"We can talk about it at lunchtime. Where d'you want to go? Caffè Fiorio again?"

"Just somewhere to get a sandwich. I can't afford to eat there every day."

"Tell me about it! Especially if the bonuses are to be low this year."

"They are. Did you have your meeting with the boss man yet?"

He shook his head. "With me being out of the office yesterday and then what's been going on this morning, there hasn't been a chance." He frowned at me. "How's that going to work, if I'm babysitting you?"

"You're not babysitting me," I said, pushing his arm. "You're working with me."

"Tomah-to, tomay-to," he said, with a wink. "Whatever."

I gave him some stink-eye, then thought for a minute. "I could go and visit Charlie in Computer Support. I wanted to ask her to the karaoke night without the guys overhearing. You could meet me there after."

"Okay, I'll speak to Nick when we get back and work something out." He gazed across the office again. "As for the spy cam, if I find anything, I'll call you over and ask if you know if there's a more recent edition of this book. If I don't, you'll know I drew a blank."

Dev didn't find anything.

❄

We reconvened at lunchtime. At a tiny, brightly painted shop owned by an industrious Polish man who insisted in calling me 'Madam' and Dev, 'Sir', we bought sandwiches.

Then we took them to a park bench outside a medieval church down a narrow side street a block away from the office. With walls made from irregular ancient stones, two wide stained glass windows above two solid wooden doors, and a small clock tower peeking above the roof, it was an intriguing building. Why two doors? One of these days I'd need to explore inside and find the answer.

Above our heads, a breeze rustled the leaves of an old oak tree. It also brought the scent of garlic from a nearby Italian restaurant. Dev's stomach rumbled, and I sneezed.

"Bless you," Dev said, automatically.

A bandy-legged grey-haired man shuffled down the steps from the church, turning his hat in his hands. The creases on his face and the stoop of his back made him look like he carried the cares of the world. I had an idea of how he felt.

"So," said Dev, taking a bite from his chicken sandwich. "What do we do now?"

Watching the old man shamble along the pavement, I pulled out my falafel wrap, and thought about the audiobook mystery I was listening to on my commute to work. "Hamish Macbeth always seems to investigate the backgrounds of his suspects, and he gets clues that way."

Dev looked at me like I'd grown an extra head. "Hamish who?"

I waved a hand dismissively. "He's a policeman in a mystery series. But you're missing the point. If we check out our suspects' backgrounds and find out who's got programming skills, we can see who might have been able to set up those shell accounts. Or we could go from the other end, see if anyone is spending lots of money—new car, new house, whatever."

Chewing on his sandwich, Dev's head bobbed slightly. "You might have something there. But... should we not keep following the trail of the bank accounts? It sounded like you'd got close to the last of them."

"That's true." We both ate in silence for some time while we mulled things over. "How about I carry on with the accounts, and you start investigating the list of suspects?"

Dev wrinkled his nose. "If I'm honest, I think you'd be better doing the social media stuff. Have you seen my FaceBook profile?"

I hadn't. But a few taps on my phone screen later, I was looking at an anonymous grey icon. "Looks just like you," I teased.

"Ha, ha," he said mirthlessly, taking a swig from the bottle of water he'd bought with his sandwich.

"What about Twitter? D'you do that?"

"Not me. I can't be bothered with all that phoney stuff, people trying to make their lives sound exciting." He looked sideways at me. "I prefer face-to-face. Real people."

I swallowed. The conversation seemed to be venturing into dangerous territory again. "Okay," I said brightly, "You follow the money, I'll spy on our colleagues."

There was a beat of silence. A muscle jumped in Dev's cheek. Then he said, "Talking about that, we still need to work out how the hacker knew you were leaving last night."

"Yeah. Maybe *they're* tracking the network, and they saw me logging out?"

"It could be. I'll look and see if there's a way to identify network scanners, check if anyone else is doing it apart from you."

I hesitated for a second, then blurted out, "There's something I need to tell you." My 'follow the money' comment had reminded me of the Secret Santa poem.

He stiffened.

"There's someone else who knows about the hacker. Apart from Nicholas, I mean. And Antoine."

Dev deflated a little. "Antoine?"

"In the Paris office. They were the first to notice the irregularities in the network. Anyway," I raised a hand impatiently, "at the Christmas party, my Secret Santa gave me a rhyme. A clue. That's how I knew to look for Robin Hood."

"Oh-kay." His forehead creased. "How come you never said at the time?"

"The rhyme said to keep it a secret."

"And you're telling me now because...?"

"Because you're off the suspect list."

He clutched his chest theatrically. "Moi?"

"I couldn't be sure. Until the tripwire thing. You were at that conference that day. So we figured you were innocent."

"We?"

"Me and Nicholas." I turned my palm up. "I suspected him, too, for a while."

"My, but you're the mistrustful one. So he's in the clear now?"

"He was out of the office when someone logged in to my computer."

Dev breathed out slowly. "Right. But Manda was there."

"In body. She had her headphones on, so she saw nothing. Or so she said."

"Hmm." Dev scratched at his designer stubble. "So, what do you think? Has she been taking out shares in 'Hello' magazine recently? Or buying her boots from Jimmy Choo?"

"Not that I've noticed."

He scrunched up his sandwich wrapper and dusted crumbs from his trousers. "Still, might as well start somewhere."

It felt yucky, investigating my colleagues. But Dev was right. We had to start somewhere. I just hoped we weren't stirring up a hornet's nest.

CHAPTER TEN

When we got back to the office, Nicholas wanted to meet with Dev about his bonus, so I phoned down to Charlie Thwaite in Computer Support and arranged to visit her.

My minder—Dev—parted ways with me outside the door. "I'll come and find you after my meeting. Stay with Charlie till then."

"Yes, Sir!" I clicked my heels together and saluted him.

His eye roll would've made a great internet meme, if only I'd had my phone out in time to video him. I resolved to catch him at it some day, then pushed into the support department's office.

Charlie waved when she saw me. "How's it going?"

I made a face. "Long story. What about you?"

"Fine." She picked up two mugs from her desk. "Let's go get a drink."

Charlie led me over to their kitchen area. It had a

similar layout to ours, but there were shouty notes posted on the fridge and cupboard doors reminding colleagues to 'clean up after yourselves' and 'if you didn't bring it, don't take it'. I had an idea who the passive-aggressive note poster was. "Frank's handiwork?" I asked Charlie, pointing at the Post-its adorning the refrigerator.

She snorted. "How d'you guess?"

A few minutes later we both had coffees, and I'd told Charlie about the karaoke night on Friday. "Want to come?" I asked.

"Will Dev be there?"

I blinked at her, my mouth falling open. "Dev? But he's—"

"I know, he doesn't look like my type. But I think he's cute. And funny. He reminds me of Chris O'Dowd."

"From *The IT Crowd?*"

"Yep."

Now that she'd said it, I couldn't get it out of my head. They weren't quite doppelgangers, but they *could* be distant cousins. "I'd never have guessed. Is that why you come to our floor so often when things need fixed?"

She held up her hands. "What can I say?"

"Well, Friday night was his idea, so I think it's safe to assume he'll be there."

"Friday night?" said a loud voice behind us.

"Oh, hi Lee." Charlie tilted her head at me. "Izzy's team Christmas night out," she lied.

"Really. Where you going?" He shuffled past us, all

starched shirt and lemon aftershave, then reached into the fridge, pulling out a can of Coke.

"A pub," I answered. "Nowhere special."

He waggled his eyebrows. "A pub is *always* special."

"Lee," Charlie made a shoo-ing motion with her hand, "we're having a girly chat here, and you're short an X chromosome."

Muttering under his breath, he sloped off.

Charlie shook her head. "He's only been here three days, and he's already getting on my wick."

"What's his story?" I asked, thinking that I could kill two birds with one stone, and do some information gathering on the new start while chatting with my friend.

She wrinkled her nose. "Silver spoon, if you ask me. Mr Oxley is his step-dad, and he got the job without so much as an interview. Although, to be fair, he knows his stuff. He's just a bit loud and obnoxious with it."

"Ah!" Light dawned. "That explains why we saw him having lunch with Oxo on Monday."

Charlie shrugged. "Probably."

"So what does he do when he's not at work?"

"Irons his shirts, most likely," she said sarcastically. "I dunno. We've not chatted much."

I didn't dare ask any more, in case she thought my interest in Lee was more than professional, and was about to change the subject, when Dev appeared round the corner. Beside me, Charlie sucked in a breath.

Catching my eye, he jerked his chin at the ceiling. "Nick wants you for a meeting."

I feigned surprise. "Oh, okay." Stepping over to the sink, I emptied the dregs from my mug and rinsed it under the tap. "Thanks for the coffee, Charlie." I winked at her. "See you on Friday."

Quietly opening the door of the gym at the Community Centre, I tiptoed along the back of the room and found a space to unroll my exercise mat.

I was late, courtesy of a signalling fault on the District Line. Before I copied the rest of the class and lay down, I made a 'sorry' face to the Pilates teacher.

Queenie, a statuesque black woman in figure-hugging turquoise Lycra, was at the front, helping another client with their double leg stretch. She gave me a thumbs-up and then announced the next move to the class.

For an hour I contorted my body and flexed my limbs in an effort to build control in my 'core'—the muscles in my mid-section.

Although I quite enjoyed the classes, I didn't do Pilates solely for fun, but also to help with my horse riding. I'd realised a couple of years ago that the better balanced and controlled my body was in the saddle, the better Leo performed for me. So really, the Pilates was cross-training for my dressage.

However, another benefit to the class was that it

gave me time to think, and tonight's topic was the Robin Hood mystery.

Unfortunately, we'd got little further that afternoon. Dev had hit a brick wall tracing the deposit accounts, when he'd discovered that the next link in the chain was an account at a different bank. It wasn't impossible for him to trace, but it was a *lot* harder than finding information within Bleubank.

And I'd had no luck either. After hours spent surfing people's FaceBook profiles, hunting for evidence of extravagant spending, my eyes felt like they were crossing. But I'd found nothing. Could it be that we were looking at the wrong people? Or was the miscreant a master at hiding their tracks?

However, I wasn't done there. There were still the other social media channels to try. So that would be tomorrow's job.

I was just deciding where to start, when the door of the room burst open, and the janitor came clomping in. "Miss Queenie," he cried.

Everyone's heads turned to the back, then to Queenie at the front, like the spectators at a Wimbledon tennis match. "Yes, Eric?" Her voice was deep and melodious.

"You'll 'ave to stop the class, miss, I'm sorry." Murmurs of protest broke out at this pronouncement. "We're 'aving problems with the plumbing again, an' I'm going to 'ave to shut the place afore we get flooded." He swiped a hand across his bald head.

Queenie clapped her hands. "Ladies! You can all practice your spine flexes and your scissor holds at home. We were almost finished with tonight's class, anyway. So let's stand and do one forward fold before we go, to stretch out our bodies, ready for the days ahead."

Dutifully, we all clambered to our feet and reached our fingers towards our toes. The grumbling died down as we all concentrated on lengthening our backs.

"I shall see you all next week!" Queenie's voice was bright as she sent us on our way. Unfortunately, her optimism would prove ill-founded.

It was still dark when I arrived at the livery yard early on Thursday morning. A sheen of rain made the street lights sparkle like diamonds and the tarmac glistened like anthracite. Away from the main road, tall trees absorbed the traffic noise, and it was relatively quiet in the car park when I got out of my Corsa.

Inside the barn, however, was a hive of activity. Obviously, I wasn't the only one who planned on riding before work. Straw flew in the air, horses nickered in anticipation of their breakfast feed, and people chatted briefly before scurrying off to complete their tasks.

With my saddle over my arm, I was returning from the tack room and wondering whether I'd have time to clean the saddle after I finished riding, when Veronica Rothwell hustled across the barn. Veronica was the American lady whose horse had the stable opposite Leo.

"Izzy, dear," she said, touching my elbow and looking at me intently, "I need your help."

On the wrong side of forty, Veronica had one of those timeless faces that belied her age, and, even at this time of the morning, she somehow managed to look immaculate. With caramel-streaked hair cut in a sleek bob, an expensive quilted jacket and spotless beige jodhpurs, next to her I felt like a scruff. Then a waft of her Calvin Klein perfume made me sneeze.

"Excuse me," I said, then deposited my saddle over Leo's half-door and found a tissue in my pocket. "Sorry about that. What's up?"

"It's... you see... well, I heard, I heard you can find things out. About people. On FaceBook and suchlike."

I sighed inwardly. Trinity must've been talking. "Uh, perhaps. Tell me more?"

"Well, it's a trifle delicate..."

Giving her an encouraging smile, I reassured her. "Don't worry, I won't tell anyone." But I hoped she'd tell *me* in the next few minutes. I was on a schedule here, and if I wasn't in the saddle soon, I'd not have time to ride properly.

She pursed her lips. "It's like this. I met a man. On Tinder. You know, that swipe left, swipe right app?"

I nodded. I'd heard of it, just never had the inclination to use it.

"He seems like a lovely person—very caring, very intelligent—but I'm..." she cast her eyes down, as if searching for the right word, "There's just something about him... I'm not sure. I guess I'm worried he's only interested in me for the wrong reasons."

My brow scrunched. "Why would that be?"

"Well, for my money of course." She brushed an imaginary hair off her jacket. "After I lost my second husband, I—Well, let's just say, I've got a gold card and I know how to use it." She looked up at me again, her expression hopeful. "But Kenneth, well, I wonder if he might be number three. I just need to be sure about him. You understand?"

Something tickled at the back of my nose, and I had to turn away so I didn't sneeze all over her. "Sorry," I said, my eyes watering. "Uh, yes. But wouldn't you be better with a private investigator?"

"Oh, I might. But I don't want someone following him around the place. He may spot them." She put her hand over mine, briefly. "You would be *much* more discreet, darlin', I'm sure. Check him out for me, see if he is what he says he is."

With a sweet smile, she added, "And of course I'd pay you for your time. I've heard these PIs charge one hundred pounds per hour. Would that be sufficient?"

It took a lot of effort to stop my jaw dropping. If that really *was* the going rate for detective work, maybe I should think seriously about starting 'Izzy Investigates' after all. In the bank, I'd need to be promoted to the Board of Directors to earn that sort of money.

"Um, do you have a timescale in mind? It's just," I scuffed my boot on the concrete, "I'm pretty busy at the office just now and I've got a dressage competition next weekend with Leo. So I'm not sure how much spare time I'll have. I don't want to let you down."

"Well, it would be nice to have an answer before

Christmas—he's asked me to go away with him to a country hotel," she added in a hushed voice. "But really, anything at all that you can find for me would be just wonderful."

I swallowed. "I'll see what I can do." I motioned towards my stable. "Leave me a note of your phone number and his details, and I'll get it once I've ridden." I told her the information I needed about Kenneth, then checked my watch.

The conversation with Veronica had knocked me behind schedule, and I *really* had to get going, so I'd have time to work on my dressage.

Tack cleaning would have to wait.

CHAPTER ELEVEN

Thursday's investigations at work were almost as frustrating as Wednesday's. When it got to five o'clock, Dev plonked himself on a clear piece of desk in my workspace, and we had a pow-wow.

He had worked out which bank the Robin Hood money was going to—a small, privately owned bank in Switzerland—but, to find out more, he would basically have to hack into their systems. This was exactly the thing he was trying to prevent in his current job at Bleubank. So, if they had staff anywhere near as good as him, it would prove impossible.

"But you never know," he said, ever the optimist. "Their security might not be on par with ours. After all," he raised a cheeky eyebrow, "they haven't got *me* working for them."

"Let me scratch your head for you," I said, holding up my fingers. I was about ten feet away from him, but I reckoned his head was at least that big.

For my part, I was still trawling through social media, and had seen more photos of babies and cats than one person needed for a lifetime. It was enough to make my forehead feel like someone was squeezing it in a vice. But I hadn't yet found anyone buying luxurious yachts, dripping with diamonds or jetting off on expensive holidays.

"Perhaps I need to look somewhere else," I suggested, as I rooted in my bag for painkillers. "I'm searching for the results of their ill-gotten gains. Maybe I should try to narrow it down, and find out who's got the appropriate computer skills to do this in the first place."

Dev rubbed his chin. "You may be right. There's no point flogging a dead horse." His eyes widened when he saw my face. "Sorry, rotten choice of words. There's no point banging your head against a brick wall," he amended. "If you're getting nowhere, maybe now's time to try something new."

Taking a gulp from my water bottle, I swallowed two tablets. "So, I need to hack into our personnel files, d'you think?" The idea of that was almost as icky as snooping on people's social media.

He screwed up his nose. "It seems to me that a quick search there for degrees in computer science might save us both a lot of time and hassle."

"Have you any idea how well secured the Human Resources database is?"

"I'm sure it's pretty old—pre-Y2K technology. So probably not that good."

"Okay. I'll have a look at that tomorrow." I looked up at him. "Time to call it a night?"

"Sure," he said, swinging his legs off the desk he'd been sitting on. "I'll just go get my jacket."

Fifteen minutes later, Dev was waving me off outside Monument tube station, on his way to the Bank station where he'd catch the Docklands Light Railway to his shared flat on the Isle of Dogs.

Pushing through the barriers, I made my way down to the District Line platform. It was the height of rush hour, and everywhere was crowded and noisy.

With a whoosh of warm, smelly air, a Circle Line train arrived. Almost as one, the throng of commuters pushed forward and into the domed carriages with their sliding doors. I kept to the side, but with more people arriving every second, the platform quickly filled again and I found myself near the front.

A glance at the information board told me that my train would arrive in two minutes. *Time for some Hamish Macbeth.* With the station this busy, I reckoned I was bound to be standing for most of the journey.

From my pocket, I produced my earbuds and pushed them into my ears. It dulled the surrounding noises, but I'd wait till I was in the carriage to switch the audiobook on, so I'd be certain to hear the train coming.

Sure enough, a minute later, lights appeared in the tunnel entrance, and I stepped forward, preparing to board my train. But suddenly, something pushed me from behind—hard. Hard enough to force me to the very edge of the platform.

Dimly, I heard the crowd behind me gasp, as I teetered on the concrete lip above the tracks, illuminated in the headlights of the approaching train.

Throwing out my hands for balance, I tightened the core muscles I'd been working on at Pilates last night, and threw my weight backwards.

Just in the nick of time.

The engine of the tube train missed my nose by inches. Someone grabbed my arm, and someone else hauled on the back of my coat, and somehow I was standing there, upright, not lying splattered on the rails beneath.

"Are you okay?", "What happened?", "That were a near miss!" Voices filled the air, but I was still in action mode; reaction had not yet set in.

I spun around, searching the crowd behind me for anyone—or anything—suspicious. It was so busy that it was hard to be certain, but I was sure that I glimpsed a black-clad figure pushing through the mass of bodies and heading back toward the stairs. Was that my attacker? Or had it just been an accident? My brain was spinning.

Someone took my arm and led me into the carriage. Magically, a seat was free, and they ushered me onto it. "Are you all right, miss?" asked a young chap in an Arsenal top.

Nodding, I put my head in my hands and puffed out a loud breath. My heart was hammering, and I didn't trust myself to speak yet. But a question kept running through my brain.

Had I just been in the wrong place at the wrong time, or had Robin Hood tried to kill me once again?

Rather than walking from the station as I usually would, I decided to take a taxi to the stables to collect my car. It was an expense I generally avoided, but tonight it seemed prudent. I didn't think that my attacker—if that's what it had been—had followed me, but I couldn't be one hundred percent sure.

As I paid the driver, I saw with relief that there were other cars in the car park. I wouldn't be alone here. The headache that had been brewing all afternoon had come back, and my eyes felt like they were being squeezed together. My throat had got in on the act too, and was prickling like I'd swallowed a cactus. Unfortunately, it was too soon to take more painkillers, so I'd just have to survive till I arrived home.

Before I did that, though, I needed some Leo therapy.

A nicker of welcome greeted me as I approached my horse's stable. He seemed to know there was something amiss, and stood quietly when I circled my arms around his shoulders, hugging him tight.

Warm breath tickled the back of my neck, and the comforting smell of horse soothed my soul. After only five minutes, I felt better. My head was still sore, but I was ready to face the world again. And I'd realised that I had a phone call to make.

Standing with my arm draped loosely over Leo's back, I dialled Nicholas' number. "Are you okay to speak?" I asked when he answered.

"For a minute, yes." I thought I could hear tension in his voice, perhaps because it was unheard of for me to contact him after hours.

"It's just—" in a rush, I told him about the incident at the tube station, how it *might* have been an accident, but that I was suspicious it had been deliberate.

"Where are you right now?"

"At the stables with my horse."

"Alone?"

"No, there are a few others here."

"What about when you get home?"

"I have a flatmate, she'll be back soon." And then I remembered—tonight was Trinity's hot date with Theo Yourdis the firefighter. So she probably wouldn't be in until late.

Nicholas had ploughed on, though, unaware of my inner dialogue. "All right, so tomorrow you'll work from home. I'll send Devlin over to yours with your incognito laptop. You can both dial in to the secure network and carry on your enquiries from there." There was a slight pause, then he added, obviously as an afterthought, "If that's okay with you?"

"It's fine." It would be weird to have a co-worker in my house, but I'd cope. "So I'll see him at, what, ten o'clock?"

"Maybe a little earlier. I'll phone him now and see if he can get into work a little earlier than usual."

"Right. I have to go to the stables early doors, but I'll make sure I'm home from nine onwards."

"Perfect."

"Oh—one more thing."

"Yes?" Nicholas' clipped tones told me that he'd considered our conversation ended.

"Could you ask Dev to please bring coffee?"

Parking my car in its space near the door of the apartment building, I stepped out and checked nervously all around me, before hurrying to the main entrance and letting myself in.

Briefly, I considered calling on Mrs Lacey, so I wouldn't be alone in the house. But then I suddenly realised that, even if the Robin Hood hacker somehow had my address, we were in a different flat now!

Relief flooded my body. Nobody knew my new location apart from Trinity, my landlord, a few firefighters and a couple of neighbours. Certainly no-one at work would be aware I'd moved house. Dev could just find out when he pressed the buzzer to get in.

But that thought made me cautious again. I knocked at Mrs Lacey's door.

My neighbour answered quickly, wearing a lilac twinset and pearls over a tweed skirt and low-heeled shoes. She reminded me of one of my great-aunts in Scotland. "Why, Izzy, it's lovely to see you." She opened the door wider. "Come on in. I baked some scones this afternoon."

I held up a hand. "I'll not, thanks all the same. It's been a long day, and I've got a splitting headache. I just want to get home and put my feet up. But first I have a favour to ask."

"Of course, dear, of course. You know I'll always try to help you, if I can."

"It's not much. It's just—if anyone presses the entry phone and asks for me or Trinity, will you not let them in? Even if they say it's a delivery? I'll let you know if I'm expecting someone." At her quizzical look, I explained, "Trinity's ex is stirring up trouble. But nobody knows I've moved upstairs, and I want to keep it that way."

She raised her eyebrows, but, bless her, she didn't question my garbled explanation. "Anything for you, dear. Now," she held up a finger, "wait there just one minute, and I'll get you some scones to take away with you."

Before I had time to protest, she was pressing a plastic container of home baking into my hands. "You're an angel," I said.

"Don't be silly," she said, then made a flapping motion with her hand. "Now, off you get and tuck yourself up."

Raising my palm in farewell, I clambered up the stairs, desperate to get hold of some pills to rid of this headache. The tickly throat had been joined by a thick nose, symptoms that my fuddled brain eventually pieced together as potentially being a winter cold, rather than just a mere headache. I rolled my eyes. That was all I needed.

By the time Trinity arrived home a few hours later, in a cloud of happiness and Dior perfume, I was coddled on the couch with a big pack of tissues, a large mug of hot lemon and honey, and the TV playing CSI-Miami box sets.

"How was the date?" I croaked, putting my laptop onto the coffee table.

"Aw, it was lovely," she said, almost glowing with joy. "He's such a nice guy. But," her face clouded, "what's up with you?"

"I think I've caught a chill."

"Well, you should be in bed, then, Izzy, not out here getting cold."

I pointed at the electric fire, which had both bars blazing. "I'm nice and warm."

She put her hands on her hips. "Hmmm. Right, tell you what. I'll make us both a hot drink, you can tell me all about your day and *then* you get off to bed?"

"Yes, Mum," I said, then dissolved into a fit of coughing.

Her eyebrows rocketed heavenwards, but she refrained from responding to my cheeky comment. Instead, she came back a few minutes later with tea and sympathy. "So, fill me in," she said, "what's the latest on the hacker?"

I shook my head. "Nothing, sadly. Except..." in my groggy state, I'd actually forgotten about the tube platform incident. But I couldn't face explaining it all to her, it would take more energy than I could muster right now. Instead, I changed tack. "Except, Dev is coming over here to work tomorrow."

"Really?" Her eyebrows started climbing northwards again. "Is something going on between you two?"

"Nothing like that. But we think we're being spied on at the office. Hopefully, it'll be more secure here."

Trinity's eyes fell on my laptop screen. "Isn't that Veronica?"

It was my turn to raise my eyebrows at her. "Yeah. She asked me to investigate her new man. Somehow," I gave her a pointed look, "she knew about me finding things on social media."

"Ah." Trinity had the grace to blush.

"It's okay, she's paying me. And I found something out. I'll tell her tomorrow."

My friend's eyes widened. "So what did you find?"

I tapped the side of my nose. "Client-investigator privilege." The side of my mouth twitched upwards. "But she'll probably tell you if you ask."

"So you're an investigator now?"

"Seems so." As if I didn't have enough else to do...

CHAPTER TWELVE

The next morning, Trinity took one look at my flushed face and bloodshot eyes, and ordered me back to bed.

"But I've got Leo to ride," I protested.

"No way, Jose. I'll make sure he gets looked after for you."

I wanted to object and say that I was fine, but my body wasn't cooperating. My shoulders had an anvil pressing down on them, and my ribs were wearing a corset one size too tight. Plus, my throat was on fire and my head was full of wool. Really, I was in no fit state to go anywhere.

"Okay," I said weakly, and thirty seconds afterward I had collapsed back on my bed and into a dreamless sleep.

A persistent buzzing woke me two hours later.

"Wha—" I groped around on the bedside table for my phone.

"Izzy!" Dev's tinny voice boomed out of the speaker. "I'm outside. Let me in!"

"Urgh." I groaned something unintelligible at him, and almost turned over and went back to dreamland. But before I could do that, he squawked some more, and I forced myself to swing my legs out of bed. By some superhuman effort, I managed to stagger to the other side of the room, into my dressing gown, and out to the front door. I pressed the entry release button and said, "Top floor. Flat B."

"Oh. Okay." Dev's voice sounded even weirder on the intercom.

While he was climbing the stairs, I hurried back to my bedroom and swapped my pyjamas for jeans and a warm fleece. I was just pulling wooly socks onto my feet when the doorbell rang.

"Would you look at you!" was his greeting when I let him in.

I ran a hand through my medium-length brown hair, which was no doubt sticking out at all sorts of angles, as it hadn't seen a hairbrush since yesterday. "Sorry," I croaked. "I've got a cold."

Dev took a step back and made the sign of the cross with his fingers. "Just my luck," he said, "I forgot my garlic."

"That's for vampires, silly." I opened the door wider and ushered him in.

"Where shall I put these?" He indicated the cardboard tray he was holding, containing two large takeaway cups.

"You're a lifesaver." I pointed him at the kitchen

counter. "Drop stuff on table. Put fire on. I'll brush hair. Be back one minute." Somehow, my glue-like brain could only construct short sentences. This was going to be a long day.

The coffee Dev had brought was hot and *very* strong. So strong that it actually permeated some of the fog in my head, enough to let me work a little.

And a little was all it took.

Dev's prediction from yesterday that the personnel database would be easy to crack proved correct, and within half an hour I was looking at search results showing all of our colleagues with computer science qualifications.

"Look at this," I called him over. He peered over my shoulder, and I pointed at the list on the screen.

It contained all the usual suspects, the ones I'd been checking for days. But there was one extra name we hadn't expected:

Walter Oxley.

It seemed that Mr Oxley had obtained a First in Computer Science from Brunel University, then changed tack and done a Master's degree in Business, finishing off with an Accountancy qualification. Those later achievements were what had allowed him to climb the corporate ladder, eventually ending up as Deputy Financial Officer at one of our rival banks, and then CFO at Bleubank.

Dev sat down in the chair next to me with a thump, and we stared at each other.

"Could it be him?" I asked, not believing the answer could be so simple.

"It could well. Let me check—I'll use the Robin Hood password and his email as a username, and try to log in to that Zurich Privée Bank account."

While Dev tapped away on his computer keyboard, I pulled out the Secret Santa rhyme, and chewed my lip. The person who'd written it had known Oxo's password, and they'd obviously known something was going on.

"D'you think," I interrupted Dev, "that my Secret Santa could've been Iris, Oxley's secretary?"

He looked, up, green eyes roving around the room as he turned that over in his mind. "You might have something there. It would definitely fit. She wouldn't have the computer skills to investigate, but she'd likely realise that things were out of whack."

"I can't think of anyone else it could be." I smiled. "Hopefully that's one mystery solved. I'll try to speak to her once everything has died down." Rolling my neck, I stood and went to put the kettle on. My head was starting to thicken again, and I needed more paracetamol and cold remedy if I was to carry on working.

"Bingo!" Dev shouted as I carried two steaming drinks toward the table. Then his jaw fell open. "Would you look at that!" His index finger touched the screen. "I don't think I've ever seen that many zeroes on a bank account before. The man's minted."

My mouth fell open too, and I quickly put the

mugs down, before I dropped them. "It's not his money, though," I pointed out. "He's been stealing it from Bleubank. It's no wonder the profits were down."

Dev's jaw tightened. "That's right. And with the amount those managers earn, you'd think he'd be happy, and not be trying to embezzle more. It makes me mad."

"Some people never have enough," I said, and then my mind made a little connection. "Or maybe he has an expensive ex-wife. Remember I discovered that Lee Isaacson was his stepson?"

Cogs turned in Dev's brain. "I'll bet it was Lee who tried to sabotage you." His voice rose. "Ginger-headed mongrel. Just wait till I get him." He slammed his fist onto the table, then got up and stalked round the room like a caged bear.

"Cool it, Dev," I said in as calm a tone as I could manage with a throat that felt like sandpaper. "He'll get what's due to him, and I'm fine. No harm done."

He growled. "More by good luck than anything." But his posture relaxed a little, and he thumped down into his seat again. He took a gulp of the tea I'd made him, then frowned. "So, what do we do now?"

While thoughts tried to free themselves from the treacle that was my brain, I picked up a pen and turned it end over end. "I think all we can do is tell Nicholas," I said eventually.

"But we can't just leave the money there. He might move it again."

"We need it as evidence. Otherwise he could just deny everything."

"We could take screenshots?"

I fiddled with the pen some more, thinking. "Okay, how's about you do the screenshots, then we'll make a new, secure account at Bleubank and move all his money into that. *Then* we tell Nicholas and let him inform the police and the board of directors."

His face brightened. "I could live with that. Let's make it so!"

I grinned. "You're such a nerd!"

Half-way through the afternoon, Dev and I had moved more money that either of us was ever likely to see again, Nicholas was cock-a-hoop that we'd solved the mystery, and my body had decided that it'd done more than enough for one day.

"I need to get back to bed," I groaned.

"But it's the karaoke tonight. You've got to come!"

My watch said it was only three thirty. Trinity was seeing Theo the firefighter again tonight, so I'd be on my own in the flat. But I really was *not* feeling sociable.

"I couldn't face the journey into town, Dev, if I'm honest. My body feels like I've run ten marathons back-to-back. I need some sleep. Plus, I'll just infect everyone else with my cold." I grimaced. "You've probably got it already."

He made a face. "So, if I've got it already, I'll pass it on to everyone else tonight, anyway."

There was some logic in that.

"I have an idea." Raising a hand, he cast his eyes around the room. "Do you have a DVD player?"

"Uh, yes." I pointed at a silver box on a shelf underneath the telly.

His expression lit up. "How about *we* take the karaoke to *you*?"

My brain couldn't make sense of that. "What? How?"

"I'll get the gang to come round here," he must've seen the look on my face, because he added, "in a few hours, once you've had some sleep. We'll bring some beers and a carry-out, play karaoke on a DVD, then leave you to get your beauty sleep by ten o'clock. How's that sound?"

I stared around the room, wondering if I had enough energy to do housework. But then I realised that, since we'd just moved, and half my stuff was still downstairs, the place was actually pretty clean and tidy.

"Okay. As long as you won't be offended if I have to take myself off to bed before the evening's over."

He held up a hand, three fingers pointing in the air. "Scout's honour."

"Another condition. Make sure Charlie Thwaite gets asked along. But *don't*, under any circumstances, invite Lee, or let him get wind of it or find out where I live. I don't want my flat torched."

"Right. Need-to-know basis only. I can do that. I'll head off now and start organising things."

A couple of hours sleep and an invigorating shower seemed to be sufficient to revive me enough to enjoy the party. And I used my dodgy throat as an excuse not to sing, which was a kindness to everyone else, given how tone-deaf I was.

We were half-way through the evening, and even Nicholas was starting to loosen up, when the door of the flat opened and Trinity walked in, her face pale. With a frown, she looked around the room, obviously not understanding what was going on. "Have I got the wrong place?" she asked.

I hurried over. "Long story," I said, "it's my workmates. Since I wasn't well, they decided to bring the night out to me." I jerked my chin back. "Are *you* okay? You don't look right."

"I—" she shook her head. "I'll tell you in the morning." Her eyes lit up. "Is that roasted peanuts over there?"

"Yeah. Come and join the party." I ushered her into the throng. "Everyone, this is Trinity, my flatmate." I started telling her everyone's names, but she stopped me with a laugh.

"I'll forget," she said. "I'll just call you all Bleu One, or Bleu Two or whatever. Okay?"

In a corner, Dev was deep in conversation with Charlie, oblivious to all that was going on around about. I smiled. Maybe this impromptu event would have an unexpectedly good outcome.

CHAPTER THIRTEEN

On Monday, Dev came round to my apartment again, and we spent the day watching vintage Star Trek episodes and drinking cold remedy. It felt decadent, but we'd agreed with Nicholas on Friday afternoon that it would be politic for us to keep out of the office until the repercussions of our discovery had died down.

Officially, we were both on sick days—which was true anyway, since Dev now had man flu and was practically dead on his feet, and I still hadn't recovered from my cold.

Staying at home also made me feel safer, as we weren't sure if the board had done anything about Oxo and Lee on Friday, or whether they'd wait till things opened up on Monday before telling the police. Either way, we should both be clear to go back into the office the next day.

When I woke up on Tuesday, my cold had subsided enough that my brain was feeling more normal, although my lungs were still clogged and I was coughing a hundred times per hour.

Nicholas had ordered me to take a taxi in, and charge it to the firm's account, so I arrived in style. It was a luxury I knew I shouldn't get used to, but I figured I perhaps deserved it.

After all, between us, Dev and I had solved the mystery of the anomalous data, and, in the process, had discovered lost revenues that would bolster the bank's profits and keep the shareholders happy.

I'd made the driver take a detour via the coffee shop, so I was clutching my re-usable cup when I entered the office. Things seemed strangely subdued. Or was it me? Was I expecting some kind of fanfare or celebration, like a victorious hunter returned to camp? I laughed at myself. We British didn't *do* things like that.

Reaching my desk, I said 'hello' to my colleagues, switched on my computer, then groaned at the sight of my Inbox. It would take me most of the morning to sort that out.

Squaring my shoulders, I took a slug of coffee, and applied myself to my emails.

Dev arrived a short time later, looking pleased with himself. He reached over the partition and gave me a high five, before disappearing behind his computer monitor. I assumed that he, too, was fighting his way through an ocean of emails. I didn't expect to see him this side of Christmas.

When my eyes were starting to cross from the

amount of junk in my email folders, I decided it was time for a change.

There was one more thread of the mystery that I needed to tie up.

In deference to my struggling lungs, I took the lift to the top floor. Plush carpet absorbed every footfall and framed artworks hung on the walls like trophies. It was a different world up here. Even the air seemed rarified.

Near the end of the corridor, I knocked on a solid mahogany door. "Come in," called a thin voice.

Behind her desk in the reception area before the CFO's office, Iris Hooper flushed bright red at the sight of me. I didn't need to say a word to know that she was my Secret Santa. It was written all over her face.

"You found out," she said tremulously, a small hand patting nervously at her grey curls.

"Yes, thanks to you." I smiled reassuringly. "But if you hadn't given me the Robin Hood connection, I might never have solved the mystery."

"Silly man," she shook her head, silver earrings twinkling as she did so. "He thought he was so clever, yet he used the same password for everything."

My forehead scrunched. "What was the fourteen fifty-four thing?"

"His birthday," she said simply. "One, four, fifty-four."

"Oh! I thought it was something to do with Robin Hood." I pointed at the inner sanctum behind her. "He's gone, I assume?"

Her chin lifted. "Yesterday."

"Well, thanks for the clues," I said, "and thanks for the voucher. I'll use it to get some new riding gloves." I smiled at her. "I'll not keep you any longer."

I'd got as far as the door when one further errant thread popped into my brain. "Oh, another thing—was it you that told the 404 hacker group?"

She pressed her lips together. "You mustn't tell, but my nephew is a member. At first, I thought he would be able to work out what Mr Oxley was doing, but the security here was just too good for the hackers to crack it."

That made my heart glow. I'd have to tell the others that what we were doing was making a difference.

"So then I tried you," she continued, "You seemed like an honest, clever girl. I was sure you'd decipher it."

"It was lucky you got me as your Secret Santa, then."

Stifling a smile, she waved a well-manicured finger at her computer. "Not so lucky, really. It's me that organises the list!"

At lunchtime I popped my head round the corner and attracted Dev's attention. "Lunch?" I asked. "Sandwich at the church?"

"Could do." Then his cheeks coloured. "Er, would it be okay if Charlie joined us?"

I grinned. Looked like Charlie had got her man. "Of course."

Tuesday after work was the first time I'd felt well enough to ride Leo in days.

My lung capacity was still abysmal, so I had to keep it simple, but it was just great to be back aboard my boy again. The partnership we had was so special to me, and when he was going well, it truly felt like we were dancing together.

Trinity had been doing the majority of the cooking since the weekend, although I'd not had much of an appetite, so mostly I'd been eating soup or toast. But on Tuesday night, she had promised to produce another of her tasty Caribbean dishes.

I walked through the door of the flat, nostrils flaring at the amazing scents wafting toward me, glanced at the kitchen, then stopped in surprise. "Trinity! Your hair!" Stepping closer, I turned a circle around her to get a better look.

Gone were her long dark tresses, and in their place was a stylish pixie cut that made her look like a younger version of Halle Berry. "Wow!" I said. "I love it." I wrinkled my brow. "But what inspired you to get it all cut off?"

She spooned food onto two plates and angled her head at the table. "Sit yourself down and I'll tell you."

Over another delicious meal, she explained. "I never told you, did I, about Friday night?"

"Friday?" I felt like I was missing something. "At the karaoke?"

"No. Before that. Remember—I was out with Theo."

"Oh, of course! I was so bunged up with the cold I forgot. Sorry." I frowned. "You came home early, didn't you?"

"Yeah." Her eyes narrowed. "I walked out on 'im." She took another mouthful of food, then carried on with her story.

"We went to the pub, and then when I asked for a second Prosecco, he refused. Said that I'd had enough, that I'd end up making a spectacle of myself if I had too much to drink. I ask you," she lifted a hand in the air, "how long had 'e known me? About three days. And had 'e ever seen me drunk? No. Me, I don't *get* drunk. I know when to stop. And besides which," she gave a wry smile, "I can't afford it."

"So what happened then?"

"Well, next thing 'e was criticising my clothes, telling me that my skirt was too short and that I'd be giving other men the wrong impression. Do you know what I did then?"

I shook my head.

"I stood up," her cheeks flushed as she remembered the altercation, "slapped his face, and stormed out of the pub, straight into a taxi, and back here."

"Oh, wow. No wonder you seemed upset. I'm sorry I forgot to ask you on Saturday."

"Don't you worry. You weren't well. And I were hardly here."

I felt a bit guilty at that. Trinity had looked after Leo for me at the weekend, free of charge.

"So, I decided, I've 'ad enough of men. I'm going it alone. I'm not 'aving anyone control me." She ran a hand through her trendy, short hair. "An' this is like me saying to the world, I'm a new woman."

I fingered a lock of my own shoulder-length hair, wondering if I should follow her lead and get mine cut off too. But I didn't want to seem like a copy-cat.

"How shall we celebrate?" I asked. "I got some more ice-cream."

"And *CSI*?"

"Perfect!"

CHAPTER FOURTEEN

On Wednesday evening, I turned up at the Community Centre for my Pilates class and found a throng of people crowding around the door, talking nineteen to the dozen. Spotting the tall figure of Queenie at the front, I pushed my way through. "What's going on?" I asked.

In answer, she pointed at a poster stuck to the glass. 'Closed until further notice', it declared.

"The plumbing finally gave out," she said, "and the council hasn't got any money to fix it."

"So the class is off?"

"I'm afraid so. Until I can find us somewhere else, anyway."

"Let me know. Thanks. And Merry Christmas!"

"You too," she replied, but I could tell her mind was elsewhere.

It was still early evening, but I'd ridden Leo in the morning—as best I could, with my lungs only working at fifty percent capacity—so there didn't seem to be anything left to do except go home.

When I walked through the apartment door a short while later, I discovered Trinity sitting at the kitchen table, her head in her hands.

"What am I going to do?" she moaned.

I blinked at her for a minute, then light dawned. "Are your classes off too?"

She nodded. "All I've got left are a couple of measly Salsa sessions in Wimbledon. Everything else were at the community centre here in Putney. The stables don't pay me much. How will I ever afford the rent?" She went back to staring at the table.

I put a hand on her shoulder. "Don't worry about it for now. The rent's covered, remember? And Queenie said she was going to find somewhere else to run Pilates. Maybe you can find another place too."

With a sigh, I slumped down on the couch. Things had been going so well. But now my friend was in trouble, and it was affecting me too. With a start, I realised, for the first time, that I really *liked* having her stay here. In fact, I preferred it to being on my own.

That was quite a revelation to me.

I'd always seen myself as an animal person, not a people person. And yet, here I was, worrying about losing my flatmate, and trying to work out if there was anything I could do to help her.

They said that people didn't change. But they were obviously wrong.

It was Thursday morning before I saw Veronica again, to give her the results of my investigations.

"Veronica," I said, leaning over her stable door, "I haven't seen you all week, but I wanted to tell you what I'd found out in person, rather than on the phone."

She finished wrapping an exercise bandage around her horse's leg, then stood up. "My dear, that's just wonderful. I never expected you to find anything out so quickly."

I refrained from telling her that it had only taken me a little over an hour last Thursday evening, and that pretty much anyone who could use FaceBook or Google could have found out the same information. "I'm afraid it's not the best news," I said, concerned that her expectations would be dashed.

"Is that so?" She shook her head. "Why is it I'm not surprised?" Leaning against her horse's side, she gazed intently at me. "Tell me everything."

A short while later, I was two hundred pounds better off—"You've saved me more than that in heartache, darlin', I can't thank you enough"—and Veronica had discovered that Kenneth Yates, alternatively known as Ken the Pen, was a skilled con man with a long history of fleecing rich women.

With a feeling of satisfaction, I turned to my own horse. Maybe I could get him that new bridle after all.

But, with only two days to go before the final of the Parkside League, I was getting a bit twitchy about how little riding I was able to do. By the time I'd groomed him and tacked him up, I had limited energy left to ride. It seemed like this cold would never go away.

"Coo-ee!" Suzie popped her head over the door just as I was struggling with Leo's girth.

"Oh, hi Suzie. Are you on a back shift today?"

"Yes, I did a swap with someone else." She frowned at me. "Are you having some difficulty there?"

"It's just this cold. It's wiped me out. Even the simplest jobs are an effort."

"Aw, that's not good. Are you managing to ride?"

"Barely. I'm going to try again now. I need to practise for the dressage on Saturday."

"Oooh, of course. I remember you said you was going to that. I'll let you get on, then."

"Thanks." I led Leo out of the stable and went off to the arena.

Thirty minutes later I was back, feeling like a wet dishrag. I'd done more than I had for a while, and it had wiped me out.

Suzie took one look at my face and grabbed Leo's reins off me. "I'll untack him for you. You sit yourself down, love, get your breath back."

I didn't have the energy to argue with her. Sitting on an upturned bucket, I put my elbows on my knees and my chin in my hands, waiting until my head stopped spinning.

It seemed like only moments afterward that a bright voice said above me, "I'll just take him out to the field for you." It was Trinity.

"Are you sure?"

Suzie appeared at that point with a mug of sweet tea. "Drink this," she instructed, "I think you need it."

Twenty minutes later, after the ministrations of my two friends, I was feeling a lot better, and ready to face a day at work. Before I left, they sat me down.

"Firstly," said Trinity, "you've to get a taxi to the station today. Okay?"

Pursing my lips, I remembered the two hundred pounds in my pocket. I supposed I could afford it. "Okay," I agreed.

"Secondly," this time it was Suzie, "Trinity and I have made a plan. We'll be your grooms for Saturday, for the competition. We'll do your horse, so all you'll have to worry about is riding."

"But I thought you were on night shift at the weekend?"

"I'll swap shifts again so I can be there. We want you to do yourself justice. And that'll not happen if you're still unwell and having to do everything on your own."

Tears pricked my eyes. "Are you sure?"

"We're sure," said Susie.

Trinity nodded her agreement. "Team Leo is behind you."

I had to fight hard not to cry. "Thanks. You guys are the best." It would be lovely, for a change, to be at a competition with friends, rather than on my own. What was it they said? Teamwork makes the dream work? I hoped they were correct.

Now all I had to do was manage to ride for longer

than half an hour on Saturday without collapsing. I could do that, couldn't I?

I'd only just arrived at the office that morning when Dev and Nicholas came striding toward our team's section. Dev had a spring in his step and a smile on his face. He stopped at my desk and asked, "Audi or BMW, Izzy, what d'you think?"

Taken aback, my forehead puckered. But before I had time to ask him to explain himself, Nicholas called me over. "Join me in meeting room two," he said, and marched off. Dev gave me a thumbs up.

Running a hand through my hair, I stared after our team leader. Then, with a shake of my head, I grabbed my coffee and followed him out of the office. Nothing was making much sense this morning.

Five minutes later, I understood why Dev had looked so happy.

The Bleubank executive team, Nicholas explained, were so pleased with the outcome of our investigations, that they were going to increase our bonuses. He named a five-figure sum—a significant amount of money, almost life-changing. I gulped.

But I wasn't to brag about it, Nicholas cautioned, because Dev and I were the only ones whose bonuses had increased.

"In return," Nicholas continued, "they have asked that you sign this non-disclosure agreement." He pushed a sheaf of papers across the table at me. "We don't want anyone else to realise how easy it was to subvert our systems."

"But, I'd never tell a soul," I protested. "Why would I?"

Nicholas shrugged his thin shoulders. "I believe you. But I know you. The board don't. It's merely... extra insurance on their part. You understand?"

Pulling my coffee towards me, I took a mouthful. I needed time to think, and I needed caffeine to lubricate my brain.

"Let me just have a read." I picked up the paperwork and began to scan the paragraphs of text. But it was all in corporate jargon and legalese, and difficult for a lay person to decipher.

As much as I could understand, it was exactly as Nicholas had said. They were asking that I never disclose any details of the fraud perpetrated by 'a member of senior staff'. That seemed to be it.

"Okay," I said, and signed at the bottom. Twice, since there was a copy for me, and one for the company.

Nicholas also signed, as witness. "That's that then," he said, putting the cap back on his pen. "The money will be in your account by Christmas. Good work."

And that was it. Just like that, I was tens of thousands of pounds richer.

❄

It was about two o'clock when Dev and I returned from a celebratory lunch. He'd decided on an Audi; I'd decided to buy a young horse to train, and maybe a lorry to take me to competitions as well. Or a deposit on a flat. I needed to think about that one.

Passing through reception on our way back to the office, we noticed all the smartly-dressed people heading up the stairs. Dev tilted his head. "Must be the shareholder meeting."

"Oh, that's right, it was today, wasn't it?" Spotting a pile of glossy brochures on the reception desk, I picked one up and leafed through it idly as we climbed the stairs. Dev had opened the door to our floor and was holding it for me when I stopped dead. "The toe rags!" I exclaimed. "The scumbags! The total shysters!"

Dev shut the door again and looked furtively around. "What's up?"

I held out the brochure—Bleubank's Annual Report—and jabbed my finger at a section of text.

Reaching for it, Dev read the paragraph, and his jaw fell open. "They're taking the Mick, aren't they?"

"Nope. This is the annual report, Dev. It's there for the whole world to see."

"The ratbags! That NDA they got us to sign, that was—"

I put my hand up, suddenly aware of how our voices were echoing in the concrete and metal stairwell. "Let's take it outside," I said, feeling not a single shred of guilt at extending our lunch hour. I think I'd subconsciously realised I was going to leave. I just hadn't verbalised it yet.

A few minutes later, we were sitting under the oak tree by the old church once more. Dev had calmed down slightly, but he was still fuming. "So that NDA was to stop us telling the police. I can't believe they let that crook away with it. And with a golden handshake as well!" He looked me in the eye. "Especially since he tried to kill you."

"I've been thinking about that. I think it was perhaps Lee that went after me. Remember they were plotting in the coffee shop. But have you noticed Lee's not around any more?"

"That's as maybe. It was still Oxo who put him up to it."

I sighed. "You're probably right."

He got up off the bench and stomped about. "Why would they do that? Why would they let such a cheating criminal walk away scot-free?"

Crossing my legs, I wrapped my arms around my knees and rested my chin while I thought. "It's all about the shareholders," I realised, thinking out loud. "They don't want to admit to being defrauded, they don't want to admit to the poor judgement that elected him onto the board, and they don't want to admit how close they came to insolvency."

"So, it's all about saving face?" Dev had stopped his pacing and faced me, his hands on his hips.

"Looks like it."

He growled. "That's it, I've absolutely had enough. As soon as that money hits my bank account, I'm done.

I'm handing in my notice. PayPal or no PayPal. I'll find something else, so I will."

I gazed at the concrete jungle around us. This peaceful church with its ancient tree was like an oasis of calm in a crazy city. But I was sick and tired of the rat race. "I'm getting out too."

"What will you do? Dublin?" He looked hopeful for a moment. Maybe Charlie hadn't totally bewitched him. I felt sad for her.

"Nope. I don't know exactly what yet, but I've had it up to here with cities. I want to live in the country again. Somewhere everybody knows your name."

CHAPTER FIFTEEN

It was Saturday before the answer came to me.

I'd survived my two dressage tests, and my gorgeous Leo had behaved impeccably. While we waited for the results to be announced, I was once more sitting on an upturned bucket, and Team Leo were doing their thing around me, sponging my horse down and preparing him to travel back to the stables.

Suzie had given me a copy of Horse & Hound magazine to read while I waited. I was scanning the classifieds, wondering if anyone had a nice youngster for sale, when a block advert caught my attention.

My eyes widened and I rocked back, almost tipping the bucket over in my excitement.

But before I could say anything, the tannoy crackled and a voice boomed, "Could all the prizewinners in the Parkside League please come to the main arena for the prize-giving. In first place, Miss Isobel Paterson and her horse Leo—"

I didn't hear any more, for Suzie and Trinity pulled me up and danced us round in some kind of demented polka, screaming and laughing and crying all at the same time.

My insides felt all fuzzy. Teamwork really *had* made the dream work!

When they finally calmed down enough for me to speak, I clutched Trinity's shoulder. "Look at this." I pointed at the advert, then handed the magazine over. "D'you fancy it?"

Wanted: *Horse trainer*

To work with young horses using Natural Horsemanship methods.

Live-in position. Small salary. Own horse welcome.

Would possibly suit couple as groom's position also vacant.

Apply to Lady Alice Letham, Glengowrie Stud, Perthshire.

She read the text, then looked up at me, her face shining. "You think there's much call for Salsa classes up there?"

I grinned. "Why don't we write to her and find out?"

❄

THE END

FROM THE AUTHOR

Like my amateur sleuth, Izzy, I'm a dressage-riding computer geek who loves coffee - but there the similarity ends. She is far smarter than me, and a lot younger! I hope you'll join me in discovering where her curiosity leads to next...

Find my books here: books2read.com/rl/RBMarshall

Sign up for my newsletter to find out when the next *Highland Horse Whisperer* story is ready: rozmarshall.co.uk/newsletter

JINGLE BONES

ROSIE MELEADY

Irish wedding planner Daisy Dell is an international expert on everything weddings, especially in Italy. But sometimes, a dash of murder and mystery finds its way past her up the aisle...

Note: British English

CHAPTER ONE

"Daisy, me old flower, how good to see you again," the grinning, jolly face of my distant cousin Michael greeted me at the door before he threw his arms around me in a warm embrace. It had been many years since a blood-relative had embraced me and it felt warm and comforting, like a cup of thick Italian hot chocolate.

"You haven't changed a bit. You're taller and you've got less hair than I remember," I said, rubbing his bald head playfully.

"And it's great to see you grew up pretty enough to capture a husband," he retorted. It was like we were back being teenagers, having our long-distance calls between Canada and Ireland again.

"Hey less of the husband stuff, this is Paolo, he's just a friend."

"God bless you Paolo, for putting up with her as your friend." Michael shook Paolo's hand with great vigour. Michael had definitely not lost his sense of humour in the near forty years we had not seen each other.

"How did you find me Michael?" I asked as we followed him into the back room. "Or should I call you Father? Actually, that's a bit weird. Can I just call you Michael?"

"Of course, it is better than some names I am sure I get called... Finding you was an absolute miracle. Some people would call it a coincidence, but as you probably guessed by my profession, I don't believe there is any such thing as coincidences. They are miracles," he said, ushering us to a table.

"This is Guiliano," said Michael, introducing a guy in his early thirties who stood wearing a tool belt and paint splashed overalls, scratching a bit of paint off a door frame with his nail. "He's the miracle worker around here. He can fix anything and he keeps everything ticking over and in shipshape. It's because of Giuliano I found you," Michael explained as he placed mugs and wine glasses on the table. "I was looking for a wedding planner in Italy and there you were. I couldn't believe my eyes when I saw your name, and that you were in Italy. Who would have thought we would both end up in Italy?"

Giuliano didn't seem the type to call on a wedding planner should he find himself in an engagement predicament.

"Tell my cousin your story Giuliano," Michael urged, not that he felt Giuliano would tell it better, but it gave Michael time to tuck into a slice of warm apple cake his housekeeper had just brought in along with a full coffee pot and a bottle of wine.

Michael lifted the pot, ready to pour for me.

"No coffee for me thanks," I said. "I wouldn't touch the stuff, too bad for my health. I'll have the wine instead."

As Michael poured my wine and Giuliano helped himself to a coffee, he explained his story. "Father Michael wanted my help to clean up and repair the loft above the refectory. And while doing it, we found a box of unopened letters from Daniela addressed to me. Daniela and I were childhood sweethearts."

"Not like me and you," Michael interrupted laughing, his mouth half-full of cake, referring to our childhood pact that if I didn't grow up to be pretty enough to capture a husband by thirty, Michael would marry me out of the goodness of his heart. It seemed perfectly logical to our five-year-old minds. We would have forgotten it, but we had told our parents and they never let us live it down—every family event and phone call tears rolled down their faces, laughing while recalling Michael's 'romantic' proposal.

"These two are the real deal." Crumbs were flying everywhere.

Giuliano continued, "Daniela moved with her family to Canada when she was 15... My parents both passed when I was young and I lived with my grandmother on the pasta street. My uncle was the parish priest, Lord have mercy on his soul, and he lived here in the refectory. He wanted me to follow in his footsteps and join the priesthood, so he must have hidden the letters from me. I thought she wasn't bothered with me anymore and, well, I didn't have an address for her, so we hadn't been in touch for 15 years. But after we found the letters and thanks to Michael, we found people who knew them when they lived in Toronto. They moved back to Sicily three years ago. So we met up again last month for the first time and, well, it was like we never had parted, the feelings were the same... so I proposed and now we have a wedding to plan."

"Her family moved to Toronto," chipped in Michael, picking up the crumbs from his plate with a licked finger. "The same as my family did, only two parishes away. Can you believe it?

"I found them through the church network. The power of the Catholic Church is mighty," said Michael in his best Irish accent, with an undercurrent of a chuckle.

"Powerful at keeping love apart, do you mean? Without his uncle's interference, they wouldn't have missed 15 years together," I said, jibing him with sarcasm.

"Not at all. We are all about love here at San Nicola! You know St Nicholas is the patron saint of women wanting to be married? Tomorrow happens to be la Festa delle Zitelle—the feast of unmarried women. It's when single women come to the church and put three coins in the box and wish for a husband. The local council give them a symbolic gift along with a wish for them to find a husband."

"A wish? That sounds more like a curse! Who in

their right mind thought up this idea?" I said, now helping myself to the cake I could no longer resist.

"Well, it comes from the story of St Nicholas... the one of the three sisters and the coins?"

My blank look encouraged him to explain.

"St Nicholas was young when his parents died during an epidemic. He inherited a lot of wealth and he believed in giving to the poor and in need. He heard of a poor man with three daughters, who had no dowries for the girls, which meant instead of getting themselves a good husband, they would be sold into slavery.

"Mysteriously, on three different occasions when each of the daughters was going to have to leave the following day, a bag of gold appeared in their home, providing the needed dowries. The bags of gold, tossed through an open window, are said to have landed in stockings or shoes left before the fire to dry."

"Is that where the custom of children hanging stockings or putting out shoes for Santa Claus came from?"

"Exactly! The Basilica has a special wedding donation box, called the Sposi box. It is emptied every year on the 7th of December, the day after the feast day and the money is given to one couple each year who can't afford their wedding. It usually adds up to quite a substantial amount. So, this year we have decided Giuliano and Daniela should have the funds as Giuliano has a big, adopted family of pasta grannies he wants to treat to a party... somewhere."

"Somewhere?" I ask, curious that they had not even thought of a wedding venue yet.

"Well, that is why we were looking for a wedding planner—to give us guidance, as neither Giuliano nor myself have any notion of what to do. And Daniela had to go back to finish work in Sicily. She will arrive tonight, but time is ticking by—we empty the box in two days and then we will book whatever is needed for the wedding. We were hoping to decorate the parish hall and have the reception there after the ceremony next weekend?"

"Next weekend? Are you kidding me? That is only days away!"

"It's only a simple wedding. The pasta grannies are looking after the food and the nuns who supply the altar wine are supplying the wine. I'm doing the ceremony. What more is there to organise but a few bits and pieces? We just don't know if we are missing anything and we want to make it special for Daniela."

"What about a photographer, cake, music, flowers, decoration?"

"Hmmm... yes... I hadn't really thought of that. But thank God you are here, my prayers are answered, all those services are here in Bari and I am sure they will all be willing to help as Giuliano and Daniela have become quite the celebrity couple, they'll be giving Kim Kardashian and that fella Kanye a run for their money soon, hey!"

"Michael, I usually spend at least a year planning a wedding, not just a few days, I can't do this!... And I think Kim and Kanye have divorced so not the best example to pull on."

"Oh please, at this time of year I have no time to spare. There is something happening in the parish every day between now and Christmas Day. Such as tomorrow's festival, you should come along and put your three coins in the box. Santa Claus might bring you a husband!"

He winked at Paolo, who chuckled away, leaning back in his chair, watching me squirm. He knew too well how much I hated the idea of getting married. After 600 weddings in forty different countries during the last twenty years of running my wedding planning business, I had experienced enough weddings to last me a lifetime. But that wasn't the only reason. Growing up with parents who were constantly arguing, I couldn't see why two people so in love could then hate each other so much, other than marriage being the cause and marriage being the only reason they felt stuck with no free will to leave a situation they hated.

"No thanks, I won't be attending. I don't want any such wish made over me."

"There will be great food including bruschetta made with oil from this year's olive harvest, which was particularly fine, and plenty of wine."

"Puglian wine and olive oil? Now that sounds worth coming to the festival for, so much more attractive than finding a husband."

Paolo is giving me those eyes that burn into the back of my skull, as if he knows how to flip through my mind. It was best to change the subject back to the reason we were here, and it was not about me finding a husband.

"Giuliano, do you have any photos of you and Daniela together when you were younger?"

"Yes, I do somewhere, not many, a few school trip photos and the likes."

"Okay, gather them up along with the letters she wrote to you and we'll meet tomorrow morning to work out a plan for decorations."

"Fantastic!" Michael slapped his hands together as if to kill a mosquito. "I've got to run and do confessions, and I know you have to drive Paolo to the airport. It's a shame you can't stay Paolo, but perhaps next time?"

"Yes, I am sorry that I have to get back to Florence. The idea of a church full of single ladies looking for love appeals to my heart more than getting back to work," he laughed, flashing a big smile and winking at me. He was such an Italian.

"It was very kind-hearted of you to drive all this way from Trasimeno with Daisy and then have to fly back in the same day," said Michael, walking us to the door.

"How could I resist? She rarely lets me get behind the wheel of Mabel Carr. Daisy did most of the driving, but she let me have the honour for the last four hours of the journey. I always wanted a Morgan convertible. Now I have a gorgeous woman who owns a Morgan convertible, which is an even better deal!"

Outside sat Mabel Carr, all shiny and red, recovering from her long journey, with Shadow in the back seat on high alert. There was never a fear of anyone stealing Mabel with my fierce looking, long-haired black, German shepherd in the back who in reality wouldn't hurt a fly and was afraid of creaking doors and the dark.

"I bet you are sorry you don't live here," said Paolo as I walked him to the departures area at the airport. I didn't need to ask him why. My scrunched-up eyebrows were doing the talking.

"Think of all the gifts you would have accumulated over the years from the single woman festival."

He fell exaggeratedly from my playful push and bounced back to wrap me in his arms. I sank in and enjoyed the moment, but then pushed myself away from him gently. I had work to do, a wedding to organise and I could do without the distraction of his fit body.

CHAPTER TWO

The following day I was up early to take Shadow for a walk. We wandered along the back streets near the cathedral. The local papers had the news of Giuliano's and Daniella's love story on the front page. Apparently, she had put coins in the Sposi collection box as a teenager and wished for a good husband. It said her letters had been lost. It didn't mention that Giuliano's priest uncle threw a spanner in the works of their relationship.

We strolled down the hidden streets of old town Bari. In a small alley, a dozen grannies had already set up their wooden pasta tables outside their front steps, ready to make fresh pasta as they did every day. They were carrying forward a tradition passed down from mother to daughter as generations had done before them. Cutting and moulding their orecchiette by hand. Already some early birds had their first batch of golden nuggets of pasta drying on fine wire stretched on a wooden frame like something a pan-handler sifting for treasure in a gold rush river would use. I kept Shadow on a tight rein. Pasta was one of her favourite dishes. Well, anything slightly edible was her favourite dish. I knew she wouldn't be so rude as to help herself, but her table manners wouldn't stop her from sticking her big wet curious nose into a drying frame and probably knocking it over.

"The ear-lobe-styled pasta depends on the size of the thumb of the pasta maker," chimed up a familiar voice from behind me. It was Michael, as cheery and as jolly as someone who has had their morning coffee laced with happy hormones. "They are traditionally served with turnip tops. Can you imagine our parents trying to get us to eat turnip greens with pasta? I don't think I would have been able to become a priest after all the hateful thoughts and bad language that would have induced," he said, stopping to give a drive-through-style blessing to one of the pasta granny's grandkids.

The front door was open and I could see into the little terraced house. A narrow hallway with a staircase that resembled more of a ladder to the right and an open door to a small room that seemed to be the TV room, dining room and kitchen combined. No wonder the women worked outside their front doors. There was nowhere big enough to fit their pasta tables inside.

"Giuliano lives down there." Michael pointed to a rambling cobbled narrow alley off the street, which was only wide enough for a moped or small car to fit down.

I knew it was Giuliano's place by his 'car'. A three-wheeler traditional ancient olive grove 'ape' I had seen him in the day before.

"If he had been female, his fate would have been sealed and he'd be out here making pasta like the other women, instead, his uncle had him do odd jobs around the church and for parishioners to earn his keep and he became quite the handyman."

The women called out greetings to Michael as we passed. He seemed to have time for everyone, throwing a personal greeting and introducing me as his cousin, without stopping.

"They are all busy making pasta for the wedding now. We'll have ten courses of pasta by the looks of it, so you have to be diplomatic. They all played a part in bringing up Giuliano. It is like he had twenty nonnas. That is why they all have to come to the wedding, he can't leave any of them out."

One lady with chubby cheeks, sparkling eyes and an apron sprinkled with love hearts and sheep handed me a bag of dried pasta.

"A gift for your cousin," she called. The others looked peeved that they had not thought of that to win favour with the priest. Michael and I nodded a 'grazie'. I felt like royalty doing a tour of my subjects as we continued walking.

"I've a good recipe for sauce for orecchiette, remind me to email it to you," said Michael, popping a hard-boiled sweet in his mouth. "Do you want one? They help me stay off the cigarettes."

"No thanks, can't have candy this early or I'll be

sick... So this is a big day for the Basilica?" I said as we rounded the corner onto the main street leading to the cathedral.

"Well, I'm afraid that will happen today. You will probably meet a candy that will make you sick... you'll see what I mean," he chuckled into his bag of pear drops. "It is a big day, but it is not the biggest festival for St Nicholas. You should come here on 9th of May—that is a truly spectacular festival."

"So if the 6th of December is the day St Nicholas died, then I am guessing May 9th, is his birthday?" I wasn't expecting any awards for this sleuth analysis.

"No, it is the day St Nicholas' bones arrived here from Myra," explained Michael. "A big statue of St Nicholas is brought from the Basilica in a boat and we go on a day-long sea voyage with a flotilla of dozens of boats. Thousands of people line the harbour in the evening to welcome the statue's return. The statue is then carried on the shoulders of costumed men with flower poles and torches. Then there is a big mass in the Basilica and, as the mass comes to an end, the choir chants and a priest crawls into the crypt of St Nicholas under the altar, and brings out the manna—it is a sacred liquid that always accumulates around the relics which are the bones of Saint Nicholas, and the congregation get anointed with the sacred manna."

"Myra is in Turkey, right? Maybe that is why we eat turkey at Christmas, because it is where Santa was born?" I was, of course, joking and Michael knew it.

"Well, smarty pants, Myra was actually part of

Greece at the time." We had turned off the pasta street and walked towards the Basilica.

"Greasy turkey for Christmas should be the traditional meal then. I've been talking to my assistant Sophia and she is going to work on getting the photographer, florist and cake today. I'll focus on pulling it all together, the decoration and the music, there must be a local band that would be available?"

"Ah yes, talk to Giuliano about that. He's a great accordion player. He knows all the musicians in town."

As we turned down another street, we walked directly into a group of men dressed in long black robes and upside-down top hats, but with a smaller rim. Each had a long white beard, red cape and a beautiful ornate cross resting against their black robe on a long chain.

"Gosh, I wasn't expecting to see so many Greek Orthodox here. I thought they were a bunch of Santa impersonators for a moment."

"We get a lot of Greek Orthodox priests visiting the Basilica to participate during the festivals, especially in May. It's a very inclusive celebration."

"So if Nicholas' tomb is in Myra, how did his bones end up in Italy?"

"His tomb was a popular place of pilgrimage. Because of the many wars and attacks in the region when it became part of Turkey, some Christians were concerned that access to the tomb might become difficult. So for the religious, and, I will not lie, also the commercial advantages of gaining a major pilgrimage site, Italian cities tried to get the relics of Saint Nicholas.

"In the 11th century, sailors succeeded in 'spiriting' away the bones, bringing them here to Bari. The Saint Nicholas shrine that they built for the crypt then became one of medieval Europe's great pilgrimage centres."

"You mean they stole Santa Claus's bones?"

"The church prefers the word 'spirited'."

"Stolen."

"Spirited."

Our childish jibes at each other went on until we got to the Basilica. Huge frame structures had been constructed to light up the whole of the outside of the cathedral and the surrounding buildings in the piazza. It was still very early in the morning, but preparations were well underway inside for la Festa delle Zitelle. Beyonce's "All the Single Ladies" song started up in my head again and stuck annoyingly on replay.

A gaggle of giggling nuns were setting up tables with the gifts from the commune for the single ladies. There were a few people dotted around the church praying. Three older women sat huddled in a whispering prayer line doing a decade of the rosary. Perhaps one of them had a pesky daughter at home who needed to find a good husband and needed some extra early prayers on the day of all the single ladies.

A monk knelt but seemed to be watching the festivities set up rather than praying. Two Orthodox priests stood near the altar above St Nicholas's crypt and a backpacker sat in contemplation on one of the side altars where my cousin was leading me. As we approached, Michael muttered, "Oh no, she's here," as the clack-clacking of determined high heels against marble tiles came from the side. "It's that sickening 'Candy' I warned you about. Quick, we can outrun her."

CHAPTER THREE

Michael sped up towards the door of the sacristy where he would find sanctuary, but only reached the front pew before he could no longer ignore the fifth hiss of "Father, Father, Father we really must talk," in a Californian accent.

"Father, as a member of the board that supports the charitable events of this church, I really have to put in a last plea for you to reconsider the decision of this year's Sposi box."

A festive jumper with a protruding red bobble on it for Rudolph's nose, clashed somewhat with her shoulder-length dyed, red hair. "From a PR point of view, the couple Claudia and Antonio are younger and, well... she's better media bait. We would get a much-needed boost in international media coverage with the Romeo and Juliet story of theirs. This church needs more visitors and more donations if we are to get that roof fixed next year, it needs to become a must-visit place in Italy. You and I, Father, may both be blow-ins to this community, but I have been here 30 years longer than you and I know that—"

"Candy," exclaimed Michael, interrupting her. I could have guessed her name by the fifth attempt. "Romeo and Juliet were star-crossed lovers, Claudia's and Antonio's families get on wonderfully and they are not short of money."

"But I have created a wonderful story around them that the media would love and I have fabulous photos of them."

"Thank you for your concern and for doing your PR job so well. But the Sposi box is not about PR, it is about helping a couple in need. Giuliano and Daniela could not get married without the donations from the box. You know the church's actions have already kept them apart for nearly twenty years, it's time to fix that. We have talked about this before and the decision is final. Their story is beautiful and I am sure you will make the best of it."

I caught the eye of the backpacker. It was hard not to as his eyes were piercing blue, something I would normally find very attractive, but they were like saucers, staring eyes that were chilling rather than thrilling. Hollow cheeks emphasised his gaunt face and greying stubble, combined with a disheveled comb over, did not add up to an attractive look. He seemed to listen in on the conversation. I have seen Italians do this before when I am talking in English to someone.

They are doing the same as I do, trying to catch snippets they understand, but the backpacker didn't look Italian. He was definitely a tourist and probably just enjoying a conversation in a language he understood.

Candy turned on her heel, muttering, "You are making a big mistake," and waving her hand in the air.

Michael watched her strut down the aisle, "She's not even Catholic, but loves telling me what I should do to get more visitors to the church... and to her guesthouse in town, the one you are staying at. It's her husband's family business," Michael said, rolling his eyes.

I had no time to respond. The two orthodox priests made their way over.

"Father Michael, how are you?" The older priest greeted Michael, as he gripped both arms and they bobbed heads to each side.

"Very well, Padre Alexander, and you and your wife are keeping well too, I hope?" responded Michael warmly.

"Yes, very well, thank God. Alicia is here somewhere helping the sisters. I am sure you will bump into her at some point. But I would like to introduce Padre Bartholomew. He has joined our parish and was keen to come and visit the crypt of St Nicholas," he said with his hand outstretched toward the younger priest who looked like a sketch I once saw of Rasputin. Long grey beard and dark circles under his eyes. He nodded and did a semi bow of his head.

"You have a busy day ahead," smiled Padre Alexander, "but I look forward to catching up with you during the refreshments later in the day," and with a swing of their capes, the two swished away without further ado.

"He has a wife?" I asked, perplexed at my ignorance of the rules of the orthodox church.

"Yes, he was married before becoming a priest, so in that circumstance, they are allowed to be married. Which is unfortunate as it stops him working his way up the ranks in the church and they need good men like him. But he's right, it will be difficult not to bump into his wife. She's the size of a small roundabout, too much Greek cheese... Oh there she is." Michael nodded in the direction of the altar that sat above the crypt of Saint Nicholas.

As the words "Michael don't be so ungracious" tripped off my tongue, I saw who he meant. Being shorter than me and rounder, I could see how you could draw a perfect imaginary 360-degree circle around her from the top of her head. She was awkwardly getting down on her hands and knees, picking up invisible lint from the cream carpet that led to Santa Claus's crypt and bones under the altar cloth skirts.

She was trying to push Shadow away, who was over licking her face after doing the rounds to greet everyone in the church with a friendly tail wag.

"And don't be deceived. She's not a jolly woman. I think she sucks lemons for breakfast to set her face up for the rest of the day. Talking of which, let's have a quick cup of tea and some toast at the refectory and then I'll walk you to Giuliano's house. I won't be able to stay as I'll have to get back here. I am going to have a stream of single women flowing through the aisles today so I won't have much time to help, but Daniela will be back and I'll see if I can assign anyone else to you to assist."

"Do you regret not getting married?" I asked curiously as we munched into our toast at his kitchen table.

"Now, I know the pact we made and I know it is the festival of single ladies, but it's no time for you to propose to me," chuckled Michael.

"No, I'm serious. Do you have any regrets?"

"Not at all. I had fun at college, but I like to dedicate myself to a bigger love and helping people find their way. People tell me their troubles now and how complicated their lives are. Mine is simple. I can stay focused on loving God and his people and I love it."

I was beginning to see my childhood friend Michael in a different light.

"You haven't lost your wit Michael, but I don't think you should say your next confession to Padre Alexander, as I am sure your attitude towards his wife is sinful. Anyway, time is ticking on. I need to meet Giuliano to start planning this wedding before his bride arrives and then get Shadow back for breakfast."

"And what about you? It was unfortunate Paolo had to leave so soon. I would have liked to get to know him. What does he do?"

"Oh, this and that, he just came with me to share the driving. He'll come back when I am going home and drive back with me."

"Wow, that is some dedication, it must be serious?" Michael smirked as we walked from the back of the church to another side street where the late morning December sun was turning the ochre terraced buildings into bright orange.

"Don't be getting ideas, I will only ever be arranging other people's weddings, never my own."

"Famous last words," laughed Michael.

As we arrived, Giuliano was sticking paper over the lights and windows of his car.

"Ciao! What are you up to Giuliano?" called out Michael.

"I'm going to spray paint it white for the wedding. I've been meaning to paint it for so long and so doing it for my new wife seems like a good start. Oh Daisy, I have the photos ready for you." His enthusiasm was endearing.

"I know it needs a woman's touch, but it is clean and tidy," he said, opening the door to his quaint little narrow house. It was cute, but he was right, it definitely needed a little pizzazz. On the table, a small pile of letters lay beside nine or ten photos. "Daniela has some photos too which she is bringing with her from Sicily today."

"I know you prefer tea than coffee, so I will make you one." He continued to walk into the kitchen.

"Daniela is very excited, she has not changed." He babbled as he filled a kettle, but I was not listening. Something distracted me in one of the photos.

A photo of a younger Guiliano and Daniela I recognised from the newspaper with her shock of red hair and two others sat on top of the pile. The date at the bottom told me it was nearly twenty years ago. One guy stood close to Daniela with his arm around her awkwardly. His piercing blue saucer-like eyes and gaunt look hadn't changed. There was no doubt it was the backpacker I saw in the church.

CHAPTER FOUR

The following morning was more sombre in the town after the previous day's celebrations, but not in Guiliano's apartment. Daniela had arrived back the previous evening from her dress collection venture to Sicily and we had arranged to meet before breakfast.

"It is all a bit too much for me up in the apartment, so if you don't mind, I will stay down here with the excuse of preparing the wedding car. Daniela is up there and looking forward to meeting you," said Guiliano after greeting me while he re-stuck already perfectly placed masking tape.

"It must be exciting to have her back."

"To be honest, I have hardly seen her. She arrived back yesterday evening and had to run out to meet a friend who had turned up unexpectedly. She missed dinner, and she was a bit upset when she returned, but I didn't ask her why as I think it was women's stuff about the wedding." He shrugged his shoulders and then climbed into his three-wheeled car.

"All the fluffy stuff, I have no interest in. I'll leave that to Daniela. I will focus on this," he said, rubbing the steering wheel. "I am taking it to my friend's garage where we will paint it today."

"The ape is going to look great for sure," I said, tapping the front window screen. It was best to stick to stuff he liked rather than expecting him to be interested in cake and flowers.

A petite but strong looking woman with long red hair tied back in a ponytail opened the door to me, a very unusual hair colour for an Italian. Her smile was that of someone trying to suppress a laugh during a funny incident at a funeral. Her eyebrows were wobbly, as if she wasn't too sure whether I was going to hit her or hug her. "Hi, I'm Daniela, you must be—"

"Daisy." I reached my hand out to give hers a friendly shake. She skipped the handshake and threw her arms around me, kissing me on both cheeks. "Oh thank God. I thought you were another one of the church helpers Father Michael sent to help me."

With those words I heard a squawk of approval coming from inside, followed by deep, loud tutting. The squawking voice was the familiar sound of Candy.

The Rasputin-looking priest was sitting on an armchair in the corner looking slightly terrified as Alicia, the large Greek priest's wife, walked rocking from side to side as if her knees couldn't bend, across the room to him carrying cake and coffee.

In the small kitchen area, was Candy with her

phone stuck to her ear. On seeing me, she threw her free hand up in the air then slid her glasses from her nose up to grip her hair back with them. Her hand waved towards a flower arrangement on the kitchen table and then in the direction of Alicia. I say a 'flower arrangement' with grace. It was more of a red plastic bow collection, wired and stuck in a large square of florist's oasis, along with the odd plastic lily and a plastic bunch of grapes.

"We can't have this!" she hissed. "She want's to create these hideous arrangements for the wedding from left overs found in the sacristy and attic. The same attic where the letters were found. She thinks this dusty mess is romantic because it was in the same attic. She has awful taste, it won't do at all."

I'm horrified at how loud Candy is speaking about Alicia the Greek.

"Maybe keep your voice down a little," I encouraged.

"Oh, she doesn't understand a word of English, we can say what we want about her. I've just got a bridal magazine in Illinois to agree to do a feature on the wedding if we have wonderful photos. But there is no way they would feature something like this. We need to use the budget to secure an excellent photographer and a great florist. Who are you getting?"

Someone giving me orders about how I should do my job really gets my back up and someone taking for granted that I am going to work for free also really gets my back up. She was doing both.

Between my assistant Sophia and myself, we already had a decoration theme worked out, and getting a photographer and a florist to do a contra deal for the publicity they would get in the local newspapers would be a little easier now with a feature in a US wedding magazine onboard, but we were still on a tight deadline and we were going to have to pull in a lot of favours. I had been invited to Puglia to meet up with an old friend and give some guidance about a wedding. No one had asked me to find service providers, and no one seemed in charge, which was normally the bride or bride's mother. I hadn't even had a conversation with the bride yet to see what she wanted, but all of a sudden, this woman had put herself in charge.

"Daniela, can I have a quick word somewhere quiet?" I asked, taking the girl's arm and not giving her a choice as I angled her down the hallway.

"You seemed to have gained two bridesmaids," I joked.

"I don't know who they are, I thought they were with you at first, but then Giuliano said your assistant is a German shepherd, which I think would be more useful at this point." She looked nervous, rearranging a cushion on a chair in the bedroom.

"The American woman keeps shouting orders at me and telling me what is going to happen on the wedding day. She says it needs to be a dramatic event.

"And the Greek woman just keeps feeding the priest the food we got in for my parents. She's here to alter my dress. She's supposed to be a great dressmaker."

"And the priest?"

"I think he got lost and ended up sitting in Giuliano's sitting room or he is chaperoning the Greek woman to protect her from the American, perhaps."

"Okay, first things first. How about we deal with the dress and get the Greek doing what she is here to do? I'll deal with the American. But before all that, I'd like to know how you would like your wedding to be..."

Daniela flopped down onto the cushion she had just puffed. "I just want to get my mother here. She'd know what to do about... about complications. I just want a simple day with Giuliano and me and my parents and some old friends. I want it to be special, you know? But it has all got ... complicated." Tears started running down her face.

I had heard this so many times from brides before. Wanting something simple but people getting involved and making things complicated.

"Don't worry, I am here to help. Come on, dry your eyes. I'll stay for a couple of days and sort things out for you. It's all going to be fantastic. We're already working on a getting a photographer, florist and have ideas for the decoration."

"Oh yes, Giuliano said you wanted some photos. They are over there on the dressing table."

"Okay, I'll take these. You go wash your face and I'll get Alicia in here and started on your dress."

Outside in the living room area, Candy was still marching up and down in the kitchen on her phone giving orders. And the Greek had a pot of water on to boil and had her head stuck in the fridge. Shadow was happily lying under the kitchen table chowing on a marrow bone the Greek had given her. She couldn't be too bad if she loved Shadow. I went over to Rasputin, who still looked terrified. "You speak English, don't you?"

"Yes, yes, I spent three years in Oxford."

"Okay, can you tell Alicia to go and see the bride urgently and start working on her dress? She needs to know this is the most important job to be done."

"Gladly. I really cannot eat any more food."

He propelled himself up off the low chair that had nearly made his knees level with his shoulders and with two or three long strides he was over in the fridge beside Alicia, muttering away a Greek explanation to her.

"Ah si, si. I am very importanto," she said, her chin up, glancing at Candy and drying her hands on a tea towel before shoving it into the hands of the American, who held it at arm's length like a pair of dirty socks. The Greek rocked on down to the bedroom like a Wobbly Weeble.

Just as Candy hung up, I started talking before she could give me orders. "I was wondering if you could put together a Pinterest board of the style of images the American magazine would want. Your guidance on this would be most helpful to me finding a photographer."

"Of course. I will need to go back to my house to put it together and it may take some time, but I would be happy to mentor you on what the US magazine market would require."

I didn't tell her I have had weddings feature in

Cosmo, Vogue and the top wedding magazines in the US. Besides, it wouldn't matter what she came up with, I would take any offers I could from photographers who would be interested in doing the shoot for free in exchange of the publicity. That is if I could find one available in time.

"I'll get started on that now. Getting the shots right is the most important thing," Candy said, packing up her bag on the counter and whisking her way out the door. My phone was buzzing persistently, but I didn't want to even look at it until Candy was gone in case she involved herself in the call if it was about the wedding.

As soon as the door shut, I saw Rasputin's shoulders mirror mine in going down two notches with released tension.

"If you don't need me anymore. I think I will go back to my hotel."

"Just hang on. Let me check if there is anything needing translating in the dressing room." I knocked gently on the door, before easing it open. Daniela stood with her back to me on a stool, draped in a cream lace Victorian-style dress with a zillion pearl buttons going from the end of the train right up to her neckline. The Greek looked like a human pin cushion with a boxload of silver pins jutting out from between her lips as she zipped around, pulling and easing the darts and sides.

In the full-length mirror Daniela faced, she looked like the perfect bride. "You look amazing," I gulped. Seeing brides in their dresses for the first time was always a waterworks explosion ready to happen for me.

"Is everything going okay, or do you need anything translated?"

"No we are doing fine. She is doing an amazing job already."

"Well if you need anything just call me. I'm going back to my hotel to start working on things. I'll leave my card on the kitchen counter."

My phone was buzzing again. I glanced at the screen and saw it was Michael. "It's okay Padre, they seem to be doing fine, you can go now," I said, pulling the bedroom door closed after me as the Greek Padre hurried out the front door.

"Hi Michael," I said accepting the call.

"Where have you been, I have been trying to catch you?"

"Sorry I have been at Giuliano's trying to organise all the helpers you sent over."

"Never mind that. Something dreadful has happened."

"What?" I couldn't imagine what he was going to say but Shadow's eyes locked onto mine, she could always sense any stress building in me.

"The money is gone. Someone stole the Sposi collection box. If we can't get it back then we cannot get Daniela's parents over on a flight or pay for anything, the wedding won't be able to go ahead... But that is not the worst..."

"What else?" I said still in eyeball lockdown with Shadow.

"They also stole the relics... the bones of Saint Nicholas."

CHAPTER FIVE

I wanted to keep the news from Daniela as she seemed to have just relaxed about her wedding again. So I slipped out the front door with just a cheery 'ciao' and headed straight back to Michael's house next to the church.

The housekeeper let me in. Her eyes and the way she was fidgeting with her handkerchief told me she was worried, very worried.

Michael was pacing the kitchen floor tiles. "Thank God you are here. This is why people get married, to have someone to talk to in times of trouble, I get it now. I talk to God, but he's not exactly vocal at the moment about what to do about this mess. I understand someone stealing money, but holy relics... bones... why?"

"Sit down before you wear a track in the floor tiles. I'll put the kettle on. We'll have some tea and figure this out. Tea always helps... So, when were the bones last seen?"

"We don't check on them that often. They are in the crypt under the altar, so I am not too sure. I noticed they were gone this morning after we saw the collection box had been stolen. I checked just in case they had hidden it under the altar, and that is when I noticed the crypt had been opened."

"So they could have been taken anytime, not just yesterday?"

Before responding, Michael took a gulp of the hot milky Irish tea I had put in front of him. Like every other Irish person abroad, his family kept him stocked with tea parcels to quench our insatiable habit of drinking black Irish tea with a drop of milk.

"Well, I confided in Padre Alexander this morning when I discovered they were gone. We were due to have a meeting, and I had to share the awful news with someone. He told me his wife had told him she had looked into the crypt yesterday and saw the blessed bones. They are not buried, they are just down a little under the altar. Easy to access for the manna each year."

I meditatively twirled my tea around with the spoon. "But there were a lot of people in the church yesterday for the festival so it could have been anyone."

"Not exactly. It couldn't have happened during the festival as the altar was cordoned off and the front pews were taken up with nuns and priests doing a prayer vigil, so if anyone had got past the ropes, they would have noticed them. No, it must have happened before or after we opened the church to the public for the festival."

"Okay, so who does that narrow it down to... a few hundred?" I said hopelessly.

"Well, they stole the collection box, so they must have needed money. Perhaps they think they can sell the bones for money or magic cures or something?"

"If we don't find the collection box, there probably won't be a wedding. There was several thousand euro in it and the church cannot afford to pay for the wedding."

"So we better find that collection box fast then. Let's think of who else was there..."

"The nuns... the Greek priests...the priest's wife.... the American... you and me...."

"We could probably eliminate the nuns and the priests."

He stirred his tea again thinking out loud, "Someone who wants or needs money and...bones?"

"That weird looking backpacker!" I exclaimed as if I had the answer to the million dollar question.

"Which weird looking backpacker?"

"He was sitting near the altar of the crypt, he was gaunt looking but had unmistakable eyes. I think he's a guest at the wedding, as... hang on, I have a photo of him. It's out of date but he hasn't changed much," I rummaged around in my Mary-Poppins-style wedding planning carpet bag before finding the bundle of photos Daniela had given me that morning. After shuffling through the pile, I found the one I had seen the day before in Giuliano's. "He's in a picture with

Daniela and Giuliano when they were in school...Here it is...oh no..." The one of Giuliano, Daniela and... he had been cut off. The guy with his arm awkwardly around Daniela had been snipped off the end of the photo. Eliminated. Before I could explain Michael's mobile started to hum "We wish you a merry Christmas". He glanced at the screen but there was no caller ID. "Pronto?" he answered and then switched to English.

"The Daily Mail?...How did you hear about the relics? We've only just discovered—" His eyes widened. "An American woman called you? ... No, the church doesn't have a PR agency, just an interfering old bat." He pressed his screen hard several times trying to hang up the phone.

"Maybe it wasn't someone after money, maybe it is someone who wants publicity?" he said with a flavour of anger... which was a flavour of Michael I had not experienced before.

"She wouldn't." My mouth genuinely fell open at the thoughts of Candy picking out the bones from under the altar and 'spiriting' them away for a headline.

"Oh, she would. She has come out with the craziest ideas in the past. Like having the bones out on display and letting visitors rub them to make a wish. She was calling it Project Wish Bones. Could you imagine?"

His phone was buzzing again. He took a deep breath and looked at the caller ID. "I need to take this, it's the detective that was here this morning." My heart went out to my poor friend, who was looking far from his usual jolly self as he pressed the speakerphone.

"Good day Father, this is Detective Nutella here. I'm afraid we need your services down at the Hotel Rossa..."

"That's where I am staying," I mouthed across the table to him.

"We have found a body. The victim's backpack has a religious badge on it, so I think the last rites or a prayer would be appreciated before we move him to the morgue. I should tell you, we are treating it suspiciously. We think it was a murder."

"I'll be right over."

"Michael, that's the backpacker I was just talking about. I remember seeing a Vatican flag felt badge sewn onto his backpack. The guy in the church yesterday... The one Daniela or Giuliano cut off from their school picture..."

The ticking of the cuckoo clock became louder as silence fell on the room. Our eyes met across the table and neither of us wanted to admit what we were thinking.

"My car is outside. I'll give you a lift to the hotel. I need to bring Shadow back there for her breakfast anyway."

CHAPTER SIX

"So if it is the backpacker, and he's dead, then that eliminates him as a suspect as the thief," deduced Michael, clinging on to the sides of the passenger seat. I know I tend to drive fast but so does everyone in Italy, I couldn't believe he found my driving a white-knuckle experience.

"No! Quite the opposite," I screeched. "Have you never read or watched a mystery story?" I looked at his shaking head in disbelief and made a mental note of what to get him for Christmas—an anthology of stories by mystery writers.

"Whoever murdered him wanted the money or the bones. He must have been working for someone." Walking to the hotel would have been faster as the driving route was through a series of one-way streets that took us away from the hotel and back again. There was an uneasy silence between us, and I had to mention the elephant in the room. "It was definitely him in the photo with his arm around Daniela... he was cut out of the photo in the same 24 hours that he was murdered. Do you think Giuliano or Daniela would... you know?"

"Noooo," Michael said rearranging himself in the seat. Even though he had said 'no' I was sure the same thing had crossed his mind and now that I had verbalised it, it diluted the thought somewhat. "They were getting the money anyway, so why would they kill him for it? And what interest would they have in taking the bones?"

He had a point and my fear that the wedding venue would need to be moved to the local prison eased. I parked Mabel Carr in the small car park to the rear of the hotel and we walked in the back entrance. Through the front revolving door beside the reception area, we could see the yellow crime tape fluttering in the rising breeze. A wide figure of a man in a long black overcoat and bright green scarf stood with his back to us.

"Detective Nutella," called out Michael.

"Ahh Father there you are. A busy day for us, what?" He sounded a little too cheery for a day that involved a major robbery and a murder in a normally a quiet town. He was bobbing from side to side as if preparing himself for taking a header during a soccer match. "The body is outside, under the balcony. He fell from three floors up. I just thought it would be the Christian thing to do and give him a few words, what? There's no blood and gore. It looks like it was a clean snap of the neck, poor chap. I'll bring you out, what?"

"My room is 311 on the third floor, detective," I

interrupted before they headed out to the crime scene. "Is it okay if I go to it?"

"You must be Signora Daisy Dell, what?"

I thought it was just me translating what he was saying incorrectly, but I now knew that he was in the habit of ending each sentence with the word 'what?'

"We have been looking for you. Please wait here at reception while I bring Father Michael outside. We can then go to your room together. I have a few questions I would like to ask you. What?"

"What?" I said back indignantly. "Are you treating me as a suspect?"

"As your room is next to the victim's, I merely want to ask you a few questions. Please take a seat. I will be back in a moment. What?" He eyed me up suspiciously and said a few words to the policeman standing beside the door in the foyer while twitching his head in my direction. The policeman nodded and gave me a stony stare as I took a seat with Shadow leaning against my knees to comfort me.

"I think there's a storm picking up. What do you think, what?" he said cheerily to Michael who glanced back at me with a worrisome look on his face as they revolved through the door.

I watched as Michael opened his kit bag, took out his long priest's stole and a small bottle of oil before he placed the stole around his neck and knelt behind the shrubbery where the body lay out of sight. The police and forensics in white, along with the waiting morgue crew, stood with their hands clasped in front and heads bowed as Michael did his thing.

He was back on his feet and folding his stole back up in no time at all. "God, he has an easy job compared to mine, and so much more respect," I muttered to Shadow, her stomach growling for her breakfast. The policeman looked at me even more suspiciously.

"Sorry for keeping you Miss Dell," the detective said politely walking back towards me with Michael. "Is it okay if Father Michael comes too? My Italian is okay but just in case, I don't want anything misunderstood," I said.

"Of course," Detective Nutella agreed as he clicked his heels and held his hand out, directing me to the elevator.

"Who was he?" I nodded my head in the direction of the corpse to Michael.

"A French national of the name John Paul Mercer. One of the police recognised him as he used to come here during the summer as a student many years ago."

On the third floor, the corridor to my room had tape across it. There was a flurry of activity around the entrance of the door next to mine as we approached. A guy in a white paper boiler suit came out, his face a shade of orangey-red and a shock of black curls squeezing out from under the elasticized hood around his face. He resembled a tall version of an Oompa Loompa in Willy Wonka's chocolate testing lab.

"One moment please," said the detective to us as he stood aside, out of hearing range. I watched their lips closely. "I think they have found the collection box," I mumbled sideways towards Michael's ear.

"How do you know?"

"Lip reading. My assistant Sophia was semi-deaf as a child so she is much better at it than me. Her father is from Ethiopia and her mother is Italian American. She can speak and lip read in five different languages and can tell where someone is from in US or UK by their lip movements. I've developed the skill myself from watching strained families at weddings all these years. A wonderful skill to pre-empt a fight or a drunken uncle saying something he shouldn't during a speech."

Shadow let out an audible sigh and groaned as she lay down, prepared for another long wait for her breakfast. She was expressing how both Michael and I were feeling. We were both standing with our arms folded, put out at having to hang around with so much to do.

"Good news, we have found the collection box under his bed," smiled the detective returning to us.

"And the relics?" asked Michael hopefully.

"There is no sign of them in the room. I am sorry. But at least we have one part of the mystery solved, what? Now if you would like to go to your room Signora Dell, we'll have a quick chat and then I will be on my way."

As we walked past the crime scene, I could see inside where there were two other Oompa Loompas, a knocked over table lamp and an empty bottle of scotch lying on the floor with two glasses on the table. The brief glance inside didn't allow me to gather much more detail.

The hotel was small and surprisingly old-fashioned for something that Candy was involved with. The guest room doors still had a physical key with a large brass fob attached rather than a swipe card. I rattled the door and Shadow led the way in and nosed the mini bar fridge, knowing I stored her breakfast in there.

As she wolfed down her food, Detective Nutella sat pensively at the desk on the only chair in the room, while Michael perched on the side of the unmade bed. I stayed standing by the kettle, waiting for it to boil. I brought it with me to every hotel, along with tea bags. Electric kettles are not the norm in Italian hotels and I needed my regular cups of tea for my brain to function.

"We still don't know the time of the murder exactly, but I would like to establish if you heard any commotion from the room next door last night or this morning?"

"I'm afraid I am going to be very unhelpful. I came back at about 11pm and went straight to sleep. I was at the airport and then I went for something to eat and took Shadow for a late walk down to the marina. If there had been any commotion during the night, Shadow would have woken me. This morning I left at dawn. I didn't even hear a key in the lock next door to be honest, nor a toilet flush or shower running."

"Nothing, what?"

"Nothing at all."

"Hmph... well that is helpful in itself. So the crime must have happened either before 11pm last night or after dawn this morning. And from my experience of bodies, I would say it was this morning. What?"

Was he expecting me to agree at the time of death of a corpse I hadn't even seen? Even if I had seen it, how would I know?

With that there was a crisp rap on the door, which the detective automatically presumed was for him. He presumed right. The Oompa Loompa stood holding up a clear plastic bag up.

I watched his lips closely and walked over to Michael. "They have found some significant evidence. Several strands of hair on the victims' clothes and in the room. Long, red hair."

Michael gripped his mug. "There's only two people I know in this town who have long red hair... Candy and Daniela."

CHAPTER SEVEN

Detective Nutella had followed the Oompa Loompa into the hallway.

"Daisy, give me the photo. I need to give it to him," Michael hushed at me.

"No way, that would be a betrayal of trust," I hissed back.

"They could charge us for withholding evidence."

"Forget you saw it Michael, keep it for the confessional. It can't have been Daniela. She's not the type." Although while saying the words, I was thinking about my morning with Daniela. How distressed she was over small things and wanting her mother to be with her as things had got 'complicated'. But it was also odd that Candy had a new interest in the wedding considering she had written off the couple the day before as a PR disaster.

"Oh and you have met so many murderers in your

day that you would know one if you saw one?" Michael hissed mockingly.

I hadn't had a chance to tell Michael about my past summer of murders. "Well sort of..."

"Let's wait and see what she has to say first," I hissed back.

In walked Detective Nutella. "We have a suspect. A redhead. There are only two I know of in this town. The DNA test will show which to pursue but I will be calling on both for questioning."

"You don't have to wait until a DNA result. Just stick the hair under a microscope and shine a light on it," I piped up while finishing off my tea, my back still resting against the mini fridge. Detective Nutella looked blankly at me.

"One is a natural redhead, the other is dyed so under a microscope a natural red hair will reflect the colours of the rainbow." They were now both looking at me in disbelief.

"What? I am Irish, I know about redheads, alright? What?" Now I was at the 'what' thing. It was contagious.

"We are finished here for today but we will keep the room sealed off until we are finished questioning suspects. I'm afraid there is no sign of the relics being in the victim's room or in his bag. Perhaps that is what the fight was over? After we have questioned the women, we may have some more hope of where to find them. I will be in touch, Father, if we hear anything." And with a swing of his coat, Detective Nutella was out the door.

We both semi held our breath while we listened for his footsteps disappearing down the corridor and heard the bing of the elevator going down taking him out of earshot.

"We need to give him the photo," urged Michael, still in semi-whisper.

"We are not giving him the photo," I responded in a similar tone, "And why are we whispering?"

"I understand it can't have been Daniela," he said, trying to get his voice back to normal. "I mean, why would she want the bones? And the money is theirs anyway."

"Maybe it was nothing to do with the money or the bones, Michael. He had his arm around her in the photo. Maybe it was a crime of passion?"

Michael's phone started to wish us a Merry Christmas again. "It's Giuliano," he said, looking at the screen.

"Father Michael, they have taken Daniela to the police station. I am just back from the garage and someone said the police took her in the back of a car. A neighbour has said it has to do with her robbing the church and another said she has murdered someone. Daniela did not murder anyone. I don't know what they are talking about and I don't know what to do." His voice was loud and frantic.

"Calm down Giuliano. I have seen the detective today and attended the crime scene. The Sposi box was stolen from the church. But that has now been found. A French man named John Paul Mercier stole it. Do you know him?"

"No... oh wait... You can't be talking about... there was this guy...a student, he was older than us... he stayed with Daniela's family the last summer I saw her before they left for Canada... he came between us. His name was John Paul, I think they dated for a short time, but he was not a nice guy, she never liked to talk about him. Is that the guy you are talking about? Has he come back? If so, I'll kill him."

"No need, someone has already got there before you," commented Michael.

"Oh no, are you saying it was him who was murdered? ... Oh no... did Daniela... is she involved? She told me she was going to see a friend last night and when she came back she was quite upset... it must have been him... oh no."

"She is just helping them with their enquiries. They are talking to other people also, so don't worry Giuliano. Maybe get down to the station? By the time you get there they may be finished and I'm sure Daniela would be glad to see you."

Michael rocked himself into standing off the side of the bed. He looked a little weary even though it was not yet 11am.

"I must go, I have duties to attend to. I need to start confessions in 15 minutes. Maybe someone will come in with information. It has happened before for crimes, but I can't do anything about it as what is said in confession stays in the confessional."

No one seemed to take into account that my time in this town was limited. I was supposed to be leaving the following morning having seen my friend and given a little guidance on how to plan a simple wedding, not be part of a murder investigation and trying to find the real Santa Claus. The sooner this was solved, the sooner I could get back to my beloved villa Brigid Borgo, Sophia and Paolo. I caught myself sighing at the thought of him which made me jump. I missed him. I missed him a lot and it made me very uneasy.

As soon as Michael left the room, I took out my notebook, drew a line down the centre of the page and began to list the possible suspects for both crimes. 'Bones' was on the top of one column and on the top of the other 'Murder'.

Under 'Murder' I had:

1.Candy the American

Motive: Accidental but robbery was a PR stunt.

However, there was no sign that she knew him in the church. And she didn't have a plan as she was complaining and annoyed. If she had a PR plan which involved stealing the money, she wouldn't have bothered harassing Michael about switching couples.

2.Daniela

Motive: She was going to use the money to run away with her old flame John Paul and things got sour? Or he knew something about her that would cause Giuliano to cancel the engagement. Or he stole the money, and she wanted it back?

3. Giuliano

Motive: Crime of passion. He found Daniela with John Paul. Or he heard he was in town, heard the backstory from Daniela and lost control.

4. Someone unknown

Motive: Unknown.

Next I moved onto the 'Bones' column.

So the suspects were those who were at the church yesterday morning when I arrived.

1. Candy the American

Motive: Publicity. But would she dare move something so sacred and lose favour in the community?

2. The murdered guy, John Paul

Motive: Just out of badness to get back at the community? His focus was money and Daniela so it seems to be unlikely he would go to the trouble of taking the bones.

3. The Greek Wife, Alicia

Motive: Can't think of one... other than for making broth?

These all seemed unlikely... who else was there... who else would have an interest in bones?

My shoulders suddenly went rigid and my hand trembled enough for me to drop my pen. My eyes shot towards Shadow who was lying in front of the fridge looking at me curiously with her big chocolate eyes and head tilted to the side, one ear up and one ear flopped over.

"Ooh no Shadow... Did you eat Santa Claus?"

There was only one thing I could do.

CHAPTER EIGHT

I fidgeted while waiting. Looking around in the darkness, I saw a piece of paper to my left. Hating litter, I picked it up. It was a receipt for two bottles of grappa and a chocolate bar. I stuffed it in my pocket. The small eye-level door slid back. Through the grill, a dim orange glow of light surrounded him while I stayed in darkness.

"Bless me Father for I have sinned."

He physically jumped at the sound of my voice.

"Are you sure you want to do this?" he muttered, leaning his ear closer to the grill and looking straight ahead. I ignored him.

"It's been about 10 years since my last confession.... Actually, I just lied about that, you can count that as my first sin... it's been about 35 years since my last confession... I'm not getting off to a good start, am I?"

He nodded meditatively. He was in priest mode

rather than jokey friend mode. Silence fell. I took a deep breath.

"I think my dog may have eaten Santa Claus."

"Holy Mother of God," his body jerked, causing his bible to fall off the shelf with a thud and he banged his head off the same shelf on the way back from picking it up. Holding the back of his head with one hand and the bible in the other, he squeezed out the words, "Are you sure?"

"No I am not sure, but she was up on the altar that day when the Greek wife was having a nose at the crypt. So she knew there were bones there and... and I didn't see her for a while, while I was helping you set up."

"Jesus, Daisy."

"Are you allowed to say that?"

"I'm saying it in prayer."

"It didn't sound like a prayer."

"It was."

"No it wasn't."

"Oh come on, we're not going to do this now.... Should we get her x-rayed?"

"Well she had a marrow bone since and how would we know the difference? And she wouldn't have eaten them whole."

"Lord almighty."

"You seem to be in pain, turn your head around and I'll check if it's bleeding."

"It's not bleeding," he took his hand down and double checked. "But I am in pain, my whole body is in pain. How am I going to explain this to the bishop? To the Pope? He has already been on the phone with the bishop."

"Maybe I should get you some ice?"

"Hold the ice and just bring me a straight whiskey..." He took a deep breath and there was enough of a pause for me to count to six. "If it was Shadow, you probably need to get out of Puglia, I can imagine some people will be very angry and may call for her extermination."

"No... would they?" I started to sweat. I hadn't thought of the backlash. "Okay, I am getting out of here. You can come visit me in Trasimeno if you get excommunicated."

We both bundled out of the confessional at the same time. There was no one in the church except for one person. Rasputin, sat waiting outside the confessional.

"Ehh I thought you were leaving this morning. We said goodbye?" said Michael.

"I decided to take a later boat as I need to talk to the police... I heard the bride Daniela has been charged with the murder and I could not let that be. I saw what happened..."

"Not charged, just questioned, she—"

"I was staying at the hotel.... He was not murdered. He fell, he was very drunk. Will you take me to the police station? I do not speak Italian so I need a translator."

"I don't have a car, just a bike, but Daisy could bring you. Can't you Daisy?" Michael looked at me pleadingly.

"But I need to leave!" I glared at Michael.

"There's a bride and a groom at the police station. Their happiness is on hold. You can help them. What difference will an hour make?"

"Okay then, but you keep your mouth shut. What is said in confession stays in confession, remember?"

"I'll follow on my bike," said Michael, knowing Mabel Carr was really only a two-seater with room for a big dog in the back but not a big priest. I think it relieved him to not have to experience my fast driving again.

I'm sure it was a weird sight. Me driving my red Morgan convertible with my sunglasses on and the ends of my colourful silk scarf skipping in the wind behind me and a worried looking Rasputin dressed in black with his black, funny hat sitting in the passenger seat beside me.

"I saw him come out of the confessional, he must have stayed in there all night," launched Rasputin. "I was there early, and I heard the rattle of coins and then when I looked over I saw him shove the box into his bag. I was in shock. I watched him hide in the shadows as the sacristan opened the doors. The thief then hurried out the door and I went after him. I looked around for the sacristan to get help, but she had already gone around to the side of the church, so I thought it best to pursue him. I followed him back to the hotel, where I had just come from. It was just getting light, and he was slugging a bottle of grappa. By the time he got back to the hotel he was wobbling all over the place. He was very drunk but he managed to make it to the hotel. He went in the backdoor and I lost him.

"I went to my room and waited a short while, trying to think what to do. I decided to come and find Father Michael. I was walking away from the hotel when I saw him on the balcony. He dropped something and leaned over to catch it and fell. I ran to him but it was obvious he died on impact."

"Padre, you don't have to tell me this. Save it for the police. I really don't want to be involved any more than I already am. I have other things on my mind now and I can do without being involved with this case." I'd had my fill of this mystery and I needed to get Shadow out of here before someone let the cat out of the bag and a lynch mob came for her.

The rest of the brief trip around the series of one-way systems was in silence.

"There is Father Michael now, he could take the direct route." I pulled up to the steps of the station where Michael was just finished locking his bike.

"I wish you a safe trip home, Padre. You are going by boat?" I looked towards the marina where the boats were clanking against each other with the rising wind.

"Yes I don't like flying and it's only a few hours by the ferry."

"Okay have a safe trip back."

As he unfolded himself from the car, he leaned over from the pavement as he closed the car door. "I heard what you said in the confessional about your dog."

White noise started screeching through my head.

He had heard. How could he not have heard when we were loud whispering and Michael was bashing around in the box, I'm surprised they didn't hear us out on the street. I wondered as a priest overhearing a confession, outside a confession box to another priest, would the rule of not being allowed to tell what was said in confession still apply? I didn't want to wait to find out.

"Got to go." I screeched off in Mabel Carr, while he was still talking and still leaning over. If it wasn't a convertible his head would still be in the car and the rest of his body waving like a windsock on the other side of the window.

It took me at least 20 minutes to find my way back to the hotel after my sweaty, flustered self, took a wrong turn. Every moment was precious. I knew Michael wouldn't say anything about Shadow, but I wasn't convinced the Padre would not feel obliged to open his mouth. It would not take long for the word to spread like bush fire. I needed to get Shadow out of there, fast. They were all so crazy about the bones they would definitely want to open her up or put her down or something.

I couldn't pack my bag quick enough. Shadow tried to help by gathering her things in a pile. And then my phone rang. It was Michael.

"Daisy," he said breathlessly, "The Padre told them about the bones."

I didn't expect what he said next.

CHAPTER NINE

"What are they going to do to Shadow?" I held my breath while holding half the contents of my underwear drawer in the air, mid hurried bag packing.

"Shadow? ... did he not tell you in the car what happened?... The thief had another bag. The Padre saw him hand the bag into a black car on the corner of the street near where the pasta grannies live. The car skidded away towards the motorway, like it was in a hurry. He said it was like a Starsky and Hutch scene. But the police think they know who it was by the description of the car. So don't worry, Shadow did not eat Santa Claus! And they have released Daniela. Come over for a cup of tea and I'll tell you all about it. Stay another night, we'll have dinner and catch up properly."

I exhaled loudly and dropped my underwear. I could breathe again, but not stand up, apparently, as I crouched down and sat on the floor to recover. Shadow came over tail wagging, causing devastation in the process as she knocked over the glass of water on my bedside locker and caught her tail in the cable of my laptop charger and nearly pulled it off the table. But I didn't care about that, I just cared about all the licks she was smothering my face with and that she was safe. "I think we both could do with a walk and some fresh air. Let's go see Father Michael."

I strolled down the pasta street and nodded 'hellos' at the women busy creating their earlobes of pasta. The street was sheltered from the chill wind that hit us as we turned the corner where the bones had been handed over. I found myself looking at the ground in the hope of finding a few of them but nothing had changed. The waves were rising and the boat masts were waving back and forth. In the distance I could see Padre Rasputin waiting on the dock for his boat to arrive. It was kind of him to miss his earlier ferry to help save the couple's wedding day.

As Shadow and I walked, I thought about everything that had happened in the last 24 hours. It all seemed too much to fit into that short space of time, and my brain was now trying to sort it into logical order.

"Daniela went to see John Paul as he had said he was going to stop the wedding happening no matter what it took," said Michael, recounting Daniela's words at the police station while he poured me tea from the teapot.

"He had stayed with her family for a summer as a

student and became obsessed with her. He was a devious and violent type but she never told her parents as she knew they needed the money from his room rental. He stalked her the following year and so when they went to Canada, she was relieved to be that far away from him. That's how bad it was. Years later, when social media started, she went on it to try to reach Giuliano but John Paul found her and stalked her on there too. And then turned up on her family's doorstep in Canada. Of course, her parents invited him in as they didn't know about him being strange. Can you imagine the fright she got when she returned home from work? They left Canada soon after and moved to Sicily. Not because of him, of course. But again Daniela was relieved he no longer knew where she was."

"And her hair, how did so many strands end up in his room?"

"She went to see him to tell him to leave her alone. He grabbed her arm as she was walking out of the hotel room and his hand got tangled in her hair, so some strands were left as she pulled away. She left the room and could hear him throwing things around in anger, which explains why the room was trashed and it looked like a crime scene.

"This is where the Padre helped with the enquiries. John Paul must have gone to the church after Daniela's visit. He knew that was the way they were paying for the wedding from the conversation he overheard us having in the morning. So, by stealing the money he thought the wedding wouldn't happen. That was what he was referring to when he said to Daniela that he knew a way to stop the wedding. We were lucky the Padre was there, otherwise there wouldn't have been a witness to all this and things would have got very complicated for Daniela. Anyway both she and Giuliano will be at the church shortly, they want to push on with the rehearsal and the wedding plans. I just pray to God that a Christmas miracle happens and the bones are found soon."

The tea had kicked my brain into action. Everything suddenly fell into place.

"I'll be back in a moment Michael. I have an idea." I grabbed my coat and hot-footed it out the door with Shadow at my heels.

"I didn't get a chance to say goodbye," I called out over the noise of the increasing waves that were turning from lapping to slapping and soon to be crashing. Padre Rasputin was still down at the dock.

"The ferry has been delayed due to the weather. But it's coming now," he said nodding at the growing shape of the ferry cutting across the waves in the distance.

"Thank you for clearing Shadow's name. Father Michael told me what you said about the relics being taken and the car skidding away."

"Yes, like Starsky and Hutch. Wheel spins and everything."

"Hmmph, I just walked down that street. Thankfully the wheel spins did not leave any skid marks on the pale flagstones. Because that would normally happen with such violent wheel spins, I think?"

Rasputin shrugged awkwardly.

"I was just thinking back to what you said about seeing the thief before sunrise in the church... How come you were in the church that early?"

"I was praying of course."

Shadow started to gently claw at the smaller bag that sat beside his suitcase.

"How did you get into the church?"

"Through the door of course," he sputtered, laughing in disbelief that I could be so stupid.

"But only the sacristan and Father Michael have the keys and, as you said yourself, the sacristan only arrived and opened the doors after you saw the thief take the collection box. And how come the thief didn't see you, I am sure he checked around for witnesses?"

He didn't respond.

Shadow's gentle clawing turning into proper digging motions, told me all I needed to know. It was the same motion she used when digging up bones in my lovely garden. "Shadow stop," I ordered.

Rasputin looked relieved but Shadow had stopped perfectly still mid digging motion, knowing there was another order coming. Her tail wagged slightly.

"Bag to Michael" I ordered.

In a nano-second Shadow had the knapsack in her mouth running down the pier towards the church.

"NO stop," shouted Rasputin, but Shadow didn't respond. "You can't do this... they were stolen," he said, distraught.

"This is not your decision. Do you think your church would be happy with you stealing them back after nine hundred years? Two wrongs don't make a right, as my grandmother always said."

"They should be returned to their rightful home in Myra, that is where St Nicolas's home was, where he was born, that is where his remains belong."

"Leave it for the churches to decide on what's best. Work your way up to being the big guy of your church and then get the relics back the proper way if you still feel so strongly about it... but home is not always where you were born and lived. It where you are most loved, and he is very much loved here in Puglia. It's how I feel here in Italy. Loved. I understand what you were trying to do, but you need to go home now on the ferry so you don't get into trouble. Go back to where you are loved."

He calmed and, as if by some miracle, the waves calmed too as the wind eased. The ferry had docked and its passengers were spilling out, while others who were waiting in the ticket office, avoiding the wind, filed in.

"How will you explain it?" he said picking up his suitcase.

"Simple. Shadow found the abandoned bag on the dock and 'spirited' it back to the church. She deserves the praise after I accused her of eating Santa Claus."

CHAPTER TEN

"You're not going to believe it Daisy. A Christmas Miracle has happened!" exclaimed Michael as I walked down the aisle of the church. "Shadow arrived into the church with a knapsack and inside, carefully wrapped in a towel, were the relics. The driver of the car must have been expecting money and threw them out the window somewhere along the way and Shadow found them."

"That's a miracle indeed, that's great, you can relax now and enjoy Christmas," I said.

Over near the crypt, Shadow was feasting in the praises of hugs and petting from Giuliano and Daniela who had arrived to finalise their ceremony.

"Oh my goodness, this is going to be the best Christmas feel-good news story ever! It will definitely go viral and international," cried out Candy trotting down the aisle past me, "I've got to go and spread the news and get ready for the cameras."

"Please stay for the wedding. We would love Shadow to be a special guest," said Daniela, who was also much more relaxed and glowing like a bride should be just before her wedding day.

"Of course, I would love to. And I am sure Shadow would love to too."

"She'll be getting lots of bones from Santa in her stocking for sure this Christmas," chuckled Michael.

"Just as long as they are just bones from Santa and not the bones of Santa." I laughed and rubbed my girl's fluffy ears. I'm sure she winked at me about our secret.

My phone chimed the tune "All The Single Ladies."

"God darn—"

"Daisy, you can't say that in the church," scowled Michael.

"Sorry, this is Paolo's idea of a joke, changing my ringtone for his calls, and I'd just got it out of my head. I'm just going to take this outside."

"That ring tone! You know I have no idea how to change it back and now that tune is stuck in my head again," I scolded as I stood out on the steps. In the distance, on the calmer sea, I could see the ferry getting further away.

"So how are things going in Puglia?"

"Good! Well, the money has been found and Shadow found Santa, and she has been invited to be a VIP at the wedding at the weekend."

"So are you staying?"

"Yeah I think so..." I said, looking at the people

coming towards the church to see Shadow as the news of the return of the bones quickly spread.

"Why don't you come down for the wedding and stay the night and we'll leave the next day rather than rushing?"

"Daisy, are you asking me to be your date?"

"No!"

"You know what they say, Daisy, one wedding is the making of another... this might be your lucky day."

"Don't push your luck!" I smiled.

I went back into the church and watched Michael reinstate the bones back into their resting place. Quietly, I took a chance on Candy's idea and made a secret wish on the bones that this would be my lucky wedding. In that moment, for the first time in my life, I felt ready. It was a real Christmas miracle.

THE END

FROM THE AUTHOR

I moved from Ireland to Italy in 2018 and when I am not writing humorous stories about life in Italy or killing people in my books, I am a destination wedding planner like my main character Daisy Dell.

I keep myself busy renovating a 22 roomed derelict villa near Tuscany, which I bought by accident when shopping for bananas, but that is whole different story which I write about in my humorous *A Rosie Life In Italy* book series.

All the books in my *Deadly Wedding Cozy Mystery* series are based in different regions of gorgeous Italy. I enjoy sprinkling my mystery stories with some real history of Italy and sometimes a flavour of something that has happened at one of my weddings over the last 20 years.

If you liked '*Jingle Bones*', you might like to explore other books in this series and my *A Rosie Life In Italy* series.

Find out more about Rosie and her books here: linktr.ee/rosiemeleady

Free Gift Recipes for 'A Cozy Italian Mystery Feast' click here: https://dl.bookfunnel.com/vke1d9exhu

DECK THE HALLS AND MURDER

PATTI LARSEN

A corpse on the town's Christmas tree? Talk about holiday spirit...

CHAPTER ONE

I shifted the shining red ornament in favor of the crocheted white angel with the gold halo and stepped back, eyeing the difference. Sighed and put the decorations back the way they'd been, instead unclipping the cord of the light string and moving the row of colored bulbs down just a smidge before smiling, satisfied.

The tree looked amazing, I had to say, glowing star at the top alight with new, white bulbs, the evergreen dominating the sitting room shining out the window and casting a lovely, multi-colored festive wash over the grass in the front yard. Yes, grass. No snow, not yet, but I had hopes for Christmas, a mere week away.

This was the Green Mountains of Vermont, after all. While unseasonably warm so far, a storm could blow in at any moment and blanket my picturesque little hometown in a thick bed of white that would take months to melt.

A girl could dream, right?

I hummed along to a popular carol playing from the speakers in the dining room as I exited into the foyer and checked my computer for late arrivals. From the looks of things all of my guests were present and accounted for, which meant the plans I had with Daisy for tonight were a go after all. The scent of evergreen and cinnamon dominated the entry of my bed and breakfast, sweeping banister to the second floor wound with real boughs—Mom insisted and I agreed whole heartedly with her trek into the woods dragging Dad along for muscle—and the gorgeous, antique decorations my Grandmother Iris so carefully preserved and used year after year.

Last year had been a whirlwind and while I'd done some adornment, I hadn't had time to sort through all the boxes of delights she'd left me along with her beautiful B&B. This year, I took the time, recruiting Mom and Daisy to assist and, a day spent oohing and ahhing and reminiscing over old treasures ended in the truly stunning and merry look we'd achieved.

From the sleigh bells hanging from the front door ready to chime their cheer at every opening to the holiday themed tablecloths and napkins, to the Christmas centerpieces and glass angels and Christmas trees set about in every room, Petunia's had been transformed into its own little winter wonderland.

And I couldn't have been happier about it.

I beamed down at the fat fawn pug sitting at my feet, her own decorative red bandana with the fur lining giving her that happy holidays panache I had already photographed and posted on social media ad nauseum because, oh my goodness, wasn't she just the cutest? While I'd always loved Christmas, this year just felt... different. Maybe it was how settled I felt in Reading finally, how happy and confident in my place here, how comfortable running my bed and breakfast. Whatever the reason, this holiday season was bound to be amazing and I couldn't wait for the big day and Ho Ho Ho.

Don't tease a girl for being thirty going on twelve.

I bolded the note I'd left for the staff NOT to book the four days I'd marked off for any reason, just in case. As of December 23rd until the 27th, Petunia's was all mine. Mom and Dad and Day were even coming for the holidays, to stay over, a little mini vacation for all of us. My mouth watered at the thought of Mom's amazing turkey dinner, her epic stuffing.

Best. Christmas. Ever.

And just the beginning.

The front door opened right on time with that lovely ringing I was sure I'd be sick of before Christmas was over. Daisy swept through, looking all kinds of cheery in her red wool flare coat and matching mittens, an adorable Santa hat perched on her dark blonde curls, those gray eyes sparkling with delight and her beautiful face a wreath of smiles.

"Are you ready?" She bent to scratch Petunia behind the ears when my pug waddled to her side looking for attention.

Was I. "All set," I said, fetching my coat, wishing I'd thought to get a hat of my own, feeling a bit drab in my long, black coat and boots. Even as Day, beaming a smile, whipped out a second hat from inside her own and handed it to me before liberating two strings of lights from her pocket, clicking the buttons on the necklaces of bulbs so they flashed into life.

"I couldn't resist," she giggled while I laughed and hugged her.

"This," I said, slipping the garland of lights over my jacket, tugging the hat firmly over my red hair, "is only one reason I love you so much."

Daisy dimpled while I slipped Petunia into her harness. The door to the kitchen swung open, April—or Andy? Hmmm... Ashley?—waving at me as we exited the B&B for the fun ahead.

"I'm just so happy you're home." She linked arms with me, Petunia leading us across the street as if knowing exactly where we were going and why. More likely, she thought we were heading to Sammy's Coffee for a donut hole, but she was waddling in the right direction, so I let her have her head as we strolled. "This has been the most amazing eighteen months."

"Aside from the murders, you mean." I winked at her, laughed. "Day, I agree." I inhaled the crisp air that surely felt like snow, right? "This is going to be an amazing year, I just know it."

Oh, Fleming. I had to learn to be careful what I said. The Universe was always listening. Especially knowing said Universe had a rather interesting sense of humor.

I brushed off the trepidation I'd created in my own mind and chose to enjoy the evening with my best friend. What was the worst that could happen?

Fee. *Seriously*.

CHAPTER TWO

The center of the massive metropolitan downtown (snort) that was Reading's Main Street was already lined with residents, many faces I recognized blending together into a sea of smiling humanity topped in many cases in antlers, Santa and elf hats, the jingle of bells and flashing of personal light strings evidence Daisy hadn't been the only one unable to resist the call of the festive.

I tucked in closer to my bestie, shortening Petunia's leash to keep her out from underfoot, though from the snuffling she did on the pavement, the way the odd child turned to squeal and hug her and stuff something clandestine and definitely not on her diet into her eager mouth, made me groan over the epic farting I'd be dealing with all night and likely well into tomorrow. I loved my adopted pug, the fourth in a long line of Petunias named for the very B&B I managed, but if the guests and everyone else who thought she was adorable (she was, darn it, part of the problem) didn't stop feeding her various treats that fired up her intestines to tragic result, I wasn't going to survive her. Being gassed at two in the morning was getting old.

"Look, there's your folks." Daisy tugged on me, waving and beaming at Mom and Dad where the former sheriff of these here parts and the retired principal who knew everyone by name stood near the corner of Main and Poplar. Dad towered over my petite mother, as usual, though I looked enough like her with her heavy red hair and blue eyes I knew I'd age gracefully, ever so grateful for that fact. I did, however, welcome some of Dad's height, though my 5'7" wasn't exactly Amazonian. Still, at least that meant I didn't have to ask anyone to reach for things on high shelves or feel intimidated by those bigger than myself.

Not that Lucy Fleming was intimidated by anyone. If anything, the small, beautiful redhead who hugged me when I joined them had that air of someone who could take on the whole world and never flinch.

As for the stoic and yet kind male side of the Fleming duo, his own eyes sparkled, Dad's grin almost boyish as he let me go before hugging Daisy and then crouching to ruffle Petunia's ears.

"I do wish it had snowed," Mom said, hands clasped in front of her tucked into velvety soft gloves, her hair held back behind her own Santa hat. Dad's reindeer antlers flashed, the tiny embedded bulbs sure to give me a headache if I looked at him for too long, though I had to admit, the fact Mom talked him into them made me giggle.

I wrinkled my nose at my mother, and though I'd had the exact same thought earlier, shrugged. "It's winter in Vermont, Mom," I said.

"It'll snow when it snows." Dad finished that line, one that I was positive every single person in Reading had uttered at one point or another since the dawn of freaking time.

Daisy sighed with complete contentment. "At least the parade won't be held up," she said. Waved across the street with that same enthusiasm she showed for everyone she met. While my gaze followed her excitement and I caught myself grinning and waving, too. Deputy Jill Wagner waved back, a single motion of her wrist, clearly on duty if her uniform was any indication. Never mind that, even as I smiled at her, my gaze drifted sideways to the tall, handsome man who joined her, his dark curls covered in a knitted cap instead of the cowboy hat he liked to wear, blue eyes lifting to meet mine from the opposite corner.

I know my smile shifted. I couldn't help it. Not because I wanted it to. Sheriff Crew Turner had that effect on me. The mishmash of emotions that ranged from irritated frustration to hormonal va-va-va-voom never failed to make interactions with Captain Handsompants about as awkward as possible.

Didn't help I had a bad habit of solving his murder cases for him, either. Something he was always very careful to point out in that annoyingly calm and confident way of his. That was, until I stirred his temper, his very long and patient fuse, to the point the under eye tic showed up along with that vein that stood out on his forehead.

Well, you know what? I was in a great mood and decided to let bygones be bygones. Waved and grinned at him, too and, to my surprise, caught the slow and sexy (so sexy) smile in return as he mimicked Jill's single gesture.

Friends, then. Or, at least, not enemies. I had no illusions. Things had been rather tense since Halloween and the death of Sadie Hatch. While I hadn't set out to yet again poke my nose in where it wasn't wanted and failed to mind my own business (yes, that was Crew's voice you just heard saying those things), I just couldn't seem to follow through. Not my fault people brought me clues and information and dumped things in my lap that ended in cases being solved though, right?

There was only one thing that could shift my mood (okay, two, but the likelihood a dead body was going to drop out of the sky was slim to none, so let's narrow things down, shall we?) to the worse and that particular thing chose that particular moment to do his particular brand of yuck and make himself known.

By stopping next to me, hocking up a nice load and spitting on the ground next to my boot. I looked up—barely—into those eyes empty of anything but contempt and baseless judgment and did my best not to punch my truly horrendous cousin Robert in the face. Since he was a deputy after all. Hitting him might get me arrested. Might, because, truth be told, I knew the sheriff didn't like him either and would likely give me a pat on the back behind closed doors for a job well done.

"You make sure to run home to bed after this, Fanny," Robert sneered. "Little girls out past their bedtime are just asking for trouble."

Okay, there was nothing not gross about Robert Carlisle, but that comment? Went further even than he and his 70's porn star mustache had ever gone before. I think he knew it, too, because he backed off, shooting me with his thumb and index finger before carrying on to torment other people for no good reason.

So tempting to follow him down a dark alley and do all of Reading a permanent favor.

Instead, I chose the high road and, when he passed the stand as a reminder of its presence, a cup of hot chocolate.

I left Petunia with Daisy and headed for the cart, standing in line for my turn, hugging myself against the chill though my heart was full. This was the first time I'd get to see the Reading Christmas Parade since I was a teenager, my ten years in New York City kind of a blur of college, working and being cheated on by my ex-boyfriend. Yes, the holidays in Manhattan were epic, from the tree in Rockefeller Square to ice-skating in Central Park, how the big retailers went all out with decorations in the stores not to mention the lights everywhere courtesy of the city. But there was something so deliciously lovely about the more economical—but no less enthusiastic—decorations that adorned my beloved hometown, an air of not just festivities but of community and caring during the holiday season that I'd missed out on for a long time.

Had taken for granted and wished away. Until I came home. Realized what I'd given up. Decided to embrace and, to my internal delight, knew I'd never turn my back on again.

I caught sight of Mayor Olivia Walker near the tall set of red curtains that had been set up in front of town hall, just a block away. She was impossible to miss, even from a distance. With her smooth, black bob tucked into a white fur hat and her entire body decked out in white wool, she snapped commands I caught the tail ends of despite the fact the local high school band was tuning up nearby and drowned out most of what she had to say.

No doubt the later parade date and town tree reveal was part of some master plan she had to increase Reading's tourist trade since that was all she seemed to think about. Not complaining or anything, but I wished, for once, she'd stop and enjoy what she created. As for me, unlike my first year back when I still felt disjointed and rather out of place, struggling to sort out who I was and why I'd come home, this year I chose to make the very most of being with my family and friends.

Felt amazing, actually.

"You said you'd help me sort through everything." I glanced sideways at the young woman standing close by, her face unhappy despite our surroundings, the tall man with her hunching his shoulders inside his jacket.

Neither of them seemed to have embraced the Christmas spirit.

"I told you," the man said, "just throw it all away. It's been over a long time, Tracey. You need to let this go."

It was clear that wasn't the answer she wanted to hear from him, the rebellion on her face pinking her cheeks past the chill of the air, jaw set, full lips a thin line and, despite her tiny self up against a much taller and bigger man, she seemed ready for a fight, trembling inside her puffy blue jacket and knitted hat.

"I knew this was a mistake," she snapped. "Thanks for nothing, Uncle Kenny." And spun before he could stop her—which he tried to do, to his credit, one big hand reaching for her too late—and marched off through the crowd, pushing people out of her way aggressively. The man she called uncle sighed and turned his back, slouching off in the opposite direction.

I meeped a little when someone hooked their arm in mine, Daisy joining me, face sad.

"How tragic," she said. "It's Christmas. Family is so important this time of year."

Was she talking about the fight between the girl and her uncle or her own sad circumstances? It was no secret Daisy's absentee father was a piece of work, nor that with her mother's passing, she was rather alone in the world. I hugged her then, refusing that bit of so-called logic. Because while I might have walked away from her, too, when I left, she welcomed me back with open arms and, forevermore, Daisy Bruce would not just be my best friend, but my sister.

Day helped me with the hot chocolate, both of us turning back toward Mom and Dad, practically running headlong into the ivory clad iron fist who ruled our little town. Olivia looked out of breath and rather peaked, but she paused in her headlong march to the hot chocolate stand to say hello.

"Hope you're enjoying tonight so far," she said in about the darkest and least welcoming tone I'd ever heard.

"It's great," I said, weak smile seeming to mollify her. "Everything looks fantastic."

"It's so beautiful, Olivia." Leave it to Day to gush in her genuine and authentic way that put everyone I knew at ease. Including, apparently, our frazzled and strung-out mayor who flashed my best friend a smile that was more grimace than joy, but it landed anyway.

If the mayor was going to say something to add to that expression, however, she didn't get the chance. Because, before she could speak, a lean, angry woman in a ski jacket with her dark hair tucked under a fur hat—complete with ear flaps—stopped next to us, glaring at Olivia like she'd offended her somehow.

"Where's my money?" Like the mayor was a prostitute and this chick her pimp. She didn't quite hold her hand out for the cash, but she might as well have, while Olivia's expression flattened out and her jaw clenched in response.

"The invoice is with finance," the mayor said. "As I told you earlier, Marion."

"You ordered that tree three weeks ago," the

woman Olivia identified as Marion snapped. "Payment was due December 1st."

"If there was a mix up in the payment, I apologize," Olivia said, though she really sounded like she hated having to do so. "Please stop by the office tomorrow," no stress on that word or anything, "and I'll see to it personally."

"No need." The tall man from earlier appeared out of nowhere, tugging on the woman's arm. "It's fine, Olivia," Kenny said, nodding to Daisy and myself, clearly embarrassed by his companion's attitude. "I'm sure it was just an honest mistake. Right, Marion?"

Marion snorted like there was no such thing when it came to the mayor while Olivia pointedly ignored her and nodded graciously to Kenny.

"Mr. Beckett," she said. "So nice to see you in town for the holidays."

He cleared his throat. "Just here to sort out some family business."

Olivia didn't seem to register that. "I assure you, and Ms. Jackson, the account will be cleared tomorrow. Now, if you'll all excuse me, I have a parade to start." Olivia spun and marched off.

I have no idea what possessed me but seeing her leave without the very thing she'd come for made my heart ache. I chased her, grabbing her elbow. She turned back to me, expression tight, until I pressed one of the cups of hot chocolate into her gloved hand.

"You're doing an amazing job," I said, keeping my voice low. Olivia and I didn't always see eye-to-eye but it was clear she was struggling and doing her best for our town. Someone needed to appreciate her, even just a little. "Thanks for this, Olivia. I'm really looking forward to it."

Her eyes widened just a little and for a moment I wondered if she would speak. Even cry, if the moisture gathering there was warning of impending tears. Instead, she squeezed my now empty hand with her free one before leaving me there to finish what she started while my heart grew a few sizes.

Ah, the Christmas spirit. I really needed to find a way to carry it with me all year.

CHAPTER THREE

When I rejoined Daisy, she was beaming at me, already in line for another cup to replace the one I'd given to Olivia. She didn't comment, but she didn't have to, that sweet expression of hers speaking volumes for her while I felt myself blushing over the simple act of kindness that now had me a bit uncomfortable.

All the more so when I noticed Robert smirking in my direction. If he caught my act and was judging it? He could suck it. Being a nice person who thought of others *would* trigger his sense of bully, the jerk.

Which cut the rest of my odd disquiet over feeling weird about what I'd done out from under itself and restored my happiness.

Arm in arm with Day, I returned to my parents and, after handing over a cup of steaming cocoa to my Dad, took back the leash to my chubby pug and, with a heave and a grunt, lifted her into my arms, my own hot chocolate at my feet, so the dear girl could see better.

I really was becoming a softy.

The opening song the band played announced the beginning of the parade, though I knew "parade" was a rather generous term for what was about to unfold. Since the entirety of the offering was visible in the square in front of town hall, all the excitement and preparations for the big event were likely to take all of ten minutes—and that included the lighting of the tree behind those ridiculous (and had to be expensive) red curtains.

Instead of my typical cynical eyerolling for the affair, however, I found myself cheering along with the crowd of Reading residents and visitors alike as the marching band started the show, their truly painful renditions of Christmas carols only making me all the happier. Since I'd once lugged a snare drum in one of those exact white and blue uniforms up Main Street and to all the football games we always lost, nostalgia was a welcome friend at the memory of doing my uncoordinated best to use my sticks and walk to the beat without tripping and falling on my face.

Good times.

The band paused at least two minutes, running through several different carols all strung together (I think I recognized "O Holy Night" and "We Three Kings" before "Little Drummer Boy" marched them on). When they finally started moving again, they didn't go far, splitting up at the top of the corner, forming a wall of music as the cheerleader club took the street, bouncing and leaping and throwing one another in acrobatic moves that actually had me gasping at their skill. And the fact the poor girls in their skimpy costumes had to be freezing as I shivered inside my heavy coat. They didn't seem to care, smiles wide, and not a mistake made before they, too, gave way to the happy and cheerful selection of locals dressed as elves, jingling their way through the crowd, handing out candy canes and tweaking noses.

But no one paid attention after the fanfare began, everyone stopping to watch, my own heart pounding, my face aching from smiling, as the red painted sleigh came into view from behind yet another red curtain, pulled by horses with reindeer antlers on their harnesses, the driver slouched over, a cigar hanging from his lips, elf costume rather rumpled and exceedingly hilarious, considering. Because, despite his disgruntled appearance, it was the gorgeous couple in the sleigh itself that had everyone screaming in delight, calling out and waving rather excitedly, as our very own Mr. and Mrs. Claus—Dr. Lloyd Aberstock and his lovely wife, Bernice—threw more candy canes into the crowd, their stunning suits, I knew for a fact, custom made just for them.

There was a reason they had that particular job to fill. I'd always thought Dr. Aberstock looked like the jolly old soul himself, and his lovely and adorable wife, Bernice, was so much his perfect partner in the North Pole gig it was impossible to think St. Nick and his bride could look like anyone else.

"Ladies and gentlemen," Dr. Aberstock boomed

over the crowd, "hes, shes and theys," I beamed at his inclusiveness, "and my very darling boys and girls," the kids lost their minds. "Christmas is at hand. Join Mrs. Claus and myself, won't you, for the lighting of our tree. Let's welcome the holidays together!"

The sleigh started up again, horses clip-clopping their way to the corner before doing a slow turn to follow the band, cheer team and elves back the way they'd come to town hall. As I waited for the crowd to thin, I set Petunia back on her feet, noticing as I did the young woman from the earlier argument at the hot chocolate cart was standing next to me. She didn't seem to notice I was there, staring into the crowd like she was all alone in the world and, with that same Christmas spirit that had me stop Olivia (and a healthy dose of busybody thrown in for good measure, because I knew myself better than that), I smiled and spoke up.

"I don't think I've seen you in town," I said. She jerked a little, surprised to be addressed, perhaps. But she didn't frown or move away so I stuck out my mitten. "Fiona Fleming. I own Petunia's, the B&B."

She blinked at me, her brown eyes distant, before she finally smiled a little, shook my hand rather perfunctorily. "Tracey Beckett," she said. "Sorry, I'm not really in the mood for this." She stuck both hands in her pockets, looking away again. "I don't even know why I came."

"I used to feel that way," I said. "Took a while, but I finally figured it out."

She grunted softly, shrugged inside her puffy ski coat. "I don't even live here anymore," she said. "Just here to sort out some... family business." Her lips twisted, unhappiness apparent. Funny how she said the exact same thing her uncle did.

I wanted to ask more, but before I could, an older woman in a long winter trench, her narrow head stuffed into a plaid hunting cap and big, heavy boots clomping on the pavement, stopped next to Tracey, glaring at the girl while the younger backed off a half step at the intrusion.

"What do you want, Olga?" Tracey seemed intimidated but angry at the same time.

The older woman's lined face screwed into a grimace before she repeated Robert's act and spit on the pavement, though her offering wasn't quite so impressive.

"You go back to the city," she growled at Tracey. "If you know what's good for you." Shifted her beady, dark eyes to me, overgrown eyebrows wriggling as her deeply wrinkled mouth turned down into a crevasse of unhappiness. "What are you looking at?"

I didn't comment, to which she snorted and then marched on, brushing past Tracey hard enough she clipped her shoulder before carrying on. Then again, as I watched in growing annoyance, the woman Tracey called Olga didn't seem to pick favorites, practically mowing over a pair of little kids before their mother jerked them out of harm's way and kicking the tire of the hot chocolate cart with one boot hard enough to make it wobble.

"Pleasant woman," I said.

Tracey glared after her then shrugged again, the

favorite gesture of the twentysomething set. "Olga Nowak is a nutcase," she said, as if that explained everything. "I used to live next door. My dad's..." she paused. "But she's right. I should never have come back here."

"Please, gather round!" That was Olivia on a loudspeaker, microphone in her hand, standing on the little stage next to the red curtains hiding the tree. The sleigh had stopped near the stairs to the platform and Dr. Aberstock had already joined her, helping Bernice with a hand up. When I glanced back to Tracey she'd already gone, though where I couldn't say. None of my business, but Daisy was right. Christmas was no time to be sad and alone.

Leading the happy Petunia toward the tree, I joined my bestie and my parents near the far side of the curtains, close enough I could touch the heavy vinyl if I wanted to. Dad might not have been sheriff anymore, but he knew how to work a crowd. While I was positive a more distant view would give the full picture, the idea of standing right next to the tree as it was lit made my little girl's heart go pitter pat. With a wicked grin, I ducked past my dad and winked up at him, Petunia hanging back at Mom's feet.

"My fellow Reading residents," Olivia said, "I am delighted to welcome Christmas to our town!"

Something was supposed to happen then, apparently, though it took some hissing whispers from Olivia to the young man standing next to the ropes who tugged furiously on them several times, before the curtains finally dropped to the tittering laughter of the crowd. At that same moment, Dr. Aberstock connected the heavy extension cords that would light the tree in our very high-tech Reading celebration.

I loved my town.

Looked up at the towering spectacle lit with multicolored bulbs and hung with sparkling ornaments.

Froze. Inhaled sharply. And was on the move without thinking, because one of the decorations was not like the others.

Pretty sure Olivia's orders to hang things on the tree didn't include a body.

CHAPTER FOUR

There was something incredibly creepy about a sweet-faced man in a Santa suit crouched over a dead body that would have ruined Christmas for me if said suit wasn't worn by one of my also favorite people, Dr. Aberstock. He, for his part, seemed unphased by the fact he still wore his furry hat and fluffy coat, that his gleaming buttons reflected back the oddly mummified face of the dead man lying on the ground under the glowing Christmas tree.

Someone had failed to turn the lights out even after Crew quickly and efficiently cleared the scene, having Jill and the grumpily compliant Robert herd parade goers and cheer squad members and crying band mates out of the square so an investigation could begin. Mind you, said gathering stopped dead (no pun intended) at the corner and, *en masse*, chatted and pointed and made comments about the fact there had been, only a moment ago, a dead guy swinging from the town tree like our very own angel.

Of death, however. Which wasn't really in keeping with the holiday, so whoever put him there? Had a very sick sense of humor. Or something to prove.

"He's not fresh, that's for certain." Dr. Aberstock leaned back on his haunches, wrists resting on his knees. I had trouble balancing that way myself, let alone with a rather portly tummy in the way. The doc never ceased to amaze me. "I'd estimate he was embalmed maybe a decade ago?" He looked up at Crew who had, as yet, to chase me or my dad, the two of us lurking (hey, I called it what it was, because *lurking*) where we'd both come to a halt under the place the body had hung. Either it was Dad's presence that kept the sheriff from giving us the boot or the fact my father helped lower the corpse or even, maybe Crew had grown tired of telling me to mind my own business while not saying so in as many words to Dad but meaning them.

Whatever his reason(s), our sheriff took note of the doc's findings before looking up and meeting Dad's eyes, the inappropriate flashing of my father's antlers remaining unmentioned. The fact Crew pointedly ignored me could have been on purpose, a nod to my being there. Or could have been his unwillingness to deal with me just yet. So many options hovering around, so little time.

"Would have been on your watch, John." That could have come out like an accusation, but Dad took it as Crew meant it while I bristled a little. What was he implying?

Nothing, Fee. He wasn't implying anything. Just stating fact.

Dad, for his part, frowned and nodded. "This is Brian Beckett," he said. "Used to own the Christmas tree farm. I think his brother took it over, Kenny?" I twitched at that, couldn't help it. Wait, the same Uncle Kenny who I'd seen and then met earlier? Tied to that nasty piece of work, Marion, who'd made Olivia uncomfortable and the nice girl, Tracey, I'd just met?

Their mention of family business now had my head spinning.

Crew seemed to notice my reaction because he finally met my eyes, his own guarded, the deep blue catching the flashing lights of the tree and Dad's antlers and reflecting the glow back to me. "You have something?" How careful, that tone, words clipped but not enough for me to call him out on rudeness.

"His daughter and brother are both here," I said. Okay, blurted. "And his neighbor." Don't forget Olga, the creepy old lady. "And someone named Marion Jackson who works at the farm."

See, I didn't set out to upset him, did I? He asked, didn't he? Came out and asked and it wasn't my fault I encountered all of the above said people tonight. If anything, one would think he'd be appreciative of my presence, of the fact I had information to share.

One would think.

Except, we had a history of butting heads and it

appeared that wasn't about to change anytime soon, Christmas being the reason for the season or not.

I did give him credit for not losing his crap and storming off, though the jaw jump and the tic had started, so I knew he was already at a slow sizzle. As long as the forehead vein held off, we might be okay. I also considered it a miracle I didn't mutter, "You asked," and for falling silent after delivering the above which, to my amazement, was harder than I thought it would be.

I'm nosy, okay? Get over it.

Olivia's sudden appearance cut off any chance Crew might have had to respond to me, if he even intended to. She huffed so loudly, her face furious and entire being trembling, I decided keeping quiet was probably for the best anyway.

"This is a disaster." She hissed that at no one in particular before spinning on Crew and planting an index finger firmly in his chest, staring up at him like he'd dug up the man on the ground and hung him on the tree personally just to make her life miserable. "I want this taken care of immediately, Sheriff Turner, and I mean *immediately*." She wiped at her mouth with one glove, red lipstick coming off on the ivory wool. It was testament to Olivia's upset she didn't seem to notice, though I flinched a little at the visual, as though she herself had suffered a fatal blow, and was about to fall before us, another Christmas tree victim.

Hush, imagination. I had more than enough complications in my life at present I didn't need fake ones too.

Instead of dropping like my mind whispered would be just my freaking luck, she spun and marched toward the crowd again, leaving the rest of us to stare after her a moment.

Her attention hadn't eased Crew's own mood, however, so when he fixed that blue-eyed gaze on me one more time, I knew his fuse had finally burned down to the caldera inside him and one false anything would have me kicked out of the scene.

Well, maybe I didn't want any part in his little body problem. So there.

"You said Kenny Beckett." I nodded at Crew's question, his pen almost tearing the paper of his notebook he pressed so hard. Wasn't helping Dad noticed, grinned a little before covering his mouth with one big, gloved hand. Crew realized his temper was showing, cleared his throat. Spoke into his shoulder mike. "Jill, Kenny Beckett, please."

It was only a moment later she was gesturing from the edge of the crowd to the tall man I'd met earlier, his lean, lanky form covering ground in long strides. Pale faced and trembling, he glanced down at the body before averting his eyes.

"Sheriff," Kenny said. "This is horrible. Is that really Brian?"

Crew pointed at the body. "I need you to make a positive ID, Mr. Beckett," he said.

Kenny looked down again, swallowed hard as though his stomach threatened a second coming, then jerked his gaze away, nodded. "That's my brother," he whispered. "Who would do such a thing?"

"I take it Mr. Beckett was buried here in town?" Crew's usual soft questioning wasn't present, the harshness of his tone seeming to surprise even him, though Kenny didn't seem to notice.

"He was," Kenny said. "Reading United Methodist Cemetery, attached to the church."

Crew made a note. "Can you tell me, how did your brother pass?" There was the kinder, softer sheriff, the one I was used to even when I participated in investigations without his approval. He usually reserved such tension just for me or for those who angered him, never for the victim's families.

"He hung himself," Kenny said, voice now dull and empty. "Nine years ago today, in fact." That made his presence a sign of something more than a prank, then, perhaps? "On the farm."

The same farm where the evergreen above us, still glowing its happy holiday cheer, had come from? There had been a possibility this was a prank, aimed at Olivia or the council. A sick joke, probably a drunken choice made by some yahoos who didn't know better. Except it was pretty clear to me—and hopefully to Crew—that the possibility of such had died its own death. Yeah, no coincidences here. Someone was sending a clear and unhappy message that likely had nothing to do with Reading and everything to do with Brian Beckett's passing.

But who and why?

"Any idea why someone would do this, Mr. Beckett?" Crew was in full-on professional with a solid side of compassion mode again, though it had no impact on the victim's brother.

Kenny, for his part, didn't snap out of his dull and empty state. "I have no idea," he said. "Why anyone would do this to Brian?"

"I remember the case," John said then, that equally kind and grave tone almost a perfect match for Crew's. Did they go to the same cop school or something? I knew they hadn't. Which made me wonder if they butted heads because they were so much alike or maybe that was just me and I needed to admit I was the problem. Yeah, I already knew the answer to that. "Doc, there was a temp coroner in the office that week. You and Bernice were on a cruise, I think."

"Yes, John, to Fiji. As usual, you have an excellent memory." Dr. Aberstock stood and hooked his thumbs in his thick, black belt, looking so Santa-like while the emaciated corpse laid out at his feet gave me chills. "You found no evidence of foul play, did you?"

Dad shook his head, frowning down at the dead body. Only then did he seem to realize he still wore the flashing antlers, sliding them from his head and turning them off, all the holiday cheer gone in that one act I hoped wasn't a bad sign of Christmas disaster to come. "I didn't," he said. "I spoke to his daughter, Tracey." He glanced at me. "Right? You said her name is Tracey?" I nodded, stayed silent, while Dad went on. "Poor thing found her father hanging from the rack where they wrapped the trees for transport. Two empty whiskey bottles." Dad shook his head then. "There was no indication it wasn't suicide."

"Of course it was suicide," Kenny said abruptly. Stopped, stared at my father. "What else could it have been?"

I didn't say murder. I swear I didn't. But I was thinking it, you better believe it. And from the grim expressions of the two lawmen in front of me, they were, too.

"I told you!" The young woman appeared beside me, shoving me out of her way though I took no offense, considering. Held my ground as Tracey Beckett pushed past Crew too and stared down at the body of her long-dead father. Tears poured down her face when she spun on Dad. "I told you he didn't kill himself." I wasn't expecting her to punch him, but she did, both fists hitting Dad in the chest. He didn't flinch, didn't try to stop her, though she only managed one solid hit and a second more feeble one before her uncle reached out and pulled her away from my father.

"The coroner said there was no evidence that it was murder." Dad paused and I hated the doubt that crossed his face. He was an amazing cop, had served Reading as sheriff for a long time. I trusted and believed in him and so did the rest of our town. To think he'd made a mistake? Crushing, to be honest, though he'd never know it.

We were all human and you know what? I had to accept my dad wasn't a superhero.

"Miss Beckett," Crew said, "did you have something to do with your father's appearance tonight?" He said it softly enough, in that same compassionate voice he'd found for her uncle.

Instead of letting it soothe her, however, Tracey snarled in response to his tone. "You're disgusting," she said. Sobbed twice, barely breathing, before collapsing to the ground where she wailed her heartbreak.

I went to her immediately, her uncle seeming at a loss, Crew's face tight with whatever he was fighting off at her response. He'd had to ask, I knew it, he knew it, we all did. But the way Tracey crumbled? If she had anything to do with this, I'd eat the damned tree in front of me and call it Christmas dinner.

"John." Crew cleared his throat again, tucking his pen and notebook away, looking up at the tree, squinting into the glow. "I'm going to have to reopen the case."

"Of course you are," Dad said immediately. "And I'm coming back to the office with you to show you what I have. If this wasn't suicide, if I missed something, I'll make it right." He met my eyes where I hugged the still weeping Tracey. "I promise, Miss Beckett. I'll make it right for you."

Tracey ignored him, jerking free of me, staggering to her feet while Dr. Aberstock spoke.

"It's my honor to review the autopsy," he said. "If something was missed on my counterparts end, I'll find it."

The EMT's had arrived, making their way through the crowd, heading for our little huddle. I stood, staying close to Tracey, hanging back with her as Crew and Dad left for the sheriff's office, Dr. Aberstock leaving for his car to follow the ambulance, Jill and Robert finally dispersing the crowd while Kenny hovered, looking like he wanted to say something to his niece but not knowing what. Finally turning and walking away in that same hunched and defeated way while Tracey stared at the tree with tears rolling down her face and I took a chance, like I always did, and poked my nose in where it wasn't wanted.

CHAPTER FIVE

"I'm so sorry about your father." I didn't try to touch her again, but felt her sway next to me, looking down at the pavement where Brian Beckett's body had lain only a moment ago.

"No one believed me back then," she said, bitterness and fury mingling with grief as she vibrated with it, so much emotion aging her past her biology. "I was only fourteen. Just a kid. I told the sheriff Dad didn't kill himself. He wouldn't." She spit out that last word with venom. "My father was a jerk, a real ass. No one really liked him, not my mom, not Uncle Kenny. But he was my dad." She sniffled, wiping at her running nose and wet cheeks with the cuff of her jacket. Turned to stare at me with the hurt, lost expression of a little girl who the world let down in the worst way possible. "Promise me you won't let them stop until they find out what happened to my dad."

She didn't have to ask. I'd already made myself that

assertion. "I swear," I said. "Tracey, John Fleming is *my* dad." She flinched at that, glanced the way Crew and my father had gone. "He's a good cop. And he meant what he said. If something was missed, he'll find it. He and Sheriff Turner." Not to mention Dr. Aberstock. And yours truly.

I didn't expect Daisy to join us, though I was happy to see her. She held out her hands to Tracey who glanced at me as if unsure of my bestie's intentions before I half-smiled in sorrow and encouragement.

"Daisy Bruce," I said, "Tracey Beckett. It was her father."

Day let out a soft cry of compassion and hugged Tracey. The shock on the girl's face almost made me laugh, if the clear lack of anything resembling familiarity with being comforted hadn't made the whole moment even more tragic.

"Don't worry, Tracey," Daisy said. "Whoever did this, Fee will figure it out. Won't you, Fee?" I opened my mouth to caution my best friend not to go on, but she barreled in, didn't she? Both feet and guns of support blazing. "She's solved four murders so far," well, six if you counted the young man haunting Sadie's house and the professor, but who was counting, "and I'm sure she'll be able to find out what happened."

Tracey spun on me then, eyes huge. "You meant it," she said. "You really meant it."

Crew would be pissed but I nodded. "Every word."

She seemed mollified, wiped at the last of her tears. Sagged against Daisy when my bestie went in for an arm around the girl's shoulders. Mom's appearance, Petunia in tow, seemed to have an even lighter influence on Tracey. She knelt and hugged the pug who licked her wet cheeks happily before groaning a deeply satisfied sound when the girl rubbed her ears.

"It's been quite an evening," Mom said, meeting my eyes with concern there, but keeping her tone even. "Why don't we all head back to Petunia's for a cup of tea?" She smiled sadly down at Tracey who looked up, startled. "You too, Tracey. I think it would do you a world of good. And if my husband and daughter are going to solve this case, find out what happened to your father," Mom had clearly been eavesdropping, and now you know where I got it from, "Fee is going to need all the information you can give her." Tracey looked down at Petunia who meow-yawned at her before panting her sweetness in the girl's face. "Do you think you're up to it?"

Tracey stood, nodded slowly. "Thank you," she said. "For believing me."

If she'd said another word, one more broken and aching syllable, I would have burst into tears myself. Instead, Daisy's arm linked through hers and leading the way, I fell in step with Mom and Petunia and headed home, the evening not quite the happy holiday celebration I'd hoped for.

The cheery decorations at Petunia's seemed slightly less so as we entered the foyer, though I forced myself to shake off the looming doom that had followed us home from town square. Besides, this wasn't about me, the tiny young woman under the big ski jacket looking in need of a solid meal or ten as I relieved her of her coat and stored it in the front closet before following Mom, Daisy and Tracey into the big, bright kitchen, Petunia huffing along in search of treats.

I settled the young woman on a cushion with a bowl of cut up strawberries and left her to feed the wriggling porkchop who loved every second of their interaction, eyes bulging while Petunia awaited each morsel, corkscrew of a cinnamon bun tail wagging energetically, Tracey's heavy melancholy lifted briefly while she giggled over the pug's antics. When she was done and my fawn creature had licked the bowl clean to her dissatisfaction (that there wasn't more), Tracey joined us at the kitchen island, perching on a stool and leaning into the counter, accepting the tea Mom offered. She'd definitely improved in her mood, even smiling shyly at my mother, at Daisy who patted her hand before Tracey cupped the mug in her tiny fingers and blew on the steam.

"I remember you, dear," Mom said, setting a plate of scotch cookies on the counter, perfectly piped in stars and trees and snowmen, glazed icing artistically applied to the point I always felt guilty biting into them and ruining what Mom made.

Tracey helped herself to one, nibbling a corner. "You do?" She seemed surprised by that. "I wasn't the kind of student you'd remember, Mrs. Fleming."

Mom made a tsking sound. "You loved art to the point Mr. James asked me to give you a free class last semester before graduation so you could focus on applying to art schools." Tracey's face lit up a little. "I was so sorry to hear you moved to Montpelier. I never got to find out if you were accepted, though I'm sure you were."

Tracey nodded then, sipped her tea, much more at ease. "I was," she said. "Went for a year. But Mom got sick, so I had to drop out." She shifted in her seat. "Cancer. Was a long battle." She sighed. "seven years of it. Mom died a week ago." Another fidget, as though she couldn't get comfortable. "That's why I'm here. She had a storage locker, left a bunch of stuff behind she was too sick to deal with when we moved. I'm here to clean it out finally. Move on." Tracey sniffed, wiped at her nose with her cuff even as Mom passed her a tissue. "Nothing was the same after Mom and Dad split. I was eight." She loved to shrug as though such truths would simply roll off her back. "I thought maybe when he married Marion everything would settle down. But they only lasted five years." A deep sigh seemed to deflate her, pale face drawn with worry and weariness and enough grief for a lifetime lived in barely two decades. "Now, maybe, I can figure out what I want to do. But I have to clean up this mess first." Jaw tight again, she pushed her mug away. "Thanks for the tea."

It felt like she was going to bolt, but I had to keep her here if I was going to fulfill my promise.

"You found your father." Yes, it was callous, but a slap in the face might have been what she required to bring her back to the moment instead of losing her in the past, as her distant stare seemed to have done.

She flinched, met my eyes while Mom sighed. Had I gone too far? But Tracey just nodded.

"In the barn," she said. "Where we kept the harvested trees. We'd cut them down then bind them in twine to keep the branches from getting broken." Her hands lifted and seemed to shape something, as though acting out of old memory. "Dad built this machine to do the wrapping because it was really hard to do by hand." Tracey's eyes brimmed, but her voice didn't change, didn't crack or warble. "He drank a lot. Like, a whole lot. I used to find him out in the barn passed out with a bottle in his lap. He never hurt anyone, wasn't that kind of drunk." She used the tissue Mom had handed her on the tears escaping, on her nose, but still maintained that level tone and matter-of-factness that hurt me far more than blubbering would have. How much hurt did one have to endure to create that amount of detachment, to make such a performance possible? I didn't want to know and wished she didn't have to carry it with her. "It was Christmas and I was helping out. Mom hated it, but it was the only time I had to spend with him so I'd take December every year and move back to the farm." Tracey hesitated a long moment, took another sip of tea, then spoke. And, when she did, she finally let me hear the pain she bore. "I went outside to check on him. I heard a noise and figured he'd gotten drunk again, was sleeping it off. But when I turned the lights on..." Tracey shook, closing her eyes, unable to speak for a moment while I sat and let her have the time she needed, Mom and Daisy and myself all holding space for her to grieve as, likely, she'd never done before. "He was wrapped up in the rigging, hung." Tracey took the new tissue Mom pressed into her hands but didn't use it yet. "He was already dead, there was nothing I could do. But I still wonder, if I'd just gone out to check on him sooner." She shrugged one last time, stared at the tissues in her hands like she had no idea what they were, the jagged edges of her chewed nails showing the remnants of black nail polish chipped to bits.

"There's nothing you could have done," Mom said.

Tracey didn't respond.

"Could he have accidentally been caught up in it, Tracey?" I had to ask that question. She looked up when I did but I didn't stop, needing her to hear me. "It was off when you arrived?" She nodded. "Could the safety switch have turned it off?"

She startled me by barking a laugh. "Um, no offense, but Dad built the thing," she said. "Trust me, there was no such thing as a safety anything on the farm."

"That's why you thought it was murder and not suicide," I said.

She leaned toward me, lips a thin line of determination. "There's no way he could have gotten in that position on his own, couldn't have reached the switch to shut it down. And I didn't do it. Someone had to have put him on the rack and waited for him to die before turning it off again."

Only one thought crossed my mind and from the way Mom frowned and Daisy went pale they were wondering the same thing as me.

How did Dad miss that?

CHAPTER SIX

Tracey accepted a fresh dose of hot water for her tea when Mom offered up the pot, though she didn't drink much of it as she went on, staring into the steam like it might offer answers she'd never been able to uncover.

"I know you're going to ask me why you think someone would murder Dad." She didn't look up, but the anger on her face told me she was lost deep inside it and had been a long time, didn't need outside affirmation to let it show or build. "Like I said, he wasn't the nicest guy. Actually, he really was horrible to a lot of people." So clear-cut, and without judgment. "But he loved me and was always good to me, even when he was drunk." Dads. I got it. Glanced at Daisy who seemed enraptured by Tracey's unfolding story, my bestie's eyes shining with unshed tears of her own. So much empathy in one lovely package. Made me wonder why she'd never gone into psychology, though if Day ended up a therapist she'd be the one in need of drugs because she'd absorb every patient's pain as her own in an attempt to fix them.

"My ex-stepmom," Tracey said then, fingers tightening around the mug so much her knuckles whitened and she finally did meet my eyes again. Hers flashed fresher anger than what had held her just a moment before. "The divorce was messy, super messy. Went on for months, fighting back and forth. But Dad held his ground and she only got what was promised in their prenup. Bad enough she had shares in the farm." She sat back now, ignoring the cup of tea, the cookies, running her hands over her brown hair, shaking out her ponytail that hung over the shoulder of her knit sweater and clung with static to the pale blue fibers. "She threatened him all the time, even before they divorced." Tracey paused, a flicker of guilt passing over her face. "Thing was, he threatened her back." Sounded like true love. "I don't know if it was enough for Marion to want to kill him, but they got into it pretty bad sometimes. And when Dad died, just before the divorce was finalized? She talked Uncle Kenny into letting her manage the farm. So even though Dad wanted her out, Marion's still there, has been ever since." No bitterness about it, though, nope. Just a heaping pile of steaming resentment that made Tracey's cheeks pink. "And then there's Olga," she rushed on. "That crazy old bat, she was always sneaking onto the farm, snooping around. She and Dad fought all the time. She even has a shotgun she carries with her everywhere." I hadn't seen it tonight, though

Vermont did have an open carry law. "I remember him saying one time if he caught her on our land again, he'd shoot her." Tracey's entire being flinched. "He didn't mean it, not really. But maybe something happened and she decided it was him or her."

I nodded so she'd know I wasn't judging—well, not much—and gestured for her to go on.

"That's pretty much it," she sighed, sagging inside her bulky sweater, tiny hands folded on the counter in front of her, thumb nail picking at the remains of her black polish. "Dad didn't deserve to be dug up like that, no matter what anyone thought of him."

"Of course he didn't," Daisy said, reaching forward to squeeze Tracey's hand before letting her go again. "We're so sorry."

Tracey seemed surprised all over again. "You're all so kind," she said, hugging herself. "Thanks."

"So, Marion owns part of the farm and manages it?" How did that happen? Shouldn't Tracey have ended up with her own stake in it? Or had her father cut her out of the will?

Tracey's face twisted again, this time in disdain and accusation. "That's right," she said. "When Dad died, Mom assumed I'd get a stake in the farm. Dad always said I would. Except, it turns out the will gave Uncle Kenny and Marion equal stakes in the operation. And they decided to team up against me." Wow, what a family. "They stole the farm out from under me, forced me to sell my shares. For pennies." Tracey hunched tighter like she was defending herself against an enemy we couldn't see. I wondered how she could have survived so long with so much vitriol running circles in her head. "It was supposed to be my future and now I have nothing."

If Kenny Beckett ended up murdered? Or Marion Johnston for that matter, I'd be having a serious conversation with the young woman beside me. But it was clear she had no motive to kill her father. The opposite. Though I was sure if she had the option, she'd raise him just to kill him herself for the position he'd put her in.

"The farm is more than just history and connection to your father," Mom said like I'd missed something.

Tracey nodded then, reached for the mug, sipped. "Dad wasn't a nice guy, but he was a good businessman. He had arrangements with the state government, supplied trees to almost every town in Vermont, not to mention out of state contracts. The farm is worth millions."

Okay then. That was a giant motive she finally laid out on the table.

"Tracey," I said, "you know I have to ask you this, but not because I think you had anything to do with it. To exclude you."

She didn't react, though clearly knew it had been coming. "I found him, remember?" The bitterness was back, retreating when she visibly relaxed at my silence. Maybe she was learning to trust and maybe she was just tired of the whole thing but whatever the reason, when she went on her tone had changed to weary. "I was in my room, had gone to bed early. I was asleep, heard a noise outside from the barn." She shivered. "It must have been the rig running that woke me, but by the time I went out to check, it was quiet again." Tracey's hands started shaking, tea sloshing around a little until she set the mug down with a firm thump. "That's it."

"And the exhumation?" I tried to be gentle, but the question had to be asked.

Tracey smiled, surprising me. "You know what? I wish I'd thought of it. Kind of fitting, finding Dad on one of our trees on the same night he died nine years ago. Whoever did this wants the truth to come out." She wrinkled her nose. "More than I did, I guess." When she sighed this time it was as though she expelled all the emotion she'd shown us in the last few minutes, leaving behind the shell of a young woman trying to fit the pieces of her life back together. "Now that Mom's gone, I just want to put this all behind me. But if there's a chance we can solve Dad's murder," no question in her mind, he was killed, and I was leaning toward believing her, "I'd have gladly gotten a shovel and done it myself."

CHAPTER SEVEN

I left Tracey in the tender care of my mother and best friend, retreating with my phone to dial the church office. To my surprise, someone answered after the second ring.

"Sorry to call so late," I said to the huffy woman's voice on the other end, clearly unhappy to have to answer at eight in the evening. "I'm looking for whoever manages the cemetery."

"This is she," the woman clipped, her crisp tone firmly cranky. "Gertrude Ennis. How can I help you?"

"Ms. Ennis," I said, "my name is Fiona Fleming."

"I've already spoken to your father," she snapped, "and the current sheriff on the matter. I can assure you, Ms. Fleming, I have no idea what happened, how our cemetery could have been desecrated in this manner." Like she herself had been accused of digging up Brian Beckett and displaying him on the town's tree. Either Crew gave her a going over or she was one of those people who jumped to guilty conclusions no matter what was said to them.

"I'm positive you weren't involved, Ms. Ennis," I said in my most soothing Lucy Fleming tone. It seemed to work, the woman expelling a loud a sigh at the other end of the line.

"I should think not," she said. Paused. "I'm here in my office right now looking at the plot map. I've agreed to meet Sheriff Turner," she said his name like he was now a pariah in her view and deserved nothing less than whatever punishment the Lord almighty delivered for being rude and accusatory toward her, "at 8am tomorrow morning to investigate the site."

"Thank you, Ms. Ennis," I said. "I'll see you then. Please, try to get some rest. I'm sure this will all be sorted out tomorrow."

"Thank you, Ms. Fleming," she said, tone shifting further from affronted to sympathetic. "I look forward to meeting you."

I hung up the phone, not so sure Crew would have the same reaction when I showed up at the cemetery but determined to do so regardless.

When I returned to the kitchen, it was to Mom and Daisy insisting Tracey stay for the night.

"Fee, the poor dear is in that horrible little place on the edge of town." I knew The Summit Motel, wasn't a fan, either, hated sending overflow guests to stay there when Petunia's was full. As it happened, I did have a room free and instantly agreed to the arrangement.

"I don't want to intrude," Tracey said. "I'm just here a few nights."

Daisy was on her feet, pulling the girl up beside her. "Let's take a drive," she said. "We'll gather your things and get you set up, cozy and safe, here at Petunia's. That way you don't have to worry about a single thing."

I really loved my best friend. Tracey went with her without further argument, though she did pause to squeeze my hand on the way past, looking a bit dazed to be taken care of like this. I let them go, returning to sit next to Mom who handed me, not a tea this time, but a cup of coffee, bless her.

It wasn't much of a surprise Dad joined us a minute later, also accepting a hot java, in the middle of our discussion over the case. My father's typical unreadable and granite like expression seemed cracked around the edges and, when he hugged me before taking a hearty sip from his cup, I saw the doubt once again surface.

"This isn't your fault, Dad," I said.

"John," Mom said, leaning in to kiss his forehead, "what did you find out?"

Dad exhaled a long and heavy sigh, rubbing at his cheeks with one big hand before leaning into the counter over his coffee. "Just what I remember," he said. "Coroner's report said Brian Beckett was drunk, but that the hanging couldn't have been accidental, that he had to have purposely stepped up onto the rig when it was running. No defensive wounds on the body, history of alcoholism."

"Dad, Tracey said the rig he was hung on didn't have a safety switch." I hated to prod him like this, but he had to know if he'd missed something. "Shouldn't it still have been running when she arrived if it was suicide?"

But my father was no slouch when it came to investigating. His eyes held no deceit or evasion as he nodded. "I thought of that, kid," he said. "But what she didn't tell you—or forgot in her grief or even never knew—is that the breaker to the rig had tripped. Which meant it had to have been on purpose, that Brian getting caught up in it overloaded the circuit and shut the thing down before she made it to the barn."

That was a huge piece of information that changed a lot.

Dad wasn't done. "Without any evidence to the contrary, I had to close the case. With the coroner's report ruling it suicide, I didn't have much choice. I did argue with him, though. Wanted the final report to read accidental. But the young doctor, Montrose, insisted there was no way Brian could have been caught up in the rig without doing so on purpose."

"Did you agree with him?" One last poke at the old bear.

My father took a long drink of coffee before answering. "I examined the rig," he said. "From what I could tell, Montrose was right. The twine feed was just too high, the platform elevated. The only way Brian Beckett could have been caught up in the wrap to hang himself was to put himself in harm's way on purpose."

I sat back then, crossing my arms over my chest. Even as Dad's phone rang. He answered it immediately, putting it on speaker, setting it in the middle of the triangle the three of us made before speaking.

"Hey, doc," he said. "Fee and Lu are here with me."

"I expected no less," Dr. Aberstock's cheery voice replied. "I assume you've reviewed the case from your end by now, John?"

"I have," Dad said, tone heavy. "What did you find?"

"From what I can tell," the doc said, "your notes were complete. As always, John." Dad didn't respond to that, though I could tell Dr. Aberstock wasn't just blowing smoke but being his eternally genuine self. "As for my counterpart, I'm afraid Dr. Montrose wasn't as thorough as I would have been. I blame youth and inexperience, though from what I hear, he's moved on to other specialties so I hope he's more rigorous in his focus than he was in this case."

"I take it you found signs leading away from suicide," I said.

"Indeed, Fee, that I did." The sound of papers shuffling and a few keystrokes preceded his findings. "Whoever embalmed the body was equally inefficient. Fortunately for us, as it means the fluid didn't make it to all the veins. Leaving me sufficient blood for testing. As you are aware, Mr. Beckett was an alcoholic, suffered from early stages of cirrhosis of the liver. There was enough residual trace in the blood I extracted to suggest Mr. Beckett, despite his built-up tolerance, would likely have been unconscious, and that's just from the amount of whiskey he'd drunk." And unable to do as Dad suggested, since being passed out meant there was no way he could have hefted himself up and onto the rig without help. "Even more importantly was the missed substance that he'd ingested as part of his night's imbibing."

"He was poisoned?" Dad perked at that.

"More like knocked out," Dr. Aberstock said. "With enough sleeping pills added to his intake to take out a gorilla."

CHAPTER EIGHT

As I expected, Crew wasn't excited to see me when I joined him and Gertrude Ennis the next morning. To his credit, however, he didn't immediately demand I march my redheaded self back to my car and go home to mind my own business, so I took that as a welcome to join the investigation because that was, apparently, all I needed to reassure my inner busybody she had free rein.

I was a master of making all kinds of excuses given the right circumstances,

"You can see," Gertrude said directly to me after a handshake she obviously hadn't offered to the sheriff if his deep frown and agitation told me anything, "Ms. Fleming," another dig that drove his jaws together hard enough I heard the squeak of his molars grinding together from five feet away, "Mr. Beckett's plot isn't exactly in the center of everything." An understatement, considering the empty grave sat on the very edge of the cemetery, with barely a low fence of chain link between it and the woods on the other side of the plot. "We don't employ cameras in this area, I'm afraid, so finding the culprit will be difficult."

I kicked at the ground with the toe of my boot, noting the surface seemed softer than I expected. "How hard would it have been to dig up the grave, Ms. Ennis?"

She tucked her mittened hands inside her wool coat against the chill of the morning while Crew crouched and stared down into the hole in the ground.

"As you are aware," she said, "it's been unseasonably warm this December. Certainly not cold enough to impede digging."

"May I ask," I went on when the sheriff didn't interrupt or try to stop me, "who embalmed Mr. Beckett?"

Gertrude stiffened instantly, Crew's head snapping up, blue eyes now crinkled around the edges and the vein in his forehead making an appearance.

"I did," she said with so much offense in her tone I let it go immediately. Not because Crew had straightened and was glowering at me, instant guilt I'd gotten the doc in trouble silencing me where nothing else would. "Now, if you'll excuse me. Ms. Fleming." She glanced at Crew, nodded, didn't speak again. Instead, she spun and marched off toward the church, leaving me alone with the sheriff.

Not my first choice, at least when he was in this kind of mood.

"What is it about this town," he said, that gravel in

his voice even rougher than usual, "that every single person in it seems hell bent on ensuring even the most sensitive information is common knowledge?"

Now, if I hadn't already been in a rather defensive position, I might have been able to rein in my temper and my tongue. However, knowing me as you do, surely you understand how hard it was for me to restrain myself in that moment. No, *impossible.*

As evidenced by my snippy retort (and I claim snippy without guilt).

"Hardly common knowledge," I said. "Just me and Dad."

That didn't mollify Crew in the least. Probably made things worse. Definitely made things worse. And I really needed to learn to keep my mouth shut.

Only one thing would make this right. I had a single shot at it and, in true Fiona Fleming fashion, gave it my all while knowing things could either bend to my favor or go so badly I'd regret even considering what I did next.

Chose to err on the side of sharing and told Crew everything Tracey told me.

There were times I knew I irritated Sheriff Crew Turner to the point of near apoplexy, that I drove him around the bend and back again and, one day, I might be the cause of an aneurysm if he didn't learn to just let me do me and not get so worked up over it. Thing was, the best part about Crew was his willingness to listen, even when he was angry, to take what I learned and fold it into his own investigation without arguing or pulling the mansplaining card. In fact, despite our differences, he more times than not weighed everything I'd uncovered against what he knew and shifted gears in favor of the truth and justice instead of his own ego, which always raised him in my estimation despite our continuing conflict.

Case in point. When I wrapped up what she'd unfolded the night before, informing him of Tracey's whereabouts to his short nod of thanks, finishing with Dad's addition of the circuit breaker and Dr. Aberstock's findings, Crew stared at the ground a moment, brows furrowed over his remarkable blue eyes, hands in the pockets of his sheriff's jacket, before speaking in a low and careful voice.

"From the looks of the ground the body was just dug up last night." He kicked at the dirt, cascade of it loosely falling into the hole. "There's still enough moisture in it that it couldn't have been earlier, considering the above-freezing temperatures we had overnight." Fog when I'd woken confirmed that, though it had burned off already under the lovely warmth of the morning sun, feeling more like late spring than December. "And, if Ms. Ennis can be believed, the grave was intact when she left at dusk."

Wait, he was sharing information back? I held still and waited for more. Wasn't disappointed.

"Which gives us a very narrow window of time." He looked up then, at me, no sign of his anger visible though I doubted it was completely gone just yet. He was just a good actor and a good cop.

"Without any kind of video footage, it's going to be hard to identify the culprit." I pointed at the ground.

"Though there's at least a few footprints that might help."

He nodded, careful and precise. "I'll have Jill look into it," he said. Drew a deep breath. "Fiona." Paused, exhaled. "Fee." Crew shook his head then, smiled, though without real humor. "As always, your input is... helpful." That was a complement. I took it. "And, as always, uninvited." Hard to hold that gaze when I knew he was right. Except Tracey kind of invited me, hadn't she? No, wait. She'd only come back to the B&B because we'd asked her to. But she'd needed us, needed to talk. To have someone listen to her and believe her. All sophistry, though, and I knew it. Crew seemed to watch the facts spin out into truth in my head before speaking again, this time kindly. "I'm taking this very seriously," he said. "And carefully. For obvious reasons." Dad. He was talking about Dad, wasn't he? I opened my mouth to respond, to deny the need to tread lightly, but Crew was already speaking again. "Your father was an excellent sheriff and still is a brilliant investigator. I value his work and his ethics. I promise I won't twist this against him. If it hadn't been for the coroner's mistake, I'm positive John would have gotten to the bottom of things." Wait, was Crew worried I'd be mad at him for looking into one of Dad's old cases? Had I misread him? "But I need to have the chance to do that without a giant dog and pony show." Ah, the rub. "You have a tendency toward your father's brilliance but without his... finesse." My lips twisted into a wry smile while Crew grinned at me. "You understand what I'm asking?"

"You're trying to protect Dad's reputation and my bull in a china shop methods make that harder." I wasn't stupid.

"I'm glad we see things the same way." Crew chuckled. "I never thought I'd say that about you and me."

I laughed too, though with sadness behind it. There had been a time I hoped we might connect on a more personal level. And, if it wasn't for my penchant for being nosy and solving murders, maybe that would have been possible. Seeing this side of Crew raised that hope again, despite knowing the chances of ever having a relationship with him that wasn't based in conflict and confrontation were pretty slim.

A girl could dream about such things though, right?

"Thank you for sharing what you know," he said, turning and walking off. Stopping a moment, looking back over one shoulder. "I'd appreciate it if you did uncover anything else if you'd let me know." Crew left me there, staring after him, before forcing myself to turn back to the empty grave and the odd sorrow at the lost opportunity.

When I finally pulled myself together, silly girl, I did one final walk around the plot, pausing near the fence to look out into the woods.

Spotted the footprints and drag marks just inside the tree line.

And, in true busybody fashion, acted before I could think about what Crew just asked of me, hopping the chain link to investigate.

CHAPTER NINE

I could have called Crew, of course I could have. Wouldn't have been a huge effort to just turn and yell his name, even. He wasn't entirely gone from the parking lot yet when I hopped the fence. I even heard the rumble of his truck engine starting when I ducked into the undergrowth onto the path just a few feet from the edge of the trees.

Thing was, he didn't notice I'd gone, wasn't paying attention, obviously, because despite the fact I half expected him to show up out of the blue because he'd been watching me and noticed I'd already reneged on our so-called bargain (wait, had I agreed to it in a way that could be upheld in a court of law?) I followed the tracks and drag marks alone and on my own, not a sniff of Crew Turner to be found.

The soil was soft on the edge of the path, led right to a dirt road behind the church. Wait, I knew this road. It led around the property and to the other side of town, one of those local bypass roads tourists never used but those of us from around these parts used as shortcuts when necessary. Mind you, the bumpy and rutted way wasn't exactly photo shoot ready, nor kind to shocks and car undercarriages, enough puddles skimmed with ice thanks to the cool shelter of the trees lowering the temp to just freezing and heaves to make even the most hearty Reading resident wary unless in possession of a 4X4.

I paused at the edge of the road, noting tire treads that looked more rugged than the average car. The footprints ended there, as did the drag marks. So, whoever did the digging up of the corpse had a vehicle waiting to transport the uncovered goods.

Which led to a dead end (what was with the puns already?). The trouble was, the road itself was hard-packed enough the tire indentations vanished the moment they left the softer edge and carried the body away. At least I knew now how and where, which meant the possibility of some kind of trail after all.

I reached for my phone as I hopped the fence yet again and headed for my car. The number I dialed, however, wasn't Crew Turner's.

"Hey, Jill," I said when the deputy answered, my friend's greeting happy enough. "I need to tell you something and I don't want you to get mad."

She laughed on the other end of the line and I could almost see her tall, broad-shouldered self with her blonde ponytail bouncing under her knitted hat, grinning at her phone.

"Let me guess," she said. "You found something out about the case and if you call Crew he'll be pissed."

"We just had a conversation," I said carefully. "I don't want to disappoint him."

Her chuckle made me grin in return. "Just tell me," she said. "I'll make sure he finds out from me."

I filled her in on what I'd stumbled over while she grunted softly in reply.

"I'm on my way there now," she said. "I'll take a look. Thanks, Fee. Very helpful."

"Happy to hear it," I said. "At least you appreciate me."

She laughed one more time, the sound of her car door closing and engine firing up in the background. "You make me look good," she said. "I'll keep you posted." And hung up.

Okay then.

I was just pulling up to Petunia's when my phone rang, Dr. Aberstock's number flashing. "Hey, doc," I said.

"Fiona," he said in that cheerful tone of his. "I tried to reach your father but he's not answering. Can you pass something along?" Which was code for here's some information Crew likely wouldn't want me to have but Dr. Aberstock, on the other hand, wasn't even hesitating to hand over.

I loved that man. "Sure thing," I said, grinning all over again. "I'll make sure he gets it."

"Just confirming it was sleeping pills," the doc said. "And since Brian Beckett didn't have a prescription for such medication, I'm calling it murder."

"I'll make sure Dad knows," I said. "Thanks for the confirmation."

"Fee." Dr. Aberstock cleared his throat on the other end of the line. "You know I adore your father. John Fleming is one of the best cops I've ever worked with. His record is stellar. This isn't his fault."

I sighed and nodded though he couldn't see me. "I know, Dr. Aberstock," I said. "Mistakes happen to the best of us. But you know Dad's blaming himself."

"I do," the doc said. "Because that's the kind of man your father is. No matter what the circumstances, he holds himself accountable. Please, if you can talk to him, assure him if I'd been in the office the night Brian Beckett was brought in, he'd have had a case to pursue instead of this unhappy revisit. And also assure him," his tone changed to firm and almost angry, "I'll be reviewing each and every case Dr. Montrose oversaw during my vacations, under a microscope."

"I'm sure he'll be relieved to hear it." I thought about it a moment, then asked a question. "Doc, how would I go about finding out who in Brian Beckett's life had a prescription for sleeping pills?"

Dr. Aberstock didn't hesitate. "The investigating officer should be able to look into that, even after the fact," he said. Suggesting loud and clear I talk, not to Crew, but to my father. The fact the doc suggested I bypass the sheriff wasn't lost on me, nor was his then cheery goodbye.

I hung up then, grateful for Dr. Aberstock and his kindness. Knowing it wouldn't matter, not to Dad, but hoping it might at least give my father a modicum of comfort.

Yeah. Because John Fleming was forgiving of himself when he dropped the ball. Time to give him a shot at making things right once and for all.

CHAPTER TEN

If I expected to find Dad in a funk, I was sorely mistaken. In fact, when I arrived at my parent's house (Petunia in tow and the staff left in charge), I found my father at the kitchen peninsula, Mom making coffee and Dad on the phone.

"Thanks, Don," Dad said, hanging up as I stopped to hug him, then circled to hug my mother, accepting the mug of coffee from her while she poured another for Dad.

"Dr. Aberstock called," I said.

Dad nodded, pushing a notepad toward me, his heavy handwriting legible for once. "Already had a chat with Lloyd," he said. "That was Don Pierce, at the pharmacy. Looks like we have two suspects to chat with."

"They both had scripts for sleeping pills?" I arched an eyebrow at the list. That meant Tracey's suspicions about her uncle were correct, Kenny Beckett having been prescribed the pills. So, it turned out, had her mother, Jayne. With Tracey's mother dead, was there even a way to find out if she was a viable suspect?

And, if she had killed Tracey's father, would it serve anyone to deliver that news to her still grieving and now orphaned daughter?

"You're thinking what I'm thinking," Dad said, grimacing and shaking his head.

"Surely you don't think Jayne had anything to do with it?" Mom seemed shocked by the suggestion.

"We can't rule her out yet, Mom," I said. "We only have Tracey's story to go by at this point. And, if truth be told, while I believe her, this means she had access to the murder weapon herself. Since she found the body..."

Dad didn't comment on that. "The timing is rather telling."

I sighed, hating this line of thought but knowing better than to let it go. "Considering Jayne just passed, Tracey and Kenny are back in town at the same time... yeah, Dad. There has to be a connection."

Mom tsked softly, but more out of pity and sorrow. "That poor girl," she said. "She's had a hard life, dear thing. I can't imagine what she's going through."

Dad pushed back from the counter, slapping both big hands on his thighs. Any outward appearance of guilt over fumbling the case had been smothered in my father's typical confidence. "Then let's either get her the answers she's looking for. Or."

"Put her in prison where she belongs." I set down my own cup. And told him what I found at the cemetery along with what I learned from Gertrude and Crew.

"We need to go back to the scene of the crime," Dad said, heading for the door. I followed, slipping into my coat and boots while Mom hovered, looking worried. When she hugged me, Dad's brief kiss to her cheek preceding his march out the door to his truck, she whispered in my ear. My mother didn't hesitate when I arched an eyebrow at the panting pug sitting on her feet, babysitting the least of her concerns. "I'm worried about him," she said. "He blames himself."

"I know," I whispered back. "We'll figure it out, Mom. That'll help."

She blinked at me, tears brimming, but forced a brave smile and a wave for Dad.

I had amazing parents.

I followed him rather than going with him, wanting my own car. It was a short ride to the farm, the large "Evergreen Acres" sign pointing me in the right direction even if I wasn't on Dad's heels.

The long drive, flanked by Christmas trees in training, ended abruptly in a large, open yard, big, white house wrapped in a veranda across from the entry, far left filled with a huge warehouse, the steel roof shining in the sun. But it was the tall form of Kenny Beckett standing next to the company truck, clearly arguing with the smaller and yet no less fierce Marion that caught my attention.

They didn't seem to notice we'd arrived, were still shouting at one another when Dad and I got out of our respective vehicles and headed their way. Kenny finally realized they had visitors, looked up as Marion said something about a payment, the angry owner now contrite and almost embarrassed, though the woman who managed the farm didn't seem to care if we saw them fighting.

"John Fleming," Kenny said, shaking Dad's hand. "And Fiona, correct?" I nodded, shook as well, though when I turned to offer my hand to Marion she ignored the gesture, hands tucked into her pockets, face grim and cheeks still flushed from the words they'd been having.

The sound of another truck pulling up had me wincing. Impossible not to guess who might be behind the wheel, though when Crew joined us he didn't seem upset, merely polite when he, too, shook Kenny's hand.

"Mr. Beckett," the sheriff said. "I have a few questions."

"Of course," the farm owner said.

"I understand you take sleeping pills." I almost gaped at Dad's audacity, the blunt way he just blurted that out. Caught the clench of Crew's jaw and, on impulse, reached out and tugged just a fraction on the sheriff's cuff. His gaze slid sideways to me, and I bit my lower lip, hoping he got the message.

Dad needed this.

Wouldn't you know? Crew was smarter than the average bear. Let my father carry on, while Kenny stuttered.

"I used to," Kenny said. "But I've been doing hypnosis for my insomnia the last few years." Frowned finally, as though trying to resume control. "Why is it any business of yours?"

"Because," my father said, "your brother," he nodded to Kenny, "was murdered and it's time the truth came out."

They both gaped at him. Kenny's face crumbled, Marion's eyes filling with tears. Their anger gone, they turned to one another, Kenny hugging his brother's ex-wife who cried on his shoulder a moment before they pulled free and got themselves together.

Quite the act if Tracey was to be believed. "I'd heard your divorce was less than amicable," I said before I could stop myself.

Marion jerked like I'd slapped her. "We might not have survived our marriage, but I still spent years with the man," she said. "I loved him once. To find out he didn't kill himself, that he was murdered..." Marion looked away, wiped at her eyes.

"Didn't stop the two of you from undercutting Tracey's part of the farm," I said. Well now, there you were, righteous rage for the little guy. I wondered when it would show up.

Kenny looked distinctly uncomfortable, ashamed, even, but Marion just shrugged.

"That's business," she said. Wow, classy. "How did Brian die?"

I managed to stay quiet, Dad, too, while the sound of a car pulling up, a door opening and closing behind us, distracted me. Leaving it to Crew to fill in the gaps.

"He was drugged," the sheriff said. "Sleeping pills laced in his whiskey. Whoever killed him dosed him first to make sure he wouldn't wake up when they hung him in the rig."

While I wasn't surprised when Crew showed up, I have to admit I wasn't expecting the next person who joined us, though perhaps it shouldn't have been a surprise when Tracey pushed her way past me, almost throwing herself on Kenny.

"You killed him!" She screamed at her uncle before spinning on Marion. "You both did." She threw a photo at her ex-stepmother before collapsing into sobs. "I hate you!"

Dad caught Tracey, supporting her, while I relieved the shaking Marion of the photograph her former stepdaughter used as a weapon against her. Glanced at it, eyebrows rising in surprise, not just at the content (that was revealing enough, as in lacking clothing and decorum between Kenny and Marion) but the date stamped on the corner from the camera that took it.

"Looks like you two were closer than you let on." I handed it to Crew who frowned down at it before looking up to meet Kenny's now guarded gaze.

"You were having an affair," the sheriff said. "And this photo is proof of that." He looked back and forth between the two of them, both becoming more visibly uncomfortable by the minute, Kenny barely able to meet the sheriff's eyes, Marion's face bright red. "Since this image is dated a year before Brian's death and was in the possession of Tracey's mother," Tracey had to have found it in Jayne's storage locker, there was no other explanation for its sudden appearance, "I can only assume at the very least she knew of the affair." Neither of them spoke. "The question is, did she tell Brian?"

Because, like it or not, here was yet another motive for murder.

CHAPTER ELEVEN

"You were here that night." Tracey had pulled herself together sufficiently to throw that at her uncle. Kenny didn't argue as she went on. "That's why I went to bed early. You and Dad were arguing again. And drinking." She pushed my father away, but not roughly, as though she needed to stand on her own two feet. "Did you kill him, Uncle Kenny? Did you murder my father?" She choked on that question, jabbing an index finger at Marion. "For her?" Tracey didn't even look at the woman now staring at her own boots like her guilt wouldn't let her face the girl she'd once called stepdaughter.

Kenny didn't answer, though Crew didn't seem to take that as a reason not to act.

"Mr. Beckett," the sheriff said with grim intensity, "I think you'd better come to the office and answer a few questions there. Shall we?"

The fact Kenny didn't argue, seemed dazed and

almost confused, meant he didn't fight Crew's request and, a few minutes later, the two were driving off in the sheriff's truck.

I was surprised when Marion broke her frozen stance and guilty hover and made a move for Tracey, trying to hug her. "Tracey, honey, I'm so sorry—"

But whatever it was Marion was going to apologize for—cheating on her father, having knowledge of his murder or just plain grief over how things turned out—she didn't get the chance to finish. Tracey spun and ran off, heading for the big warehouse, while Marion covered her face in both hands and started to cry.

I left Dad with the grieving woman and headed after Tracey, finding her, a moment later, just inside the door to the tree storage. The dim light and almost overpowering scent of evergreen made me pause, my eyesight adjusting slowly to the change in illumination. Tracey hadn't turned on any lights so by the time I'd blinked away the bright sunlight she had closed the distance between herself and the large rack in the middle of the room, staring up at it with tears running down her cheeks.

I winced at the sight of the monstrous thing, twine running from large spools on one end, winding through rings down the center of the long machine, a completed tree trussed like a Christmas goose standing on the far end. And, upon examining it and the height at which the twine began, had to agree with my father and the otherwise slacking Dr. Montrose. No way could Brian have accidentally been caught up in it. He had to have been placed there, like one of the very trees he harvested.

"I haven't been back here since Dad died," Tracey whispered. "I thought I could do this, go through Mom's stuff. But it's so hard, Fee." She hugged herself and I hugged her, too. "What am I going to do?"

"You're going to accept more help," I said. "Day and Mom and I will come to the unit with you. We're happy to sort things out." She almost fought me, but I turned her to face me. "You don't have to be alone, Tracey. There are people in the world who really want to be there for you."

"But why?" She almost wailed that. "You don't know me. Why do you care?"

"Mom knows you," I said. "And even if she didn't, it's... just the way we are."

A little snuffling, some dabbing at her face with her sleeve and she nodded. "Thank you," she said, voice cracking. "I've never had anyone I could rely on. Mom was so sick all the time and no one seemed to care."

My heart broke for Tracey and, in that moment, even if she confessed to me she'd killed her own father I would have moved heaven and earth to make sure she got away with it. Because no one should have to feel so alone they didn't know how to accept help.

"Let's go," I said, guiding her to the still-open doorway. "The past lives here, Tracey. But you don't have to anymore."

I had just waved her off, seeing her drive away with the promise she was going back to Petunia's to lie down, when I noticed movement near the corner of the building. Dad had disappeared though his truck remained, so I could only assume he was inside the house talking with Marion. Curious, I headed toward the motion and, on doing so, spotted a startled face that I recognized before the woman spun and disappeared.

Olga Nowak was living up to Tracey's accusations of snooping, apparently. Since I, too, shared that particular moniker, I figured following her was the most logical option, one busybody to another.

Trouble was, she knew the terrain and I didn't, so it wasn't until I was red-faced and panting, wishing I'd worn a lighter coat despite the descending chill now replacing the spring-like warmth of the morning, that I realized I'd come to the edge of the tidy evergreens and into some heavier underbrush.

The only way I knew I'd reached the property line? One, a barbed-wire fence that had a section cut out of it—not the owner's choice, I was sure—and the business end of a double barrel shotgun pointed at me as Olga turned to level her weapon with threatening intent.

"Take one step past that fence," she said, "and I'll shoot you for trespassing."

I gaped at her audacity. "Considering I just chased you off someone else's property," I snapped back, "you might want to think that option over."

"Prove it," she snarled.

Oh, she did not just go there. "Listen, crazy lady," because I was in no mood to deal with this right now, thank you very much, "you either put that gun away or

I'll make sure you never get a chance to cross onto this property again, let alone your own."

Maybe an empty threat, but she seemed to take it seriously, lowering the weapon, grimacing at me in return. Even as my phone buzzed, a text coming in.

I checked it despite the furious and clearly cracked walnut with the shotgun still staring in my direction like she was looking for a reason to pull the trigger. Was very glad I did, since the text was from Jill and held some very interesting information I felt rather vindictive about considering the circumstances.

Wildlife cam on the road caught the perp, my deputy friend sent. Along with a photo. Of none other than the woman I faced right now, driving an ATV with a trailer on the back, the corpse of Brian Beckett in clear view.

I looked up, met her squinting eyes. Turned my phone toward her. "Looks like the odds of my threat are about as real as yours." She grimaced, the gun barrel rising again. Oddly, I wasn't afraid, more furious than anything. "You do know digging up bodies is a felony?" What in the heck possessed her to exhume her neighbor's corpse nine years later?

"Olga." I hadn't heard Dad approach, saw the woman flinch, the gun pivot in her hands. But when she saw it was my father, she lowered the weapon again, turning her head as if embarrassed for him to find her like this. "Have you met my daughter, Fiona?"

Olga grunted something that might have been hello but likely wasn't. "I didn't hurt nobody, sheriff," she said. "Minding my own business."

My father didn't correct the use of that title. "You dug up Brian from his grave, Olga," Dad said, slightly amused. She grinned at him suddenly, showing gaps in her teeth. "That's hardly minding your own business." Okay, clearly Dad had history with this whackadoodle, so I let him deal with her. Since my methods had more than likely been leading me down a path that would have ended up with buckshot and blood. "Why did you do it?"

She abruptly repositioned her gun, opening the stock, tucking it under her arm in a practiced move that proved to me she not only knew her way around it but was probably a better shot than my dad. "It's personal," she said.

"You and Brian had a relationship?" Dad seemed surprised by that.

But when Olga snort-smiled and he-hawed a braying laugh, it was clear he'd missed the point.

"I want access to the land," she said, eyes bright. "He said I could use it. I used it all along." Tracey said she'd been trespassing. That Brian fought with her over it. But I didn't call her on that, let her continue. "And then he died and that moron," she snarled, shifting back to furious and mad, "and the woman he was banging," so she knew about the affair, "went and ruined everything."

"What's on the land you want, Olga?" Dad's gentleness shouldn't have surprised me, his easy nature with the old woman.

Worked, too, how she went all soft and sweet on him. "You won't tell nobody?" Dad shook his head while she glanced side to side like someone might overheard before whispering loudly enough I was sure they heard back on the farm, "Mushrooms."

Dad's eyebrows shot up while I choked on a laugh. "The magical kind, Olga?" He tsked at her but she shook her head.

"The expensive kind," she retorted, digging something out of her pocket, showing us a small, thin strip of white and dark. "The kind chefs in New York pay hundreds of dollars for. Each."

Holy heck.

Even Dad was floored by that. "They grow here?"

"On my land," she sounded proud of that. "And over there." She grunted then, pointing over the fence. "Brian let me pick his, kept the oaks and beeches intact. That's what's needed, oaks and beeches and a certain kind of soil and mountain air." She scowled into the woods toward the main house. "Then Brian died and his brother and his little whore started cutting them all down and putting in those ridiculous evergreens." She spat on the ground. "No more mushrooms." She pointed to the right. "They're planning to dig up the last grove in the spring. I had to do something."

"Olga, do you know something about Brian's death?" Dad sounded sad. "You could have told me then, you know. When I asked you."

She shrugged, though she did seem ashamed. "Didn't hurt me none," she said. "Just kept picking. Except it's hurt me lots since and it needs to stop." She grit what remained of her teeth. "If he goes to jail, will they leave the trees alone?"

Dad inhaled very slowly before answering. "Olga," he said, "do you have evidence that Kenny killed Brian?"

She blew a raspberry into the chill air. "Saw them go in the barn that night," she said. "Kenny came out. But Brian never did."

CHAPTER TWELVE

I sat on a plastic container filled with kitchen contents (according to the masking tape strip on the top) and sorted through the file folder Tracey handed me, Daisy perched nearby going through a box of assorted items. Mom hadn't been able to join us, still home with Petunia in her possession, but promised to come later that afternoon, not that it mattered. Having us there seemed to have lightened Tracey's spirits somewhat. She didn't seem surprised or all that upset when I told her what I knew, though hearing from me that it was more than likely her uncle killed her father that night should maybe have been more impactful.

Except, of course, she'd already reached that conclusion on her own.

"You're sure he did it?" Tracey's tone wasn't empty enough for me to worry she was stuffing her emotions down, just sad and curious.

"Crew seems convinced," I said. "And Dad. There's a lot of evidence."

"Yes, but are you convinced?" Tracey seemed intent on that question, so I rolled it over before replying.

"I don't know," I finally said with a sigh. "I wish it was cut and dried for you, Tracey. But sometimes the best we get is mostly sure."

She nodded at that, went back to her own sorting.

Daisy had thought to bring her music and portable speaker so we had Christmas tunes to listen to while we worked. I smiled as Daisy called Tracey over and the two leafed through a photo album, the young woman pointing things out to my best friend as they went. And I realized this wasn't actually about going through Jayne's stuff to get rid of it, but a chance for Tracey to reconcile herself with her past and move on.

Something I was enthusiastically in agreement with.

I flipped through the folders, came to one marked with Brian's name, opened it while the strains of "Hark the Herald Angels Sing" melded with Daisy and Tracey's giggles, and felt the entire world come to a heaving stop. Forced myself to breathe while I read the contents. Glanced at my bestie, knowing shock had to be the only expression registering on my face, caught her surprise and quick nod.

Message received. I had something I needed to look into, and I didn't want Tracey involved until I knew the truth of it.

"Sorry," I said, standing quickly after tucking the

file into my coat, "I have to run to Petunia's for a minute."

"It's okay," Tracey said, Daisy waving me off. "Thanks, Fee. For everything."

I fired up my car in the gathering dusk come early this far in December, hoping to add to that gratitude of hers. Because if what I'd just read was correct? Cut and dried might be her Christmas present after all.

So, I know what you're thinking. Calling Crew, calling Dad, calling Jill, heck, calling anyone would have been the smart thing to do. Except, I had this weird worry that I was wrong, jumping to conclusions, and, if I was going to be honest, needed to prove it to myself before I dragged anyone else into my guesswork. Because the faster I drove to my destination, the more I doubted I was right and the further along the path of questioning my reasoning I walked until I was climbing out of my car in the yard at the farm.

To the sight of Marion hastily shoving suitcases into the back of her car.

And had my guesses confirmed after all.

She gaped at me a moment as I closed the distance between us, a deer caught in headlights she knew were going to be her end. Everything in her expression, in the fear and darting panic in her eyes, screamed guilty while I fished out the file and showed it to her.

"You had a prenup," I said, Tracey's mention of it brought into evidence physically in the papers I showed her ex-stepmom. "One that stipulated if you cheated on Brian you'd lose all your shares in case of a divorce."

Marion snarled at me. "Where did you get that?"

"Jayne had it," I said. "Turns out she cared about Brian more than you ever did." Had Tracey's mother ever stopped loving him? No way of knowing now, though she'd certainly done her best to keep an eye on him despite their parting. "Just like she had evidence you broke that agreement with Kenny long before you filed for divorce."

Marion didn't have the right to so much anger, not after what she'd done. "You have no idea what he was like," she said.

"Never got the chance to meet him," I said. "Alive that is. Since you murdered him." I tsked at her. "For money, Marion, really? Shares in the farm? Did Kenny know what you were planning? Did the two of you set this up so you could control the farm and cut Tracey out?" Despicable, horrific.

"Tracey had controlling shares without Kenny's help." Marion's eyes darted left and right. Looking for a way out? I was between her and the driver's seat of her car, so there was no exit that way. Though I had her where I wanted her, what exactly was I going to do with her? Way to think things through, Fleming. "I knew Brian had the photos, said he had proof of the affair. He was going to cut me out, after putting up with him for years." She thought he owed her, huh?

"This farm worth his life, Marion?" Yes, I was baiting her. I needed her off balance, at least long enough to figure out a plan to corner her and take her in. Or talk her into turning herself in. Like my life ever went that easily.

Oh, and by the way, the whole *what was the worst that could happen* question from last night? Regretted it, down to my toes.

She didn't answer that question, rage turning to cunning as she spoke. "I heard him fighting with Kenny that night," she said. "I snuck onto the farm to talk to Brian, to make him see reason. He didn't say anything about the affair. They were fighting about other things, stupid things. Contracts and planting. The usual." She shook then, trembling all over, staring at the suitcases she'd managed to cram into the trunk of her sedan. "I waited until Kenny left, offered Brian a bottle. An olive branch." Marion barked a laugh. "Laced with Kenny's sleeping pills." Of course she had. She might have had an affair with her husband's brother but it was clear she held him in about the same esteem as she did the man she murdered. "Didn't take long to knock him out. Though it was an effort to get him on the rig." She wasn't a big woman, and all that dead weight (puns, oiy!), I could only imagine. "It did its job when I turned it on. I watched him hang." Zero remorse there. The woman was a monster. "I tripped the breaker on the way out, so it would look like suicide and slipped out just in time. I almost ran in to Tracey." Wait, there was grief, but for the girl. And when Marion met my eyes, hers were wet. "I love that child," she said. "I never wanted to hurt her."

"But you were fine stealing her part of the farm from her," I said.

Marion flinched. "That was Kenny's idea," she

said. "I couldn't afford to rock the boat. Not after what I'd done."

Leaving the door open for Tracey to lose her legacy along with her father.

"Why didn't Jayne use the photos against you to trigger the prenup?" If she had cared about Brian...

"She didn't have the prenup," Marion said. Pointed at the file folder. "Those papers were Brian's. She must have had some of his things mistakenly transferred to her when he died. I lost track of them when the house was emptied after his death. I was going to burn them. Didn't get the chance." She shook her head. "Just bad luck."

"And about to get worse," I said. "When you come with me and tell the sheriff the truth."

I saw it in her face the instant she made the choice, but I was still too slow to stop her. Which meant, the moment Marion Jackson leaped into action and ran for the barn, I was swearing my fool head off and racing in pursuit.

This time when I passed through the door into the warehouse, it was so dark I stumbled, and that saved my life. As I fell to one knee, I heard the swish of something passing over my head, caught the reflection of the light from the yard on metal and lunged forward, catching Marion at the knees and sending her falling backward with a shriek. The ax she'd tried to decapitate me with clattered to the concrete floor, her own head hitting hard enough I heard it bounce.

Panting, leaning against the unconscious woman

beside me, I pulled out my phone and dialed a familiar number, knowing for once I wasn't going to mind hearing Crew yell at me for not minding my own business.

At least I still had the ability.

CHAPTER THIRTEEN

Petunia trotted through the healthy two inches of snow that had fallen overnight, her little paws stirring up the fluffy fall, her cute little red coat barely fitting her girth despite the fact she was on a continual diet.

The afternoon air carried the scent of the town's tree toward me, the lights already glowing though dusk was just settling around us, the main attraction looming over the square. Snow definitely made things feel more festive, despite the fact Olivia had, dead body adorning it only a few days ago or not, decided to leave things as they were. Which meant, of course, lots of chatter about bad luck and corpses at Christmas that I found oddly amusing despite the gravity of the situation.

It wouldn't have been Reading if there wasn't drama, after all.

I'd only this morning attended the reinterment of Brian Beckett, Daisy holding Tracey's hand on one side while I did the same on the other, my parents flanking us, even Crew there as the minister said a few words. I'd been a bit surprised Kenny joined the ceremony, though Tracey informed me she and her uncle had a long talk about the past and, in doing so, came to an agreement.

Turned out now that Marion was going to prison for murder, her shares reverted to Kenny. Who, in turn, gave them—without asking for payment—to Tracey, restoring her legacy and, it seemed, giving both of them a new start.

"I guess I'm staying in Reading," Tracey told me in the parking lot after the service, her uncle lurking nearby. She seemed the most content and even happy she had since we'd met. "Since I'm suddenly half owner of the farm and Uncle Kenny lives in Atlanta."

He joined us then, arm around her tentative but not rejected. "It's my biggest regret," he said, "choosing business over family. I finally get a chance to rectify that. We're still working things out," Tracey nodded but smiled, "but I can't think of anyone better to run the farm for both of us."

When I considered that, according to Dad, Olga had her own happy ending, I couldn't help but wonder about the magic of the holidays. Crew agreed not to press charges when Kenny and Tracey insisted, instead pairing up with their neighbor in the mushroom business. Amazing how such solid wins could come out of sorrow.

I had run into Crew on my way to my car outside the cemetery, paused to talk where he leaned against his truck, watching my father shake Kenny's hand.

"All's well that ends well, I suppose," he said. Met my eyes, tense and still unhappy, though his anger had lost its edge since he arrived at the farm to take Marion into custody.

"You're still mad," I said.

He shifted his weight from one foot to the other. "Someone I know has difficulty with boundaries and agreements."

"Someone I know," I said rather archly, "assumes the boundaries and agreements he dictates are actually mutual without confirmation."

Crew grunted then. "You're saying I want to believe you listen to me."

I didn't comment, not even when he sighed and shrugged, turning to open his truck door.

"I'm having a gathering at Petunia's tonight," I said, my mind stumbling over my heart's weird impulse to bring it up. Crew hesitated while I went on, cheeks pinking and brain chastising me for even mentioning it because no way was he going to say yes. "Friends and family. A little Christmas party." Crew's silent staring made me even more nervous. "You're welcome to come, if you want. 6pm." And I'd clearly lost my mind because the last place Crew Turner wanted to be was anywhere near me.

"I'm not family," he said then, voice oddly soft. Paused, eyes quiet and curious.

"No one should have to be alone at Christmas," I

said then, more abrupt and sharp than I meant to be, put off by his attitude, by my own continuing attraction to him despite the fact we would never, ever see eye-to-eye. "Come if you want. The invitation stands." I walked away then, head high, heart pounding and internally berating for putting myself into a position where he could reject me.

Hurt more than it should have, frankly.

I paused by the big tree, smiled up at it, memory of that moment with my burning cheeks as I drove away and refused to look at Crew still giving me the uncomfortable train wreck sensation I seemed to cultivate when it came to the handsome sheriff.

Whatever might come, I was home and whether he liked it or not, I wasn't going anywhere. Or changing a single thing about me.

So there.

We were home in lots of time for a shower, to give Petunia a thorough brushing and tie her cute Christmas bandana around her neck before Mom and Dad arrived, Daisy right behind them. I took a moment to admire the deep emerald dress I'd chosen for the evening, loving the color's complement to my hair color. Not my usual shade, tending toward jeans and flannel or t-shirts, but it was Christmas, so a little extravagance was acceptable, right?

Jill was next to arrive, looking amazing in a dark suit, the Aberstocks caroling their way through the front door, the bells jingling them inside. Daisy had already fired up the music, the appearance of Tracey and Kenny a nice surprise, a few other friends rounding out the seats at the dining room table while Mom whipped up a delicious meal and the festive spirit I'd been longing for filled me to the brim.

I was just passing out champagne when the door jangled one last time, turning me on the ball of my high heel, smile already in place. Drank in the tall, dark-haired deliciousness who'd decided to join us after all and felt that smile I'd been wearing turn to something a little bit more satisfied.

Left the others to their own recognizance to join Crew at the door, taking his wool trench coat, a dusting of falling snow on his shoulders, in his dark hair, trying not to stare at the rare sight of him in a suit, dark blue shirt the color of his eyes open at the collar two buttons, black curls swept back from his forehead.

He held out a wrapped box, the beautiful red bow sparkling with glitter. "I heard there was a party for friends and family," he said. Waited.

I took the present, and, on impulse, tippy toed up to kiss his cheek.

"Friends and family are always welcome," I said, surprised to hear my voice had dropped a little, to feel the tingling zing inside as he smiled that slow and sexy smile of his, eyes sparkling.

I let him pass, entering the sitting room to place the gift he'd brought under the tree before returning to the foyer to watch him. He shook Dad's hand, Mom hugging him while he laughed and hugged her back. Which had my heart softening and my mind spinning over possibilities, wishes and hopes.

I couldn't help but wonder if maybe we might have a chance after all.

Christmas miracles, right?

THE END

FROM THE AUTHOR

Patti Larsen is a USA Today bestselling, international multiple award-winning author with a passion for the voices in her head. Now with over 150 titles in happy publication, she lives in beautiful Prince Edward Island, Canada, with her plethora of pets.

Find her at https://www.pattilarsen.com/home

And her newsletter at https://bit.ly/PattiLarsenEmail

SLEIGH BELLS WING

HILLARY AVIS

Peck the halls with boughs of holly...

CHAPTER ONE

Ruth Chapman was going to miss this old farm. Yes, even the pothole at the end of the gravel driveway that threatened to crack her Honda's front axle every time she turned off the highway. She'd made the turn so many times that she knew to slow to a crawl before cranking the steering wheel and easing her tires through it, like a secret handshake that allowed her entry to the family property unscathed.

The car crept down the narrow, gravel driveway, past the bare-branched apple orchard, toward the little yellow house her grandparents lived in from the day they married until the day they passed on. Amos and Louise Chapman had been frugal folks, children of the Depression who didn't need much to be content. They raised four kids in a tiny, two-bedroom cottage and hosted every holiday meal in the minuscule kitchen, even when their brood burgeoned with grandchildren and great-grandchildren.

For her whole childhood, Ruth assumed that everyone ate Christmas dinner sitting on the living room floor with a plate balanced on their knees. That's just how it *was* when family gathered together. Squishy. Packed with love.

She'd miss that, too.

It's not that she wanted to sell the farm, Ruth reflected as she parked the car and mounted the porch steps, noting that the railing wobbled on her way up. Rotten post. She'd have her brother, Rusty, replace it before the home inspector caught the problem and delayed the sale for the repair.

It's just that two years on from Grandpa's death, the orchard was getting expensive to maintain. The mowing, the pruning, the harvest. Plus, the cottage roof needed attention, and the barn was going to fall down if somebody didn't get in there and prop it up. And none of the Chapman clan, scattered across the state and down into California, had extra cash to sink into a property that they visited only once or twice per year.

Ruth and Rusty, the only Chapmans still in Honeytree, had done their best to keep the farm from decomposing, but they had lives to lead, too.

Nobody wanted to sell it, but nobody wanted to take it on, either. It was time.

Speaking of time...Ruth checked her phone. Her client, Donna Hughes, was due to arrive in a few minutes, just enough time to turn on the lights and open some windows to air the place out.

It was chilly inside the cottage, the thermostat set as low as possible to save money, just warm enough to keep the pipes from freezing during the recent cold snap, so she kept her coat on as she moved room to room, flipping on the light switches and pushing curtains open to let the weak, December sunlight stream in.

Lighting sold properties, especially this time of year, when most days were gray and gloomy and the sun set before five o'clock. It was real estate sales 101. Plus, Ruth knew for a fact that Donna, whose lucky slot machine pull had resulted in a million-dollar windfall and an early retirement, dreamed of a space where she could set up a painting studio. The attic bedroom would be the perfect spot, with its picturesque view of the old barn and the blueberry farm next door.

Ruth headed upstairs, planning to move the furniture to show how an easel would fit by the window, in case Donna didn't have the imagination. Most homebuyers didn't. She put her weight behind the old desk under the window and shoved it into the corner, dusting her hands and standing back to admire the room once the space was clear.

The room was dirty, she realized. Bits of fluff littered the bare floorboards, and a layer of dust coated the top surfaces of all the furniture. There was even some kind of *animal* dung dotted here and there, maybe from a bat or other small creature that had taken up residence.

Irritation prickled her scalp, the kind that made her silver-streaked curls feel even tighter than usual. Rusty was supposed to clean the house yesterday. She'd *paid* him to clean it, actually hired him from the small budget she'd set aside as the listing agent for the property. She'd cut him a check last night!

Fifty-six years old, and the man still didn't know what "clean the house" meant. *Every room, Rusty.* Not just some of them.

She couldn't show it like this. She ran downstairs, thankful that no one had bothered to empty the kitchen cupboards yet, so all the good flannel cleaning cloths were still stacked underneath the sink beside a gummy bottle of dish soap and half-empty jug of Pine-Sol—the only cleaners a person needed, according to Granny Lou, who'd cooked up her own furniture polish and window cleaner from pantry ingredients.

When she retraced her steps through the living room, Ruth realized with horror that the dirt wasn't confined to the upstairs.

The dust lay thick on the living room mantel, too, blanketing the shepherdess figurine and the clock and the candlesticks, the graduation photos and wedding photos of her father and his siblings, the baby pictures of their grandchildren, all now in their forties and fifties.

She swiped her dust cloth hurriedly, getting the worst of it. And that's when she found it. Under the 3-D decorative ducks that hung, wings outstretched, beside the fireplace, a tower of bird droppings topped a large ceramic elephant like a decorative ornament. Perfectly placed on its head, like if you spray painted the whole thing gold, it might look like an exotic souvenir, the pile of poo-poo was a feat of fecal engineering. A monument of manure.

Generations of Chapmans had ridden on the elephant as toddlers, held on its slippery back with loving hands and a chuckle by Grandpa Amos, and to see it desecrated like that!

Rusty would pay.

Ruth stormed outside, glad that Donna was late. It was saving her bacon instead of burning it like it usually would.

"Ruston Darrell Chapman!" she hollered from the porch toward the barn. Strains of AC/DC, which had been drifting out the half-open barn door, shut off, and Rusty emerged, wiping his hands on a red shop rag as he ambled toward the house. "You told me you cleaned the cottage!"

He pulled a face at her as he shoved the rag into the back pocket of his jeans. He reached the porch and leaned on the post that wobbled under his weight. "Huh," he said, wobbling it even more until Ruth heard a faint *crack* as some of the rotten wood gave way.

"Stop it," she snapped. "We're trying to put things together, not break them apart."

He raised one eyebrow in that annoying older-brother way. "That so?"

Ruth planted her hands on her hips. "Yes, that's so. And the house is disgusting, Rusty! There is *doo-doo* on the *doodads*! You know I can't sell it like that."

He looked her straight in the eye, the blue color so similar to hers that it was almost like looking into a mirror. "Maybe I don't want to sell it."

Her voice hardened along with her resolve. "We

have to, and you know it. Don't make me the bad guy here. We all agreed it was the best thing for everyone."

"I could do it. You know I could." His jaw worked underneath his salt-and-pepper stubble. He jerked his thumb over his shoulder, indicating the barn. "I just got one of the tractors running. And I worked under Granddad for years, paid attention, learned all the orcharding. I could do it," he repeated stubbornly.

She softened at the look on his face, sympathetic as his sister even though she was still ticked off as the one who cut him a paycheck for work that wasn't done. "I know you could. But the fact is, you can't afford to buy the rest of us out. It's not a cheap piece of property. The best thing for everyone is to sell the place, split the proceeds, and use your share as a down payment on the next phase of your life. Whatever it is."

Rusty kicked his toe in the gravel and ran his hands through his unruly curls so they stood out from his head like the halo of a naughty angel. "All the memories here, though. You can't put a price on those. We'll never get those back once we sell."

"I know." Her voice cracked a little. "Memories packed into every corner. Like when Grandpa would put us up on his shoulders so we could reach the one apple we wanted. Always a high one."

"Hiding between the sheets when Granny Lou hung the washing over there." Rusty grinned, pointing to where the laundry line used to run from the cottage to the shed. "Remember when we found the possum family living under the pump house?"

Ruth nodded, her eyes filling with inexplicable

tears. Thickly, she said, "They were so cute, and we didn't tell a soul because we wanted the babies to grow up before they lost their home. You rode your bike out here every day so you could check on them."

"Making popcorn garlands at Christmas, and then hanging them in the orchard for the birds when we took down the tree," Rusty reminisced, gazing out at the apple trees and their gnarled branches. "It's a Chapman family tradition, Ruth. How can we just give that up?"

She sighed, resignation settling into her bones, soft and cold like snow. She *did* have to be the bad guy. The adult, even though he was the older one. "We can make popcorn garlands anywhere. We'll still carry on our traditions, even without the farm. And like, Gloria's kid needs braces? Cheryl's oldest is headed to college next year, and you know she's not getting any scholarships. They need the money, and they're not the only ones. *You* need the money. You don't want to live in the trailer behind my house forever, do you?"

"No," he admitted reluctantly.

"And Mom could finally afford a power chair, so she and Dad could do more stuff together. Make *new* memories instead of just hanging onto the old ones. That's what Grandpa and Granny Lou would want for us."

Rusty hung his head, silent. Finally, he mumbled, "You're right. I just—"

"What?"

"Do we have to sell it *now*?" He looked at her with pleading eyes, and she knew the exact pressure squeezing his heart, because it was constricting hers, too. This *didn't* feel like the right time, but the farm had been sitting empty almost two years now. The timing was never going to feel right, whether they sold today or in ten years.

"If not now, then when?" she demanded. The question was rhetorical, but she could tell Rusty was trying to work out an answer, one that satisfied him, if not her.

"After Christmas," he said finally. "Please, just...let us have one more. Let's be honest, it's going to take us a while to clean out the barn, anyway."

"You were supposed to be doing that, too," she grumbled, but he had a point. They weren't in that much of a rush. Donna might wait if she really loved it. And if she didn't, another buyer would come along eventually, even if it meant selling to a Californian refugee.

Plus, she might be able to list it at a higher price later in the spring, when the orchard was blooming and the mud wasn't so deep. "Fine, one more Christmas, and the farm goes on the market in the new year."

Rusty's face brightened, and he swept her up in a hug, squeezing her too tight as he spun her around. "You're the best, Ruthie!"

She held up her finger once he set her down. "You're not off the hook, though. You better march your butt in there and clean the excrement off the elephant, or I'm stopping payment on that check."

"You're so bossy," he grumbled, the same way he

had when they were eleven and twelve instead of fifty-five and fifty-six.

"Newsflash! The person who signs your paycheck is *literally* your boss," Ruth tossed back over her shoulder on her way to the car. "And find whatever critter is living in there and get it out!"

CHAPTER TWO

Ruth sent Donna a text message asking to meet her at the new café next to the drugstore. Maybe if she broke the news over a nice lunch, Donna wouldn't be peeved to hear that the farm wasn't going on the market just yet. Especially if Ruth came prepared with some other options—cottages that needed less work, maybe, or that had a lake view.

She stopped by the Do or Dye, her little salon on Main Street in Honeytree's quaint downtown, to print out some new listings on the way to the café. Hairdressing was her *other* part-time career that didn't make ends meet unless you counted split ends, and she conducted her real estate business out of the salon's back room. Between the two jobs, she earned a good income, but it'd taken a lot of hard work and long hours to get to this point.

She was surprised when, as she waited for the printer to spit out the listings, she checked her phone and didn't find any return texts from Donna. Either she hadn't read them, or she was ignoring them.

Maybe Donna forgot about the showing. Or overslept. This was Ruth's usual sleep-in day, the one day a week the salon was closed, but it was also the day she usually scheduled showings. Wasn't that often she had to wake up early, given the slow pace of the Honeytree real estate market.

She dialed, imagining Donna's groggy voice answering and how they'd laugh about it. It'd be a good segue to an apology for not showing her the farm after all.

Ruth waited, tapping her fingers on the empty manicure station, the printer silent in the back room after its final, stuttering buzz. No answer.

A little bead of fear shook loose in her chest. Though only a few years older than Ruth, Donna wasn't a healthy woman. She smoked and had a rattling cough. Ruth had heard through the salon-chair grapevine that the slot machine windfall had been a blessing because it meant she could retire from her job doing cleanup at the sawmill. The sawdust wasn't good for her lungs, either.

Hopefully, Donna was OK. Maybe just lost track of time.

Ruth called Tambra, the salon's manicurist and receptionist, whose house happened to be directly across the street from Donna's.

"You need me to come in?" Tambra asked when she picked up, the sound of something frying in a pan and her two little boys bickering in the background.

"No, hon. Just peek out your kitchen window and tell me if Donna's home."

The crinkle-snap of blinds being bent made Ruth wince. "That car of hers is there. Want me to go knock?"

"No, I'll drive over, thanks. See you tomorrow. We've got a full day booked." She swiped the ink-damp pages from the printer tray and locked up the door on her way out, fanning and blowing on the pages to dry them so they wouldn't smudge on the front seat of her car.

Donna lived over by the high school on a tidy little side street in a peach-painted ranch with a postage-stamp front yard. When Ruth pulled up, she spotted Donna's recent splurge, a screaming yellow Corvette, occupying both spots in the double driveway, so Ruth parked on the street.

Someone else hadn't, though. Judging by the deep rutted tire tracks that interrupted the uniform green of the lawn, someone had recently parked on the grass. Ruth picked her way around the mud on the way to the front door. It was slightly ajar, so she cautiously pushed it open a couple more inches.

"Hi Donna, it's Ruth!" she called through the crack. "Your realtor?" She waited a few beats, during which it seemed like the gray sky darkened an equal number of shades.

A faint, pitiful meow came from inside the house. Fearing the cat might escape, Ruth stepped inside onto the plush, blue carpet and shut the door behind her. Immediately, she noticed something off.

A pair of sneakers, pink with sporty squiggles on the sides, stuck out between the couch and the coffee table. Deeper blue wet spots splotched the carpet around them, and large shards of glass bristled in the pile like teeth. Red poinsettia petals pooled nearby, so convincingly bloody that they made Ruth feel faint.

It looked like a shark attack had taken place in the middle of Donna Hughes's living room!

Ruth rounded the couch and confirmed that the shoes belonged to feet, and the feet unfortunately belonged to Donna, whose pale, waxy skin and vacant stare confirmed that she had not, in fact, read those text messages.

Ruth's stomach turned, and she ran for the porch.

Outside, rain had begun in earnest. Ruth huddled under the small overhang as she dialed the sheriff's department, praying Eli was in the office today. Sunday was his day off, too, but he was usually working anyway, and he was the kind of person who would answer the phone even when he wasn't on the clock simply because he liked talking.

"Yellow?" he answered cheerfully.

"It's Ruth," she said. "I'm at Donna Hughes's place, and you better get over here. I think she's—well she definitely is."

"Is what?" Eli asked, popping his gum in that annoying way he had since middle school. Sometimes Ruth just wanted to grab it right out of his mouth.

"Dead." The word caught in her throat.

"Well, OK then. Hang tight."

Ruth sat on the porch and tried not to hyperventilate. Donna, who she'd just talked to last night to confirm the showing, *dead*!

Her phone buzzed and she hardly noticed it, only glancing at it half-heartedly to make sure it wasn't Eli. *Leona Davis*, the caller ID proclaimed, jolting Ruth out of her self-pitying horror. Her childhood best friend, one of those friendships that had never faded, despite the decades and distance.

"Leona!" she exclaimed into the phone. The rain turned to a downpour so loud she could hardly hear the voice on the other end of the line over the spatter on the sidewalk.

"Hey." Leona's voice didn't have her usual brash confidence. "I don't think I can make the visit, Ruth. I have to cancel. I'm so sorry. I just can't."

"What? We've been planning it forever!" Ruth slumped down on the concrete steps, hardly even feeling the cold, fat raindrops hitting her legs where they stuck out into the weather.

"I know," Leona said miserably. "You understand, with the TV thing...it's just too much for me to see people now that it's gone viral. This is the end of my marriage, I swear. I called my attorney. Filing papers tomorrow."

Ruth's head spun. Leona and Peterson had been married for thirty years, at least. Peterson, a successful Beverly Hills plastic surgeon, lavished Leona with diamond bracelets and luxury vacations and anything else she wanted. They'd raised their brilliant daughter, Andrea, and spoiled their two grandbabies, and from the outside, seemed blissfully happy. The idea of them splitting up was bewildering. "What TV thing?"

Leona groaned. "You haven't seen it."

"Seen what?"

"The clip from *America Today*. Don't google it. Please don't. Swear you won't. It's bad."

"Fine, I won't google it. You're sure it's over?" Ruth nibbled her lower lip, watching the tire tracks in the lawn begin to fill with water. A thunderclap sounded overhead, making her flinch.

"What was that?! It sounded like a gunshot," Leona said.

"Thunder. A winter storm blew in. Must have rained a half inch in the last five minutes. I'm going to send you a picture." Ruth snapped a quick shot of the rain filling up the ruts on her phone and sent it to her. "Those were empty when I got here. It's all come down while we've been talking."

"Wow. Guess I'm not missing out on the beautiful Oregon weather by cancelling on you," Leona joked, her tone bittersweet. "And yes. It's *over*-over for me and Peterson. This is the last straw on a very large camel's back. Honestly, the camel croaked a while ago and was starting to stink."

"What are you going to do?"

"I don't know," she admitted. "I talked to Andrea about possibly moving to Chicago to be near her and the kids, and she didn't think it was a good idea. She's probably right. I hate deep-dish pizza, and Chicago winters?"

"Worse than Oregon mud," Ruth agreed. "Well,

you have a lot of options. You live in a dang mansion, Leona. Even if you only get half of it—"

"I get none of it. Pre-nup." Leona sighed heavily. "This whole thing would be so much easier if he were dead."

Ruth sucked in her breath, thinking of poor Donna inside, stretched out on the carpet. "Don't say that."

"I know, I know. I'm just rankled by the unfairness of it all. Because he's an insufferable jerk, I walk away with chicken scratch. I should get a bonus for tolerating Peterson for so long!"

"I one-hundred percent agree." That was the main reason Ruth had never bothered getting married. With two businesses to run on top of all her volunteer work, she was too busy to put up with anyone else's nonsense.

Ruth spotted Eli's black SUV marked with the sheriff's department seal pull around the corner and park behind her Honda. "I should go. Listen, keep me updated."

"I miss you, Ruth."

Ruth's eyes watered. "Miss you, too."

"Boyfriend?" Eli joked as she hung up, snapping his infernal gum. The water dripped off the brim of his hat onto his jacket, but he didn't seem to mind. Both his uniform and his chipper mood appeared impervious to the weather.

"No, just catching up with Leona." Ruth tucked her phone into her purple tapestry purse and stood.

Eli perked up, moving to join her on the porch. "Did she say anything about me?"

"Why in the world would she say anything about you?" Ruth squinted at him and then shook her head. "Never mind, don't answer that. You have work to do."

She led him inside and, shielding her eyes so she didn't have that jarring red-on-blue image in her vision again, pointed in the direction of Donna's prone form.

"Well, this is a new one," Eli said.

"Surely you've seen a dead body before."

"I meant the cut poinsettias. I thought they only came in planters." Eli snickered at his own joke.

"A woman died!" Ruth said tartly. She didn't have the patience for his brand of humor right now. A tiny gray streak ran by them and out the front door into the storm.

Oh no. The cat she'd heard was a kitten, and the kitten had officially gotten out. She rushed out to the porch just in time to see the poor thing, already sodden, splash off the curb into the gutter and then stumble into the relatively dry safety of the space under her car. It shook the water off its head irritably and crouched there, barely visible in the shadow. It gave a tiny, miserable mew.

Eli spoke behind her. "Sorry about the cop humor, Ruth. I was trying to lighten the mood, and I forgot you found the victim. Friend of yours?"

"Client," she corrected absentmindedly. How was she going to coax the kitten out? She couldn't stomach walking through Donna's living room to her kitchen to get the cat food, passing by those sad poinsettia petals.

"That had to be upsetting. Do you want me to call someone to give you a ride home?"

Ruth didn't answer. She was too stuck on a word he'd said before. *Victim.* Did he mean that Donna had been killed? She hadn't really considered *why* or *how* Donna died. Just that she *was* dead.

Her head felt like the inside of a washing machine, a dozen thoughts churning and splashing together. Donna was dead. The cat ran into the storm. Donna was murdered. The kitten was under the car, almost in the street. Someone had killed Donna, smashed a vase of flowers into her forehead. Who could kill a woman and then just leave a little kitten behind? Just a baby! It was the height of heartlessness.

"I'll take that as a yes."

"No," Ruth said quickly. The rain was only getting worse, the runoff coursing along the curb, a rushing river compared to the tiny cat. There was no way the kitten could cross it to get back to the safety of the house.

There, the water marring the carpet was soaking in further, sinking away into the pile, taking whatever had happened with it, and Eli was just standing there, staring at *her*. Doing *nothing*. "Shouldn't you be solving the crime or something?"

"Ruth," Eli prodded gently. "I'm calling your brother."

CHAPTER THREE

By the time Rusty arrived in his cherry-red dualie pickup, Ruth was soggy down to her underpants from lying in the street, but she had a fluffy, gray, blue-eyed kitten tucked into her purse with the zipper undone partway so it could breathe.

"I heard you killed your client," Rusty said cheerfully, walking around the vehicle to open the door on the passenger side for her. Strains of Christmas carols from the truck's radio wafted out into the rain. "Guess she's not going to make an offer on Granddad's place now."

"What is wrong with you people, cracking jokes about a murder?" Ruth shook her head as she heaved herself into the seat, careful not to bang the purse around. "Donna was a *person.* She had a *cat*, for goodness' sake." She settled the bag on her lap and opened the zipper a little wider to show him what was inside.

"Laugh or cry, Ruthie. That's how you survive."

Rusty leaned into the truck to get a better look at the kitten. "Will you look at that? What's his name?"

"I don't know. He doesn't have a collar, and I can't exactly ask Donna."

"How about Tinsel?" Rusty suggested, then shut the door before she could answer.

When he slid into the driver's seat, she poked him in the ribs. "I'm not naming a cat that doesn't belong to me."

"Doesn't seem like it belongs to anyone, now." Rusty put the truck in gear and pulled out, flicking on the wipers a few seconds later when the windshield became too muddled by raindrops to see through. "Home or other home?"

"Other home," she said automatically. Eli had promised to drop her car at the salon after he finished up at the crime scene. "Actually, on second thought, swing by Shelly's shop on the way. If she's there, we can hand off the kitten."

Shelly, Donna's daughter, ran a florist shop a few blocks away from the salon. Ruth had overheard Eli's heart-wrenching call to inform her about her mother's death, one that had instilled new respect in Ruth for Eli's compassion and gentle approach to his job. It made up for the gum snapping and bad joke cracking.

She could *almost* fathom what Leona had seen in him when the two of them dated back in high school. At the time, they'd made sense in a superficial way: head cheerleader dates football quarterback. But maybe there was more to it. Ruth wondered if Leona had kept in touch with him over the years, too.

Rusty pulled the truck into the tiny, three-space parking area of the florist shop, a yellow, shingled building with a sharply peaked roof and gingerbread trim. The front window was decked out in a holiday display. Sparkly silver garlands criss-crossed it, punctuated by hanging, glittery snowflakes. Inside, on risers pillowed with cottony "snow," holiday-themed floral arrangements enticed passersby to enter. *Deck Your Halls with Boughs of Holly*, read a hand-lettered banner above the flowers.

The delivery van was still parked at the shop, so Ruth got out and went to the door, hoping that meant Shelly was inside. The sign was turned to "Closed" and underneath it, a piece of paper was scotch-taped to the inside of the glass. Scribbled in Sharpie was the message, "Sorry, Family Emergency."

She knocked anyway, crossing her fingers as she peered through the glass. A minute later, Shelly poked her ponytail out of a back room, and then, when she saw it was Ruth, came to the door. She had her phone in one hand and a soggy Kleenex in the other as she opened it.

"You heard about Mama?" she croaked, her eyes so puffed up that they were little more than slits. She swabbed at her nose with the tissue.

Ruth nodded. "I found her. She missed her appointment with me this morning, so I went to check on her. So sorry for your loss."

That sent Shelly into a fresh round of tears, the poor woman.

Ruth stepped inside the shop and was immediately

enveloped in the scent of pine boughs and cinnamon. She made sure the door was shut behind her before she unzipped her purse and extracted the sleepy kitten. He licked his still-damp tail a few times and settled into Ruth's arms, purring. "I didn't want to leave him at your mom's," Ruth explained.

"Rotten rosebuds, I forgot about the kitten," Shelly snuffled. "I told her not to get one, but that casino money went straight to her head. She went and bought herself everything she ever wanted. The ridiculous car, the ridiculous kitten. Just frittering her winnings away. Now what am I supposed to do with all that stuff?" She grabbed a couple of fresh tissues from a box by the register and blew her nose into them.

"Well. Sell the car, keep the cat?" Ruth held out the kitten to her, but Shelly stepped back, hands raised.

"Oh no. I can't. Ansel is horribly allergic to pet dander. Gives him terrible rashes. That's why I didn't want Mama to get one. It meant we couldn't go over to her house anymore. Maybe that was the whole point." Shelly swiped the tissue under her nose again and then tucked it into the kangaroo pocket of her gray hoodie. "She never did like him. She refused to come to our wedding, did you know that? I was so mad at her, I didn't talk to her for a year."

Ruth stroked the cat and shook her head. She'd never met Shelly's husband, Ansel, but it was hard to imagine anyone not getting along with Donna, whose personality was summed up well by the yellow Camaro and the darling kitten. Spunky, bold, and lovable. "I'm glad you were able to reconcile."

"Me too," Shelly said. "I regret wasting that time. I thought I'd have her longer, but I guess no matter how long you have your mom in your life, it's never long enough. A shame we couldn't have one last Christmas together, though."

Ruth swallowed and nodded, thinking of her own family, spread across the state. Thank goodness Rusty had talked her into one last Christmas at the farm. The family traditions would help heal all their hearts, at least a little bit. She wished she could do the same for Shelly.

"I'll find a good home for the cat," she offered.

Shelly stared mournfully at the ball of gray fluff in Ruth's arms. "Mama loved him," she said. "Named him Huey, after her dad. I hate to see him go."

"Can't Ansel get an allergy shot or something? Surely he won't make you give up Huey when your mom just passed."

Shelly's face stilled, and she gave a swift shake of her head. "No, he'd kill me," she said flatly. "As much as I want to, I just can't risk it."

Ruth was suddenly twice as glad that she'd never chained herself to a husband. Between Leona's devastating divorce and Shelly's fear of bringing home a harmless little kitten? The single life looked better and better.

"Can I hold him one last time to say goodbye?" Shelly looked longingly at Huey. The goodbye was clearly for her mother, not the kitten. Ruth promptly handed him over with a lump in her throat, averting her eyes so Shelly could have a private moment, and perused the shop instead. She admired the bunches of red roses in the cooler case and then moved to the wreaths and table arrangements, mostly made up of evergreen branches and holly peppered with red berries.

A sideways glance revealed Shelly nuzzling her face into Huey's fur, tears pouring down her cheeks onto his little head. At least the kitten was already damp and didn't seem to mind, purring and kneading the shoulder of Shelly's sweatshirt with his tiny claws.

Ruth looked away again, toward the front window where she could make out the red truck parked outside. Rusty was probably wondering what was taking so long, so she went and waved at him. He gave her a thumb's up, but then he started drumming impatiently on the steering wheel. She turned back to Shelly. "I should let you get back to it. I'm sure you have a lot of details to arrange."

Shelly croaked an agreement and tucked Huey into the depths of Ruth's proffered purse. "I can't thank you enough. Make sure he goes to a family who loves him as much as Mama did," she added. Impulsively, she turned to grab something, thrusting it into Ruth's hands. An arrangement of cut poinsettias in a glass vase, tied with a red ribbon. "Here. Merry Christmas."

Ruth stared at it in her hands, stunned by the gesture, and her mouth went dry. It was the same as the one in Donna's house—or what it must have looked like before it was smashed over Donna's head. Did Shelly know her mother had been murdered with an identical arrangement?

No, of course she didn't. Ruth had overheard Eli's call. He only told Shelly that Donna had passed away and that the body would be released to a mortuary of her choice pending the county cause-of-death inquiry. It sounded so benign when he put it that way, but it hadn't looked benign.

Red petals on blue carpet flashed vividly in her memory, like blood in water.

She couldn't mention it to Shelly, so she just clutched the vase tighter and took it out to the truck, where Rusty leaned across the cab to push the door open for her when he saw her hands were full.

"Pretty," he grunted, waiting to back out of the lot until she was buckled in and had tucked the arrangement between her knees so it wouldn't fall over during the drive.

"You can have it for your place if you want. I can't even look at it without seeing Donna's corpse—it's the same flowers that killed her."

He raised an eyebrow. "You don't think Shelly did it, do you?"

"No, of course not!" Ruth snapped. "Why would she kill her own mother?"

Rusty stared at her like she was as thick as a thesaurus. "I'd think that was obvious. She inherits all the money, right? Donna's big win?"

Oh. Ruth hadn't considered that. As Donna's only child, Shelly *would* get everything. The money, along with the "ridiculous car and ridiculous cat" as Shelly had put it.

That reminded her...Ruth unzipped the purse a

few inches, and Rusty made a noise of surprise when the kitten popped his head out. "You're keeping him?!"

"His name is Huey, and no. Shelly can't have the cat because her husband's allergic, so I said I'd find him a good home."

"I'll take him," Rusty declared as he put the truck in reverse.

Ruth snorted. "You can't even remember to feed yourself. And no, beer does not count as food."

Rusty grumbled, but for once, he didn't argue.

CHAPTER FOUR

A few days later, and the cottage was coming together. Rusty had done his doodoo-duty and cleaned up after the critter that'd been roosting in the living room and nesting in the upstairs bedroom, although he still hadn't managed to find and evict it.

Now that the place was clean—or at least, clean enough—it was time to decorate. Huey prowled around Ruth's ankles, attacking her toes through her cozy wool socks while she unpacked the dusty boxes of Christmas stuff from the barn and sorted it into piles.

There were strings of lights, both indoor and outdoor. A wooden Nativity set that must be a century old and probably belonged to her great grandparents, if not an even earlier generation. Shoeboxes of ornaments for the tree. Serving dishes painted with cute holiday scenes. Needlepoint stockings, one for every Chapman descendent. Even a decorative sleigh and horses for the mantel, complete with real jingle bells.

Speaking of the tree, Rusty was busy cutting a young Doug fir from the back corner of the property. When Ruth heard him thumping the trunk against the porch surface to knock off the dead needles before he brought it in the house, she hurried to open the door for him, careful not to let the kitten out.

The fresh scent of fir boughs wreathed them as he hauled the tree over to the tree stand already set up in its usual spot. He held the trunk steady while she laid on her stomach, huffing and puffing, to tighten the stand around its base.

"You picked a nice one," she said, once it was secure and she could stand back to look at it. It was close to symmetrical, with only a few crooked branches that would require some creative ornament placement. She spit some stray needles out of her mouth and then picked a few others out of her curls, before brushing some stragglers from the shoulders of his wool jacket.

Rusty swelled with pride at her praise before scooping up Huey, who was already trying to climb the lowest branches. "Think Mom would like it?"

"Mom will love it," Ruth said confidently. "It's perfect. Let's flip for who has to untangle the lights. I hate doing lights."

"I meant the kitten," Rusty said. "He looks so cute under the tree. We could wrap a box and sneak him inside and give it to her." His eyes sparkled at the thought of their mother opening up the box, and Ruth was almost taken in by the fantasy, too.

But Mom still had limited mobility, which would make pet care difficult, and Dad didn't need the extra responsibility caring for a cat. He had enough to do with caring for Mom.

"Animals aren't good gifts," Ruth said. "It's like, 'Merry Christmas, here's a fifteen-year commitment that you didn't ask for.'"

"Who are you going to give him to, then?" Rusty asked, pouting a little as he rubbed Huey's head. "Or are you just trying to keep him to yourself? Don't tell me you haven't thought about it."

She had, more than once. But that was the holiday lull talking. People weren't selling houses or booking hair appointments right now, so the kitten was a pleasant distraction. But the clients would return after New Year's, and then Ruth would be back to her seven-day-a-week work schedule. Poor Huey would be lonely, stuck at home without anyone to cuddle. He needed a family.

"I put an ad in the paper to run after Christmas," she said. "I'm sure the right person will turn up. Maybe a nice retired lady like Donna."

Rusty kissed Huey on the nose and set him down with a pat on the rump. "Go catch that chicken for me, little tiger."

"Chicken?!" Ruth asked, as Huey scampered off.

Rusty rolled his eyes. "What'd you think was roosting in here, a reindeer?"

"I don't know—a wild something. A pigeon. A turkey. A bat? How in the world did a chicken get in here?" Rusty didn't answer, and Ruth thought something like guilt was creeping into his expression.

"Guess I better go put up the lights on the porch." He grabbed a box and headed for the door.

"Did you put a chicken in this house to scare off my clients?" Ruth demanded, planting her hands on her hips.

"I'll do the lights on the tree, too," Rusty said over his shoulder. "Don't worry about them."

"Answer me, Ruston Darrell Chapman. Is this chicken situation your fault or not?"

"What? Didn't catch that." He banged the front door closed behind him, cutting her off before she could repeat herself a third time.

CHAPTER FIVE

The tree hung with ornaments and the mantel with stockings, Ruth rustled up the old air popper from the top shelf of the pantry. The cottage's kitchen had been built before the era of most electrical appliances, so outlets were few and far between, and there was nowhere to set it up on the countertop. She made a spot for it on the table amidst the holiday décor and located Granny Lou's biggest mixing bowl, the one she'd always used as a baby bathtub when her grandkids came to visit, to catch the popcorn.

It was a couple days out from Christmas still, but it was easier to string garlands with stale popcorn, so it seemed prudent to pop it now rather than later.

She poured in the kernels and paused before she plugged in the machine. "Brace yourself, young man," she admonished Huey. Then she shoved the plug into the outlet. The popper roared to life, causing Huey to leap about two feet in the air.

Ruth giggled, wishing she'd videoed the reaction so she could post it online to give her friends a chuckle. It was the kind of thing that might even go viral, it was so cute and funny.

That reminded her...what was it Leona said about a viral video clip? Something so bad, it precipitated her divorce?

She'd promised not to google it, but she had to know. What could be that terrible?!

A quick search later, and she found it. An *America Today* segment, with both Leona and Peterson appearing for a short interview about Peterson's new TV pilot for a reality makeover show. Leona looked so classy and festive in a snug pencil skirt and red twin set, her curly blonde hair straightened into sleek waves that nodded along with the anchor's introduction.

Ruth smiled, seeing her best friend's face, the familiar features softened with time's artistic hand. Leona looked great. Hopefully she'd be able to reschedule her visit to Honeytree once the furor over the video died down. Ruth had missed her more than she'd realized.

This segment didn't seem too bad. A little awkward, maybe, when Peterson revealed that Leona was going to be the star of the new show. She seemed completely taken by surprise.

Oh wait.

Oh no.

The popcorn started popping, kernels erupting out of the popper into the bowl and drowning out the audio from her phone. It didn't matter; Ruth could witness the horror without hearing what was being said.

It was bad. So. Bad.

Bad enough that Ruth couldn't watch any more. She shut off her phone before the end of the clip.

Leona's claim that it'd be much easier if Peterson were dead was true, because then Ruth wouldn't have the overwhelming urge to bash him over the head with a vase of poinsettias. How in the world was Leona able to suppress her homicidal instincts and continue to cohabitate with that monster?!

The last few kernels whizzed out of the popper, missing the bowl entirely and landing on the floor. Huey leaped delightedly after them, batting them around the kitchen linoleum with his soft little paws. Ruth unplugged the empty popper, and its roar sighed into silence.

She eyed the overflowing bowl of popcorn. It'd take at least twice that much to create enough garlands to satisfy the Chapman clan. She emptied the still-hot kernels into paper grocery bags and repeated the whole procedure to fill the giant bowl again.

This time through, she caught the little cat jumping on camera, popping straight up into the air just like a piece of popcorn when she turned on the machine.

"You have to see this," she gushed to Rusty when he came inside and went to the sink to wash the grime off his hands from hanging the outdoor lights.

"Smells like Christmas in here," he commented, a funny thing to say since the house smelled like popcorn and not gingerbread or cranberry sauce. He dried his hands on a dish towel and took the phone from her. The short video was cued up already, and he watched it several times, laughing harder each time Huey boinged in the air.

"Best movie of the year," he declared, and Ruth wanted to kiss him. He wasn't such a bad egg, her big brother. He tossed a few pieces of popcorn into his mouth and crunched them noisily. "Bet if you put this online, someone would adopt him in a second."

Ruth nodded. "Good thinking."

Rusty watched the video again, chuckling. Then he raised his brows. "You gonna put snow tires on the Honda?" he asked her.

She wrinkled her nose, confused by the sudden change in topic. "Should I? Are we supposed to get bad weather?"

"I accidentally scrolled your photos instead of hitting play again." He turned the phone screen around to face her, displaying the picture of the muddy tire tracks in Donna's front yard. "Snow tires," he repeated. "I thought maybe you had a picture because you wanted to get some."

"Oh, no—I just snapped that to show Leona the downpour," Ruth explained. "The tire tracks were empty when I got to Donna's house, but while I was talking to Leona and waiting for Eli to show, they filled up. They were totally underwater by the time you got there."

"This is from Donna's yard?" Rusty asked, like she

hadn't just said that exact thing. He handed her the phone, shaking his head.

She tucked it away in her purple purse. "Yeah, why?"

"Well, it rained the night before. And then it rained while you were there. She was killed sometime in between. And those tire tracks were left in between, too. Stands to reason that the person who left them might have been the killer."

She sucked in a breath. "You know, you are full of good ideas tonight."

Rusty buffed his nails on his shirt. "Wait till you see what I did with the lights outside."

"Go on, show me," she said, following him out into the night, still distracted thinking about those tire tracks. Rusty walked out well into the large gravel parking area and pointed up at the roof. She had to crane her neck to take it all in.

A huge, illuminated star was outlined against the house, the peak of the upstairs dormer forming the top point, the arms of the star stretching out along the gutters and the other two points staked to the ground in front of the porch. A dozen long strands of lights stretching away into the orchard like a brilliant, glowing tail. It was enormous. Breathtaking.

"I made it out of zip ties and junk from the barn," Rusty explained. "I wanted to do something special for our last Christmas on the farm."

"That's just extraordinary. Really, Rusty. It's so special." She squeezed his arm. "I'm so thankful for your help in all this."

He got a little glint in his eye. “If you’re *really* grateful—”

She groaned. “What do you want?”

“Buy me dinner. It’s prime rib night at the Greasy Spoon.” He rubbed his belly.

“You’re such a child!”

“A child that can eat a 24-oz prime rib,” he shot back. A bold claim he backed up once they dropped Huey off at her house and went to the restaurant. Rusty finished his prime rib and then her steak with gusto, too, and sat back in his seat, groaning.

“Pig,” she said affectionately.

“Cow.” He smirked at her across the table.

“You folks want dessert?” the teenage server asked them in a perky voice. “It’s included in the price, but most people don’t eat it.”

“Oh, we’re going to eat it.” Rusty pushed his empty plate toward her to make space for new, full ones.

“You can have mine,” Ruth told him, after the server bused their dishes. Her belly was tight but comfortable, and she didn’t want to push her luck.

Two slices of cranberry cheesecake were delivered from the cooler and topped with a puff of canned whipped cream. While Rusty ate both pieces, she stared out the window, enjoying the sparkle of holiday lights that decorated the businesses across the street.

Wilds Gas and Go had red and white lights wound around the posts, so it looked like giant candy canes were holding up the canopy over the gas pumps. Two animatronic reindeer on the roof of the drive-thru coffee hut pawed their hoofs and bent their heads to graze on the shingles. Shelly's florist shop was swagged with white lights that reflected off the glittery window display, making it almost look like it was actually snowing inside. Even the delivery van was decorated for the holidays with a huge silver bow on the front grill.

"Think she's got studded tires on that thing? For making deliveries up in the hills?" Rusty asked, his mouth full of cheesecake.

Ruth only caught the last half of his question. She dragged her gaze from the festive view to focus on her brother across the table. "What's in the hills?"

He paused to finish his bite and then swallowed. "Shelly's van," he said more clearly, nodding to the window. "I was thinking, she drives that thing all over. Maybe she got snow tires to handle the back roads." He widened his eyes meaningfully.

"You're not still stuck on the idea that she had something to do with her mom's—" Ruth broke off as the server returned to the table with the check. She gave the girl a tight smile and her credit card.

Rusty shrugged. "Idle thought."

"Well, stop." Poor Shelly had enough to deal with. She didn't need Rusty spouting off nonsense and starting rumors that might dog the woman for years.

But once they were outside in the crisp, clear night, Ruth couldn't help thinking that the van, which had looked adorable from inside the restaurant, now hunched menacingly in its parking spot, the metallic ribbon above the front bumper glinting like teeth in the harsh streetlights. It reminded Ruth of the shards of glass that'd been stuck in Donna's carpet.

When did Shelly give Donna those cut poinsettias? Was it that morning, before Ruth arrived? Had Shelly parked her van on the lawn to deliver the arrangement, then started some kind of argument with her mother inside? About the kitten, maybe, and how it meant she and Ansel couldn't visit anymore?

Ruth pictured Shelly with the vase in her hands, incensed at her mother's impulsive decision. Maybe she didn't even mean to hurt Donna, just lashed out in frustration, flung the vase. How had she felt when the glass shattered, when her mother collapsed on the blue carpet, when the soft, red petals fluttered to the ground?

Even if the rumor didn't get started, *Ruth* would be wondering for years.

"I guess we could check," she said aloud, her hand on her car door. "Just to rule it out. Since we're right here."

"Atta girl," Rusty said, grinning. "Watch my back." He jogged across the street, barely glancing both ways, and Ruth scurried after him, clutching her purse to her hammering heart.

There was hardly any traffic, but Ruth's stomach clenched every time a car passed as Rusty kneeled beside the van to get a better look at its tire treads. He hopped up again just as fast. How did he still have so much *bend* in him? Ruth's knees protested just watching him.

"Regular old all-season," he announced with a little shrug.

Now she felt silly, hugging her purse like it was a teddy bear and jumping every time a pair of headlights hit them. "Told you," she snapped.

Unperturbed by her crabbiness, Rusty changed the subject. "What do you want for Christmas, Ruthie?"

"Little late to be asking. Christmas Eve is tomorrow," she added, following him back to her car.

"Last-minute shopping is part of the fun." Rusty drummed his fingers on the dashboard and hummed the first few bars of "Winter Wonderland" as Ruth pulled out of the Greasy Spoon parking lot and headed toward home. "Really, you can't think of anything? If you don't give me a hint, I might buy your present at the auto parts store. New windshield wipers or something. Is that what you want?"

"What I *want* is that chicken out of the cottage before Mom sits in something." She shot him a grin when he snorted.

"So bossy."

"I'm serious, Rusty! You put that bird in there; now you get it out!"

She could see his impish expression out of the corner of her eye as his picked up the carol where he'd left off. "*Gone away is the chicken—*" he sang. He stopped, waiting for her.

"*It better be,*" she sang, not keeping to the tune at all.

CHAPTER SIX

The next afternoon, Chapmans poured in from around the state, a steady stream of cars and cousins filling up the parking area and then leaving their vehicles in the orchard alongside the driveway when that filled up. They brought food—casseroles and hams and fresh-baked bread and pies that lined the counters—and eggnog and bottles of brandy and sparkling cider for the kids. And presents, too, a pile of them by the tree that were already losing their bows and tags and getting mixed up.

The little cottage was packed like a tin of sardines, the way it should be when family gathered. A little too warm, a little too crowded, a little too noisy. Just right, Ruth thought.

She passed out dental floss and Granny Lou's collection of tapestry needles, and they all took turns stringing popcorn garlands, the kids flitting around the edges of the group and alternately nabbing stale popcorn and playing with Huey, who thought the whole holiday had been staged to provide him with more legs to scale with his tiny talons.

"At least he's not climbing the tree," Rusty joked as they watched the kitten inching up the left leg of Uncle Earl's polyester slacks. Rusty still hadn't managed to get the chicken out of the house, but a couple of glasses of eggnog had put Ruth in such a good mood that she didn't even feel like ribbing him about it.

"I'm glad we did this," she said, bumping her shoulder against his as she added a few cranberries to her popcorn garland. "I like filling up the cottage with more good memories. We're not leaving it sad and empty for the next person. We'll pass it on full of joy and hope and all the things it *should* be instead of letting it sit here like a memorial."

Rusty's face still held a hint of regret, but he nodded in reluctant agreement.

"Since you didn't get me a chicken eviction, what *did* you get me?" She elbowed him, trying to draw out a smile.

"Didn't have time to shop! I spent the whole morning chasing that thing around!" he protested.

Ruth giggled indulgently, remembering how earlier, before everyone arrived, he'd squawked louder than the poor bird when it'd flapped away upstairs and he couldn't locate it. Kind of how she couldn't locate the next popcorn kernel. She kept missing it with her needle.

Phew, she was tipsy. Whoever made the eggnog sure hadn't been stingy with the bourbon. She felt herself sag against Rusty's shoulder.

"Watch it!" he said, alarmed, stopping her wrist before she stabbed him. "I'll finish your garland for you, how about that for your present?"

"That, plus scoop Huey's litterbox until I find him a family, and you've got a deal."

"Fine." Rusty grimaced. "Anybody call for him yet?"

Like he was going to get out of litter box duty that easily! No, she had to give Rusty some credit. As much as he complained, he always did what she asked—eventually, anyway. He had a good heart, even if he was a little impulsive and irresponsible sometimes. Maybe once the farm sold, he'd figure out what he wanted to do in life.

She shook her head and scooted out of her chair, dropping a peck on his cheek before going to make the rounds.

"You, sir!" She picked up Huey, who clambered up her arm to her shoulder and curled up against her neck. "Maybe I'll rustle up a new family for you tonight instead of waiting for a stranger to call."

She relaxed in the Christmas cacophony, weaving and mingling and talking up Huey's sweet, playful personality to anyone who would listen. She almost had Uncle Earl convinced at one point, until Cheryl swooped in and reminded him that his little Schnauzer liked nothing better than chasing gray squirrels, which bore a remarkable resemblance to the little cat's fluffy gray tail.

So no new home for Huey, but between the cookies and casseroles and crackling fire in the fireplace, not to mention the gifting and gabbing and general good cheer, it was a perfect, satisfying Christmas Eve. And in the morning, after an uncomfortable night in a sleeping bag on the floor, Ruth woke up to two things:

1. Snow sprinkled all over the living room.
2. A very loud *cock-a-doodle-doo.*

She rubbed her eyes and blinked a few times, yawning. At first she thought she was imagining both. But then the errant chicken crowed again from its perch on the top of her beautiful Christmas tree!

"Good morning to you, too," Ruth muttered, brushing some of the "snow" off her sleeping bag. It wasn't snow after all—it was tiny bits of popcorn. The rooster bent its head and pecked a few times at the garland wound around the tree, sending another shower of white flecks flying over the rows of still-sleeping Chapmans, who were wedged into every available bit of furniture and floor space.

Huey, who'd been curled up on her chest, stretched and needled the puffy sleeping bag. Ruth cradled him and reached to nudge Rusty, who was snoozing upright in Granddad's easy chair by the fireplace. Behind him, stockings for the kids bulged with gifts.

"Rusty!" she hissed. He grunted and stirred but didn't open his eyes. She inched closer and pinched his big toe. "*Rusty.*"

He jerked awake. "Oh. Merry Kishthmuth," he mumbled, closing his eyes again. She repeated the pinch, and he cracked his eyelids. "Ow, Ruth. What?"

She pointed at the Christmas tree. As if on cue, the rooster let loose with another blast of his version of the morning reveille. Rusty rocketed out of the chair and waved his arms at the rooster, trying to herd it toward the front door. It startled, flapping his powerful wings directly into Rusty's face, and sent popcorn flying all over the kids who'd been woken by the ruckus and had piled down the stairs from the attic bedroom.

Rusty, blinded by the cloud of popcorn particles, tripped over an unsuspecting second cousin and pinwheeled his arms as he fell. He crashed into the base of the tree, sending it toppling over. The water reservoir splashed over a handful of sleepy relations as the tree's force launched the rooster halfway to the kitchen.

Rusty vaulted the sofa and lunged for the bird, managing to grab one tail feather and extract another ear-splitting squawk. Ruth groaned. "You can't chase it! We already know it's faster than you!"

"I'm trying!" Rusty protested, attempting another capture. He grunted at the impact of his body against the floor, his arms empty. The kids, who were rooting for the rooster, shrieked with glee, drawing their parents from other rooms and adding to the Christmas chaos.

The fugitive flew up to the mantel and teetered on

top of the decorative sleigh, every beat of his wings making the sleigh bells jingle like Santa Claus himself was coming down the chimney. Then he hopped onto the back of one of the miniature horses and let out another trumpeting crow, sending the kids into gales of giggles.

Rusty rolled over, holding his stomach and shaking with laughter until Ruth tossed a throw pillow from the sofa at his head. He caught it and asked, "Do you have a better idea?"

She pulled herself up on the arm of the sofa and plucked the popcorn out of her hair. "Well, it obviously enjoys the Chapman family tradition. Why don't you tempt it outside instead of trying to tackle it? What's the old saying? 'You catch more chickens with popcorn than with pouncing'?"

He rolled his eyes but dutifully unwound yards of popcorn garland from the tree and dragged it outside, leaving the door open behind him so Ruth could see that a picturesque dusting of *real* snow had delivered a white Christmas for their last holiday in the cottage. The orchard looked like it came straight off the front of a holiday card.

The rooster sprinted after the end of the long, starchy snake, out the open door, and well into the orchard, leaving little prints across the frosty grass that a bunch of pajama-clad Chapman children followed like dotted lines on a treasure map.

Rusty flung the end of the garland into the high branches of one of the apple trees and strung it between a few more so it wouldn't get soggy in the dew-damp grass.The rooster, indignant over being chased but clucking with pleasure over his bounty, flapped up into the top of the tree, dislodging a shower of fresh snowflakes onto Rusty's head. Rusty shook it off like a dog and then pounded his chest.

"Now that's how Chapmans do Christmas!" he shouted into the low, early morning clouds. A crowd joined Ruth in the doorway to share in his success, and a round of applause began, followed by a few hoots and cheers. Ruth joined in as much as she could with Huey still in her arms.

Rusty beamed, flinging out a Vanna-White arm toward the rooster, and burst into the final refrain of "12 Days of Christmas," hollering at the top of his lungs, "And a *rooster* in an *apple tree*!" He launched into a new verse of the song, waving his fingers like an orchestra conductor, ending it, "Two spoiled kids and a *rooster* in an *apple tree*."

The whole crew obliged and joined him in a few more verses with Chapman tweaks as Rusty added his own words to the lyrics and conducted the choir. The kids ran barefoot in the orchard, hollering at the cold and doing their best to make snowballs out of the scant snowfall, and Ruth's throat squeezed, she was so full up on family.

Cradling the kitten, she smooched her mom and dad on their cheeks on her way by and found a quiet corner of the cottage to message her friends who weren't so lucky. She knew both Shelly and Leona were having lonelier holidays and probably could use a little extra love.

Leona shot back a text right away. "Merry Christmas to you, too! I'm visiting the grandbabies, so life's not all bad. Talk soon."

Shelly's reply took a little longer, and it came in the form of a phone call. "R-ruth?" Her quavering voice came over the line so quietly that Ruth could barely hear her.

"Yeah?"

"D-do you still have Huey?" She sounded downright miserable. Ruth guessed every holiday was hard when you were missing someone special. She hoped that by next year, Shelly would be able to remember the good times with her mom and find comfort in them.

"He's right here in my arms, doing fine. Doesn't sound like you are, though, hon. Anything I can help you with?" Ruth gnawed her lip, plugging her ear to hear Shelly's voice over the raucous clamor of Chapman kids tearing into their stockings in the living room and Chapman grown-ups clanking coffee cups in the kitchen.

"I know I said I didn't want him, but can I have him back? Please?"

Huey's purr swelled, and Ruth felt a little twinge. She'd gotten attached; he was a sweet little fluffball. But she couldn't keep him, and that was that. Besides, he'd belonged to Shelly's mom, so if Shelly wanted him, she should have him.

"I'll pick him up," Shelly offered thickly. "I just—I think I need him."

Of course, she needed a piece of her mom with her on Christmas.

"Don't you worry about a thing," Ruth said. "I'll bring him to your shop right now."

CHAPTER SEVEN

After a careful, icy drive to town, seeing Huey in Shelly's arms was heartwarming to say the least. She cradled the kitten, cooing over him and petting him until he was a boneless, drowsy puddle.

"I'm glad Ansel changed his mind," Ruth said, reaching out to stroke Huey's whiskers one last time before she returned to her family's fray.

For some reason, the comment made Shelly's eyes well up again. "He didn't," she croaked. "Not about the cat anyway. He changed his mind about *me*. He served me with divorce papers yesterday. I'm staying here at the shop now, until I can find my own place. That's why I can keep Huey after all."

Ruth felt like she'd been hit in the back of the neck with a snowball, icy disgust sliding down her spine. "He's divorcing you the same week your mom died?" she blurted disbelievingly. Who would do something like that—during Christmas, no less? That was just...cruel.

"He's divorcing me *because* my mom died," Shelly snuffled.

Ruth shook her head. "I don't follow. I thought they didn't get along, anyway."

"The inheritance from her became joint marital property. He gets half if we divorce, and I guess half of it is enough for him to buy his freedom." Shelly plucked a Kleenex out of a box and dabbed her eyes. "He said he's been wanting to split for a while, but he hasn't been working so he couldn't afford it. I honestly had no idea he was unhappy, but he's apparently been seeing someone else for the last three years."

"No!"

"Yep. I thought he was going snowboarding all the time, but he was actually shacking up with some elderly lady. He had the gall to say I shouldn't be upset he cheated, because he"—Shelly made air quotes with her Kleenex hand—"'doesn't love her or anything.' He's hoping she will leave him some money in her will if he hangs around long enough."

Ruth's jaw dropped even further. "How low can he go?!"

"Low enough to win a limbo contest," Shelly said, cracking a smile through her tears.

"Well, good riddance. In real estate parlance, he doesn't even sound like a fixer-upper; we call that a total tear-down. You need a whole new husband, hon."

"To heck with husbands. I think I'll be a cat lady instead." Shelly grinned down at the kitten in her arms and let out a shuddering sigh. "I just hope Ansel doesn't ask for spousal support on top of the inheritance. He can probably get half my business, too. He can make my life really difficult if he wants."

Ruth couldn't help remembering what Leona had said about Peterson on the phone, that it'd be easier if he were dead. It certainly would be easier on Shelly if Ansel would keel over. How convenient for *him* that Shelly's mother died and provided him with half an inheritance well before it was due. She could have easily lived another twenty years if someone hadn't bonked her on the head.

She sucked in her breath at the realization. If anyone had a motive to murder Donna, it was Ansel. "Can I ask you an odd question?"

Shelly nodded, only half paying attention because Huey had roused himself and was batting at the nose of the light-up Rudolph on her questionable Christmas sweater.

"Does Ansel have studded tires on his vehicle?"

"Yeah, how did you know? He has them for driving up to Willamette Pass to snowboard—well, he wasn't doing that, turns out. But I guess for appearances, he had them. Why?"

Ruth shook her head. "It's probably nothing, but I saw some snow-tire tracks on your mom's lawn the other morning, before I found her."

"You think—" Shelly paled, stumbling backwards to sit in a chair next to a tiered display of blooming orchids, leaving the end of her question hanging. "*Would* he?"

"You know him better than I do. You tell me."

"Ansel wouldn't go to Mom's house on his own. He'd barely go with me when I begged him. So if those were his tire tracks...he might have done something to her," Shelly admitted. "He's always had a temper."

Ruth pulled out her phone and found the photo she'd taken. "Is this his tread pattern?"

Shelly stared at the image a few seconds and shrugged. "Maybe? If you text it to me, I can go over to the house and compare it to his tires."

"Not on your life! You should stay as far away from Ansel as possible until that divorce is final," Ruth said. "Until he's no longer your husband, the only thing standing between him and the other half of that inheritance is—"

"Me," Shelly breathed, her eyes wide.

"Yep. If he's willing to kill your mom for half the money, he might be willing to do the same to you for the other half. The safest thing for you to do is stay here with the doors locked and the sheriff on speed dial in case he comes by. I'll go check his tread pattern. Your house is the beige one on Date Street, right?"

Shelly's hand snapped out and grabbed Ruth's wrist. "No, what if he sees you? I don't want him to do anything to you, either."

Ruth patted her hand. "He won't."

"He *might*, if he thinks you're on to him. You haven't seen him explode, Ruth. One time, when we were out on the lake and a fish slipped his line, he blamed it on me because I was singing along with the radio. He got so mad, he pushed me out of the boat and left me there. I had to swim to the shore and call my mom to come pick me up. He didn't even check to make sure I was safe before he drove away."

Sobered by the anecdote, Ruth had second thoughts about visiting Ansel's place alone. "How about I get the sheriff to check the tires for us? And in the meantime, hunker down and don't let anybody through that door. You and Huey just have a nice cozy Christmas Day. Eat some chocolate and watch a movie, anything to keep your mind off it, OK?"

Shelly gave a faint smile and even fainter nod, holding Huey close to her chest.

The snow had melted by the time Ruth found Eli. She spotted his SUV parked in the lot between the library and the covered bridge, and when she neared, noticed him sitting inside it, wearing a white costume beard and a red Santa hat.

He rolled down his window when she parked next to him. He grinned through the beard. "Ho, ho, ho, Merry Christmas."

She smirked at him. "What did you just call me?"

"Sorry, just got back from a Gifting Tree delivery, so I'm still Santa," he explained, plucking at his red-and-white suit. "I've been instructed not to break character as long as I'm wearing *the beard*."

"Good advice. I'm here to speak with the sheriff, not Santa, though. It's about the murder," she added. "I was hoping you'd check on something for me before I go pointing fingers at a possible suspect. I know I have a reputation for dealing gossip out of my salon chair, but I hate to pass along bad information. Are you working today or should I call someone else?"

Eli stilled. "You shouldn't be investigating anything, Ruth. If you have a tip, you can give it to me, and I'll look into it."

Ruth felt awkward shouting her suspicions out the car window, so she stepped out of the Honda and into the passenger seat of his SUV. "Can you please take off the hat and beard? I can't keep a straight face looking at you."

He tugged them both off, hanging them on the mirror, and she pulled out the tire tread picture again. "I took this at Donna's house on the morning she was murdered. I think the tracks might belong to the killer's car. Rusty says they're snow tires. You know, the studded kind? And I just found out that Shelly's husband, Ansel—well, soon-to-be ex-husband—has studded tires on his vehicle. He and Donna hated each other, and he'll inherit half her estate now that she's gone. Shelly says he's got a terrible temper, too."

Eli frowned at the phone screen, looking deep in thought. "I noticed tracks at the scene, but they were so washed out by the time we processed them that we didn't get a good tread pattern."

"I'll email it to you," Ruth offered, already doing it.

"Well. Don't think it'll help much. Sorry to say," he said hastily. "Your photo is clear, but it doesn't have any context—can't see her house or anything. You could have taken it anywhere, any time."

“Don’t phones record that info?”

He nodded. “If you have location services turned on.”

Ruth checked her settings, and her shoulders sagged. “I guess I turned it off. Great. The one time I actually figure out some techno-thing, and it comes back to bite me in the britches.”

Eli patted her shoulder. “Don’t beat yourself up. It’d be a stretch to get a warrant based on the tracks alone, anyway. A lot of people have the same kind of tires.”

“But you believe me, don’t you?” Ruth asked, her heart mired in helplessness as sticky as a melted candy cane.

He nodded. “I’ll keep an eye on Ansel. See if he’s acting strange or if anything else comes up that points to him.”

“Shelly could be in danger!” she protested. When Eli didn’t have an immediate reply, she started to get out of his SUV. “Well, if you’re not going to check his tires, I will.”

He hauled her back by her purse strap. “Oh, no you don’t. Let’s say you’re right. It’s the same kind of tire treads. Then what?”

She crossed her arms. “Then you arrest him.”

“I already told you, that’s not enough for a warrant. We’d need corroborating evidence.”

“Fingerprints from the scene. You *must* have found fingerprints.”

“He’s family. Of course his fingerprints will be in her house. Still not enough.”

She tossed up her hands. "Well, how in the world is anyone ever arrested, then?"

He looked at her with kind amusement. "Killers are never as smart as they think they are. Especially ones who kill in anger, like in Donna's case. It was a snap decision to use that vase of flowers. That means whoever did it made mistakes. We'll flush 'em out. And I'll make sure Shelly is looked after, too." Eli grabbed a pack of Doublemint from the cupholder and offered her a stick. "Here, it helps me relax and takes the edge off."

She took the gum and popped it into her mouth. A burst of sweet, minty flavor spread over her tongue as she chewed. It reminded her of being a kid, roller-skating around the barn with Rusty and her cousins, chewing gum as they chased each other in circles. "I didn't know they even made this kind anymore."

"Only us old fogeys chew it, I guess." He winked at her. "Reminds me of the good ol' days, back in school when you and me and Leona and Rusty all hung out together. I miss it. Feel like I took a wrong path somewhere along the way."

She raised her eyebrows, surprised at his admission. "You're so good at what you do, though! Hard to say that was the wrong path."

"Oh, I don't mean professionally; I love my job. But look at me. It's Christmas Day, and I don't have anywhere to be except work, Ruth." He turned to her, and she was surprised to see his warm, brown eyes were a little too shiny.

"Thank goodness," she said stoutly. "Where would

our town be without you? Those Gifting Tree kids wouldn't have their presents delivered by Santa. Shelly's mom might not get her justice. We need you."

He brushed his eyes with the furry white cuff of his Santa suit and gave an embarrassed cough. "You probably should get back to your folks. Don't mean to keep you from your family."

She punched him in the shoulder like she would Rusty if he were acting so dumb. "You're coming with me. We have enough ham to feed half of Honeytree. Maybe all of it. And the kids will love it if Santa comes for dinner."

The corner of his mouth quirked up. "Can't say no to unlimited ham, even if I have to eat it through this thing." He pointed to the beard hanging from his rearview mirror.

"Good. Then you won't mind if we happen to cruise by Ansel's house. It's on the way."

He puffed out an exasperated breath.

"Ham," she reminded him.

"Fine. I'll follow you over," he grumbled good-naturedly.

CHAPTER EIGHT

Ruth looked up at Eli from her crouch next to Ansel's Subaru Outback, dread ringing in her ears. "It's the same."

"Well. You sent me the picture already, right? I'll add it to your witness statement, and you can submit an addendum about when and where you took the photo. It can't hurt."

"Hey!" a sharp voice came from the other side of the car. "What's going on out here? If there's a scratch on my paint, I expect you to make good on the damage! Insurance or cash, I don't care, but I'm not paying for—"

Ruth stood and saw Ansel storming toward them, a raggedy bathrobe open over pin-striped flannel pajamas. A tall man in his mid-forties with shaved-bald head, he had a nasty-looking rash crawling up the side of his neck and decorating the backs of his clenched fists.

He cut his rant short when he rounded the station wagon, and Eli tugged his fake beard down to reveal his face. His bony shoulders rounded, like he was trying not to loom. "What brings you out here, Sheriff? Is there a problem with my parking job?"

Eli made an apologetic gesture to his Santa suit. "Oh, I'm not on duty."

"I just dropped my phone?" Ruth fudged, holding it up since it was already in her hand.

"Well, maybe don't hang around my tailpipe like a coupla hemorrhoids, then, or I'll have to call someone who *is* on duty to come boot you off my property," Ansel snapped, furiously scratching the back of one hand. He turned on his slippered heel and stomped back into the house, slamming the front door so hard that the window beside it rattled in its frame.

"Merry Christmas to you, too," Eli muttered under his breath. "I wouldn't mind arresting that guy, now that I've had a chance to talk to him."

"Did you see the creeping crud on his face and hands?" Ruth asked. "Shelly said he gets rashes from pet dander. Maybe he got it from going to Donna's house."

"Good eye. I missed it." Eli stared at the tires on the Subaru, looking meditative. "If Ansel's the killer, I'm a little worried he might circle the wagons now that he's seen me nosing around. Might start destroying evidence, starting with these tires. Can you snap a picture of them with the license plate in the shot, just in case he decides to ditch 'em before I come back with a warrant?"

"Does this mean you're passing up the unlimited ham offer?" Ruth asked, eyes on her phone while she did as he asked. They both moved to the sidewalk to avoid drawing more of Ansel's ire.

"'Fraid so. Not the first Christmas dinner I've missed and won't be the last, either." Eli popped his gum absently, clearly off somewhere in investigation-land. "Gonna drive down to the county office and do the paperwork myself so it doesn't wait the weekend."

"Well, too bad. Stop by the farm if you get done early, and we'll be glad to have you. Don't forget to assign someone to watch Shelly's shop in case he comes after her," she reminded him before she got back in her car.

He scrunched his face up and groaned. "Whoever gets to babysit on Christmas is going to *love* me."

"Better babysitting than investigating a second homicide."

Eli tilted his head, like she'd said something smart instead of snarky as she'd intended. "Actually, now that you mention it, could be a good thing if he shows up at her shop with ill intent, and we have someone there. It'd be the nail in his case, proving he did it."

"You can't use Shelly as bait. Not unless you're going to protect her twenty-four seven," Ruth insisted. "He might not have premeditated Donna's death, but this one he'd have more time to plan. Which means fewer of those mistakes you were talking about. It can take months to finalize a divorce, so he has all that time to think of how to go about it."

Ruth glanced over her shoulder at the house. The

curtain in the living room window twitched, like someone had been watching them. "I think we better go," she said in a low voice, even though the person in the house couldn't possibly overhear.

Eli nodded. "Listen—can you maybe coax Shelly to participate in your Chapman ham-stravaganza until I get things worked out at county? I'm concerned this guy might lash out, based on how he reacted to us."

"You mean calling you a hemorrhoid?" Ruth giggled, giving his red, padded belly a tickle like he was the Pillsbury doughboy.

Eli grinned. "Pretty sure you were included in that characterization."

Ruth squawked in mock indignation. "In that case, let's nail this guy as fast as possible. I'll 'babysit' until you're done with paperwork, and we'll keep Shelly out of harm's way." She stuck out her hand, and they shook on it before heading in opposite directions.

It wasn't hard to convince Shelly to come to Christmas dinner once Ruth said that Huey was welcome, too, and Eli turned up late in the evening to collect her, when everyone over forty was sleeping off a food coma and everyone under forty was playing a board game.

"Nice lights," Eli remarked as he wiped his feet on the mat. "What's all the junk in the apple tree out there?"

"Tradition," Ruth said, yawning against the back of her hand as she steered him to the kitchen. Shelly was still drying the dessert dishes with Cheryl and her teenage daughter while Huey snoozed on the rag rug by the sink, one of Granny Lou's creations. "Your government taxi's here, Shelly. Thanks for pitching in on the cleanup."

Shelly smiled over her shoulder. "Almost done and then we can go."

"Kicking us out already? I was promised ham!" The twinkle in Eli's eye that said he was joking was belied by a loud growl from his stomach.

Ruth ducked her head into the fridge to get out the leftover ham and some fixings and slapped together a thick sandwich for him stuffed with cranberry sauce and pickles. She even stuck an olive on top with a toothpick, to make it fancy for Christmas. Eli dug in with his elbows on the table, mumbling appreciatively through the giant bite.

"We're having sandwiches now?" Rusty sidled into the kitchen to peer over Eli's shoulder. "Dang, that looks good." Ruth rolled her eyes and made him one, too. He really was a bottomless pit.

A few minutes later, Shelly folded her dish towel and sat down at the table with them, Huey on her lap. She stroked the kitten until he began making biscuits on her knees, wincing as his needle-sharp claws punctured the fabric of her pants. "Ready when you are. Ruth said you'd have someone watch the shop tonight?" she finally asked, a thin, worried crease appearing on her forehead in contrast with her light tone.

He nodded. "I have a deputy scheduled to park outside overnight, and then tomorrow I suggest you stay with friends out of town. Preferably someone your husband doesn't know. And while your shop is open, I'll make sure to swing by a few times per shift."

"I don't want to put you out," Shelly said, sounding miserable. She had every right to be, after the week she'd had. "I'm sure you have better things to do than mediate ugly divorces."

Eli cleared his throat. "Well, I wanted to ask you. Would you be willing to...I don't know how to put this nicely, sorry. The longer we wait, the less likely it is we catch who killed your mother. So I'd like to draw out the killer, make them come to us rather than chasing after them. Set up some bait."

"Hang some popcorn in the tree," Rusty added, nodding along.

"Is that what was outside?" Eli asked. "I wondered."

"Yup. Bird bait." Rusty's cheerful tone didn't stop Shelly from going slightly pale.

Eli gave her a sympathetic grimace across the table. "It's not comfortable. But I can assure you, the department would be right there every step of the way to keep you safe."

Ruth squeezed Shelly's shoulder reassuringly. "You don't have to do it. That's why Eli's asking, to make sure you're OK with something like that."

"I'm—I'm just not sure," Shelly said, voice shaking. "It's hard to think straight with everything that's going on. It's so nice being here with all of you, and the idea feels fine now, but when I'm alone in my shop? Every drip of the faucet makes me jump a mile in the air."

The image made Ruth think of the video she had

of Huey on her phone, his utter shock at the sound of the popcorn popper turning on. She pulled it up for Shelly, hoping to lighten the mood a little, calm her jitters. It worked well enough. Shelly lost the gray pallor and sat forward in her chair to watch as Huey boinged up on the screen, the fur on his back puffing out even more than usual.

On the second time through, she smiled, and the third pulled out a laugh. The fourth time through, Huey popped his head up over the edge of the table to see what had distracted Shelly from petting him. He looked like a little meerkat in one of those nature documentaries.

"I thought it might get him adopted by a nice family if I posted it online," Ruth said, reaching to scratch him between his downy ears. "But I guess we don't need to worry about that now. That reminds me, I should cancel the newspaper ad I placed, otherwise I'll have people calling all next week."

"He's lucky you were there," Shelly said softly. "I don't know what would have happened to him if you hadn't found Mom when you did. The poor thing, stuck in the house with her."

Ruth didn't think that was the time to mention that the door had been left open, too.

"Do you really think Ansel did it?" Shelly asked abruptly, her lips suddenly tight as she cuddled Huey despite his wriggles.

"Now that was a ham sandwich." Eli pushed his empty plate a few inches away and sat back in his chair before turning his attention to Shelly's question. "I can't speculate about Ansel's guilt or innocence. But a few things put him at the top of the suspect list in my mind."

He began counting them off on his fingers. "One, his dislike of your mom. Two, his track record of angry outbursts. Three, his tires match tracks at the scene. Four, he has a rash, which may have come from exposure to Huey. Five, I reviewed the forensics report this afternoon, and all the prints in your mom's house were knowns. Family members and close friends," he explained.

"And realtors," Ruth added. She'd provided her fingerprints to Eli for comparison when she'd given her witness statement.

He nodded. "That pretty much rules out a stranger unless that person wore gloves. Since it's clear the killer didn't come to Donna's house with the intent to commit murder, we can assume there was not that level of premeditation. So five fingers point to Ansel, and as we say in my line of work, five fingers make a fist."

"Meaning?" Rusty asked.

"Meaning strong enough to potentially close the case," Eli explained. "And you're the person closest to him, Shelly, so he's likely to tell you things he wouldn't tell others. He might even believe that, because you're his wife, you can't be compelled to testify against him."

Shelly took a deep breath. "Then I want to help as much as I can. What do I need to do?"

"I'll draw up a plan with the deputy detective assigned to the case and let you know your part," Eli said. "We'll design something that will put pressure on him to act—something that will play on his fear of being caught, maybe. We'll spin a good story for you to tell."

"I'm not a very good liar," Shelly said worriedly.

"What about his greed?" Ruth blurted out. "Could you play to that?"

Eli nodded. "That could work. But he might be content with the payout he's already guaranteed."

"That's not what I'm talking about." The video of Huey had given Ruth an inspired idea about how to goad Ansel into action. Not by dangling Shelly's half of the inheritance in front of him, but by threatening *his* half. Ansel might be satisfied without doubling his payday, but surely he wouldn't be content with losing everything, not after he'd *killed* for it. "I'm talking about taking away that guarantee, so his crime might have been for nothing."

Eli tapped his chin as he thought it through. Then his posture energized, and he sat forward. "You know, if the money was his objective, that could be the most powerful motivator out there. Putting it in jeopardy might be the key to the whole thing. Not a lot of people could simply walk away in that situation."

"Then you'll be happy to hear that I already have a plan in motion, and it doesn't put Shelly at risk, either. Merry Christmas to you." Ruth grinned at Eli and waved at him across the table. "Meet your new bird bait. It's me."

CHAPTER NINE

To Ruth's surprise, Eli agreed to every aspect of her scheme. He called it "downright elegant."

A few days after Christmas, Shelly made the preplanned call. She'd practiced it a dozen times before Ruth took the script away from her so she wouldn't read from it while she was on the phone. Better if it sounded natural.

"Ansel?" The quaver in Shelly's voice came off one-hundred percent real. "I'm sorry to bother you—no, this isn't about that. I don't care what you do with the drapes. It's about Mom's will. I just heard from the lawyer, and apparently, she left everything to the damn cat! Whoever has custody of it inherits everything, so one of us needs to—" She broke off, rolling her eyes as she tolerated an explosive interruption that was audible even though the phone wasn't on speaker.

"You getting this?" she mouthed to Eli, who was operating a digital recording device attached to the phone, another wire running to his earpiece. What Ruth wouldn't give to hear the tantrum Ansel was throwing!

"I know you're allergic. That's why I told the sheriff to find it a new home instead of keeping it. Obviously, I had no clue you were going to divorce me at that point nor the faintest idea Mom would make the cat her beneficiary. I'm not saying you have to keep it. Just that we have to find it by Thursday when they read the will, or neither of us is getting a dime." She paused, Ansel's voice rising enough that she had to hold the handset away from her ear. "No, it's microchipped; they'll know if it's the wrong cat. That's just it, I don't know who has it. And if nobody turns up at the lawyer's office with the darn thing, Mom's whole estate goes to the animal shelter. House, car, cash, everything."

A smile spread across Shelly's face as Ansel's garbled shouts filtered out of the phone's speaker into the florist shop. "Uh huh. You do that."

She hung up and set the phone back in its cradle, and Ruth held her breath. Eli pulled the earpiece out of his ear. "Well done. That was seamless."

"I forgot to mention Ruth's name," Shelly said reflectively, gnawing her lower lip. "I should have used the script."

Ruth turned on the ringer on her phone. "I wouldn't worry about that. I plastered Huey's cute jump-scare video and sob story all over the local online groups, plus his adoption ad ran in the paper on Sunday. It's gone viral already, judging by my voicemails. I bet Ansel will call me today."

Her estimate proved right. He called within the hour, his voice sickly sweet as he expressed interest in the "darling" kitten and described his lifelong love of cats.

"Great!" Ruth chirped as she spun in her salon chair. "Come on down to the Do or Dye for a meet-and-greet, see if you get along with the little guy."

Ansel couldn't keep his impatience out of his voice. "That's not necessary. You can just drop him off at my house. I'm sure he's perfect."

She pinched her lips, trying not to giggle. He was falling for this like rain through a gutter downspout. "Uh huh. Well, several other potential adopters are coming by to meet him, too, and then at the end of the day, I'll choose the best family for him."

Ansel *snarled*. "Fine. I'll be there in five."

He hung up, and Ruth shivered. She texted Eli to let him know Ansel was on his way and saw him give a thumbs-up out the window of the sheriff's office across the street. He was poised to take action if and when Ansel lost his temper. She trusted Eli to keep her safe if the plan went sideways.

As soon as the Outback pulled up in front of her salon, she hit the "record" button on her laptop, angling it just so, and then pretended to be busy sterilizing combs and brushes at her station. The bell over the door jingled as merrily as Santa's sleigh, and she looked up, pasting on a pleasant expression.

She hardly recognized Ansel with a baseball cap

pulled low on his forehead and a puffy green jacket disguising his bony frame. But his rash, fading but still visible, like the impression of an angry slap to the side of his neck, gave him away as the same man.

"Hi! So glad you could make it."

He grunted, avoiding eye contact and instead scanning the salon. Looking for the kitten, she realized. "Where is it?" he demanded. He straightened his shoulders and loomed into her space. She took a step backward, a hair-thin thread of fear coiling in her stomach. This was a killer. She'd never been more sure.

"Why don't you have a seat and tell me about your previous pets?" she suggested, patting the back of a chair that was in view of the laptop's camera.

His tongue flicked out, wetting his lips, before he reluctantly sat. "Fine. Um. None recently, but you know. Cats. Dogs." He waved his hand dismissively, still barely looking at her as he searched the room for any sign of Huey.

"Tell me about your most recent kitty," she pressed, taking a seat across from him and folding her hands in her lap.

A muscle in his jaw flexed, and his eyes hardened into a challenging stare. "It was...cute. I liked it."

"How nice," she said pleasantly, like he'd given a satisfactory answer. "What did you feed it?"

He leaned to peer under the counter where Ruth kept the extra stock for the shampoo shelf. "Uh...Cat food."

"You're so funny!" She forced a laugh. "Why are you looking to adopt a kitten right now?"

Ansel scratched his neck. "What do you mean? I just want a cat. Where is he?"

She ignored the second question and answered the first. "Well, some people want mousers, some want playmates. Some people are looking for lap kitties to cuddle and love. Some people like to relax with their pets or even take them to work." Ruth was really warming up now and getting into character. But she needed to tighten the screws on Ansel. He was a suspect, not a potential adoptive pet parent.

She lowered her voice and tried to sound conspiratorial. "Huey lost his owner under very tragic circumstances, you understand. The owner's extended family should have taken him in, but they rejected him outright, can you believe it? Such a shame. Now it's my job to make sure Huey is going to a loving home that will keep him forever, so he doesn't experience any more trauma in his young life."

She could practically see the wheels turning in Ansel's head as he tried to work out whether to confess that he was part of Donna's family or risk losing out on kitten custody. She held her breath. *Would he take the bird bait?*

"Actually..." he began, and Ruth worked hard to keep the triumph off her face. "I believe his original owner was my mother-in-law. My wife—"

The word seemed to catch in his throat; at least he had that much conscience.

"Doesn't want him," Ruth finished. "I heard. I'm afraid all family members should agree before adopting a pet. I'm not comfortable releasing Huey to you if she's not on board. Sorry, I think it's best if I find him another home."

"We're getting divorced!" Ansel shouted, rising from his seat and practically vibrating with anger at being denied. "Where's the stupid cat?"

He stepped toward her so she had no room to stand up, and Ruth suddenly wished her chair wasn't up against the window. She couldn't even scoot away.

Please, let Eli have a good view of what's going on.

"Wait a minute," he said, leaning down and putting his face so close to hers that she could smell the onion on his breath. "I know you. You were the one poking around my property the other day."

She froze in her seat, her heart flapping and crashing around her ribcage like a rooster caught inside a cottage.

A sick calm infused Ansel's expression. He reached out and tugged one of her curls, pulling it out straight and letting it spring back. His rashy face inched closer. "You were with the sheriff," he murmured. "I knew you two were up to something. He thinks I did it, doesn't he?"

"I don't know what you're talking about." Her voice came out high, breathy, false even to her own ears.

He grabbed her blouse, the fabric popping in protest as his grip strained a seam, and yanked her to her feet. "The cat, and nobody gets hurt."

"Nobody else, you mean?" Ruth babbled, trying to stall him while she waved her hands behind her back in the desperate hope that Eli could see her through the salon window. "Donna already got hurt when you hit her with that vase."

"Shut up," he said, sounding almost amused. "I know that fleabag's not here, or I'd have fresh hives already. Where do you have it stashed?" He twisted his fist so the fabric tightened around her neck.

"Home," she lied, and he loosened his grip, allowing her to fall back in her seat. She rubbed her neck, relieved until she saw him pick up a pair of her shears. "N-no, that's not necessary."

"I think it is." His voice was glib as he moved toward her, stripping off his jacket one arm at a time...so it wouldn't get her blood on it, she realized with no small amount of terror. She couldn't take her eyes off the glinting silver scissors as he moved them from one hand to the other. "You know too much."

"Just let me go," she begged. "I won't tell. Anyway, if you kill me to get the cat, they'll know it was you." She injected as much confidence as she could into her words.

Ansel picked up her purse, riffling through it to remove her wallet, and then reached behind the counter for her cash box. "No one will make the connection," he said. "Who would kill someone over a cat? It'll look like a simple robbery gone wrong. Where's the key for this thing?"

A flicker of motion outside the salon door caught Ruth's eye as she described the key's hiding place amid her collection of crystals and shells. She turned her head enough to spot a tiny scrap of brown fabric peeking out from behind the exterior doorframe. It had to be Eli's sheriff uniform, the rest of him hidden, ready to make a move. Relief surged through her, and then fear—had Ansel spotted him, too?

No—he was still cleaning out the cash box. She cleared her throat, hoping to draw his attention and give Eli the best chance to intervene. "Why'd you do it, anyway? Kill Donna, I mean."

"Because she was a selfish broad." Ansel's pale eyes glittered underneath the brim of his cap. "I went over there to ask her to share the wealth, toss a little my way since we were family. But she claimed I didn't deserve it. Like *she* did? She didn't work for that money—she just got lucky! And then she got *real* unlucky," he added with a chilling chuckle. He pocketed the cash and then tucked Ruth's wallet into his shirt pocket, patting it. "Home address."

What was Eli waiting for?

"Why didn't you take her kitten after you murdered her, if you wanted it so much?" Ruth stalled, panic narrowing her throat, making the words thin and reedy. "Kind of stupid of you to leave the door open so your cash-cat could run out into the rain."

"Kind of stupid of her to leave her money to an animal," he mocked. "Just like it's kind of stupid of you to invite me to your salon when you already knew I was a cold-blooded killer."

Ansel's unsettling eyes bored into hers for a split second, and then, shears gripped like another kind of weapon, he lunged. She slammed her eyelids shut, too cowardly to watch her own demise, just as the bells over the door crashed like thunder.

Ruth opened her eyes just in time to see Eli tackle Ansel from the side, bringing him down in an incredible flying leap that disarmed him and pinned him to the tile floor in one smooth motion.

He certainly hadn't lost his football tackle skills since they graduated. Thirty seconds later, Eli had Ansel trussed up like a turkey and was reading him his rights. While Eli called a deputy to come transport Ansel to the county lockup, Ruth couldn't help reflecting that, unlike the itinerant rooster, this jailbird had required both popcorn *and* pouncing to apprehend.

"Better late than never, I guess," Ruth said to Eli when he finished with the call.

Eli grinned. "I wasn't late. I was right on time!"

"Well, you showed up when it counted, although it was a little too close for my taste," she said wryly. "I owe you one. A big one."

"About that," Eli said, eyes twinkling like he was Santa Claus passing out the presents again. "I know just how you can repay the favor."

CHAPTER TEN

There were a lot of things to celebrate this New Year's Eve, Ruth reflected as she put the sparkling wine on ice in preparation for the big toast.

A murderer was behind bars, for one. Ansel's recorded confession was damning enough that his lawyer indicated he'd enter a guilty plea in exchange for a lenient sentence. Donna's soul could truly rest in peace because justice would be served.

Two, Shelly was safe now that her evil soon-to-be ex was out of the picture. His crimes made him ineligible to receive her assets in the divorce, including the inheritance, and the paperwork would be fast-tracked as a result. Shelly would be free of him in weeks instead of months. She was still devastated by the loss of her mom, of course, but with Huey's help, she would heal, Ruth hoped. The kitten, for his part, had already taken to his new life as the florist shop's mascot.

Third, the so-called Last Chapman Christmas had been such a success that the family email list was buzzing, not about the sale of the farm, but about where and how they'd gather next year. The current vote was for a beach rental with an ocean view.

"We'll feed the popcorn to the seagulls," Mom had joked in one message.

Fourth reason to cheer—the property would be ready to list as soon as Rusty hauled the more valuable items in the barn to the January farm auction. He'd even replaced the porch post, bless him, although he hadn't managed to capture the wily rooster.

Fifth but not least, Ruth was feeling pretty darn good about herself. She'd caught a killer, saved a kitten, hosted a happy holiday, and most importantly, avoided marrying any awful people who'd eventually ruin her life. Instead, she'd invested her energy in family, friends, two rewarding careers, and her own personal fulfillment.

Five fingers made a fist. Case closed on a year well-lived.

Cheers to that. She poured herself a sparkling flute of champagne. She just had one thing left to do before the clock chimed midnight.

She dialed her best friend.

"Got your glass ready?" Leona asked when she picked up the phone.

"Sure do. It's pink, too." Ruth eyed the clock. Two minutes until the new year. Two minutes to repay Eli for saving her life. "I've heard you should begin the year how you intend to go on. Got anything figured out now that you've had a couple weeks to breathe?"

"Not really," Leona said. "All I have figured out is what I *don't* want. And what I don't want is what I always thought I did: this glamorous, plastic life in the big city. Give me a homestead and my two hands, and I'd be happier. Sometimes I think I should have stayed in Honeytree all along. I've never been able to stop missing the small-town life, even when I was on a private plane to Paris. Somewhere I took a wrong turn, I guess. Got off on the wrong I5 exit."

"You know, Eli said something similar to me recently," Ruth said.

"Eli Ramirez?" Something new colored Leona's voice.

"Of course, Eli Ramirez. Do we know any other Elis?" Ruth giggled. "He talks about you all the time, by the way. Says dating you in high school was the best time of his life. He regrets letting you go."

She could practically hear Leona's eyes roll. "That was a long time ago. We missed that boat by about forty years."

"It's never too late to have the life you want. It's always just the right time," Ruth said knowingly. *There, Eli. Debt paid.*

The clock caught her eye, and she started counting down. "Nine...eight...seven...six..."

"Happy New Year!" Leona chorused with her when the hands hit midnight. "To lifelong friendship."

"To living the life you love," Ruth added, taking a

sweet sip from her glass. "Speaking of which, if you're serious about homesteading, I know of a place coming on the market soon..."

THE END

FROM THE AUTHOR

Happy holidays! Want to follow Leona's Honeytree homestead hunt and learn exactly what's in that viral video? Read the *Clucks & Clues* series, cozy mysteries full of felonies, friendship, and fun. Oh, and lots of chickens.

Hillary Avis writes farm mysteries with humor and heart from her home in Oregon, which she shares with a menagerie of kids, dogs, cats, and chickens...and one very patient husband. When she's not writing stories, she's staying up until the wee hours of the morning reading them.

You can learn more about her and her books at hillaryavis.com, or join her newsletter at www.sendfox.com/HillaryAvisAuthor and get cute chicken stories delivered straight to your inbox.

CHRISTMAS IS CANCELED

CARLY WINTER

Will her favorite time of year bring her joy...
or tears?

CHAPTER ONE

As I stepped out of the shower, the off-key voice of my dead grandmother's ghost, Ruby, singing "Holly Jolly Christmas" filtered into the bathroom. I loved everything about Christmas: the food, the decorations, the way my heart felt just a little lighter and kinder than it did the rest of the year. I even loved Christmas carols—except when Ruby sang them. Nails on a chalkboard or a chorus of drunk monkeys would have been preferred.

"Ruby, could you please keep it down?" I yelled as I wrapped my hair in a towel. Just as I cleared the steam from the mirror, she appeared behind me and our gazes met in the reflection. She'd died wearing a purple muumuu over her thin frame and her long gray hair pulled back into a ponytail. She was stuck that way for eternity.

In an attempt to appear frightening, she raised her hands above her and rolled her eyes into the back of her head. In her best ghostly voice, she said, "I am the Ghost of Christmas Past, and you are a party pooper."

"And you aren't scary."

Ruby furrowed her brow and crossed her arms over her chest. "Is that the Christmas spirit? Telling someone not to sing Christmas carols? I suppose you put pee in the punch instead of tequila during your holiday parties?"

"Gross," I replied, rubbing lotion on my arms. "You're just a little loud for this early in the morning."

"And you, my dear one, are a Grinch." With a wave, she stuck out her tongue and faded away.

When Ruby had died three years ago, she'd left me her house in Sedona, Arizona. I'd spent a lot of summers with her while growing up doing all sorts of things my uptight mother wouldn't allow me to do—watch R-rated movies, eat cookies for breakfast, and stay up all night if I so desired. While my own mother, Ruby's daughter, was conservative and rigid, Ruby was all about fun. The more rules there were to break, the happier she was.

Both thrilled at my new start in life and saddened that Ruby and I had lost touch as I entered adulthood, I'd left my house in Louisiana and moved to Sedona. Soon, I realized working as a yoga instructor wasn't going to pay the electric bill, let alone the mortgage, so I turned the big home into a bed and breakfast. After running it for three years, imagine my surprise when I was hit by lightning and discovered that my house was haunted... by my dead grandmother.

"Let's go, Bernie!" Ruby yelled. "We've got so much to do!"

She wasn't wrong. My to-do list for the Christmas party grew each day as it drew near. I'd spent hours upon hours decorating the house and I still wasn't done. Thankfully, my friend, Darla, was going to bring most of the food. She owned the local diner and loved to cook, so she'd volunteered and I'd gladly accepted since I hated cooking and most recipes I attempted were inedible. I still had to shop for the white elephant gift exchange and stop by the liquor store. Ruby also wanted more lights on the outside of the house, but I wasn't going to take my life in my hands to climb a ladder. My handyman, Henry, who helped me with odd jobs around my home, had agreed to come over this afternoon. The ugly Christmas sweater I'd ordered was also late, so I figured I might have to improvise there.

I opened my closet. An impressive array of 80s movies t-shirts hung in a neat row—everything from the *Breakfast Club* to *Working Girl*. Even though I had been born in the middle of that decade, I had a deep appreciation for the movies of that time. What did one wear for Christmas gift shopping? *National Lampoon's Christmas Vacation*, of course. The best Christmas movie ever made.

For good measure, I also wore my Santa cap, red scarf, and jingle bell earrings. No one could ever accuse me of not having any Christmas spirit.

"Don't you look cute?" Ruby said as I entered the kitchen.

"Thank you."

"Can you turn on the lights in the living room and we can take a quick peek before we go?" Ruby asked. "Just to make sure we don't need to pick up any bulbs."

"Sure."

In her ghostly state, Ruby couldn't move inanimate objects, which led to her bossing me around and me complying most of the time. After plugging everything in, I stepped back and admired my work.

The twenty-piece Christmas village sitting on the erected table behind one of the sofas looked as though it might come alive at any second. Ruby had collected pieces during her life and I'd added a few as well. Figurines of kids running through the snow and adults shopping at the various stores scattered across the town. "I love this thing," Ruby said quietly as she bent over and stared at the shops. "The dog groomer was always my favorite."

I smiled and walked over to join her. "I also like the church and the cookie factory," I said.

"You know what it's missing?" she asked, standing upright. "A Santa figurine. We should add that to the list of stuff to pick up."

I pulled out my phone and typed it into my notes.

"Let's check the banister," she said. "I want to make sure all the lights are working."

As I followed her up the staircase, I inspected each white bulb embedded in the garland. Red bows had been placed at every measured foot all the way up to the top. "Looks good to me."

"Now the tree." Ruby pointed back downstairs.

"It's easier to look at it from up here," I replied.

The fifteen-foot fake fir tree stood in the corner also covered in white lights, a few bows, and many ornaments, some of which I had made as a child. Others had been given to me by special people in my life. All had deep meaning for me. I'd also found some lemon-scented car fresheners to hang on the bottom branches. My hope had been they would repel my cranky tabby, Elvira, and to my utter shock, it seemed to be working. She'd approached the tree a couple of times but turned the other way once she got close. Not a very holiday-like scent, but it was better than her climbing the tree and taking it down.

As I looked over my living room, a sense of peace blanketed me and I smiled. I loved Christmas.

"You need to invite more people to the party," Ruby said. "We want to have the biggest rager in town!"

"I'm fine with our small guest list," I said. Ragers were *not* my thing. "Besides, I don't know that many people."

I tended to be an introverted homebody, but while alive, Ruby had been the life of every party and had known everyone in town.

"Just get out more!" she urged. "Go to the bar! Join a club!"

"I like my life just the way it is," I replied as I hurried down the staircase. "I'm not arguing with you."

"You better not leave me here!" Ruby yelled from right behind me. "Don't even try!"

"Have I ever left you behind?" I asked, grabbing my purse. "Besides, we agreed we'd go together today."

"That's a dumb question. Of course you've left me. Or at least, you tried."

I stared at my ghost for a long moment and recalled she was right. When we were inside our home, Ruby roamed freely. Once we left the four walls, she couldn't go more than fifteen feet away from me. Somehow, we were tethered together by an unseen "leash," as she liked to call it.

Sometimes I raced out of the house in order get a little time to myself. Guilty as charged.

"Let's go!" Ruby yelled as we made our way to the back door where I stopped to don my coat.

We headed to the SUV and I slid in. The drive to town remained uneventful, except for Ruby's singing. Once we arrived, finding a parking spot became a nightmare.

"Everyone's doing their shopping!" Ruby squealed. "I love this time of year!"

I finally discovered an empty space behind Joyous Jewels, the local jewelry store featuring a lot of turquoise, silver and Native American pieces.

As Ruby and I walked over to the main drag, she hummed and spun around in circles. "We need to find some good gag gifts for the white elephant exchange," she said. "That's always a hoot when someone ends up with something ridiculous."

I stopped at the Joyous Jewels window which had a painting of a Christmas tree and twinkling lights around the frame. The glimmering pieces of jewelry caught my eye even though I never wore any. I glanced down at my mood ring—the only piece I did wear besides my earrings—and noted the color as dark blue. Happiness. Yes, things were going well for me. I waved at the owner, Merry, and continued on my way.

All the stores had participated in the decoration festivities and some even had Christmas music piped out onto the walkways in front of their stores. Ruby gave a running commentary of her opinion on the decorations, what people were wearing, and anything she found interesting.

"Oh! Look! A Santa figurine! It's perfect, Bernie!" Ruby exclaimed as she pointed at a store window. "But that man's sweater... ugh. I bet his grandma knitted that thinking she was doing him a favor. He's probably wearing it to be nice to her. I bet that ends up in a donation bin."

Yes, the jolly Santa figurine would fit in with the village perfectly. And frankly, there were a lot of men around with awful sweaters, so I wasn't sure which one she meant. "Let's go in," I murmured.

We went inside to purchase the figurine and I picked up a few decoration replacement bulbs just in case one did go out. My motto: better to be prepared than sorry.

After waiting in line for a bit, we exited the store. A man I'd seen earlier at Joyous Jewels stood outside and we exchanged smiles as I passed. Tall with dirty, dark hair, his overly large coat hung on his thin frame.

Ruby and I walked by a few other stores and she continued her running commentary. This store did a beautiful job of decorating. That store should have tried harder. Why was that woman wearing flipflops in winter? The man over there was going to have back problems from carrying all his wife's packages. I half-listened as I took in the window displays.

As we strolled by Fiona's Flowers, I caught a glimpse in the window. The tall guy I'd noticed earlier was following me. "Let's go in here," I whispered as I opened the door.

"Why? No one wants flowers for a white elephant gift exchange! Where's the fun in that?"

As I pretended to study the different bouquets, I glanced up at the window. Sure enough, he stood just outside as if he waited for me.

"You're right," I whispered. "No one wants flowers. Let's leave."

"That was fast," Ruby said. "Glad you listened to reasoning. Where should we head to next?"

"Let's keep looking," I whispered, checking over my shoulder every few minutes. The man was still present, although he didn't seem to be paying me much attention. Was he following me or not? After being mixed up in several murders, I'd learned to always be aware of the happenings around me.

"Pizza socks, Bernie!" Ruby exclaimed, pointing at a window display. "We need pizza socks!"

I couldn't agree more.

We found a plethora of quirky gifts in the store, aptly named Perfect Presents and Parties. A Public Toilet Survival Kit that included wipes, latex gloves, and a toilet seat cover. Elephant Salt and Pepper shakers. A Dinosaur Kale Growing Kit.

"Can you imagine Gunner wearing the pizza

socks?" Ruby asked. Despite being surrounded by people who couldn't see or hear my ghost speaking to me, I laughed and received a few odd glares. Gunner, a cop who'd been undercover for five years with a biker gang, stood over six feet tall and had the build of a military tank. Pizza socks on him would be hysterical.

After grabbing all my finds, I walked over to the checkout and stood in line, Ruby right next to me.

"Do we have everything?" she asked. "I think we do."

I checked my list, mentally counted my gifts and nodded, but didn't answer. It would appear I was having a full conversation with myself to everyone else in the store.

After paying cash, we headed back to the car. I glanced over my shoulder a couple of times and didn't see my stalker. Right before we reached Joyous Jewels again, I found myself face-to-face with him.

"Excuse me," he grumbled as he tried to side-step me while looking over my head at the crowd behind me.

I attempted to move out of his way, but we ended up stepping the same direction, then engaging in the awkward dance of two people trying to avoid each other, but only succeeding in remaining in each other's path.

His focus remained beyond me and I finally stood in place. Our shoulders bumped as he hurried by, not bothering to apologize.

"Rude," I muttered, determined not to let him ruin

my perfect day. When we arrived at the car, I slid in, glad to be free of the throngs of people.

"That was so much fun!" Ruby squealed. "I adore Christmas shopping!"

Usually I did as well, but despite my attempts to forget the man and enjoy the day, I couldn't stop thinking about him. Had he been following me? It certainly seemed that way. The fact I'd spotted him outside almost every store we visited caused me worry.

And my worry turned to panic when I arrived home to find my wallet missing.

CHAPTER TWO

"That guy I thought was following me must have taken it!" I yelled as I glanced at the contents of my purse scattered across the kitchen island. "When he bumped me! He must have somehow grabbed my wallet!"

"It's okay, honey," Ruby said, running her hand over my arm. Goosebumps appeared as she did so and a shiver ran down my spine. Her touch always felt like ice had been laid on my skin. "It's just a few calls to the bank and a trip to the Department of Motor Vehicles to get a new license."

"I should've known he'd pull something like that," I said, groaning. "The DMV is the worst."

Ruby smiled and blew me a kiss. "Maybe with the holidays getting a new license won't be such a long wait. People are concentrating on other things."

As the scent of lavender and marijuana—what Ruby had smelled like while alive—engulfed me, I sighed. The trip to the DMV would have to wait until after the party. Until then, I'd have to be extra careful while driving so I didn't get pulled over or end up in an accident.

"Besides, I went seven years with an invalid license without a problem," Ruby said. "No one checks the date on those things anymore. It's not like you have to do it right away."

Of course, this bit of advice came from the woman who was arrested for streaking down a golf course. And drinking tequila naked at the Bell Rock Vortex. All while in her seventies. The list of laws she broke while younger stretched extensively.

A knock sounded on the front door, thankfully bringing the conversation to an end. I hurried over and opened it to find Henry, my handyman.

"Hi, Henry," I said. "Come on in."

"You should consider dating him," Ruby said. "Handymen are very good with their hands, if you know what I mean."

Pursing my lips, I did my best to ignore her and the blush crawling up my cheeks. She'd died of a heart attack while in bed with her handyman. Relief swept through me when she disappeared, laughing hysterically at my embarrassment.

In his thirties and very married, Henry's black hair sprouted from his red baseball cap bearing his company name, Handyman Henry. Not very creative, but there was no doubt about his profession. A thick black beard covered his jaw. His weathered, calloused hand gripped mine as he smiled. "Nice to see you again, Bernie."

"You too. Thanks for coming on short notice. How're the kids? And Judy?"

"As good as four kids under the age of eight can be," he replied, glancing around the living room. "And Judy's fine, thanks for asking. Looks like you're in the Christmas spirit."

"Oh, yes," I said. "My favorite time of the year. I tend to go overboard with the decorations."

"It appears Santa came early, too," he said, pointing at the couch where I'd dumped all my presents.

"Yes. I'm having a party and a white elephant gift exchange."

"Sounds nice," he murmured, then turned to me. "Do you need anything done in here?"

I shook my head. "Only outside."

"Why don't you show me and I'll get started?"

After stepping out and explaining where I wanted the lights to go, I hurried back to the kitchen and phoned the bank to cancel my credit card. During that time, my friend Darla had called.

"Hi!" I said when she answered, putting her on speakerphone.

"Hey, Bernie. I was wondering if you could come by the diner for a bit. I'm working on new recipes for the party and I wanted you to do a taste test."

I glanced at my packages that needed wrapping. They could wait until I got home. Henry would leave an invoice for me, so there was no reason for me to hang around. “Sure. I can be there in about twenty minutes?”

“Perfect. Oh, and can you bring Ruby?”

Darla was one of the few people I had told about my ghost. Bonus points to her for not thinking I was out of my mind. “Of course.”

“I understand I’m in high demand,” Ruby said, appearing next to me. “It’s exhausting being so dang popular.” She raised her hand to her forehead and sighed dramatically.

“See you in a bit, Darla,” I said. After hanging up, I turned to my grandmother. “Come on, drama llama, let’s go.”

I admired the red rocks of Sedona as we drove to Darling’s Diner. Tall, rugged and the color of rust, they provided a beautiful landscape to our town and I couldn’t imagine going a day without appreciating their magical splendor.

After parking in the lot between Darling’s Diner and Jumping Jack Jeep Tours, I exited the vehicle and headed into the restaurant. The hostess waved and motioned for me to head to the kitchen where I found Darla among the stainless-steel tables, gas stoves, and fryers.

“Hey, Bernie!” my friend greeted me as we embraced. In her thirties—the same age as me—we’d been friends since I moved to town. “How are things going?”

“Good. Everything’s coming together nicely.” Despite the party being my idea, the butterflies of anxiety still tickled my belly. I wanted everything to be perfect.

“And now we need to go over the party menu,”

Darla said, tucking a blonde lock of hair behind her ear as she looked to my right, then my left. "Hi Ruby! I keep hoping that one day I'll be able to see her."

"Hey, Darla!" Ruby replied, smiling, then she turned to me. "I just love it when your friends speak to me."

Darla suffered from schizophrenia but seemed to be doing well. In all my time knowing her, I'd never seen her so happy and peaceful. Besides her medication, Jack, who owned Jumping Jack Jeep Tours next door, most likely had a lot to do with her calm disposition. They'd been dating a few months and both were very happy.

"I know you wanted to keep things simple, but I was hoping you'd say yes after tasting the Beef Wellington with grilled asparagus," Darla said shyly.

"Beef Wellington!" I exclaimed. "Seriously?"

"Yes! I want to do a big sit-down dinner, Bernie! The planning and cooking... it's been so much fun. I know it's your party and we agreed on a simple meal, but I wanted to try something different. Something a little fancier."

I had imagined appetizers and finger sandwiches. After mentally tabulating the chairs at my dining room table, I didn't find a problem. Everyone would fit and I'd never eaten Beef Wellington before. "If you're up for it, Darla, then you can serve whatever you'd like."

"What about our dance party?" Ruby asked. "Is this going to turn into some hoity-toity thing where everyone sits around sipping after-dinner tea?"

"No, we'll still have our dance party," I said.

When I visited Ruby in my younger years, she'd pull out a chest of clothes and we'd dress up for a specific time-period, move the furniture in the living room, and blast music until late at night. We had more disco parties than I could count.

"Oh, good." Ruby sniffed. "Since I can't eat, I find all this talk of food particularly cruel."

"Then just ignore us," I said. "You wanted to come and you knew we would be discussing the food."

"I know, but I can still feel sorry for myself."

Turning back to Darla, I smiled. "Let's see what you've got."

She reached into the oven and pulled out a prepared plate of Beef Wellington, grilled asparagus, and mashed potatoes. My mouth watered as I inhaled the delicious scents.

"That looks amazing," I murmured, wiping the corner of my mouth, afraid I'd drool.

"Take a seat," she said, pointing to the small table in the corner.

I sat down and she placed the plate in front of me, then took the chair across from me. As I cut into the Beef Wellington, she studied my every move. I suddenly feared it would be awful and I wouldn't be able to hide my disdain.

Thankfully, the food almost melted in my mouth and before I knew it, I'd cleared my plate.

"I'm going to take your silence and the fact you practically inhaled everything as a good sign," Darla said, chuckling.

"Yeah, she reminded me of my Hoover vacuum I

used to use," Ruby said. "That thing would suck up a small child if needed."

"That was delicious," I said, slightly embarrassed at my lack of etiquette. "Amazing."

"So I can serve it at your party?" Darla asked, her eyes dancing with excitement.

"Of course you can!" I replied. "Now that I've tasted it, I'd be upset if you didn't!"

"I can't wait for this shindig," Darla said. She took my plate and walked it over to the sink, then poured two cups of coffee and set them on a tray with cream and sugar. "It's going to be so much fun."

"Yes. It's going to be small, but I think it will be great." In total, I had six guests including myself. If you counted the ghosts that would be present, there'd be eight. My boyfriend, Deputy Adam Gallagher, had a ghost living with him as well. Fortunately for him, his spirit, Ned, was nothing like Ruby. Instead, he liked to keep to himself and Adam couldn't see or hear him—but I could. Ever since I was hit by lightning, I'd become some sort of ghost whisperer and I'd yet to decide if it was a good or bad thing. On one hand, I could see ghosts! On the other hand, could I really? Or had the lightning strike scrambled my brains and I was imagining all these spirits? This was a question I pondered often.

Darla took a sip of her coffee. "What have you been up to today?"

"We went shopping for the white elephant gift exchange," I said as I poured cream into my coffee. "And, I had my wallet stolen."

"Oh, no! How did that happen?"

"I swear this guy was following me," I replied. I gave her a blow-by-blow of where I'd seen him and how he hung outside the flower shop as if he waited for me. "Then he disappeared. A little later, Ruby and I were walking back to the car and he bumped into me. When we got home, I realized my wallet was gone."

"So you think he took it when he knocked into you?"

I nodded. "It's the only time I could've lost it."

"That's too bad. Did you call your credit card company?"

"Yes. Now I need to get a new license and I hate the DMV."

Darla laughed and shook her head. "I've never heard anyone say they enjoyed going, Bernie. It's one of the ugly things in life one must do."

As we chatted, Ruby remained so quiet, I almost forgot she had come with me. However, when Darla's boyfriend, Jack, walked in, Ruby came alive. Well, as alive as she could, considering she was dead.

"Hello, there, Mr. Dimples," she purred. "Aren't you looking sexy today in those greasy jeans?"

Jack owned Jumping Jack Jeep Tours next door, which, aptly named, offered Jeep tours of the Sedona area. He did most of his own repairs and could be found covered in grease or dirt at any given time. Ruby also considered him the best-looking man in Arizona, and she might be correct. With his wavy brown hair and deep green eyes, he was handsome. Combined with his bright smile where his dimples became more pronounced—hence her nickname for him—he became magazine-worthy material.

Darla stood and kissed him. "I should've realized you'd show up in time for dessert."

"Oh, she's so lucky," Ruby said, sighing. "If I were alive, I'd give him a kiss he'd never forget."

"I've never missed dessert, Darla," he replied, his eyes twinkling. "How are you doing, Bernie?"

"Good," I said, so thankful he couldn't hear my ghost. "Your girlfriend is going to make me put on weight."

He grabbed his taut stomach with each hand. "You and me both."

I rolled my eyes as Darla opened the fridge and pulled out three plates. "We've got a chocolate tart, a cinnamon apple pie, or a creme brûlée."

"Can't we have all three at the dinner?" Jack asked, sitting down at the table. "After all, it is a Christmas celebration."

Darla handed us each a fork and the three of us tasted each treat.

"They're all delicious, Darla," I said, groaning. "I can't choose."

"You have to vote for one," Darla chided. "Which one was your favorite?"

I really couldn't answer. "I'll let Jack decide." As I stood, I stretched my arms over my head, suddenly exhausted. Must have been all the calories I'd consumed. "So, I'll see you two tomorrow night?"

"I'll be there around four, if that's okay," Darla said.

"Of course. Are you still planning dinner at six?"

"Yes."

"We'll see you then!" Jack said. "Oh, wait! Is Ruby with you?"

I nodded and grabbed my purse off the back of the chair.

"Tell her I say hello."

"And tell him those jeans hug his tush nicely," Ruby said.

"I will, Jack," I said before hurrying out of the diner with my ghost in tow. Would there ever be a time when she didn't embarrass me? And why did I allow it? Only I could hear her. Perhaps I feared that one day, they would.

Adam, my boyfriend, called as I drove through town.

"You shouldn't be on the phone while driving, Bernie," he said after we exchanged greetings.

"I'm on Bluetooth. Totally hands-free."

"You should still be concentrating on the road. I've seen a lot of accidents with Bluetooth in use."

"I wanted to talk to you," I countered. "Besides, I'm almost home. I could drive this road with my eyes closed. Are you coming over?"

"Yes. I was calling to let you know I'll be there in about half an hour."

I pulled into the lot behind my house and turned off the car. "I'll see you then!"

"Let's go around front and see what Henry did!" Ruby exclaimed as I ended the call.

When we reached the front of the house, I examined the area where I'd asked him to string the lights. They hung evenly and would be pretty once lit. Everything was on a timer and previously when I'd messed with the settings, I'd accidently programmed the device to go off at four in the morning. I'd leave it alone for now. I went inside and made a mental note to check the display after dark.

After grabbing my wrapping paper and locating my scissors and tape, I went into the living room, turned on some Christmas music, and sat down to wrap my presents.

I gasped as I sank into the cushions, panic constricting my chest while my stomach curled with disgust.

They were gone.

CHAPTER THREE

The good thing about dating a cop was that he arrived right away. The bad thing was that he went directly into what I called "cop mode" and started interrogating me as if I wasn't his girlfriend but some criminal he'd arrested.

"Have you checked out the rest of the house?" he asked, his voice brisk and all business. "To make sure no one's hiding?"

"Ruby made me sit down here and she went through all the rooms upstairs," I mumbled. "She couldn't find anyone."

"I'm going to do a quick sweep for myself," he replied. "No offense, Ruby. I believe you looked, but I'll feel better if I do as well."

"None taken, copper," Ruby said when Adam ran upstairs. "Do what you need to do to unknot your boxers."

A few moments later, Adam returned. "Do you

know where they entered from?" he asked, examining the front door. "Did you lock up before you left?"

"I think so," I grumbled as I took a seat on my couch and stared at the Christmas tree. "I don't know how they got in, but I know who did it."

"Who?"

"The guy who stole my wallet downtown," I said. "He had my license, so he knew my address. He's probably been watching the house and waiting for me to leave so he could break in uninterrupted. He saw I had a bunch of packages."

Adam hurried over and kneeled in front of me. "Your wallet was stolen?"

Angry tears welled in my eyes as I told him the story. "He was following me and probably saw a lone woman out loaded down with shopping bags as an easy target."

He sat down next to me and pulled out a notebook. "Can you describe this guy?"

"Tall, thin, greasy dark hair," I said. "He resembles the grinch. Except he was white, not green."

Adam sighed and jotted down my description. "I'm going to check the back door and downstairs windows."

"There weren't any broken windows when I looked," Ruby said, sitting on the couch across from me. "I think if that jerk had gotten in that way, you'd feel a breeze. Do you?"

I shook my head. "Nothing."

"He must've gotten in through the back door, then."

My tabby cat, Elvira, stalked into the room from the kitchen and meowed to announce her presence.

"Come here," I said, patting the cushion next to me. "Come give me some love. I need it."

Instead, she narrowed her gaze, lifted her nose in the air, and walked up the stairs. I swear the only reason the cat stuck around was because of Ruby, whom she loved. On the other hand, I—the one who fed her, cleaned her litterbox and desperately wanted to snuggle her—was someone she barely tolerated.

"The party will be fine without the gifts," Ruby said. "Tell everyone what happened. No one will care."

"I know," I muttered. "But *I* care. I wanted the party to be perfect."

"There's no such thing, Bernie." Ruby sighed. "I don't know how many times I need to tell you to stop aiming for perfection because it's never going to happen. Just accept things as they are, throw your shoulders back, smile, and take it all in stride."

Easy for her to say. She hadn't been planning the party for a month.

Adam strode back into the room. "They came in through the door in the kitchen," he said, jotting down something in his notebook. "There're scratches on the lock and the doorframe I don't recall seeing before."

"Did they pick it, or just bust it?" I asked. Did I need to call Henry back to fix the lock?

"It'll hold, but definitely replace it." He sat down next to me and took my hand in his. "In fact, I'd like for you to swap out all the locks for something with a deadbolt. They all look pretty old. I can do it for you, if you'd like my help."

Laying my head on his shoulder, I took a ragged breath. Another thing to add to my to-do list.

"I'm going to have to grab my laptop and make a report," Adam continued. "I'll also check if there are any other similar incidents. Maybe he's got other houses he's hit. It's probably a good idea to send someone to patrol downtown and see if they can spot this grinch guy."

Elvira stood at the top of the stairs watching us through a narrowed gaze, her tail swishing back and forth.

"I'll be right back," Adam said. He stood and kissed my forehead, then strode out the front door to his car to retrieve his laptop.

When he returned, he sat down next to me again and typed up the report. "I don't see anything in here resembling your experience," he murmured. "A couple of drunk drivers, a small fire from a candle, and a couple of cars broken into. Nothing about a woman being followed and her wallet being stolen."

"He'll do it again," I said. "He was a pro. Otherwise he wouldn't have been able to lift my wallet from my purse without me knowing it."

"It was unzipped?"

I nodded.

"You should always keep your purse zipped when in a crowded area," Adam lectured. "In fact, just keep it zipped at all times so it becomes a habit."

"A little late for that advice, copper," Ruby muttered. "And just a bit patronizing if you ask me."

Biting my tongue, I stood and hurried into the kitchen to fetch a glass of water. I agreed with Ruby. If I didn't put some space between the two of us, I'd most likely say something I'd regret. Adam and I had dated for months, then broken up because of my own dumb actions. I didn't want to rock the boat anymore now that we were back together, especially over something so stupid.

Of course, I knew my purse should've been zipped. It was like telling someone who had tripped to watch their step. Irritating and unnecessary.

When I finished my water, I returned to the living room and smiled. I'd bring the conversation up another time.

"So everything else is ready for the party?" he asked, closing his laptop.

"Yes. Darla's making an amazing meal and all the lights are finally hung outside."

"We're all looking forward to it, Bernie," he said, wrapping his arm around my shoulder. "The house looks great, by the way."

Elvira meowed and I glanced up at her again. She stalked over to the banister, keeping her gaze firmly on me.

When she jumped onto the railing, I shot to my feet and yelled, "Don't even think about it!"

"Uh oh," Ruby said. "It's a test of wills and I know who's going to win. And it's not the lemon-scented air fresheners."

"Elvira!" I screamed as she readied herself, her tail swishing again as all the muscles in her hindlegs twitched. "Don't! Please... don't do it!"

Time seemed to stop as my cat lunged through the air Superman-style and hit her mark—my Christmas tree—with incredible precision. The ornaments rattled, some crashing to the floor and breaking into pieces. The tree swayed as Elvira batted at the lights and other decorations.

"Dang it! You stupid cat! Get down from there!" I yelled.

Adam raced over and reached to steady the tree, but it was too late. It came crashing down on top of him, taking him to the floor. Elvira leaped again and cleared the disaster, then sat down to admire her handiwork.

"Copper down! Copper down! Mayday! Mayday!" Ruby yelled waving her hands in the air while I pulled the tree off Adam.

"Are you okay?" I said, dropping to my knees beside him. Spatters of blood surrounded his head, seeping into my rug.

"I think so," he muttered, closing his eyes. As he reached for the back of his head, I noted blood on his knuckles.

"Run, cat, run!" Ruby yelled. "She'll make you into a pair of gloves for this debacle!"

"You're bleeding," I said. "Let me get a cloth."

I strode into the kitchen and noted Elvira had taken Ruby's advice and gone to hide. A good thing, because I was so angry, I debated taking her to the shelter.

With a slew of curses, I wetted a towel and hurried back into the living room. Adam had stood but I noted blood pooling at his neck.

"I think you need to head to the emergency room," I said, placing the cloth on the back of his head. "You may need stitches. You're bleeding pretty bad."

Glancing around the floor, I found so much glass and broken ornaments, I was surprised more damage hadn't been done to him.

"I'll be fine," he muttered, bending over to grab the tree. As he tried to set it upright, the plastic core snapped in half.

"Uh oh," Ruby said. "Between the broken tree and the stolen gifts, I have a feeling Christmas is canceled."

"You need to go get that cut checked out," I said as tears welled in my eyes and I ignored my ghost. "Let me drive you."

"Really, it's—"

Tired of my day and everything that had happened, I snapped. "Quit being such a man!" I yelled, my hands clenched at my sides. "I can practically see your brains that cut's so deep! You need stitches!"

"Well, someone's not happy," Ruby scoffed. "You need to calm down."

"Don't tell me to calm down!" I screamed.

"I didn't," Adam said, his eyes wide. "You're scaring me, Bernie."

"I wasn't talking to you!" I marched into the kitchen to retrieve my purse and coat, then I returned to the living room and pointed toward the back door. "Now get in my car!"

"I'll stay home," Ruby called as I followed Adam. "This doesn't seem like a fun trip, and I hate hospitals."

My hands shook as I jammed the key into the ignition. Thankfully, Adam remained silent as I drove. I took some deep breaths and tried to calm myself. Of course, I worried about him. Glancing over, I could see the soaked cloth was leaking all over my car seat. Just another thing to deal with.

I pulled up in front of the emergency room and walked him in even though he insisted he didn't need any help. The on-duty guard told me to move my car but I just glared at him and muttered for him to mind his own business. Hopefully he wouldn't ask for the ID I no longer possessed.

"We'll get you in quick," the nurse said, eyeing the bloody rag with distaste. "Just take a seat for a minute or two."

"You'll need to go park your car now," the guard said, his voice gentle and quiet as if trying to talk a toddler out of a tantrum. "Or I'll have to have it towed."

I strode out of the building feeling like a child about ready to throw myself down on the ground and scream and cry. First the gifts had been stolen. Then my cat had destroyed my living room. A trip to the emergency department. Not to mention the blood I needed to clean up in my house and car.

Laying my forehead against the steering wheel, I allowed the tears to flow freely. My Christmas spirit seeped away like water through a crack in the pavement. Anger at my unknown burglar and my cat replaced it and consumed me, along with utter exhaustion. I didn't have the fortitude to put any more energy into the holiday.

Ruby was right: Christmas was canceled.

CHAPTER FOUR

Late that night, I drove Adam back to my house. I'd been right: he'd required stitches and the doctor also wanted me to watch him for a concussion.

I had set my phone alarm to repeat every two hours, but despite my exhaustion, I didn't need it. I barely slept as I worried for Adam. From the white rocking chair in my bedroom, I wrapped myself in a blanket and monitored him closely as he lay under the yellow comforter, his soft snores filling the room. As the morning sun rays peeked through the window, he woke with a light headache and soreness around the stitches but seemed happy once he was up and settled in the kitchen while I made coffee and toast.

Since arriving home the previous evening, I'd avoided the living room and hadn't seen my horrible cat. Even though I wanted to strangle her, I set out her food. Ruby had also disappeared. Most likely she'd gone to her tunnel, a place she said led to

Heaven. It was dark except for the illumination at the end of it. According to her, she'd tried numerous times to get to the light, but she never could. It remained out of her grasp and both of us figured Heaven wasn't quite ready for Ruby, leaving her trapped on this plane.

As Adam and I sat quietly in the kitchen sipping our coffee, I tried to pretend yesterday never happened, although I'd have to face the mess in my living room at some point.

"How are you feeling today?" Adam asked.

"Tired. I barely slept."

"Thanks for watching out for me. I think I'm fine, though."

"I'm glad," I said, grabbing his hand. "I was worried."

A knock sounded at the front door. With a groan, I hauled myself up from the barstool and shuffled over to answer it. I'd closed my reservation app and hung out my No Vacancy sign, both virtually and physically, until after Christmas. Some people obviously didn't pay attention to such things. Or perhaps my ugly Christmas sweater had arrived just in time for the party I was about to cancel.

I kept my gaze firmly on the floor as I walked through the living room, not quite ready to face the disaster. More coffee and a hardening of my heart would be needed before I could take a broom to the mess and scrub the blood out of my carpet and hardwood floors.

To my utter shock, my friends Jezebel and Gunner graced my doorway.

"What are you guys doing here?" I asked, stepping aside to let them in.

"Adam texted us," Jezebel replied as she took me into a firm embrace. "Said you had a bit of an accident here and needed some help cleaning up."

I finally turned around and studied the scene of the cat-crime.

The tree lay in the middle of the living room, the top half crooked at an odd angle while the bottom half still had a few lights blinking. Broken ornaments and glass surrounded it. Some decorations remained intact on the upward facing side of the tree and scattered around the living room, but not many. I hadn't noticed it the previous night, but some picture frames from the fireplace mantel had also gotten caught up in the melee. Adam's blood dotted the crime scene. My stomach turned as I took it all in. My Christmas tree and its ornaments had been precious to me because of the memories they held. As I studied the mess, I had the urge to vomit and cry all at once.

"Wow. Elvira did that?" Gunner asked as he crossed his thick arms over his chest. "I'm a bit impressed."

"Yeah, it kind of looks like a tornado came through here," Jezebel agreed. "Maybe some hurricane force winds. At least she left the Christmas village alone."

But she hadn't. At some point, she'd gotten into the Christmas village and knocked over my new Santa figurine, which lay shattered on the floor.

I realized that Elvira had been angry at my attempts to keep her away from the tree by hanging lemon car fresheners around the bottom branches. And it had worked. She hated the lemon scent. However, I never imagined she'd go to such lengths for revenge and I didn't know if I could ever forgive her.

"She was definitely going after the tree," Adam said as he strolled in. "Dang cat jumped from the upstairs railing to the tree and everything came down."

"Let's see *your* damage," Gunner said. Adam turned around to reveal a bald spot where the doctor had shaved him and a nice line of stitches. Gunner studied them a moment then shook his head. "All from a cat. Who knew they could cause so much destruction? What did you hit?"

He'd obviously never owned a cat if he didn't know the level of damage they were capable of.

"I'm not sure," Adam said. "Maybe the table on the way down? Or it could've been any of the broken ornaments. They did find glass in the cut. I didn't feel anything until Bernie noticed I was bleeding."

"And now?" Gunner asked.

"Slight headache," Adam said with a sigh. "And my pride's hurt for being bested by a cat. I should've been able to save the tree."

Jezebel turned to me. "How are *you* holding up?" Her brow creased with concern as she tucked a blonde lock behind her ear.

"I'm tired. I was really worried about Adam last night. I had to watch him for signs of concussion."

"From the looks of it, he's going to be fine," she said, patting my shoulder. "Trust me. I've had worse injuries."

Jezebel had once wanted to become a professional MMA fighter, but she was never quite good enough. As she strode into the kitchen, her jeans hugged her thick, muscular legs. She'd kept up her physique even though she'd quit fighting. Instead, she ran Tip 'Em Back, a dive bar on the edge of town, and taught self-defense. With my yoga-loving peaceful ways, I found it strange to have a friend who embraced violence so easily, but I'd learned that sometimes, violence needed to be met with violence... or at least the ability to defend myself. After almost being tossed down a stairwell headfirst, I'd signed up for her class and we'd quickly become friends.

Ruby appeared next to me and grinned when Jezebel returned with a glass of water. "Hey, Jezzy! In spite of what it did to you, don't you love nature?"

"That's mean!" I scolded. "Be nice, Ruby!"

While alive, Ruby had been friends with Jezebel's grandmother. The two spent a lot of time together and had a tradition of greeting each other with insults.

"Tell her what I said!" Ruby yelled, jumping up and down, clapping her hands. "She'll love it!"

I repeated the offense and Jezebel burst out laughing. "Ruby, I refuse to have a battle of wits with someone who's unarmed."

"Oh! Good one," Gunner called. "She got you there, Ruby!"

Despite the mess and my profound sadness, I found myself chuckling along with everyone else. Having been under a cloud of despair since yesterday, the levity of the moment was a much-needed reprieve.

"Can you grab us a few brooms, a vacuum, and some garbage bags?" Gunner asked. "We'll have this cleaned up in no time."

As I hurried into the hallway to fetch everything from the closet, tears sprang into my eyes. I was so grateful for my friends. The mess wouldn't have taken me long to clean up, but emotionally, it would have been difficult at best. Many of the ornaments carried great memories for me. My heart ached at the thought of trashing them.

"Go sit down in the kitchen," Jezebel instructed when I returned with the supplies. "Take a load off and try to relax."

Gunner winked at me as he took the vacuum. With his thick black beard, bald head, and sheer size, he'd frightened me the first time I'd met him. As a cop, he'd been undercover in a motorcycle club, but I hadn't been aware of that little detail. I'd accused the gang of being involved in a murder and Gunner had threatened me in hopes of protecting me by making me stay away from the club. When I hadn't, Adam and Jezebel had to tell me his secret. Even though I'd almost blown his cover, we'd become fast friends once the murder was solved.

As my friends and Adam cleaned up my memories, I checked my email in the kitchen and had another cup of coffee.

My insurance was due. Did I want to renew my home warranty? Then a customer begging me to open for Christmas so she didn't have to have her in-laws stay at her house over the holiday. I typed back a nice, but firm, note. My bed and breakfast would be closed until the twenty-eighth.

Jezebel walked in moments later with a large garbage bag and headed out the back door to dump it in the bin. When she returned, she sat down. “It looks like someone tried to break into your house. The back door’s all scratched up.”

“They tried and succeeded,” I said. “And stole all the gifts for the white elephant exchange.”

“Oh, no! Were you home?”

“They waited until I was gone. I know who did it. Some guy was following me while I was shopping, and then he took my wallet.”

“You really did have one heck of a bad day yesterday,” Jezebel said, shaking her head.

Gunner entered carrying half the tree. “We couldn’t resuscitate it,” he said. “The middle is snapped in half. You’ll have to get another one.”

“I set all the ornaments that survived on the couch, Bernie,” Adam said, hauling the other half. “We’ll get you a new tree today.”

No, we wouldn’t.

“Should you be doing that?” I asked. “The doctor told you to take it easy for a few days.”

Adam smiled and rolled his eyes. “Honey, I’m fine. Really.”

Not listening to doctor’s orders... Typical man.

As the two men made their way out the back door, I said, “I just want to cancel the party, Jezebel. I don’t have a tree. I don’t have any gifts. My Christmas spirit has fled the building.”

"We don't need all that stuff," she countered. "Christmas is about spending time with friends and family, not about the decorations and the gifts. Besides, what's Darla going to do with all the food if we don't eat it?"

"Donate to a shelter," I grumbled. "I'm not in the mood for a party."

"That's because you're tired and you had one awful day yesterday," Jezebel replied. "You'll feel differently after you get some sleep."

Ruby appeared directly behind the woman, her hands on her hips. "And now I'm the Ghost of Christmas Present. Quit with the pity party. So some stuff went wrong. That doesn't mean Christmas should be canceled."

I didn't have the energy to argue with either of them.

When my phone shrilled, I almost dropped it on the floor, it scared me so badly.

"It's Darla," I said when her name popped up on the screen. I answered quickly. "Hello?"

"Hey! It's me!"

Although she sounded chipper, I knew something was wrong. I could hear her trying to disguise it in her voice. I placed my elbow on the table and my forehead in my hand. Another wave of exhaustion rolled through me and I sighed while closing my eyes. "What's wrong, Darla?"

"Why do you think something's wrong?" she asked, her voice high and tight.

"Just tell me," I said. "What happened?"

CHAPTER FIVE

"You're never going to believe me, but one of my refrigerators went down last night," Darla said. "It was the one that held tonight's meal."

Pursing my lips, I stared at the floor, believing every word. Obviously, the universe did not want me to have my Christmas party. It wanted me miserable during my favorite time of the year.

"No problem, Darla," I said. "I'm going to cancel the party anyway."

"No! Don't because of this! I can put together the original menu—some finger sandwiches, chips, dip... I'll have everything whipped up in no time."

"It's not just the food," I said, sitting back and meeting Jezebel's gaze. "After I got back from your place yesterday, I discovered my house had been broken into and they took all my white elephant gifts."

"Oh, my word!" Darla exclaimed. "Do they know who did it?"

"I think it was that guy I told you about who followed me and stole my wallet. He had my address and probably waited until I left before breaking in. He saw me carrying all my gifts and knew I had a big haul."

"That's terrible," Darla replied. "What's happening to people's Christmas spirit?"

Really good question. "Then last night, Elvira took down the tree." Despite my efforts, I couldn't hold back the tears. "She jumped from the banister onto the tree and it toppled over. Adam tried to rescue it, but he fell and I had to take him to the hospital to get stiches in his head."

Darla remained quiet for a long moment. "I'm so sorry, Bernie. I know how much those ornaments meant to you."

"Yes." I wiped my cheeks as Jezebel fetched a box of tissue. "Jezebel and Gunner are here cleaning up for me."

"Is Adam going to be okay?"

When he and Gunner strolled in from outside, they spoke in low tones, then returned to the living room. "He seems fine. They had to shave a strip of his hair to clean the wound. It looks pretty silly."

"I'm glad he wasn't hurt worse. What a relief."

"So, as you can imagine, I'm not in any mood to celebrate Christmas," I said. "In fact, I'd like to go to bed and wake up after New Year's."

"I'm working on changing her attitude," Jezebel said loudly so Darla could hear her. "We're *all* going to celebrate Christmas."

"No, I'm not," I said. "If you guys want to get together, fine. I'm staying home. Christmas is canceled."

"Put Jezebel on the phone," Darla said. "I need to plan with her. I know you've had a rough couple of days, but you're acting like the Grinch. You planned your little heart out and now Jezebel and I will take it from here. "

I handed the phone to my friend and announced I would take a shower. They didn't seem to understand that I had absolutely no intention of participating in any type of celebration. Forgetting tomorrow was Christmas Eve sounded like the best course of action for me. Perhaps Darla was right. *I* was the Grinch, but I couldn't seem to get past my string of bad Christmas luck.

After my shower, I slipped on my sweats and sweatshirt. Staring at my bed, I suddenly became so tired, I didn't think I could take another step. I slipped under the comforter and closed my eyes, inhaling Adam's scent on the pillow which consisted of his shampoo and disinfectant. Just before sleep overtook me, Elvira snuggled into my neck and purred loudly.

"I hate you," I whispered, yet I reached up and stroked her back.

She meowed and darkness engulfed me.

When I woke, I wasn't sure of the time, the day, or even my name. Vibrations of excitement hummed within me, but then reality crashed around me. Tomorrow was Christmas Eve and I'd canceled my party. I'd canceled Christmas. I'd canceled my favorite holiday.

As I rolled over, Elvira groaned and stalked out of the room. Adam came in a few moments later.

"How're you feeling?" he asked.

"Miserable."

He walked over and sat on the bed, handing me my phone. "There was a call, but we didn't answer it. They left a voicemail, though."

I took the device and played the recording.

Hi, I'm looking for Bernadette Peterson. This is Terry from Perfect Presents and Parties downtown. I have your wallet. Unfortunately, since it's the day before Christmas Eve, I can't bring it to you. My store will be open late, and then I need to head home. If you could stop by today, I'll have it here for you. If you can't make it today, I'll be here tomorrow until three. I've got to get home and celebrate with the family Again, it's Terry from Perfect Presents and Parties.

"That's great news!" Adam said.

Finally. Something good had happened to me. At least I could cross the DMV off my to-do list. "I wonder where he found it?"

Adam shrugged. "If that man did steal it, he probably dumped it after cleaning it out and getting your address."

"I'm going to head down there," I said.

"Let me come with you."

"Are you up for that?"

"Sure. I'll even wear a baseball cap so you aren't embarrassed by my snazzy new haircut."

I snickered despite my depression. "Let me get ready."

Ten minutes later, I had run a brush through my hair and changed out of my sweatpants, into my jeans. After pulling on my boots, I was ready to go.

"Gunner and I changed the locks on your house," Adam said. "You now have some deadbolts that Superman would have a hard time destroying."

"That was sweet," I replied, giving him a quick kiss on the cheek. "Thank you."

"Wait! Wait!" Ruby yelled as we walked toward the back door. "I want to go!"

Of course. "Sure, Ruby. Come on."

"Let's stop and get Ned, too. He'll love being out and around."

"You make him sound like a dog," I muttered.

"All men are to a certain extent," Ruby whispered as we followed Adam out the door. "Trust me on that one."

Once in the car, I drove to Adam's to fetch his ghost. The three of us entered the condo and Ruby yelled, "Ned! Hey, Ned! Do you want to go?"

Ned appeared. I'd spent so much time with him, the bloody shirt no longer fazed me.

"Where're you headed to?"

"Downtown. We're going to look at Christmas lights," Ruby replied. "And you get to ride in the car!"

While alive, Ned had never traveled in a vehicle.

While dead, he liked to play chicken in the road with them.

"All right," he said. "I suppose I'd like to join you."

Interestingly enough, Ned couldn't leave his house without my presence—the same as Ruby. Somehow, I'd become a ghost 'pied piper' after being hit by lightning all those months ago.

As we drove, Adam found a radio station playing Christmas carols and Ruby sang along at full volume. I quickly turned it off, finding the music—and my grandmother—only made my mood worse.

"Why did you do that?" Adam asked.

"Yeah," Ruby chimed in. "That's just wrong, Bernie. Just because your mood resembles the poop in a punchbowl doesn't mean you have to make things miserable for the rest of us."

"I just don't want to listen to Christmas music," I grumbled. "Besides, we're almost there."

We found a parking spot off the beaten path. Swarms of people hustled about looking for their last-minute gifts. A chill hung in the air and I wondered if snow was in the forecast until I saw a thermometer outside one of the stores—fifty degrees. Well, it was chilly for Arizona, anyway.

My attitude didn't improve as we weaved our way through the throngs. Just yesterday, I had relished in the crowd, the Christmas music, and the decorations. Today, I found it all annoying as heck. When a man bumped into me, I elbowed him in the ribs and glared at him despite his apologies and wishes of a Merry Christmas.

Ned and Ruby trailed behind us, chatting away about the decorations while people passed right through them. Linking my arm with Adam's, I sighed and leaned my head against his shoulder. "I wish I could find a way out of this funk," I said. "I hate feeling like this."

"You can," Adam said. "Allow the Christmas spirit to seep into your bones."

"It sounds like an infectious disease," I said, chuckling.

"In a way it is... a good one, though. One that should be spread throughout the world."

We stopped at a few window displays and I appreciated not being in a rush. Since Thanksgiving, I'd been going a hundred miles per hour, putting together my party and decorating.

The store Boots and Bags carried custom leather goods. I admired one of their purses in the window and debated mentioning to Adam how much I liked it in case he needed to pick up a last-minute gift, but then I remembered I wasn't celebrating Christmas.

As I glanced up, I caught a reflection in the window of a man passing by behind me.

The very guy who had stolen my wallet!

Anger swelled within me as I turned around and reached out, grabbing his arm. "Hey! You took my wallet!"

His brow furrowed as he pulled out of my grasp. "Excuse me?"

"You took my wallet yesterday!" I yelled. "Then you broke into my house!"

"Get him, Bernie!" Ruby yelled. "Give him a quick kick and make him sing soprano so the copper can arrest him!"

"What's this all about?" Ned asked. "This man stole from Miss Bernie?"

As I tugged at the perpetrator's coat again, I wished for the hundredth time Ned would quit with the formalities. The ghost always addressed me as Miss Bernie, and it irritated me to no end when my mood was good. I wanted to kick *him* in the nether regions, but that would be a waste of effort since my foot would slice right through him. Instead, I focused my wrath on my thief.

People began paying attention and stopped to watch. Some pulled out their phones and filmed. I didn't care. My fury boiled.

"You must have me mistaken for someone else," my robber said. "If you'd like to talk about it, we can go inside the store."

He pointed to Boots n' Bags and I shook my head. "The cops are going to arrest you. I've got one right here! Are you out here looking for more innocent victims?"

"Ma'am, I—"

"You're a sorry sack of a human being for ruining Christmas, you slimy jerk!"

Adam placed his hand on my shoulder. "Bernie, stop!" he whispered harshly. "Please calm down for a minute and listen to me."

"Don't tell me to calm down!" I shouted. "This guy—"

"Is a cop," Adam muttered under his breath. "Please remember you're being filmed."

Slowly, I released the thief's jacket and gazed around at the crowd that had formed. I loved my phone. I appreciated the efficiency. Yet, as I stared at all the cameras filming me, I desperately wished the technology had never been invented.

"I'm so glad I made a fool out of myself before FaceTwit and Insta-Toc—or whatever they're called—came around," Ruby said with a heartfelt sigh. "At least back then we could laugh and move on. Now, it's preserved for all eternity on someone's device."

"Let's walk this way," Adam said, placing his arm around my shoulder and turning me away from the crowd. I stared down at the pavement as he led me away, my cheeks flaming with embarrassment.

When we rounded the building and ended up in a parking lot, I glanced up to find the man I'd just accused of robbery following us, along with a few people still filming on their phones.

"All right," Adam said, placing himself between me and the looky-loos. "The show's over. Merry Christmas, and go along with your day, please." After they left, he turned to me. "Bernie, this is Max. He works for the Sheriff's office with me and was put on foot patrol for the holiday shopping season to help prevent thefts and pickpocketing. Max, this is my girlfriend, Bernie. I'm sorry about all of this."

"Why aren't you wearing a uniform?" I asked.

"I'm trying to blend in," he replied with a shrug. "Why did you think I stole your wallet?"

I sighed and explained the happenings of the previous day. "You were the one constant during the afternoon. I actually thought you were following me, and then when we bumped into each other, that's when I was sure you grabbed my wallet."

"And I followed you home and stole all your gifts when you left the house?"

I nodded.

"Nope. Sorry. Not me," Max said, smiling. "I don't even recall seeing you yesterday."

How fitting. He'd been on my radar, but he hadn't even noticed my existence. My embarrassment seemed to have no end.

"She received a phone call that a store owner had picked up her wallet," Adam said. "We're heading that way. Again, I'm sorry about this, Max."

I swallowed back tears of humiliation. I'd acted like such a fool. Grabbing a cop, screaming like a banshee and accusing him of stealing from me while at least a half-dozen people filmed... it didn't get much worse. Well, I supposed I could've been naked, but thankfully not.

Max smiled again and waved. "No worries, Adam. Have a good one, and Merry Christmas."

As he walked back to the stream of shoppers, I wanted the ground to open and swallow me whole.

"Let's go get your wallet," Adam said.

Following him quietly, I was mortified by the scene I'd made and a sick realization that curled my stomach.

I knew who must have stolen my presents. I just didn't understand why.

CHAPTER SIX

As I walked into Perfect Presents and Parties, I scowled at all the people lined up waiting to checkout.

"It would be rude for me to cut in line," I said. Adam nodded in agreement.

Ruby, on the other hand, believed it may be a good thing. "You're already all over Face-Tok or whatever it's called for accusing a cop of stealing your wallet. Might as well make it a home run and anger all these people, too. Remember, there's no such thing as bad press!"

Ignoring her and silently disagreeing, I stepped to the back of the line and patiently waited. Ruby and Ned discussed the tables of gifts surrounding us.

"What in tarnation is that thing?" he asked. I glanced behind me and found them huddled over a nose hair trimming kit.

"Men in particular get a few stragglers out their

nose and this helps them keep the strays in line," Ruby explained.

"That's ridiculous," Ned scoffed. "We didn't worry about such things in my time."

"Yeah, I figured as much. Were you aware some men actually shave around their stick and berries as well?"

"Stick and berries? What exactly is that?"

I groaned and tried to tune out the conversation.

"What's wrong?" Adam asked. "Are you okay?"

"I'm trying not to listen to the ghosts' conversation," I whispered. "Ruby's trying to educate Ned on some men's choice of hygiene."

"There probably wasn't a lot of that around during his era," Adam replied. "In any form."

"Well, I'll be darned!" Ned shouted. "What kind of nonsense is that?"

"At least they're getting along," I muttered. Sometimes they fought like two siblings.

The line moved slowly until finally, I stepped up to the cash register.

"What can I do for you?" the man asked with a jolly grin as he glanced at my empty hands. Short and round, he wore a red Santa cap and a red shirt and could've passed for one of Santa's elves. The Christmas spirit was in full swing within his heart.

"I'm Bernadette Peterson," I said. "Someone phoned me and said you had my wallet."

With a snap of his fingers, he replied, "Oh! Yes! That was me! I'm the owner, Terry. Hang on just a second. I set it in the safe in back."

The woman behind me groaned, and I shot her a glare but kept my mouth shut. I didn't need any more confrontation for the day.

"Here you go," the man said a few moments later. He opened it up and glanced at my driver's license. "Yep, that's you."

As he slid it across the counter with a chuckle, Adam asked, "Can I ask where you found it?"

"Right here! She left it on the counter after checking out. I tried to find her when I realized it, but there were so many people gathered outside, I couldn't see her."

"Thank you," I murmured. Every single dollar was still wedged in there along with my credit cards. "How did you get my number?"

"Good thing you had a business card stuffed in the side pocket," he replied with a wink. "When my brother and his wife come to visit, I'm going to suggest they stay at your place. I looked up the reviews and they're really good. She fancies herself a psychic, so she'll be into the hauntings people mentioned." He leaned forward as if he were about to share the biggest secret I'd ever heard. "She drives me a little crazy."

Great. The annoying psychic would be staying with me. "I look forward to meeting them," I replied, forcing a smile.

"I can't wait to haunt them!" Ruby squealed. Ruby and I had a rule: she couldn't haunt any of my guests without my permission. She really never followed the directive, but if this woman ever checked in, she could do whatever she wanted to her. Considering Ruby's ghostly abilities were so limited, the haunting wouldn't consist of anything very noticeable. But as a self-proclaimed psychic, Terry's sister-in-law would most likely revel in Ruby's feeble attempts.

"Thanks for calling me about this," I said, stuffing the wallet into my purse. "I appreciate it."

"Can you move along?" the woman behind me asked. "We still have a big line back here and I've got other places to be."

Her Christmas spirit had obviously gone down in a heap of flames, just like mine, and I held my tongue.

I thanked the owner again and we walked out the door.

"At least we've got the wallet mystery solved," Adam said. "Now on to the gifts."

"Oh, I know who took them now." Glancing to my left, in perfect kismet timing, Henry, my handyman, walked toward us, his arms loaded with bags. I pulled Adam to the right about ten feet. "Let's stay here just for a minute."

"What are we doing?" Adam asked.

"We're watching my thief and gathering evidence."

Henry strolled into Perfect Presents and Parties without noticing us. Ruby and Ned continued to chat while I stared at the man through the window.

After waiting in line, he got up to the counter and unloaded all my gifts from the store bag he carried, handing over the receipts. The owner yakked with him for a moment as he processed the refund, then handed over the cash to Henry.

"Henry stole my gifts," I whispered to Adam. "Did you see him get the money?"

"Are you sure those are yours, or is this another incident where you may be jumping to conclusions?"

Touché. I seemed to have done exactly that a lot lately. I shook my head. "No. He noticed the presents on the couch. We actually talked about them. He also knew when I left. Then he picked the lock on the back door and stole them. Look—the owner is holding the pizza socks I bought. And there's the Public Restroom Survival Kit."

"Those are some great gag-gifts," Adam replied. "I'm impressed with your choices."

"Thanks."

"Was anything else missing from the house?"

I shook my head. "Not that I noticed."

"Why do you think he did it?"

"I have no idea," I replied, shrugging. "Let's go find out."

I followed Henry, my heart aching with betrayal. Dozens of times over the years he'd been in my house fixing things for me. I thought I could trust him, that we had a sort of friendship and mutual respect.

How wrong I'd been.

Just as he was about to enter another store where I'd purchased some items, I hurried behind him and tapped him on the shoulder. His face paled and his eyes widened when our gazes met.

"B-Bernie," he stuttered. "Hi!"

"I know what you did, Henry," I said. My voice

sounded tired and weak. I didn't have the energy to be angry any longer.

"What? W-what do you mean?"

"You stole the gifts for my party. I just watched you return them and get cash back."

"Sorry, Bernie. I don't know what you're talking about. I—"

"Please don't make this any worse by lying," I said.

He smiled, but guilt shone in his eyes. "I'm not lying."

"Henry, I know what I saw." Pointing to Adam over my shoulder, I said, "I believe I've introduced you to my boyfriend, Adam, who's a sheriff's deputy."

"Yeah, we've met."

"You want to tell us what's going on, buddy?" Adam asked. "Why you're stealing from Bernie?"

Tears welled in the man's eyes and he couldn't meet Adam's hard gaze. "I don't know what you're talking about."

"Maybe we need to go to the station and discuss it," Adam growled. "Would that be better?"

I didn't think Henry would have stolen from me unless absolutely necessary. He never had before. "It's okay, Adam," I said, placing my hand on his forearm. "We don't need to do that. In fact, I'd like to buy you a cup of coffee, Henry. Then, I'd like to hear why you took my presents."

Finally, his shoulders sagged and a couple of tears tracked down his cheeks. "I'm so sorry, Bernie," he whispered. "I had no choice."

"Come tell me about it," I replied. "Canyon Coffee is just a block away. They've got great scones."

"Well, I never saw this one coming," Ruby said, trailing behind us with Ned. "Henry? Of all the people, I never would've expected that. Always watch out for the quiet ones, Ned."

"Why's that?" he asked.

"Because the quiet ones are the most trouble."

"I tend to be fairly quiet, Ruby. I don't feel I'm much trouble."

"Ned, you were a dang bank robber who took a bullet to the chest!" Ruby scoffed. "If that's not trouble with a capital T, I don't know what is!"

Once inside Canyon Coffee, I spied a table in the back corner and hustled through the crowd to claim it while Adam spoke with Henry, then got in line. He didn't need to take my order; we'd frequented the store often enough for him to have memorized exactly what I wanted.

Henry sat down next to me and placed the rest of my purchases on the floor between us. We waited in silence except for the ghosts arguing about what tasted better: chocolate or cherry pastries. Personally, I loved both and wouldn't turn either away, but chocolate had my vote.

When Adam returned with our coffee and scones, I took a long sip of my vanilla latte, then met Henry's gaze. "What's going on?" I asked.

He sighed and sat back in his chair. "Business has been slow," he said. "There's a new guy in town who has rates I can't meet. I'm not sure how he works for so cheap, but he's been draining my business the past few months."

I nodded, following where the story was headed.

"As you know, I've got four kids, Bernie. And... and I don't have enough money to give them a proper Christmas. Heck, I don't have enough money to give them *any* Christmas. The oldest was on the trampoline last month and broke his arm. My wife, Judy... well, she's got cancer. She's got a fifty-fifty chance of making it. The medical bills are piling up."

"I wasn't aware Judy was sick," I said, now fully comprehending the depth of his predicament. Judy being ill was worrying enough. Add on the cost of getting her well, and the stress Henry was under—this could drown anyone. I'd been in the hospital after being forcefully given an overdose of flunitrazepam, a drug given to insomniacs and also utilized as a date rape drug. The bills were ridiculous.

"When I saw all your presents and the decorations in your house, I wanted to be able to give my kids something. Anything. So yes, I took your presents. I felt awful about it, but I also didn't want to have to explain to my kids that there is no such thing as Santa. I didn't want them to wake up to nothing on Christmas Day. If Judy... if Judy isn't going to make it, I didn't want her last Christmas to be one where the kids found out Santa isn't real. She loves this time of year, and I want it to be happy for her. She's been under such a cloud with the cancer treatments. Watching the kids open presents just warms her heart."

I still couldn't find it within myself to be upset. In

fact, just the opposite. I wanted to help Henry. "I don't want any of that either," I said, pointing at the presents on the floor between us. "Take the rest of the gifts you have and return them. Use the money to get those kids some presents."

Adam smiled as Henry's eyes widened. "I... I don't know what to say."

"'Thank you' would be a good start," Ruby muttered.

"Just don't steal from anyone else, okay?" Adam grumbled. "You're lucky Bernie doesn't want to press charges. You could be in jail for Christmas."

"I won't," Henry said, standing and grabbing the bags. "I can't... I can't tell you what this means to me, Bernie. I'm a proud man and I've never done anything like this before. I'm disgusted by the levels I've sunk to in order to give my family a Christmas."

"Just go do the best you can, Henry."

"You're a wonderful human being. Thank you."

As he hurried out of the coffee shop, Adam and I finished our drinks. Suddenly, my heart sprouted wings and I grinned. It seemed my funk had disappeared. "I feel good for what I did."

Adam grabbed my hand. "It's nice to see a smile instead of the scowl you've been wearing since yesterday."

"I was pretty miserable," I replied. "But now, the tree, the gifts, the dinner... it all doesn't seem to matter."

"That's not what Christmas is about," Ruby chimed in. "The Christmas spirit has touched your heart again because you did something nice for someone."

I glanced at the two ghosts standing over my shoulder. "You're right."

"And, you can do even more," Ruby replied, smiling.

"Like what?"

"Don't worry," Ruby said, rubbing her hands together. "Let's pretend I'm the ghost of Christmas Future, and I have a plan."

CHAPTER SEVEN
CHRISTMAS EVE

In the past, when Ruby mentioned a plan, it always meant trouble for me. However, this time, she had concocted an idea I could really support. My heart felt as if it would burst right open with joy.

"Okay, are we ready?" Adam asked.

My friends had gathered in my living room, all of them agreeing to participate in Ruby's scheme.

Gunner had put dibs on becoming Santa. We'd found a suit to rent, even though it was about four sizes too big for his fit frame. We'd tied pillows around his midriff, dyed his black beard white and I'd dug up an old pair of dress up glasses from Ruby's chests in the attic. His girlfriend, Jezebel, had opted to be Mrs. Santa. Thankfully we were able to find a red and white suit for her and once again, Ruby's collection of old clothing and wigs came in handy. Jezebel looked great with gray hair.

Jack, Darla, Adam and I did our best to come up

with elf costumes: our ugly Christmas sweaters we were going to wear to my party and jeans. I did discover some elf hats at Perfect Presents and Parties while out shopping earlier in the day.

Darla had pulled together a meal: turkey, gravy, mashed potatoes, and all the fixings. It sat out in her car packed in a warmer. The back of my vehicle was stuffed with presents and my fingers were bandaged with papercuts from all the wrapping.

"I think we're set to go," I said. "Gifts, food, and the Christmas spirit is in full swing."

"Let's head out!" Ruby yelled. "Woohoo!"

We piled into our respective cars, Adam and I riding with the ghosts in my SUV.

As we drove across town, we sang along to the Christmas songs playing on the radio. "Deck the Halls." "Jingle Bell Rock." "Santa Claus is Coming to Town." By the time we reached our destination, my Christmas spirit was at a fever pitch.

I pulled out the bags of Christmas gifts from the back end of my car and brought them up to the front door of the small, two-story home. No wreath. No lights. A small Christmas tree had been set up in the window, its white bulbs blinking on and off. Being aware of what the family was facing inside, it seemed downright depressing.

As I stood on the step, I glanced behind me at my crew. Excitement crackled in the air around us. When I'd shared Henry's story and Ruby's plan, they'd all jumped on board, ready to pitch in.

I rang the doorbell and held my breath while we

waited. Yes, I was excited, but also nervous. What if Henry's family didn't want us to spread our Christmas cheer? Yet, something inside me told me I was doing the right thing, that our visit was desperately needed.

A small, rail-thin bald woman opened the door, her gaunt brow furrowed in confusion. "Can I help you?"

I'd met Henry's wife, Judy, once about a year ago and I barely recognized her. I cleared my throat. "We're here..."

To do what? Give the kids a nice Christmas? Feed the family? Give them a good memory of the holiday in case she died?

"What's going on?" Henry asked, coming to the door. His eyes widened in shock when he saw me. "Bernie, what are you doing?"

"Let's go in," Ruby said, marching past me and the owners of the house. "Come on, Ned. Let the living work things out while you and I explore as far as our leashes allow."

"Merry Christmas, Henry," I said.

"Ho! Ho! Ho!" Gunner yelled, stepping up next to me. "There're four children on my good list living here and I'm here to deliver their presents!"

"Is that Santa?" a child's voice called from inside. "Is Santa here?!"

Squeals of delight filtered outside along with the patter of little feet hurrying toward the door.

"And I'm Mrs. Santa!" Jezebel said cheerfully. "It's lovely to be out with the big guy and seeing all the kiddos!"

Two girls and two boys burst outside and stared

up at Gunner with wide eyes and open mouths. All under the age of eight, their surprised little cherub faces confirmed my friends and I were doing the right thing.

"He's so *big*," one of the younger one said.

Jezebel bent over and whispered not-so-subtly, "That's because he eats too many cookies!"

As the kids grabbed Gunner's hands and dragged him inside with Jezebel trailing behind, Darla introduced herself, "I'm Santa's chef. Have you and your family eaten tonight?"

Judy shook her head as tears tracked down her cheeks. "I'm... I'm so tired. I don't have the energy to cook. We were about to throw in a frozen pizza."

"That's my specialty," Henry muttered. "I'm not good for much else in the kitchen."

"It's great," Judy said. "It's all we need."

"Well, as Santa's chef, I've whipped up a turkey dinner with all the fixings for you," Darla said, taking Judy's hands in hers. "May I bring it in?"

Judy glanced at me and back to Darla. "Why are you doing this?"

"Because we'd heard through the grapevine that this family was in need," I said. "We wanted to help give you a wonderful Christmas."

Judy turned to her husband. "Did you have something to do with this?"

He shook his head. "If you're asking if I planned this, the answer is no."

I wouldn't go into the facts. Henry had stolen from me to give his family a decent Christmas. He'd made it clear they were overwhelmed with bills and worry and I wanted to make it better.

"Come in," Judy said, shrugging. "A home-cooked meal sounds wonderful, and the kids are too excited for me to send away Santa. Excuse the mess. Like I said, I've been tired."

After Darla and Jack fetched dinner from her car, we entered the modest home. The only sign of Christmas besides the small tree in the window were stockings hanging from the fireplace mantel. Gunner had sat in a chair by the living room window and Jezebel stood behind him. The kids had gathered at his feet as Jezebel read "'Twas the Night Before Christmas."

Adam and Jack helped Darla and me get dinner ready. There wasn't a table large enough for us all to sit at, so we decided to place the food out buffet-style and have everyone self-serve. Ned and Ruby stood at the halfway point between the kitchen and living room, watching us all.

"Ned, this was one of the best ideas I've ever had," Ruby said, obviously very satisfied with herself. "Those kids are happier than pigs in mud."

"I agree. This is a very kind thing for everyone to do. Even the mom seems to be enjoying herself. I'm glad I'm here to witness this."

Peeking around the corner, I found Judy sitting on the couch with Henry, her head resting on his shoulder. Both smiled as they observed the kids listening to the story.

Darla tapped my shoulder and motioned me back

into the kitchen. "I know I run a restaurant and I'm a clean freak, but this kitchen is pretty dirty," she whispered. "I used the bathroom, and there's dirty laundry overflowing in the basket. This family needs more help than one meal and us in costumes."

For the first time, I took a good look around. The small kitchen had bits of food on the floor and little handprints on the refrigerator and cupboards. I imagined with four small children, it was tough keeping things clean.

I considered running down the hall and throwing in a load of laundry, but it seemed like I was invading their personal space. I'd already pushed in on the family. "Let's clean after dinner while we do the dishes and the kids are opening their presents," I whispered. "I'll talk to Henry and see if they'll be okay with us coming in once a week to help out."

A few moments later, Darla called, "Dinner!"

Adam and I helped the kids pick out what they wanted to eat and got them settled at the table. Judy claimed everything looked delicious, but she'd only be able to eat a bit of mashed potatoes because her stomach was so sensitive from her treatment.

We all gathered in the living room, plates in hand. Henry walked over to the old stereo and found a radio station playing Christmas music.

"I didn't know Santa liked gravy!" one of the children shouted as Gunner stuffed a huge spoonful of mashed potatoes and gravy into his mouth.

"Yes!" Jezebel replied. "Besides cookies, mashed potatoes and gravy are his favorite!"

I snickered and continued shoveling turkey in my mouth. Gunner and Jezebel worked hard to maintain their physiques, and that included a good diet, if one didn't count their love of beer. I bet he hadn't touched mashed potatoes since last year's holidays.

"When can we open presents, Santa?" one of the children asked.

"Soon!" Gunner replied. "After we finish eating. Make sure to clean your plate so you have lots of energy to play with your new toys!"

After dinner, Darla and I cleaned the kitchen while the kids opened their gifts. I peeked around the corner every now and then to see if they liked our choices, and I was thrilled when they screamed and yelled about the pizza socks while sliding them over their tiny feet.

Once we had cleaned up, Santa announced his departure.

"We've got a lot of presents to deliver tonight," he said, hugging each of the children. "We've got to get on our way."

As the kids waved goodbye and asked why Santa was getting into a Ford F150, Adam and Jack explained that the reindeer were hungry and eating some hay at a farmer's field outside of town. The farmer had loaned Santa the truck to come see them. I appreciated their creativity and ability to think on their feet.

"Wait until I tell my friends that Santa and Mrs. Santa ate dinner with us!" the oldest one yelled.

As they gathered around the tree again to study their gifts, Darla, Jack, Adam and I packed up the car and wrapped the leftovers, leaving them for Henry and his family.

"I'm not sure what to say, Bernie," Henry whispered when he caught me alone on the stoop. "I never imagined I'd hear from you again about work, and then you did this. I was horrible to you. Why?"

Laying my hand on his forearm, I said, "I'll be honest, Henry. When you took those gifts, it put me in a foul mood. Well, that and the fact that I thought someone had stolen my wallet and my cat ruined my Christmas tree. But then I realized your actions weren't malicious, but a cry for help." I skipped the part about my ghost coming up with the plan we'd just executed. "And when I told my friends, we all agreed this family needed a little love."

"It's the nicest thing anyone has ever done for me," Henry said, stuffing his hands into his front jeans' pockets. "I was so worried thinking how I'd give the kids a proper Christmas... Thank you."

I embraced my handyman and hoped the Christmas spirit bursting from my heart would somehow envelop him as well. "We want to help more," I said. "Let us come in to clean and do some laundry every week."

Henry stepped away and shook his head. "I can't do that."

"You're busy trying to keep food on your table and Judy needs to rest. Let us help you out."

"I can't pay you."

"That's good because I don't want to be paid."

"It doesn't feel right."

As we bartered and finally came up with an arrangement that was acceptable to both of us, Jack, Darla, and Adam filed out of the house.

"Are we set to go?" Jack asked.

I nodded and explained that Henry would do some odd jobs around the house and at Darla's diner while she and I came in and cleaned and kept up with the laundry.

"That sounds like a perfect compromise," Adam said.

"I appreciate you all," Henry replied. "Thank you again."

As I turned, I found Ruby and Ned staring at us, grinning like two Cheshire cats. I didn't acknowledge them because Henry had had enough surprises for one night.

"Well, I'd say that was a big success!" Ruby said as we pulled away from the curb and waved at the family standing outside.

"Agreed," I said, sighing. "A perfect Christmas."

"And there weren't any dead bodies!" Adam said.

"With any luck, it'll stay that way," I replied. Although considering my recent history, I had my doubts.

But one could hope.

THE END

FROM THE AUTHOR

Carly Winter is the pen name for a USA Today best-selling and award-winning romance author.

When not writing, she enjoys spending time with her family, reading and enjoying the fantastic Arizona weather (except summer - she doesn't like summer). She does like dogs, wine and chocolate and wishes Christmas happened twice a year.

For more stories about Bernie and Ruby, please visit: carlywintercozymysteries.com/sedona-spirit-mysteries

To grab your copy of *The Fraud is Found,* another short story featuring Bernie and Ruby, download it here: dl.bookfunnel.com/f7ne2kay63.

THE TOY PUZZLE

VICTORIA LK WILLIAMS

The Tattletale Café is known for great drinks and the latest gossip... can Leigh-Ann use the gossip to save Christmas?

CHAPTER ONE

I looked up as the holiday wreath of silver bells attached to the front door jingled to see two of my favorite patrons walk into the cafe. Most of the lunch crowd had left, but Nora and Liz always arrived at this time of day. They jokingly had told me it was the best time to get our full service and not feel rushed to leave. And they never left fast; these two women could make their lunch break last for two hours without even pausing.

"Hi, Leigh-Ann, we'll just grab our normal table at on the boardwalk," said Nora

I gave a wave of my hand in agreement to the pretty young woman. I couldn't help but smile as I noticed the two women were laden with bags from their earlier shopping. But what brought the smile to my lips were the festive Santa hats that were perched on their heads. I always wondered if the two women thought they were British on their way to tea with the Queen because they always came dressed to perfection, and always with a gorgeous hat.

A movement to my right made me turn my head to see one of the newer waitresses start toward the two women. But her movement was arrested by a more seasoned waitress, and I heard her explain to the new hire in a hushed tone," Don't even bother. Those two are Leigh-Ann's customers."

"But the tables on the boardwalk are mine today—"

"You'd better learn pretty quick. Leigh-Ann has seniority, and that gives her the pick of the customers. Besides, if you go out trying to take those women's orders, they're just gonna ask for Leigh-Ann and give you a brush-off. Save yourself the hassle."

The more experienced waitress turned the young girl by her shoulders towards another table and then looked at me with a wink. I gave her a thumbs up; my way of thanking her for avoiding an unpleasant scene.

I would make it up to the newbie later in the day by steering her towards another customer that I knew was a good tipper, but there were certain patrons that I didn't share. And Nora and Liz were on top of my list.

Grabbing two iced water glasses, I added a lemon into the rim of each glass and filled it with sparkling water. I gave the women a moment to set their bags down and get themselves comfortably seated before I headed out to the boardwalk.

"Hello, ladies. It's good to see you both." I gave the nod at the stash of bags sitting around their chairs. "Did you save any sales for the rest of us?"

The two women laughed and thanked me for the

glasses of water. I knew better than to take the order right away. They would need a few moments to study the menu, even though they generally ordered the same thing every time. What they always order differently was their afternoon cocktail. It would depend upon their mood and the season, and today was no exception. Some days it was alcoholic, other days it was a tasty brew of coffee or one of my special blends of tea. Today, they ordered the specialty of the day, which was hot chocolate. There was just enough nip in the December air coming off the Atlantic Ocean to put any Floridian in the holiday spirit.

"That's a popular drink today. I'll put your order right in."

The two women thanked me, but their minds were on the shopping they had yet to do. As I walked away, I heard them laying out plans for the rest of their shopping day.

A few minutes later, I returned to their table with the tray holding two festive mugs of hot chocolate, whipped cream piled so high it almost equaled the size of the cup. I had to admit it was pretty good, and I contemplated getting one for myself when my shift was over.

Nora and Liz paused in their gossip long enough to give me their lunch order, and I was right; it was the same salad that they always ordered. I closed my orderpad and turned to walk away. This was a signal for the two women to start the conversation again.

"Did you hear about the toys?" Liz asked Nora.

My ears perked up when I heard the question. It

wasn't something I would typically expect the two women to be talking about. Neither woman had a child that would need toys, and their conversations usually ran around what was going on at the country club. My curiosity was aroused, and I almost turned back to listen more carefully. However, I knew the women would still be talking about it by the time I returned with their meal, so I kept going. I heard the women's voices behind me, but I couldn't make out the words as I walked away. Subconsciously, I gave a nod of approval. The restaurant was living up to its name, the Tattle-Tale Cafe.

By the time they finished their lunch and I had cleared the dirty dishes, most of the café was empty. The other patrons out on the boardwalk had given up sitting in the nippy air and left. But Liz and Nora didn't seem to notice. They were too busy talking. Without asking, I ordered them another round of hot chocolate and on impulse grabbed one for myself. I would take my break after I finished serving them and go sit in the corner out of the wind and relax.

Approaching their table, I found they were still talking about toys, and my curiosity piqued. I placed the cups in front of them, and they looked at me with a smile, as if noticing for the first time the chill in the air.

"Oh, thank you, Leigh-Ann. This is just what we need. I hadn't realized how cold it's gotten out here," Liz said.

Nora agreed as she looked around, noticing that it was only them sitting on the deck. Then she saw the third cup on the tray.

"Leigh-Ann, sit down with us. We never have time to talk to you." Patting the seat next to hers, Nora insisted I join them. I hesitated. It was one thing to sit at the bar with the customer, but their invitation to join them at their table made me feel uncomfortable.

"Nora's right. Leigh-Ann, join us. We're all friends here. Sit down and let's catch up with each other."

Liz's words caught me by surprise. It was like a voice coming from my past, and I looked at her in shock.

It was as if they knew my secret. In another life I had been one of them—one of the ladies who lunch.

CHAPTER TWO

Nora pushed out the chair she'd been patting for me to sit in. If I didn't join them, it would be rude, and the women had always been so nice to me. I couldn't do that to them. Putting the tray I had in my hands on the table next to me, I grabbed my cup of hot chocolate and tentatively sat on the edge of the seat next to Nora.

The women included me in their conversation as naturally as if I had been sitting at the table since their arrival. For a moment I felt out of place. They were dressed for a day of shopping, whereas I wore a pair of jeans, one of the cafe's polo shirts and a thick sweater to ward off the chill. But regardless of the outward differences, the two women seemed to know we were cut from the same cloth, and in a matter of moments, the three of us were chatting up a storm. It took me a few moments to feel comfortable, but Nora and Liz treated this as an everyday occurrence, and soon my past came to the surface, and I relaxed.

We talked about some of the new shops in the plaza, and the women showed me a few of their purchases as if they were displaying great treasures. It was easy to fall back into this habit of gossiping harmlessly, just spending an afternoon with friends.

You see, this is a secret that I kept to myself. I had been part of this life for years. Working a high-end job, shopping at high-end stores, spending afternoons shopping and taking late lunches with friends to catch up on the duties of their lives. But I had given it all up. I had to. That way of life killed my husband, and I didn't want it to kill me.

"Did you hear about the toy theft?" Liz's voice broke into my thoughts, and I glanced at her in surprise. There wasn't much I didn't hear about; it seemed all gossip in the town ended up at the Tattle-Tale Cafe. But I had not heard about any toy theft, and I shook my head.

"It's just awful, Leigh-Ann. All those toys that had been collected to donate to the children who needed them most have been stolen."

"Somebody just went into the warehouse and emptied it. It was as if the Grinch had come in to get the toys from Cindy Lou's house. There wasn't even a crumb for a mouse left in the warehouse," Nora added.

I was shocked. The toy drive was one of the most significant holiday events in our small town. It was so big that a warehouse was rented every October to store the toys for children in need. It seemed as if everybody in town took part. Even those who didn't have money to spare did their share by volunteering. It was a massive community effort. To think that somebody had undermined it by stealing the toys not only shocked me but angered me.

"When did this happen?" I asked. "This is the first I've heard of it."

The two women exchanged a look and seem to realize they had let something slip that maybe they shouldn't have.

"Well, there aren't too many people who know about it," Nora said. "We just came from the warehouse. We were with the coordinator of the toy drive when the theft was discovered. I don't even know if the police have finished the report."

Liz was nodding her head vigorously, and she jumped into the conversation to fill me in with all the details that they knew.

"We were there with the coordinator to discuss the possibility of renting the warehouse next-door. With two more weeks until Christmas, we were still hoping to get a lot more toys in one final push, but we had nowhere to put them. That's how full the warehouse was."

"I thought the poor man was going to have a heart attack when he opened the overhead warehouse stores and found an empty room staring at us," Nora told her. "It was as if nothing had ever been in that storeroom. He ran back out into the driveway to look and make sure we were at the right place, but we were, of course. Somehow, between yesterday when the group of volunteers was there sorting and this afternoon, all of those toys and packages were stolen."

"Oh my gosh, that's just awful. Did the police have any clue what might've happened?" I asked.

The two women shook their heads. We were silent for a moment as we each took a sip of our hot chocolate.

"So now what happens?" I asked.

Liz and Nora looked at each other. It was clear they hadn't thought beyond the fact that the toys were stolen. But on instinct, they both began making plans for what needed to be done next. These women weren't the head of committees for nothing. They spent the next few minutes making notes and plans for how they could start collecting toys so that not all the children would go without. But while their thoughts were focused on how to be constructive and replace the missing toys, my thoughts went down a different path. I wondered what could be done to find the missing toys and bring the heartless person to justice.

CHAPTER THREE

Liz and Nora kept busy for the next fifteen minutes, making lists and writing down contact names they could call to help put things into motion. I added a bit here and there, but my mind was still thinking about the cruel person who could have pulled this off.

"Leigh-Ann, do you have a moment?"

I looked up to find Dee, the manager of the café, hanging her head at the door, making a motion for me to come back into the restaurant. With a guilty jolt, I realized I had been sitting out here for over half an hour, much longer than my fifteen-minute break should have been. But Dee didn't look upset.

"Listen, ladies, I need to get back to work, but if there's anything I can do, you make sure to let me know. We'll get this figured out somehow and make sure not one child goes without a toy this Christmas."

The two women barely looked up at me. They

were so involved in their list-making. Nora waved me off to indicate she'd heard me, so I pushed back my chair and walked in to see what was going on inside the cafe.

Nothing seemed out of the ordinary. There were only a few customers left before we closed for the afternoon. I love the hours of the café. We are open early in the morning for breakfast and close at 4 o' clock after lunch. We are closed for dinner hours, allowing the other restaurants in town to accommodate our customers before reopening the cafe in the evening, usually with a live band. No meals were served at this time, just drinks and snacks. It was perfect, and I knew Dee loved the fact that she didn't have to prepare evening menus.

"Hey, Leigh-Ann, where's your Santa hat?" One of the regulars pointed to my head as he asked the question.

"Oh, it's somewhere around here."

I had forgotten to put it on before I went outside. I looked around and saw that the other waitresses still had theirs on, and I grinned. This is what I love about the Tattle-Tale Cafe. Everybody enjoyed the hometown feeling and felt comfortable enough to wear things like silly Christmas hats. As I looked around, I noticed we were missing a waitress, and I raised my eyebrows as I looked over to Dee. Giving a jerk of her head, she indicated for me to follow her to the office.

"Is there a problem, Dee?" I asked, closing the office door behind me.

"Not anymore. Funny how things work themselves out, isn't it?"

I gave her an inquisitive look, not quite following what she meant. Dee must've realized that she needed to explain.

"We're down one waitress now. We had one with a bit of an attitude, and she seemed to have a problem getting along with the rest of the staff. She was very put off that you got the preference of tables and customers and was getting rather vocal about it. A couple of the other girls tried to tone her down, but it wasn't working—so I let her go."

I gave her a quick look, trying to judge whether she was upset about losing a staff member. But judging from her grin, she seemed pleased about it.

"Well, thank you for taking care of it. I'm sorry you were put in that position. I forget the new staff doesn't always understand the dynamics of the café."

"Well, you have to admit our dynamics are different and although they may not know the complete story behind what goes on here, our regular staff accepts it. And there's no reason to apologize. I'm doing my job isn't that what you hired me for?"

She gave me a wink, and I thought back to the day I had hired her. You see, our dynamics are genuinely different. I'm not only a waitress. I'm the owner of the Tattle-Tale Café. And Dee wasn't just my head waitress, she was the former owner. We kept the ownership secret because it worked out perfectly for us.

"Will this cause a problem for staffing the next shift?"

"Not at all. Some of the girls were asking for extra hours to get them through the heavy holiday shopping they have planned and are more than happy to fill in. I've got it all under control. There's no reason for you to worry about it."

We exchanged smiles, and I knew Dee was remembering that day I walked into the restaurant to find her sitting at the counter crying into her teacup. The café was closing within five minutes, and Dee had a sign in her hands ready to post on the window that they were closed for good.

I could still remember the heartbroken look she'd given me when I had asked about the sign. It was so easy to see that her heart and soul belonged to the café, but she just couldn't keep it going. I don't know if it was fate or just a wild piece of good luck, my walking into the café, but I wasn't gonna turn my back on it. I seized the opportunity and quickly laid out a plan. I would purchase the café, close it down for a few months for revamping, give it a new name, new staff, and a new image. Dee would function as the manager. No one was ever to know that I was the owner, only that I was a privileged waitress, who could make her own hours and pick her customers.

Dee had been meticulous in picking the staff and I had so much fun reinventing the café. As I listened to her tell me stories of how the café had been in the community for so long, the one thing that I noticed the most was that the café was a meeting place. As she told her stories about some of the wild gossips that had been spread there over the years, I knew the new title for the café. The Tattle-Tale Cafe was cute, clever, and catchy. Exactly what I needed for people to remember and want to come and see what it was all about.

As if she were following my thoughts, Dee elbowed me in the ribs.

"It's worked out well for us, hasn't it?" she asked.

Impulsively, I reached over and gave her a quick hug.

"Our guardian angels both knew we needed each other that day. I'll always be grateful for needing a cup of coffee at just that time on that particular day."

"Not as grateful as me, Leigh-Ann. You've given me the best of both worlds—I manage the restaurant, and I don't have to worry about the bills," she laughed.

"And I found a new career. One far removed from the high-powered lifestyle I used to live. Yes, it's definitely worked out."

The older woman reached up, dabbing a small tear at the corner of her eye, and quickly changed the subject.

"So, what was all the hoopla going on out there on the patio? The three of you seemed pretty intense."

I quickly filled her in on the latest gossip, and she was just as horrified about the theft of the toys as I had been. I recognized the look in her eyes, and I knew, without a doubt, she would get active in replacing those toys. She had enough connections in town that she could help pull it off without a problem. Yes, it seemed like people would get behind rescuing Christmas for the charity. But I wanted answers. I wanted to know how something like this could happen in our small town with nobody knowing about it.

"I'm going to head back out and see if I can move those last stragglers out the door so we can get cleaned up for the evening hours," Dee said.

"That's fine. I am going to stay here and make a few phone calls. Let me know if you need anything."

Giving me a thumbs up, Dee left to shoo out the last of the stragglers so she could close the doors so we could prepare for the evening. A new band was coming in that she was excited about, and I knew she wanted to oversee to every detail to make sure they would want to return.

Rather than picking up the phone, I grabbed a pad of paper and started writing down the questions that were nagging me.

1. *Who had access to the warehouse where the toys were stored?*

2. *How had the thieves gotten tons of toys out without being noticed?*

3. *What was going to happen to the toys that were missing?*

4. *Who benefited from this awful act?*

5. *What had the police found out?*

I looked at the last question and tapped on the paper with the end of my pencil. I had a source who could give me the answers to the last question, and I knew just what to do to get Corbin into the café to talk to me.

Picking up the phone that was half hidden under a

clutter of paper, I dialed a number I knew by heart. It was answered by a gruff, impatient voice.

"Yeah, this is Corbin. What do you need?"

"Geez, Corbin, what happened to the phone etiquette?" I joked.

"Sorry about that, Leigh-Ann. I'm just kind of busy right now. What can I do for you?"

"Well, I figured you would be pretty busy and wouldn't bother to take time to eat a proper meal. Why don't you swing by the café, and I'll fix you something along with your favorite coffee?"

There was a moment of hesitation, and then I could hear the laughter in his voice as he answered me.

"So, the gossip has reached the Tattle-Tale Cafe already, eh? Actually, that sounds like a pretty good idea. I need a break right now. I can be there in fifteen minutes."

"Come around to the kitchen. Dee is locking up the front doors as we speak."

Barely thanking me, the police officer hung up the phone. I shook my head. Yes, I was going to pump him for information, but I knew that if he didn't stop by, he would go all evening with nothing to eat as he worked on the case. And I was a firm believer in looking out for the men in blue, as well as my friends. And if that meant fixing him a meal, then that's what I would do. Getting the information I wanted was just a bonus.

CHAPTER FOUR

I was waiting at the back door as Corbin pulled up in his unmarked police car. I had a large mug of his favorite brew of hazelnut coffee in my hands. There was a to-go cup filled with the same blend sitting on the counter, but I knew if he saw the mug, he'd be more inclined to stay for a while. And that would allow me to pump him for some information about the toy theft.

"That smells like heaven, and it's desperately needed," he said as he took the mug from my hands, barely clearing the threshold of the door.

He didn't take a sip. The steam was coming off the cup, giving him a clear indication that the coffee was piping hot, but he took a deep breath and gave a sigh of appreciation.

"Go have a seat at the side table. I've got a plate already for you. Let me just grab that and my cup of coffee, and I'll be right there."

I pointed to the small bistro table that we had set

up in a corner of the kitchen for the cook to take a break when she needed it. More times than not, this is where Corbin would sneak in to grab a hot cup of coffee and a few moments of peace.

"Hope you don't mind. I just fixed another one of today's specials for you. It's hot roast beef and a side of fries."

I set the plate down in front of him and reached overhead to grab a set of silverware wrapped in a napkin.

"Mind? Why would I mind? No matter what you put in front of me, it's gonna taste good."

Like a greedy kid, he grabbed the sandwich with both hands, ready to take a bite. He hesitated when he saw I had nothing but a cup of coffee in front of me.

"You're not having anything?"

I shook my head and pointed to my coffee, indicating it was all I wanted. As I pulled up the chair, he dug into his sandwich, and the grin across his face was all I needed to see to know that he was enjoying it. After a couple of bites to quench his immediate hunger, he put the food back down and looked across the table at me, one eyebrow raised.

"So, I suppose in payment for this fine meal you're gonna want to talk about the toy theft?"

I didn't even bother to try and hide my ulterior motive. With a brief nod in agreement, I waited for Corbin to provide me with some information.

"There's really not much to say. Sometime between last night after the last of the workers left, and this morning when a few of the committee ladies arrived, the entire warehouse was emptied. The security cameras had been dismantled and being after hours, there was no one in the neighborhood to notice anything."

"That sounds to me like somebody thought it through. And with the number of toys that were in that warehouse, it must've taken some coordination to pull it off in that short span without being seen."

Corbin took a sip of his coffee before answering me, his forehead furled in worried wrinkles.

"You're right about that, Leigh-Ann. And the chief has put me in charge of making sure we find out what's going on as quickly as possible. Not only does he not want the kids to go without a Christmas, but he also doesn't want the adverse publicity for the town either. So, it will be my head on the chopping block if we don't find those toys."

"Let me help, Corbin. Maybe if I poke around and ask questions, people might be more inclined to answer them. No offense, but most people are a little nervous talking to a cop."

"None taken," he said. "I know you're right. Most people are nervous around a cop. But I don't know about asking you to get involved..."

"Well, let's put it this way. I'm going to ask questions and snoop anyway. Either we work together, or we will be butting heads over this."

Corbin gave me a funny look, and I realized I'd never spoken so forcefully to him before. Some of my corporate background must have been coming out. But it seemed to convince him I meant what I said. He shrugged his shoulders before answering me.

"I've got nothing to lose by having you help. But I don't want the chief to know. You got that, Leigh-Ann? The only reason I agree with this is that I trust you, and I know you tend to analyze things and come up with some pretty good conclusions. Maybe if the two of us work together, we can figure this out quickly."

Picking up my cup, I held it up, and he raised his to meet it, tapping mine, and we formed a partnership to solve the toy puzzle.

We sat and went over the facts of the case while he finished his dinner. By the time he'd finished, he had agreed to meet me the next morning and go to the warehouse.

"I don't know what good it will do. It's just an empty warehouse," I heard him mumble, but I ignored him.

He was just finishing the last of his coffee when he got a call on his radio that he was needed at another location. We got up together and walked to the door. As he went to leave, I handed him the second cup of coffee in the to-go cup. He grinned at me in thanks and then left.

CHAPTER FIVE

It was a beautiful crisp, clear winter day when I woke the next morning, and I grabbed my sweater on my way out the door. I knew to dress in layers because in the next couple of hours the sun would peek through, and it would quickly warm up to the mid-70s. While the tourist might think that was glorious weather, and many of them would flock to the beaches, for me it was still a little on the cool side.

Corbin had planned on swinging by and picking me up on his way, but as luck would have it, he got another call. So, I agreed to meet him at the warehouse. Since it was such a beautiful morning and I had plenty of time, I decided to walk the mile to the warehouse's location and enjoy a few quiet moments to myself.

When I arrived, Corbin was pulling up in his car, and together we walked to the front door. He held the door for me as we walked into the main office. The reception desk was empty, and the place felt abandoned. I wondered what was going on.

"Hello? Anyone here?" I called out.

I was expecting to hear a woman's voice coming from the lunchroom area, but instead, I heard a man's deep voice coming from behind the warehouse door. A few moments later, the door opened, and a worried-looking man entered the reception area. His eyes locked on Corbin first, and I saw him frowning.

"I hope there are no more problems, officer? I told you everything I knew yesterday."

"No, no problems, Mr. Ross. I just want to take another look around."

Corbin took a step forward, and now the man could clearly see me.

"Mrs. Hackett, I didn't know you'd be here."

"Oh, you two know each other?" Corbin asked.

"Just from the cafe," I was quick to answer, as I gave the other man a warning look. Thankfully, he was smart enough to catch on, and he didn't contradict me.

There was no reason for Corbin or anybody else to know that I had paid for the rental of the warehouse for the Christmas season to hold the toys. It was listed in the books as an anonymous donor. And that's the way I want it kept.

"Yes, I'm a regular at the Tattle-Tale Cafe. Best coffee in town, you know." With a wink, Dan Ross kept my secret.

Corbin looked from one to the other of us as if he was going to say something and then, with a slight shake of his head, kept his mouth quiet and started looking around the room. I followed his line of sight, realizing he was searching for the security cameras.

"Mr. Ross, did you ever figure out what happened to the cameras on the night of the theft?" he asked as he walked from one corner of the room to the other, looking at each camera and the angle where it was aimed.

"Yes, as a matter fact, your security team found one wire had been cut in a discreet place where you wouldn't notice it. Apparently, he actually had to take the housing off the unit to find the problem."

"Won't that mean that whoever did it had to take extra time? And wouldn't that also takes special knowledge?" I asked.

Mr. Ross shrugged his shoulders, not sure himself of the workings of the security system. But Corbin gave the nod to indicate I was correct in my assumption.

"That's one reason I think whoever did this had knowledge not only of the inventory in the warehouse but also of the inner workings of the office and your systems. Mr. Ross, you said it's just you and the receptionist who works here?"

"Yes, the receptionist is here most days by herself. I open and close the office, but I'm gone most of the day with other duties for the business." He hesitated for a moment and then continued, "But she's the most trustworthy woman I know. She's worked with me for years. She probably knows the business better than I do."

Corbin didn't respond to Dan Ross's assessment of his receptionist's character. Instead, he pulled out a small notebook and flipped it open. He looked through the pages for a moment, and then seemed to find what he was looking for.

"Was there anything of value being stored here other than the toys? Anything else that a thief might want?" he asked the manager.

"No, not at all. The warehouse was rented specifically for the toys. As a matter fact, we cleaned it completely from top to bottom before the first toy was brought in to make sure no dirt would get on the gifts."

Breaking in, I asked a question I thought I knew the answer to but wanted it clarified.

"What was the process with the toys, Mr. Ross? Were they just stored here?"

"No. The volunteers would come in daily. Each gift was inventoried and then wrapped. Then, they were assigned to different bins according to the age and gender of the gift." He gave me a funny look, as if puzzled I would ask this.

"That's what I thought. But I wanted to make sure. Do you have a copy of the inventory of the toys that have been brought in?" I asked.

Rather than answering me, he walked over to the reception desk and pulled a folder out. Opening the folder, he pulled a stack of papers and handed each of us a few pages.

"I asked the receptionist to make copies of this. I thought it might be needed both by the police and the insurance company."

As I took my copy from him, I thought to myself that it was odd that they stole all the toys but none of the office equipment. I knew there was an expensive copier, as well as computers, inside the office. It was apparent to me that the thieves were only interested in the toys.

"Am I missing something?" Corbin asked. "There doesn't seem to be any overly expensive toys on this list. No big-ticket items that could be sold for easy cash."

"No, that's the complete list," Dan answered. "And no, there won't be any expensive gifts. The donations were all supposed to be under fifty dollars."

I didn't say anything, but I did agree with Corbin that something wasn't right about this theft. We walked out into the warehouse and looked around, trying to find a piece of evidence that might have been missed the day before. But there wasn't anything.

It wasn't until we'd said goodbye to Mr. Ross and were standing outside the warehouse office that I realized what was nagging at me.

"Corbin, the value of the gifts wasn't what was important."

He looked at me and raised that one eyebrow—a habit he had that worked well when interrogating suspects. But I ignored it as I explained.

"This was more about the emotional damage that could be caused. It almost seems as if somebody wants to ruin Christmas."

CHAPTER SIX

There wasn't much more Corbin and I could see at the warehouse since it had been emptied. I poked my head into the office, but nothing looked unusual or out of place. With a frown, I noted the time. Still, the receptionist wasn't in. Before I could think more about it, Corbin called out to me from the warehouse. Leaving the office, I walked to the doorway of the warehouse to see Corbin had the overhead doors open.

"These doors are well maintained—there's not a squeak to them. No one would have heard them opening, even if there'd been somebody around to hear."

Reaching over his head, he grabbed the rope to pull the door back down to demonstrate what he meant. The doors landed on the floor, making a little noise only when they touched the concrete pad.

"I see what you mean," I said.

I heard Corbin's phone, indicating he had a text

message. After he read it, he glanced at me, and I knew he had to leave.

"Stop back at the café after the lunch rush," I suggested. "Maybe, between the two of us, we'll discover some ideas or more information."

"That sounds like a plan. But I don't know what you're gonna find out that I can't."

"You be surprised what I can find out, especially at the café. I did name it the Tattle-Tale Cafe for a reason, you know."

I gave him a wink, and he smiled back. Then briskly, he turned back to Dan Ross, thanking him for his time and the printout that he had given him. A few moments later, Corbin was in his car, driving off to his next call.

"Dan, thank you for keeping quiet about who rents the warehouse," I said.

"It's not a problem, Leigh-Ann. I understand you want to remain anonymous. I just hope this isn't going to be a problem with the insurance company."

"It shouldn't. We made sure we have full coverage. Besides, that's why we have insurance. Theft is no different from a fire, and we need to cover our assets in case of emergencies. But with theft, we still could get the toys returned. We simply need to solve the crime."

"I think that might be easier said than done," he replied. "Well, at least we have an inventory of what was lost, and the insurance inspector was here last week so he will verify the contents of the warehouse as well."

I patted the man on the shoulder, hoping to give

him a little reassurance. Then I glanced at my watch and realized I had enough time to make a trip into the city. I dreaded the thought of seeing some of my old contacts, but I needed to put things in the works. I was going to call old friends and acquaintances to help raise the awareness of the need for the toys. Our small town would not be able to raise the exact amount of toys all over again without help. There are only so much small businesses could donate.

I arrived back at the Tattle-Tale Cafe in time to help with the lunch rush. Dee jokingly referred to me as her floater, and she never put me directly on the schedule, allowing me the freedom to choose when and where I worked. I was there most days, anyway, working the lunch shift and helping where I could. Once the rush was over, Dee and I sat down at one of the tables on the patio to grab a quick lunch for ourselves.

"Well, you came back looking quite self-satisfied. I take it your morning was productive?"

I openly grinned at my friend, giving her a nod.

"Yes, I called in a few favors, twisted a few arms, and reminded a few people of past help I've given them," I was happy to tell her. "I've got quite a list of people willing to donate to help replenish the toy drive."

"We've been pretty busy back here, too. The girls put up posters wherever they could think to, and they each started putting the word out that we were going to be collecting toys again."

Dee took a sip of her hot chocolate and looked at me over the brim of the cup before she expressed the same concerns that I had before going into the city.

"We have to be honest, there's only so much the community can give. Everyone was so generous the first time around. And who knows when the insurance will reimburse us."

"I agree, Dee. We can't rely solely on the donations from our local businesses. That's why I called in favors. But I think what we really need to do is to find the original toys and bring the thieves to justice."

"Leigh-Ann, you know that's going to be easier said than done. Those toys are probably long gone, along with the culprits who took them. I mean, I know Corbin, and the police department will do their best, but let's face it, stealing toys isn't a high priority."

"Well, it is to me. And I intend to do everything I can to find those toys."

Dee's eyes widened at my proclamation, and she gave me a look of concern.

"Let's just be careful, Leigh-Ann. There's no reason to step on the toes of the police. Let them do their job the way they're trained."

I gave a slight shrug, not deterred by her warning.

"You just said yourself they're busy and this may not be high priority. So, why shouldn't we jump in and help? After all, the Tattle-Tale Cafe is the best place to find information about what's going on, and people love to talk. Eventually, somebody's going to say something that will lead us in the right direction."

The door of café opened, and a group of women came in to find a table.

"And speaking of the gossip mill..." Dee mumbled, eyeing the door.

CHAPTER SEVEN

I turned my head to see what she was looking at. This wasn't the group of women that I usually went out of my way to wait on. They reminded me too much of the women I had come across when I worked in the city. Unlike Liz and Nora, this group of women gossiped with malicious intent. Their style of gossip could cut you to the bone and shatter you. I usually made it a point to avoid them.

They were noisy today and buzzing about something that interested them. I fully intended to ignore the women, but they sat at the table right next to us, and their voices were loud. It was hard not to hear their conversation.

"She just didn't show up for work. That must be a sign of guilt."

The other woman around her agreed, and it was clear that she was the ringleader. I didn't want to listen, but I couldn't help myself.

"And you know she's really tight with Allison Peters. I wouldn't be surprised if the two of them weren't in it together. And Allison's been the head of the committee for some years, so who knows what else might have disappeared in the past."

When I heard the name Allison Peters, my ears perked up. She was the toy drive coordinator, and I was astonished at what I was hearing. As adamantly as Stan Ross had proclaimed that his receptionist was honest, I firmly believed the same thing about Allison.

The women's discussion was interrupted by the waitress. As the ladies gave their orders, I noticed Nora and Liz had also arrived. I wanted to talk to them without the other women overhearing us, so I hurried over to the door to greet them as they walked out onto the deck.

"Liz, Nora, it's great to see you. Do you have a moment to talk? I have some news about the toy drive, and some questions to ask."

"That's perfect," Nora replied. "We've got news too. Let's pick a table that's little more private if you don't mind."

I saw her make a face as she answered me and turned my head to see what she was looking at. Her gaze was directly fixed on the table of women I had only moments before left. I had the feeling my two friends were not all that friendly with the other group, and I steered them to a table in the corner under the overhang.

Pulling out our chairs, we sat down at the table, almost instinctively with our backs to the other women, as if trying to hide what we were going to discuss from them. Liz motioned for me to talk first, so I opened with the news of the contributions I had scored during my trip into the city.

"That such good news, Leigh-Ann. You were smart thinking outside of the box," Liz said.

"I agree. It's going to take more than just the same people donating for this to work," Nora added, as she pulled out her tablet from her over-sized purse.

We spent a few moments going over the donations I had secured, and Nora added them to a list she had already started on her tablet. Once we were finished going over the list, I looked at the two women expectantly, wondering what they had to tell me. It was Nora who leaned forward, almost as if she was telling the secret.

"Rumor has it that you were planning on trying to find out who stole the toys."

I was surprised. I hadn't realized anybody else was following my train of thought, but then I realized Dee was just as much of the gossip as these two women I was sitting with, and she was probably the one who had disclosed the information.

"I'm going to try and do what I can. It doesn't seem right that somebody should get away with destroying Christmas for innocent children caught in the cross-hairs."

The two women nodded in agreement, and then Liz slid an envelope across the table to me she'd pulled out of her purse while we talked.

"What's this?" I asked.

"We have no interest in pointing fingers, but we made a list of everyone who takes part in the charity or had access to the warehouse. Maybe this will give you a place to start."

I glanced at the list as I thanked Liz. Most of the names I knew, but there were a few that took me by surprise. One of them was the woman sitting a couple of tables behind us. Without saying a word, I pointed to the name and raised an eyebrow as I looked at Liz and Nora.

"I thought that name might take you by surprise," Liz said.

"I wasn't aware she was involved. She hasn't been to any of the meetings," I responded.

"That's because she's in a huff," Nora said. "She thought she was going to head the committee, and she's been doing everything she can to sabotage Allison Peters' efforts. And you know as well as I do how well everything is going under Allison's leadership."

I glanced discreetly over my shoulder to the other table as I thought about Nora's comment. My eyes met the woman in question, and Marcia Cameron looked down her nose at me—until she realized who I was sitting with. Then she got the biggest fake smile I've seen in a long time. I knew what was going to happen before she even pushed her chair back, and I turned quickly to the other two and warned them.

"Speak of the devil, here she comes now," I hissed.

Ignoring me, she approached the table and did the traditional air kiss to Nora and Liz. Neither woman invited her to join us, and it was clear they were uncomfortable having her stand beside our table with her back to me. Without giving either woman a chance to say a word, she interrupted our conversation.

"I'm so glad I caught you two. It's just tragic what has happened to the toys. I want you to know that I'm here to help. I can easily jump in and do whatever needs to be done to make sure that the toy drive is a success. There's no reason to let Allison screw it up—"

Nora interrupted her before she could say another word. "Now, wait a minute. Allison didn't do anything wrong."

But Marcia shrugged off Nora as if she hadn't spoken. "Whatever. I just know none of this would've happened if I had been the head of the committee. But that's unimportant. We need to get this solved, and I want you to know I will do whatever I need to make sure things are righted."

Marcia heard her name called by one of the women she'd been sitting with and, with barely a glance in my direction, said a quick goodbye to Nora and Liz. Then she rushed back over to her table as if afraid she would miss out on a bit of gossip. Whatever the other women at her table had to say, their reaction was to pick up their bags, leave money for their check, and walk out.

CHAPTER EIGHT

"Well, what was that all about?" Liz asked.

The three of us exchanged looks, each wondering what was going on with the women who had just left.

We were silent for a moment, caught in our own thoughts. It was the approach of another waitress to clear the now empty table behind us that shook us out of our reprieve.

"I think with the donations Leigh-Ann has secured, we've got a good start in refilling the warehouse," Nora said.

"I agree," Liz added. "And I like your idea of going outside of town for donations, as well. Most of our husbands work in the city, and many in big companies. I think it's time to put the word out for the other women on the committee to start hitting up their husband's office for donations."

Nora's comment about filling up the warehouse set

a spark to my thoughts, and I slowly grinned at the two women sitting next to me.

"I'll be honest. I am going to find out who did this. And I think refilling the warehouse is a perfect place to start. Someone stole those toys for another reason other than their value. It's obvious because enough expensive things in the office were left behind. Things that would bring in some pretty good money from the pawnshop. No, I think this was done with malicious intent."

I watched as they each reacted differently to my words. Nora's mouth dropped open in surprise, and it was apparent she hadn't thought of that angle. Liz, however, smiled along with me. And I think if her face was green, I could've called her smile Grinchy.

"I like where your thoughts are going, Leigh-Ann," Liz said as she swallowed the last of her water.

Nora still looked a tad confused, so I hastened to explain my thought process.

"If those toys were stolen for a reason other than profit, then whoever stole them isn't going to be happy to find we're filling the warehouse back up. I think we need to make the refilling of the warehouse a huge deal. Let's get as many people involved as we can and really get the word out. The more it's talked about, the angrier the person who stole the toys in the first place is going to be."

"And what could that possibly accomplish?" Nora asked, still confused.

"Oh, that's a devious idea, Leigh-Ann." Liz gave her approval, and I continued to explain to Nora my thought process.

"If they took toys the first time and we refill the warehouse, then their first theft accomplished nothing. Can you imagine how angry they're going to be? It's a sure bet that they're going to try and steal the toys again."

Looking at my friends, I saw that they both knew exactly where I was going with this idea, and the three of us raised our glasses in a toast.

"And when they try to steal the toys for a second time, we'll be ready for them. We'll catch them red-handed."

Our glasses clinked together as if sealing the deal, and we exchanged smiles, smiles that hinted at a darker side to each of us.

"Can I get you ladies anything else?"

I looked up to see another waitress standing at the table. I hadn't even noticed her walk up. With a quick glance at my watch, I saw that we'd been sitting there for over half an hour. I was surprised at how fast time flew.

"Oh, thank you, sweetie. But I think we need to get going." Nora answered the server, who gave a nod of her head and walked off to another table. As she walked away, Nora and Liz began gathering their bags, and I stood up, ready to go back to work.

"We don't have a lot of time to accomplish a great deal. Why don't we meet again here tomorrow? Let's get a phone chain going tonight and get as many women committed to raising more toys as we can," Liz said.

Nora and I agreed with Liz. But I planned on

doing more than just making phone calls for donations. I planned on making a few phone calls to help me figure out who the thief was. And I also had set in motion a trap to catch them.

"I can see the wheels turning in your head, Leigh-Ann. Whatever you are planning, please be careful. There is no sense of anybody getting hurt over this," Nora cautioned.

"Well, I disagree," I replied. "If we don't pull this off, there will be some innocent children who will be hurt, and I can't have that."

Liz nodded at my words, and Nora gave a sigh. I think she knew my mind was made up and there would be no deterring me. I walked the two women to the door of the Tattle-Tale Cafe and said goodbye. Then I headed to the office to talk to Dee.

CHAPTER NINE

My talk with the two women had set things in motion in my mind. I knew I had to make some phone calls myself, but they weren't the type of phone calls asking for donations. I had already done that. It was time to move on to solving a crime. I had some pretty good contacts from my old life who I planned on calling. Plus, I knew I could pump Corbin for more information on what was happening with the case.

When I reached Dee's office, I knocked on the door frame of the open door. Dee looked up from her paperwork, and I had to hide my smile. There was a pencil sticking out at each side of her bun, making her look like she had antennas shooting out of her head. It was clear she was in the middle of ordering supplies, so I didn't want to take a lot of time.

"Dee, I wanted to let you know that I'm going to be in and out for the next couple of days, so don't count on me for the schedule."

My friend looked up at me, a worried frown creasing her forehead. "If I'm here, of course, I'll chip in, but I want to keep my attention on the toy drive," I added.

With a sigh, Dee put down her pencil on the pad she was working on to give me her full attention.

"You know you don't have to explain anything to me, Leigh-Ann. But I want you to be careful. Not only could you put yourself in harm's way, but if you dig too deeply, you may find your own secrets start to come out."

I shrugged my shoulders. I knew Dee was right, and I really didn't want my secrets out. But I felt called to solve this and to make sure the children had the toys they deserved for Christmas.

"I'll be careful. And if the truth comes out, well, I can't control that." I gulped and thought about what my next step was. "I need to go back into the city. There are a couple of people who might have some information for me about this theft. At one time, they were good friends, so I'm hoping they can keep a secret. But if not..."

"You're going to keep Corbin informed of everything you do, right?"

I heard the worry in her voice and hastened to assure her I would talk to Corbin.

"As a matter of fact, he's probably going to be here fairly shortly for a late lunch. After I talk to him, I'm heading back to the city. I don't know what time I'll be back today, so I'll see you in the morning."

Walking around the desk, I gave her a hug and

pressed my fingers against her forehead, trying to smooth her worry lines.

"It'll be okay, Dee."

Giving a sigh as she shook her head, Dee turned back to the paperwork in front of her, and I left her office.

Walking past the kitchen, I noticed the enormous clock and was amazed at the time. Thinking quickly, I realized Corbin would be here within the next ten minutes, and I detoured into the kitchen to prepare him a sandwich and a cup of coffee. If I was going to pry information out of him, I could at least offer him a good meal.

Sure enough, Corbin was there within ten minutes, right on the dot. I swear sometimes that man was more predictable than the tides. I could see he was tired, yet his eyes lit open when I held up the cup of coffee and pointed to the plate sitting on the counter.

"Oh my God, you don't know how much I need that coffee. That sandwich looks great, too. Thanks, Leigh-Ann."

I shrugged off his thanks and pointed to the chairs. Grabbing one for myself, I waited until he sat down for his first bite of the sandwich before I asked him how the investigation was going.

"Not well. Nobody seems to know anything, and I still haven't been able to question the receptionist. If it wasn't such a headliner, I don't think my boss would be letting me spend so much time on it. After all, murders are a little more important than stolen toys."

"Not to those little kids!"

Corbin held his hands up as if defending himself, and I realized how sharp my words must sound to the tired man.

"You're right, Leigh-Ann, of course, it's important to the kids. It's important for all of us. But theft always takes a backseat to murder."

"Has there been a killing in town that I haven't heard about?

Corbin took a sip of his coffee before answering.

"No, of course not. I guess I just get a little annoyed when some crimes get more attention than others depending upon who is affected."

"Or are you just frustrated?" I asked, figuring that was the real reason for his comments.

"Yeah, you're right. I am frustrated. Sorry about that. I've never seen a burglary where there's absolutely no trace of evidence."

"It'll all get sorted out. Someone had to see something."

I offered words of comfort, but I don't think Corbin really heard me. He seemed miles away.

We didn't talk much while he ate, both of us wrapped up in our own thoughts. Before I knew it, the man beside me was pushing his plate away with one hand, while the other lifted his coffee cup to his lips. After draining the last drop, Corbin pushed back his chair and grabbed his gear. It was clear he was going back to work.

"Look, Leigh-Ann, I know you're cooking something up, and I appreciate that you want to help. But don't put yourself in any danger or impede the investigation. There's not much you can do. From this point, it's a lot of tedious work and following up on leads that will probably lead to nothing."

I didn't bother to argue with him. I just nodded to show I understood. I had my own agenda mapped out in my mind, and as soon as Corbin left, I planned on putting it into motion.

CHAPTER TEN

For the second time in one week, I was driving back to the city. I had called ahead to let the few friends I intended to see know I was on my way. They all knew how much I hated the city and had set aside time to meet with me so that I could be in and out of their offices without delay.

It felt uncomfortable to drive the streets I once knew like the back of my hand. I had my car valet parked, and the attendant recognized me from my years of working in the same office building.

"You coming back here to work, Miss Leigh-Ann?" The older man smiled at me as he asked the question, showing a couple of missing teeth. He'd worked at the building since the beginning of time and was as much a fixture as the pillars that graced the entry.

"No, I gave this up a long time ago, George," I answered.

"Well, whatever you're doing, it seems to agree

with you. You look relaxed and healthy. That's a good thing, Miss Leigh-Ann."

As I joined his laughter, I realized he was right. I was happy with my new life. I was living a much healthier lifestyle without the stress of working in this building. Promising to take good care of my car, he hung the keys up on the valet rack, and I gave him a wave as I walked into the building.

The receptionist was waiting for me, and she directed me to one of the small conference rooms. There I found my two old friends waiting for me. We spent just a few moments catching up and then I explained why I was there.

"So, you see, it's a small-town police force. They're good, but they're not used to crimes that have no meaning or clues left behind. I thought with your connections we might be able to find out if this is more than just a random theft." When I finished speaking, I looked at the man and woman sitting next to me.

"Well, we took the information you gave us when you called, and we did a little digging. Your instincts are still sharp, Leigh-Ann. This is not a random act." The older man leaned forward, and I could clearly see he was excited about what I had brought them into. Before I could answer him, the woman next to him jumped into the conversation.

"We scoured our contacts, both in the police department and some of the local businesses. Quite a few corporations have been complaining about warehouses being emptied of their inventory with no trace. But this is the first time they've taken something as nondescript as a warehouse full of toys," she said.

What she said surprised me. "Really? I had a feeling something was up, but I had no idea it was going to be this big." I looked at my old friends and remembered a time when my husband would have been sitting right next to me, the four of us planning our next promotional campaign or company function. Sam and Mary had been our partners in the business, but when my husband died, I'd sold off my share to them and walked away. They had always been like family to my husband and me and continued to keep in touch with me. It was only natural I would turn to them to help solve this toy puzzle.

"If it weren't for the method of the theft and the fact that it matched exactly the other thefts in the city, I would say they were random acts. But everything points to it all being done by the same people," Mary said.

"This needs to be reported to the police, but we wanted to talk to you first," Sam said. "I know how important it is for you to stay incognito in your little town. If we report this to the police, they're going to get in touch with your police department and it's going to come out that you are connected to the investigation. What do you want to do, Leigh-Ann?"

I thought for a moment before answering.

"Can you hold off just for a couple days? If I can set a trap and catch the robbers in the act, then everybody will be happy. And no one will need to know my connections."

Sam protested, but Mary hushed him and gave me a nod before she answered.

"I don't see why not, Leigh-Ann. After all, these robberies have been going on for over six months and the police are no closer to solving them. What's another couple of days going to matter?"

I grinned at my friend, and it felt like old times, the two of us conspiring together. With a sigh, Sam seemed to give in, and he pushed a thick envelope across the table to me.

"This is all the information that I could find about the facts. Maybe it will help you," he said.

I didn't stay much longer; I had gotten the information I needed. Besides, I was feeling closed in as I noticed the hustle and bustle of people in the hallways outside the conference room. It was time to head back to my little coastal haven. My friends seemed to notice my nervousness, and we ended our meeting with hugs and promises of staying in touch.

CHAPTER ELEVEN

I made record time to get back to the shore, driving like the devil was on my heels. By the time I got my keys from George, I felt like the city was closing in on me. I was so anxious to get back where I could smell the salty air and walk down the sidewalk without bumping into somebody every couple of feet.

I pulled into the parking lot of the Tattle-Tale Cafe, even though it was after hours. This was because I had a small apartment above the café. It was perfect for my needs and with a wraparound porch, I could enjoy the salt air and the view of the ocean anytime I wanted. And that's just where I wanted to be tonight. I was eager to look over the reports that Sam and Mary had given me. I could tell from Sam's expression that there was something in there that would interest me. But knowing Sam, he expected me to find it myself.

When I entered my apartment, I pushed the sliding glass doors open so the breeze coming off the ocean would fill the room. Then I grabbed a bottle of wine, a glass hand-painted with bright pink flamingos, the folder Sam had given me, and a tray of cheese and crackers. Setting everything down on the little bistro table I had set up in the balcony's corner, I realized it was a little cooler than I expected, so I rushed back inside and grabbed the blanket to wrap up in. I was ready to start leafing through the papers.

I went over that paperwork two or three times while dusk settled, and the lights automatically went on, allowing me to continue to read. I saw nothing the first couple of times going through the information, but then I connected one name on all the reports. It would never raise a red flag with me except that I had met him and hadn't liked him at first sight. It was the insurance adjuster for the warehouse. But unless you looked closely, you wouldn't easily find his name because most of the reports only listed the insurance company and for each warehouse, and there seemed to be multiple companies listed.

Sam had been thorough. He not only had given me the police reports, but he'd given me the insurance claims as well. It was when I went over the insurance claims that I noticed the name. Most people probably wouldn't have noticed because the name was spelled differently, and the signatures were different on each of the forms. It was only a letter or a different middle name, but it was enough for me to catch.

David R. Leine

Dave C. Lennie

D.R. Leni

and finally, the name I recognized, *Dave R. Lenny.*

"Got you!"

I snapped my fingers as I pointed at the name on the paper. I was sure this was the key that would connect all the thefts together. But I still didn't understand why he would be interested in stealing cheap toys that were meant as gifts for underprivileged children.

I reached for my glass of wine and realized it was empty. Yawning, I stretched my arms over my head and glanced at my watch, surprised at the hour.

"Time to put this away for a bit and get some proper food in me," I said to myself.

An hour later, my stomach was full, and I had a second burst of energy. Whether it was from the simple meal I had just consumed or the fact that I had taken a break and allowed my brain to clear; I was ready to tackle the next pile of papers waiting for me.

This time I grabbed a cup of hot tea along with the paperwork and headed to my desk. It was too cold to sit out on the balcony now, and I wanted to spread out the paperwork on my desk without worrying about the wind blowing the papers away.

I picked up the folder that Dan Ross had given me at the warehouse. It was time to look over the inventory to see if I could find something that would have been worth something to the thieves.

I took a quick glance through the paperwork before settling in to go over the details. I was impressed by the thoroughness of Allison Peters, the toy drive coordinator. Not only had she listed every single donation, but she included a description, a dollar value, and who had donated it. If the information wasn't available, she left it blank. The woman sure knew her way around an Excel spreadsheet.

It didn't surprise me that many of the gifts had been donated anonymously. I had given quite a few that way myself. But Allison had listed everything else about the toys, including a potential match for a child who might need that toy. As I went up and down the list, I grinned at some of the toys listed. Old favorites were there—Tonka trucks, Lego's, Lincoln Logs, board games, books, Barbie dolls, and stuffed animals were in abundance. It pleased me to see not only toys for children but also for teenagers. I knew these kids were often forgotten, and they deserved gifts just as much as the younger ones did.

I got through half the sheets when I realized I was working on another list of the same toys. But this list grouped the toys according to age group brackets. Yes, Allison was thorough.

I was working my way through the second list when I came across a toy listed with no dollar value, no designation for the child, and had multiple question marks for a description. I didn't remember seeing the toy listed on the first list and quickly went back to the paperwork. This time I found it Allison had labeled it as an electronic toy. It was the question marks on the second list that made the toy jump off the page for me.

"What's the matter, Allison, not up on your Nintendo games?" I muttered to myself.

I reached over and took a sip of my tea, grimacing when I realized it had gone cold. Still holding the papers, I stood up and went to the kitchen to refresh my drink, reading as I walked. I went through the rest of the pages as I waited for my tea to brew, but my eyes kept jumping back to those question marks. It was clear to me that the toy had annoyed Allison with her inability to identify it.

I glanced at the clock, hoping it wasn't too late to call Allison to ask her about the toy. I decided to go ahead, but I didn't get an answer. I left a brief message asking her to call me. As I hung up, I remembered the unpleasant woman from the café who had commented snidely about the receptionist being missing. And then I remembered Corbin mentioning he still hadn't talked to the receptionist or Allison. I wondered if it was all connected somehow to that toy.

Once I was back in my office, I pulled out a sheet of paper and wrote down a few ideas to pursue tomorrow. There was nothing else I could do tonight, and no matter how many times I read over the files I had been given, the words would not change. It was time to give it a break until I could do something the next morning.

CHAPTER TWELVE

The next morning was a blur. Phone calls startled me out of bed and continued for most of the day. Liz and Nora were in full gear, along with the rest of the committee members, in their quest to replace the missing toys.

It was about 10 o' clock before Allison returned my phone calls from the night before.

"I'm so sorry it took me so long to get back to you," Allison began. "I just got back from the police. They had a lot of questions for me, but I think they're convinced I had nothing to do with the robbery. Why would I?"

"I'm sure they're just covering all the bases. And of course, not being able to talk to you on the day of the robbery—"

"Well, like I explained to the detective, I had a family emergency. I spent most of the day in the hospital with my nephew. He broke his foot skateboarding."

"Oh, that's awful. I hope he's okay," I told her. After being assured her nephew was fine, I asked Allison about the toy in question.

"That toy bugged the heck out of me. I have no idea what it was, what age child would want to play with it, or even how it works. I had decided not to include it in the giveaway. The worst thing we could do is give an inappropriate toy to a child."

I could clearly hear the frustration in her voice. In my mind, I could picture Allison standing there with the toy in her hand, trying to figure out how to categorize it.

"Can you describe it?" I asked.

"That's the whole problem. I've never seen anything like it before. It was electronic, and judging from the coloring and shape, it was meant for kids. Although I tend to think for older kids. It had a small computer screen, several buttons to click, and it could fit in the palm of your hand."

As Allison describe the toy, I drew a rough sketch of it. I could see why she had a problem with it.

"Did it have the manufacturer's name?"

"Yes, but it was not a toy manufacturer which threw me for a loop. It was an aviation company. But maybe they're getting into toys now, too. It seems like everybody is."

The rest of the conversation was about new toys that had been collected. I was informed that the warehouse was already beginning to fill, and I agreed to meet with Allison the next day to go over our progress at the warehouse.

The rest of my day was taken up with picking up toys and making phone calls. I managed to talk to Corbin and told him about the name I had found in the paperwork. I didn't fill him in on how I had found the name, and he didn't ask. It was easy to hear the frustration in his voice, and I knew the case was starting to get to him. We arranged to meet at the warehouse with Allison the next day. Something was nagging at me about that toy, and I thought maybe it might make some sense to him because it certainly didn't to me.

When I pulled up to the warehouse the next day, the overhead doors were up, and it was easy to see there was already a considerable accumulation of toys. Allison and Corbin were there waiting for me, and I waved to Dan and his assistant, Debbie, as I walked past the office, indicating that they should come out and join us.

Once we were all together in the middle of the warehouse, I waved my hands toward the toys and grinned.

"This warehouse is going to be full in no time. I think it's time to set the trap."

I heard Corbin groan but ignored him as the others agreed with me.

"Dan, has a security team gotten here and set up all the new systems we talked about?"

Dan confirmed everything was set up, and there would be no getting away with so much as a marble out of that warehouse without somebody being caught. Thankfully, Dan kept quiet about who paid for the new system, as well as the fact that there was a new owner of the building. I had considered it a wonderful investment.

I looked at the two women standing next to me and knew they were going to pull their weight without even asking.

"Has anyone been putting up a stink about having to raise new toys or the use of the warehouse?"

Debbie cleared her throat, giving Allison an apologetic look before she answered me.

"The only negative thing I have heard at all about this is from Marcia Cameron. I'm sorry, Allison, but she keeps insisting that you should not be involved in this. She seems to think it was your fault that the toys were stolen in the first place. She's done everything she can to take over the collection of toys, but she's getting shot down at every level."

Allison gave a weary shake of her head and sighed.

"You know I would have gladly turned over the chairmanship of this if I'd thought Marcia would honestly do a good job. But I'm afraid the only reason she wants to be a coordinator is for the recognition, not for helping the children."

The rest of us agreed with her and reassured her

not to worry about Marcia. Then I proceeded to lay out my plan.

"I've arranged for media coverage Saturday morning to be here at the warehouse. We're going to make a big show about the toys being replaced in time to get to the children for Christmas. I'm also going to mention that a few toys were recovered, and we are on point to duplicate every other toy that wasn't."

Corbin looked at me, startled. He knew as well as I did nothing had been recovered yet. I held my finger up for him to wait a minute before he raised the question and then I continued.

"I'm doing this on the off chance that there was something in this warehouse that the thieves specifically wanted. If they think we may have recovered something, they will try to get it back. And if they were doing this just for malicious intent, they'll want to try again, anyway. Whoever these thieves are, they're making the Grinch look like a saint."

The others began to talk excitedly about my plan, and after a few moments, I saw Corbin smile. I knew he agreed with me and would support me. With the security measures that we had taken and Corbin's cooperation, there was no way the thieves would get away with the toys again. Hopefully, we could catch them before anything was destroyed or anybody got hurt.

Turning the planning of the media party over to Debbie and Allison, I motioned for Corbin and Dan to follow me back to the office. I knew the two men would want the details of my plan, and I was pretty sure that Dan was excited to show Corbin the new security system. Within an hour, the five of us were satisfied with our plans and felt confident that it was a fail-proof endeavor.

CHAPTER THIRTEEN

The week flew by. Before I knew it, it was Friday, and we were making the final preparations for the media blitz the following morning at the warehouse.

Toys had poured in from both corporate sponsors as well as the generous shops in town who once again dug deep into their coffers and donated duplicate toys. I was amazed at the generosity of the shop owners. Word had spread quickly on what we were doing, and I was making daily runs to the warehouse with my car full of toys that had been dropped off at the Tattle-Tale Cafe. Tourists were even getting in on the action, and many were buying toys at the toy store and then dropping them off at the Tattle-Tale Cafe when they came in for lunch.

Allison was once again keeping meticulous details on everything that came in and assigned it to a child. It even looked like there might be extra toys, which we made sure would go to the national toy drive so that other children could benefit.

Liz and Nora were in their glory planning for the big holiday party where the toys will be distributed, as well as the media conference. They had taken over the warehouse and decorated the entire office area where the media would meet. It looked like a winter wonderland, and when you opened the door to look into the warehouse overflowing with toys, you would've sworn you were in Santa's workshop.

I'd been busy as well. Besides running around with toys to be delivered, I was making sure all the security details were dealt with and getting in touch with the insurance company. I'd had an interesting conversation with the insurance adjuster who made a claim for the first batch of missing toys.

"Mrs. Hackett, this is quite the endeavor you've taken on. And you're sure that this list duplicates all the toys?"

The insurance adjuster had questions of his own, and this was just one of them. Somehow the man was involved, but I wasn't sure how, so I went out of my way to give him details, not quite knowing where it was going to lead.

"Oh, yes, every single toy has been duplicated. Of course, I have no idea what some are. The kids seem to know how to use everything now, so I'm not worried about it. There are even a few electronic toys that, to be honest, I couldn't make heads or tails of. There was one, in particular. I swore I knew what it was, but when I showed it to one of the teenagers, he wasn't sure what it was, but he was quite interested."

I knew I was pouring it on thick, but I wanted to make sure I had his attention. Sure enough, he took the bait.

"You showed this to one of the kids? You mean from the first batch of toys, right?"

I clearly heard the anxiousness of his tone, and I couldn't help the smugness in my voice when I answered him.

"Oh no, this is from the second batch of toys. And since it was from an anonymous donor, we have no idea of how to contact anybody to find out what the toy is or how to use it. I'm thinking of pulling it aside until we can find the donor. I would hate to give an inappropriate toy to a child."

"That sounds like a good plan. You wouldn't want to a child getting hurt with a toy that isn't for their age group. If you want, you can put the toy aside, and I can see what I can do to find the donor."

In my mind, I could see him wiping the sweat off his forehead when he realized I was going to hold the toy out from the rest of the giveaway.

"Oh, that won't be necessary. I'm just going to leave it here in the office and deal with it after the holiday. Now, you will come on Saturday morning for the media blitz, correct? I know the media is going to want to be reassured that your company will stand behind the safety of for the toys. After all, you did such a fine job the first time. Why not take credit for it?"

The man hemmed and hawed, but I finally got him

to agree to come to the media blitz. I wanted him where I could see him when the toys were exposed for everyone to see. Although to be honest, I had a feeling something was going to happen before Saturday morning, but I didn't know what.

After seeing to all the last-minute details throughout the day on Friday, Corbin and I took time off and had a late evening dinner. It felt good to relax for a moment and talk about anything except the toy drive. It was by mutual agreement that we steered away from the topic.

After dinner, we still weren't ready to go back to the warehouse. Instead, we went to a local coffee shop and sat out on the patio by the fire pit.

It felt good to talk to somebody who wasn't involved in the Tattle-Tale Cafe or knew about my past life. To be honest, it was the first time I'd sat and talked to a man for any length of time since my husband died, and I was pleased with how naturally Corbin and I got along. I realized we had developed a strong friendship, just one of the many I had formed since moving to the shore.

We finished our coffee and walked back to the warehouse, giving us the chance to enjoy the festive holiday lights that were up around town. There would be nobody at the warehouse. Everyone had left hours ago, so there was no reason to rush.

It wasn't until we were almost there that I got a tingly feeling along the back of my neck, and I knew something was wrong. I glanced at Corbin and pointed toward the warehouse.

"We need to get there quickly. I just have a bad feeling that something is happening."

Corbin didn't question me. He just grabbed my hand, and we rushed toward the warehouse. Before we reached the front door, he came to an abrupt stop and pulled me off the main sidewalk to stand behind some bushes to hide us from view. That's when I saw a light moving around inside the office area of the warehouse. Somebody was in there, and they were using a flashlight to find something. And I had a pretty good idea of what they were looking for.

Corbin pulled his gun out of his holster and told me to stay still. I let him take a few steps ahead of me and then I followed, foolishly disregarding his instructions. He didn't even realize I was behind him until after he'd entered the office. He raised his gun and commanded the person in the office to halt and put their hands above their head.

"Keep your hands above your head and turn around and face me," he commanded.

I couldn't help but gasp when the man turned around, and I saw it was the insurance adjuster. Even though I had been expecting him, it still took me by surprise. I saw Corbin tense when he heard my gasp, but he didn't take his eyes off the other man. Instead, he told me to step out of the way and then instructed the intruder to get down on his knees with his hands above his head. In a swift movement, Corbin slapped a pair of handcuffs around the intruder's wrists. Then, with not too gentle movements, he pulled the man to his feet and pushed him into the office chair. While he did that, I walked over to the wall and turned on the light switch.

It was clear the man had been in here for a while searching. Debbie's files were scattered across the room, and opened drawers in her desk showed he had also rummaged through there. He glared at me, clearly angry and frustrated.

"You said you were gonna put that electronic toy in the office. Where is it? I searched this place high and low."

Surprised by his question, I replied, "What's so important about that toy? You stole it once before, didn't you? And this isn't the first time you stole items from warehouses. You left a trail. It may have been hard to find, but I did. And once I found the first clue, it was easy to find every single warehouse you've emptied."

At my words, the man's shoulder sagged, and he seemed to realize there was no getting out of this situation.

"I'll tell you about that toy, but I'm gonna want something in return. I can give you the names of big-time corporate spies. But I'm gonna want leniency."

Corbin and I exchanged looks, and then he gave a shrug of the shoulder and told the man to provide him with all the information he had, and he would be sure to get his leniency. I knew Corbin was lying—I could tell by the twitch of his eyebrow—but the insurance adjuster didn't. He was just looking for a way to save his own hide.

CHAPTER FOURTEEN

I was exhausted the next morning, and if I could've gotten away from not going to the warehouse for the media blitz, I would have. But I knew that would not happen, and, besides, there were still some questions to be answered about the toy theft.

Corbin and I had stayed up late into the night listening to the insurance adjusters' long list of thefts and shakedowns.

It seems he was in the business of insuring corporate warehouses, often stocked with new products that hadn't even gotten their product patents yet. It gave him easy access to steal the ideas and prototypes and sell them to the highest bidders. Corporate espionage at the highest level from one of the lowest men on the totem pole.

It seems the electronic toy that none of us could figure out how to work was no toy. It was a prototype for one of the big computer companies—their next innovative product ready to come out on the market within months. Losing this product would have been devastating to the company. But the insurance agent wasn't selling this one to the highest bidder. Instead, he realized what a gem he had, and he planned on holding it for ransom. That's why he was so panicked when I told him there was a second one. When he found out I had lied, he almost looked relieved.

But that still didn't explain why he had stolen all the other toys. When he told us his reasoning, I was flabbergasted. And this morning, we're going to use that information to bring another person to justice.

The warehouse parking lot was full of cars. Some were even parked along the side streets when I arrived. Apparently, the theft of children's toys right before Christmas had become a big holiday story.

I debated on how I wanted to confront the person working along with the insurance adjuster. When I saw the line of cars, I knew I couldn't do it publicly. I didn't want to take away from the wonderful things the toy drive had accomplished.

When I entered the office, I could barely move around there were so many people. I quickly found Corbin and whispered to him what I wanted to do. He nodded in agreement and then left to round up a couple of the people that we need to talk to. I went in another direction to get the remainder.

Five minutes later we were standing in the middle

of the warehouse with all the toys around us. Corbin had brought with him Dan, Debbie, and Allison, while I had grabbed Liz, Nora, and Marcia. We gathered away from the ears of the media, in a spot where we could talk without being overheard. We were silent for a moment, staring at those gathered around us, and I noticed one person get nervous. Corbin gave me a nod, indicating I was to do the talking. I cleared my throat and began.

"I have good news. Last night, we caught the thief who stole the toys the first time around. He had quite the story, and it seems he also had a partner in crime. Someone who didn't necessarily want to hurt the children but wanted to see the downfall of a rival for their own glory."

Debbie, Dan, and Allison looked confused, not understanding what I was talking about. But I noticed that Nora and Liz immediately caught on to what I was saying.

"Oh, Marcia, please tell me you didn't do something stupid," Liz said, not bothering to hide her disgust.

Nora didn't say a word. Instead, she shook her head and gave Marcia a look that a parent would give to a child they were very disappointed in.

"I don't understand. Leigh-Ann, what is this all about?" Allison asked.

Before I answered her, Marcia seemed to break. She looked at Allison and sneered.

"Of course, you wouldn't understand what this is all about, Allison. Everything falls in your lap, everything works out perfectly for you, everyone loves Allison. I wanted to be the head of the toy drive, but you took that away from me again this year. So, I decided that if you failed miserably, you'd never be asked to be on any committees or help with any of the fun things that go on around this town again. It was my turn. But you, Leigh-Ann! You had to go and stick your nose into things. You, Liz, and Nora all had to collect all new toys and make this big production out of it, and again I got excluded."

By the time Allison finished, her voice was screeching, her face was red, and she looked like she was ready to attack someone. Corbin and Dan each grabbed one of her arms to keep her in place. Then Corbin looked at me expectantly.

"So, what do you want me to do? Do I arrest her?"

I looked around at the other women standing around me, trying to judge what they would want me to do.

"I think if Marcia can tell us where all the toys are that were stolen, and we can recover them, then there's no reason to arrest her. You have the person who took the toys, there's no reason to drag Marcia into this. I think she's learned her lesson. I don't think we'll have any more problems with her. What do you all think?" I suggested.

I looked at the women around me, and they each nodded in agreement. I was amazed at how generous the women were and how quick they were to forgive. Whether it was the season or their nature, it didn't matter. Marcia was getting a second chance. It would be up to her if she changed her way of doing things or fell back into her old habits. But one thing was for sure; those of us in the room knew what she was capable of and would be sure to avoid getting her involved in anything in the future.

Before anything else could be said, one of the other committee members within stuck her head out into the warehouse and yelled that the event was ready to begin. Walking over to a side door of the warehouse, I held it open and looked directly at Marcia. Her shoulders slumped, but she didn't cry, and after a few moments she raised her head and, without looking at any of us, walked to the door I held open. As she passed me, she whispered the words "I'm sorry" before she left.

CHAPTER FIFTEEN

"Oh, Leigh-Ann. Can we get three cups of that wonderful hot chocolate, please? And join us out on the patio."

I looked up at the voices as they walked by me to see Liz and Nora, their arms full of shopping bags once again. I grinned at the jaunty Santa hats on their heads.

It was a week after the media blitz and the excitement at the warehouse. All the toys had been distributed, and things were winding down as people spent time with their families for the last few days before Christmas.

Liz and Nora had obviously been shopping again and, if I knew those two, they would right up until Christmas Eve. Our friendship had been bonded over the toy event, and I no longer felt uncomfortable joining them out on the deck to enjoy a beverage and chitchat. After all, this was the Tattle-Tale Cafe, and that's what we do here—meet with friends and chitchat. And just maybe spread a bit of gossip.

A few moments later, I set three cups of steamy hot chocolate, whipped cream piled high in the cups, on the table. The three of us talked about our plans for the holidays. The time passed quickly, and before I knew it, they were getting ready to leave. But before they did, there was one more piece of gossip that had to be spread.

"Did you hear about her husband?"

THE END

FROM THE AUTHOR

Christmas is all about the kids, and when someone tries to spoil that wonderful holiday spirit, Leigh-Ann is fighting mad. Taking the toys away from children is cruel and heartless. Getting help from friends and the community to save Christmas brings the patrons of the Tattletale Café together with purpose.

I love that Christmas brings people together to work side by side to help those less fortunate. I live in a small town with my husband and two cats, and charity work is a huge focus of so many who live and work here. Especially during the holidays. I have been active in many toy drives and charity auctions and love being part. It's hard work, but worth it when you witness the results.

Christmas in Florida may look different but the special warmth that comes with the holidays is universal. Merry Christmas!

If you enjoyed The *Toy Puzzle* then be sure to check out *Killer Focus*, the first book in the Mrs. Avery's Adventures series.

www.VictoriaLKWilliams.com

www.victorialkwilliams.com/contact.html

MARRY CHRISTMAS

JOANN KEDER

A mysterious death puts Nova's epic Christmas wedding in jeopardy.

CHARACTERS

Chloe Merlin–hair stylist and long-suffering cousin of Nova

Doris Buckley–employee of Cosmic Cakes and Antiquery, lover of *Danforth Dudley Mysteries* and Chloe's unlikely best friend

Bryce Davidson–Chloe's handsome longtime boyfriend

Nova Merlin–Chloe's demanding cousin who insists her wedding will be the event of the year

Jeffrey BonVova–Nova's fiancé

Beverly Thomas–hotel guest with a mysterious past

INVITATION

Nova Leighanne-Mauve Merlin and Jeffrey Thomas VonBova III invite you to our special holiday celebration!! Join us on Christmas Eve as we say our vows at the Piney Falls Cannery Conference Center and Resort. Guests are asked to wear their finest Christmas attire. Our ceremony will begin promptly at 4:00 p.m. with reception following. Please refer to our online gift requests as we have very specific tastes.

DECEMBER 1ST

"I don't know, Chloe. It don't seem normal to have a weddin' on a holiday. Folks have other concerns at Christmas. Besides, all those shiny decorations and whatnot always give me a headache. Maybe your cousin could do a nice Easter wedding instead? I could make an egg-themed cake."

Chloe Merlin studied her friend's weather-beaten face. "You're serious? Doris, we talked for hours about this. You were in favor of helping Nova out. You said 'Christmas is the best for a last-minute weddin', Chloe. Everyone'll be in a festive mood and forget just how awful your cousin, Nova is.'"

A balding, portly man appeared from behind the counter of Weebly Wedding Wares and More and wiped his brow.

"The Oregon Coast is supposed to be pleasant in the fall, not in the nineties. Just atrocious. You girls decide on anything yet? I'm going to close up shop early today and go sit in front of my brand new air conditioner."

"We just started. Haven't even had a chance to pick out a cake yet." Doris placed her hand on the side of her face, as if she were whispering a good secret. "Chloe promised she'd let me make a tall cake. Never done one over two layers before. It's kind of surprising, given Cosmic Cakes and Antiquery is the only bakery for forty miles."

The man fiddled with his name tag displaying the name Tim Thatcher and the words, *ask me about our local tacos.* "I'd really like to get out of here. I don't do well in the heat, Ms.—"

"MISS Doris Buckley," she huffed. "Also Chloe's best friend in Piney Falls. The forty-year age difference don't matter." She tapped her skull. "Up here, we're as connected as bread and butter."

Tim touched the river of sweat running down his neck and beginning to dampen his crisp, white collared shirt. "Next week the temperature should be lower. Could we wait till then?"

Doris put her hands on her hips. "Won't work. This event is taking place in less than a month." She shook her head. "Nobody was more surprised she was getting married than Nova herself. He's some kind of rich kid with lots of money and no sense, I'll bet you. I suppose she wants to hurry up and get this done before he changes his mind."

"Could we take a couple of magazines with us? Just to look over?" Chloe asked. She smiled, displaying dimples on either side of her heavily-freckled face.

Smiles were her secret weapon. "Doris only has a book of birthday cakes at the bakery, so we'd like to get some ideas."

"I don't normally lend them out, but today is an exception." He slid *Holiday Cakes For the Discriminating Bride* across the counter to Chloe, but Doris intercepted.

"I'll be taking that. And then we'll need one with decorations, and I'd like to plan the dinner, something with peas..." Her voice trailed off.

"Slow down, please. Nova hasn't mentioned her dinner ideas or peas." Chloe put a slender, pale hand on her forehead. "I wish she hadn't given me this responsibility. The last thing I want to do is plan someone else's wedding, let alone my very particular cousin's. I wish she'd fly out here from Iowa and do it herself, but she insists she's too busy."

"Ladies, I don't want to be rude, but I'm going to have to insist we continue this another day. I don't know how you two are able to stand this heat." He walked over to his door and turned the sign from "Sashay on in!" to "See Ya Soon!"

"Well, that's a fine how-de-doo! I'll be leaving a snippy review. No one throws Doris Buckley out of a store." Doris picked up the magazines and jammed them under her arm. "You comin' Chloe?"

"I'm a stylist over in Tellum. Come get a trim on me." Chloe grinned and handed Tim a light pink business card with a pair of scissors in the corner. "We're air conditioned."

He chuckled. "I'm not sure I want to make the

forty-mile drive just to get the few hairs I have left trimmed." He was removing his keys from his pocket just as a woman banged the door open, shoving his body against the wall.

"November Bean, what's going on?" Chloe's wiry-haired yoga instructor was breathless, despite the fact that she was more fit than anyone over forty Chloe had ever known.

"It's just awful. I was on my way to get mud for my detox bath when I heard the news. Someone has been murdered at the Piney Falls Cannery Conference Center!"

DECEMBER 4TH

"Mr. Lumquest, Officer, can you tell me more about the murder?" Chloe pulled a section of his dark hair between her fingers up tall and cut off the ends. "My cousin is getting married at the Conference Center soon and I'm worried there is a killer on the loose."

"You can call me Boysie. I've been coming here since you started cutting hair." His broad comforting smile reminded Chloe of her own father.

"Chloe, you should know by now that I don't give away details of an investigation." Officer Boysie Lumquest smoothed the edges of his mustache, resting his arm on the armrest.

"Please sit up tall so I don't get this crooked. I'd hate for you to have to drive back to Tellum for a few wayward hairs." Chloe was used to his wiggly nature. She'd learned from each of her customers how to tell when they had a confession to make. His was mustache smoothing.

"Sorry. You know my mother-in-law would fix it. She thinks it's a waste of time for a man to pay for a haircut anyway."

Chloe snipped another section, pausing just the right amount of time. "She wasn't from around here, was she?"

"Huh? Oh, the murder victim. No, she was just passing through, far as I can tell. We couldn't find much in her room. Beverly was a pretty woman. It was a real shame to find her all bloodied in the bathroom like that."

Chloe's pulse quickened. "I'm sure her family is anxious to hear what happened. Unless you think one of them did it?"

"The door wasn't forced open, so I'm fairly certain she knew the alleged killer and willingly let him in. I say 'him' because there were two muddy shoe prints coming out of the bathroom. Some real fancy brand according to my deputy. Funnel cakes, or something like that."

"Funello? Those things cost at least five-hundred a pair!"

Boysie Lumquest, as if waking from a trance, sat up taller in his chair, causing Chloe to cut one section crooked. "I can't tell you anything more though. On-going investigation, you understand."

"Completely."

As Boysie left, he dropped two twenty-dollar bills on the counter. "For you. I know I'm not the easiest client." He winked as he walked out the door and she waved. Chloe watched until he was in his police cruiser before she went to the break room and called Doris.

"Boysie doesn't have a clue what's going on. You spend all of your spare time reading crime novels. I think we should investigate for ourselves. I'd feel better planning this wedding if I wasn't worried about a killer lurking around."

"Are you sure, honey?" Doris didn't try hiding the glee in her voice. "I have every *Danforth Dudley, Private Eye* book memorized. Did you know that when they made it into a television series, they left out two major characters? I tried calling the studio to tell them. Nobody seemed to care."

"Let's check it out tomorrow. Come over to my house in the morning." Chloe held the phone away from her ear. "Oh, shoot. Nova's calling. See you then!"

Chloe took a deep breath before answering. "Hello! I was just going to call you!"

"Everything is on schedule, right Chloe? I don't want any surprises." Nova Merlin's high-pitched nasally voice was so loud Chloe had to hold the phone six inches from her face.

"No surprises, I promise. Your wedding is the most important day of your life. I'm honored you would trust me with the details." She couldn't remove the image from her brain, of a beautiful woman lying in a pool of her own blood.

"I'm trusting you with the most important day of

my life." Nova sighed. "I don't trust easily, you know. Since I don't have a mother to help me, it's nice to have you in my corner."

It was unusual for her bristly cousin to offer a compliment. "How nice of you—"

"Oh, and Chloe? Could you make sure you get some highlights in your hair before the ceremony? That brassy red look will really mess up my pictures."

Chloe smiled. There was the Nova she'd handled delicately since childhood. "Of course. I'll ask someone else in the salon to mute my hair. Just for you."

"Wonderful. I'll check in with you next week."

DECEMBER 5TH

The doorbell rang as Chloe pulled her sweater over her head. Fall was her favorite season and she was glad the weather was finally behaving appropriately. She waited patiently, knowing Doris always walked in with or without an invitation.

"Chloe? You ready? We're gonna get to the bottom of this. I re-read *Danforth Dudley and the Case of the Murdered Mistress* last night. You have to wonder if her lover came to break things off, and then—" she made a slicing gesture across her neck. "I asked Officer Lumquest this morning when he came in for his mocha and cinnamon rolls and his lips were sewn up as tight as a drum. One of the other regulars who works nights at the hotel told me when she checked in, this Beverly woman told him she was here on business. Seemed real serious. The maid found her when she went in to clean, still wearing her fancy clothes from the night before. The poor maid said she was holding a handful of dark brown hair. Other' n that, I don't know anything."

"My mom always said you were meant to be a sleuth," Chloe said wistfully.

"I miss your mom. She was a good friend." Doris sneezed and took a tissue from her pocket. "Got that nasty virus that's going around. Cosmo wants me to stay home from work tomorrow."

Chloe looked at her with surprise. "I can't believe you have anything nice to say about my mom anymore. She ran off with your husband. I'd think you would be bitter."

Doris patted Chloe's shoulder. "It brought us together though, didn't it, honey? We've been friends going on ten years now, thanks to the both of them. It also gave you a way to relate to Nova too, since her mother up and did the same thing." She sneezed again, this time into her coat sleeve. "Oh golly. This ain't what I wanted today."

Chloe shrugged her shoulders, thinking of her conversation with her cousin. "I didn't tell Nova about the murder. I don't want to tell her unless it's absolutely necessary. She's kind of, well, delicate, and this news would throw her over the edge."

"No need. We'll have this figured out before her big day."

By the time they reached Piney Falls Cannery Convention Center and Resort on the edge of town, the only thing that remained of the investigation was yellow police tape strung across the front of the only nice hotel in town. Formerly the location of one of many local canneries, the property had been revitalized a decade earlier. Now the green trim was peeling and three windows had tape over the cracks.

The two women ducked underneath and walked up to the double glass doors. Chloe cupped her hands around her eyes and pressed her face against the glass. "It's closed. I don't see anyone at the reception desk and everything looks dark. I don't know how we'll get in."

"That's a fine how-dee-do. Who closes a hotel over one murder? Good thing I came prepared." Doris pulled a room key from her pocket. "Let's see if this still works. My brother, Lester, stayed here last month and forgot his key. I found it when I was vacuuming my couch." She put the key in the slot and the door clicked open.

Chloe paused. "What if someone sees us?"

"Don't be silly. The lookie-loos have already been here and we've only got two police. We've got a nice window of about a day before things heat up again."

"You're amazing, you know that? I can't believe we're friends some days."

Doris blushed and patted her on the back. "Let's get our cute selves inside before someone sees us now."

Taped to the front of the darkened reception desk area was a note that read, "Closed due to illness."

They walked down the dark hallway, illuminated only by Chloe's phone light. "How do we know which room?" she whispered.

"Number eighteen. That's what I heard anyhow.

Gossip's usually pretty accurate with the six a.m. crowd. The ten o-clocks tend to be off the mark."

When they reached the end of the hallway, the door to room eighteen was propped open with a trash-can. Chloe slid it out of the way and made a sharp right turn when she entered, opening the bathroom door. "There's no blood on the floor." She bent down close and touched the linoleum, trying to imagine what horrid event happened there.

Doris began pulling fluffy white towels from the shelf underneath the sink. "Just what I thought." She stood and proudly displayed her find. "A credit card."

"How did you know?" Chloe stared at her in amazement.

"In *Danforth Dudley and the Case of the Canoodling Crossing Guard* one of the victims hid her credit cards in her hotel room when she arrived for her tryst with the drug dealer. She knew someone was after her and if they killed her, they'd have access to all of her bank accounts. She wanted to make sure her kids still had money. It was really touching. I think I watched that episode six times even though they forgot to add the part about Danforth's handsome nephew getting snuffed." Doris touched her short, grey hair absently. "Such a good show."

"What's her name?" Chloe asked impatiently.

"Oh, sorry. Let me see..." Doris squinted, unwilling to remove her readers from her pocket. "Beverly Thomas. She must've been doing okay for herself. It's a Venus Platinum card. They only give those out to the big spenders. One time we had a tourist come into the bakery with one." She tapped the card on the edge of the counter. "He just oozed money. Only left a two-dollar tip. Lousy rich people." She grumbled.

"Do you think she hid anything else?" Chloe stood and made her way into the bedroom, where she began opening dresser drawers. "These are all empty."

"Too obvious." Doris raised her foot and shoved the mattress hard. When it moved against the wall, several more cards and photos came into sight.

Chloe picked them up and began reciting as she read. "Hanley Department Store, preferred guest card, Cross Pique Coffee frequent user card, Pumped Up gym membership...and a bunch of pictures of her cat."

Doris took a close look at the gym membership card, which displayed a picture of a dark-haired woman with full lips smiling broadly. "Pretty woman. She's had some work done. The natural brow don't make that kind of a question mark. Looks to be about thirty. She's got a red nose like she just came in from the cold. Serious cold."

"Chicago, maybe? I'd be willing to bet we can pinpoint her home for sure by calling these businesses." Chloe reached underneath the part of the mattress still concealed. She pulled out a passport. "I guess I spoke too soon." She opened the blue passport book and a folded up one-hundred-dollar bill fell out. "Beverly lived in Des Moines. She's got stamps in here from all over the world."

"Now we have to wonder what brought her to little old Piney Falls, Oregon. Was she on vacation and ran into a stranger who looked for random people to harm?

Or was she running from someone in particular?" Doris went over to the curtains and pulled them open, causing the room to flood with light. "Danforth likes to use different light sources in the room to see what might show itself." She scanned the space for anything out of the ordinary. When she didn't find anything, she sat down at the small round table and folded her hands in front of her.

"This is strange." Chloe came over to the table and tossed the passport in front of Doris. "Look at the fourth page. A sticky note with the name Jeffrey Von-Bova and his phone number. That's Nova's fiancé."

DECEMBER 8TH

"What do you think, Bryce? Should we go with this one?" She pointed to a cake with six tiers, each one covered in tiny, gold packages and red balls of holly.

Her dark-haired, muscular boyfriend leaned forward in his chair, shaking his head. "That's too much cake for a small wedding. Seems to me that they'd want something simple. You said nothing complicated, right?"

Chloe tried hiding her disappointment. She'd been hinting for months that three years of dating was long enough. She'd hoped including him in Nova's wedding planning would be the incentive he needed. "You haven't been paying attention. There will be one hundred fifty people at this wedding. Jeffrey's parents are flying their entire country club in from Iowa."

"Me and Chloe have important things to discuss, Bryce." Doris picked bits of the marbled chocolate and white sample cake she'd made from her teeth and stood. "I'll go heat up the kettle. Just made a new blend of mint and green tea. Keeps the brain alert. You want some?"

They both nodded. "Thought you might be leavin', Bryce." She shuffled behind the counter of Cosmic Cakes and Antiquery without waiting for his response.

Chloe leaned over the table, sniffing the musky scent of his aftershave that drove her wild. "You know we're doing this for Doris, remember? The fancy cake and decorations?" she whispered.

He kissed her gently. "I thought it was your snooty cousin who was at fault?"

Chloe giggled and lightly pushed him away. "If Doris catches us, she'll turn on the hose. It's too cold for that right now."

Doris returned with two steaming cups on a tray. "You know, I've got other thoughts for this wedding now that I think about it. I'm warmin' up to this Christmas idea. We could go over to Piney Falls High and recruit them theatre kids to act as ushers, dressed up as elves. Course we wouldn't want the tall ones."

"Doris, you've made your point." Bryce stood. "I'm not discussing elf ushers. Call me later, okay?"

"I will." Chloe smiled as her boyfriend walked out the door.

"Thought he'd never leave. You haven't said anything about our investigation, have you? We don't want word getting around. Boysie might think we're trying to step on his turf."

"I'll have to tell him eventually. Bryce and I don't

keep secrets." Chloe brought the steaming mug to her lips. "Ooh. That's good."

"You mean other than the fact that you're lookin' for matrimony and he thinks you're gonna date till you're my age?"

Chloe decided to skip this argument. Doris never thought Bryce was good enough for her. "What do we do now, according to your books?"

"I don't need no book to tell me what to do. We're gonna call those places with the cards and pretend like we're this Beverly who lost them. Maybe she's got a friend working at the gym or the department store. Somebody knew her."

"I want to contact Nova's fiancé and ask why Beverly would have his information, but I'm not sure how to go about it. If he gets defensive, he might tell her I'm nosing around and then she'll be angry too."

"First things first, honey." Doris rubbed her shoulder. "Let's call these places, them are easy. Then we'll worry about the boyfriend."

"It doesn't seem right to keep these from Officer Lumquest. What if this information could break the case wide open and we're hiding it? Won't we get in trouble?"

"Psssht." Doris pushed the air with her hand. "Boysie came in for two scones and a vanilla latte this morning. He said they were waiting on the forensics team before they went any further. With a two-man police force, they don't get things done quickly. We wait for them and your cousin's whole wedding party'll be in danger."

A look of concern crossed Chloe's face but she said nothing. "Okay. Let's get busy. Do you have the cards?"

"I'll do you one better. I took the liberty of doing a search for these phone numbers. You call the gym and I'll call the department store." Doris handed her a piece of paper with Cosmic Cakes and Antiquery written in swirly letters across the top.

Chloe took the number and walked outside, buttoning her coat to keep the brisk wind out. "Brrr." She hoped the predictions for a harsh winter were incorrect. She turned her back to the wind and dialed.

"*Pumped Up,* this is Carol, can I interest you in a spa add-on package?"

Chloe cleared her throat. "Hi, Carol. This is...Beverly Thomas. I've lost my wallet and I'm worried someone will try to use my cards."

"Oh, Bev. While you were on vacation? Such a bummer." Carol put her hand over the phone while she coughed. "Sorry, everybody here has some kind of illness. It's a good thing you took some time away."

"Yes, on vacation. On the coast."

Carol chuckled. "I didn't think Arizona was on the coast, but maybe my map is different from yours. I can send you a new card. Are you still at 405 Bent Light Avenue? That's the address we have, but I remember your telling me you were moving soon."

"I'm in the process of moving. Could you send it to my office instead?" Chloe held her breath, hoping she wouldn't have to provide any more information than that.

"The Mundley Security Company? Is that still over on Fourth?"

"Umhm. Thanks." Chloe thought quickly, trying to make sure she'd wrung every bit of information from this conversation. "Carol, my boyfriend is worried that they'll steal my identity."

"If you don't mind my saying, I'd be more worried about him than a complete stranger. I'm sorry, but you know me, Bev. I'm always real with you."

"Why do you think that? He's a good guy."

"Good guys don't hide from the women they love. I was hoping you would come home from this trip and realize he's bad news."

Chloe wasn't sure where to take the conversation from here. "That's what my sister says too."

"Your sister? Are you feeling okay? I know those Oregon people like their marijuana, but your entire family died in that fire six years ago. Put down the pot and come home. There's nothing positive for you there."

"Thanks, Carol."

DECEMBER 9TH

"I'm just here to get my hair cut," Doris announced louder than necessary. "Holidays are coming up soon, you know."

Chloe glanced over to the waiting area and rolled her eyes. "I'll be with you in a minute, Doris. Look at those magazines and see what style you want."

The lady in Chloe's chair leaned forward and stared in the mirror at her stylist. "You get some strange ones here, don't you?"

"She's like a mom to me and not strange at all," Chloe answered defensively. She ran the comb through her client's hair and pulled harshly when she got to a tangle.

"Ouch!" The woman put her hand to her head. "I didn't mean to offend you, Chloe. Just stating the obvious." She sneezed, spraying all over Chloe's mirror. "Sorry, think I'm coming down with that nasty virus. I sure hope you don't get it."

"We're finished here, Nan." Chloe spun the chair around and ripped the cape from her neck. "See you next month!"

Chloe didn't pause for Nan's reaction. Instead, she walked over to the waiting area and motioned for Doris to follow her. The two women headed to the break room where Chloe closed the door behind them. "Well? What did you find? Something more than the snippy woman at the department store who hung up on you, I hope."

"Is that how you greet your favorite scone maker?" Doris pulled a Pluto Peach scone from her oversized black purse and set it on the table. "Woulda brought you more, but we had a school bus full of hungry animals and they cleaned us out." She took a tissue from her purse and blew her nose so loud it startled Chloe.

"Thanks! You always know what I need. I didn't eat breakfast." She picked up the square pastry and bit it hungrily. "Tell me what you found. Someone is bound to take their break soon and then we'll have to go outside. When it's raining sideways, I prefer to keep my sleuthing indoors."

Doris pulled out a chair and sat down, removing her rain coat and patting her straight, grey hair. "Had some nice curl when I left home." She opened her purse and handed Chloe a crumpled document.

Chloe's mouth hung open. "How did you get this? Did you go to the police station and steal it?"

"Well, it's a funny story. I was visiting with my neighbor, Lance, who works the front desk at the police station. He said, 'Doris, we'd like us some scones. If you'd bring some to the station someday, we'd all be so pleased.' That's just what I did. While he was handing them out to the other people there, I took a look at his desk. Poor Lance, he ain't so good with the filing. He left this forensic report right there on top of a stack of papers. Just askin' for me to take it."

Chloe scanned the paper briefly. "Beverly died of poison? She let her boyfriend into the room and he brought her an iced latte laced with cyanide? Not what I expected."

Doris took the paper from Chloe's hands. "It don't say that."

"I'm speculating. It says she died of acute poisoning."

"One more thing I found out. This Jeffrey character stayed across town at the Spruce Bark Motel. Ed Junior says he stayed four nights. Snooty sort, askin' for room service and a 'Do Not Disturb' card. Who does he think he is? The king?"

"Nova's fiancé was in a relationship with Beverly Thomas. I can't believe it. How am I going to tell her?" Chloe put the last bite of scone in her mouth and chewed slowly. "She'll be devastated. She's prickly on the surface, but underneath, she's still a hurt little girl who wants to be loved. Her dad spent two years coaxing her out of her shell after her mom left."

"We don't know for sure what happened yet, so I'd wait. We need to get all of our ducks in a row before you go telling your cousin anything." Doris wrapped her arms tightly across her chest and then abruptly stood and began chewing on her fingernails.

"Next for us is finding out everything we can about Jeffrey and his family. Maybe he's not the only one in that bunch of richy riches who is capable of murder. In *Death at Dag's Drive-In,* the entire family was behind a string of murders. They volunteered to work the concession stand to poison the popcorn. Everybody in town thought it was so nice this family of upper crusts was donating their time, when in reality they were just there for easy access to victims. Gets you wonderin', doesn't it?"

DECEMBER 10TH

Chloe spun around, allowing the ruby red skirt on the floor-length chiffon bridesmaid gown to swirl around her. She watched with satisfaction in the full-length mirror. Her slender body didn't fill out the dress, especially the top part, but she actually looked good.

"Can you turn sideways one more time?" Nova instructed from her kitchen in Iowa.

Chloe turned obediently. "My only complaint is the skirt is so full, we bridesmaids may trip."

Her cousin's perfect face twitched, a sign there was a blowup coming. "I didn't ask for your opinion, Chloe. This is MY wedding and I'll be making all of the decisions. I've been waiting my entire life to have a wedding fit for a princess. Guys have been begging to marry me ever since I was in tenth grade and my braces came off. I'm a goddess in this town and this wedding is going to be a manifestation of all of that. Got it?"

Chloe bit the inside of her cheek. "Got it. I just thought—"

"You'd better make sure every detail is perfect, cousin. Any foolish mistakes may send me over the edge. It IS the most important day of a woman's life. Next to her first full-body wax." Nova paused, overcome by emotion. She brought a tissue to her face and sighed.

Chloe waited patiently, as she'd learned to do with her cousin's dramatic downs.

After a few minutes, Nova put her tissue down and stared hard at the screen. "I want to go over my list to make sure you've covered everything so far. We've booked the D.J. and the caterer. When I spoke with the flower store, the owner became very snippy when I explained I wanted three-hundred Hawaiian orchids flown in for my ceremony. Can you believe that? It's like she's never had a bride with exquisite tastes before."

Chloe breathed deeply.

"Jeffrey's family bought out the entire convention center. Take this down–I want you to go over there and inspect the rooms. Jeffrey's mother has an allergy to mold and his sister doesn't like the color green. I don't know how well they clean their rooms, so make sure they are spotless too. I don't care to find any surprises."

"Of course. It's a very nice place. I'm sure they'll clean everything up before you get here."

Nova took a long drink of her Seventeen Greens juice, a new multi-level marketing product she'd begun selling. "What does that mean? Don't they clean every day?"

"Oh, sorry." Chloe blushed and turned her head away from the computer screen. "I was just thinking out loud. I need to clean up my place before you arrive." She thought quickly, trying to come up with a good reason to find out more about Jeffrey.

"I'd like to prepare a speech for your reception. Can you tell me how you and Jeffrey met?"

Nova's face softened. "It was so funny. He came into my dad's coffee shop, Jack's Beanery. He was just passing through Sandy Salts, on his way to Des Moines for a business meeting. He said I took his breath away."

Chloe cringed. She'd heard that line before and immediately went the other direction. "What is his job again?"

"He's very important. He's a regional sales manager for Mundley Security. He travels all over the country selling alarm systems to businesses. Jeffrey was their top salesman three months in a row. My fiancé is very good at what he does."

"I'll bet," Chloe quipped. "I mean, he'd have to be exceptional to catch your eye."

"You've been acting very strange this morning, Chloe. Is there something you're not telling me?"

"I..." She could bring up Jeffrey's relationship with Beverly, but Doris warned her to wait until they "had their ducks in a row." Nova wouldn't believe her anyway, unless she had indisputable proof. "I was just thinking that it can be a little breezy here on the

Oregon Coast in December. Do you have a back-up plan for pictures if the weather doesn't cooperate?"

"Ha!"

Nova's laugh was so loud and sharp Chloe stepped backward and lost her balance when her foot caught on the surplus fabric. Her head hit the floor-length mirror, causing it to shatter.

"Did you tear it? Please tell me you didn't tear it. Now we have to worry about bad luck. You should never break a mirror, Chloe."

Chloe looked at the shards of glass on the floor and touched the top of her head. "Ouch!" A welt was forming on her head. "The dress is fine, Nova. I can't imagine this will have any effect on your wedding."

DECEMBER 11TH

"He works for the same company as Beverly."

"I heard you the first time, girlfriend." Doris took another sip of her latte and looked around Cosmic Cakes and Antiquery. "Sure don't seem like we should be this slow. The tourists usually hang around till January. Did you see if there was a storm coming?"

"Have you been listening to anything I've said?" Chloe touched the spot on her head where, a day earlier, she'd received four stitches. After she hung up from her frustrating conversation with Nova, she realized her head was bleeding. Bryce came over and drove her to the hospital, taking extra care to ensure all of the fabric from the dress made it into the car.

"I heard every word! Our victim and your cousin's fiancé both work for Monday Security."

"Mundley," she corrected, "and yes, they both worked there. I'm guessing that's where their affair began. When I spoke with Carol at the gym, she seemed to think Beverly and Jeffrey were here together. I wonder why he stayed in a different hotel?"

"Motel, really. The Spruce Bark is a dump." Doris took one last drink of her latte. "We need to find out why those two were in town." She got up and put her mug on the counter. "Can I get you a scone, honey?"

"No, Doris, thanks. I'm just not sure what to do next. We need to find out if Jeffrey was involved with Beverly's murder and we need to do it soon. What would they do in your mystery series?"

Doris put her hand on the counter and cocked her head to the side. "Well, let's see. There was an episode of the television show, not the book mind you, but the television show, where Danforth Dudley was investigating an affair and he got the low-down from the people working at the front desk. We could see Ed Junior at the Spruce Bark Motel and ask what he knows about Jeffrey."

Chloe pulled out her phone and began typing. "I don't know why I didn't think of this sooner. I'm going to search a business page I belong to and see if his name comes up." She typed on her phone for a few minutes while Doris got herself a Pluto Peach scone and sat down.

"Oh, interesting. Jeffrey worked for his family business prior to this job. VonBova Bathroom Fixtures LLC. He was a salesperson."

"How are you gettin' that from the internet?" Doris pulled Chloe's hand over close and squinted at the screen. "Can it tell you why he left?"

"No, this is a site where people post their work experience. They don't want you to know the reason they left their job. But isn't it curious that his girlfriend was killed in a bathroom and he worked for a bathroom supply company?"

"Don't think that means much," Doris huffed. "How 'bout I call that business and pretend we're looking for a new bathroom?"

Chloe slid her phone over to Doris. "Do it now. Let's see what they say." She typed in the number for the store and then pressed the speaker button.

"VonBova Bathroom Fixtures, it's a Bo-tastic day! How can I help you?" A cheerful voice answered.

"Yes, um, I'm lookin' to do a remodel on my fancy house. Got three floors and a pool out back."

Chloe frowned at Doris. *"Too much!"* she mouthed.

Doris shrugged. "Your salesman came to me a while back and showed me your fixtures. Jeffrey something?"

"Oh." She couldn't hide the disappointment in her voice. "He's not with the company anymore. I could get another salesman to help you though."

"Well, how's about I talk to him? Nice young feller and so handsome. Where could I find him if I wanted?"

"I...uh..."

She paused and both women held their breath.

"This is a family business and he's part of the family. But he had personal problems so they had to find him a different job."

"What kind of personal problems? Did he refuse to

wear deodorant? Put his hair in one of them ponytails?"

"No, it's not like that." There was a commotion and then the sound of a door shutting. "I couldn't talk out on the show floor. Jeffrey and another employee got into a nasty fight and she threatened to turn him in to the employment commission for harassment. His dad, bless his heart, found Jeffrey another job right away."

Doris raised her palms and looked at Chloe as if to say, '*What now*?'

Chloe quickly pulled a pen out of her purse and wrote on a napkin. 'Ask who the disgruntled employee was!'

"Oh, um, can you tell me who that employee was? The dismembered one?"

Chloe mouthed *dis-grunt-led* as carefully as she could.

"I mean disgruntled. I'm an old lady and I'm allowed to make some mistakes."

"It was Beverly Thomas. That's all I can say right now."

DECEMBER 14TH

"Remember, let me do the talking. You've pushed his buttons one too many times, Doris."

"I don't like that guy. He's lazy and unmotivated. I don't mind telling him that."

Chloe ran her fingers through her thick, red hair as they stood in the lobby of the Spruce Bark Motel. She turned around to look out the picture window, which framed the rolling Pacific Ocean. "It's going to storm soon. I can feel it."

"That's what old people say. I don't feel anything."

A tall, beefy-looking man appeared behind the counter and said nothing. Chloe noticed his eyes looked dead. Just like she remembered. "Ed Junior? I was wondering if I could ask you some questions about a recent guest."

"Why?"

"Huh?" She wasn't expecting that answer. "Because, um—"

"Listen here, your mother is a friend of mine." Doris marched up close to him and put her finger in the air. Because of their height difference, she wagged her threatening appendage in front of his chin. "She's told me about the ruckus you caused at the family reunion last summer. You'd better answer this little gal's questions, or I might be inclined to talk to Officer Lumquest about some missing furniture."

Even though she'd asked Doris to keep quiet, Chloe was glad for this moment of intervention.

"Never said I wasn't gonna help. I just wondered why you'd be asking."

Chloe smiled so wide her cheeks felt like they might fall off. This was going to require what Doris always called, "some sugar."

"Well, I had a friend in town recently. Her name was Beverly. Funny thing, Beverly's boyfriend came to surprise her and he stayed here. He just raved about this place. He said you were the best host and he would come back again. He said we should come ask you about it because the two of you had real serious conversations late at night. I was hoping you could shed some light on things."

"Oh, you mean that Beverly who was murdered at the Piney Falls Cannery Convention Center, Spa and Resort?"

"How'd you know about that? Boysie was keeping it all under wraps?"

"That's a silly question, Chloe. Everybody knows everything here. It's a small town," Doris chided her.

"He said that about me though?" Ed Junior relaxed

and put his arms on the counter. "I really like Jeff. He's been all over the country. He told me funny stories about people in Nebraska. How they wear corn cobs on their head. I was bummed when he left."

"That's not what Jeff said. He told me you guys had late-night talks about dark secrets."

"Oh, about that woman who was blackmailing him you mean?"

Chloe concentrated hard to keep her expression from changing. "Yeah, I guess so. What did he say about that?"

"I wasn't supposed to tell anyone. But I guess if he's already told you this much, it's probably okay." Ed Junior sneezed three times. "Darn virus going around."

"Better tell us now then, just in case you keel over," Doris quipped. Chloe frowned and shook her head.

"He had a serious girlfriend in high school. He had to break things off when she got weird, or something like that. She showed up at his work and got a job there."

"What did he say? Was she still in love with him?" Chloe doubted this lost love was Beverly. She wouldn't seek out a man who abused her, at least in Chloe's mind.

"Jeff said he told her he didn't want nothing to do with her, but she wouldn't listen. He did something bad back then and she knew. We all do dumb things in high school. Heck, I stole the school mascot, Sappy, and hid him in my parents' garage for a year."

Chloe's eyes widened. "That was you? People were still talking about it when I was in school. How the

Savage Saplings had to play all of their football games without their good luck mascot statue for three years while the band members saved up to buy a new one."

"What did this feller do, Ed? He must've told you."

Ed Junior hiked up his pants. "Not really. Just said he was ashamed of it."

Chloe re-attached her best smile. "He really liked you, Ed. He didn't confide in just anybody."

"Yeah, I s' pose you're right about that. Jeff may have mentioned that he buried a body. That's all I know."

DECEMBER 22ND

"Doris, it's been weeks and we haven't uncovered anything else about Jeffrey or Beverly. I'm beginning to think we're never going to find out who Jeffrey really is and he'll marry my cousin anyway." Chloe pulled a tissue from her pocket and blew her nose. She'd succumbed to the nasty virus going around and spent a week in bed with her phone off, trying to avoid her cousin's persistent phone calls while she recovered.

"Nova's going to be here in a few days and I'm starting to get worried. We haven't found any evidence that someone went missing when Jeffrey was in high school. Beverly is even more mysterious. What are we going to do?" She walked over to the sink and washed her hands. They were raw and red from each time she'd blown her nose today, but she didn't want to take the chance of infecting any customers.

"Nothing more to do. We've covered all the bases that we can. Everything in the Danforth Dudley Mystery series ends with a big surprise that we didn't see comin'. I'm all outta suggestions and I've got Christmas on my mind now."

Chloe swallowed hard. "I wish I was better at this. I've been meaning to ask, Bryce says you two have suddenly hit it off. What did he say to change your mind?"

Doris shrugged. "Don't know what you're talking about. I don't spend my time conversing with young fellers. Hey, I've got a surprise for you, honey. Wait right here." She disappeared out the front door of the salon and returned a few minutes later with a large box. She plunked it down on the empty chair beside Chloe and smiled with satisfaction. "Don't make me wait too long before you open it. An old lady's only got so much time to spare."

Chloe ripped the brown paper wrapping and opened the box. She reached in and pulled out wads of paper. "Did you forget whatever was supposed to be in here? It's understandable, we've all been so busy lately."

Doris stuck her head in the box. "Nope. It's on the bottom. Keep lookin'. This was the only box I had so I made it work."

Chloe reached in one more time and pulled out a piece of jewelry. "This is stunning!" She gasped. The brooch was made to resemble a wilted, white daisy with tiny stones lining the petals and four pearls in the center. "Why are you giving this to me?"

"It came from my great-grandmother. Her mother gave it to her on her weddin' day to bring her good luck."

"Oh, she must've had a wonderful marriage." She sat it on her counter and continued blow-drying her client's hair. Chloe was still confused as to what this all had to do with her.

"Not really." Doris clucked her tongue. "My great-grandfather was a philanderer. Known as a cheater three counties wide. Four years after the wedding, great-grannie put the brooch on to do her house cleaning, just to feel special about herself. By then, she was fed up with her husband and all of the gossip. She made his supper and waited for him to come home. Darkness fell and there was a knock on the door. The sheriff said her husband drove his horse team off the road on the way home from a night of drinkin' and carousin' and he ended up drowning in the river. Best day of her life. She decided that brooch was the cause of her good luck."

"If I'm following you, this is to make sure that if I ever get married, Bryce will end up at the bottom of a river? I thought you liked–tolerated–him?"

Doris shrugged noncommittally. "He's all right. This is to wear on your dress at your cousin's wedding. We haven't been able to find out why Beverly was killed and neither has Officer Lumquest. I'm worried, what with your awful Nova and her no-good fiancé showing up tomorrow, that'll be a recipe for more drama."

"Bryce has been so good to me while I was sick. He offered to do some checking on Jeffrey. He hasn't found anything yet, but it's so nice he's been helping me." Chloe motioned for her next client to come sit in her chair. "The usual, Marlene?" She pulled a plastic cape around the woman and fastened it at the neck.

"Just a cut today, Chloe. No sense in getting it styled in this weather."

Doris moved the empty box to the floor and sat down in the chair. She swiveled around until she saw her reflection and smiled.

"It's odd that everyone we spoke with said the same things about Jeffrey, don't you think?" As Chloe snipped, large tufts of rich, brown hair fell to the ground.

"S' pose so. But if he's the bad guy we think he is, he's probably paid them well. In *The Case of the Canned Clam*, Detective Dudley tracks down a millionaire who pays everyone in his life to say he's a wonderful person. Made it hard to believe he'd killed his next-door neighbor."

She pulled the blow dryer out of its round holder and looked in the mirror. "I'm going to get rid of the stray hairs on your neck. Are you okay with that, Marlene?"

The woman nodded.

"Is that why you have such an aversion to rich people, Doris?" Chloe yelled, now on the other side of her client's head. "They're not all that awful."

"You say that now, but what about your cousin?"

"What about me?"

Chloe put her blow dryer down and ran to the reception desk, throwing her arms around a stern-faced woman wearing a thick layer of orange-tinted makeup.

A good foot taller than Chloe, she looked irritated when Chloe embraced her middle section.

"Nova! I'm so glad to see you! I thought you and Jeffrey were coming tomorrow?"

Nova pulled away from her cousin. "I see you haven't done anything with your hair like we discussed." She took off her grey and black fake fur coat and hung it on the coat tree, removing the other coats that were already there and placing them on an empty chair. "Jeffrey is coming tomorrow. I wanted to surprise you a day early and make sure everything was ready."

Doris crossed her arms and walked up to the counter. "Nova. Haven't seen you in Piney Falls for at least five years. Don't you think you should visit your kin more' n that?"

"I lead a very busy life managing my father's coffee shop. I don't have time to galavant around," Nova replied dismissively. "That face could use some moisturizer, Doris. You're not looking well."

"Humph." Doris picked up her coat off of the chair and put it on. "You might regret your mean behavior, Nova. Your little cousin here has worked her fingers to the bone getting your wedding ready to go. I've got to finish your six-tier cake and poor Wendy from Flower Friendly is beside herself trying to make sure your snooty flowers arrive in time. Seems you've got everybody in a tizzy and you don't even know it's you who should be—"

Chloe stepped in between her best friend and her cousin. "That cake won't frost itself, Doris." She widened her eyes, hoping her friend would take the hint. "We'll be down to take a look tomorrow morning."

"Never seen so much makeup on a woman who wasn't on display in a coffin," Doris muttered as she walked outside, into the rain and wind.

"I've struggled to understand why you spend time with that old lady. Can't you find someone your own age to hang out with?" Nova pursed her dark red lips.

"She was kind to me after my mom left," Chloe replied defensively. "She's been more of a mother to me these last ten years than my mom was my entire childhood."

Nova shrugged her shoulders. "I need to check my makeup before you take me to our venue. Everything has to be absolutely perfect. This will be the best Christmas anyone in this little town has ever had!"

"I'm so happy to see you, Nova. It has been too long." Chloe beamed. "We had so many fun times at the family reunions here."

Nova ran her hands up and down Chloe's arms. "Make sure no one steals my coat while I pull myself together. Daddy paid three hundred dollars for it online."

DECEMBER 24TH, 10 A.M.

"I've not seen wind this intense since the year we lost power for two weeks." Chloe's dad, Mark, pulled on the neck of his tux. "Surprised we can't hear your cousin complaining from here." Chloe adjusted it for him and stood back.

"You look wonderful, Dad. You realize that you didn't have to get dressed until this afternoon though, right?"

"You know my rule. Only get dressed once every day. I like to keep my life simple."

Chloe stared out the front doors of the *Piney Falls Cannery Conference Center and Resort,* watching as someone's trash blew down the street. "Even though it was her idea to get married here, I feel guilty. I should have told her the weather at Christmas can be iffy in the Pacific Northwest."

"It's not your fault, sis."

Though Chloe had no siblings, she loved it

when her father used that term of endearment. He always tried hard to make sure she felt good about herself.

One of the other bridesmaids came running down the long hallway and into the lobby. "Nova sent me to tell you it's time to start on our hair," she said breathlessly.

"Bet she didn't word it like that," Mark replied with a grin.

"Dad, you could be helpful by making sure the Christmas lights are on downtown. Jeffrey's family paid to have new decorations made just for this occasion."

Mark looked at his daughter, incredulous. "In this wind? There's no way those things are going to survive the night."

"Nova's asked me twice about them." She and her father exchanged a knowing glance.

"Okay. I'll check on them. Anything else?"

"Let's see. The caterer should arrive soon and Doris is bringing the cake around noon."

Another bridesmaid came barreling down the hallway. "You need to start on our hair, Chloe! Nova's getting upset!"

Chloe kissed her father on the cheek. "Let's put everything we've got into this wedding. Nova deserves some happy memories."

As she walked down the long hallway, she paused in front of room eighteen. Beverly's death haunted her. She put her hand on the door, trying to feel Beverly's spirit. If Jeffrey was responsible, she'd failed in proving it. "I'm so sorry, Beverly. I wanted to bring your killer to justice."

"There's still time, babe."

Chloe spun around defensively, throwing her arms in front of her.

"Ow!" Bryce grabbed his face and bent down. "You got me good."

"I'm so sorry!" She put her arm around his back and bent down to his level. "Let me see the damage?"

He looked up and smiled devilishly. "Gotcha!"

"Bryce Davidson! That was nasty!" Even though Bryce was known for his tricks, he always managed to catch Chloe off guard. "I was here for a reason! This is the room where Beverly died."

"I'm sorry. You asked me to keep working on this and I've found something."

"I hope it's something definitive. Otherwise, this whole day will be awkward."

Bryce looked puzzled. "If by 'definitive' you mean did Jeffrey and Beverly actually date in high school, then yes. I went through old yearbooks online for Glen Campbell High School in Tubley, Iowa where Jeffrey went to school. There are pictures of him and Beverly together in the drama club." He pulled a folded paper out of his pocket and gave it to Chloe.

The black-and-white image showed a group of awkward teens in torn jeans. Beverly, a stunner from a young age, posed with her arm draped over the shoulder of a stone-faced Jeffrey. The next picture on the bottom of the page was labeled "Prom King and Queen, real-life couple Beffrey!" Each one bore the same expression they had in the other photo, though this time they were dressed in formal wear.

"Well, I'm glad you found the connection, but that doesn't prove that he killed her." Chloe rubbed Bryce's back lovingly.

"I did a little more snooping around. Jeffrey and Beverly broke up right before graduation. His parents sent him away to get his high school equivalency. The whole thing was pretty hush-hush, but the school secretary told me she'd heard he'd gotten a girl pregnant and they didn't want him to marry her."

"He got Beverly pregnant? Is that why he followed her out here? A love child that she was blackmailing him to keep secret? It all makes sense. Oh, Bryce! What am I going to do with this?"

"Chloe Merlin!" Nova barked. "Why are you standing there making goo-goo eyes at your boyfriend? We've got to stay on schedule!" Chloe had placed large curlers in Nova's hair earlier that morning and several were now hanging on by a few strands. Her face was smeared in a thick, yellow crème and she wore a fuzzy robe with the words, 'Caution, Bridezilla!' embroidered on the back.

"I've got to go," Chloe whispered. "I'll be done with everyone's hair and makeup in two hours. Let's meet up for lunch and talk then." She kissed Bryce on the lips and noticed a red welt from their violent encounter. "Sorry about that," she said as she walked away. "You need to put some ice on that cheek."

DECEMBER 24TH, NOON

Nova turned her head from side to side, admiring her reflection. A thick strip of eyeliner reached from her eyes upward toward her brow like a freshly oiled road. Her rose eye shadow was intended to match her bouquet, but coupled with her dramatically tall hair it made her resemble a victim from an '80s summer camp slasher film. "I think just a little higher though. My veil is going to push my hair down and I want it to be eighties bold. That was a decade when people truly understood style."

Chloe had already teased Nova's hair up to its full potential. Getting it much higher would require expertise beyond what she'd learned in two years of beauty college. "I'm just about out of root lifter and hair spray. I was thinking we should save what's left to use right before you walk down the aisle."

Nova sighed. "You're probably right. Is there any

sign the rain is letting up? It never rains for long here, right?"

"I'll check with my dad. He was going to make sure the Christmas lights are all on for your cruise down Main Street. The carolers are scheduled to stand at every corner as you drive by." Chloe thought about the poor townspeople who had been paid a measly $50 each to stand in the wind and rain, waiting for the precise moment when the newlyweds drove down the street, waving as if they were a celebrity couple.

There was a knock on the door frame and all ten of the bridesmaids stood in unison. "You're not supposed to see us before the wedding!" one yelled. Nova's dismissive attitude was rubbing off on everyone.

"I'm not in the wedding. I just came to bring Chloe her lunch." Bryce waved a brown paper bag in the air.

Chloe smiled and met him at the door. "I'll be back in a few minutes, Nova. Sure you don't want anything?" She regretted those words as soon as she'd said them.

"How many times do I have to tell you, a bride never eats before the wedding? The last thing I need is to have stomach bloat in my twenty-five-thousand-dollar wedding dress!"

"Right, I forgot, sorry. I'll be back soon."

Chloe rolled her eyes as soon as they were out of Nova's view. "I can't imagine how she'd react if something went wrong."

"You're probably not going to want to see this, then." Bryce held a green and red plaid napkin in front of her face. The curly gold letters spelled, "Nora and Jemmy, Marry Christmas!"

"Oh no! She's going to lose it. I had Nova on speaker as we were ordering. How could this happen?"

"Poor old Mrs. Thatcher is mostly deaf. She was in for her son that day, remember? He was home with the virus."

"That's right. Well, I suppose we could replace them with plain white napkins and tell her these never came in? Would you mind running to the store?" They sat down in the lobby, where Chloe opened her sack and pulled out an egg salad sandwich she'd made the night before.

"Sure, no problem. But there is another thing I wanted to mention."

"What now?" Chloe asked through bites of her sandwich.

"Jeffrey's worked in three different businesses in the last two years. I called them and found out that Beverly worked there too."

"This affair was intense. That settles it. I'm going to confront him before the wedding. If nothing else, he's going to admit to my cousin that he cheated on her."

The double doors to the conference center blew open and Doris stumbled through. She held one door open and waited while her assistants brought in many boxes. "Had a little issue on the way over. That wind caught us and jerked the van, so I've got to work my magic on layers three and four." She smoothed her hair. "What're you two staring at?"

"It looks like a hurricane out there. I wonder if the guests will make it?" Chloe asked.

"You know how it can be this time of year. Surprised your cousin didn't think about that ahead of time." She took off her coat and set it on the reception desk, much to the dismay of the woman working there. "Did you tell her?" She glanced at Bryce.

"Tell me what? Is there more? I don't know how much more of this I can take!" Chloe stood and began pacing back and forth. "Just pull off the bandage. What's happening?"

"You've been sick, so I've been consulting with Doris about Jeffrey. She thinks we need to stop the wedding and show Nova what we have." Bryce tilted his head down and smiled hopefully. "You wanted us to get along, didn't you?"

Something about this seemed off to her, but they were two of the three most important people in her life, so she said nothing.

DECEMBER 24TH, 2 P.M.

"These candles were for the ceremony," Nova whimpered. "Now they're going to be drippy and disgusting before I even walk down the aisle."

Chloe took the candle from Nova's hand and sat it on the table. "Let's keep that away from your head, okay? I don't want to think about what might happen when that much hair product meets fire."

After two hours, there was still no power in the *Piney Falls Cannery Conference Center and Resort*. Chloe tried calling the power company, but it became obvious after an hour that they weren't going to answer. "I'm sure it will be back on before you know it," she said cheerfully, for the fourth or fifth time.

"Can you go check on Jeffrey? I haven't heard a peep from him or his family since the rehearsal dinner. I don't want him to worry about me."

There was no easy way to back out of this uncomfortable conversation. "Sure, Nova."

Someone knocked on the door and one of the bridesmaids, who had been involved in a serious game of poker, jumped up to answer.

A wiry-haired woman in a festive, one-piece red jumpsuit with matching glasses frames bounded in.

"Chloe called me and said you might be in need of relaxation." She saluted to no one in particular. "November Bean, at your service. Yoga, howling, and relaxation. Whatever you need."

Nova looked her up and down with skepticism. "You really know how to do all of that?"

"We can start with a shoulder massage. I can see your shoulders are up so high, it's a wonder they're not blocking your ears."

Nova went over to the mirror and touched her ears. "Oh no. My ears ARE a mess! No one will see my five-thousand-dollar earrings!"

Chloe was relieved to have someone else help shoulder Nova's drama. "I've got to check on Jeffrey. Will you take care of this, Mrs. Bean?"

"Certainly!" November Bean took Nova by the waist and guided her to the yellow-velvet couch. "You'll be a brand new woman when I'm done here."

Chloe closed the door and wondered what she might say to Jeffrey.

She hadn't gone more than ten feet when she saw Doris trudging down the hall. "Got some good news and bad news. Well...and maybe another bad news."

"Tell me quickly. I have to go talk to Jeffrey."

"The first bit of bad news is that I've run out of

toothpicks and this cake is on life support." Doris scratched her head. "First time in all of the years I've been making cakes for weddings. Need to get my shocks checked on the van, I guess."

"Can you spin it around so the ruined part is in the back?"

Doris's face hardened. "That might be a problem. There's a definite slant going on. Never had that issue before, but this is the first time I've done a cake this tall. You should've talked me out of it."

Chloe sighed, exasperated. "Have we gotten to the good news yet?"

"The next issue is the minister you hired."

"Pastor Wendell? Don't tell me the weather will keep him away. Is he having car trouble? Bryce could pick him up."

"No." Doris shook her head. "His car is working just fine."

"Whew!" Chloe punched her fist in the air. "Finally something is going right!"

"I didn't say that. His car is working fine but his lungs are another matter. Checked himself into Piney Falls General Hospital this morning. That nasty virus has got him down."

Chloe gazed at her stoically. "I think you owe me one bit of good news, if I counted correctly."

"Well, just so happens, I'm an ordained minister. Church of the Coffee-Making Goddess."

"What? You've never mentioned that before. Is that a real thing?"

Doris grabbed her arm and Chloe noticed her fingers were covered in frosting.

"My granddaughter wanted me to officiate her weddin'. I told her I'd need to be affiliated with a church first, so she started this one, just for me. You don't need to worry, honey. I've got this covered."

With everything that had gone south today, this seemed like a little problem. "I'm not going to worry about it for now. I'm supposed to talk to Jeffrey and make sure he's not worried about Nova."

"You'd better not ask him anything about Beverly on his weddin' day. Wouldn't be right."

Chloe didn't answer, but continued walking down the hall, waving goodbye with her frosting-covered arm. Even as she rounded the corner to the groom's bank of rooms, she wasn't sure what she was going to say.

She knocked on the door. "Jeffrey? How are things going in there?"

With an unexpected whoosh, the door flew open. A man who looked so perfect he must've walked out of a clothing magazine smiled at her. She hadn't noticed at the rehearsal dinner, but he had a dimple on one side of his face. He'd barely aged since high school.

"Um...Nova didn't want you to worry about her. She's fine."

"Do you want to come in?" He moved aside and opened the door wide.

Normally, engaging a groom on his wedding day would be awkward, but today was anything but normal. She moved to the center of the room and squeezed her palms together. "Jeffrey, I have to ask you an uncomfortable question."

He sat down on the bed and crossed his legs. "Shoot."

Chloe began pacing, both to keep her train of thought flowing and to be ready to run if he tried doing to her what he did to Beverly. "I know that you have been in Piney Falls before. I also know that Beverly Thomas, the woman who was murdered in this very hotel, was your high school girlfriend."

The relaxed expression on his face tightened. "How did you know that?"

"Does it matter? You're going to marry my cousin in a few hours and she has no idea you cheated on her, let alone murdered someone!"

Jeffrey rose and stood toe-to-toe with Chloe. "I didn't cheat on her and I didn't kill anyone!"

She could feel his hot breath on her face and she trembled. Afraid to look him in the eye, she stared at the top of his head, where she noticed a small patch of hair was missing. "Tell me now, or I go straight to Nova."

"I can't. This is my wedding day and those details need to wait for another time." He moved back a step, easing the tension in the room. "I promise, if you want the whole story, I'll tell you tomorrow."

They had reached an impasse and Chloe wasn't sure how to proceed. "What am I supposed to say to Nova? She's out of her mind with worry about this wedding and you've got a huge secret you're keeping from her."

"Hold on." He sat down at the desk and pulled out a piece of hotel stationery. As he was writing, Chloe glanced around the room, noting a pair of brown Funello shoes sitting in the closet.

"Why isn't your best man here with you? It seems odd you'd be alone."

Jeffrey looked up from his note. "I don't trust anyone. My friends know that and give me my space."

"How are you going to make a marriage work if you don't trust? Nova has trust issues too and she can't be hurt again."

Jeffrey's eyes filled with tears as he stared down at his feet. "I know what she's been through. That's what made me fall in love with her. She was betrayed by someone she loved too."

"Just like Beverly betrayed you?"

He nodded and wiped his eyes with the back of his hand. "I never wanted things to end this way."

"Now what do we do, Jeffrey? Can you really just get married like nothing happened?"

"I'm going to marry Nova today. This is her dream and I'm not taking that away from her. Do you want to break her heart?"

An urgent knock at the door startled them both. "Is Chloe in there? We've got a crisis."

Chloe rolled her eyes as she opened the door. "What?!" she snapped.

"There's a problem with the flowers. They've been trying to get ahold of you all day. The plane that was supposed to arrive from Hawaii this morning with the flowers wasn't allowed to land at the airport, due to the weather. She had to make do with what she had in the shop."

"Nova is going to freak." Chloe looked over her shoulder at Jeffrey, who was lost in his own world. "Did you hear that? Just about everything has gone wrong. Don't you think you should take that as a sign?"

DECEMBER 24TH, 4 P.M.

Candles placed on the windowsills illuminated the garland-lined ballroom of the *Piney Falls Cannery Conference Center and Resort*. There was a Christmas tree in the corner with shiny foil-wrapped boxes underneath. Conference Space B was magically transformed into a cozy Christmas scene. If it hadn't been for the sound of branches beating against the window, the wedding party could easily forget there was still a storm raging outside.

Nova's eleven bridesmaids, including Chloe, stood patiently at the front of the room in their full-skirted red evening gowns.

Jeffrey, dressed in a black tuxedo with hunter green-trimmed lapels, beamed as he waited for his bride to appear.

Chloe leaned over to Doris, who was standing close by, and whispered, "Did all of these people fly in from Iowa?"

She shook her head. "Only twenty of Jeffrey's relatives. The rest were supposed to come in this morning and they closed the airport. Jeffrey's daddy told me to find stand-ins."

A quick scan of the room showed familiar faces filling the seats. Curiously though, they all looked like they'd picked up the nasty virus. Many were wiping their noses. The scent of cough drops filled the air.

"How did you—"

"Yesterday was my volunteer day at Piney Falls Speedy Care. I kept the check-in sheet by mistake and it had all of their phone numbers. Easy peasy." Doris smiled with satisfaction. "Never thought of myself as a weddin' planner, but I'm feeling pretty good about things."

"Why would they want to come out in the middle of a storm if they're sick?"

"Jeffrey's father offered to pay each of them two hundred dollars. If you were gonna get that much money to eat cake, wouldn't you do it?"

The pianist began playing the bride's march–extra loud to drown out the sound of the branches pummeling the windows, per Nova's request. Nova appeared on the arm of her proud father, Jack. Her hair looked even taller than ten minutes ago, when Chloe used the last of the hair spray. As if on cue, the lights popped back on.

Nova's dress swished as she walked down the aisle, catching a purse and a cane as she passed by. She smiled and waved at the guests as though she were a contestant at a pageant.

When she reached the altar, where Doris was standing dressed in her best purple pantsuit, she beamed at her husband-to-be. She handed her bouquet of red roses, pine cones and small pine branches that had blown under the awning of the hotel during the storm to her maid of honor and took Jeffrey's hand.

"Friends, Jeffrey's kin and everyone with a touch of the nasty virus, welcome to this weddin'." Doris looked around the room. "This is only my second time at the wheel, so be kind."

The bridesmaid holding Nova's bouquet brushed off the pieces of branch and looked around.

"Today, Nova and Jeffrey wanted to read their own vows."

"Oh crap. It's bugs. This thing is full of bugs!" The bridesmaid dropped the bouquet and scratched her arm. "They're all over me! Somebody do something!" She walked to a row of guests and thrust her arms in the face of the first person in the row.

Nova leaned forward and scowled at Chloe. "This is your fault! You were supposed to handle everything today and it's been one giant disaster! I told you to make sure there were no mistakes!"

Chloe shook her head and turned away from the guests for a moment. Ever since they were children, she was the only one who knew how to handle Nova. She kept her from losing her cool at every family reunion and whenever they played games with the other cousins. It was her soothing touch that brought Nova out of her funk when her mother ran off.

Nothing compared to today, however. "Nova, I've

had it!" She threw the single rose she'd been holding down and put her hands on her hips. "I've worked myself so hard, I got sick trying to make sure your wedding was perfect." Her voice echoed in the large room. "I even tried to prevent you from marrying a murderer, but I guess I failed at that too, right Jeffrey?"

There was an audible gasp.

"What? I know you're stressed, but don't take it out on Jeffrey."

"Your boyfriend has been seeing someone behind your back. He was here with her last month and they got into a horrible fight. She pulled out some of his hair and the next time anyone saw her, she was dead on the bathroom floor."

Nova's chin dropped.

"I can explain. I just didn't want to do it today." Jeffrey took Nova's hands in his. "Can we go somewhere private and talk?"

Nova pulled her hands back with such force she lost her balance and fell into the second bridesmaid. Luckily, the bridesmaid caught the bride before she hit the floor. When Nova stood upright once again, she smoothed her enormous dress and took a deep breath.

"Tell me now, Jeffrey," she demanded. "In front of your parents and my dad. I want to hear this!"

"It's true. I dated Beverly Thomas in high school. She was my first girlfriend, and I was head over heels in love. I would have done anything for her."

Nova sniffed. "I thought I was your first love."

"You are, my darling. My first adult relationship."

Jeffrey took a step forward and Nova took a step back, avoiding his touch.

"Better get on with it. This ain't likely to end well," Doris remarked.

"One Saturday afternoon, she called me and her voice was shaking. She asked if I was serious about doing anything for her. I told her of course I was, and she said, 'Then come here now and don't question anything I ask you to do.'" Jeffrey took a deep breath and glanced at his parents. His mother was visibly shaken and his father's face was beet red, like he was about to explode.

"She was pregnant with your child," Chloe stated simply. "She's been holding that over your head all of these years."

"No, that's not it at all. When I got to her house, she took me to the basement. There was a homeless man lying on the floor. She said he'd broken in and attacked her and she hit him over the head with her mom's mixer. I bent down and checked his pulse. He was dead."

Jeffrey's mother got up and ran out. "Mom!" he called after her. "I'm sorry! You knew this was going to come out at some point!"

"Finish up, I want to hear the rest of this," Doris urged.

He gave her a dirty look, but continued. "I could see she was terrified, so I did my best to calm her down and then took the body out in the country and buried it. We had this horrible secret between us and the guilt ate at me for a long time. I finally confessed to my parents and when Beverly found out I'd told them, she hit the roof. She threatened to kill them and me before she'd go to jail."

Nova's eyes widened. "What did you do?"

"My folks sent me away. They figured time would ease her anger. For eight years, I heard nothing, so I came back and started working at the family business. Beverly found out I was there and blackmailed my parents into giving her a job." Jeffrey choked back a sob. "Every day was worse than the last, and I realized if my family was going to have any peace, I'd have to go somewhere else and start over. I thought maybe this time she would have found something in her life to distract her, so I let my guard down. I went out in public, joined social media and lived like any other single guy."

Someone sitting directly behind Nova's father sneezed so loud, Jack Merlin turned around and glared at them.

"Then one day," Jeffrey continued, "I'm at work and I hear there's a new employee who's already told the staff we're an item. That evening, I found her in the parking lot and I begged her to leave me alone. She said, 'You ran out once and I'm never letting you go again.'" Jeffrey started to cry.

Doris pulled a crumpled tissue from her pocket. "Here. I don't think it's used." He took it without hesitation and blew his nose.

One of the newly-recruited guests started coughing and had to get up to leave, causing two more to follow.

"You're not walking out on my wedding!" Nova yelled.

"They'll be back, honey. I promised them cake," Doris assured her.

Chloe cleared her throat. "If she was blackmailing you, why did you follow her here?"

"It's the opposite. *She* was following me." He stepped forward once again and grabbed Nova's hands. This time, she didn't resist.

"Nova's always talked about how beautiful the Pacific Northwest is. I knew she had special memories of family reunions here and that's why she chose this location for our wedding. So, I decided to surprise her and buy a vacation home. I was here looking at houses. I stayed at a seedy motel where I thought she wouldn't find me."

"What happened that day in her room, Jeffrey?" Doris asked. "Ed Junior already told us you two were fighting."

Jeffrey looked at the floor. "This is hard to tell you, my love. I did go to her room to threaten her. I was sick of living in fear. We got into an argument. I told her I'd found the love of my life and she hit me. I grasped her arm and with her other hand, she pulled out a chunk of my hair." He touched his scalp. "Something snapped in me. I grabbed her arms and held them down as I told her I was done. I wasn't afraid of her any longer. For the first time, she realized she'd lost control over me. That's when she reached into her pocket and pulled out the pill. I don't know what it was."

"Cyanide," Doris and Chloe said in unison.

"She smiled and put it under her tongue. I ran out of there so fast. I didn't want to be there when she...you know."

"Why didn't you call the police?" Boysie Lumquest, drenched despite being cloaked in rain gear, walked down the aisle and stood in front of Doris. He removed his hat, allowing the accumulated rainwater on the brim to spill onto the floor. "Here for two reasons. First, I wanted to check on you folks. I knew today was a big celebration and the electricity's out. I can see you're all doing fine, though I didn't plan on hearing a confession to murder."

"He was scared! He loves me and he was worried I wouldn't understand!" Nova touched Jeffrey's cheek.

"Second, we finally got the full autopsy report back on Beverly Thomas. I've been on the phone with medical personnel in Sandy Salts, Iowa." He scanned the room full of coughing and sneezing guests. "Beverly had a highly contagious virus they've named Salty Sinus Syndrome. This nasty virus that's been going around came to town with Beverly. You folks are gonna be quarantined here until I hear back from the Health Department. Could be a day or so."

It happened so quickly that the bridesmaids, in their full-skirted splendor, had trouble moving out of the way. The largest oak tree in town came crashing through the window, its branches reaching out to grab everything in its path. Being bridesmaid number eleven and the furthest from an exit, Chloe had no way to move out of its path.

Like a slow-motion game of dominoes, the thick,

heavy branches toppled the giant Christmas tree. Chloe watched in horror, wondering if Piney Falls Cannery Conference Center and Resort Christmas tree was the last thing she'd ever see.

"Chloe! I love you!" At least she'd heard his voice one more time.

A small fire, created when the candles in the windows fell on the wedding greenery, was quickly extinguished by heavy gusts of rain. There was screaming and crying while most of the wedding guests tried to exit as quickly as possible.

Doris moved in the opposite direction, fighting her way over the mess of broken ornaments and branches where the tree landed. She pulled away debris until she saw her friend's pale, freckled face.

"Oh no. Chloe, I can't lose you, honey. Talk to me." She continued pulling branches until she uncovered the bottom half of her body.

"My chest hurts." Chloe tried moving her arms, but they were stuck under the oversized Piney Falls Cannery Conference Center and Resort commemorative 2015 merchant ship ornament. Boysie joined Doris in removing branches.

When Chloe was completely uncovered, Doris sat back on her haunches. "Well, doesn't that beat all."

"What's wrong? Am I going to lose a limb?" Chloe asked fearfully. "Tell Bryce I love him!"

Doris yanked on the Christmas star until it unattached from Chloe. "Open your eyes, honey. I've got something to show you."

Chloe looked up and saw Doris holding the jagged

edge of the once-beautiful decoration. “Was that stuck in me?”

“No. Not stuck in you.” Doris poked the jewelry on Chloe’s chest, causing her to wince. “In my great-grannie’s brooch. I knew it was going to be as lucky for you as it was for her.”

DECEMBER 24TH, 8 P.M.

With the lights on, the guests were treated to a visual wonder. The second largest room of the *Piney Falls Cannery Conference Center and Resort* was set up with round tables covered by red cloths. In the middle of each table were round pieces of pine from a recently felled tree in Friendly State Park. On top of each piece of wood was a beeswax candle made in an old coffee cup with holly berries decorating the base. The ceiling was covered in tiny, sparkling lights making the room look like a winter wonderland.

Nova and Jeffrey, who had exchanged vows with Doris at the reception desk, stood together at the head table. In front of them sat the last two napkins that Bryce had neglected to collect. Nova glanced down and dug her manicured fingers into her palms when she read them. She glared at her cousin. "This is unforgivable! Can't you spell?"

Chloe shrugged her shoulders.

"She really lost it earlier. Do you want her to cause a scene again?" Jeffrey whispered in his wife's ear. Nova nodded and smiled, relaxing her fingers.

"Besides, I asked her to make something special, just for us. Look around–we're the only ones with these." Jeffrey winked at Nova's cousin.

Chloe frowned, unsure of his message. Nova had been right about one thing: this Christmas was one they would never forget. She felt a poke on the shoulder and whipped her head around. "I'm off the clock!" she snapped.

Bryce looked tentatively at Chloe. "I haven't been entirely honest with you. Doris and I have been talking about things besides the murder. She was putting me through a series of tests, including learning your entire family history, back to the seventeen hundreds. I think I passed."

"Oh?" She took a drink of champagne and touched her chest where she was almost impaled by the Christmas star. "That sounds like something Doris would do. But why would she test you?"

"Careful!" he cautioned, pushing the glass away from her face.

"Hey!" she protested. "I deserve the entire bottle after the day I've had."

"No, look at your champagne!"

She brought the fluted glass up to eye level. At the bottom was a round, gold object. When she looked at Bryce again, he was on one knee.

"Chloe Merlin, will you marry me?"

Jeffrey stood at that moment and raised his glass and the guests raised theirs in turn.

"To my beautiful Nova, and to this wonderful town of Piney Falls. Marry Christmas to all!"

THE END

FROM THE AUTHOR

Doris and I share an affinity for television trivia—just ask the social media games that proclaim me, "brilliant." While my memory isn't as good as hers, I do love to sink my teeth into a good mystery, especially one with lots of twists and turns.

You can find Doris, along with all of the quirky residents of Piney Falls, in the *Piney Falls Mysteries Series*.

For a story set in midwestern United States, read *The Story of Keilah* and *Secrets and Sunflowers*, where Nova finally meets her match!

Website and newsletter sign up: www.joannkeder.com

THE PURLOINED POINSETTIA

CATHY TULLY

Christmas is almost here, and the search for pilfered plants leads to a deadly discovery.

CHAPTER ONE

Dr. Susannah Shine straightened the star on the top of the Christmas tree, dislodging a shiny, red Christmas ball. The ornament tumbled, bouncing off two branches before it rolled across the waiting room with a *tink, tink, tink.*

"Dr. Shine, no." Tina Cawthorn squatted, scooped up the ornament, and tottered across the waiting room, one hand on her pregnant belly. "No touching my work of art."

Susannah stepped back, grinning. "Just trying to help."

"That's okay, boss." Every year, her chiropractic assistant took charge of decorating the Christmas tree and was very protective of her creation. "You can help by seeing to Miss Larraine. She seems upset."

Susannah crossed the waiting room, frowning. Larraine Moore, the office manager of Peach Grove Chiropractic, was like a grandmother to her. In the insurance room, which twinkled with Christmas lights, Larraine stood with her hand on the phone receiver.

"Are you okay?"

Larraine turned, her lips pinched together, and sighed. "Seems we won't be decorating the church tonight. The poinsettias and wreaths aren't ready. Somehow, the order was misplaced." She smoothed her Christmas cardigan. Usually dressed in solid white, Larraine wore a sweater speckled with green Christmas trees. "Miss Shirleen's madder than a wet hen. And I don't blame her."

"That's awful. How did that happen?" Tina appeared behind the front desk.

"I have no clue." Larraine gave Tina a half-smile. The two women were a study in opposites. Twenty-something Tina was petite and dark-skinned, with a heart-shaped face that had filled out during her pregnancy. Larraine, well into her sixties, stood a few inches taller, with white hair and barely enough pink in the complexion of her long face to convince you that she was alive. "All I know is, Miss Shirleen is all in a tizzy because the order isn't at the florist."

Larraine squeezed through the doorway and Susannah stepped to the side, elbowing the model spine that Tina had adorned with tinsel and a Santa hat. Strands of tinsel floated to the floor as Larraine passed. A quick tap of the keyboard and she had clocked out.

"Are you using the new florist in downtown Peach Grove?" Susannah asked. Twisting to grasp at the silver ribbons that fluttered just past her reach, she felt a sudden wave of vertigo and quickly straightened.

"Yes, she gave us a discount." Larraine pulled a business card from the pocket of her white scrub pants and stared at it. "Not that it matters now."

"I just met the owner at the Peach Grove Business Association meeting last week." Susannah paused. "She seems like a reasonable person. You should go talk to her."

"I'm fixin' to." Larraine pressed her lips together and sighed. "I don't want to have to tell Pastor Ron."

"Maybe Miss Shirleen got the order number wrong," Tina offered. "She is getting older."

Larraine raised her brow. "Shirleen and I are the same age."

"Er, I just meant..." Tina's eyes widened, and she looked at Susannah for help.

"Why don't I go with you?" Susannah asked.

"You don't have to do that. I can put on my big girl britches and do it myself."

"Nonsense. We can go and then have lunch. She should remember me from the meeting. I might be able to help smooth things over." Susannah turned to Tina. "You coming?"

"No, I have a doctor's appointment." She patted her belly.

"Let me grab my purse, Larraine." Susannah strode down the hall to her office. Henry the Eighth, her betta fish, swam silent circles around the green Marimo moss ball at the bottom of his tank. She tapped a few flakes of fish food out of the canister, and he wig-wagged his tail at her. Satisfied that he was well fed, she grabbed her purse, turned off the light, and called, "*Ciao, bello.*"

In Larraine's Mercury Marquis, they trundled down Highway 42 past the municipal building and the church. Gliding into a spot right in front of the True Blooms Florist, Larraine hopped out of her car and entered the shop, one fisted hand on her hip. A dark-haired man wearing a black-and-white geometric print sweater over a black skirt stopped sweeping and turned to her.

"I'm looking for the order for the Peach Grove Baptist Church." Larraine reached into her pocket and pulled out the card. "My friend was here earlier, and she said y'all don't have it in."

"No, ma'am." The young man moved behind the counter, leaning the broom against the wall.

"But I ordered it weeks ago." Larraine pointed to the number on the card.

There was a noise in the back of the store, and Susannah saw the owner come around the counter carrying a vase of roses. A name tag, which read *Shannon*, was affixed to the top of her knee-length forest green apron bib. She nodded a greeting and opened the door to the refrigerator case.

"Yes, ma'am," the clerk behind the counter said. "But like I told your friend, I don't have any order with that number on it. Maybe you wrote the number down wrong?"

"Young man," Larraine said, peering at him over her readers, "I may be some dumb, but I'm not plumb dumb."

"Ma'am?" The man blushed.

The refrigerator door shut and Shannon approached. "Can I help you ladies?"

"Yes, please." Larraine turned toward the woman, who towered over her. "I placed this order weeks ago for the church, and your assistant tells me he can't find it."

Shannon walked around the counter and touched her assistant on the shoulder. "Why don't you go to lunch, Conrad?"

The clerk nodded and left his perch behind the computer. Susannah watched as he entered the back room and picked up his keys from a long workbench that was covered with ribbon and small white tags. The floor creaked as he made his way out the back exit. The True Blooms shop was right next door to the Peachy Things boutique, owned by her best friend, Bitsy Long, and Susannah was familiar enough with the condition of these units to be duly impressed with anyone who could modernize these arthritic 19th-century brick-and-wood buildings.

Shannon pursed her lips. Susannah noted her impeccable makeup as she tapped the keyboard. "May I see the order number?"

Larraine pointed at the order number written on the business card in her spindly handwriting. Shannon frowned as her fingers danced across the keys. "Hmmm. I think I see the problem."

"Oh?" Susannah leaned in, stretching to see the screen.

"Yes." Shannon regarded her. "Do I know you?"

"Dr. Susannah Shine." Susannah offered her hand.

"We met at the Peach Grove Business Association meeting last week."

"Yes, I recall now. You're Bitsy's friend." Her larger hand swallowed Susannah's hand. She paused and looked at Larraine, then back to Susannah. With a conspiratorial grin, she asked, "How exactly are you involved here?"

"Oh, I'm just along for the ride. Miss Larraine is my office manager." Susannah hoped Larraine wouldn't object to a little white lie. "We were on our way to lunch when she asked if I would mind going along on her errand."

Suddenly the door to the shop blew open with a bang, drowning out the bing-bong of the electronic doorbell, and Bitsy Long fell into the room. She winced, shrinking back a bit as she waved, fluttering her fingers. "*Hola.*"

"Hey, Miss Bitsy," Shannon said, unfazed by the Cosmo Kramer-esque entrance.

"What all is going on in here?" Bitsy crossed the shop in two springy steps. The red pom-pom nose of the Christmas moose on her sweater bobbed. She winked at Shannon and encircled Larraine and Susannah in a two-person hug. "I've been waiting a dog's age for y'all to come next door and invite me to lunch."

"We're almost done. Shannon is trying to clear up a problem with Larraine's order." Susannah turned from Bitsy back to Shannon. "Right? You said you found the problem?"

"Well yes, I did." She turned back to the computer and pointed to the screen with a long lacquered nail.

"You see, Conrad doesn't have access to this data, so he couldn't see the order number."

"What data is that?" Bitsy pushed between Susannah and Larraine.

"Canceled orders."

CHAPTER TWO

"Canceled?" Larraine blinked, taking the card back and staring at the number. "This order was canceled? Who canceled it?"

"Someone from the church." Shannon grabbed the mouse and clicked. "I remember now. I took this order over the phone."

"Yes. I called it in weeks ago."

"When I got in touch with the church to verify the order and get payment, I was told you all had changed your mind."

"Well, I'll be." Larraine put a finger to her lips. "That's not right. Do you remember who you spoke to?"

"It was the financial secretary. A woman."

"I wish someone would have contacted me." Larraine sagged. "And the financial secretary is a man. He has a new assistant, Olivia Franklin, but, still, it must be some kind of mistake."

"I apologize," Shannon said, her smile fading for the first time. Her eyes landed on Bitsy. "Things haven't been going as smoothly as I led you to believe at the business association meeting."

"Spill it, girlfriend." Bitsy had been elected president of the Peach Grove Business Association only a few weeks before, and she had a grand vision of her role as president. Her dreads bounced as she nodded encouragingly. "I'm here to help."

"Well, to be honest"—Shannon looked at Larraine and then down at the keyboard—"I've had plants stolen from the shop, and my Christmas display was all torn up."

"What in the world?" Larraine whispered.

"Did you report it to the police?" Susannah asked.

"Yes, the chief came himself and took the report. But there's not much they can do. He thought it might be teenagers."

Susannah nodded. She remembered Randy Laughton, the Peach Grove police chief, taking the report of a broken window in her garage, and squirmed. He'd been wrong about the teenagers then, and she wondered if he were wrong now. She swallowed back a comment. She and Randy had an uncomfortable history.

"But what does that have to do with the church?" Larraine asked.

"The vandalism?" Shannon shrugged. "I can't prove anything about that. But I think the canceled orders are connected to one person from the church who doesn't approve my lifestyle. I just assumed this was another one of those issues."

"It wasn't that *unmarried women shouldn't run their own business* thing? Was it?" Bitsy asked, pointing to herself and then Susannah. "We've heard that before. I think Olivia, er, Livvy Franklin is the only one who cares about that."

"Uh, well, it might have been a woman called Livvy. But the problem wasn't so much about me as about my assistant, Conrad."

"What's wrong with Conrad?" Bitsy jabbed Larraine. "He's not a Methodist, is he?"

Larraine drew her brows together at the reference to a well-known rivalry that bordered on antagonism between the two congregations.

"I think there's gossip because he's an unconventional dresser." This time, Shannon held Bitsy's gaze and then shifted her stare to Susannah. "And, er, he's not married. If you know what I mean."

Larraine's face pinked. "That might could be Livvy. She's good at heart, but sometimes needs a nudge in a more loving direction."

"Well, nudge away. At this rate I'll be lucky to make my mortgage payment, what with the losses on the plants that were damaged in the display and the slow sales. Not to mention the poinsettias that had already gone missing before the display was completely demolished."

"I doubt Livvy could have had anything to do with that." Larraine pressed her lips into a firm line. "But I promise you this. I'm marching right over to the church and I'm not leaving until I get approval for this sale. This is the business of the decorating committee. The office of the financial secretary has no right to cancel our orders."

CHAPTER THREE

With a nod to Bitsy, Susannah followed after Larraine as she jogged out of the florist shop and to her car. The door locks popped open and Susannah slipped in.

"What could have gotten into Livvy?" Larraine asked, jabbing her key into the ignition and checking her mirror. "Saying those things."

Susannah remained silent. She had often congratulated herself on hiring Larraine to manage her practice. The woman was honest, hardworking, and loyal. Her devotion to her church was one of the things Susannah admired the most about her friend, but Susannah had met Livvy and could explicitly picture her saying those things.

"Love the sinner, hate the sin." Larraine frowned as she pulled into traffic. Livvy, an accountant, had been a student in Larraine's Sunday School class twenty-five years earlier. “I just don’t believe Livvy could be so ugly as to destroy Shannon’s floral display.”

“If you say so.” Susannah bit her lip. She had only spoken to Livvy once; though mousy in demeanor, she had been judgmental and bitter. Susannah wouldn’t put some petty vandalism past her.

“I do. And I’ll deal with her later,” Larraine said, tapping a finger on the steering wheel. “But right now I need to clear this up with Albert.”

Susannah opened her mouth to ask how, but Larraine interrupted her. “Alexa, call the church.”

“Calling,” Alexa’s robotic voice replied through the car speakers.

Larraine sent a quick glance Susannah’s way. “You have to understand, the decorating committee has a budget authorized by Pastor Ron. We can spend it any way we want.” The sound of ringing was amplified by the stereo speakers. “Within reason, of course.”

A woman’s voice came on the line, and Larraine greeted her. “Charleen, darlin’,” Larraine drawled. “Can you put Albert on?”

Charleen Barnes was Pastor Ron’s wife. If she was answering the phone, the church must be short-staffed during this busy Christmas season. Susannah imagined that everyone was doing double duty getting ready for the big day.

“He went home for lunch,” Charleen replied.

“Thank you, darlin’.” There was a click as Charleen hung up and the stereo speakers went silent. Larraine’s eye twitched as she glanced into the mirror, knuckles white on the wheel.

Susannah's stomach rumbled. "Let's get lunch, we—"

The car made a sudden lurch as Larraine stomped on the brake and spun the wheel in a tight U-turn. Susannah was hurled toward Larraine and then back, shoulder harness clenching her torso as she reached wildly for the grab handle above the door. Larraine completed the turn and gunned the engine.

"What's happening?" Susannah shouted, glad she had taken a pee break before she left the office. "Where are we going?"

"We're going to see Albert Calloway. He's the financial secretary and he's the only one who has the authority to deny my charge." Larraine glared at Susannah. "I'm gonna give him a piece of my mind."

Susannah's heart had barely stopped palpitating when they cruised to a stop in front of Albert's house. It was no surprise that at a little after one p.m. on a weekday, the streets were empty and sidewalks deserted.

"Maybe it's just a mix-up," Susannah said.

"There might could be a very reasonable explanation," Larraine agreed. "And I intend to find out what it is. Or I'm gonna raise a ruckus with Pastor Ron."

A car in the driveway told Susannah that Albert had indeed come home for lunch. His two-story brick-front house was the picture of Christmas cheer. Lights were strung across the eaves, and red and white plastic candy canes lined the path to the porch and trailed both sides of the driveway. A large wreath with a huge red bow adorned the front door. With two identical six-foot nutcracker-soldier banners flanking the entrance, the house had a *Babes In Toyland* vibe. Nothing pointed to Albert being a poinsettia pilferer.

Larraine grabbed her purse and got out of the car. She settled the strap on her shoulder, and Susannah thought she saw her bare her teeth. "I'll be right back."

"I'm not going to miss this." Susannah was out of the car in a flash. "I mean, you might need me."

"Thanks." Larraine led Susannah past plastic candy canes that were posted like pickets. "You're sweet."

"You're just saying that 'cause we're surrounded by candy canes." As they made their way along the curved concrete pathway to the porch, a shriek sounded from inside the house. Both women stopped in their tracks.

"Nooo!" a howl emanated from somewhere inside.

Miss Larraine's face blanched. "What the—"

Susannah bolted to the porch, flattening a plastic confection as she went. The door flew open and Susannah staggered back as Santa barreled past, hitting Susannah's shoulder, carrying short twin daggers covered in blood.

"Stop!" Larraine cried.

Santa, who wobbled as he ran, raised the daggers up as if to strike Larraine. Susannah, her hand buried in her purse, felt for the easy-access holster that held her pistol in place. She grabbed it, hands trembling, and brought the pistol out of her purse. "Freeze!"

Santa—who Susannah now realized wasn't Santa at all but a chubby white-haired woman in a red tracksuit—stopped. There was a thunk as the daggers hit the walkway. Susannah stared, trying to make sense of what she saw. It wasn't twin daggers but some kind of a metal snowflake covered in blood.

"Dr. Shine, it's okay!" Larraine hollered at her. "Put down your gun."

Susannah raised her eyes from the pathway. The red-clad woman moaned, turning toward Susannah, hands now high in the air.

Susannah gasped.

Miss Shirleen Carter did indeed freeze, hands as red as the candy canes that surrounded her. "Albert's dead."

CHAPTER FOUR

Susannah lowered her weapon and shoved it back into her purse. In two long strides, she was face to face with the tear-stained cheeks of Miss Shirleen.

"Are you sure he's dead?" Susannah asked.

Shirleen shook her head as she wept. "I don't know," she hiccupped. "I tried to see if he was breathing, but there was so much blood. The smell was awful. I took off runnin'."

Larraine stared at the blood on her friend's hand and then at the metal snowflake on the path, and swayed slightly. Susannah steadied her.

"What is this thing?" Susannah nodded at the snowflake. Its pointed, knifelike edges were covered in blood. "And what were you doing with it?"

"It appears to be a Christmas stocking holder," Larraine said mechanically.

Susannah squinted. The snowflake had a hook jutting from its rectangular base for hanging the stocking.

When not covered with blood and gore, it was something you would find quaint, not menacing.

"I don't know," Miss Shirleen blubbered. "I don't even remember picking it up."

"Was anyone else home?" Susannah asked.

Miss Shirleen shrugged.

"You two stay here." Susannah strode to the porch and paused. The innocence of *Babes In Toyland* was gone; instead, she felt she was entering *The Nightmare Before Christmas*. The wooden soldier banners swayed in the light breeze, their mustachioed faces now ominous.

"I'm calling 911," Larraine said.

Susannah stepped inside the house. A hole in the plaster where the doorknob had slammed into the wall testified to how terrified Miss Shirleen had been as she made her escape. Drops of blood speckled the entryway. Thrusting her hand into her purse, Susannah again removed the pistol, and she stood for a moment, listening.

Susannah had to make sure Albert was dead, and not just injured, but she didn't want any more surprises. Her training as a law enforcement officer with the New York City Transit Patrol came back to her, and she scanned the hallway and the staircase, then glanced into the kitchen before entering the living room.

A man she assumed was Albert Calloway lay sprawled on the white carpet in front of the fireplace, one foot on top of an old-fashioned wooden fire engine. Susannah dropped her Glock into her purse, then bent to feel for a pulse at his neck. There was none.

"Is he...?" Larraine had crept into the house without Susannah hearing.

"Yes." Backing up toward Larraine, Susannah grabbed her phone, fumbling to get the video engaged.

"What is all this?" Larraine whispered.

Susannah glanced at Larraine, who was staring at the ten-foot Fraser fir surrounded by potted poinsettias. She focused the phone and panned it to take in the whole room. Against the white walls and off-white furniture, the shiny cellophane coverings of the pots and the bright, perky leaves were a veritable riot of red. "Looks like he's the vandal."

"I reckon." Larraine's voice was muted, and Susannah went to her side. Her complexion was positively ghostly, probably from the shock of seeing Albert. She murmured, "This is the exact decoration scheme we had in mind."

"Who had in mind?"

Larraine glanced at Susannah, eyes moist. "The decorating committee at the church. We wanted a glittery-gold theme for the tree in the fellowship hall, surrounded by red poinsettias." She pointed to Albert's tree. Susannah raised her phone to record what she observed: Gold-toned Christmas balls twinkled with an iridescent shine. A wide gold ribbon was interwoven among the branches. Nestled in the topmost branches, an angel in golden skirts with her wings unfurled looked down upon the scene, harp in hand. "It's exactly the same, down to the angel with the harp."

A siren grew louder as it neared the house. "Let's get out of here before Randy shows up." Susannah wanted to avoid seeing the police chief.

"Amen to that." Larraine shivered as Susannah guided her through the hall.

At the doorway, Susannah paused and took Larraine's hand. "We're too late."

In the driveway, Miss Shirleen leaned against a car, which Susannah now realized belonged not to Albert but to Miss Shirleen. She held one hand against her chest; the other pointed the way to the front door. Next to her, Detective Varina Withers stood scowling. Her eyes met Susannah's and opened wide before they narrowed down into angry slits.

CHAPTER FIVE

"Dr. Susannah Shine." Detective Withers trotted down the candy cane pathway toward Susannah. Her kinky blond hair fell loose across the shoulders of her navy windbreaker. "Why am I not surprised?"

The detective shifted her gaze to Larraine, and Susannah felt her office manager's hand tremble as the detective assessed them from head to toe and then scanned the front of the house and doorway. Her eyes lingered for a second on the nutcracker soldiers before she glanced back at Susannah. She jerked her head over her shoulder, which Susannah took to mean, *Get out of my way*.

Susannah and Larraine sidestepped onto the brick porch as the detective paused and removed her weapon. Larraine leaned away from the woman, then hurried down the path. Susannah raised her hands in a *Who, me?* gesture and followed Larraine.

"Y'all come over here." Miss Shirleen motioned to them.

As the blare of sirens grew louder, Susannah glanced across the street where someone peered out from between the slats of the mini blinds. Just then, blue lights strobed from down the block as two Peach Grove PD patrol cars sped closer. As they flew past, a man in blue jeans walking his dog did an about-face, yanking on the leash to get his dog to change direction.

One patrol car swerved to the curb. The other skidded into the driveway behind Detective Withers's sedan, and Police Chief Randy Laughton vaulted out of the passenger side and scrambled up the walkway, uprooting plastic candy canes as he ran.

Detective Withers emerged onto the porch and held up her hand. Randy slowed as she pointed to the snowflake stocking-holder on the walkway. "Watch the evidence."

Randy stopped and peered at his shoes. He stiffened and retreated to his patrol car. As the detective circled the bloody implement and snapped pictures at various angles with her smartphone, Randy removed yellow crime-scene tape from the trunk and hurried back down the path. The detective pocketed her phone and glared at Susannah. Without looking back at Randy, she said, "When you're done here, secure the premises. Do not let any of those women inside."

Chief Laughton nodded. With an angry stare at Susannah, he handed off the yellow tape to his junior officer, then entered the house with the detective.

Keith Cawthorn, who had hung back as Randy and

Detective Withers took charge, now approached the women, one hand on his utility belt. "Miss Larraine. Miss Shirleen. Dr. Shine."

Susannah pulled her gaze from the house. At six-foot-five, Keith towered over Susannah, and Miss Shirleen looked positively petite next to him.

"Are y'all okay?" Keith motioned to Miss Shirleen, whose hands and wrists were coated with reddish-brown stains, then to Susannah, who had a smattering of stains on her fingertips.

Miss Shirleen sniffed, her light blue eyes dull, and mumbled something unintelligible.

Susannah nodded. "I checked Albert's pulse."

Keith drew his brows together in an expression that clearly said, *Tell it to the detective.*

"Officer Cawthorn. Allow me," Detective Withers interrupted. Keith stepped aside as she withdrew a neatly folded white handkerchief from her pocket and handed it to Miss Shirleen. She addressed Miss Shirleen, "Did you find the victim?"

Miss Shirleen nodded, took the handkerchief, and rubbed at her fingers and nails. Behind the detective, Randy cut across candy cane lane, his lumbering gait uprooting another plastic candy cane, which he dragged into the driveway.

"Gentlemen," the detective began, "let's get their statements sorted out. I'll start with..." Her voice trailed off.

"Miss Shirleen Carter," Larraine offered.

"Very well. Randy, will you please take a statement

from the doctor?" Randy nodded to the detective. "Keith, you talk to Miss Moore."

Keith put his hand on Larraine's shoulder and guided her down the driveway toward his cruiser.

Randy's steel-gray eyes bored into Susannah's. She had known Randy for many years; he was a consultant to the Peach Grove Business Association, and at one time she had considered him a friend.

"Dr. Shine." Randy nodded. "Come this way."

Susannah could see his jaw muscles working, never a good sign. In the past, there had been some antagonism over her office cat, Rusty, setting off the burglar alarm, but over the last year, a spate of sudden deaths had thrust Susannah into the limelight of a police investigation too many times. With her past training as a police officer in one of the largest police forces on the planet, Susannah had never asked for special treatment, but she expected a modicum of respect from Randy. She didn't get either.

Susannah followed as he pushed past his cruiser, stopping a few paces down the sidewalk in front of the house next door. A *For Sale* sign was posted on the lawn, and Susannah wondered if that were the reason no one had come out of the house to rubberneck, like the dog walker who now stood at the bottom of Albert's driveway staring openly, oblivious to his dog lifting his leg and peeing on a plastic candy cane.

Before Randy could ask her anything, a brownish-silver Yukon SUV with a Christmas wreath strapped to its grille careened down the block.

It swerved wildly, heading right toward them.

CHAPTER SIX

Randy grabbed Susannah by the shoulder and pulled her off the sidewalk and onto the lawn. The driver of the Yukon hit the brakes, continued on the wrong side of the road, and angled the car up to the curb, scraping the tires against the concrete with a squeal. The vehicle bucked as it stopped, coming to rest so close to Randy's patrol car that a plastic candy cane would barely fit between the two.

Randy stepped forward, hands outstretched. "Hold it."

A blond woman threw open the driver's door and sprinted past him so fast he was left grasping at the wisps of tinsel that hung from her Christmas sweater. Up the lawn and onto the driveway she ran, with the police chief a step behind. When she squeezed her hefty frame between the detective's and Miss Shirleen's cars, Susannah wasn't sure she saw her feet touch the ground. The woman threw herself in front of the detective and engulfed Miss Shirleen in a hug.

"Mama," she huffed. "What happened? Are you okay?" The woman bore an undeniable resemblance to Shirleen Carter.

"Charleen." Miss Shirleen was clearly flustered.

Susannah realized the woman was Charleen Barnes, wife of Pastor Ron of the Peach Grove Baptist Church.

Miss Shirleen wiggled loose of her daughter's grasp. "I declare."

As Randy shuffled between the cars, he reached out for Charleen but whacked his shinbone so hard Susannah heard it from where she stood on the grass. The bump stopped him cold, and Detective Withers reached the woman first.

"Ma'am." The detective curled her fingers around Charleen's arm. "Step back, ma'am. You can't be here."

Charleen disengaged from her mother and spun on the detective. "I don't see why not. Albert works for me." Charleen blushed. "Well, he works for my husband. For the church."

The detective pursed her lips before she asked, "What are you doing here?"

Charlene waved at the house across the street where the mini blinds again fell into place. "Harriet Goolsby called me. She saw Mama go into Albert's house. Then she saw Mama run out." Charleen paused and turned toward Miss Shirleen. Her hands flew up to her mouth and she gasped. "Mama! How did you get that blood on you? Are you hurt?"

"Your mama is fine," Randy said, reaching Charleen and gently prodding her shoulder, turning her away from her mother and the detective.

Charleen wriggled her shoulders, dislodging a small red Christmas ball from her sweater. It bounced down the driveway and became wedged between the grass and the first plastic candy cane. Randy's thick hand remained firmly on her shoulder, and she was forced to change directions. Spotting Larraine on the sidewalk with Keith Cawthorn, Charleen called, "Miss Larraine? What happened? Is someone going to tell me what—"

Randy interrupted. "Our investigation is ongoing. We don't have any information right yet." He led her down the driveway.

Susannah followed discreetly behind, suddenly curious about the pastor's wife. Susannah had never realized that she was Miss Shirleen's daughter. What were the chances that the woman across the street only today happened to notice who came and went from the financial secretary's home? Susannah bit her lip. Did Charleen use the woman to spy on her employee? What reason could she have for that? Susannah paused, then pulled out her phone and pretended to read.

At the Yukon, Randy glanced at Charleen's parking job and shook his head, then opened the door. Leaning his elbow on the door, he faced Charleen. "Now Mrs. Barnes, I appreciate you were upset, and I'm not gonna give you a ticket for parking on the wrong side of the road, but you have to leave."

At the mention of a ticket, Charleen's voice went up an octave. "A ticket!"

Susannah saw the back of Randy's neck redden as he asked her, "Who was it that called you?"

"Harriet Goolsby." She nodded her head at the house across the street, and this time the mini blinds didn't budge. "She doesn't get out much since Herbert died. She never learned to drive, bless her heart." Charleen put her hand up to her mouth so Harriet Goolsby couldn't read her lips and stage-whispered, "I reckon she has nothin' better to do than to sit at the window and watch the world go by."

"Uh-huh," Randy said.

Larraine, now finished speaking to Keith, joined Susannah on the lawn. They watched in silence as Randy nudged Charleen into the driver's seat. Larraine elbowed Susannah and tapped her watch.

"Tell Pastor Ron, 'Hey,'" Randy said, pushing the door closed with his palm.

Charleen nodded and reversed the Yukon, her left front tire scraping against the curb.

Susannah, hoping Randy would be busy interviewing Harriet Goolsby, took Larraine's hand and quietly walked toward her Marquis. Before she could open the car door, she felt a tap on her shoulder.

"Not so fast, Doctor." Detective Withers smiled. "I don't believe the chief is finished with you."

"I have to get back to the office." Susannah tried to sound reasonable. "Can't I make my statement later?"

"I'll tell you what we can do." The detective looked pleased with herself. Her lip curled as her soft Louisiana drawl took over. “Mrs. Moore here can go back to your office and let your patients know that you are going to be late, while you and I have a chat. Then, when we are done speaking, I will personally carry you to your office.”

Susannah smiled sheepishly and stepped away from Larraine’s car.

CHAPTER SEVEN

True to her word, Detective Withers pulled her Ford Taurus into the back lot of Peach Grove Chiropractic and dropped Susannah off, only thirty minutes behind schedule. Susannah muttered her thanks and dashed across the gravel lot for the back door. By text message, Larraine had assured Susannah that she had rescheduled her first couple of afternoon patients, but Susannah was anxious to get inside nonetheless. She was in the kitchen, slurping at a bottle of water, when Tina found her.

"Dr. Shine, not to worry." Tina smiled, one hand resting on her pregnant belly. "Miss Larraine pushed your patients back so you have a few minutes to collect yourself."

Susannah bit a chunk out of a gluten-free protein bar and chewed for a moment before answering Tina. "Thank goodness for Larraine." She leaned out of the kitchen and peered down the hall. “How is she? Is she very upset?”

“Why?” Tina took a step out of the kitchen, her black scrub pants contrasting with the festive penguin and holly decor of her top. She glanced down the hall. “She did look a mite paler than usual.”

Susannah frowned and sipped at the water.

“She didn’t tell me what happened, only that it was something terrible, and I should ask Keith.” Tina turned her dark heart-shaped face to Susannah, her black eyes large, questioning. “What happened? Did Miss Shirleen burn a batch of cookies?”

Susannah inhaled sharply, and water slid down the wrong way. She sputtered and coughed. Water dribbled down her blouse.

Tina patted her back.

“She didn’t tell you?” asked Susannah.

Tina shook her head. “No.”

Susannah pulled her out of the kitchen and down the hall, into her private office. “Then, what is she telling patients?”

“I heard her say that you had a family emergency. I thought Caden got sick, and you had to pick him up at school.”

Susannah’s sister, Angela Rossi, and Angela’s eight-year-old son, Caden, lived with Susannah. She frowned. As far as she knew, Caden was perfectly fine, along with Angie and any other members of the Shine clan. It wasn’t like Larraine to tell a lie, not even what other people would consider a white lie.

“What really happened, Dr. Shine?”

Susannah closed the door to her office and approached the fish tank where Henry the Eighth swam, content in his ignorance of the world outside his tank. She watched him for a moment, then turned to Tina and motioned to the chair across from her desk. "You better sit down."

Susannah cleared her throat and took a sip of water before she rehashed the story of the canceled poinsettia order. Tina nodded along as Susannah explained what the florist had said, and how Larraine wanted to see if she could catch Albert, the financial secretary, at his home. "That's where it all went south," Susannah muttered.

"How so?"

Susannah watched Tina's expression fall as she detailed how they had pulled up to his house to find Miss Shirleen fleeing with a bloody iron snowflake in her hand. Tina's hands left her belly and flew up to her face. "That's just awful. What did Miss Shirleen say?"

"She didn't say anything at all." Susannah exhaled, then glanced at the protein bar she had dropped on the desk. "We didn't have any time to talk to her before Detective Withers showed up."

Tina looked like she was going to cry. She was fond of Miss Shirleen and her baked treats, but Susannah thought it was her gift of a hand-crocheted baby blanket that caused Tina to tear up.

"We barely had time to get out ourselves."

Tina shot up in her chair. "Y'all what?"

The intercom buzzed and interrupted their conversation. Larraine's voice sounded strained as she asked, "Is Tina with you?"

"She is."

"Tell her to get her tail out here, we're ready to go."

Susannah took a last bite of her protein bar and rolled her eyes at Tina.

"Dr. Shine, you're a mess." Tina stood. "You never said how Miss Shirleen is doing with all this."

"I'm gonna guess, not very well."

"What do you mean?"

"It means that while the detective was still questioning me, Randy put Miss Shirleen in his patrol car and took her away."

CHAPTER EIGHT

As deep as her complexion was, Tina paled. "Do you think Miss Larraine knows?"

"I don't think so." Susannah moved to the fish tank and shook a few flakes out for Henry the Eighth, her lips pursed until they almost puckered. "But it might depend on how well she knows Harriet Goolsby."

"Harriet Goolsby?"

"She's the woman who lives across the street from Albert. She seems to keep tabs on him, or, er, his house. She called Miss Shirleen's daughter to let her know that Miss Shirleen was there. I don't know if she saw Randy arrest Miss Shirleen."

A *blam* sounded in the hallway.

Susannah spilled a pile of fish-food flakes into Henry the Eighth's tank. She spun and saw Larraine in the doorway, one hand at her throat, a pile of files at her feet. Tina hurried to Larraine, holding her belly.

"Lord have mercy," Larraine said. "Did I hear you right? Randy arrested Shirleen?"

Tina picked up the files and escorted the office manager to the chair she had just vacated.

"That's how it looked to me."

Larraine's eyes welled up. At sixty-four years old, tall and fair, Larraine was the picture of good health, but Susannah worried about her. Her light blue eyes had lost their usual luster. Tina stood behind the chair and placed her hand on the older woman's shoulder. Susannah couldn't bear to watch.

"Let me get you some water." Susannah rushed out of the room and returned quickly, twisting the cap off a bottle of Dasani. Handing it to Larraine, she saw the fear in her eyes.

"Thank you." Larraine sipped at the water, then tugged on the collar of her cardigan. The cheery green trees that just a few hours ago had added to the holiday spirit now cast a pall of ill health over Larraine's complexion.

"Miss Larraine, you don't think—"

"Absolutely not," Larraine interrupted Tina. Pressing her lips firmly together, she looked down and shook her head. "Shirleen Carter is my oldest and dearest friend. She just is not capable of something like this."

Tina stared at Susannah over Larraine's shoulder, exhaling through her nose. "I can't wait. I'ma call Keith right quick."

"Make it fast." Susannah flicked her eyes after Tina as she wobbled out of the office. Nudging the water bottle toward Larraine's lips, Susannah furrowed her brow. "Drink."

Larraine's hands trembled as she brought the bottle up.

"Good." Susannah moved around the desk and pulled her phone out of her purse. "Why don't you take the afternoon off?"

Larraine stood. Though the water bottle bobbled as she rose, her complexion no longer had a greenish sheen. "I'd rather stay. I want to keep busy."

Susannah nodded. "Tina is calling Keith, and I'll call Bitsy." Everyone knew that Bitsy had cousins all over the county, including at the Peach Grove Police Department.

"You don't have to call her," Larraine said. "She's coming in with Roman in a little while."

Roman Broady, one of the clinic's on-again, off-again chiropractic patients, was dating Bitsy. Roman was retired military and had just opened his own security firm. Between Roman and Bitsy, Susannah knew there would be plenty of information to go over.

"Well then." Susannah put her phone down. "I guess we'll have some answers pretty soon. You'll see—Miss Shirleen is going to be fine."

It was close to six when Roman strode through the front door and checked in for his adjustment. Larraine viewed him over her readers as Tina came around the counter to escort him to the treatment room.

"Where's Miss Bitsy?" Tina asked, searching the waiting room for her. "I thought she was coming with you."

Susannah met them in the hall, craning her neck to see into the waiting room. "I thought Bitsy was coming with you."

Roman lifted his hands palms up as they walked toward the treatment room. "I am not my girlfriend's keeper." Roman's deep voice and relaxed way of speaking always put Susannah in mind of James Earl Jones with a touch of Sam Elliot. "She was here, but when I tried to park, she told me she had to get food for the meetin'. Then she grabbed my keys, pushed me out of my own truck, and took off down the road."

"She did?" Susannah lifted her brows and glanced at Tina, who gave her a tiny shrug and then turned and retreated down the hall.

Roman smiled, shook his head, then winced. "Ow, my neck. Hurts to turn. Or laugh." Roman spoke in a clipped manner, sometimes hacking the ending off words. Hurts became *hurh*, or sometimes became *hah*. Susannah nodded as he rubbed his trapezius muscle with long, slender fingers. "When you have a girlfriend who is a hot mess, you find yourself doing both. A lot."

"I understand your pain," Susannah said, observing his posture and movement as he hung his black hoodie on a hook. "In more ways than one."

Roman turned back to her. "Do y'all know what Bitsy's up to? Looked to me like she had something on her mind, but she wouldn't say what."

"It might have something to do with what happened this afternoon." Susannah motioned to Roman to lie down on the adjusting table. "But let's get you adjusted. If she went to get food, I think she's planning on a long sit-down about it."

Roman complied, and Susannah palpated his neck. Then she placed one hand on the right side of his spine and stretched his head gently to the left with the other. "Breathe," she told him as she thrust down, causing a series of resounding pops.

"Lordy, lordy," Roman said, turning his head first to the left and then to the right. "Most of the stiffness is gone. I really needed that."

"Good." Susannah helped him up and motioned him to follow her into the therapy room. In the hall, Susannah spied Larraine behind the front desk. Typically always in motion, she stood staring at nothing, her hands at her sides.

Tina appeared at Susannah's side. "I'll help Mr. Roman get on the traction table." She cut her eyes toward the front desk, and Susannah took that as her cue to change direction toward Larraine.

Halfway down the hall, a loud banging filled the office.

CHAPTER NINE

Larraine looked up curiously.

"You okay?" Susannah peered at her office manager. "Why don't you go home early? Tina and I can finish up."

"I just may do that."

Blam, blam.

Tina came behind the front desk. "What is that noise?"

Susannah reached the window and pushed the window treatment aside. A black Range Rover Sport was idling outside the entrance; Roman Broady had recently purchased the gently used Sport for his business. The noise came again, and this time Susannah recognized it as a thump on the door. She pulled it open to find Bitsy with her hands clutching three different takeout bags, and her chin perched atop a tray of paper cups.

"Don't nobody leave," Bitsy said, shooting a glance to Larraine as she crossed the waiting room and trotted down the hall. "I got us a fast-food feast."

Susannah glanced at the Range Rover that Bitsy had left with the passenger door open.

Roman appeared in the hall with a chuckle. "That my chill girl makin' all this noise?"

"Uh," Susannah said, as the ex-Marine squinted, noticing his SUV outside. "It is."

"Just like Bitsy to leave my baby unattended," he said as he cut across the waiting room to where Susannah stood with her hand still on the door. He quirked a brow. There was a sparkle in his eye that told Susannah he enjoyed Bitsy's eccentricities just as much as she did. "Eh, Doc?"

Susannah nodded and closed the door, stepping into the waiting room and then coming to a dead stop as Bitsy careened past. "That was fast."

"Tina helped me get the food into the break room so's I could get Roman's car parked right quick."

"Why didn't you just drive around back?" Susannah waved her hand before Bitsy could answer. "Never mind. I know. Poltergeist."

"Whenever you get that back parking lot exorcised, I'll use it again."

Susannah shook her head.

"And I been doing a smidge of research." Bitsy smiled. Dark freckles stood out on her rich brown skin and trailed across her cheeks and nose. "I found out that Catholics are all up on the whole exorcism thing."

It was Susannah's turn to chuckle. "What did you use for research? The movie?"

"And what if I did? Some movies are historically accurate, you know." Bitsy moved to the window and pushed the curtain aside. "That's your tribe, right? Rosaries, ancient artifacts, and all that."

Susannah was forced to agree, but it was technically more her mother's tribe. The woman wore her rosary out. "Sure, sure. I'll look in the parish directory."

Bitsy sidled past Susannah and opened the door as Roman re-entered carrying a tray.

"You left this." Roman held a red metal tray covered with plastic wrap. The tips of plastic utensils poked out from under the wrap.

"You're a genius." Bitsy gave Roman a peck on the cheek and took the tray, then shut the door with her foot. Bitsy's contributions to their non-sanctioned investigations were not just food related. With a sharp mind and keen wit, it also helped Susannah's sleuthing that Bitsy's cousin Little Junior was an ear on what happened at the Peach Grove PD.

"Miss Larraine." Bitsy approached the front desk where Larraine had just picked up the phone. Larraine tugged the chain to her readers between her fingers as Bitsy said, "You put that receiver down. I got all the information you need right here."

Larraine returned the receiver to the cradle and lifted her brow. Tina was right; usually pale as baby powder, Larraine's skin was positively translucent, a blue vein prominent at her temple. "I can't stay. Charles is expecting me directly."

Bitsy stopped and lifted the tray. "You can bring him one of my hot chocolate stirring spoons. It's a brand-new recipe I found on Pinterest. You can use them for hot cocoa or coffee."

"A recipe for spoons?" A tiny smile raised the corners of Larraine's mouth. "This I have to see."

Bitsy smiled and made two quick clucks with the side of her mouth, as if she were calling a horse. Only when Bitsy did it, it sounded encouraging and fun. Larraine gave a soft chuckle and tailed Bitsy down the hall, listening to her describe dipping plastic spoons in melted chocolate. Susannah gave a side eye to Roman and repeated the clucking sound, jerking her head in the direction of the break room. "Let's go."

In the break room, Larraine grabbed the chair closest to the back door and surveyed the bags with a frown. Bitsy stood beside her and quickly unpacked while Tina set out plates and napkins. Soon the table was filled with wrapped and boxed items. Bitsy pointed with two fingers. "We got tacos and nachos, chicken and biscuits, and burgers and fries." She frowned at one of the scoop-shaped french fry holders whose contents had obviously been disturbed.

"I sense a disturbance in the Force." Susannah gave a short snort and pointed to the cardboard container.

"If by disturbed you mean half-eaten," Roman deadpanned, hands on his hips. "I sense it, too."

"Alright, I snitched a few fries," Bitsy said, waving her fingers. "Don't give it no nevermind."

"Oh, I mind." Roman reached out and picked up

the container and handed it to Bitsy. "Those're yours, bae."

At the sound of the endearment, Tina glanced up, teary-eyed. "You so cute." She wiped her eyes with the back of her knuckle as she left the room, returning momentarily with the swivel chair from her desk, which she rolled to the head of the table next to Bitsy.

Bitsy gave Tina a quick hug. "You cute too." She slid the chair out of Tina's hand and stationed it next to hers. "But not as cute as my man." She patted the chair, and in one step Roman was beside her and they both sat.

Tina laughed. "Well, that shows me."

"*Mangia*, everybody," Susannah said. "Let's get down to business."

"That's Noo Yawk Italian for 'eat,'" Bitsy explained to Roman, then pointed at Tina with a handful of french fries. "Sit."

There was a hurried hubbub of arms and shoulders as the women chose their meals. Roman quirked an eyebrow and joined in.

"Okay," Susannah said, biting into a hard-shell taco and catching shreds of tortilla and cheese as it crumbled. "Bitsy, you start."

Bitsy shook her head with a deer-in-the-headlights look and mumbled. "Oo goo." Which Susannah took to mean, *You go*. She swallowed. "Start at the beginning."

"Larraine wants to get home," Susannah looked at Larraine, who was picking at a biscuit. "I can fill you two in after."

"'Kay." Bitsy picked up her cup and slurped at her soda, gazing at Larraine over the plastic top. "Er..."

"You can say it." Larraine sniffed. "Dr. Shine already mentioned that Randy took Shirleen in."

"Well, they've arrested her for killing Mr. Albert," Bitsy said. "They found her fingerprints all over the murder weapon."

Larraine paled. "You mean the Christmas stocking thingy?"

"Christmas stocking?" Roman asked. "Was he strangled?"

"He was smashed with a snowflake." Bitsy took an extra-large bite of her burger and looked up. "'At's what Little Junior said."

"Wait, what?" Roman looked confused.

"A snowflake-shaped Christmas stocking holder. One of those heavy iron pieces you put on the mantelpiece," Susannah explained, shuddering as she remembered the blood on it and Albert. "Someone hit him in the head with it."

"Shirleen told me she found Albert like that. When she got there, he was already on the floor, bleeding. She only picked it up because it was in the way." Larraine folded her arms and swallowed, though she hadn't eaten a thing. "Just 'cause your fingerprints are on something, that doesn't mean you're a killer."

"Apparently Randy thinks it does. Just be grateful this one is still walking around." Bitsy tipped her cup toward Susannah. "Detective Wisters is chompin' at the bit to arrest you, too."

"It's Withers," Larraine and Tina said simultaneously.

Susannah felt the blood drain from her face.

"You're lucky Miss Larraine could vouch for you," Tina added.

Larraine grunted. "Well, I never."

"Yes, you did, Miss Larraine," Tina piped up. "We've been through this before with those two. Haven't we?"

Susannah and Bitsy nodded, remembering the times Susannah had been high on the detective's list of suspects in other investigations.

Larraine sat back, deflated, tugging at her sweater. "Why in heaven's name does that woman hold a grudge against you?"

"She doesn't like alternative treatments is what I heard. Thinks they do more harm than good," Bitsy offered, leaning in and lowering her voice. "I heard her mother ran away with an osteopath, and she never got over it."

"I heard it was her father," Tina said. "He had an affair with an audiologist."

"Ladies," Susannah said, "can we get back on track?"

Bitsy gave Tina an almost imperceptible nod and Tina returned it, then stared at her plate, apparently refusing some kind of a challenge. Bitsy stared at Susannah with innocent eyes and then slunk low in her chair and kicked her under the table.

"What?" Susannah put her taco down.

Larraine straightened, her eyes on Bitsy. "She wants you to ask me if I think Shirleen did it."

There was silence for a beat. Roman leaned forward and asked, "Do you?"

"No." Larraine's mouth formed a thin line as she pulled her biscuit apart. She looked around the table and sighed. "But it won't look good for Shirleen if it gets out that she and Albert had a fling back in the day."

CHAPTER TEN

"Say what?" Bitsy blurted.

"Mind you, I'm not certain." Larraine snatched a biscuit from the middle of the table and picked at it. "And I don't want anyone here mentioning it. At least not until I can speak to Shirleen."

"Miss Larraine," Tina asked softly, "do you think hiding that kind of relationship is even possible?"

Roman shook his head. "Probably not."

"*Tsk.*" The noise Larraine emitted was short and sharp. She raised her chin. "When did *he* become part of the Ladies' Crime-Solving Club?"

"I swore him in this afternoon," Bitsy said.

Tina giggled.

Larraine dropped her shoulders. There was more than a little pink in her cheeks when she mumbled, "Sorry."

"Maybe I overstepped my bounds," Roman apologized. "But you know, secrets have a way of coming out when something like this happens."

"He's right." Susannah sat back and mirrored Larraine's folded arms. "We can keep it between us for now."

"Yeah, on the down low," Bitsy said, lifting the plastic wrap on the tray of chocolate-covered plastic spoons and popping one in her mouth.

"It's not common knowledge," Larraine said, "and I don't think it has any bearing on what happened today."

"Why not?"

"Albert left town after—"

"—they finished baking their cookies?" Bitsy grinned, pointing at Larraine with the plastic spoon.

"Uh," Larraine squinted at Bitsy. "Sure. You could say that. Then Shirleen married someone else, and I never heard her speak of Albert again."

"Until he came back to town," Susannah said.

"Even then she didn't talk about him. He's been with the church for years and this is the first time we've had anything to do with him. Someone else did this."

"Someone who was very angry," Susannah said.

"Why do you think that?" Tina asked.

"You don't plan a murder using a Christmas stocking hanger as a weapon." Susannah paused. "I mean, it was someone he let into his house. Someone he must have trusted. He let them into his family room with all those poinsettias he probably stole. He must have felt comfortable that they wouldn't care where he got them from."

"Lord knows, he wasn't well liked," said Larraine.

"Did you know him well, Miss Larraine?" Tina asked.

"I didn't, but plenty of other people did. He had final say on all financial matters, including salaries and benefits. It never affected me, but people gossip. From what I heard, Albert could be petty and selfish. Like stealing those design ideas."

"What ideas d'ya mean?" Bitsy, who had finished sucking the chocolate off the spoon, was now busy piling some of Roman's fries on a biscuit and drenching them with ketchup.

"The design ideas for the church Fellowship Hall," Tina replied, pushing her chair back and heading toward the kitchen. She glanced at Susannah. "Right?"

"Yes," Susannah answered. "Apparently he refused to approve the orders for the flowers and decorations, and then used the exact decoration scheme in his house."

Tina returned from the kitchen, sipping at a bottle of water. "But how would that affect anyone else?"

Larraine huffed, her nostrils flaring. Susannah had rarely seen her so annoyed. "First off, he stole the design ideas from Emma Lee Satterfield. She's a sweet young woman who just graduated from design school."

Bitsy, who herself had graduated from the Savannah College of Art and Design, started to say something; she reached for her cup and shoved the straw into her mouth in a vain effort to clear her palate of the carbohydrate bomb.

Tina giggled. "Miss Bitsy, don't try to talk."

Larraine continued, "She's building a website and presence on social media. She wants to be an Instant-gram influencer."

Susannah nudged Larraine. "Insta-gram."

"Oh." Larraine was too annoyed to blush. "Insta-gram. At any rate, she was going to take pictures of the Fellowship Hall and put them on her website and Instagram. Social media is important to businesspeople. Her idea is less than half done. He took that away from her."

Bitsy had sufficiently cleared her mouth so that she too could make *tsk, tsk* sounds.

"And that's to say nothing of Shannon Ellis, the florist." Larraine brought her fist down on the table with a thump. Going over all these details was upsetting Larraine, not helping her. Perhaps Susannah should have insisted that she go home early. "He stole from her and vandalized her shop and displays."

Tina got up and made her way around the table; she put her arms around Larraine's shoulders and gave her a hug. Larraine clasped Tina's hand, and a single tear slid down her cheek.

"Mr. Calloway did that?" Bitsy said.

"From what we could see." Susannah nodded. "We had already spoken to Shannon and found out that someone had stolen poinsettia plants from her shop and broken her displays. Well, Albert Calloway's home was wall-to-wall poinsettias."

"Couldn't he have gotten them somewhere else?" Tina asked.

Larraine lifted one shoulder in a halfhearted shrug. "I expect."

"More importantly"—Roman pointed at Larraine with a french fry, and Susannah held back a chuckle because of how much he reminded her of Bitsy—"why would anyone want to kill him for that?"

Larraine sighed and spread her hands flat on the table. "Y'all know I don't abide gossip, but over the years I've heard some very disturbing things about Albert. Of course I didn't give them much attention, but maybe there was some truth to the stories."

"What kind of stories?" Tina stepped out from behind Larraine's chair to look at her.

"Well, there was a rumor that he let someone's health insurance policy lapse on purpose when they were in cancer treatment. Naturally he claimed it was an oversight, and at the time, I thought that was probably the case."

"That's cold," Bitsy said.

"I know," Larraine murmured, staring at her hands. "There were other things like that. And one time, I overheard a conversation between two women." She glanced around the table and bowed her head. "I've always felt awful about this. I didn't mean to eavesdrop. I was in the supply room in the kitchen, and they were in the entryway by the doors. They couldn't see me and I couldn't see them and I didn't recognize the voices. One of them said a man had forced himself on her. I thought she said Albert's name, but I couldn't be sure. I couldn't hear clearly."

"Oooh eee," Roman said, adding a whistle.

"I should have said something to someone."

"How could you, Miss Larraine?" Tina crouched down to eye level with her friend. "You didn't have much to go on."

"Tina's right," Susannah said. "You couldn't accuse someone without being sure you heard correctly. If you knew who was speaking, you might have been able to help."

"Even so," Roman added, "she might have denied it. If the victim was confiding in this other person, there might have been a reason she didn't report him to the police herself."

"Roman Broady." Bitsy turned to him, all jest out of her voice. "What kind of macho double-talk is that?"

Roman wrapped a long arm around Bitsy's shoulder. "Listen, bae. The dynamics of abuse are complex. If Albert was as despicable as he seems, this woman might have been afraid for her job, or her children, or other family members her disclosure might have affected." He gave her a squeeze. "I'm not saying it's right. I'm just saying without even hearing the name properly, and not having the victim report the assault herself, what could Miss Larraine have done differently?"

There was silence around the table.

Susannah cleared her throat. "I agree with Roman. This guy sounds like a class-A rat. But, legally, you had no leg to stand on making any kind of accusation. Ethically, I understand why you feel bad about it."

"Spoken like a true subway patrolwoman," Bitsy said.

"I know whereof I speak." Susannah quirked a

brow at her friend. "Where do you think all the rats in New York City live?"

Bitsy gave her a smile and stuck her hand under the plastic wrap of the tray of chocolatized spoons. "I think my cousin Denise just moved into Albert's subdivision. I'm gonna chat her up about this. She might have some 411."

"So how do the purloined poinsettias fit into all this?" Susannah asked. "Was it just to mess with the decorating committee? Or did he have some other reason?"

"Maybe he still had feelings for Miss Shirleen," Tina offered.

"Hard feelings, I would say." Larraine shook her head. "A power trip, maybe? To make Shirleen come to him and ask for the money in person? If that was the reason, it worked."

"If he was doing that to her just for fun, what was he doing to other people?" Susannah asked, more to herself. No one replied. "If we're going to help Miss Shirleen, then we have to gather some information at the church."

"I don't think I'd be the best one for this job," Larraine said. Her position on the welcoming committee had put her in the position of meeting many parishioners, and Susannah had used her in the past to gather information. "Every time I think about poor Shirleen, I just tear up."

"You're probably right." Susannah glanced around the table. Tina and Keith attended the Methodist Church, and Bitsy was more of a spiritual person than a churchgoer. "Roman?" Susannah asked.

"Not me, but—"

"—Iris Duncan." Susannah finished for him.

Iris Duncan was a medical tech at Henry County Hospital. She had served in the Marines with Roman and helped him get his job at the hospital. Over the summer, at Larraine's invitation, Iris had attended a picnic at the Peach Grove Baptist Church and later became a member.

"But she's still a newcomer." Larraine stood and reached into her purse. "What am I thinking? It just shows you how rattled this whole thing has made me."

"What do you mean?" asked Susannah.

"Tomorrow night is the annual Christmas pageant. Y'all take my tickets." Larraine took the red tickets out of her purse, stared at them, then dropped them on the table. "Shirleen and I were fixin' to go."

Her face, which was already splotchy, pinked even further. Turning, she reached the back door and, before anyone could respond, slipped out. Tina reached for the door but Susannah stopped her. "Let me go. I'll just make sure she's okay to drive."

Bitsy piped up, "She forgot her chocolate spoon."

CHAPTER ELEVEN

When Susannah returned to the table, the takeout boxes and bags had been cleared except for one white paper bag, which Bitsy had torn open and was using as note paper. She looked up at Susannah with a plastic spoon hanging out of her mouth. Susannah raised her eyebrows.

"'Is onesh pepperment."

"I'm not going to ask," Susannah said.

"We putting together our plan, Dr. Shine," Tina said.

"I spoke to Iris," Roman said, pointing at his smartphone, which sat on the table. "She's got her own tickets to the Christmas pageant and she'll meet us there tomorrow night."

"Did she say anything else?"

"Just that she couldn't recollect Albert." Roman tapped his phone. "But she had good things to say about Miss Shirleen, especially the pumpkin chocolate chip cookies that she got in her welcome basket."

"Welcome basket?" Bitsy removed the plastic spoon from her mouth.

"Hush, you chocolate hound." Roman waved a calloused hand in front of her face. "We got work to do."

"I'm working." Bitsy pointed to the paper bag where she had written: *Albert, poinsettia poacher?* Under that, Iris's name was scribbled next to the words, *ticket* and *plus one?*

"Okaaaay," Susannah said looking back at Roman.

Roman said, "You're in luck, Dr. Shine. The pageant is sold out, but Iris has an extra ticket. She said you can have it. She'll text you." He indicated Bitsy with his thumb and dragged the tickets that Larraine had placed on the table to his place. "Me and Bits will take these 'uns."

"Excellent." Susannah sat. "Hopefully Iris has gotten to know a few people and we'll get a feel for who else might have wished Albert Calloway harm."

"And maybe someone can tell us a thing or two 'bout a thing or two." Bitsy wiggled her eyebrows at Tina, who giggled.

"You trippin', Miss Bitsy." Tina turned to Susannah. "That's an old southern way of saying we're lookin' for gossip."

"I got that." Susannah reached for the tray with the spoons. "Don't forget, we need information on Miss Shirleen and Albert and also about Olivia Franklin. We need to find out if the thefts and vandalism of True Blooms are related to the church or not."

Bitsy removed the spoon, the bowl of which still held remnants of dark chocolate and crushed candy cane, from her mouth. "That's easy. Most folks should know that you and me represent the Peach Grove Business Association. So it will be natural-like for us to ask questions." She paused. "But I don't think anyone will open a conversation with, '*Doesn't little Jason look precious dressed as a wise man, and by the way I nipped some poinsettias from the florist the other day.*'"

Susannah rolled her eyes, and Roman patted Bitsy's hand.

"That's where Iris can help. People will be more apt to open up with someone they're comfortable with." Susannah turned to Roman and asked, "Did Iris mention anything about the autopsy?" Iris worked in the medical examiner's office at the hospital.

"No, they're backlogged," Roman said. "I wouldn't expect any answers today. Maybe tomorrow."

"You know the drill," Susannah said to Tina. "See what kind of generic information you can get out of Keith. Next of kin, children. Things like that. And, Bitsy, find out from Shannon if she has any kind of cameras or surveillance equipment."

"I know she doesn't. Neither do I, but I'm thinking about getting one of those doorbell cameras."

"Miss Bitsy, can't Mr. Roman here set you up with some surveillance equipment?" Tina asked.

"I could, but my bae wants to be an independent businesswoman," he said.

"I do." Bitsy smiled at Roman, then rubbed her chin. "But that's not the whole reason. Roman is just setting up his business and I don't want to take away from his bottom line. Besides, in fifteen years in downtown Peach Grove, I've never had so much as a Halloween pumpkin go missing. I believe Shannon when she says someone has some kind of an axe to grind against her."

"I agree with you," Susannah said. "All the more reason for us to find out what's going on and who's doing it."

CHAPTER TWELVE

When Susannah arrived at Peachy Things, Andrea, Bitsy's niece, was leaving with Priscilla, Bitsy's pet pot-bellied pig. Priscilla snuffled up to Susannah, rubbing her snout on Susannah's slacks like a cat.

"She must smell Whippy," Andrea said.

"Probably." Whippy was Susannah's dog, so named by Bitsy for his love of whipped cream. He and Priscilla had fallen in love at first sight. "Where's your auntie?"

"She's in the back room getting ready for the Christmas pageant." Andrea had to restrain Priscilla, who was angling for the door. "She's trying to pick out the perfect Christmas sweater."

"That shouldn't be too hard," Susannah said.

"It's easy for her," Andrea said, as Priscilla strained at her harness. "It's a problem for Roman."

As if on cue, the curtain that separated the storeroom from the sales floor flew to the side, and Roman strode into view, shouting over his shoulder as he went: "That's not happening!"

"Come back, boo," Bitsy called.

"Oh." Roman stopped, looking at Andrea. "I thought you'd left."

"We're goin'," Andrea said, waving to Susannah. "Have fun at the Christmas pageant tonight. I'll be pig-sitting for Miss Priss."

The porker snorted, and Susannah shook her head, smiling. Bitsy and her niece had no shortage of nick-names for the hog. Before the door could fall shut, Bitsy appeared, stopping short to prevent herself from crashing into Roman. The Christmas holly motif cur-tain settled on her shoulder.

"Hey." Bitsy's voice rose and fell. "Why—" She fol-lowed Roman's gaze. "Oh, Susannah."

"Please don't say that." Susannah grinned, holding the smile, as an awkward silence grew between her friends. She backed toward the door. "Uh, maybe I'll come back."

"Don't leave on my account," Roman said.

"N-no," Susannah stuttered. "I meant to, uh, go talk to Shannon about some flowers for my Christmas table. See ya later."

Susannah waved at them through the display win-dow, pointing to True Blooms and making an exagger-ated grab for the door handle. She barely noticed the door chime as she entered the shop. The fragrant scent of flowers filled the air.

"Can I help you?" Conrad was behind the counter, watching Susannah curiously.

"Yes." Susannah straightened, feeling foolish. "I was thinking about ordering a display for my Christmas table."

Conrad raised a brow. "Did you have anything special in mind?"

"Well, not really," Susannah could feel her face flush. Talk about a lamebrained idea. They must be sold out of everything remotely Christmas-y at this late date. "It's a last-minute idea. I don't cook, so I have to set the beautiful table and I thought..."

"Yes?"

"Well, I guess I didn't really. Think, that is." She cut her eyes to Bitsy's shop and lowered her voice. "I really just stopped in to get away from an awkward situation next door."

Shannon poked her head out of the back room. "Is Bitsy still trying to get Roman to be the back end of a reindeer?"

"How's that?"

Conrad jerked his thumb at the wall. "They've been at it all afternoon."

"Really?"

Shannon nodded. "Roman won't agree to wear the couples sweaters Bitsy chose. The reindeer goes across both sweaters. She would get to wear the sweater with the face of the reindeer. He would be the rear end."

"Ouch," Susannah said. No wonder the man was mad. "Sounds outrageous, even for Bitsy."

"Girlfriend," Shannon said in a singsong voice, moving to the side of Conrad and putting her elbows on the counter and her chin in her hands, "you have no idea."

"Well, it must be love." Susannah shook her head.

"Must be." Shannon stood up. "Now, how can we help you?"

"I was wondering if you have anything for my Christmas table, but I'm afraid I don't really have a good idea of what I want."

"Let's start with size? A table display?" Shannon came around the counter, motioning toward a shelf that held different-sized vases. "Or a perhaps a vase?"

Susannah knew the center of the table would be laden with a huge platter of Angie's antipasto. The second course would be a big tray of pepperoni lasagna. "How about two smaller vases? One for either side of the table."

Susannah pointed out two simple glass vases, and Shannon stepped behind her and removed them. The woman was a few inches taller than Susannah's five-foot-ten frame and easily collected the vases off the top shelf. After reviewing the options for flowers, Susannah selected some fragrant lilies and roses. As Conrad processed her debit card, she said, "Angie's going to love this."

"Is Angie your partner?" Shannon asked.

Susannah laughed. "No. She's my sister. She and her son live with me."

Shannon nodded, pausing a moment as if debating something. "So, Bitsy tells me that you were there when they found the body of that man from the church."

"Yes. Albert Calloway."

Shannon gave a little shiver. "Terrible."

"As far as I'm concerned," Conrad said, handing Susannah her debit card, "it couldn't happen to a nicer guy."

"Conrad Jones," Shannon said slowly. "A man has been murdered."

"He wasn't a nice man, he was a bad man. A vile, unpleasant man."

Shannon looked puzzled. With her voice barely above a whisper, she said, "You didn't know him."

Conrad's mouth twisted. "I didn't have to."

Susannah thought he looked like he might break down and cry. She knew she should leave, but she was riveted.

"How can you defend him?" Conrad asked Shannon. "You've told me yourself we might not make this month's mortgage payment because of what he did."

"Now listen here," Shannon said. "We don't know for sure that he did anything."

Susannah cleared her throat. Shannon and Conrad stopped arguing and looked at her. "I might have some information that could clear things up."

"How?" Shannon asked.

"I, uh," Susannah said, pulling her phone out of her purse. "I took some video when I was in Albert's house."

"What?" Shannon asked softly.

"How is that going to help us?" Conrad said brusquely.

"Well, there were quite a few poinsettias in the house."

"I knew it." Conrad banged his forefinger against his breastbone. His black eyes deepened.

"But I don't know if they were yours. Is there a way you can tell?"

Shannon reached behind her to a small work platform and grasped a couple of thin, tapered pieces of white cardboard. "I special-ordered these."

On closer inspection, Susannah was looking at a small plant label, thick white plastic with a round head. In raised red lettering, it read: *Merry Christmas*. Along the tapered end, which would disappear into the soil, were the words *True Blooms*.

Susannah brought up the video and advanced it to where the plentiful poinsettias were in the middle of the screen, and then she enlarged. Shannon dipped her head toward the phone as Susannah zoomed even more. Peeking around the red foil of one of the pots, the plastic *Merry Christmas* label was evident.

"I told you," Conrad swore. "I told you. People like him are everywhere. They want to feel superior to people like you and me. And what do they do? Take our work and pass it off as their own."

Shannon opened her mouth to reply, then slowly closed it.

Susannah was surprised at how dead-on Conrad was about Albert. She stayed silent and continued staring at the image on her camera. Sitting against the leaves of a particularly large poinsettia, something red glittered. Susannah hadn't noticed it before. She pointed it out to Shannon. "Is this another kind of tag?"

Shannon tore her gaze from Conrad and glanced at the image. "No. That must be from his tree."

"I'm leaving." Conrad turned to go, but Shannon grabbed his wrist and he stopped.

"I'm sorry I talked you into coming here with me." Shannon said to him. "I knew it would be hard."

"I knew it would be hard too, but I didn't think it would be like this. These people don't know us. They haven't even given you a chance." He grasped her hands and brought them to his lips. His tone became softer. "You're really, really good at this. You're gifted."

Shannon met his gaze.

"So, if some guy wants to cancel orders and upset a lot of people, and maybe even steal our plants or ruin our business, I'll be devastated for you."

"Conrad."

"But don't expect me to cry for him."

With that, the young man stood up, snatched his hoodie off the back of the chair, and walked out the door.

CHAPTER THIRTEEN

Iris Duncan strode across the Fellowship Hall of the Peach Grove Baptist Church, swerving around a little girl dressed as an angel singing "Jingle Bells." Iris's blunt bangs dusted the top of her eyebrows, which gave Susannah the urge to blow her own bangs out of her face. The style on Iris looked windswept and sexy.

Susannah shot a guilty look at the Christmas tree, which was decorated with gold ribbon and topped by an angel playing a harp, as Larraine had described. Pushing away worldly thoughts about hair and fashion, she found herself pondering the same question that had plagued her since she left True Blooms. Had Conrad Jones been involved in the murder of Albert Calloway?

The young man certainly seemed angry. Could his feelings toward Albert have caused him to confront the financial secretary at his home? It was possible that

Conrad could have found out where Albert lived, but knowing that he was killed in his living room, Susannah hesitated to think that Conrad was the killer. Given that Albert had been the one to cancel the order for the flowers, Susannah doubted he would have wanted to argue about it with an unknown man who showed up on his doorstep. Even if had claimed to be from True Blooms, Susannah was skeptical that Albert would have let him in.

Iris handed her a paper plate with some Christmas cookies. "Still obsessing about what's-his-name? Conrad?"

Susannah nodded. "I get it. The odds are against it."

"I wouldn't let some strange guy into my house. Just common sense." She tapped her purse, where she kept her Sig Sauer, and lifted one shoulder. "I've seen Albert on the firing range. I don't think he would either."

"I know. I know," Susannah frowned at the cookie sampler. Not a gluten-free one in the bunch. "What about you? Did you overhear anything?"

"Nothing." Iris cut into a piece of triple-layer chocolate cake with a plastic fork and gave a quick jerk of her head toward Charleen Barnes and three other women deep in discussion at the beverage table. "That's the event planning committee. They're complaining to the pastor's wife about someone in the food service ministry. They think the food quality has gone downhill recently."

Susannah exhaled her distaste.

"I know," Iris replied, as she cut a large swath out of her piece and offered it up to Susannah, who declined. Iris shrugged and shoved the piece into her mouth. She paused, an expression of delight crossing her face. "Backbiters. Obviously none of them tasted this cake. It's fantastic."

"Have you seen anyone who's on the list?" Though too upset about Miss Shirleen's arrest to attend the pageant herself, Larraine had sent Susannah the names of the other members of the decorating committee.

"No." Iris motioned to the corridor that led to the auditorium. "They're probably in there, saving a row of seats."

Susannah glanced at her phone. "I guess it's time."

Iris cast a longing gaze to the dessert table and tossed her plate in the trash. She looked elegant in a Christmas sweater with a montage of classic holiday motifs on a black background worn over a pair of black leggings. It sure beat out Susannah's Frosty-the-Snowman sweater and blue jeans for class and style. Iris flipped her hair and said, "Let's go."

In the back of the assembly hall, Susannah asked, "Is there a restroom around here?"

Iris nodded and pointed to a set of double doors on the opposite side of the hall. "Go out those doors and make a left."

Susannah gave her a thumbs-up and hurried across the room, scanning the crowd for Livvy Franklin as she went. As she pushed through the door, her phone vibrated, and Bitsy's name came up with a text message.

Where you goin?

She replied: *Restroom*

Bitsy replied with an emoji of a tidal wave. Susannah grinned as she thumbed the laugh-cry emoji, then looked up, disoriented. She had never been in this part of the church campus before, and the hallway she'd been walking down emptied into a new corridor. She turned the corner, expecting to see the restrooms, and was surprised to find Charleen Barnes, holding hands with Conrad.

He looked up, jerking his hand away from Charleen as if he had been burned. Blushing, he buried his fists in the kangaroo pocket of his hoodie and hustled away. Charleen nodded to Susannah, an artificial smile plastered on her face. "Can I help you?"

"Restroom?" Susannah managed as the young man disappeared around a corner and an unseen door opened and then slammed shut.

Charleen pointed in the opposite direction and Susannah pivoted, wondering what she'd just witnessed.

When she came out of the restroom, Charleen was gone. The halls were deserted. In the packed auditorium, Susannah squeezed her way down the row of parents with their camera phones and iPads at the ready, and took the empty seat next to Iris.

Bitsy leaned around Iris and poked Susannah's thigh. "Took you long enough."

"I got a little turned around." As Susannah answered, the lights went down and a murmur rose from the audience.

"You found a hound?" Bitsy asked. "Not again."

"No, no." Susannah and Bitsy had rescued a stray

dog only a few weeks ago. She raised her voice over the noise of the crowd, just as the curtain opened and a hush fell over the room. "Not a hound." Her voice carried throughout the room, and heads turned. Charleen's blond bob swung as she, too, gave a quick glance over her shoulder, then tapped Pastor Ron's arm and pointed at the side of the stage.

A woman in front of Susannah turned and glared. "Shhhh."

She slid down in her seat and muttered, "I'll tell you later."

Through verses of "Hark! The Herald Angels Sing," Susannah scanned the crowd as Iris and Bitsy nodded along to the choir of preschoolers. The only person on Larraine's list she would know for sure was Livvy Franklin, and Susannah worried that the accountant could be sitting behind her. With the pastor and his wife busy with the recital, Susannah thought this might be a good time to look around.

When a seven-year-old stepped on stage to announce, "Behold, a virgin shall conceive a son," Susannah felt a tap on her shoulder.

Bitsy was staring at her from behind Iris's back. "They're talking about you!"

The woman in front of Susannah glared again. "Shhhh."

Susannah gave the woman a sheepish smile and shot Bitsy a look. Now that everyone was preoccupied with the program, it was time to do some snooping. She got up from her seat, now facing the other parents seated in her row and was immediately blinded by the flash from a camera-phone. She stumbled into the aisle. Halfway down she spotted Livvy, and a plan began to form.

On her way back to the Fellowship Hall, she composed a group text to her friends: *See you later at the dessert table.*

CHAPTER FOURTEEN

Susannah looked around the Fellowship Hall, which was empty and still, except for a wisp of tinsel that blew across the beverage table. Not unexpectedly, everyone had decamped to watch the precious babes of the congregation sing Christmas carols.

Susannah paused. The only other time she had been at the church was for an outdoor picnic. She would have to try and find the pastoral offices by herself, without Larraine's advice. She crossed the Fellowship Hall and tiptoed into the older section of the church campus. The original sanctuary was now a chapel that smelled of mildew and furniture polish. She held her breath as she passed by the chapel and stole down a dim hallway to a door marked with an exit sign.

Susannah stepped through the door and into a large common area furnished with two sofas and a coffee table. Beyond the seating area was a desk with a phone and a toy elf holding a small chalkboard. On the chalkboard, the words *The Pastor Is Out* were written in a shaky cursive.

"If that's the pastor's office, then where..." Susannah whispered to herself, as she turned toward a Christmas tree heavy on the gold rope garland. She glimpsed a staircase that hugged the wall and sprinted up the steps two at a time.

The upper floor was ringed by an interior balcony that overlooked the waiting area. A polished railing was wrapped with more gold garland, and a number of doors lined the balcony. The whole upper floor was dimly lit by a small light fixture on the vaulted ceiling.

In the silence, Susannah could hear the muffled singing of children. She darted across the balcony, reading the signs on the doors, and then hurried around the corner, careful to stay close to the wall. The financial secretary's office was at the end of the hall, and she pushed through the outer door and was met by darkness. There was a soft click and she stood stock still, frozen in place.

After a few minutes of breathing with her mouth open wide so she wouldn't be heard, Susannah finally engaged the flashlight app on her phone and panned the light around the room. Directly in front of her was a desk, which she assumed was Livvy Franklin's station. Behind the desk, the door to Albert Calloway's office stood open, and she dashed inside.

Heart pounding, Susannah wondered how many more times she would find herself skulking around the office of a recently departed victim of murder. Had she had taken a wrong turn in life? Gone off the rails somehow and lost her moral compass? The image of Miss Shirleen in handcuffs came back to her, and she pushed those thoughts aside.

On Albert's desk, she saw the usual accoutrements: a phone, a computer and keyboard, a cup of pens. Covering the surface of the desk was a desk blotter. Shining her light on it, Susannah realized it was a calendar with a *Jesus Is the Reason for the Season* sticker at the bottom. She narrowed her eyes, quickly scanning the rows of dates in the month of December. Christmas was framed in red Sharpie. A few other dates were highlighted. Albert had made notations and doodles. Susannah glanced at today's date, then brought up the camera app and snapped a picture.

A door softly closing caught her attention. Hands trembling, she doused the flashlight and wished she hadn't had that demitasse of espresso after dinner. Footfalls on the staircase were unmistakable. She flew out of Albert's office to the door and opened it a crack. Livvy Franklin was heading up the stairs, her phone to her ear.

"Yes," Livvy said into the phone. "I know."

Susannah began to sweat. Had Livvy followed her? She peered out the door again. Livvy seemed distracted by her phone call, and Susannah quietly closed the door and searched wildly around the room for somewhere to hide. She could dash inside Albert's office and hope for the best.

She shook her head. If Livvy had left the door to

Albert's office open, seeing it closed now would make her suspicious. "Think, Susannah."

No sooner had the words left her lips than a hand covered her mouth and someone dragged her backward.

CHAPTER FIFTEEN

"Dr. Shine," a familiar voice whispered. "It's me, don't scream."

Susannah spun, causing a rush of dizziness. She blinked twice and found herself face-to-face with Larraine Moore, her eyes white orbs in the darkness.

Larraine put her fingers to her lips and tugged at Susannah's shoulder, pulling her into a closet she had not previously noticed. Confused, Susannah backed into some wooden shelves, and Larraine reached out and pulled the door closed. As she slowly released the knob, the latch hung up on the strike plate, making a soft click.

Susannah raised her eyebrows. Suddenly whirling around had aggravated her Meniere's disease, and it took her a few seconds to realize that Larraine had been in the closet the whole time she was snooping around Albert's desk. Susannah inhaled again.

The door to the balcony shook, and Livvy stepped

heavily into the office, still on her phone. "I'm here. Just give me some time. I'll find it."

The accountant continued through her office, and then the door to Albert's office closed. Susannah felt for Larraine's wrist with one hand and quickly twisted the doorknob with the other. She pulled her friend out of the closet and through the door to the balcony walkway, where she felt Larraine gently tug her wrist in the opposite direction. At the corner of the building there was a door lit with a red exit sign.

Susannah followed Larraine into a stairwell, where the sound of their movements was amplified by two stories of air. A safety light dimly illuminated their escape down steps whose anti-slip mats muffled their footfalls. At the bottom of the staircase, Susannah swung the fire door open and held it for Larraine as they veered around the corner of the building into a small parking lot where Larraine's Mercury Marquis was waiting. For the second time in as many days, Susannah rode shotgun.

"Goodness gracious," Larraine panted, leaning over the steering wheel as she exhaled, trying to catch her breath. Her normally perfectly coiffured helmet hair was undone in places. "What were you doing in there? You scared the life out of me. I have a crease in my derriere from squishing against those shelves."

"You scared me, too," Susannah said, touching Larraine lightly on the arm. "I heard that closet door latch close and I felt like I was frozen in place for an hour."

The women looked at each other and burst out

laughing as Larraine patted her hair into place and engaged the engine.

"What now?" Larraine asked. "Back to the Christmas pageant?"

"Oh, no. You're not getting rid of me that easy. It's only seven thirty and we have a lot to talk about." Susannah pursed her lips and tapped at her phone. "There. I sent a text to Bitsy, Roman, and Iris telling them to meet us at the office. I rode with Iris, so I don't have to worry about the Jeep. You're stuck with me for now."

"Coffee?"

"Coffee."

Before Larraine could leave her parking spot, a dark blue Ford Taurus pulled up beside her. Detective Withers stepped out, closing the door quietly. She folded her arms and approached Larraine's window.

Larraine smiled and lowered the window. "Detective."

Detective Withers bent forward, staring past Larraine to Susannah. "Well, well. Will you look at this."

Larraine glanced at Susannah and then back to the detective.

"What might you too lovely ladies be doing here?"

"Tonight's the Christmas pageant," Larraine said.

Susannah nodded in agreement, giving her office manager points for answering the question without telling a lie. "Right. The annual Christmas pageant."

"And the pageant takes place in the staff parking lot?" asked Detective Withers.

"We were just leaving," Susannah said.

"Hmmm. Doctor, you certainly have a way of saying something without saying anything."

Susannah forced herself to stay still, even though she felt like a specimen wriggling under the detective's magnifying glass.

"Nice speaking to you, Detective." Larraine raised the window with a friendly wave and pulled out of the spot. Before she could drive ten yards, a Peach Grove PD cruiser drove into the parking lot and stopped across her path.

Randy Laughton scowled from behind the wheel. Susannah wondered if his foul mood was because he ran into them or because he had to drive himself tonight. He stalked over to the Mercury and put his hands on his hips, staring at Larraine until she lowered the window again. "I hope I don't have to remind you ladies not to meddle in the investigation of Mr. Calloway's death."

"No, sir," Susannah said.

"Now, Doc, there's no reason for sarcasm," said Randy.

"Of course not," Susannah replied. "And there's no reason for you and Detective Withers to treat us like suspects. It's well within reason that we would be at the church on the night of the annual Christmas pageant. Now if you don't mind, we'd like to go home."

Randy narrowed his eyes, as if daring Larraine to move her car. She put the Mercury in reverse, and drove away.

CHAPTER SIXTEEN

At the Starbucks drive-through window, Susannah handed Larraine some cash and asked, "Does Charles know where you are?"

"I told him I had some shoppin' to do," she said, retrieving the cardboard drink holder from the cashier and handing it to Susannah. "He never asks for details when I use the 'S' word."

A few minutes later, Rusty dashed across the gravel lot of Peach Grove Chiropractic as Susannah unlocked the rear door. The tabby figure-eighted her legs, depositing the requisite amount of cat hair on her jeans, before he circled his kibble dish and sat. Larraine placed the coffee on the break room table and hurried down the hall to let the others in. Susannah spilled some dry food into Rusty's dish, gave him a scratch on the chin, and shut the door.

Bitsy led the way down the hall, followed by Iris and Larraine.

"Where's Roman?" asked Susannah.

"He got a call and had to scoot." Bitsy reached for a coffee and sat, entangling her fingers in the plastic wrap and wrestling a chocolate-laden spoon free. "I'm glad I left my collection of stirring spoons here. I need me a snack."

"Girl," Iris said, "I saw you slip some of those Krispy Kreme donuts in your purse when you thought no one was looking. Pony up and share."

"So long as you take those chocolate-covered Oreos out of yours."

Iris winked and purred, "I didn't think you noticed."

They both laughed and piled their paper napkin-wrapped treats on the table.

"Okay, ladies," Susannah mock-scolded. "Get a hold of yourselves and your blood sugar issues. We need to break this down."

Larraine nodded. Iris slipped into a chair and flipped back the plastic wrap on the tray of chocolaty spoons; she nabbed one embedded with tiny pieces of mini marshmallows.

"What's goin' on?" Bitsy asked. "Why did you flat leave me at the church?"

"Miss Larraine and I ran into each other." Susannah explained how she and Larraine had the same idea: to search Albert's office while everyone was preoccupied by the Christmas pageant.

Iris raised a brow.

Bitsy clapped.

"But I didn't find anything," Susannah continued. "And I don't even know what I was looking for."

"Maybe proof that Albert stole those poinsettias," Bitsy said.

Susannah perked up. "I have that. I stopped by True Blooms this afternoon and Shannon showed me a plant tag that she had special-ordered to put in the Christmas plants." Susannah bent to retrieve her bag; she found the plastic *Merry Christmas* tag and tossed it on the table. "Shannon identified it in the video I took of the plants in Albert's living room."

Bitsy snapped her fingers. "I knew he stole those plants. Poinsettia pilferer!"

"I can't believe a man of the church would act so ugly," Larraine murmured.

Iris muttered her agreement, then added to Susannah, "You took video of the crime scene?"

"Uh-huh."

"Well, quit hogging the evidence. Let's take a look."

"Sure." Susannah got her phone and pulled up the camera app, which displayed the last picture she'd taken, that of Albert's desk blotter.

Bitsy glared at the picture. "That doesn't look like a corpse."

"No. It's the calendar Albert kept on his desk." She placed the phone on the table and enlarged the picture. Four heads bent low to look. "I thought it might hold a clue. That's all I managed before Livvy showed up."

"Wait." Bitsy straightened. "What was Livvy Franklin doing there?"

"Looking for something," Larraine said. "But we didn't wait to find out what."

Iris looked at Larraine. "Back up, you two. I think you left some things out."

Larraine explained how she had hidden from Susannah and they both had hidden from Livvy, who came in and made a beeline for Albert's office.

"Lucky she went into his office," Bitsy commented. "Got you out of the closet."

"Be careful of who you accuse of coming out of the closet." Iris chuckled, peering at the photo, then shook her head. "Let me get all this straight. I feel like we're jugglin' cats."

"Okay. From the beginning." Susannah stood and counted off on her fingers. "We found Shirleen at Albert's house holding the murder weapon, but she claims she found him already dead. We all suspected Albert of stealing the plants. Now, thanks to those little plastic doohickeys, that's confirmed. Conrad was angry enough about it that he could have taken a swing at Albert with a Christmas stocking holder, but we're not sure how he would have known where to find him."

"Or even who he was," Larraine added. "Shirleen and I knew he denied the charges because we know how the church is organized."

"Check," Iris said. "I didn't think someone like Albert would even let a stranger in his house, never mind turn his back on him long enough to get brained by a snowflake."

Susannah nodded, continuing. "Then there's Livvy. She could have been involved with the poinsettia thefts, and she's made unkind and intolerant remarks in the past."

"You can say that again." Bitsy wrinkled her nose.

"And she sneaked into Albert's office looking for something." Susannah paused with her ring finger bent backward. "Given the shameful and vile things he seemed to be capable of, we don't know if she was helping him or being exploited by him."

"Could Albert have been blackmailing someone?" Iris asked. "I might be new to the church, but I've seen how people react when his name comes up. People were afraid to cross him."

"I wouldn't put it past him." Susannah paused, looking away from Iris, her gaze migrating up to the ceiling, then back down to Larraine. "How could I forget? There's something else. I saw Charleen and Conrad together before. It looked to me like they were holding hands."

"What?" Larraine exclaimed. "Why didn't you say something sooner?"

"In all the excitement to get out of Albert's office, I forgot."

"When did this happen?" Bitsy asked.

"When I went looking for the restroom before the Christmas pageant started. I told you I got turned around. I saw them in the hallway."

"You don't think Conrad and Charleen are hooking up?" Bitsy asked.

"Now I've heard everything," Larraine said. "How could they be hooking up? I thought he was gay."

"Oh, right," Bitsy said. "I must be gettin' tired."

"This is getting plumb out of control. I know what I have to do next." Larraine stood. "I'm going to go talk to Livvy. If there was anything goin' on with her and Albert, it's over now."

Bitsy stood and stretched. "And I'm gonna stop by Peachy Things. Maybe Shannon is at True Blooms and I can discreetly ask a few questions about Conrad being at the church."

Iris laughed. "You, discreet? Now *I've* heard everything."

"You just come with, and you'll see. I can be downright restrained."

Larraine reached for the doorknob.

"Wait, I'll go with you." Susannah walked Bitsy and Iris out the front door, turned off the lights, and followed Larraine out.

CHAPTER SEVENTEEN

Larraine pulled her Mercury Marquis into the driveway of Livvy Franklin's house. Several strings of white LED Christmas lights were draped across the hedges in front of the house. The front door was wrapped like a Christmas package with a huge red bow.

"Somebody's home," Larraine said.

The blue light of a television seeped through the sheer curtains of a bay window. Larraine knocked on the door, and the volume of the TV suddenly dropped. They waited, but no one came. Larraine knocked again, and the mini blinds lifted and framed Livvy's eyes. Susannah was put in mind of Harriet Goolsby watching the world go by. The door opened a few inches, and Livvy peered out, the rectangular lenses of her eyeglasses magnifying the surprise in her eyes.

"Miss Larraine," Livvy said, giving Susannah a side-eye glance that told her she was less than welcome. She kept her hand on the door as she spoke. "What are you doing here?"

"Olivia, who is it?" A weak voice called from deep inside the house. "Who's callin' so late at night?"

Livvy called over her shoulder, "It's Miss Larraine, Mama. From church."

"Well, invite her in."

"I am, Mama." Livvy blushed and, with her hand still on the door, allowed it to swing wide. Larraine stepped in. Livvy gave Susannah a stare and then backed a few paces into the small sitting room. "Excuse me."

Livvy bustled across the room and down a narrow hall, where she vanished into a room. In a few quick steps, Susannah stood at the end of the hallway, leaning in to catch Livvy's words. Her voice was low but clear. "Now you hush, Mama. I'll take care of this."

"Olivia Franklin, Larraine is an old friend. You give her my regrets. I can't entertain company like this."

Livvy's voice got even lower. "I said I'd take care of it, Mama. You just stay in here and don't interfere."

Susannah couldn't hear any response; then the bedroom door opened, and she hurried back to Larraine's side. Livvy made her way down the hall and reentered the family room.

"My mama sends her regrets. She is not able to receive visitors." Livvy headed toward the kitchen. "Can I get you ladies anything? Mama did some baking today for the Christmas pageant, and she always leaves a little aside."

"No thank you," Larraine said

Livvy returned to the family room. "Come on in."

"May I sit?" Larraine asked.

"Of course." Livvy shot a glance to the back of the house and added, "Where are my manners? Please."

The women sat, and Larraine said, "Livvy, we need to talk."

Livvy looked from Larraine to Susannah and gave a little snort. "What could we possibly have to talk about?"

"I think you know." Larraine looked her in the eye. "Albert Calloway."

"Not this again. I guess you only want to talk to me when your friend is in trouble." She jutted her chin at Susannah and pouted like a petulant child. Over the summer, Larraine and Susannah had spoken to Livvy about a different case, and she had been just as hostile then as she was now. "I already told the police everything I know. It's not my fault if you're in trouble."

"It just so happens we know that you were in Albert's office tonight snooping around."

Susannah thought Larraine might choke on the words *snooping around.*

Livvy jumped to her feet, hands balled into fists. "That's a lie."

Larraine ignored the outburst. "No. We all know it's true. I want to know why you were there." Larraine patted the cushion and said, "Sit down, please."

"I won't. You're just making things up to try and blame other people so she can get off." Livvy sneered and jerked her thumb at Susannah. "Well, as you sow, you shall reap. Let her take her punishment like an adult."

Larraine stood, her hands on her hips. "Dr. Shine is not accused of killing Albert. Miss Shirleen Carter is."

A gasp came from the hallway, and the three women turned to see Livvy's mother, dressed in her nightclothes and seated in a wheelchair. Althea Franklin wheeled herself a few paces into the family room. "Shirleen Carter? It can't be."

"Mama, you stay out of this."

"I will not." Althea wheeled herself to Livvy across the inexpensive carpet that had been worn bare by the burden of the wheels. "Shirleen Carter and I were schoolmates. She was such a lovely person, so caring. A perfect fit for her ministry on the welcoming committee. I just don't believe it."

"We should leave it to the police. Maybe she did do it," Livvy said. "How are we to know? A lot of people hated Albert. Why should she be any different?"

"Olivia Franklin," Althea responded, "that is not Christian talk."

Livvy deflated. "No, Mama, it's not. But Albert was not a very Christian person."

"'Do not judge, or you too will be judged.' Matthew 7:1."

Livvy's expression fell, and Susannah noticed the bags under her eyes. The young woman had lost weight since the summer, and when Larraine took her hand, Susannah was surprised at how bony her fingers were. "Livvy, tell me why you're saying this," said Larraine. "If it can help Shirleen, I have to know."

Livvy shook her head. "Always so nosy. Spying on me so that you can help your friends. Who was there to help *me*?"

"Olivia, what are you saying?" Althea studied her daughter, two large creases crinkling her forehead.

"Matthew also said, 'Let your good works glorify your Father.'" Livvy walked across the room and picked up her shoulder bag. She removed an envelope and turned to her mother and dropped it in her lap. "Albert didn't do any good works that I know of. And I'm glad he's dead."

"This is addressed to Pastor Ron," said Althea.

"It's mine. Go ahead and open it." As her mother slid her fingers under the flap of the envelope, Livvy crouched down; then, almost as if her slight frame were being compressed by its own weight, she sat heavily on the floor.

Susannah shifted on the sofa and Larraine pressed her palm heavily into Susannah's thigh.

Althea removed a sheet of paper, and two photographs slid onto her lap. With a shaking hand, she picked one up and gasped. Olivia began to sob.

"Why?" The words seemed to stick in Althea's throat.

"He told me he loved me." Olivia wiped her nose on her sleeve. "He lied. He always lied, and it caught up to him."

Althea's eyes widened, and a tear slid down her cheek. "Olivia, what did you do?"

"What did I do? I did whatever he told me to do. Picked up his cleaning, shopped for his groceries." She stood, her eyes boring into Susannah and then Larraine as she continued. "Cut checks late, undermined Pastor Ron's wishes. Even stole things. Like the poinsettias from that freak florist."

"Olivia." Her mother's voice, barely a whisper, trailed off to silence.

"That's why you're really here, isn't it?" Olivia jeered at Larraine. "You want me to confess? All right, so I stole some pots of flowers from those two heathens. What of it? Why do you care so much about them, anyway? They shouldn't be in our town. They're not welcome here."

With that, she hefted her shoulder bag from where she had dropped it on the floor, threw the door open, and left.

CHAPTER EIGHTEEN

Susannah and Larraine bade a hasty goodbye to Althea and rushed to Larraine's car. At the far end of the street, Livvy's car was just rounding the corner.

"There she is." Susannah checked behind them as Larraine gunned the engine and pulled into the street.

"What do you suppose she has in mind to do?"

"I have no idea," Susannah said. "But see if you can follow her without her noticing. No stunt driving."

"You don't think she killed Albert, do you?" Larraine touched her throat with a thin finger.

"I don't know what to think. I didn't see the pictures, but I can imagine what they showed." Susannah blinked twice and exhaled. "Maybe she went to his house on one of her tasks, and he did something that pushed her over the edge."

"Good grief." Larraine placed her hand back on the wheel, twisting her wrists as she drove. "I really hope not. That would be tragic."

Larraine followed at a distance as Livvy drove into Peach Grove and turned into a shopping plaza not far from Main Street. A sidewalk Santa rang his bell for spare change in front of the supermarket entrance. "I'm not sure about this." She squeezed the Mercury into a spot between two other cars and threw it into park. "I think we've invaded her privacy enough for one day. If she wants to go shopping, I say let her be."

Susannah rubbed her fingers along the sides of her mouth. At first she had been afraid that Livvy might do something drastic. Perhaps even hurt herself. But a little retail therapy, such as could be had at the Shoppes at Peach Grove, surely couldn't be detrimental to her health.

"You're right." Susannah hesitated. "But I want to make sure she didn't stop here because she's on to us. Let's wait until she goes into one of the stores."

Larraine nodded and sat back as Livvy drove past the pizza restaurant, supermarket, and vitamin shop, then cruised down the parking lot aisle in front of a nail salon where she took the space farthest from the store front.

"What's she up to?" Susannah asked.

"Maybe she just wants to sit a spell."

A few minutes went by, and Livvy remained in her car. Susannah imagined Livvy listening to the radio or playing on her phone. She was about to suggest that they move closer when her attention was caught by a blond woman leaving the vitamin shop and making her way down the aisle toward Livvy's car. Even in the dim light, the woman was unmistakable.

Larraine asked, "Is that—"

"—Charleen Barnes." Susannah made a pitiful attempt to whistle.

"Well, I'll be."

"You and me both."

Charleen approached Livvy's car, and Susannah and Larraine watched as she slid in next to Livvy. Larraine put her car into gear and backed out of the spot.

"Wait, where're you going?"

"We have to get closer to see what they're doing."

"Hang on, Charleen's getting out."

Charleen slammed the door so hard that Susannah heard it fifty yards away. Darting between parked cars, Charleen stopped at the brownish-silver Yukon she had been driving the day before and climbed in. The engine came to life, and she backed out of the spot, then stopped short as a pedestrian walking down the aisle jumped to the side.

Susannah said, "Follow that Yukon."

Larraine nodded and watched as Charleen drove out of the shopping plaza and headed for Main Street. On Main Street, she slowed as she passed Peachy Things and True Blooms. Susannah was surprised to see a light on in Peachy Things, then remembered Bitsy's comment that she was going to see if she could catch Shannon at True Blooms. Larraine braked as Charleen slid her Yukon into a parking spot in front of True Blooms and got out.

Larraine bit her lip and frowned. "What in the world?"

"Turn here." Susannah pointed. "And go down the alley behind the shops. Maybe she won't notice us."

Larraine did as Susannah suggested and poked the front of her Mercury out onto Main Street again.

Charleen was still standing on the sidewalk. Her hands framed her face as she peered through the glass door of True Blooms. She turned and stepped back, pushing some papers down into her jacket pocket as she crouched down and picked up something from the sidewalk. Standing, she glanced around, as if looking for someone, then turned and headed back to her car. Larraine sighed, stretching her neck to see around Susannah. "Okay, I'm finished spying. This is too much. I'm going home."

"Sure, I understand." Susannah motioned to Peachy Things. "Just drop me off. I, uh, want to talk to Bitsy."

"That's fine." Larraine watched Charleen's Yukon disappear down Main Street. "Everyone deserves some privacy."

Not everyone, Susannah thought, but she said nothing as Larraine took the space Charleen had just vacated. "Good night."

Susannah sprang out of the car and tugged on the door to Peachy Things, which rattled but didn't give. Larraine sat in the car as Susannah texted Bitsy. In a moment, Bitsy appeared from beyond the holly-speckled curtain, followed by Iris. Susannah waved goodbye to Larraine.

"What are you doing here?" Bitsy said as the bells

on the door jingled. "I thought Miss Larraine went to give Olivia a piece of her mind."

"We did. It's a long story that leads to Charleen Barnes."

Bitsy tilted her head, her eyes narrowed. Susannah read the confusion in her eyes.

"What does the pastor's wife have to do with this?" Iris asked.

"I'm not sure," Susannah said. "But we followed her here. She went up to the True Blooms door, then left."

"Why didn't you keep following her?" Bitsy asked.

"Larraine got an attack of conscience."

"Glad that doesn't happen to me," Bitsy murmured.

"Uh-huh," Susannah replied. "Did you talk to Shannon and ask her about Conrad?"

"We didn't see her." Bitsy glanced at Iris. "I knocked when we got here about forty minutes ago. No one answered. Iris and I were just having some hot cocoa and talking this whole thing over."

Iris nodded. "What about you? Did you find out what Livvy was doing in Albert's office?"

"Yes," Susannah responded. "She was looking for a letter he was holding over her head."

"Why would she have to sneak around to find a letter?" Bitsy frowned. "You mean he was going to mail it for her? I don't remember seeing any mail on Albert's desk when I looked at the picture you took."

"Speaking of that"—Iris put down her mug of

cocoa—"I never got a chance to look at that picture you took of his desk. Can I see it again?"

Susannah handed her phone to Iris. To Bitsy, she said, "We didn't get all the details, but he was obviously blackmailing her. The letter had pictures she didn't want to anyone to see."

"What!" Bitsy exclaimed. "And you followed Charleen instead? If that was me, I would smash him with a snowflake for sure."

"I don't think Livvy could do this. She's too frail. Whoever killed Albert stabbed him and then bashed him," Iris said, motioning to Susannah's phone. "Can we get this on a bigger screen? It's hard to see detail."

"I think I need the charging cable to transfer the image onto a computer."

"You can borrow mine." Bitsy went to an outlet next to her coffeemaker and disconnected the USB cable from the charging cube and handed it to Susannah. "I'll get my laptop. I left it on the front counter."

When Bitsy returned, she connected the cable and opened a photo-sharing program. Susannah stared at the screen, amazed at the clarity and size of the image.

"That's what I thought," Iris said, pointing to the edge of the blotter nearest to the *Jesus Is the Reason for the Season* sticker. "There's a small piece of tinsel there."

"So?" Bitsy put one hand on her hip. "It is Christmas."

"Okay, I never said this." She tapped the date on her watch, which covered most of her wrist. "The

Peach Grove PD should have the autopsy report by now, so I guess I'm protected."

"Why do you need protection? You think there's a snowflake serial killer?"

Iris barked with laughter. "You break me up." She shook her head, chuckling. "I mean for my job. If they could trace a leak back to me, I'd lose my job."

"Oh." Bitsy looked disappointed.

Susannah elbowed Bitsy. "Please, go on."

"The medical examiner found a little piece of tinsel like this during his autopsy." She hovered her finger over the computer screen, pointing at the sliver of silver. "It was embedded in the wound that killed the deceased."

Bitsy whistled, moving her head slowly side to side.

"Dr. Shine?" Iris asked. "You still with us? You look like you're a million miles away."

Susannah retrieved her phone and brought up the video of Albert's house. "I'm trying to remember where I've seen that kind of tinsel."

"Really?" Bitsy said. "Like I said, it's Christmas. The stuff is everywhere."

"But think about it," she said, holding her phone up for the others to see as the video ran. "Both Albert and the church had predominantly gold decorations. Gold garland, gold ribbon."

"That's true, Dr. Shine," Iris said. "But Bitsy's right. It's Christmas. Tinsel is everywhere."

"Not everywhere." The video played through once. "Anyone see silver tinsel in that video?"

"No."

Susannah handed the phone to Bitsy. "See if you can get it on your laptop and let's watch it again."

The video began to play, and Susannah stepped back to the laptop. She pointed at the poinsettias. "See the plastic tags from True Blooms poking over the red wrappers?"

Bitsy nodded. Iris bent closer to the screen.

"Now look here." Susannah stopped the video and pointed. A poinsettia with large leaves filled the frame. Nestled behind the pot's red foil wrapper was a small red object. "What's this?"

Iris squinted. "An ornament?"

"Looks to me like a leaf that fell off the plant and got wedged behind the foil paper." Bitsy shook her head.

Susannah snapped her fingers. "Of course. A red Christmas ball."

"What's so special about a Christmas ball under a Christmas tree?"

"You're the design maven. Can't you tell?"

Bitsy stared at the screen, then narrowed her eyes. "There are no red balls on the tree. All the red is on the floor with the poinsettias."

"Bingo," Susannah said. "And who was wearing a sweater that had red Christmas balls and tinsel?"

This time it was Iris who answered. "Charleen Barnes."

"Charleen. But why?" Bitsy said. "It doesn't make any sense."

"I agree," Iris said. "I've never heard her say a cross word. I can't believe it."

"Of all the evidence we've ever gathered, this is the weakest, Doc." Bitsy pressed her lips together. "A maybe-red ornament and a wisp of tinsel. I have two Christmas trees myself with silver tinsel." She took two steps, pulled back the curtain, and pointed to the artificial tree in the showroom.

"It made sense to me." Susannah came up behind her and studied the tree. Not only were there slivers of tinsel hanging off every branch, but a small Christmas ball lay under the tree. Susannah's shoulders sagged. "Maybe you're right. I must be foggy from all this running around. Larraine had the right idea. I'm going home and put this day to bed."

"Me too," Iris said. "You need a ride, Doc?"

Susannah grimaced, remembering she had left the Jeep home tonight. She slapped her hand on her forehead in the classic face-palm motion. "I really am losing it."

"I'll take her," Bitsy said. "She has my casserole dish and I want to pick it up before Angie decides it's hers."

Iris nodded, said her goodbyes, and left.

CHAPTER NINETEEN

"What was that all about?"

"Just a little covered-dish concoction," Bitsy said, pushing through the Christmas curtain and grabbing her jacket and purse. She closed the laptop and handed Susannah her phone. "It was a little white lie to throw Iris off the scent."

Susannah grinned. "Are you thinking what I'm thinking?"

"If you're thinking about having a Milano cookie before we leave for Albert's house, yes."

Susannah chuckled. "What made you change your mind?"

"I really haven't." Bitsy opened a small cupboard and extracted a package of Pepperidge Farm cookies and offered the bag to Susannah, who declined the treat. "I still think you don't have any real evidence against Charleen. Conrad is more likely the Snowflake

Killer. Don't forget, he left True Blooms in a huff right before the murder. He's stronger, too."

"That's true."

"Not to mention Livvy Franklin. She has a really good motive for clobbering the creep."

"I just can't see Livvy doing that."

"Well, if you had kept track of Livvy, you might see her doing lots of things you can't imagine." Bitsy crunched her cookie and returned the bag to the cupboard. "Anyway, I want to see this alleged evidence myself. If it is there, we should be able to identify it as something that came off a garment and not the tree."

"Really?"

"You have a lot to learn about clothing." Bitsy shook her head.

Susannah sighed. "After all these years knowing you, I'm still fashion backwards."

"Yeah, you are. Let's go." She tossed her keys to Susannah and removed her phone from her purse. "You drive. I need to contact Roman and get the go-ahead from Little Junior."

In Bitsy's Explorer, Susannah headed toward Albert's house while Bitsy thumbed her phone. After several rounds of vibrations, punctuated by Bitsy's chuckles and sniggers, Susannah turned to her. "What gives?"

"Oh, Little Junior was telling me a knock-knock joke." She smiled. "Knock, knock."

"Who cares," Susannah snapped. "What did he say about Albert's house?"

"Now don't get testy." Bitsy pouted. "Little Junior's just trying to stay alert since he pulled the night shift this week."

Susannah drummed her fingers on the steering wheel.

"He said they already did the drive-by of the house for tonight. And Albert didn't have an alarm system, so we're good there."

"What about Roman?"

"I'm on that too. He's gonna meet us at Denise's house. 'Member I mentioned my cousin Denise just moved into Albert's neighborhood?"

Susannah nodded, remembering that Denise's name had come up at the office. Susannah considered Bitsy's family her adopted family, but they had so many relatives spread over several counties that sometimes she stopped paying attention to Bitsy's stories.

"She's around the block from Albert," Bitsy continued. "We can park at her house without nosy-body Harriet Goolsby noticing."

Susannah followed Bitsy's directions to Denise's home and pulled into the driveway behind Roman's Range Rover. Bitsy tapped out a text to her cousin and trotted to meet Roman at the side of the house. As usual, he was dressed in all black.

"We goin' through her backyard. Follow me. I'll pick the lock on the back door. You two get in fast and find what you're looking for. I'll stay outside." Roman stared at Bitsy. "No cuttin' up."

Bitsy stuck her tongue out at him, then took his hand. They crept down the side of Denise's house, getting their bearings. The moon was waning, but it gave them enough light to see the yards closest to Denise's house. From behind, there was no candy cane lane or six-foot nutcracker soldier banners to distinguish Albert's house from any other on the block.

"Which one is it?" Bitsy asked.

Roman shook his head. "You two just flunked spy school. Don't even know where you're goin'."

Bitsy started to respond, but Roman cut her off. "Hush. It's the one that doesn't have any lights on."

Roman started off across Denise's yard. Unlike some local neighborhoods, which backed up against stands of trees or fields, Albert's house backed up only to other homes and their backyards. A few neighbors had individual trees, but there was a lack of hiding places. Susannah's heart was pounding in her temples by the time she slipped under the sweet gum tree whose spiny seeds pods she compressed underfoot. She was grateful that Albert had never seen the need for a fence.

"It's chilly," Bitsy muttered to Roman. "And there's a storm comin'. You see that flash of lightning?"

"All the more reason to do this fast." He turned to look at the women. "Follow me and be quiet."

Roman dashed across two lots into Albert's yard, heading immediately to the back door. Susannah followed, feeling clumsy and exposed. She grabbed Bitsy's hand and together they hustled over the patio and plastered themselves against the vinyl siding. The noise of Roman working on the lock sounded impossibly loud. After a few moments, there was a click and the door swung open. Roman motioned to them, and Susannah took a deep breath and stepped inside.

Albert's kitchen took on a yellow hue from the moonlight that poured into the window over the sink. Bitsy came in and closed the door and followed Susannah as she entered the hallway. Susannah began to tremble, wondering what awaited them. Surely the family room wouldn't have changed much since Albert had been found. Had it really only been one day?

A beam of light suddenly blazed from behind her, and Susannah turned to see Bitsy using the flashlight on her phone. "Keep the light pointed down."

The light dipped to the floor, and Susannah was about to thank her friend when a loud clunk came from the kitchen.

"Roman?" Bitsy twisted, and there was thump and a groan.

The light bounced from the wall to the floor and finally went out as Bitsy fell into Susannah and dropped her phone.

CHAPTER TWENTY

Susannah managed to lower her friend to the carpet and back away. But the sudden bright light in the darkness of the hallway had made her blind.

The horrifying realization dawned on her. Someone had already been in the house when Roman let them in, and they had hit Bitsy hard enough to drop her.

Sweat broke out on Susannah's arms and the back of her knees. She took another step back and opened her mouth to scream, but the sharp prick of a knife against the softness of her throat caused her to gasp, inhaling. A gloved hand covered her mouth, silencing her.

"Be quiet," a muffled voice said. "No one is coming to help you."

Susannah struggled, shaking her head to the side and trying to bite the hand inside the leather glove. As a reward, pain lit up her skull. The world went spinning around her and she fell.

The perpetrator, apparently thinking Susannah was knocked out, rushed into the family room. Susannah's head throbbed but the spinning subsided. On the floor next to Bitsy, she spied a sprig of mistletoe framed by the white trim of the doorway. She wanted to laugh at such a mundane sight, but she couldn't. Her friend could be seriously hurt. She was able to reach out to Bitsy and feel her pulse, which was strong and steady.

In the family room, the figure bent low under Albert's tree, pawing over the gifts. Had she and Bitsy stumbled upon a robbery? If that were the case, the best course of action would be to lie quietly while the Grinch took what he wanted and left.

A frustrated groan told Susannah otherwise. "Where is it? It must be here."

The perpetrator rushed toward Susannah, who closed her eyes. The brightness of the overhead light penetrated her closed lids, and she opened her eyes to see a short, stocky person clad in an oversized black coat and ski mask run back to the Christmas tree. Susannah decided she should move while the intruder was preoccupied. She shook Bitsy, but her friend moaned, giving them away. In seconds, the person was standing over them. One gloved hand held the twin to the Christmas stocking holder that had killed Albert.

"Snowflake Serial Killer," Bitsy muttered.

No miscreant under the mistletoe was going to smash her brain and kill her best friend.

She sprang into action, propelling herself forward

as the stocking holder came down on her back, piercing her Frosty-the-Snowman sweater. Stumbling, fingertips grazing the floor, she surged ahead like a football player, her weight impacting her enemy's thighs, her head shoved into their waist.

As they hit the floor with a thump, the snowflake tumbled to the side and the oversized coat flew open.

Susannah scrambled to grab the iron weapon while staring at the figure of a heavy woman.

A *rap, rap, rap* shook the back door.

"No. You can't let them find it."

Susannah knew that voice. She reached over and unmasked the woman.

"Charleen Barnes." Bitsy had gotten to her feet; she stared down at the woman. "You're the Snowflake Serial Killer?"

A rap, rap, rap shook the door again. A siren wailed in the distance.

"Go let Roman in," said Susannah.

Bitsy wobbled away, unlocking the deadbolt that Charleen had engaged.

Roman sprinted into the family room, his pistol in hand. "She did it?"

Charleen whimpered. "I didn't mean to kill him. I just wanted him to stop bullying my sister."

EPILOGUE
CHRISTMAS EVE

"That's the last patient, Dr. Shine," Larraine said, pushing her keyboard away and sticking a pen behind her ear. Her hairdo had been shored up for the Christmas holiday and didn't budge. She glanced at her watch. "I propose a toast."

Susannah raised a brow and followed Larraine to the break room, where a bottle of sparkling cider sat on the table next to a plastic bag filled with disposable champagne flutes.

"What's the occasion?" Susannah asked.

"Just a quick toast to celebrate the holiday. Charles and I decided to drive down to Savannah and spend some time with my sister, since Shirleen won't be available." Larraine smiled. "So we won't see you again until after the New Year."

There was a knock on the door and Larraine opened it, ushering in a grinning Tina. She carried a small cube-shaped box wrapped for Christmas. Keith dipped his head under the door jamb as he entered.

"Merry Christmas," Tina said, handing Larraine the package. "Merry Christmas, Dr. Shine."

Just then, there was a loud banging on the front door. "Let me guess," Susannah said. "Y'all invited Bitsy, too."

"Of course." Tina continued grinning and bobbed her head. "I'll get it."

"No, no." Susannah placed a hand on Tina's shoulder. "You sit. I'll go. And someone open that package of glasses, uh, plastic. You know what I mean."

The banging came again. "I'm coming. I'm coming."

Susannah unlocked the front door, expecting to see Bitsy, but instead she found Shannon and Conrad.

"Merry Christmas," Shannon said. She held out a tray of homemade chocolate chip cookies. Conrad gave Susannah a forced smile and then stared down at his shoes.

"Thank you," Susannah said. "Why don't you come in?"

"I don't want to intrude. I just wanted to thank you."

Before she could say more, Roman's Range Rover pulled into the lot and came to a sudden halt. Bitsy jumped out and came over to them. She looked at the tray of cookies. "Is Miss Shirleen here, too?"

Shannon's expression changed from delight at seeing Bitsy to confusion. "Why do you say that?" she asked.

"Well, aren't those her pumpkin chocolate chip cookies?" Bitsy reached out to poke the tray, and Susannah slapped her hand. "Did she send them for the party?"

"As you can see"—Susannah waved at Bitsy —"you're not intruding. And apparently there's a party going on, so your timing's perfect."

Shannon and Conrad walked into the waiting area, as Susannah turned to wait for Bitsy, who had hustled back to the Range Rover to retrieve her own tray.

"I brought the hot chocolate bar." Bitsy shut the Range Rover's door with her foot. "Is Iris here yet? She's bringing the cocoa."

"Why am I not surprised?" Susannah eyed the tray, which was rectangular and twice as long as the one that held the chocolatized spoons. She stretched around Bitsy to see if Iris's car was nearby before closing the door. "Okay. It's a party."

As the words were leaving her lips, the waiting room was filled with the strains of "Holly Jolly Christmas." Tina stuck her head out from the insurance room. "Too loud? I can turn it down."

"Naw," Bitsy said, gesturing down the hall. "You can't hardly hear it in that break area. C'mon."

Susannah placed her hand on Shannon's shoulder. "You get used to the chaos after a while."

Shannon chuckled and nudged Conrad forward after Bitsy. Susannah was so involved singing along to the jaunty Christmas song that she jumped at the pounding on the door. "Iris."

Susannah threw the door open and was immediately taken aback at the sight of Detective Withers. Before either of them could say anything, Iris appeared, holding an electric kettle and a family-sized box of Swiss Miss. She beamed at them.

There was a momentary silence as "Holly Jolly Christmas" ended and "Jingle Bell Rock" began. Iris pushed past Susannah and bobbed her head. "Great party so far. It'll be even better once everyone has a little chocolate in their veins."

The detective raised her eyebrows and backed away from the door. "I'll come back later."

Susannah grabbed her wrist and pulled her in. "You might as well come in. Whatever you have to say to me, they'll find out about it eventually."

In the break area, Larraine was handing out plastic flutes of sparkling cider; without blinking an eye, she filled one for the detective, who waved it off saying, "I'm on duty."

"It's non-alcoholic." Bitsy said as she danced into the kitchen with the electric kettle. "But if you prefer something hot and sweet"—she gyrated her hips and touched a finger to her tongue and then to her hip and made a sizzling sound—"cocoa's coming right up."

"Merry Christmas." Keith stepped forward and shook the detective's hand. "If you have something to say, you better say it before it gets really crazy up in here. Once this lot get sugared up, you'll never get a word in."

The detective's lips curled into the briefest hint of a smile. Tina scooted past her desk, and few seconds later the music faded.

"I just came to give you an update on Charleen Barnes."

Silence descended upon the room, and the air of frivolity disappeared. Shannon cleared her throat. "How is she? I haven't been able to see her."

Detective Withers glanced at Shannon. "Her case is still within the mandatory hold period."

Shannon frowned. Upon being arrested for the murder of Albert Calloway, Charleen's mental health had been evaluated and she had been confined to a psychiatric facility.

The detective continued, "Believe me, it will be better for her in the long run. She has an attorney and she's being evaluated."

Larraine sighed and took a seat.

"But that's not all." The detective sipped at her drink, then cleared her throat. "Olivia Franklin came forward and exposed Albert's history of sexual crimes. Some of the church elders are digging in their heels, but Pastor Ron is cooperating. He wants what's best for his wife and for his congregation."

Iris stared into her hot cocoa and cringed.

"Olivia's admissions will ultimately help form a defense for Charleen." Detective Withers placed her plastic flute on the table. "We can only hope that she gets the care she needs while the wheels of justice slowly turn. That was all I wanted to tell you."

Larraine looked defeated. "I knew Shirleen couldn't have done this, but this is almost as bad."

"I'm sorry," the detective said. "I'll leave you to your merrymaking."

As the detective left by the rear door, an orange shape streaked in and Rusty materialized. Tina bent to pet him, but he leapt onto Larraine's lap and settled in.

"Awww. Rusty loves you," Tina said. "Okay, enough sulking for now. I'ma put the radio back on."

She left the room, and soon "Winter Wonderland" filled the air.

"My cocoa's cold," Iris said. "I'm gonna make another. Anyone else? It's Swiss Miss Marshmallow Lovers. Five times as many marshmallows."

Susannah groaned. "Ugh."

But Bitsy, who had just taken a bite from one of Shannon's chocolate chip cookies, garnished with a caramel from her tray of hot chocolate toppings, worked her tongue around her teeth for a few seconds, then raised her hand.

"Shannon, Conrad," Susannah said, motioning to the two empty places. "Please sit. I'll get some more chairs."

"Keith and I can't stay." Tina hugged Larraine as Keith opened the door. "We have Christmas Eve duties to attend to."

"Merry Christmas," Keith said, turning to close the door as he waved a colossal hand. "Have a wonderful holiday."

As he shut the door, Bitsy dislodged the caramel from her teeth and said, "You know what I'm wondering? Who was Charleen talking about when she said Albert was bullying her sister? I thought Miss Shirleen had a son and a daughter."

The electric kettle shrilled, and Iris could be heard in the kitchen singing along to the radio.

Susannah shrugged. "I don't remember her having a son."

Iris emerged from the kitchen, balancing a few paper cups on one of Susannah's mismatched dishes. She gave a cup to Bitsy, who immediately plunked a caramel on top of the copious amount of mini marshmallows. Shannon sat stiffly, and Conrad pushed his chair back as if to get away from the cocoa.

"He left town years ago," Larraine added, glancing around the table, her gaze landing on Shannon. "Shirleen didn't speak of him much. He wasn't happy here, so he left."

"There are some rats around town," Bitsy said, tapping the marshmallows down into the cup. "But most of us are okay."

Shannon said, "That's why I came back."

Susannah looked around the table, not sure what she had just heard. All at once she put it together. Shannon Ellis was Shirleen's new and improved daughter. Iris looked up from her cup as Bitsy reached out and put her hand over Shannon's.

"You're Charleen's sister?" Bitsy exclaimed, ripping the plastic wrap off the cookies. "I should have guessed. I'd know Miss Shirleen's recipe anywhere."

Larraine's shoulders dropped and she sniffed.

Bitsy sidled over to Shannon. "What's your mom's secret ingredient? You can tell me."

Shannon said nothing, and Bitsy looked at Conrad. "What about you? Are you in on the baking secret?"

"Bitsy Jean Long," Larraine scolded. "Behave yourself."

"Let's do that toast," Susannah said, topping off champagne flutes for everyone except Iris, who refused to give up her hot cocoa. She raised her glass, making eye contact with everyone individually. "To our newest members. Welcome to the family. I hope you like chocolate."

THE END

FROM THE AUTHOR

Cathy Tully is the pen name of E.C. Tully, a chiropractor and writer. She is a graduate of Georgetown University, in Washington DC, where she studied foreign languages and linguistics. She lived abroad in Quito, Ecuador and worked for an international trademark and patent law firm in New York City, before changing careers and graduating from Life University, in Marietta, Georgia with a Doctor of Chiropractic degree. She writes the *Dr. Susannah Shine ChiroCozy Mystery Series* and lives in small-town Georgia with her husband and rescue cats.

Website: ectully.com

Newsletter: dl.bookfunnel.com/oywdl45g4c

POISON AND POINSETTIAS

AUBREY ELLE

Madis is surrounded by poinsettias left and right, but she wasn't counting on a poisoned corpse in the mix...

CHAPTER ONE

A sea of color awaited us to the right of the supposed altar space where Rachel and Kent would say their vows. Vibrant rosy reds merged with punchy pinks. It should have brought to mind the idea of love everlasting, but in sharp contrast to the snow outside, these poinsettias seemed...too bold? Vulgar, even?

"Whoa."

My trusty worker Jon pulled up to an abrupt stop as he dragged another wheel of hoses inside. Pausing next to me as I supervised this newest delivery of poinsettias, he blinked a couple of times, flicking back his rocker hair. "That's a lot more than I thought we were supposed to get."

"Me too." But I wasn't about to correct our bookkeeper-slash-admin-genius of the company who'd handled the order. Almost two years ago, I'd welcomed my best friend to MH Landscaping on a freelance status.

Now, Rachel was a partner, a mastermind of all the busywork best done at the computer or on the phone while I was out in the field—when it wasn't winter, of course. Rach seldom screwed up, but there was *no* way she'd intentionally signed us up to get this many poinsettias to sell. The greenhouse—more like a unique conservatory—was full to bursting.

Thank goodness we cleared out the entire *greenhouse at the end of the summer.*

"They're *still* bringing them in?" Jon asked, peering to see around the wall opposite us as the women from the farm brought the flowers in.

"They're going to run out of room," I muttered, rubbing the back of my neck.

Before the end of the typical work season, Rach had urged me to consider housing poinsettias to sell. She had the space here at her large estate on the outskirts of town, and I apparently had the free time. A little something to keep us busy during the off months. It'd be fun, she said. A different thing to try, she said.

It was different, and kind of fun. I'd give her that. We'd already sold out the first week of December, and here we were, getting another shipment. Only, in her bride-to-be, pregnancy-brained state of chaos, Rachel had pulled a blooper on this order.

And there was no way I'd point out that big of a mistake just days before her wedding. Even though she had enjoyed a safe pregnancy thus far—just about to enter her third trimester, we were all walking on eggshells, determined not to trouble or upset her after she'd lost her first baby years ago.

"Maybe they'll need to figure out somewhere else to have the wedding—"

"No," Rachel cut off Jon, walking past us. Phone in hand, bud in her ear, she was clearly on hold. "No. Kent and I can still get married out here like planned. Even with all this..." She huffed a hard breath, fluffing out her blonde curls from her face. "All this excess."

I opened my mouth but she lifted a hand to cut me off. "Nope. Just no, Madis. No more worrying if I'm worrying."

"I don't want you to stress."

"And—"

She jerked her hand to silence Jon, too. "I'm not delicate. I appreciate your concern, I do. But I'm not fragile, you guys. This is on me. I *swear* we weren't supposed to get double the shipment. It's gotta be my fault, and I'll fix it. Just as soon as I get Zara on the freaking phone..." She paced, tapping her hand to her thigh.

"Why are you calling her?" Jon asked, setting the hoses down. "She's probably outside with the trucks unloading with the others who drove here."

"Yeah, that's right." I nodded my agreement.

Rach chose Zaresettia's Farm for poinsettias in a show of supporting women. Zara—the namesake, so to speak—was the owner of the all-organic co-op farm. Her three employees were females, and the rest of their staff consisted of female volunteers and young adults hoping to get out of abusive situations. All four of the women on the staff seemed equally hands-on in the delivery. During the first poinsettia delivery a couple of weeks ago, they'd operated with a close-knit familiarity, ribbing each other and seemingly finishing each other's sentences. I liked to think Kent, Jon, Toby, and Beth had that same kind of laidback attitude working on my landscaping crew, but the females running Zarsettia Farm seemed almost like sisters. All the same thirtysomething age, sharing inside jokes and in tune with each other's quirks.

"I'll grab my coat," I offered. "We'll find Zara and get to the bottom of it. Besides, if we've got double the shipment, we'll just sell double. No big."

Rachel slanted her brows at me then smiled with an eye roll. "Ever the optimist, huh, Madis? But there's no way we can sell *this* many poinsettias before Christmas. There are not enough people in Payton to buy more!"

"Then we'll sell 'em elsewhere." Supply and demand. Everyone wanted a poinsettia at the holiday times, and if we already depleted our small town's worth of customers, we'd sell them online to the rest of central Ohio. Heck, if we kept that stand stocked at the diner on Main, we'd have no problem selling straight up to the twenty-fifth.

Rachel frowned, growling at her phone. "Voicemail, again."

Jon chuckled. "Because she's got to be busy unloading the trucks outside."

But then wouldn't we hear her phone ringing in and out of the greenhouse? Come to think of it, I'd only spotted Abby, Brittney, and Claire shifting the flats of potted flowers inside the building.

"Nah. From our conversation last week, I don't think Zara was making the drive this time," Rachel said.

Really? The owner of this seasonal supplier seemed very involved in her business, even driving the trucks herself—at least she did in the beginning of the month. *Then again, what do I know? And it's none of my business anyhow.*

"I don't want to get in the way of them coming in and out." Rachel shook her head, sliding her phone in the back pocket of her maternity jeans. "Besides, I ran into Abby when they first got here and she said Zara had seemed busier than usual. I figured a direct communication via a phone call would be easiest and most professional."

"Abby's the tall one?" Jon checked as we went for the double doors that would open up to where the Zarsettia trucks stood waiting.

"No, the redhead," I corrected him. "Brittney's the tallest one."

"Ah." He nodded. "And the one with the glasses is Carey?"

"Claire," Rachel said with a chuckle. "Zara said she calls them her ABC."

"So, I should say the MH Landscaping crew is the... KJBTS?"

Rach smirked. "Doesn't have the same ring to it."

I elbowed her arm playfully. "Ha. Ha."

"But maybe the ABC will have an idea about us having too many poinsettias," she said.

What, like begrudging us for requesting they take

back half of this stock they're already unloading? All the way to Florida? No, we'd just manage and sell them one way or another.

At the double doors, Rachel snugged her scarf tighter around her neck, and Jon and I zipped up our coats. The constant back and forth between the cold of the snowy outdoors and the warmth of the cozy greenhouse had to be annoying. I wasn't surprised Abby wore jeans and a t-shirt as she hustled, carrying flats inside. Brittney was sliding trays of flowers out of the second truck, wearing a long-sleeve t-shirt and jeans as she waved at us. And at the last truck, Claire bobbed her head to whatever music she was listening to—also in a t-shirt and leggings. She wasn't alone, either.

"Tommy?" I called out to Payton's retired police chief. "What are you doing here?"

The fact he was helping out wasn't out of the ordinary. Tommy seldom sat still, a friend always ready to assist.

"Just pulled in and thought to lend a hand. I picked up Nick at the airport," the older man said as he slid more trays for Claire to grab.

"Nick?" I couldn't help my grin.

The man himself spoke up from the middle truck Brittney was unloading. Smiling wryly at Tommy, Nick groaned.

"I thought you said you wouldn't be back from visiting until the weekend," I said.

"I managed an earlier flight and thought to hurry home." He winked at me, nodding at Rachel.

"Couldn't risk missing the wedding, right? If, uh, it's still on."

Rachel crossed her arms. "Of course, it's still on."

"In there?" Nick asked, pointing at the greenhouse. "Will there be room?"

"Oh, never mind that. We'll figure it out." Rachel shook her head.

"We're looking for Zara," I said. "Seems we've made a mistake in our order."

"Z didn't have time to make this delivery," Claire said in passing. "Because she's too 'important' for something as menial as a delivery now."

I blinked, surprised at the sass in this woman's tone. Zara struck me as something of a micro-manager, but I didn't get any bad vibes from her at the beginning of the month. The woman sure hadn't suggested she thought she was "too good" for the tasks her employees completed.

"What do you mean *now*, Claire?" Brittney asked as she walked out of the greenhouse empty-handed. "She's always been the boss. Always been the same old, unbending dictator of Zarsettia's Poinsettias."

Abby joined her two coworkers as well, dusting her gloves on her jeans as she walked toward the trucks. "Come on, you two. No point whining about Z. Not like it'd change anything. Let's hurry up and get these flowers off."

Wow.

I caught Rach's attention, her brows raised just as I was sure mine were.

Jon refused to make eye contact with the three

women. Talk about awkward. And what a change from the first Zarsettia delivery. Was it because Zara wasn't here that they were so...scornful? Bickering in the freedom of their boss being absent?

"I'll, um, just call her again then," Rachel said, stepping aside and clearly uneasy about these women's attitudes about their boss.

"I'll help," Jon said, heading to Abby's truck.

The sooner they're done unloading, the better, maybe. I sure didn't want to wade into any private work-related drama. After these poinsettias were off their hands, we were clear of Zarsettia's business anyway.

"Hey," Tommy said, calling out to us. He frowned, his white brows slanting under the bright blue of his knit beanie. "Hear that?"

We all stilled, listening past Chuck Berry's "Run, Rudolph, Run" Jon had playing further inside the greenhouse.

Winds whipped through the trees, but there. It went again. A phone ringing.

Rachel lowered her phone, peering at the device.

"It's in your truck," Abby told Brittney.

"Huh? No, it's not." Brittney pointed at Claire's truck. "Is your phone in there?"

What did it matter if Abby's phone was in the back of the truck? Rachel was calling Zara right this minute...and that ringtone was in sync with the dial tone of Rachel's outgoing call.

Could Zara have left her phone in the truck? It seemed too uncanny of a coincidence.

Nick jumped into the truck. Abby shrugged at Claire, and Brittney stepped up as well. "So weird," she said. "That's Zara's ringtone. She just changed it to 'Feliz Navidad' to reflect the holiday spirit."

My stomach twisted at this not-so-coincidental detail. If Zara's phone was in the truck...wouldn't *she* be there as well? And if she was in there, why did she not show herself yet?

"I thought you said Zara didn't come on this delivery," I said to Claire.

"She wasn't planning on it," Abby replied from the packed snow-covered ground.

Inside the heated storage space, Nick followed the ringtone. He strode past the last of the tall, anchored standing racks with flats of poinsettias, stopping suddenly with a light swear.

"What is it?" I asked, peering around his shoulder. If something had our handsome police chief startled and unhappy, it couldn't be something frivolous. "Nick?"

"I think...Zara hitched a ride after all."

I gasped, spotting the lifeless woman slumped in the corner of the cargo space.

CHAPTER TWO

I held the hose to water the poinsettias, leaning to the side to peer toward the now-closed double doors to the greenhouse. Outside with the three Zarsettia trucks parked and turned off, Abby and Brittney spoke to Payton's local law enforcement. Even though Nick was on vacation, with his trustiest friend and officer, Damon, in charge, both men stood out there at the crime scene. Tommy loitered toward the side, a state detective interviewing Claire. The women huddled into coats and I couldn't help but observe how out of their comfort zone they had to be.

Out of their comfort zone. Who *wouldn't* be out of their comfort zone at a crime scene, just discovering their boss dead in the cargo space of a truck they could have driven across the country?

Here in a snowy Ohioan December, the ABC of Zarsettia Farm had to be shocked out of the usual warmth and sunshine of Florida.

Rachel had offered to have the women questioned in the greenhouse, but Nick's smirk was telling enough. He'd—rightly—assumed we'd want the interrogation to happen where we could eavesdrop. Besides, as Damon and a crime scene tech pointed out, they wanted to investigate the trucks *and* have ample space to split up the three women to question them separately yet within the same area.

Needless to say, it didn't look like Abby, Brittney, and Claire could count on leaving any time soon.

Although... I leaned over more, seeing around Rachel's shoulder as she leaned in sync with me, peering through the windows. *Although, it looks like Tommy and that detective are about to let Claire walk off...*

"Madis!" Jon shouted.

I flinched, righting myself from falling I was leaning so far over to snoop. As I faced him across the table of poinsettias, I realized I'd accidentally sprayed him with the hose.

"Madis!" Now Kent was shouting.

By correcting my grip, I'd removed my hose spray from Jon only to accidentally blast Kent.

"Sorry! Sorry!"

Kent grumbled as he shook off his arm, but Jon didn't seem as bothered, absentmindedly brushing off his sweatshirt as he too peered out the window. "Who was driving the truck Zara was found in?" he asked.

"It was Brittney's truck," I said.

"No. It was the middle truck," Rachel said. "Right?"

"Yeah, and that was the one Brittney pulled up in."

Jon wrinkled his brow. "So...she'd have to be the one to kill her?"

We all stared out the window, likely all noticing the same thing. No one seemed to be targeted for arrest, and no wonder. All three women had pointed fingers at the other.

"Why?" I asked. "When they came for the first delivery, they said they'd swapped trucks at their halfway point in South Carolina. It wasn't like they were assigned or partial to each truck."

Past the women and law enforcement working in and out of the middle truck's storage space, there were no telltale differences between each vehicle. All three half-ton cargo trucks were painted hot pink, standing out like a lost blast of summer in the snow softly falling. *Zarsettia Farm* stood out even starker, the funky cursive font on the decal screaming that Zara ran a hip business. A cartoonish logo of a poinsettia was plastered after with the name, pinpointing what product they offered exclusively. With how similar the vehicles were, and no specific woman designated to operate any which one, this couldn't be more like a game of switcheroo.

"Dang, am I cold," Claire said, coming into the greenhouse. She shut the doors, closing out the blast of chilly air. Shuddering, she hugged herself as she entered the warmth of the poinsettia-filled building. "Someone could *freeze* to death out there."

Eyes wide, she stopped and dropped her mouth open. "Oh, my goodness." She slammed her eyes shut in a wince. "Bad choice of words." Looking at us now, her lips slid into a frown and stuck there. "This is..." She sighed instead of finishing her statement. "What a morning. I can't believe she's *gone*."

"It's a shock, for sure," Rachel said.

Claire took her glasses off and wiped at her eyes. "I mean she was just— I *just* told her that—" Sniffling, she rubbed at her eyes and then smeared the condensation from her eyewear.

"Here," Kent said, gesturing for her to sit by the closest heat vent. "Warm up, at least."

We could all see her shaking, despite one arm strapped around her waist.

"Thank you, but I don't think I'll ever warm up from the shock of this." She took the seat, though, nearly falling into the folding chair we'd moved to the side.

"At least you didn't *find* her in the truck yourself," Jon said.

I shot him a look. He'd probably meant well, but still. As far as platitudes went, that one fell awfully short.

"Uh, I mean, I have. I've found a dead body on the job before," he amended. "I wouldn't recommend it. So...that's a silver lining, right? You didn't have to actually *see* her dead?"

Kent shook his head. "Just...stop," he whispered to the teen.

Jon nodded, seemingly zipping his lips shut and looking away as he blushed.

"But it wasn't your boss," Claire said.

"I should hope not." I raised my hand, not pausing from watering the plants.

"It's not the discovery of Zara being dead. It's that she was murdered." Claire shivered anew, looking at the windows where her two coworkers remained outside speaking with the cops. Still, they pointed at each other, and gestured inside the greenhouse, too, likely indicating Claire here.

"How would you know she's murdered?" I asked.

"Did they say she was murdered?" Rachel asked.

Kent groaned lightly. "Now we've got a murder *here*. Right before our wedding!" He shot me a stern, almost accusing look.

"What?" I said, setting my hand on my hip.

"Well, this is what you do," Kent said.

Now I shut off my hose and crossed my arms.

Kent rolled his hand, seeming flustered for the right words. "You can't deny that you...find dead people," he said.

"No, no, no." Jon shook his head. "It looks like Zara was just delivered here. That's hardly the same thing like we what usually deal with."

"Usually deal with? We're landscapers, not crime detectives!" I narrowed my eyes at my right-hand man, but Jon wasn't wrong. We'd uncovered plenty of murders in our little town. Silly me for thinking the off-months over winter would change that habit.

Rachel beat me to scolding him though. "Kent, that's ridiculous. Madis just happens to be in the wrong place at the wrong time."

"Well, excuse me. I'm not fond of the idea of a

dead body on our property, delivered or not," Kent argued.

"It's hardly *my* fault, though," I insisted.

Whether it was due to her bride-to-be or momma-to-be status, Rachel wasn't having this discussion. Hand held up to silence us, she turned back to Claire. "They said she was murdered?"

How could they? I peered out the windows again. Sure, the van for the closest morgue was parked out there now, but could they determine a cause of death *that* quickly?

"Well, she had to have been murdered by one of them," Claire insisted. Fingers up one by one, she gave her reasoning. "Zara was absolutely in annoyingly perfect health. She wasn't doing drugs or anything weird like that. There wasn't anything dangerous to accidentally hurt herself with in the truck."

"Maybe a flat of flowers fell off in the ride?" Jon guessed.

Claire frowned, shaking her head at him. "No. Zara wouldn't be *in* there for the ride. She didn't even plan to come on this delivery run. If she had, she would have driven in the cab, taking turns with us. Just last week, she said she was going to sit this trip out."

She'd said that before. "Because she was too busy?"

Claire scoffed. "When wasn't she too busy? She was the head honcho of Zarsettia's. The most she did with this order was check off the inventory as we loaded, but if you ask Brit, that's just because Zara's a micro-managing control freak. *Was*, I guess."

And...you're bitter about that? Did Claire want to

own the poinsettia farm? Brittney disliked Zara nit-picking as a manager? Did Abby have an issue with her boss, too? The women seemed to be on the same page of disliking Zara, but perhaps for different reasons.

"Still, it's quite the assumption to say she was murdered," Rachel said. She tried to smile, chuckling weakly. "I mean, Christmas is just a week away. No one murders people at Christmas. It's...a happy time."

Claire scoffed. "Look, Zara was murdered. She had to have been. I know she was. Because there's someone who hates her enough to kill her." Through slitted eyes, she stared at the windows. Abby and Brittney were shouting at each other now, all "separation" between the attempts of questioning lost.

Claire pointed at her coworkers, seething through clenched teeth, "She killed her!"

CHAPTER THREE

Just as Claire accused one of her coworkers, Abby stormed inside. Her face was just as pink as Claire's. From the blast of snowy winds or anger, I couldn't say.

"What?" Abby demanded. "Why are you pointing your finger at me?"

Brittney slipped in, as well, leaving Nick and his officers conversing outside. "Now what?" she griped. "You guys are at it again?"

"You!" Claire stood, no longer hugging herself for warmth or comfort. Arm raised, she pointed clearly at Abby. "You killed her!"

"Oh, for goodness' sake." Abby rolled her eyes and shook her head.

"Yeah!" Brittney jumped into Claire's accusation. "You're the only one who hated her enough to want to kill her."

"Oh? I'm the only one who hated her?" Abby

snapped and sneered at Claire. "Me? Weren't *you* the one threatening her that she'd pay for 'taking' the farm from you?"

Brittney gasped, then scowled at the redhead of the trio. "*What*?"

Smug, Abby crossed her arms. "Come on. We all knew you hated how she bought out your shares of the farm."

I blinked, unable to tear my stare from this catty fight just before our eyes. Too bad I couldn't record this for Nick, but then again, with the shouts we'd heard and the women pointing at each other, it seemed these were the heavy words they'd already told the cops.

Rachel swallowed, her mouth hanging open and her stare stuck on the unfolding drama as well. I took her hose from her, shutting the water off before she flooded the place.

"Huh? Oh, yeah." She absentmindedly registered what I was doing, not breaking her focus on the three Zarsettia employees fighting.

"Abs, that was *years* ago," Claire retorted. "That's old news."

Brittney walked up to her. "Hmmm, not so old. Just last week you told me you wished you'd never let Zara buy you out."

"It *is* old news," Claire insisted. "And even if it wasn't, it wasn't something anyone should be mad enough about to kill her!" Now she locked her glare on Brittney. "Like you should talk, anyway. You've been scheming for over a year how to 'stick it' to Zara once and for all. You can't stand how she takes all the credit when the farm was your idea to begin with."

Brittney growled. "Well, it *was* my idea! All the way back in college. But we all agreed Zara had the know-how to make it work."

"As if you're okay with her claiming all the success." Claire pivoted the other way, jabbing a finger at Abby. "And you. *You're* the one who really despised her enough to get rid of her."

Still with her arms crossed, Abby sneered. "Yeah, right."

"Yes, I *am* right. You couldn't stand it anymore. Ever since she hooked up with Tyler, you haven't shut up about her stealing your man."

Abby lowered her arms, fist clenched, but her tone cool. "I don't care who he sleeps with. He's my *ex*. That means he doesn't matter to me anymore."

"Ha!" Claire tried on the smug smirk now. "That's what you want us to believe. You couldn't stand the fact he chose her over you."

"That's—"

"All right. All right." Nick clapped his hands.

Realizing he—and the others—had come into the greenhouse, I wondered how much he'd heard. Since he wasn't immediately intercepting and following up with questions, perhaps these accusations were precisely what the women had shared outside when they were interviewed.

"Let's just take a breath. Take a step back," he advised.

"Take a step back where?" Claire asked. "You told us the truck is a crime scene. We can't leave."

"Well, Zara wasn't in *my* truck," Abby said. "Why can't I go?"

"Hey, she wasn't in my truck either, so I'm free, too," Claire said.

"Hey! I didn't put her in the truck I drove! Don't try to pin anything on me!" Brittney said.

"*No one* is going anywhere." Nick ran his hand through his sandy-blond hair. "All three of you can stick around town until this is cleared up a bit."

Abby groaned. "We're stuck here in Podunk Ohio?"

"Just before Christmas?" Claire asked, slack-jawed.

"Great," Brittney groused.

Wow. Absolutely no lack of love for Zara, then. These women had two priorities: shift the blame and avoid being holed up away from home.

"Where are we supposed to go? We were supposed to be on the road home by now," Abby said.

"There's a motel in town," Tommy said. "Perhaps we can drive you ladies there."

Nick nodded and turned at the gravel crunching and popping under tires. The morgue was carrying away Zara, it seemed. "We should be through with the trucks soon, and then we'll see where we're at."

Instead of lamenting being stuck away from home so close to the holiday, the women sighed, intermittently glaring at each other or looking away from everyone altogether.

"Hey, it's not, uh, ideal," Rachel said. "But isn't

finding Zara's killer more important than the inconvenience of staying in town?"

"I didn't kill her." All three said it in unison, even parroting the exact same gesture of pointing at themselves.

Well, someone did.

Claire shook her head. "I'm going to get a room then, if they even have any this close to the holiday. Jeez." Standing up straight, she seemed to steel her spine, saying, "And I'm *not* sharing a room with a murderer."

"What if the motel's booked? Is there room here?" Brittney asked, looking through the windows toward Rachel and Kent's large farmhouse-styled mansion.

"Uh..." Kent's eyes couldn't have opened any wider, he was so alarmed.

"Well..." Rachel rubbed her cheek. "Sure, there's room, but—"

Kent coughed, perhaps covering his sound of protest. He lurched forward, hugging Rachel to his side. "*Normally*, there would be room for a guest, but we're a full house. You know, with Christmas right around the corner."

"We're not full yet..." Rachel admonished.

Kent squeezed her close, his eyes still full of alarm, likely freaked at her being hospitable to a potential murderer. Nick wouldn't let a suspect roam too far, but did they even have any evidence to mark any of these women as the killer?

I caught Nick's uneasy frown, guessing he wasn't any more of a fan of Rachel's invitation than Kent was.

But no one wanted to be the one to turn someone down.

Hey, friends look out for friends. We all did. Rachel was just too sweet to put anyone out. Which was why I spoke up instead. "You don't have a full house *yet*, Rach, but with the wedding a few days out, you've got your hands full enough. Remember, we've got to get this greenhouse cleared enough to *have* the wedding as planned. Kent's family's coming in town and they'll take the guestrooms, so..."

Abby's brows raised. "You guys are having the ceremony in *here*?" She pointed at the surplus of poinsettias crowding around us.

"That's the, uh, goal," Rachel said.

"Why'd you order so many poinsettias, then?" Abby asked with a light laugh. "It's packed in here."

I elbowed Jon. "We can help drive you gals to the motel on Main Street. Huh, Jon?"

He nodded. "Yeah, sure. We've both got our trucks here. No problem."

Except, we still needed to clear out room for even a small ceremony. And hope that a crime scene for a murder wouldn't linger just outside the doors...

"No problem," I echoed weakly. *I hope.*

CHAPTER FOUR

In the end, my offer for Jon and I to drive Abby, Brittney, and Claire to the motel at the end of Main Street was a moot point.

Perhaps Nick wasn't comfy with the idea of his girlfriend being in a vehicle with a murder suspect because he stepped in, saying he and Tommy could easily squeeze all three women in the backseat of Tommy's SUV.

Except, Claire was adamant that she was not getting a car with a killer. Her refusal of the ride reemphasized her conviction that Abby—*or maybe it's Brittney now?*—was Zara's murderer. It seemed she flopped back and forth between her two coworkers, but she was stubborn to distance herself from any blame.

They resolved the matter when Tommy suggested I give him a ride home later, thus freeing up the front seat and Nick could drive all three women to the motel. That almost worked, but with Damon also on hand, as well as the state detective, they agreed each woman could be driven apart from the others. While no one had been outright arrested or blamed officially, the ABC of Zarsettia Farm sure looked guilty with the transportation that drove them off Rachel and Kent's property.

Once they were all gone, I all but pounced on Tommy.

"*Was* she murdered?" I asked, clutching Tommy's sleeve.

"How'd she die?" Jon asked.

"Did one of them do it?" Kent asked. "My goodness, a murderer, *here*. I don't like this one bit."

"Don't you start saying this is Madis's fault," Rachel retorted to her fiancé. "If anyone's to blame, it's all *my* fault. I was the one who found Zarsettia Farm for the poinsettias. Heck, selling the poinsettias was my brainchild to begin with. So *I'm* the one who even got them here in the first place."

"I still don't like it," Kent said. "A murder at our home."

"I bet Zara's not a fan of the events either!"

"Rach, we're about to start a new beginning in our lives." Kent waved at the bright and bold Zarsettia trucks out the window. "Feet from where someone else's ended!"

"But *was* she murdered?" I asked Tommy again.

The repeat of my question shut them all up—thank goodness. With the heaters droning in the background and the water trickling for the indoor koi pond, the clash of all of us speaking over each other at once was irritating.

Rachel blinked, shaking her head. "You... You think she just died?" she asked me.

I shrugged. "I didn't see any blood. And it'd make more sense if she just happened to pass away in the truck."

"Why would that make more sense?" Kent challenged.

Jon raised his finger, brightening as though a light bulb had clicked for him. "Because why else would she be dead in the truck?"

I nodded. That was the weirdest clue. "Let's say one of those women did kill Zara. Why stow her in the truck just before a delivery run was about to happen? Wouldn't it be easier to dump her somewhere in Florida instead of bringing her along? I can't see a murderer want to lug around the product of their murder, unless they *wanted* to be caught. Normally a criminal wants distance from the evidence of their crime?"

Rachel nodded, pointing at me. "Yeah, that's true. Boy, you really soaked up a lot of the sleuthing business in Columbus."

Hardly. I'd left a job in marketing in the city. So, the company was a studio that produced mysteries. It didn't infer I *was* a detective!

Tommy raised his hand, demanding attention. "Before we all launch into this debate, is there anything else we need to do in here?"

I scanned the greenhouse, taking in the bold reds, pinks, and whites that were so jam-packed in the space. "Well, we will need to figure out how to make room for the chairs and altar..."

Jon weaved around flats of flowers, nearing the koi pond and pointing. "If we could move these from here onto another shelving unit in the back, it could work. And those red ones over there could maybe be stacked near the white ones in the other room."

Kent blew out a sigh. "But it's pretty packed in there, too." He rubbed at the golden stubble on his jaw. "I don't know, Rachel..."

"Yeah, yeah. I know. I ordered too many. We'll make it work. We've got, what, three days?" She shook her head, walking to me and Tommy and looping her arms over our shoulders and ushering us to walk with her. "It can wait. Right now, we've got this murder to discuss. Because I'm not going to let an unsolved murder hang like a dark cloud over my wedding day!"

A half hour later, we were cozier and hydrated in Rachel and Kent's kitchen. Around the old solid oak table, we took seats to sip our hot cocoas and hot teas, but I bet I couldn't be the only one wishing for something stronger.

Tommy wasn't "with" Payton's police force anymore, but since his retirement, he'd become a fatherly figure and immediately befriended Nick. Where Nick had to be more careful about what details he shared from open and ongoing investigations, Tommy was more of a lax middleman, simply a citizen conversing with the freedom of gossip.

Just as we settled in with our drinks, though, our town's *true* gossip showed up.

Mom knocked and called out her arrival, rushing in with a box from the diner. Still in her waitressing gear beneath the thick parka I'd bought her for her birthday, she burst into the room.

"I *just* heard!" she exclaimed. "Madis, I swear, you just have a knack at finding bodies or something!"

I set my mug down hard but not with too much force that my hot tea splashed out. "If I had a dollar for every time you said that..."

"Well, it's true." She set the box on the table, easing out of her sleeves. "All summer long, you've found corpse after corpse."

Jon held up a finger. "Technically, *I* found the lady buried in the garden."

Mom shrugged one shoulder, slipping her coat sleeve out the opposite arm as Tommy stood to assist her. "Same thing. You work *for* her. I'm telling you, those old biddies in town are right. MH Landscaping *is* cursed."

I sighed, too tired of rehashing this debate.

"We've already decided Zara's murder is *my* fault," Rachel announced.

Mom blew a raspberry at her, smoothing out her apron before she took a chair. "Nonsense. You'd only be at blame if you killed her, and we all know you wouldn't hurt a fly." Seated, she exhaled a rush of air. "Now. Who did it? I rushed over as soon as Damon stopped by the diner after taking some redhead to the motel. Thank goodness my shift was over right then." She made a gimme motion with her hands. "Well? I want the full scoop!"

I gestured to Tommy. "Was Zara murdered?" I asked him.

He lowered his mug to the table and wiped his lips. "It's a preliminary investigation, of course, but I'd say so."

"How?" I asked. "I didn't see blood. Or any other immediate signs of violence."

He raised his mug again, lifting it almost as the answer. "Poisoned."

Rachel gasped.

"Really?" I asked.

Jon slapped the table. "Well, what do you expect? She was in a truck full of poinsettias! They're poisonous."

I shook my head. "Yeah, if she ate maybe a few hundred leaves. Poinsettias *are* poisonous, but it takes a lot to kill a human. At best, she'd get the runs or a rash from ingesting some of it."

Rachel scoffed. "And if she was a specialty farmer growing them, she'd know not to snack on them."

"As I said," Tommy began again. "It's early in the case, but Ford, the crime scene tech, was pretty sure the smoothie she drank was the source of poison. It's one of those..." He gestured with his hands. "High-tech shaker cups."

"A martini mixer?" Mom asked, scrunching her face as she tucked her graying red hair back behind her ears.

"No, no. Those blender cups."

I nodded at Tommy. "For making protein shakes. They have them at the gym all the time."

"Oh, right, right," Mom said.

"Ford found one with the lid closed," Tommy said. "Zara had clearly drunk some since the same liquid was found at the corner of her lips. A few drops must have dripped onto her t-shirt, too. It matches the liquid in the shaker cup, which was nestled against her leg. Of course, an autopsy will show if she consumed it, but we'll go with the assumption she drank it."

"But to know it's poisoned?" I challenged. That Zara drank from her smoothie was one thing. To jump to the conclusion it was poisoned, though? I couldn't bridge the two together just yet.

"You found poinsettia pieces in it?" Jon asked.

I slanted him a look. "It'd take *a lot* of poinsettias, Jon."

Tommy shook his head. "Nope. Something worse. Some of the smoothie must have leaked out, maybe when she was drinking it, but it wasn't mixed completely. So much so, berries were still visible, not mushed up."

"What kind of berries?" I asked, thinking of raspberries, blackberries, blueberries...

"Belladonna. A couple were intact on a spill on

Zara's pants. Ford recognized them from the five-leaved part still connected to one berry. He wrote a research paper on the plant back in grad school. Well, I guess he dropped out, but he didn't forget the research."

I nodded. "Nightshade can easily look like a blueberry. I'm not as versed with the specific petals or leaves around the berry, but they're green in a cluster, first. I can spot the leaves, for sure."

"And by the bluish-purple and green specks in the smoothie, it seems someone at least tried to blend berries and or leaves into her drink. Or maybe just added it to what she had already," Tommy said. "All three women said Zara had smoothies every morning for breakfast, so that was common knowledge of those closest to her. At any rate, Ford estimates she's been dead for probably forty-eight hours."

"Which would fit with them loading the trucks in Florida," Kent said. "None of the women said Zara was coming to make the drive on this delivery. So she was probably killed there before the women left."

"And they very well could be clueless about Zara's body in the cargo space in that truck." Tommy lifted his hands in a *who knows* manner. "There was an inventory clipboard with her body. Maybe Zara was checking off the loading process as she drank her smoothie, and then died in the truck before anyone was the wiser."

"How much would it take to kill someone?" Jon asked. "Is nightshade more toxic than poinsettias?"

"A dozen berries?" I guessed. "Belladonna's called *deadly nightshade* for a reason."

"Jeez, Madis," Mom said, rubbing her arms. "I hate to think of you near something like that during the growing season."

"It's not planted on purpose, that's for sure."

"Maybe we should make a cheat sheet of hazardous plants for the crew," Rachel said.

"Well, sure." I shrugged. "But really, it's not that common in town."

Tommy nodded. "That's what Ford said."

"Besides, I believe everyone on our crew would know better than to eat or drink anything on the ground." I smiled at Jon's *duh* smirk he shot my way.

He lifted his head from peering at his phone on the table. "And Google says it can be found in Florida."

Rachel hummed a knowing sound. "And if these women work on a farm and are, in theory, knowledgeable about plants, they'd know what it is and what it does too."

"How fast does it kill someone?" I asked. While I was familiar with deadly nightshade as a plant you didn't want to mess with, I wasn't as sure of its toxicity in a human.

"Depends on how much is ingested," Tommy said. "And Ford seemed to think her smoothie was laced with a *lot*. They'll test the evidence, of course, and like I said, the autopsy will show what was in her stomach."

"So she drank it and...passed out?" Jon asked.

"That's what Ford said. Coma to death, most likely," Tommy replied.

A quiet, mess-free way to die. *Easier to hide. And be unaware of...*

"So, assuming Zara was drinking her smoothie while the trucks were being loaded for our delivery, it means someone had to have been ready to mix the belladonna into her drink that morning," I summed up.

"Which means it'd have to be someone who'd be there before or during the loading period," Rachel said.

"Abby, Brittney, and Claire." I counted them off with my fingers.

"I thought they had volunteers working at the farm, too," Kent said.

"No. The last time I spoke to Zara, after the first delivery," Rachel said, "she told me they let the volunteers off from December eighth until after the New Year. It'd just be the four of them at the farm now."

"And who are these women, again?" Mom asked us. "The ladies who drove the trucks? I know you said you chose Zarsettia for the poinsettias because of some small-business initiative for women..."

"Abby, Brittney, and Claire," I said. "The three employees."

"And..." She cocked her head at Tommy. "Which one are you liking for the killer, huh, Tommy? Abby, Brittney, or Claire?"

Which one?

"Yes," Tommy replied.

Mom rolled her eyes. "That was an *or* question."

We all glanced at each other, seemingly entertaining the same guessing game.

"All of them?" Mom slapped the table. "All of them are suspects?"

"At this point," Tommy said. "Nick's going to have a heck of a time with how easily they blame each other."

"Okay. Who's got a motive?" Mom asked.

I huffed. "Who *doesn't*?"

CHAPTER FIVE

Since we were all at the big estate and it was nearly evening time after the chaos of finding Zara's body, Kent suggested we just stick around for dinner after satisfying Mom's gossip need to know about Payton's latest murder.

"This way, we can all keep an eye on Rachel," he whispered to me and Mom in the hallway after everyone agreed to the impromptu idea.

Mom shushed him. "She's not an invalid. Plenty of women have had challenges with pregnancies then do just fine with their rainbow babies."

"I know. But I don't want her to be stressed."

I couldn't help but chuckle. No wonder she jumped at my concerns earlier. "She's a pregnant bride. Of course she'll be stressed to some extent."

He glanced back at the rest of the group laughing and prepping for chili in the kitchen. "Not a murdered-farmer-on-her-property sort of stress."

"Oh, we'll figure that out soon enough." Mom patted his back as she glanced out the window in the direction of the greenhouse. "And those hideous pink trucks will be out of sight in no time."

"Not a fan of the color?" Kent teased.

She twisted her lips. "Meh. Pink's fine, but that kind of neon is just too..."

"Pushy?" I guessed.

"Yeah!" Mom shook her head. "I get it. Hot pink. Hello, girl power! But goodness, don't they burn their retinas with that garishly bold color day in and out?"

Kent had calmed enough to laugh along with us. "Well, they're from Florida. Everything's bright down there."

"True." I herded them back toward the kitchen. "Relax," I told him. "Mom's right. I'm sure this will be a cut and clean case to solve."

"Relax? Easier said than done," he muttered as we rejoined them.

"Boy, is he a worrier," Mom quipped to me once he walked to Rachel getting a couple of jars of tomato paste out of the pantry.

"Oh, don't tease him too much. He's just concerned."

"I know. I know. But our Rachel's no lightweight wimp." She smiled, parting to start chopping veggies with Jon as Tommy got ground beef in a pan to brown.

As I debated where I should fit in, I couldn't help but appreciate the scene. Our group of friends made a fine team in a pinch, and the comfort of knowing we could count on each other drove away a little taste of the niggling curiosity I couldn't completely shake. Oh, I'd be up all night pondering Zara's murder, but here and now, I smiled at everyone pitching in for the meal. It seemed such a simple thing. My employees, friends, and mother all getting along like this, but I didn't take it for granted. To start with, I missed out on these homey opportunities for the majority of the year, usually working late to take advantage of all the hours of sunlight.

"All we need is Toby's margaritas," Kent said.

I nodded, clearing the table since they were all crowding around the stove and counters. "I imagine he and Beth have to be near Vegas now," I said of the two landscapers who'd fallen in love on my crew.

"And Selena's been home with her family?" Tommy asked of the last missing member MH Landscaping.

Again, I nodded. "Yep. Visiting until we start back up in the spring."

"Seems like it'll be here before you know it," Rachel mused, rubbing her belly.

Mom swiped a slice of bell pepper and munched on it before asking me about someone else who'd ordinarily be included in our group. "Too bad Nick's visiting his family in Toledo, too. Missing out on a case right here in Payton."

"Nope." Tommy grinned. "He came back early—I picked him up, actually, just before we found Zara in the truck."

"Well, shoot," Mom said, giving me a woeful grimace. "You'll be lucky to see him before the holidays, Madis. Out of town, now back to a case."

As though we'd summoned him, my phone rang, showing his name on the caller ID. "Be right back," I told the others as I stepped into the hallway to answer. "Hey, Nick."

"Hey, babe. Sorry my surprise didn't pan out. I was really hoping to snag some extra downtime with you coming home a couple days early."

I smiled at his voice, appreciative of his words. Between my workaholic tendencies and his constant need to be on call, we were hard-pressed for time with each other. "You're back at the job, then, with Zara's poisoning?"

He grunted. "Sounds like Tommy's been talking with you."

"Maybe."

His sigh held enough of a note of fatigue I frowned.

"I'm still off duty, officially, but I've spoken with the mayor about assisting, being around to help Damon. I've got no doubt he can handle it, but since we're working with the local department in Florida, where Zarsettia is based, it's a little trickier than a simple case here in town."

"And that bald guy from the state cops was there this morning."

"Hm-mmm. Because this is something that's crossed state lines. Backtracking what Abby, Brittney, and Claire explained, Zara's body was in South Carolina *and* Florida."

"She couldn't have been alive then, at their halfway point of their drive to Ohio?"

"Not with the tox reports. And they've agreed she was likely killed two days ago, so that puts her in Florida."

I raised my brows. "The autopsy's already happening?" That sure was fast, especially so close to the holiday. I wouldn't stoop so low to whine that *all* governmental entities worked slowly, but...that was *really* fast.

"The autopsy's already happened. Past tense," he corrected. "Ford assisted, and it seems they didn't have anything else on hand. I just got the email of the results a couple of hours ago."

"And..." I fidgeted, dragging the toe of my shoe along the rug. "And...the results of that are too confidential to share?"

He grunted a laugh, used to my slight needling and nagging for intel. "Like I said, Tommy must have been talking to you all. I'll just say he was right—or Ford was."

"Belladonna." I shook my head. "Someone killed off a farmer with deadly nightshade. That seems so...ironic."

"How so?"

"Zara had to be knowledgeable about plants, and that was the very thing that killed her."

"I'm not sure if Zara *was* an expert of plants, despite her owning a specialty farm."

"Really? How come?"

"Those three women didn't seem to imply Zara

was an expert. At least they didn't think she was good at anything except being a bossy boss who wanted her way."

Funny. "A boss is supposed to *boss*. Aren't they?"

"That's the definition I know it as, but maybe there's more to learn from those three friends yet. We're going to talk to them separately tomorrow again, because it sure got complicated when they could see each other to toss accusations around."

"I could see that."

"Yeah. Anyway, I wanted to check in with you. So much for surprising you with my early return."

"No worries, Nick. You gotta do what you gotta do."

"How's Kent managing?"

That he was concerned about Kent's wellbeing after finding Zara was funny. "Kent? Not Rachel?"

His chuckle pulled a smile across my lips. "Well, sure. We're all worrying about Rachel being stressed, but Kent worrying about Rachel worrying has to be the most tiring concern so far."

"Well said, and very true. Mom and I were reminding him that Rach can stand on her own two feet. We're making chili. All of us are sticking together right now. We all need a distraction from the day."

"Good idea. Wish I could be there, but we're waiting on a conference call from Florida, so maybe save me some leftovers, huh?"

"If there's any left. You know how Jon gets."

With light laughter to our farewells, we agreed to meet up tomorrow. I couldn't share his optimism just yet, his easy conviction this case would more or less be a done deal with input from the law enforcement at Zarsettia's home base in Florida. But I praised him for thinking positively.

Never mind me missing out on holiday time with my boyfriend. We needed to clear the air of murder from this estate for Rachel and Kent's wedding.

After dinner, we tidied up and fell into our speculations about Zara's death again. Tommy and Jon manned the dishwasher while Kent stowed leftovers in the fridge. Meanwhile, Rachel gestured for me and Mom to follow her to the foyer at the front of the house. In other words, clearly out of earshot for the men to overhear us.

"Talk about a spanner thrown in the works. This whole day—and night—is a bust, Madis."

I sat next to her on the loveseat bench near the door. "Hey, if it's any consolation, Nick seems to think the officials in Florida will already have evidence to solve this case."

"Sure, but that won't be news until tomorrow."

"What's bugging you, if it's not the murder?" Mom asked her, propping her butt on the armrest.

"To start with, the greenhouse is packed with too many poinsettias! And there's no way Kent's going to lighten up enough to let me putz around and organize out there."

"Easy. I'll do it."

Mom elbowed me gently. "Sign me up too."

"When, though?" Rachel shook her head. "Tomorrow we've got to use Toby's van to deliver flowers to the school for that fundraiser sale. And then more to the diner. And then—"

"Hold up." I glanced at the dark sky offering light drops of snow. "How about I stay here tonight. I can work in the greenhouse, arranging the room for the wedding."

"Me too," Mom added. "We can share a guestroom so it's not a mess for Kent's family coming in for the wedding. Since Damon dropped me off here, in the morning, I can drive the cargo van Dahlia's lent you. I'll bring the flowers with me to the diner for my shift."

"Really?" Rachel asked, smiling wider.

"Yeah, why not?" Mom said. "I'll just have to pop in at home to shower and change, but it makes the most sense. Those poinsettias are only going the same place I am. Two birds, one stone. Take a look outside, anyway. You know I'm not a fan of driving on the roads when they're slick with snow. Way out here, they sure don't plow as good as they do on Main."

"What about Tommy?" she asked me. "Weren't you going to drive him home?"

I shrugged. "I bet Jon could handle that."

Rachel sighed, her shoulders not drooping as much as they were, but she still didn't seem relieved. "I don't want to ask for help. Everyone's so cautious with me, if I show a sign of weakness, I'll... I don't know. Kent will make me stay in bed."

Mom squeezed her arm. "Nonsense. He's just worried."

Rachel laughed once. "Of course, he's just worried. All he does is worry. He's hovering." Sitting up straighter, she cringed. "That was another thing I planned to do today. Wrap his present. It came earlier and I just barely got Jon to move it into the storage room off the garage without him seeing it. I doubt he'll let me out of sight to wrap it." Rubbing her lower back, she shook her head. "And honestly, I dread the idea of wrapping that big old box. Bending over is getting trickier and trickier."

Mom dusted off her hands then jerked her thumb at her chest. "I'm a master wrapper, Rach. Show me where and I'll do it. So long as you don't mind me getting a little flour and such here and there."

"Oh, I bet you've left some clothes in that guestroom you like. After one of our girls' nights over the fall."

Mom saluted her. "There we go. What'd you get him, anyway?"

"A grill."

Mom's brows shot up. "Oh. That *would* be a big box. Well, consider it done."

"And I'll go out to the greenhouse and start making room. Get ahead for tomorrow."

Rachel smiled so sweetly at us. "You sure?"

"Of course," I said.

❄

An hour later, I seriously debated if Rachel and Kent could pull it off. There were just *too* many flowers in here. So far, I'd managed to clear a walkway through the center of the bigger room, a path that was zig-zagging back and forth. Those poinsettias were stashed in the back room, and there wasn't an inch to spare. Flats stacked one on top of the other, even more plastic pots wedged into empty hanging mesh nets usually used in the summer for trapping pests when the vents were open.

For goodness' sake, we could just donate a lot of these since we're in a pinch, but then Rach would be more upset about losing the money from sales...

In the main room, where the basic wooden arbor was set up last week, I stood there, stumped.

Hands on my hips, I sighed and surveyed my slow progress.

"Already lined pots around the koi pond," I mumbled to myself. Glancing at the water, I heard the gurgles of the fish swimming and seeking food. So long as none of those hungry punks didn't knock a pot into the water...

Dang it. Jon's talk about the flower being toxic bugged me all over again. Sure, animals would be impacted by the poisonous plant, but what about fish? Could the toxin distribute in the water?

I growled. "Better not risk it. God forbid we have dead fish stink for the wedding..."

Moving all those plants nearly put me back to square one.

I stood again, roving my careful gaze over the greenhouse, waiting for an *aha* moment of genius. Nothing struck. Unless we bought more racks to tower the flats on, or moved the flowers into the house—

"Hey, that's not a horrible idea..." I turned, looking out the windows toward the estate house, curious if Mom was nearly done wrapping that grill. She was an old soul, a firm believer of a place for everything and everything in its place. I bet she'd have an idea.

A blur of movement snagged my attention. A dark coat? That had to be her now.

Only, whoever was rushed along the greenhouse wasn't heading for the side door that would make the shortest path from the house. This person was running in the snow toward the rear of the greenhouse. Toward the—

The Zarsettia trucks! It had to be one of the gals!

Damning those windows for being so opaque, and double-damning how difficult it was to see clearly from the well-lit interior of the greenhouse to the solid darkness of the night outside, I crouched instinctively, intending to follow this person back into the yard.

Before they'd all left, someone with the officers—probably Ford—strung police tape along all three trucks. As I cracked open the back doors to see who was tiptoeing to the middle truck's cab, I tried to remember which woman it could be. From this vantage, I couldn't tell how tall she was, if she had glasses, or what color her hair was, but it just had to be one of the Floridian poinsettia farmers.

Whichever woman it was, she opened the passenger door to the cab of the truck Zara had been found in. Just as quickly as she'd reached inside, she stepped back to the crunchy icing-covered snow. Her hand slid down, stuffing something within her hand into her jacket pocket.

I cleared my throat, opening the double doors wider. Risky? Maybe. But if I was going to be attacked, well, people in the house could hear me screaming.

"Hey!" I shouted when my throat clearing hadn't been loud enough. "Who's there?"

With a gasp, the woman turned to me.

CHAPTER SIX

"Madis!" Brittney exclaimed, pressing her hang to her chest. "You scared me!"

Whereas you've sure piqued my curiosity.

A thin white cord hung from between her fingers. She exhaled long and hard, her shoulders drooping as she let gravity claim her energy. A couple of yards away, she deflated, sucking in a lungful of air after her obvious fright.

"What are you doing here?" I asked, crossing my arms.

"Nothing bad."

"You're snooping at a crime scene."

She frowned, losing all pretense of being startled. "Trust me, I'm not doing anything wrong. That cop guy just barely gave us enough time to grab our things from the trucks. Talk about some crappy hospitality in the oh-so-wonderful holiday spirit. Strand us here and then not even let us have the bare minimum we've brought with us for the road trips."

"Uh-huh, I'll talk about the lousy service. Come to our place bearing a dead body to dump."

"No!" Brittney approached me, shaking her head and holding her hands out in a truce fashion. "I didn't come here to dump Zara! Heck, I didn't even know she *was* here with us like this."

Stepping closer, she glanced past me, seeming to notice something over my shoulder. When the door opened at the side of the greenhouse, I couldn't help but turn as well. Tommy entered, brows raised, but as he came inside, I also noticed car headlights backing up in the distance through the hazy windows. There was no way to determine what kind of vehicle it was, but the twin lights were unmissable.

"I wondered why all the lights were on in here," Tommy said, checking his watch. He jerked a thumb in the direction of the driveway. "Was Todd your ride out here, Brittney?"

Brittney sighed, lowering her hand with the cord. "Yeah. I swear, I just wanted to come out here to grab my phone charger cord. I was chatting with that guy Todd at that teeny bar by the motel. He offered to drive me out here to get the cord." She shivered and nodded toward the greenhouse. "Can I warm up real quick in there? I don't know how you guys handle these winters!"

With Tommy here, I wasn't as concerned about letting her in. I gestured her inside then closed the door.

As she rubbed her arms, she sniffed at Tommy.

"And now I'm stranded *again*. Clearly Todd got spooked when he saw *you* walking out here."

I rolled my eyes. Todd was a repeat offender of DUIs back when Tommy was the head officer of Payton. No surprise there that Todd still disliked being near his most frequent discipliner.

"And your only reason to come back was to get that cord out of the truck," I said.

"Yeah, I was using it in the dashboard outlet charger there and forgot it to plug into a normal outlet on a wall at the motel."

I glanced at Tommy. "The truck Zara was found in."

"Weren't Nick and the detective clear enough?" Tommy asked. "That's a crime scene." He pointed at her hoodie pocket. "And what's that shaker cup for?"

Brittney frowned and pulled it out.

Lavender and turquoise, it was the same exact size and style as the cup they'd supposedly found with Zara. The container that held the poison that killed her. Surely, Ford and the crime scene staff took that piece of evidence, but I was curious why she had something similar.

"It's mine," she said. "We all have the same ones. When I was grabbing my charger cord, I saw it in the cupholder and figured I'd bring it to the motel. I hate drinking out of those Styrofoam coffee cups. So bad for the environment." Tsking, she screwed the cup open and dumped out a teeny dribble of water. "See." I use mine for water."

Hmmm. "Still, that truck's a crime scene."

"I know. I know it is. I swear, I just wanted my dang cord!" She ran her hand through her hair, beyond flustered. "For goodness' sake, I didn't kill Zara."

"That's what all three of you ladies claim," I argued.

"Well, I can't speak for the others, but *I* didn't murder her. That's an asinine thing to even think. I wouldn't—couldn't—just kill someone, no matter how much they were annoying me."

Murder someone over annoyance? Seems so trivial of a motive, but it happens. "What was your issue with Zara, anyway?" I sat, propping my butt against the folding chair Claire had sat in hours before.

Brittney slumped against the support column post and cast her somber gaze at the ground. "What *didn't* we have issues with is a better question. All of us were on each other's case over the last few months."

Tommy settled in to stand with his feet shoulder's width apart, crossing his arms in a comfortable stance. "No one's getting along lately? Holiday stress?"

Brittney shook her head. "Nah. It's more than that."

"I'm surprised," I admitted. "When you girls made the delivery at the beginning of the month, you were all so happy. Getting along as far as I saw."

The tall brunette scoffed. "Yeah, well, that's cuz Zara was there. We might talk crap about each other, but we'd never do so in front of Zara. She's the 'image' girl. We always gotta make good in front of customers, she said." She rolled her eyes.

"Well." I shrugged. "I'd agree to an extent. Image

does matter. No one wants to hire a grouchy service provider for anything, right? I don't expect my crew to smile and be fake about it when we're landscaping, but then again, we generally get along fine. We've been together as a team for almost two years now, so practice makes perfect, maybe?"

"If that's the case, then we've had years of practice with Zarsettia's. I had the idea to start this farm since college, like, eleven years ago."

Maybe Brittney was irked with her posture against the column and stretching, but I'd say she was stiffening her spine with something like pride.

"Zarsettia Farm was *your* idea?" That was consistent with what I'd gathered from their argument earlier.

Brittney rolled her eyes again, affecting the mannerisms of a put-out teen than an adult. "I never wanted to call it Zarsettia's. That's Zara's *me, me, me* personality right there."

"So, it was your idea, but she acted on it?"

She shook her head, seeming to think on the best way to answer. "We were all eager to act on it. We had different reasonings. Different strengths to bring to the table. And it's worked, but over time, our morale kind of eroded. Maybe to counter how our success as a team seemed to just make Zara more big-headed about it all. Like it had her name and it was all her doing."

"What was your reasoning to start a poinsettia farm?" Tommy asked.

"Jeez. It never *had* to be poinsettias. That was Claire's idea. She majored in biology and took those ag courses. She said poinsettias were a hot seller for a limited time, and, well, we've done more than fine in the financial way, so that sure paid off.

"I wanted to start a non-profit farm of any kind, an earth-friendly co-op. Okay, not a complete non-profit, but something charitable in its basis. I wanted a way to give back to women because men freaking dominate *every*thing in this world."

Tommy stayed quiet, but then again, it didn't seem she was attacking him personally.

"My mom was a single parent. My deadbeat dad beat her until he left, and well, I—we—didn't have it easy. Each time someone offered us a hand, I thought, 'I'm gonna pay you back someday.' In college, I really started scheming how to do that, to pay it forward."

"So your strength in Zarsettia's, then," I said, "is the community outreach of it."

"Damn straight it is." She pushed off the column to stand even taller. "And we've done so much good, helped so many women—despite the way Zara was losing sight of that underlying business ethic."

"How so?" I asked.

"Well, she was selling us short. She wanted to make a freaking *franchise*, make the farm more about profit and the bottom line than helping women in our region. She stopped caring about the connections with shelters and schools, connections *I* spent so much time fostering. She pushed me aside when we were invited to speak at conferences and meetings, claiming we had to look at the bigger picture as entrepreneurs, not handout-providers. What she cared about in the end was how to make more damn money for herself."

Seems they definitely changed their business over the years.

"If it weren't for my ideas of this women's initiative business, we never would have even gotten started. All the accreditations and awards we earned for our impact in the community...yeah, that stuff is harder to put a price on, but that recognition got Zarsettia's out there. People wanted to support our biz because of what we stood for. But, noooo. Zara just could not get that. She'd forgotten that the success for the farm was due to *me.*" She stabbed at her chest, then sighed. "I sound so bitter."

"Hey, you're entitled to your feelings." *Just so long as you don't murder over them...*

"I still *am* bitter, but seriously, I'd never kill her," Brittney insisted.

"What did Zara bring to the table?" Tommy asked. "You said you all had your strengths."

Brittney nodded, and I wondered if she'd have the capacity to even acknowledge something positive about her former boss.

"Zara graduated in business. She was going for an MBA. So the business setup, loans, marketing, promotion...she's got a business brain, for sure."

"And Claire?" I asked. "She had the know-how of plants?"

"I wouldn't say she was an expert, but she'd at least taken more biology classes than the rest of us. At first, she'd been all about having a chicken coop rather than a crop." She huffed. "Like there's not enough chickens running around in Southern Florida. And anyway, Claire dropped out I think after the second semester of college. What Claire brought to the table was the plot of land to even begin Zarsettia's in the middle of the city. Then her dad knew someone at the water department who helped us rig the watering systems and such. She had some savings she put upfront, too, but then when we started raking in a lot of money, she had some issue with a bill or IOU, selling her shares to pool quick money for someone she was indebted to. I can't remember the details, but Abby might."

"And Abby?" Tommy asked.

"She, uh..." Brittney winced. "It'll sound bad, but she didn't really bring anything to the operation. I mean, don't get me wrong. She's just as hard of a worker as the rest of us. Maybe in the beginning, she was the cheerleader, always bright and cheering us on when things seemed impossible. She dropped out of school, too.

"When we started the farm, she was dating Tyler, and that was *all* her life was about. I was shocked when they broke up only because Abby's single goal in life seemed to be marrying him and being the mother of his children. You know, had the whole big wedding planned and such..." She shrugged.

"The Tyler that Zara was in a relationship with?" Tommy asked.

"Yeah, same guy," she replied. "And he's the whole reason we've been butting heads with each other."

"What," I guessed, "Abby's mad at Zara for dating

her ex?" *Although this morning, she insisted she was over Tyler?*

"That," Brittney said. "And he's on my bad list, too." She raised the blender cup and tapped it. "This is the product of his entrepreneurship. A company he invested in."

Tommy glanced at me, one brow kicked up in surprise.

Zara was poisoned in a cup her current boyfriend supplied? Seemed like a heckuva connection.

"I'll give him credit where it's due. He sticks to his ideas, like buying this blender cup startup way back then. He fumbled a bit and made some bad choices, but he sure learned from his mistakes. But now he's acting like an investment guru, encouraging Zara about where to take Zarsettia's." She scowled. "To make it a *franchise*!" A growl emphasized her frustration at the concept. "Then Claire, she's seemed to always dislike Tyler, especially when Abby first dated him. Claire kept telling her she could do better than him. Bottom line, she's kind of a general man-hater. I think she was bullied a lot for her glasses when she was in school, the classic Four-Eyed Freak sort of name-calling. She's always been extra-judgmental with men."

"Wonder if Tyler's been informed about Zara yet," I mused out loud.

Brittney rolled her eyes and walked up to me, pulling her phone out of her pocket. "Oh, yeah, he does. Shoot, the battery's about to die, but look. I'm not surprised that Abby just couldn't wait to tell him the news."

Like...she's happy *with the news?* Did Abby want to get Tyler back? It wouldn't be too farfetched for an ex-girlfriend to kill off competition for easier access to reclaim a lover...

I took the phone, holding it out so Tommy could peer at the screen with me.

Abby had texted Tyler, informing him of Zara's death, seemingly in a group text thread with Claire and Brittney. First, Tyler was shocked, asking for details before abruptly stopping his messages. Then, he texted that a cop from Ohio was calling him. After scrolling to the end, I saw his final input.

> Tyler: *I've got my flight and ride ready. I'll be there first thing in the morning, girls.*

"Just as well that he'll be here for questioning," Tommy said.

Because his product was used in the act of poisoning?

Or because he seemed to have driven more of a wedge between the women behind Zarsettia's Farm?

CHAPTER SEVEN

"I'm off," Mom announced at the driver's door of the cargo van we were borrowing to transplant the poinsettias to places of sales in Payton.

Last night, she'd not only wrapped the grill Rachel was gifting Kent for Christmas, but she'd also offered her present prepping skills for other items Rachel had been putting off. Odds and ends for clients, distant relatives, friends in town, all of us on the MH Landscaping crew. She wouldn't budge, refusing to tell me what my gift would be, but that was fine. I was an oddball and liked to be surprised.

As it was, she didn't end up helping me at the greenhouse. Tommy and Jon left, making good on their offer to bring Brittney back to the motel. Of course, Tommy scolded her again for the foolhardiness of helping herself to a crime scene, and I sure didn't delay in telling Nick about her showing up like that. I'd conveyed that news to him via text because he'd greeted me via messages to begin with.

Tyler must have gotten a *very* early flight because Nick, Damon, and the detective for the state were interviewing the young man since seven thirty.

Such an early wakeup on "vacation." Poor Nick. But the faster we figure out who killed Zara, the faster we can have something of a holiday break before the wedding claims all of our time.

Speaking of Rachel and Kent's ceremony, I was back at it that morning. Not even nine yet—way before my off-season wakeup time of ten or elevenish—and there I was, in the greenhouse, trying to minimize the abundance of flowers.

Nick had texted me that Tyler wanted to come see the crime scene himself, not to enter the truck or trespass the area, but to see where Zara had been found. "To find a location for closure," was the way Nick had worded it in a group text to me, Rachel, and Kent. Heck, it wasn't *my* call who could come on the soon-to-be Mr. and Mrs. Caldwell's property. Rachel was busy with laundry in the house, preparing for her future in-laws' arrival, but Kent answered.

> Kent: *I'll hang out with Madis in the greenhouse while he stops by.*

"I'm not hanging around because you need a guy to watch over you," Kent insisted.

I smiled and smirked at the same time as we carried poinsettias to the cargo van Toby lent us. "Uh-huh."

"I'm just curious what this guy looks like. With how you'd talked this morning, he must be a heck of a catch or something for all four of the Zarsettia women to be fighting over him."

"Hmm, not quite. Brittney didn't seem to *want* him romantically. If anything, she was irked at Tyler's inference with the business, his views drastically different from where she wanted the poinsettia farm to go. And she said Claire was something of a man-hater."

Kent shrugged just as a sedan pulled up along the drive parallel to the greenhouse. At least, I thought it was a sedan since it wasn't tall enough to be an SUV and wasn't shaped like a van or truck either. While it was easy to be exposed in the greenhouse with all the walls and ceilings made of semi-transparent material, it was too hazy of a view to determine details.

Knowing that the others were already busy and elsewhere for the day, I figured this had to be the trouble-stirring Tyler.

He knocked on the door, and Kent opened it.

"Miss Madis?" he asked, stepping in.

Tall, with a thoroughly sun-kissed tan and thick light-blond hair, he looked like a misplaced surfer. In jeans and a sweatshirt, he almost seemed dressed for the climate, but those sandals on his feet? Couldn't he have Googled the weather before he rushed north?

"Yes, Tyler?" I guessed, offering my hand.

"That's me."

"This is Kent. My partner."

Tyler shook his hand as well, but frowned in confusion. "You're *her* partner?"

Jeez. Was that a way of saying Kent and I would look bad as a couple? Or that I looked bad?

"In business."

"Ah!" Tyler smiled now, shaking his head. "Brittney mentioned in a text that you were hosting a wedding in here. Just thought it'd be odd that the bride and groom had to do the setup themselves."

"No, no. Not me. The bride's inside."

Kent sighed, setting his hands to his hips. "And this setup still looks impossible, if you ask me."

"Nah, nah. That's a quitter's attitude, man." Tyler scanned the greenhouse. "You're going to arrange it by the pond, I'm guessing?"

"Yep." I watched him survey the space. "Some of the flowers will be gone, but it's still a tight fit."

Tyler chuckled. "Maybe you should have thought twice about ordering so many poinsettias so close to the wedding?"

"It was a mistake," I told him, coming to Rachel's defense.

"Not that I'd wish Zara to suffer any loss of business." He bit his lip and blinked. "I wouldn't wish her to suffer *at all*." Emotions must have clogged his throat because he looked to the side, wiping at his eyes. "Sorry. It's all so...just too much to absorb. It hasn't hit me yet. It has. I know she's gone. But it's so surreal."

"I'm sorry for your loss," Kent said.

"You and Zara were close?"

Tyler wiped at his eyes again, nodding, then shaking his head. "Well, sure. We were dating. I told her I just wanted something casual. Not that it was an open sort of thing. We *were* exclusive, but we weren't—or I wasn't—at the stage of planning a long-term deal." He splayed his hand in the general direction of the pond. "I'm not rushing to get married or anything."

Casual. Committed, yet not devoted. Somehow, his interpretation of his relationship with Zara didn't match what the women hinted at. Brittney had implied he was more than merely a man Zara was dating. She'd given me the impression he was close enough to wheedle her into changing the business she'd started with her friends into a franchise.

"Did Zara share your views on that?" Kent asked carefully. "Zara wasn't seeking marriage...with you?"

Tyler didn't answer, looking everywhere but at either of us. In that awkward silence, save the heaters and water in the pond, Kent and I exchanged an *uh-oh* look.

"It's complicated," Tyler finally admitted. "I won't lie. I haven't, uh, exactly had a stellar history with women—particularly with the women of Zarsettia's Poinsettias." His chuckle was weak and cringeworthy. Was he seeking an excuse from us? An acknowledgment that would make his lousy luck with the ladies okay?

"You mean Abby?" I asked.

"Abby's... She's a great woman. Someone will be lucky to put a ring on her finger." He shook his head. "Enough about the past, especially when Zara's only been lost to us." Clearing his throat, he frowned, seeming to focus at the abundance of poinsettias. "Are you hoping to incorporate the flowers in the wedding setup?"

Kent glanced around, as did I. "I'm not opposed to having them as décor, but not to the point we are wading through a jungle of them," he said.

"They're lovely, in moderation," I added on Rachel's behalf, "but really, it's the sight of those trucks that would ruin the setting."

After he took the position at the bare arbor, Kent looked back at us and winced. "They sure stand out," he said, gesturing at the hazy, yet so-bright colors of the trucks outside the greenhouse windows.

"I can't see that they'll need to have the trucks parked there too much longer," I said. I didn't have any indication Nick and the others were any closer to solving the case and therefore no longer needed the crime scene to stay intact. But I could hope.

"If you don't mind..." Tyler jerked his thumb over his shoulder. "Can I at least walk back there? See if I could, heck, I don't know. See where she was last, I guess?"

"Sure, sure." Kent waved at him to proceed.

Tyler raised his hands. "I won't touch anything."

"Right," I said. Once he'd escaped, I turned to Kent. "You really think that's a good idea?"

"Why not?" He pointed toward the corner of the ceiling on the wall where the back doors were positioned. "Whatever he does will be on the security camera I put up at the crack of dawn."

"I knew you were a smart man."

"You talking about how Brittney just showed up last night really bothered me."

I nodded, shifting pots around the arbor. "Don't blame you. The idea of anyone just walking here would be worrisome."

"So the sooner those trucks—and women—are gone, the better. Come on, Madis, who are you liking for the murder? You've had your share of sleuthing, after all."

I shot him an insincere dirty look. "Ha. Ha."

"You haven't pinpointed a suspect yet? Can't figure which woman did it?"

"What's to say it had to be one of those three women?" Pointing at the blurred shape of Tyler simply standing in front of the middle truck, I challenged, "What if *he* did it?"

"He was in Florida, where Zara was believed to be poisoned," Kent admitted.

"Try again," Nick said as he entered the plant building, closing the door after his quiet entrance. "He has an alibi. At a meeting for one of his starter companies. Verified by several witnesses *and* the security camera."

"Bummer," I said, leaning in for Nick to kiss me hello.

"But...that's not the only evidence we've gotten on a security camera," he drawled, rocking back and forth on his feet like a know-it-all lording intel over us.

Kent and I glanced at each other, then up at the area where the new camera had *just* been installed.

"What?" I asked. "Someone's caught on there messing with the trucks or something?"

"Not that camera," Nick said, "but the one that captures someone dumping the belladonna into Zara's shaker cup."

CHAPTER EIGHT

"Get out!" I said, grinning. "You know who did it? Of course you do. You probably already arrested them, which is why you're free to tell us this. Come on, Nick. Who killed her?"

Slowly but surely, he sighed and shook his head. "Not that lucky. The video feed at Zarsettia's–granted to us from Tyler, actually, since he had Zara's password to the program–showed the person but not which person it is."

"The killer had their back facing the camera?" Kent guessed.

Nick nodded. "Yes, and since all three of the staff were wearing oversized ponchos that morning, along with enormous Santa hats, you couldn't tell which one was which."

Ponchos and Santa hats? *Huh?* Strange attire aside, their heights and body weights were all different.

"Ponchos?" Kent asked.

"It seems a volunteer made them for the ladies as a silly gag gift, like ugly sweaters, only hand-woven poncho style." Nick shrugged. "This volunteer, Juanita, already spoke with the officer helping in Florida. She'd made the gifts for Abby, Brittney, and Claire and wanted to give it to them before the delivery began. Something about her daughter being induced that day and she wouldn't have another chance to see them until well after the baby was born. I lost some of that in translation, but the three of them all put on the outfits, goofing around with Juanita and giving her their gifts for her."

"But one of them stepped aside to dump belladonna into Zara's cup," I concluded.

"Yep." Nick nodded. Unless they'd let someone else wear their festive things, one of those three slipped the poison in her cup."

"So, I'll ask you what I challenged her with," Kent said. "Who are you liking for the killer?"

"Hmmm. Dunno." Nick rubbed his chin. "They all had the means. Juanita showed the officer where she'd found belladonna along the chain-link surrounding the farm. Some had recently been snipped."

"Means, murder weapon..." I crossed my arms. "Motive, though..."

He nodded at me. "Yeah. That's the part we can't pinpoint."

"Could they have just teamed up to killed her?" Kent suggested. "A team effort?"

"Not according to Claire," I said. "She's been clear

from the beginning of all this that she should not be lumped in with the other two."

"What would be her motive?" Kent asked.

Nick wouldn't answer, but that was fine. I had been paying attention all along. "She was upset about Zara buying out her shares of the farm. I think."

"Early on, too," Nick said. "But even at that time, Brittney rounded it up to five digits."

"Wow. I wonder what she needed the cash for," I replied.

"She told us something about helping out a friend who needed money," Nick said.

"Hmm. What'd Claire get out of providing the money she'd gotten by sacrificing her shares in the farm?"

"According to the cops in Florida, it was a family thing, she was looking out for a relative who'd needed money and she was supposed to get it back eventually."

"If you're thinking one of those three poisoned her..." Kent looked back at the trucks once more. "Should that mean I can count on those trucks being parked back there as long as the women are stuck here as suspects?"

Nick's cringe was telling enough. *Yes, unfortunately. Which is all the more reason to figure this one out pronto.*

The opportunity to kill was a given—one of the ABC employees had simply walked up to the shaker cup Zara had left on the tailgate of the truck.

The weapon—poison, as concluded in the autopsy,

remnants of the smoothie, *and* this security footage at the farm down in Florida.

The motive? Hard to say. Claire was angry about having to sell her shares to Zara. Abby might still hold a torch for Zara's man. Brittney was upset with the direction Zara was taking the business...

So what was the reasoning to prompt a murder at the happiest, most festive time of the year?

Come on, Madis. What are we missing?

Before long, Rachel joined this little gathering in the greenhouse, sharing some slightly good news with me. Dahlia, at the diner, just called her to say all the poinsettias that Mom had driven to the stand were sold out. Any excuse to free up space for the small wedding ceremony was a move in the right direction.

Plenty of patrons were inquiring where they could purchase the flowers, but Mom still had the cargo van there, and doing a back and forth seemed ridiculous. *Too bad Jon already took the other van to the school fundraiser just a half an hour ago...*

Rachel suggested just having people come here and buy them directly, which seemed efficient, but Kent—and I, and Nick—vetoed the idea of too many strangers, or even just townsfolk coming to their private property. It was unnerving enough to have Brittney thinking she could be dropped off to retrieve her cup and cord.

Instead, Kent fastened some tarp to my truck and

rigged up an impromptu transport for more flowers along these cold wintry roads. Sick of the laundry and chores in the house, Rachel jumped at the idea of riding with me to bring more poinsettias to town.

I turned down Bing Crosby singing his famous yuletide tune so she could talk on the phone. First, she was confirming with Tommy that he'd fix the strings of lights that had gone out along the front windows. Kent was handling the greenhouse and Tommy had been the one to hang the lights for the busy couple in the first place.

"Kent's one aunt seems like she'll be a hard woman to please," she told me after she hung up with Tommy but not done with her phone yet. "I need the house looking perfect. I don't want any of the Caldwells thinking I'll be an unfit wife for him."

"Oh, stop. Successfully hung Christmas lights isn't an indicator of a good marriage."

"Even still. She's the one Kent worries about. She's already judged us a bit for having a baby on the way before saying *I do*. She's the only relative who's most likely to criticize us having the ceremony in the greenhouse, even though it's more like a conservatory on that side." She raised her face to frown at me. "It's not that weird of a location, is it?"

"No, not at all. Ordinarily, it would be fine." When Jon, Kent, and I first cleaned out the empty plant house rooms, it was clear how well the structure held up to the test of time. Solid, sealed tiled floors. Countless windows to let light in, all the panes held in with vintage-looking wrought-iron frames. Even the scrollwork was a little extra detail to appreciate. At the end of the summer, when we officially decided we'd use the greenhouse to hold poinsettias for sale, Mom and Rosie, a long-time friend of the family, brought over some hanging planters of pathos. In the first couple of months, those spread like crazy, offering some green bordering to the interior.

In fact, I'm going to need to either trim those or split them into new cuttings soon. Or they'll take over.

"Without the excess poinsettias, it'd be the perfect setting for a small, intimate ceremony in an almost Victorian-like room."

She laughed. "At least the koi pond was in good condition already. It's so gorgeous." Raising the phone to her ear, she continued talking to me while waiting for the person to answer. "And I'm on those flowers, Madis. Such a stupid mistake to make at the worst time. We'll get a good amount of them out today. But those trucks..."

Yeah, those were an eyesore. Neon blazing pink was just too Floridian for Ohio, especially with the backdrop of all-white snow and bare trees. The only way we could see those vehicles going was if the women who'd brought them here were free to leave... and they were all suspects—unofficially without hard evidence—in Zara's murder.

Come on, Madis. Which one did it? Think!

"Hey, Jon. We're going to do a little switcheroo." Rachel grinned into the phone, but then lowered it, setting it to speaker. "After you're done dropping off the poinsettias at the school for their fundraiser, head back and grab the flats I'd noted. Kent's there and has a list ready for how many and what colors."

"Where else are they going?" I asked, wincing at the faster rate of snowfall. The wipers squelched and carried more slush over.

Rach winked at me. "Remember that craft lady? Jody?"

Jon groaned. "How could I forget, Rach. I found a body buried in her backyard..."

"Well, she's going to some county craft thing tomorrow. At the high school in Hancock. She has a booth set up already, and she texted me, asking if we could collaborate. I guess she's trying out some new line of macrame pot cases, or something like that. The pics were cute, kind of like ugly sweaters on pots. She thought it'd look better with pots actually in them but she doesn't have any plants around. So she reached out to me, and we compromised a price, but she thinks she could easily sell a hundred. Win-win."

"Nice work," I told her.

"*Then*, when we're done taking these to the diner now, we'll grab Toby's van that your mom left there."

"And where are you guys taking another batch?" Jon asked.

"Elliot and Ursula are hosting a blood drive thing at the Y," Rachel said. "Elliot said a couple of people are going to be there doing a bake sale, so he said why not sell some flowers, too."

At a stop sign, I clapped. "We'll clear the stock in no time!"

"I just want to arrange for selling enough that the

wedding can happen and not look like an overthought in my overstocking blooper."

"Hey, we all make mistakes, Rach," Jon said.

"But I don't see *where* I made the mistake," Rachel said. "I checked all the emails, texts, and notes I'd had with Zara. I only ordered half, but they brought double. And billed us for double, too." She slid me a sheepish smile and shrugged. "And now that she's... well, it seems like it'd be bad business and karma to try to renege on the excess flowers."

I scoffed. "And it'd be hard to turn down all the flowers now, anyway. The trucks are stuck there until their drivers are cleared to leave Payton."

All talk of poinsettia plans fell to back burner as I parked next to the truck Toby was letting us use while he and Beth vacationed. As it usually was, the diner was packed with customers, and with each back-and-forth trek from my truck to inside the place, I was accosted with nothing but homey reminders of why this was my favorite time of the year.

"Jingle Bell Rock" maybe a little too loud on the speakers, still heralded over the customers chatting and laughing. Dahlia and Zoe bustling to fill coffees behind the counter, lit-up reindeer antler headbands on their heads. The smell of fresh-baked cookies and gingerbread heavy in the air among the familiar greasy scents I loved. Next to the register stood the clunky statue of Santa I'd made in art class eons ago, a gift to Mom, but she insisted it belonged at Payton's hub of traffic.

I paused long enough to sigh, inhaling a deep

breath of all this comfort, but Rachel bumped her hip to mine. "Hustle, my lady, hustle."

I smiled at her fake sass and brought the armful of poinsettias to the tables we'd had set up for the sale of them. It didn't take us long to set them up, even with people stopping us to say hello, or to ask about how the wedding prep was coming along.

Surprisingly, not many gossiped about Zara's murder. I figured that would be at the forefront of everyone's mind. When I rounded the corner of the counter, though, I caught sight of Abby coming out of the bathroom and reclaiming her seat.

"Oh!" she said in greeting at seeing us.

Aha. Maybe people weren't gossiping about the death of Zara when Abby was within earshot. Either because it was her friend whose death she was mourning, or because she was in the hot spot of perhaps being the killer.

Too much supposition. Where's the evidence? Then again, since the murder didn't actually happen *here*, it had to be a hard one for Nick and the Payton PD to conclude.

"They sell fast, huh?" Abby asked as she took her seat.

"Sure do," I replied.

She smiled sweetly. "Some days, I think back and wonder how different our lives would have been if we ran with Claire's idea to have an urban volunteer-ran chicken co-op." Her chuckle was soft, matching the warmth in her eyes. "But I won't lie. I'm proud to be a wholesale provider of those flowers."

I adjusted a pot and stepped back as she stood to check out the table with us.

"You know, they're not actually normal 'flowers,'" she admitted. "I never knew much about plants—still don't. Don't look at me for a green thumb." She chuckled good-naturedly. That seemed about right, according to Brittney saying Abby was just there working at Zarsettia's Farm after dropping out of college just because her friends were. "But I remember reading that the 'flower' parts are not petals."

I nodded. "Yep, they're just colored leaves, giving it a traditional bloom appearance."

"But so beautiful," someone else claimed, coming up behind us.

Tyler had lost some of his surfer boy look, wearing an actual coat and shoes now. He brushed the light snow off his hair as he approached us at the poinsettia table, but his gaze was locked on Abby, not the poinsettias.

She blushed, and her reaction to his comment clarified I wasn't the only one reading his words differently. He hadn't been talking about the plants, but perhaps...her.

Rachel nudged me as Tyler asked Abby if he could join her for coffee, and I didn't need more prompt to get lost than that.

Does Tyler still love Abby?

"Okay," Rach said, rubbing her gloved hands together as she stood at the tailgate for me to hand over plants. I climbed up and scooched more pots toward her. "The way Tyler looked at Abby reminds me of that picture your mom took of me and Kent at Thanksgiving."

"You mean the candid one that you used on the super-late wedding invites?"

Rachel grinned. "Well, we're keeping it so small, I sent those 'invites' to all ten people just for the sake of having an invitation in my scrapbook."

I giggled, jumping off with my pots in arm. "Yeah, but I know the photo you're talking about. When you guys were staring at each other like the world no longer existed. So stuck in those big eyes of adoration for each other."

"Uh-huh." Rachel led the way inside. "That's the way he looks at her."

"I noticed, too."

She paused at the door, her eyes narrowing in focus. "So...what was her supposed motive, again?"

"Unofficially?" I looked through the windows, stepping aside so customers could leave. "I like her for murder on the basis of revenge. She was with Tyler, and now Zara was. Maybe she hated that her friend—and boss—had taken her man. Former man."

Rachel nodded. "Yeah. That's a code no woman should break. Unless the first girlfriend *honestly* didn't harbor lingering love for the man."

I bumped the door open with my butt as I said, "And Abby's body language at the greenhouse told a different story. She might insist Tyler was old news for her, but..."

"But..." Rachel finished for me, tilting her head toward Tyler and Abby sitting closely together at the counter, their knees touching and blushing. They couldn't look any more like lovestruck souls tiptoeing past mere catching up and flirtation.

"Yeah. But that."

Could Abby have killed Zara in a ploy to get Tyler back?

After we set those poinsettias down, Mom waved me over. "Coffee, Madis?" she asked.

I slid into the space between Abby's stool and an empty one. "Nah, I'm good."

She nodded, then raised her chin at Tyler. "Sorry, you can't bring outside beverages in here," she told him.

"Oh, no worries." Tyler immediately looked sheepish, smiling wide yet nervously. "I won't drink it here. I just want to wanted to stop and say bye to Abby before I head back to Florida."

"So soon?" I asked him.

"Those officers told me I wasn't required to stay in town, and I worry about handling things at Zara's apartment."

Abby sighed. "I forgot. Who's watching her dogs and cats while you're here?"

"Her neighbor," Tyler told her, "but he's leaving tomorrow morning to visit his parents for the holiday."

Abby chewed on her lower lips. "Well, I'm allergic, but I bet Brittney can help find homes for them. The rest of us will drive back the trucks when...well, we'll head home when we can."

I almost pitied her. If she hadn't killed Zara, she was stuck here against her will. But then knowing or thinking one of your close friends and coworkers might be a killer wasn't any easier of a thought to have.

Tyler shrugged. "No rush. I mean she just..." He shook his head. "I can take over in the short term, but my pace of work isn't ideal for owning pets. Not fair to the animals to be cooped up inside all day."

"What about Claire? Does she like animals?" After all, she had the idea to start a chicken farm instead of a poinsettia one.

"I don't think she can have animals at the condo," Abby said.

"We'll figure it out," Tyler said, standing. He raised his shaker cup to drink and Mom cleared her throat.

"Oh, right. Sorry," he said. "Habit. I always have a protein shake for brunch."

Rachel pointed at the cup. "You guys all have the same brand, I notice."

She was right. The cup that held Zara's poison was the same type of container, albeit slightly different colorations. And Brittney had collected hers, too.

"Yeah!" Tyler grinned. "They're mine. Or my company's."

"You're in the blender cup business?" I asked.

"I invest in small startups. This one"—he patted the cup—"is my favorite. I bought them back when the girls started Zarsettia's. We all had the same business spirit from our college days. The cups have more of a spiked ball inside, instead of just a mesh or spiraled shape, to better mimic a utensil stirring the drink instead of just smashing the ingredients around. Makes for a much smoother shake, hands down."

"I'm proud of those cups, too," Abby said, rubbing Tyler's forearm. "I remember how you struggled to get them going at first."

He sighed, nodding. "Yeah. Lots of capital was burned on that project. Of course, I learned from mistakes, but I lost plenty of cash on it at first. I had to borrow more from my family than I'd wanted to, but it all paid off in the end. Now it's my most lucrative account."

"It's got to be so rewarding to have your own business," Mom said.

"It is," I agreed, speaking from the heart because I'd truly found my calling in running MH Landscaping. Although...I could do without the murders.

"There you are!"

We turned to Brittney entering the diner and beelining for us. Maybe not all of us, but she at least had her eyes set on Abby.

"What's wrong?" Abby stood as Brittney rushed over.

"What's wrong? I'll tell you what's wrong." She flung her arms to the sides. "Claire's gone! She must have gotten fed up waiting here in Ohio and just left!"

"What do you mean?" Abby asked. "Tyler and I were chatting with her in her room at the motel earlier."

Brittney scowled, crossing her arms. "Yeah. You guys go on and have a 'meeting' about what we should do with Zarsettia's while I was still in the shower. Way to go, leaving me out."

Abby sighed. "Brit, I'm on the same page as you. We talked this over last night."

I held up my hand. "Wait, you guys are sharing a room?"

They nodded, and Brittney shrugged. "Yeah. So? Cheaper that way."

Claire, if I recalled was adamant to distance herself from these two, though. Did it matter?

Tyler took a sip of his smoothie and caught Mom's stern look. "Sorry! Habit." He cleared his throat. "Brit, Abby spoke for the both of you. Zara and I had already started the process for me and her to shift some of the finances of Zarsettia's. I'm not trying to take over, of course not." He blinked and cleared his throat. "But with my good standing with the bank, it seemed we could invest Zarsettia's success and make it go even further."

Brittney stomped her foot. "But this isn't supposed to be about getting rich! We started this to make a living, yeah, but our mission statement was to help women—"

"Brit," Abby said. "We *know* that. Nothing's going to change. But with Zara's bringing Tyler in as a partner—"

"As a CFO," he inserted.

"—we'll have enough money to start another chapter! Another farm to start a whole new region of opportunities for women in *another* community."

"Stop thinking of this development as a franchise," Tyler said, frowning. He cleared his throat even harder. "Uh...Yeah. It's not a franchise concept like

McDonald's. More like a continuation of the farms elsewhere with the same mission statement at heart. We're not trying to sell short here. That's not my intention."

Brittney deflated, smiling at his words. "Whew. Good. Thank you for clarifying again. It's just... I know you're good with the money part of it all, and investing."

Even though he burned through money at the beginning of buying startups? And had to loan lots of money—

Lots of money.

"Tyler, who'd you borrow money from?" I asked.

He staggered, nearly missing the stool as he fell back.

"Tyler!" Abby and Brittney both went to his sides, catching him from falling to the floor.

"Tyler!" I repeated.

Rachel reached out, catching his blender cup before it fell.

"What's— Are—" Mom stood up straight. "Dahlia, call 911!"

"You borrowed money to fund that cup business," I repeated.

"Yeah." He blinked and licked his lips. "And that was all it took to make it big. I made bank with that loan."

They were all just out of college, so who could he have known that would have had lots of cash sitting there waiting?

"Who'd you borrow the money from, Tyler?" I persisted.

"Madis," Rachel admonished. "Let him be!"

"Dahlia," I shouted. "Get a warm cup of water mixed with mustard. Now, please!"

The old woman shot me a worried and confused grimace. "*What*?"

"He needs to vomit, or neutralize his stomach." *I hope Google was right about that trick...*

Still frowning, she rushed to grab the strange concoction as Zoe called for help.

There wasn't much time to connect these dots once and for all. "Tyler, who did you borrow that money from?" I asked him.

Tyler coughed, but he seemed to nod sluggishly.

I snatched the cup from Rachel. I wasn't having her remotely near more deadly nightshade.

"I borrowed the money..."

I shook Tyler's shoulder and Abby swatted my hand away.

Tyler slumped his head to the counter. "...money... from Claire," he said weakly.

CHAPTER NINE

"Claire?" Abby repeated.

Brittney gasped. "Remember? She sold Zara her shares of Zarsettia's. That was what made Zara in charge—she practically owned the whole thing."

Abby frowned while staring at Tyler. "She said she needed the money to help a friend. I thought that was code for giving it to her pothead of a cousin."

Tyler faintly chuckled, raising his hand as he closed his eyes. "Me. But I thought my assistant made arrangements...to pay her back."

Nick and a paramedic rushed in. "What's going on?"

"Belladonna." I held up the cup, urging all of them to back up so help could tend to Tyler.

"*Again*?" Damon asked, bringing up the rear after the paramedic.

"Same source," I said as Damon took the blender cup. "I'd bet on it."

Nick barricaded us from the paramedic as he checked over Tyler, and no sooner than we'd backed with the mass of concerned customers in the diner, we heard the sounds of him retching. With gloved hands, Damon screwed open the blender cup and raised his brows. "Whoa."

"Right?" I asked.

After this deadly nightshade business, Mom had nagged me about the hazards of working outdoors. To pacify her, I'd Googled it all and showed her the plant and what could happen with accidental ingestion. Keyword there: *accidental*. My crew wasn't going to snack on plants in the wild. While we'd been reading the website's information, I'd glanced at symptoms of poisoning. Sudden drowsiness headed the list. And getting the toxin out was imperative.

While Tyler threw up, we continued to back away. Damon tipped the cup to show me the inside.

"There's hardly any smoothie!" Rachel exclaimed.

It was more mushed berries than any protein shake.

"Claire!" Abby seethed. She fisted her hand, clutching Brittney's sleeve.

"I can't believe it," Brittney muttered, shocked.

"I do. Dammit, Claire killed Zara! And nearly him, too." She froze, eyes wide, staring again in the direction of Tyler on the floor now, the paramedic at his side. "He's— Oh, no. Tyler! Is he going to make it?"

"I'm—" He coughed, gagging again. "I'll be fine, baby."

Abby teared up, and Brittney hugged her side.

"She didn't like Zara owning the farm, did she?" I asked the two women.

"Claire *hated* Zara being in charge. Since she had the most shares, it made sense for Zara to lead it."

"She sold her shares to Tyler," I concluded. "And when it looked like he'd be taking over as a partner, that had to be too much irony to stomach."

Radio chatter sounded from the dispatch piece on Damon's shoulder, and he leaned his ear toward it. Nick stood, stepping back from Tyler on the ground, and narrowed his eyes as he seemed to listen over the holiday tunes still playing overhead.

Damon grinned.

"State trooper caught her on the highway," Nick said with a smile. "She'd snuck back to the greenhouse and took the truck. Kent and Tommy called it in when they saw the behemoth of bright-pink leaving the property."

Rachel whooshed out a big breath. "Well, that's *one* truck out of the way..."

And now the others will be able to leave, too.

Bye-bye, crime scene. Hello, wedding site.

CHAPTER TEN

W*edding day...*

"That was the most gorgeous wedding I've *ever* seen," Mom gushed after the ceremony.

She wiped at her eyes, smiling as Rachel and Kent stood at the koi pond, posing for just a few pictures. Of course, there had to be a photo, at the least, for Rach's scrapbook.

"And just in time," Nick added.

He looked dapper in his tux, a red and green pocket square to reflect Christmas just days away. Kent had chosen him for best man, and I'd paired up with him as Rachel's maid of honor. When she first said they wanted a Christmas wedding, I feared my dress would be a mess of *too* much festivity. No need to worry. My red dress worked well, and Rachel and I splurged on a pedi, offering red and green toenails beneath our gowns.

Jon matched the color theme as the guitarist,

playing soft Clapton ballads for the brief and sweet ceremony. Tommy, too, he sported hints of Christmas as he'd walked Rachel down the aisle. Mom and the rest of the guests shared the same dress code, heralding this marriage as a holiday spirited event.

With Rachel's masterminding to sell poinsettias, there were only a few here and there. The greenhouse no longer resembled a nursery overstock of flowers. We had plenty of room to decorate the folding chairs, and Tommy had a great idea to bring in Christmas trees bedazzled with ornaments celebrating a new couple.

Most importantly, outside the expanse of windows, there was no gaudy distraction of Zarsettia's Poinsettias truck ruining the setting with bright hot-pink. Abby, Tyler—once he recovered from his stint with belladonna—and Brittney drove the trucks home. Claire, of course, was escorted to the police station instead.

It was sweet of the remaining Zarsettia employees to send Rachel and Kent a beautiful shipment of flowers and ivy to decorate the arbor.

Zarsettia's... I bet they'll be changing the name soon.

As it turned out, Kent's aunt that Rachel was worried about had absolutely no grounds to criticize this unconventional wedding location. In short, it was small, sweet, and nicely decorated.

Rosie, in her authority as a registered marriage officiant, also added a cute touch by holding a sprig of mistletoe over Rachel and Kent when she announced them as husband and wife.

"Just in time is right," Mom told Nick as we stood off to the side, waiting to be called for the few photos.

"If they'd needed to postpone because of Zara's death, they would have had a Christmas wedding on the day of!"

"And," I added, "we were able to get rid of enough poinsettias out here that I didn't blend in like camouflage to the background of red and pink."

Laughing, Nick and Mom agreed.

"So Claire admitted that she had been deliberately messing up orders," I said, peeved still after learning that fact with the conclusion of Zara's murder.

Nick nodded. "That was what they told us from their investigation in Florida. For months, it seems. She'd been picking at this and that at the farm, hoping to make Zara look bad and want to step down."

"Of course," I said, smoothing my hands down my dress, "a simple, direct conversation probably would have turned out easier..."

Mom grunted. "But not for someone considering killing off her problem."

Kent waved at us, beckoning us to come toward the pond. "Madis! Nick!" Rachel called us for a photo with the four of us.

We stood together, adjusting where we stood and laughing as we teased each other about falling into the small pond. Smiling and posing, we did our duty to commemorate in pictures that Rachel and Kent finally tied the knot.

"Now, Madis..." Kent said slowly.

"Hmm?" I turned, making sure my dress didn't snag on Rachel's simple yet lacy gown.

"Let's try to avoid another corpse, huh? Maybe the

new Mrs. Caldwell *does* have a better handle on stressful hiccups before the milestones of our lives together. At least she takes it in stride better than me..."

Rachel smiled smugly, brushing her hand on the lapels of his tux. "Cuz women are stronger," she teased with a wink.

"But *I* hate to think of what we're going to deal with next."

I crossed my arms, not quite scowling at my business partner. "For the last time, Kent. It's not like I go looking for trouble."

He smiled, draping his arm around my shoulders and Rachel's too. "Of course not. All I'm saying is it'd be a nice Christmas gift if you could *try* to avoid any more need for sleuthing before the baby comes."

Nick chortled. "And the baby comes...?" He raised a brow at Rachel.

"Due date's in June," she reminded him.

I shrugged. "Sheesh. Who knows what the next season will bring before then!"

THE END

FROM THE AUTHOR

Madis Harrah might discover more crime, but at heart, she represents my former career. For eleven years, I weeded gardens and tended to trails in my role as a park technician and arborist in Northwest Ohio. Now, with three young, rambunctious daughters keeping me and my husband on our toes, life's certainly an adventure while I continue writing cozies. Take a gander outdoors and follow what Madis might dig up next!

See all the Madis Harrah Mysteries here: www.authoraubreyelle.com/

Newsletter Signup: landing.mailerlite.com/webforms/landing/y1z1j2

CLAUS OF DEATH

MOIRA BATES

When they promise attendees it will be an evening to remember, they mean it.

CHAPTER ONE
POPPY

Ben snagged a cookie off the holiday-themed tower and popped it in his mouth. "I can't believe my mom suckered you into this."

I shot him a withering look as I rearranged the cookies to cover his theft. "She didn't sucker me into anything. It's a paid job, and I need paid jobs. And a good catering gig can land a half-dozen more, which each has the potential to—"

He stuck out his tongue and made a rude noise. "Who are you? Where is fun Poppy?"

I elbowed him out of the way and moved to another empty dish waiting to be filled. "Trust me, fun Poppy is a lot more fun when she's not worried about paying the bills."

A young lady in a black skirt, white shirt, and black apron approached from the kitchen. One of the Rent-a-Roo crew Julia had hired to assist me and serve. An enterprising soul had created the program several years ago when he tired of eating instant ramen. Through his business, you could hire a local college student to do just about anything. This time of year, they were kept busy serving as valets and kitchen help for holiday parties. The pay was better than anything else they could get, holiday-goers are generally good tippers, and the commitment was never more than a few hours. It checked all the boxes for a busy and broke college student.

"Everything is unloaded," she said. "What would you like me to do next? I can put out the candies."

"No, I want to handle all the candies personally." Over Thanksgiving, I had told my friends in Baseless that I was going to visit my parents in Dallas. I'd told my parents I was celebrating with friends in Baseless. In truth, I watched Christmas movies and made candy. My experimentation grew out of boredom, but it blossomed into some tasty creations. I decided to serve them at Julia's Christmas party and had made dozens of little two-bite boxes to go home as party favors. It wasn't as generous as it might have seemed to a casual observer—I fully expected to go home with a handful of orders for candy gift boxes. "Take a break—things will get chaotic soon."

Ben rolled his eyes as he watched the Rent-a-Roo retreat to the kitchen. "You know my mom has to pay them whether or not they are working." I grunted a non-reply. "She hired them to keep you from working yourself to exhaustion."

"But your mom is particular," I said. Ben and I had been friends since elementary school, and he knew I meant his mom was a complete control freak. "And I'm particular. It makes no sense to have her do something if someone is going to come along behind her and change it. I need someone who is familiar with—"

"Ugh," Ben exclaimed as he snapped on a pair of kitchen gloves. "Which tray do you want filled next?"

CHAPTER TWO

JULIA

"Poppy," I called down the stairs, tightening the belt on my robe. "We're closing in—are you ready?"

Ben barely glanced up from where he was arranging delectable looking bites on a platter. "Get dressed, Mother. It's under control."

"Why aren't you ready?" I asked, as nerves rocketed through my chest. "You can't wear that—"

Ben looked me up and down with a tired glance. "I don't see why I can't wear jeans and a t-shirt if you're wearing your robe."

I opened my mouth to reply, but Poppy dropped a small, flat package into my hands before I could. "A donation for the cat rescue. You can auction it or whatever."

I stared at the beautifully wrapped package with a tag bearing her name attached to the ribbon. "Poppy, this is a gift for you."

She reached over and plucked the tag off. "Now it's for the cats."

I turned the package over, looking for some indication of what it might contain. "What is it?" I finally asked.

Poppy had returned to setting up the dessert table. "I'm not sure; it looks like it might be a necklace box. It'll be nice though."

I looked at Ben and he shrugged his shoulders as if to say, "Who knows?" I pulled off the wrapping paper and opened the box to find a beautiful emerald pendant on a gold chain.

"Oh, Poppy, this is gorgeous," I said. "Are you sure you don't want to keep it?"

She turned to look at the necklace. "Oh! I have the earrings that go with that! Do you want those, too?"

I couldn't take my eyes off the necklace, imagining what it would look like draped on my neck. Ben reached over and snapped the box closed. "Shall I tell Dad that Christmas is sorted?" he asked.

I handed him the box. "Yes, please, check made out to the cats."

"So..." Ben looked around the festively decorated room. "I'm going to go change, unless this"—he gestured at my robe—"is the official dress code."

I looked at the clock on the wall. "Ohmygosh! We need to get moving. It's almost time. Where is your dad? He should be here with Santa!" And, with a final, worried glance out the window, I raced back up the stairs to finish getting ready.

CHAPTER THREE
POPPY

I pushed through the kitchen door, startling Kenzie, the Rent-a-Roo. She slammed the refrigerator door shut, then spun around to face me with a guilty look on her face.

Visions of catering chaos swam in my imagination. "Is everything okay?"

She blushed and looked down at the floor. "I know I shouldn't have, but..." I held my breath as I waited for her confession. "Everything looks so good! I just had to taste."

A nervous laugh escaped me. "That's all? As long as it is done before the food is plated, we call that quality control."

Her lips crept into a cat-like smile. "Thanks."

A gust of unseasonably cool wind swept in the back door, bringing Ben's dad, Robby Melvin, with it. He glanced around nervously and whispered, "Where's Juls?"

I whispered my reply, although I wasn't sure why. "She's upstairs getting dressed."

He exhaled deeply. "Great, I need help. Santa is in my car and he's... well, he seems to have had a little too much holiday spirit. I'm going to get him back in my office, but we need something—"

"Black coffee?" I asked. "Maybe some sandwiches?"

"Yes," Robby nodded. "We need to take him from sloppy to jolly before the guests arrive, and, if we get a true Christmas miracle, before Juls finds out."

"I'm on it," Kenzie said, already putting together a small plate of finger sandwiches, cheese, and fruit. She added a cookie, and an amaretto cherry to the plate. "You can't put food out for Santa without including a treat."

I placed the plate on a tray and added a cup of hot, black coffee. "You're fantastic," I said. "If anyone is looking for me, tell them I had to take a phone call. If they are looking for Mr. Melvin or Santa, you haven't seen them." She nodded in agreement. "Perfect, light the Sterno under the chafing dishes. It's almost time for the real fun."

CHAPTER FOUR
JULIA

I cancelled the call as soon as Robby's voicemail picked up. It wasn't like my husband to ignore my calls, and that was absolutely what was happening. I'd called seven times in the last fifteen minutes, and each time, it flipped to voicemail after a few rings. He was screening his calls. Maybe someone else had his phone. Maybe he was hurt. Or kidnapped! Or—

"Hey, mom," Ben stepped out of his room, and I momentarily forgot that I was looking for my errant spouse. Ben had been turning heads since he was a tiny tot. In addition to a personality that filled the room, he was just pretty. There is no other way to say it. Long lashes, full lips, unblemished skin, hair the color of honey—he had everything that many women pay significant amounts of money to possess. And, best of all, he was totally unaware of it. As a result, he often had a ball cap scrunched down on his head, a three-day beard on his face, and a t-shirt that he put on the same day he last shaved. So, to see him clean shaven, hair styled, wearing slacks and a dress shirt—well, it was a rare and pleasant treat. He smiled at me. "You look nice. Is that a new dress?" And there it was. Even though he had recently refused to bail me out of jail, he rocketed to favorite child position.

"Oh, Benny." I moved to the top of the stairs. "You're the best. I don't know what I would've done if you hadn't agreed to help tonight."

He laughed as he dutifully traipsed behind me down the stairs. "I've been training for this my whole life. My earliest Christmas memories are of you telling me and Liv to 'work the crowd.'"

"That may be so, but never before has the crowd been this important."

"Ohh," he gasped in mock horror. "Nana and Pops will not like the sound of that!"

I rolled my eyes at his theatrics. "You know what I mean. This party is important. There is only one spot open on the state tourism holiday map, and we want Baseless to fill it. Can you imagine how much it would do for the town if we could start bringing in tourists for the Christmas season? We need our VIPs tonight to see that we are more than a summer destination." I found one of the Rent-a-Roos setting up the chafing dishes. "Have you seen Poppy?"

The girl looked at me like a squirrel crossing the road, unsure if she should run across or dart back into the bushes. "She... um... she had to take a phone call."

I looked around the empty room. "Well, have you seen my husb—a man with Santa?"

She shook her head in a vigorous denial.

Ben stood beside me. “Why don’t you put on that necklace that Poppy brought over? It will look great with that dress, and then Dad can see exactly why it will make a perfect gift for you. The box is on my bathroom vanity.”

I peeked out the front window at the colorful lights covering the neighborhood. “Fine,” I said, moving toward the staircase. “But when I come down, we need to find Santa. Oh, and your dad.”

CHAPTER FIVE
POPPY

I tapped quietly on the office door before pushing it open, balancing the tray of coffee and food with one hand. Santa looked up from his spot on the loveseat and wiggled an eyebrow at me. "Well, ho, ho, ho, *hello* there. Who is this little elf?"

Robby took the tray from my hands and sighed. "Ike, I can't have you behaving like that."

"It's Santa," he scowled.

I have to admit, he looked the part. He was shorter than me, and about as round as he was tall. His cheeks flushed red, and blue eyes sparkled beneath bushy white eyebrows. His hair and beard were both full and white, although he appeared to have a severe case of bedhead going on. He wasn't wearing a traditional red Santa suit. I could describe his outfit as North Pole business casual. Dark green breeches with cream-colored stockings, a long-sleeved flannel shirt the color of milky cocoa, topped by a dark green sweater vest festooned with intricate holiday embroidery. His shiny brown loafers jingled from hidden bells each time he moved his foot.

"Eat up, Santa," I said, as I handed him a holiday napkin with a roast beef and coriander chutney finger sandwich on it. Having my food truck stationed outside the brewery's taproom, and across the street from several bars, I was well accustomed to dealing with inebriated customers. "You do not want Julia to see you like this—"

I stopped talking as I heard the door click softly behind me. I waited for the screaming. After a moment, I heard Ben laugh. "It's just me. I figured something was going on, so I sent Mom upstairs to put on the new necklace."

Robby's head snapped up. "What new necklace?"

Ben, ever the diplomat, said, "Do you want to talk about jewelry or figure out how we're going to keep Santa hidden until he sobers up?"

CHAPTER SIX
JULIA

I stared at the necklace gracing my reflection. I pulled my hair back and imagined what the matching earrings would look like. I was going to have a very merry Christmas, indeed. I'm sure whoever gifted Poppy with five carats of brilliance had the best intentions, but it really wasn't her style at all. Although a natural beauty, she spent most of her time in the kitchen, so her look was simple and pared down. Even when she dressed up, she wasn't likely to have more than a simple chain around her neck. Anything more was gilding the lily. I, on the other hand, could see fifty on the horizon and would take every bit of help I could get.

My phone chirped with a message from Melanie. "Directors leaving in five."

Dang it! I wanted the party to be in full swing, and Santa in place, before the three representatives from the tourism board arrived. You impress people by bringing them to a party in full swing, not an empty house. I picked up my phone to call Deb as the doorbell rang. I opened the camera app to see Deb and several others standing on the porch as the rental valets hurriedly took care of the line of cars along our street.

I heard the chime of the front door opening as I hurried down the stairs. "Welcome!" Robby's voice boomed above the noise outside. I slipped to his side and welcomed our guests as I spied Poppy giving directions to the Rent-a-Roo bartender before she disappeared into the kitchen.

I whispered through my smile as our friends and neighbors flowed in on the frigid December air. "Where have you been? Did you get Santa?" He glanced quickly at me and then back to the unending flow of people. My husband was definitely hiding something. I continued to smile and direct guests to the coat check as I ran through the options available to keep tonight's party and parade from becoming a total train wreck. In the past, Santa was whoever they could convince to wear the red polyester suit for an hour. A poor sense of smell was preferable, since despite yearly cleanings, the suit continued to smell faintly of sour milk and cigarettes. More often than not, the job went to a high school student needing extra credit to maintain sports eligibility for the remainder of basketball season. A 16-year-old Santa in an old suit would not impress the tourism board, so this year we went all out. Ike Cumberland from Muleshoe, Texas. He wasn't just any Santa, he was THE Santa. He checked all the boxes for an authentic Santa—short, round, jolly, naturally white hair and beard. He'd appeared in nationwide media campaigns and, rumor has it, delivered a pony to seven-year-old Suri Cruise on Christmas morning. He was going to be the detail that pushed Baseless over the top to snag a spot on the holiday map.

Robby turned and smiled at me. "Oh, is this the Christmas necklace?" He lifted it lightly from my neck. "I have exceptional taste."

I kept my smile on as I took his hand, not wanting anyone to know there was an issue. "Where is our Santa? Did he miss his flight? I don't need this—"

"It's under control," he answered quickly as another car pulled up to the valet. He faced the tourism board directors as they mounted the steps. "Welcome—"

CHAPTER SEVEN
POPPY

I inspected a tray of Cranberry Brie Bites as they came out of the oven. Perfect. I quickly moved them to a serving platter and handed it off to Kenzie. "Head back to the kitchen when you are down to two on the tray. If our timing is good, you'll go right back out with something different." She nodded as she lifted the tray to her shoulder with one hand. "And make sure the bartender gets one of everything tonight."

Ben peeked his head into the kitchen and then entered. "Mom around?"

"Your dad is keeping her busy with the guests. The *contingent* just arrived, so she's probably operating at a fifteen on a one to ten scale."

"We'll know he's told her when we hear the scream," he laughed, as he reached to open the refrigerator.

I quickly moved to block him from disturbing my carefully organized supplies. "What do you need?"

Ben rolled his eyes at me. "A sports drink—the orange kind, hot sauce, and some ibuprofen. I'm not going to mess up your stuff."

"Your mom moved everything into the fridge in the garage. Nothing in here but catering stuff." I brushed a glaze on my Prosciutto-Wrapped Pears as I prepared them for their turn in the oven. "I'm assuming the drink and ibuprofen are for Santa, but I'm going to be very insulted if the hot sauce is for my food."

"The hot sauce is for Santa," he explained. "No greasy tacos, but at least the hot sauce will help him power through the headache that is about to hit."

I shook my head at him. "No, trust me, I see a lot of drunks in the course of a year. Hot sauce will just make him sick. Have him eat some cheese."

"Poppy," Ben looked at me like I'd lost my mind. "I lived in a frat house last year. Which one of us handled more drunks?"

I considered what he'd said. "Oh. Well, carry on then. Whatever it takes to get Santa sober enough to keep your mom out of jail."

He laughed, then added, "Oh, can I have a couple more of the chocolate cherries? Dude's really into them."

I plucked two from the package and handed them over. "No more after this—they're amaretto cherries. It's not enough to get anyone drunk, but it sure won't help get him sober."

CHAPTER EIGHT
JULIA

"Okay, y'all." I moved to the center of the room and put on my best Southern hostess face. "I'm so glad to see old and new faces in the crowd tonight. Even a few old friends with new faces." I paused to allow a titter to roll through the crowd. "We're going to have a quick little ice-breaker. Who is ready to Jingle Your Mingle?"

Deb circulated through the crowd with supplies as I explained the process. Unbelievably, we'd had several meetings that focused solely on whether we should have an activity at the party, followed by several meetings focused solely on what the activity should be. Actually, that is pretty much all the planning committee did. I offered to host at my house, so that I could be in charge of decorating. I hired Poppy to cater, so that she could be in charge of food. It took one meeting for me to convince the visitor's bureau to spring for Ike's travel and fees. I've got to say, it takes a lot of work to get people to do things the way you want and make them think it was their idea.

Robby took the opportunity to leave my side and slip out of the room. Shortly after he disappeared through the doorway, Ben entered the room. My husband and children like to think that they can keep secrets from me. They cannot. Even if I didn't immediately know what they were hiding, I always knew when they were up to something. The last time Robby and Ben had pulled the trick where they were never in the same room, they were hiding a laboring hedgehog in the guest bath.

The game started and people mingled, exchanging bells as they marked items off their lists. I sidled up next to my youngest child. "Benjamin."

The smile fell from his face. He knew they were caught. "Mom," he leaned in and whispered. "It's under control."

I led him over to the fireplace, gesturing to holiday cards festooning the mantle as I smiled. "You have three seconds to tell me what's going on."

He picked a card up with a questioning look on his face. "You're scaring me. This isn't a big deal, and you look like you're about to have a stroke."

I laughed and nodded my head, glancing to make sure no one was close enough to overhear our whispers. "You should be afraid. Where. Is. My. Santa?"

The surrounding voices swirled into a stretched and distorted sound, and time seemed to slow down as Ben led me out of the party and down the hallway. Maybe Ben was right about a stroke. I smelled toasted bread. *Oh, no, he was right! That's a sign!* I opened my mouth to cry for help when the kitchen door swung open, and the smell intensified as the Rent-a-Roo passed me with a tray of warm canapes.

Ben knocked gently on the door to Robby's home office, but I pushed around him and rushed into the room. I don't know what I expected to see, but it was not Santa reclining on the loveseat, scratching his... um... jingle bells... with chocolate staining his white beard.

CHAPTER NINE
POPPY

I waited for the crowd to move away before I began refilling the sweets table. My goal was to be as invisible as possible to maintain the illusion that the table was always full, as if sprinkled with North Pole magic. This was one of those times I was grateful that people rarely paid attention to staff. I loved my regular customers, but it was also nice to have the ability to disappear. I had learned to hone my skills from my friend Will, and between the two of us, we knew enough secrets in Baseless to write a prime-time drama. Not that we would ever do something like that, but it was fun to think about.

I quickly adjusted a few stray macarons, returning them to the original display pattern. I'm a firm believer that the first taste is with the eyes, so all the little details matter. As I finished, I glimpsed Kenzie in the hallway with a serving tray held to her chest; a party guest gesturing dramatically as she spoke to her.

The woman dropped her hand and stepped back as I approached, her lips held in a thin line. I smiled in an attempt to defuse her hostile stance. "Everything okay here?"

The two stared at each other for several seconds before Kenzie finally spoke. "Umm, she, umm... it's the meatballs? Yes, she wanted to know if the meatballs have pork! The meatballs."

"Melba?" Debbie Derby, one of Julia's best friends and co-director of the cat rescue, moved across the room and addressed the mystery woman. "What are you doing here?" Her tone was almost accusatory, and her normally friendly features had frozen into a frown.

The woman, Melba, brushed off Deb's reaction and stared at Kenzie. "Apparently I'm looking for meatballs." With that, she shouldered her way past us and into the crowd.

Kenzie wasted no time in scurrying off to the kitchen, leaving Deb and I staring after the two of them. Deb let out a slow breath. "I don't like this."

"Who is she?" I asked.

"Melba Marks," Deb answered as she watched the woman disappear into the crowd. "She lives in Fulfur now, but he she's from Waller's Well." She said *Waller's Well* like it left a bad taste in her mouth.

"Is that significant?"

She whipped around on me like I'd just made an indelicate suggestion. "Yes, it's significant! They're our biggest competition for placement on the map." She pursed her lips and squinted. "She's a spy."

CHAPTER TEN
JULIA

"What did you do to my Santa?"

Robby led me by the arm to his desk chair and motioned for me to sit. "This is how he came off the plane. Actually, he may be slightly less soused now... at least he's stopped telling inappropriate jokes."

"Hey," Santa sat up straighter. "My jokes are azming, amaming... pretty good!" He gazed around the office. "Where'd that saucy little elf with the cherries go?"

I'm very glad Robby had the foresight to make sure I was seated. My head spun like I'd drunk too much eggnog. It might have been the fumes emanating from Santa, but most likely it was the vision of our carefully constructed bid crumbling in front of me. I couldn't believe that all our hard work was in jeopardy from the surly sack of shame that sat in front of me.

I heard Poppy's voice rising outside the door, then a kerfuffle as the door opened and Deb fell in. "Julia!"

She didn't even seem to notice soused Santa. "Melba Marks is here, at the party. I think she is spying!" Her voice pitched up with anxiety.

I lay my head on the desk and closed my eyes in an attempt to block out reality. The blotter was cool against my cheek, and a deep breath yielded the scent of Robby's cologne.

"Is she okay?" Deb's voice had dropped to a whisper.

"Yes," Robby whispered his reply. "She's re-setting. Just give her a minute."

Deb's surprised voice broke through again, "Is that our Santa?"

A phone rang and Robby answered before he could reply to Deb. "What do you mean it's not working? No, Livi, listen to me, the luge has been running since this morning. Can they move that one to the parade route? Tell them they were hired to make snow, not excuses."

CHAPTER ELEVEN
POPPY

Melanie Perry caught my eye from across the room and gave me a questioning look. I shrugged my shoulders in reply. I wasn't about to be the one to tell her that the party hosts were missing in action because they were trying to reverse the science of excessive alcohol consumption. I made a mental note of what was lacking on the table and moved back into the kitchen.

"I don't feel so good," Kenzie spit the words out as soon as I entered the room. "I might be... I think I have... I could be contagious!"

I glanced down at the watch pinned to my apron. Rather, I glanced down at where the watch should have been on my apron. "Have you seen my watch?" I moved around the kitchen, visions of it baked into a Christmas treat, blurring my vision. "I know I had it on earlier."

Kenzie shook her head with conviction. "No. You

had a watch? Are you sure? You probably left it by the sink when you washed your hands."

"No," I tried to replay the night in my head. "It's a nurses' watch—the face is upside down and it pins to your apron. A wristwatch is just a bacteria factory in a kitchen. It must have fallen off somewhere. Keep an eye out, would you?"

"That's just it," Kenzie said. "I was trying to tell you I feel sick. Like, I don't know, I just don't think I should be here."

I placed the back of my hand on Kenzie's cool forehead. "You don't feel like you have a fever. Are you sure you aren't just nervous?" I spun to dig through my emergency box. "Here, put on this mask, just in case—"

"I really think I need to leave!"

"There's less than an hour left," I reasoned. "Just stay until the guests leave. I can handle clean up without you. One hour, that's it." Kenzie's face dropped with disappointment. "Is this about that woman... Melba?"

Kenzie's mouth formed a surprised "o" and her head jerked up. "How do you know Melba?"

"I don't," I said. "I was told she's originally from Waller's Well, and the committee members seem to think she's some kind of spy. The real question is—how do *you* know Melba? I know your conversation wasn't about meatballs."

She deflated, and her gaze returned to the floor. "I'm from Waller's Well. She recognized me and wanted to know if I knew anything about the plans for tonight." Kenzie lifted her gaze and met my eyes. "They're right. She's a spy."

Great. That's just peachy keen. This party meant so much to so many people. For Julia and the rest of the planning committee, it was a chance to literally get Baseless on the map. For me, it was supposed to be a successful and problem-free event to wash away the bad vibes of the previous months. It was going to take me into the new year on top, mentally and financially. Instead, we had a soused Santa, a scheming spy, and general chaos. It didn't appear that any of us would get our Christmas wish this year.

"So, you're not sick?"

"I'm not *not* sick," Kenzie said. "I really do feel like I might pass out."

I smiled at her innocence. She couldn't be more than a couple of years younger than me, but I'd lived a lot of years in the last two. I could've done without a few of my life lessons, but here I was, barely old enough to drink and giving counsel like I was someone's grandma. "That's stress," I said. "You have to learn to control it, or it will control you. We're going to switch places for a bit. You get the trays ready, and I'll circulate. That will keep you away from Melba. It's just about an hour until the parade starts—we just have to make it until everyone leaves." I picked up a tray featuring Christmas petit fours. "It's a piece of cake!"

CHAPTER TWELVE
JULIA

I rose from the chair behind Robby's desk, a supernatural calm enveloping me. I walked to the loveseat where Santa sat sprawled like a rejected pin-up. Sitting primly on the arm, I leaned down to gaze into Santa's bloodshot eyes. "Santa," I whispered, "the first thing you need to know is that I am not afraid to go to jail." His smile dropped, and he glanced at Robby across the room. "I—*we*—have worked too hard on making tonight perfect to have you come in and ruin it. You may have thought this to be small potatoes compared to delivering celebrity ponies, but I promise you do not want to cross a group of middle-aged Texas women who have spent the last few months dedicated to making sure every single detail of their party goes off without a hitch." He straightened up and squirmed, moving a few inches away, so I leaned in further. "You, dear Ike, are presenting as a *hitch,* and that is going to stop right now. You have ten minutes to get yourself cleaned up and jolly. You're going to work the crowd like a two-dollar hooker, then smile along the parade route until your cheeks ache. If you fail to bring joy to every child in Baseless tonight, I can guarantee this will be your last performance. Your career will be dead before you can get back to Muleshoe."

I smiled and waited for his response. The seconds ticked by, and he finally pulled himself up and said, "You can't threaten me."

I laughed. "I'm not threatening you! I'm simply telling you what a breach of contract means to me."

The silence in the room was heavy. Keeping my mouth shut was not one of my stronger qualities, but I remained steadfast, lips pressed thin and my gaze boring a hole into Ike. He glanced around nervously, as if looking for someone to come to his rescue. He finally realized that no rescue was forthcoming, and he cleared his throat to say, "I'm feeling a bit better now. Low blood sugar, you know? It can really, umm, so, anyway—where can I clean up?"

Ike followed Robby to the powder room, while Ben darted upstairs to grab an extra toothbrush and a comb. It was going to take a bit more than a splash of cold water to clean up that old coot. I stewed while I waited, unsure if I wanted to make it through the end of the night and forget everything or make it through the end of the night and then destroy Ike's Santa business. I knew the right thing, the good and honorable thing, was to move on. I also knew the good and honorable thing would be to not show up drunk to an event where you are making three figures an hour. In the end, I'd probably let it go—Christmas spirit and all that—but I wasn't quite finished being angry.

Santa emerged from the bathroom. For the most part, he looked respectable. I sauntered over and took a sniff. Deb handed me a bottle of air freshener before I could even turn around and ask. "Close your eyes," I instructed as I enveloped him in a cloud of Winter Joy. I gave it a moment to settle and then repeated the sniff test. "Good enough." I glanced at everyone waiting for instruction. "It will look weird if we all go out at once. Benny, go check on Poppy. Deb and I will dip back into the party. Robby, you follow with Ike in four minutes." I spun and narrowed my eyes at Santa. "And Ike, I want a hearty 'ho ho ho' when you enter, sparkling eyes and joyous spirit for the entire night. This has to be a party that no one will forget."

CHAPTER THIRTEEN
POPPY

Ben swept in the kitchen door as I was on my way out, almost sacrificing the perilously balanced tray of canapes. "Ben!" I screeched. "Watch it."

He took the tray from my hands and dropped it on the counter to expertly restore the bites for presentation. "Mom sent me to check on you. She had a come-to-Jesus meeting with San—"

His words were interrupted by a booming "Ho, Ho, Ho!" from the other room. Like little kids hearing sleigh bells on Christmas Eve, we ran and peeked out the door to the party. Santa was at least upright and moving under his own power. His cheeks were appropriately pink, and his eyes bright. He might pull it off after all.

Ben tipped his head to his mom standing at the bar and raised his whispered voice in imitation. "And whatever you do, do not serve Santa anything stronger than a Dr Pepper! I don't care if he offers a new car in your stocking. Do not—"

Julia's head whipped around, and she stared at Ben. Caught, we slipped back into the kitchen. "Do you think she heard you?"

"No," Ben said, "she just knows. She always knows. It's creepy."

"That is creepy," I agreed.

"What's wrong with Santa?" I jumped, having forgotten that Kenzie was in the kitchen. Her expression held genuine concern for the lecherous old elf.

"Umm, he's drunk," Ben said.

"Yes, but, he's umm..." Kenzie moved her gaze around the room as if she were afraid to make eye contact. "I mean, that's all?"

I picked up the tray of canapes and moved to the door. "That's all? It's a pretty big deal to show up drunk to a paid gig. He's lucky that Julia didn't murder him on the spot." I left Ben and Kenzie in the kitchen and moved out to the party, hoping that my smile looked sincere. If I wanted to start the new year on the right foot, I needed people to see that I was a professional, competent chef, not just the food truck girl with the bangin' breakfast tacos.

I moved through the crowd, dispensing smiles and small bites. I stopped to answer a few questions about the food and confirmed with one partygoer that I could fill a large order of candy boxes before schools let out for the holiday break. I just needed one more order before the night ended to be able to justify hiring someone to help assemble and fill all those tiny boxes.

Making the candy was the simple part. The endless repetition of the packaging was enough to drive me mad.

I spotted Melba in the corner by the main tree, drink in her hand and a scowl on her face. I sidled up with a wide smile on my face. "Are you enjoying yourself? I hope there hasn't been any further problem with the food."

One corner of her lip twisted up, more of a grimace than a smile. "It's all just hunky-dory." She looked down into her quickly emptying glass, then strode across the room to the bar without further comment.

A hand touched me lightly on the shoulder and I turned around to see Ben's dad looking worried. "Is Ben still in the kitchen?"

"I think so—"

"Look," he glanced around and then moved in closer. "I need to stay here and make sure Juls and Santa... eh, anyway, I need to stay out here. Can you ask Ben to call his sister? She called earlier and the snow machine on the parade route wasn't working. I need to know if they got it fixed."